Sarra's presence was enough to trigger the Ward.

Heat radiated from the box until she could no longer hold it. With a sudden cry she dropped it onto the carpet. The joining came apart, the hinge dropped off, and it separated into six equal pieces: the four sides, the bottom and the lid.

Collan hauled her toward the door as six translucent Mage Globes, each as large as the box had been and flashing all the colors of the rainbow coalesced five feet above the floor. They hovered, rearranged themselves into a circle, and chimed the same note in six octaves, the highest almost painfully shrill. But the voice that issued from each in turn was Glenin Feiran's.

"Greetings, Sarra!"

"Lovely weather this spring, don't you think?"

"How are your charming children and handsome husband?"

"I remember them all very well and look forward to seeing them again!"

"My regards to the Captal!"

"And here's a little gift for you!"

THE MAGEBORN TRAITOR

EXILES: Volume Two

MELANIE RAWN

DAW BOOKS, INC.

DONALD A. WOLLHEIM, FOUNDER

375 Hudson Street, New York, NY 10014

ELIZABETH R. WOLLHEIM

SHEILA E. GILBERT

PUBLISHERS

for
Nora Kathryn MacClelland Lott
and
Joanne Kathy Drucker Okumura

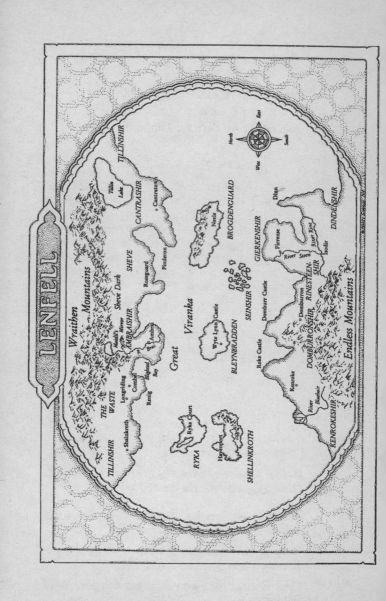

THE TALE THUS FAR:
TIMELINE

Previously I have employed the Prose Synopsis Method and the Body Count Method of reminding readers what went on in the last book. I am not particularly fond of either; the latter presupposes a bloodthirsty author (who, me?) and the former annoys me because if I could have told the whole story in three pages, I *would* have.

Below is a timeline of events in the previous volume (near as the author can recall, anyway).

YEAR	EVENT(S)
942 ♦	Collan Rosvenir sold to Scraller Pelleris
	Glenin Ambrai born
946 ♦	Sarra Ambrai born
950 ♦	Council proposes Mageborns hold government office; Ambrai leads protests; proposal withdrawn; Council proposes to register all Mageborns and offspring
	Auvry Feiran returns to Ambrai from Ryka Court; Cailet Ambrai conceived
951 ♦	Maichen Ambrai and Auvry Feiran divorced; Feiran takes Glenin to Ryka Court
	Rioting in Ambrai; Gorynel Desse takes Maichen and Sarra to Ostinhold
	First Councillor Avira Anniyas cripples Bard Falundir

Ambrai destroyed; 32,000 die

Cailet Ambrai born prematurely; Maichen dies

Desse takes Sarra to Roseguard, Collan to Falundir in Sheve Dark

956 ◆ Collan, Desse, and Falundir leave Sheve Dark

Golonet Doriaz becomes Glenin's tutor

960 ◆ Malerris Castle destroyed; Doriaz dies

964 ◆ Glenin marries Garon Anniyas; Cailet and Sarra meet in Pinderon

968 ◆ Sarra addresses the Council at Ryka Court

969 ◆ Purge begins; disturbances escalate into spontaneous Rising in Neele, Renig, Domburr Castle, Isodir, elsewhere

Cailet becomes Captal

Collan captured by Feiran at Crossroads of St. Feleris

Taig Ostin killed by Vassa Doriaz at Octagon Court; Doriaz dies

The Rising declared in Malachite Hall; Ryka Court riots; Anniyas, Garon, Feiran die in Ambrai

Sarra marries Collan at the Octagon Court

Autumn Equinox: Glenin's son is born

PART ONE

969–988

WRAITHS

1

CAILET Rille leaned back against her bedchamber door, grateful for the quiet—and the lock. Too tired to call up any additional Wards to augment those permanently in place around her Ryka Court quarters, she unbuttoned the high collar of her regimentals and wondered if she should take a nice, long, soothing bath. No, too much effort. And if Tarise—who was right across the hallway in Sarra's suite—heard the tub spigot running, she'd come in, Wards or not, to "assist" Cailet's ablutions. According to Tarise, no Lady of Importance and Position ever even trimmed her own nails.

Though Tarise Nalle was officially Sarra's personal maid (and auxiliary eyes and ears), she had set herself the task of convincing Cailet that she, too, required a servant to attend all her needs—an idea as alarming as it was amusing. There had been servants at Ostinhold while Cailet was growing up, of course—dozens of them to clean the sprawling house and cook the meals and wash and mend and clean some more. But everyone at Ostinhold made her own bed, tidied her own room, dressed herself, and did her own hair (except First Daughter Geria, whose first action on attaining her majority and a yearly allowance at eighteen was to hire a maid) Sarra, having shared Tarise with Lady Agatine, was used to having things done for her. She saw no reason—nor did Tarise—why Cailet should be made uncomfortable by similar attentions.

She was, though. And not just because it felt silly to have someone wait on her. She said nothing about the deeper reasons, the secret reasons, for wanting total privacy in her person and personal belongings. Instead she told her sister that she was perfectly capable of keeping her rooms neat, she'd been dressing herself since the age of two, and her hair was hopeless anyway. Tarise's sharp references to the exalted status of Mage Captal fell on deaf ears. Cailet wanted simply to forget her position most of the time, and the best way to do that was to be alone as much as possible.

Or so she'd thought.

She prowled the bedroom, sourly cataloging luxuries that made her feel as if she lived in a birdcage. Quite literally; sun-silvered oak furniture was inlaid with ebonwood in patterns of feathers, and fitted with golden goose heads as drawer pulls, cabinet handles, and finials on the bedcurtain rods. Thick Cloister rugs intricately figured with a whole improbable aviary splashed bright colors underfoot. The bathroom, visible through the open stained-glass door (birds splashing in a sylvan pond), was a marvel of malachite and marble and gold-beaked faucets. Birdcage it might be, but the view through beveled windows was of the gardens and Council Lake beyond, and unequaled in all Ryka Court.

Cailet stubbornly preferred her Ostinhold bedroom—which no longer existed, except in memory: bleached pine bedframe and clothes closet, cool stone floor, faded blue curtains woven long ago by some Ostin husband or son, windows overlooking the courtyard's cheerful chaos. At Ryka Court, the sight of Council Lake—so much water out in the open—made her nervous.

She knew what Sarra would say with a smile and a shake of her head: *"Waster!"* Well, she was. Bred an Ambrai in Ambraishir she might be, but she'd been born and raised in The Waste. No matter that she hated the place. It was the only home she knew.

How good it would be to return there. To sit in her old room, snuggled into the sagging old armchair, reading an adventure novel; to climb up the watchtower and gaze out on miles of Saints-forsaken wilderness beyond the security of Ostinhold. To saddle her horse and ride out completely alone. She *liked* being by herself. She'd been solitary as a child, partly through choice and partly because she was a practically Nameless orphan and such things had been very important back in the days of identity disks and Bloods and Tiers. Her new position as Mage Captal guaranteed that she continued to be set apart. But the solitude she craved was not to be found at Ryka Court. She could be anyplace—eating dinner in a tavern, shopping, sitting on a park bench, strolling the windy shoreline—and people would recognize and approach her. Most were respectful, wishing only to express admiration and gratitude. Some wanted something from her: patronage of their Web's products, her influence to settle some difficulty, a word to Sarra on their behalf. A few—and these she treasured—ventured the hope that a Mage might visit their homes to meet a young cousin/daughter/niece/grandson/friend who showed signs of being Mageborn.

But all of them, no matter how they tried to hide it (and some didn't bother), were shocked to find her so young.

They'd just have to get used to it, she told herself. And if they didn't—well, time was a sure cure for youth. Eventually she might attain as many years as she felt weighing her down now. She couldn't remember ever having felt so tired. There was something vaguely amusing about that. Not yet nineteen, and she felt older than Gorynel Desse was when he died.

Crossing to the gigantic bed (she'd tried without success to have a smaller one substituted for this silk-hung monstrosity), she lay down and kicked off her boots. Several deep breaths later, while staring at the coffered ceiling (also gilded, with birds lurking amid polished timbers), she began consciously untensing from the toes up. No one had taught her the technique—no one now living, anyway. Like everything else she had absorbed from three dead Mage Guardians and a beloved Ladder Rat, it worked perfectly.

Except on the stubborn knots in her shoulders that had been there since word came that on St. Chevasto's Day a certain cottage in Sheve Dark had burned to the ground. A little message from her eldest sister Glenin, of course; just a little reminder that the Malerrisi could still reach out from the castle in Seinshir. These last days of the old year, worry had taken up residence in Cailet's body and mind; waking, dreaming, in company or in solitude—though the Mage Captal was rarely permitted to be by herself.

She'd *needed* Falundir's cottage, damn it. When Collan had suggested a sojourn there, peace had stolen gently over her spirit. She hadn't even chafed at the winter storms that made taking ship from Ryka impossible; the cottage had been there forever, it would wait for her. Word had been sent to Sleginhold to have the place made ready; probably that was how Glenin had found out. Even in her self-imposed exile, she retained her sources of information. Which meant there were Malerrisi still at large. No one would ever know what they were unless they openly worked magic.

Sarra had been upset and Collan downright shaken by news of the fire. Falundir only shrugged, giving Cailet a look of rueful compassion. He of all people knew what it was to need a place to heal in solitude. To assess the damage, to let go of what had been lost. To work out what was possible for the future.

But the urgencies of politics made Cailet's needs unimportant. Sarra sympathized, but, truly told, she was the most insistent of those who had schemes for the Mage Guardians and their Captal. There were certain things only Mages could advise about, or do, or explain, or whatever. For Sarra, simple logic dictated that her sister the Captal thus advise, do, explain, or whatever. Full of plans and proposals was Sarra, especially for the "whatever" part—even though it had been impressed upon her that neither Cailet nor the Mages would ever work hand-in-hand with the Council.

Collan, mercifully, let Cailet alone. When she wanted company, he had the grace to just sit and talk—about music, books, his adventures as an itinerant Minstrel, anything but politics. Still, every so often Sarra would infect him with a scheme, and Cailet was too polite not to listen when he told her about it. As a grown woman, she had every right to order him to shut up; as a grown man, he had no right to take offense. As Mage Captal, she could decide what was worth hearing and what wasn't, and let people know it in no uncertain terms. But as herself, scarcely out of childhood, she had yet too much respect for her elders of both sexes to tell any of them to go away and leave her alone. And Collan Rosvenir was the very last man on Lenfell to bend his head in submission to any woman's command—even Sarra's.

"Cailet? Are you hiding in there again?"

A childish denial sprang to her lips—*"I'm* not *hiding!"* She bit it back. She didn't lower the Wards; Sarra invariably just ignored them. Cailet wasn't sure if it was determination that got her through, or if family were immune to family-cast spells. But she didn't have the nerve to make the Wards Sarra-proof. She could have; the knowledge was in her. Saints, so *easy*, even though she still didn't understand how it all worked. Did knowledge really count if you'd never really learned it?

"Come in, Sarra," she said, and sat up.

Even though she was now quite visibly pregnant, Sarra's movements were as graceful as ever. She walked to a nearby chair and sank into its green velvet depths with a sigh. Cailet knew immediately that for once she hadn't spent the day in meetings: her clothes were too casual, wide-legged black silk trousers and a loose matching tunic embroidered with a rainbow of tiny flowers. Sarra's clothes were always elegant, her hair was always tidy, and she always looked beautiful—even pregnant. Sarra did everything with grace and style. Sarra was, in fact, perfect. And for this, for just an instant, Cailet cordially detested her. The next moment, though, she smiled. Had Sarra really been perfect, Collan would never have married her.

Sarra smiled back. "Have you thought any more about what I said?"

"No," Cailet replied with a deliberately cheerful grin.

"You don't even know which idea I'm talking about!"

"And I don't *want* to know either. Whatever it is, right now I'm not interested. I think—" She broke off as Sarra turned slightly green. "Are you all right?"

"Give me a minute." Sweat pearled her brow and upper lip. She wiped it away, grimacing. "Damn Elomar!

He said this would stop once I was past my tenth week. And that was six weeks ago!"

"Are you going to throw up again?" Cailet asked warily, ready to help her to a sink.

"No. I haven't eaten anything all day, there's nothing *to* throw up. Oh, don't you start! I get enough cosseting from Col and Tarise!"

"Well, you *should* be cosseted," Cailet told her firmly. "And once we get you back to Roseguard, you *will* be. You'll be living in my house, remember, while the Residence is being finished, so you won't have any choice."

"Just what I always wanted—to be waited on hand and foot all fifteen hours of the day!"

"But you grew up that way, you should be used to all the luxuries."

Sarra laughed. "Caisha, 'luxury' is an evening alone with my husband!"

She smiled to acknowledge the truth of it, then said, "No, I meant all the things you had at Roseguard. All the wealth, and elegant living. Things like that. We live pretty well at Ryka Court, but it doesn't belong to us. Do you miss having beautiful things of your own?"

"I'm too amazed that we *are* living to worry about the *way* we live. But once we get Roseguard rebuilt, and finish decorating your house—"

"I still can't believe you did that for me," Cailet said shyly. "A whole house of my own. . . ."

"I wish you'd let me give you more. But you'll love having a place that belongs to you. You're right, I do miss that. Roseguard was so lovely. . . ."

"And Ambrai."

Sarra was quiet for a moment. "I loved the Octagon Court. It was my home. But I wasn't First Daughter, so it never would've belonged to me, and I knew it. Now it belongs to Elin Alvassy—and that suits me fine."

"Ostinhold's the only home I ever knew. I miss it, but it was never any part of it mine."

"When I think of what you should have had—it's not fair," Sarra said. "You grew up in that dust pit, while I had everything."

"Except your Name. But it doesn't matter. We both turned out to be the right bait in the end." When her sister looked startled, she arched a brow. "Hadn't you guessed? We were *meant* to come to their attention, draw them out, push them into making a mistake. It just didn't turn out the way Gorsha planned." She shrugged and lay back down, staring at the wooden ceiling timbers. "Nothing *ever* turns out the way it's planned."

Sarra said nothing for a moment, then murmured, "I'm sorry we couldn't find another place for you, Cai. Falundir's cottage would've been so perfect."

"Another place for me to hide?"

"I've never heard you sound so bitter."

"I've been doing a lot of thinking lately."

"Too much. And perhaps not enough."

Cailet turned her head to stare. "You've been playing politics too long. You're talking in two directions at once."

"And you've been sulking too long. Don't think I haven't noticed. You shut yourself up in here whenever you think you can get away with it."

Cailet rolled to her feet. "Why don't you leave me alone? Why can't *anybody* just leave me alone?"

"Because you're the only Mage Captal we've got, and like it or not, that means you have power and responsibilities and—"

"I don't want them."

"Too bad." Sarra folded her arms over the curve of her belly and glared. "What if you'd grown up in Ambrai? Would you have told Mother and Lady Allynis to leave you alone?"

"No, I would've told *Father*! At least he *loved* me!" She swung away from the shock on her sister's face. "Mother didn't want me, she wouldn't even *look* at me when I was born! But Father gave his life for me. He'd understand that I hate being on display and I hate having power and responsibility and all I want is to be *left alone!*"

Sarra rose slowly to her feet. "You didn't know him at all. Everything you say you hate, he loved and wanted more of. That's why he betrayed us."

"He didn't betray *me*."

"Maybe not at the last," she conceded. "But everything you hope to accomplish, everything you believe in—"

"Everything I was *told* to believe. Don't you see that what Gorsha did to me is as manipulative as if he'd been a Lord of Malerris? He Made me Captal—you and he decided for me, without ever asking what *I* wanted!"

"There was no one else," Sarra said quietly.

"No one you'd accept—or who could be more useful to you!"

Sarra's complexion changed again, this time to a pinched pallor of anger. "Don't you understand? Even now, after all this time?"

Cailet calmed herself and tried to explain, "I'm sorry. I don't mean it the way it sounds. It's just—Sarra, I don't understand how it all happened. I can't see the purpose of it. You, me, Glenin, the way it all came together—or came apart, I'm not even sure which— sometimes I catch a glimpse, but it's gone before I can make sense of it. And I have to know."

"You can't just accept it, and go on?"

"That's the whole point! What do I do now? *Don't* say I can do what I want—that's an option I don't have and never will."

"But you can choose any path you want!"

"As long as it provides more Mage Guardians to take the places of all those who died. Thousands of them, Sara. *Thousands.*" She circled the bed to take her sister's hands. "I envy you so much. You're so sure of yourself. What you want to do and what you ought to do are pretty much the same. It's the way you're put together inside. But what am I? I've never been just Cailet, just myself— not even when I was little. All those Wards set against my magic—"

She stopped, knowing she could talk until next Midwinter Moon and not make herself clear. Collan would understand. He, too, had been Warded; he, too, wondered what facets of himself had been lost or changed or imposed on him by those Wards. But Collan had lived longer with himself as he was; he'd be thirty-two (or thereabouts; he had no idea what his true Birthingday was) on the first day of the new year, and he had long since become used to himself, comfortable with what he had become—Wards or no Wards. Cailet suddenly wanted to be his age, to have the first of adulthood behind her with all its difficult searchings and failures and new definitions of who she was.

"You're so sure of yourself," she repeated softly.

"Don't you believe it, little sister," Sarra retorted.

"But I *have* to believe it. Otherwise I've got nothing to work toward."

Black eyes widened. "Don't tell me you see *me* as—"

Cailet smiled at Sarra's astonishment, then gave a sigh and a shrug. "Well, who else should I look up to? Glenin?"

"If you have to have an example before you, you could've chosen a much better one than me, Caisha."

"I don't think so. But do you see what I'm talking about? I know I have to find other Mageborns and replenish the Guardians, but what about *me*? What happens in *my* life? Can I even *have* a life, apart from being Mage Captal?"

Again Sarra was quiet for a time—a new aspect of her, this thoughtful silence, perhaps a result of the inward-turning of a pregnant woman, but more likely a sign of growing maturity. Slowly, she said, "As an Ambrai, your life would have *been* Ambrai. Firstborn, Secondborn, Thirdborn, we all would have had special duties. You and I could have chosen for ourselves more than Glenin, of course, but—" She shook her head, golden hair gleaming in the sun through tall windows. "Ambrai is lost to us. It belongs to Elin now. So you'd think we'd be free to make our own lives as we wished. We can't. I fight for every hour I spend with my husband. I plot and scheme for every moment I can escape my duties."

So she did understand, at least part of it. Clasping the small, cool hands, Cailet said, "Sarra, doesn't it make you feel *used*?"

"No. Use*ful*. You look at it as a curse. I see it as a

gift. How many people are allowed to accomplish even a portion of what we have?"

"Gifts don't come with price tags attached," Cailet reminded her.

"I'm willing to pay."

Her proud determination sent a shudder through Cailet. "You've paid all your life, Sasha. I haven't. I don't know if I want to."

Sarra frowned. "If you're not willing, then your life will be a bitter one."

"How can it ever be *my* life?"

Lips thin with exasperation, Sarra broke away and turned for the door. "I was right—you haven't thought *nearly* enough. When you have, let me know. Hide in here and sulk. It won't do you any good. The world's still out there—and, as you say, nothing ever turns out the way we plan."

2

RYKA Court seemed more populous than ever—or perhaps Cailet was simply growing more intolerant of crowds. Every hall and corridor and chamber was stuffed with members of the Council and the Assembly, with Ministers of this-that-and-the-other, with administrators and aides and assistants—and at least six functionaries attendant upon each.

Cailet's three rooms—reception salon, cozy office, and bedchamber-with-a-view—were a sanctuary of sorts. But Sarra was right, she couldn't stay in them all the time. Whenever she emerged, whether as Mage Captal for a meeting or social event, or as a citizen of Lenfell with private business of her own, all her movements were fodder for the gossips. And they said the most absurd things.

"Why did I buy toys for the baby at this shop instead of that one?" she fumed to Collan one afternoon. She'd invaded Sarra's rooms by a side entry after seeing a knot of people in the hall outside her own door. "What's the deep inner significance of my choosing to have lunch at this tavern instead of that? What secrets am I hiding when I'm silent during a conference?"

"Well, you could always tell them the truth." He poured another cider for her and brandy for himself. "You found a cute stuffed animal, you like the beer, and you were quiet because the conference was boring you sense-less."

"They'd never believe me. Everything I do has some ulterior motive, some mystical meaning." She accepted the cider and flopped onto a sofa. "I'm the Captal, and there's amazement enough for them. They haven't had one around for twenty years. But not only am I the Captal, I defeated Anniyas single-handed without breaking a sweat, magically speaking. I must be omnipotent, invincible, able to move mountains and change rivers in their courses—"

Collan pulled an aggrieved face. "I was there, too— with Anniyas, I mean, though I can't vouch for the other stuff. Don't I even get mentioned?"

"Stop laughing at me!" But she had to grin back at him. He was good for her, this Minstrel-turned-Blooded Lady's Lord. "They'd rather believe all those stupid spec-ulations, no matter how ridiculous."

He gave a cynical snort. "Of such lies are legends made, kitten. You might as well sit back and enjoy it."

"I don't want to be a legend. What they're saying about me has nothing to *do* with me."

Collan yawned elaborately. "You think the majority of people who get songs written about them would recognize themselves in the lyrics?"

She stared at him with genuine alarm. "Col, you *wouldn't*—"

"Oh, not me. I'm a lowly Minstrel, not a true Bard. And Falundir doesn't have time right now. He's in the middle of his opera—don't worry, it's not about you," he added, laughing again at her panic. "No, it'll be those eloquent heralds of popular culture, those masterminds of melody, those paragons of poetry—the barroom balladeers, in case you didn't recognize the colorful descriptives—who'll render your spectacular tale in song."

Cailet tucked her bare feet under her, scrunching into a corner of the couch. The level of liquor in the bottle probably had a direct connection to his eloquence. "How drunk *are* you at this hour of the afternoon?"

"Not very. Look, Cai, people believe what makes them comfortable believing. If you don't give them what they want, they'll make it up." He paused to admire the honeyed glow of sunlight through the brandy. "I'm supposed to have millions stashed in banks all over North Lenfell. And because I'm a husband with control of my own money, I'm a target for every fool's pet scheme." He snorted. "Yesterday it was an iron mine in Kenrokeshir. Iron? In Kenrokeshir? How stupid do they think I am?"

"Stupid enough to marry someone even stupider," Sarra said, plodding into the room. She lowered herself into a chair as if more than her pregnancy weighed her down. "Congratulate me. I just managed to insult one third of the Assembly, annoy another third, and the only reason the remaining third isn't insulted or annoyed is because they're at the horse races. No, I don't want to discuss it. I'll only get furious all over again, and I'm too tired. Somebody talk about something pleasant."

"If you ask me, it's talking that's the problem around here," Collan said—and flung a pillow at Cailet.

Unprepared, she took it right in the face. Retaliation was obligatory; she hadn't grown up in the rambunctious Ostin household for nothing. Soon there was a full-scale war going between herself and Collan, while Sarra pretended to cower in her chair, laughing herself completely out of breath.

"Waster, you're history!" Collan roared from behind his chair, lobbing more pillows.

"Lute-plucking scum!" Cailet yelled back. Feathers began to fly, most of them in Col's direction, which she considered only right and proper.

"No fair!" he cried, as indignant as any eight-year-old, and sneezed. "Magic's against the rules!"

Not bothering to correct his impression, Cailet

launched another pillow. "Rules?" she scoffed. "In a pillow fight?"

That was how Tarise found them: the Mage Captal and Lord Rosvenir battering each other while the Councillor for Sheve lay in her chair giggling helplessly, all three of them adrift in feathers. For a moment Tarise looked sorely tempted to join in, then grimaced with regret and announced the arrival of Irien Dombur.

"Oh, send him away," Sarra said, plucking feathers from her clothes.

"Urgent business," Tarise replied apologetically. "About as far as I can send him is your reception room. Here, let me help you get cleaned up."

"He wants to see *all* of us?"

"He does. Sorry."

Ten minutes later Cailet accompanied Sarra into the reception chamber, Collan a polite pace behind them. She felt his fingers hurriedly remove a few last feathers from her hair and repressed an inappropriate giggle. From Sarra's expression, no one would have guessed that only a few moments ago she'd been crowing with laughter. Yes, a Rosvenir was definitely good medicine for whatever ailed an Ambrai. Collan's calculated insanity seemed to have restored Sarra; she looked alert and relaxed, though mirth sparkled still in her black eyes.

Murmured greetings were exchanged, Col did his duty by serving drinks, and Irien Dombur made small talk about the dreadful rainy weather for the required length of time before stating his purpose in coming here.

"Simply put, there are rooms in Ryka Court we can't get into. All of them belong—or I should say used to belong—to former First Councillor Anniyas."

"Terrific," Collan muttered.

"Comparisons of the architectural renderings with the physical reality do not match. And these places are Warded, as confirmed by your own Mage Guardian, Captal."

"You expected them not to be?" Col asked; even though Dombur was a Councillor, Collan could get away with being rude to him man-to-man, and took advantage of it every chance he got.

"Of course not." The Councillor favored him with a
sharp glance from the piercing sapphire-colored eyes typical of the Dombur Name. "Anniyas lived in those rooms.
Naturally they would be Warded." Addressing Cailet
again, Dombur went on, "We know several things about
the Wards. They repel any attempt to cancel them or even
to determine their exact nature. Brute force is unavailing
against walls we know to be those of secret chambers—
and of course we have no intention of destroying them or
what they might contain."

"They weren't set by amateurs, in other words,"
Cailet commented. She knew about the Wards; Viko
Garvedian had told her several days ago there was some-
thing odd about Anniyas's chambers. Though there'd
been time to investigate, she hadn't. Anything to do with
Anniyas meant thinking of that night in the Octagon
Court. To Irien Dombur she said, "They were set by
someone who knew what she was doing."

"Precisely, Captal." He hesitated, then shrugged
heavy shoulders as if he might as well get the difficult
part over with. "There are also . . . sensations encountered
in their proximity."

"Fear, dread, and the occasional stomach ache?"
Viko had told her that, too.

Dombur didn't bother to conceal surprise. "Correct
again. Has the Captal already investigated?"

Cailet's turn to shrug. "Wards of that type are not
uncommon, when one wishes something to go unnoticed."

"And that's exactly the case!" he exclaimed,
abruptly human in his astonishment. "I and every other
member of the old Council guested in Anniyas's suite a
dozen times on social occasions, and not once did any of
us feel anything! It was only when your Mage—one of
the Garvedians, I believe—began to investigate that the
Wards seemed to alter in subtle ways, so that once alerted
to them, even someone not Mageborn could feel them. I
tell you freely, Captal, it was the most amazing thing."

"The touch of magic triggered them, in other words,"
Cailet said, nodding.

That's the way, Caisha, always make them think you know more than you really do.

Shut up, Gorsha.

"Where exactly are they placed?" Sarra asked—ever practical.

"One on a closet door. One seemingly in the middle of her dressing room, with the nearest wall ten feet away."

Cailet wanted badly to inquire just how often Councillor Dombur had been inside Anniyas's dressing room, but decided it was beneath a Captal's dignity to take so obvious a shot at him (though she was half-hoping Collan would). She didn't like Irien Dombur any more than Col did. The Councillor had been secretly for the Rising, like many others, but hadn't declared himself until it was clear that the Rising would win. According to Sarra, all the Dombur Blood had a streak of arrogance beyond the usual: it came from the two times Domburronshir had challenged the Council's authority. Once, long ago, the self-styled Grand Duchess Veller Ganfallin had done a frighteningly good job of conquering a large swath of Lenfell; more recently, somebody calling himself her descendant had attempted the same. Anniyas had led the battle against his forces and personally killed him—though Cailet could scarcely imagine the woman's ever wielding a sword, and to use magic openly would have given her away as Mageborn. The people's gratitude had been expressed shortly after the putative Grand Duke's death, by declaring Anniyas First Councillor.

". . . could be underneath the floor, of course," Irien Dombur was saying now, "but it's still damned odd—begging your pardon, Captal, Lady Sarra. The third is on a wall at right angles to a window, which really is the most curious of all, because there's absolutely no structural way there could be any sort of passage. As I mentioned, a Mage has explored these three areas but was unable to get past the Wards."

Cailet said nothing. She knew what he wanted, but he'd have to ask—sweetly, politely, even pleadingly if she so desired. She wasn't going to volunteer. Not this time.

"We were wondering, Captal. . . ."

"Were you?" Col asked blandly. "Wondering what, exactly?"

"As I was saying," Dombur continued, badly concealing annoyance, "we were wondering if the Captal—"

"Could do what?" Col broke in again. "Stroll on in, open the Wards, and you'd have in your eager little hands all of Anniyas's secrets?" Dombur opened his mouth to protest; Col didn't let him. "First off, what makes you think there's anything to be found? Oh, I know—why Ward something if it's not important? From what I know of the late unlamented First Councillor, she'd set a Ward just for the fun of knowing that when she was gone, everybody'd race around in circles trying to get rid of it—only to find fuck-all behind it!"

"I believe," said Dombur coldly, looking down his long nose, "that your acquaintance with Anniyas was not of an extent to warrant any presumption of her motives."

"Is that so?" Col lounged back in his chair, long legs crossed at the knees, thumbs hooked casually in the pockets of his gray wool longvest. Irien Dombur's acquaintance with Collan Rosvenir was not of an extent to warn him that this was the Minstrel's most dangerous pose. "I had the pleasure of her company for a few days a while back. They say torture brings out the truth. In my experience, that means the truth about the person doing the torturing."

"I don't see what this has to do with—"

"Killing is one thing," Col explained as if to a particularly slow-witted child. "People kill for a lot of different reasons. But you have to have a special quirk inside to enjoy causing pain. What she did to me really gave her a thrill. She'd put up Wards for the same reason."

"Even if this were true—"

"Oh, that was only my first objection. The second is this." Now he uncrossed his legs and leaned forward, blue eyes silvering to wolfishness. "Why should the Captal do this little exploration? Because the Council asks? Or is it an order? If the latter, I thought that was settled back after the elections. And if the former—what's in it for her, except a headache from working all that magic?"

"I beg your pardon?" Dombur blinked.

"You think magic comes for free?"

Cailet stirred then. Physical weakness after powerful magic was not something she wanted generally known. "He's right, it doesn't. But assuming there really is something behind these Wards, I think a headache is a small price to pay. I'll take a look at Anniyas's rooms, Councillor. But alone. If the Wards *aren't* one of her little amusements—though I think Collan's right about that—I don't want anyone around who might be injured."

Collan snorted. "That's your cue to express concern for *her*," he prompted Dombur.

"I *am* concerned," he responded stiffly. "As we all are for the Mage Captal's safety."

Sarra reentered the conversation. Col had made his point, and enough was enough. She didn't want to get a reputation for having an unmanageably uppity husband—even if he was precisely that. "I'm sure Councillor Dombur is expressing the sentiments of all Ryka Court, indeed, all Lenfell. Captal, I'd appreciate it if you'd keep us informed."

"Of course."

Collan, after a brief glance at Sarra to indicate that she hadn't heard the last of this, got to his feet and played perfect husbandly host once more. "Thank you, Councillor, for taking time out of your busy schedule to bring this matter to our attention in private."

It was dismissal, and Dombur knew it—even when delivered by another man who, moreover, had no official power whatsoever. But no one was ever verifiably impolite to Lady Sarra Liwellan's husband; she had the irritating habit of treating such lapses in manners as if directed at her. The Councillor rose, bowed importantly to the women, and took his leave.

"Not now, Col, please," Sarra said when Dombur was gone. She pinched the bridge of her nose between two fingers, as if she were the one who had worked too much magic.

He inspected her narrowly. "I'd say 'now' is just the right time for a visit from Elo. Isn't it a wonderful coincidence that I invited him and Lusira for dinner tonight?"

"I'm fine. Just tired. I don't need to see—"

"And here, in happy hour, are the Lady and her husband," he said as the door opened to admit the couple—with Tarise and her husband Rillan Veliaz right behind them. Judging by the look that passed between Collan and Tarise, they had an understanding about providing excuses to kick unwanted guests out of Sarra's rooms. Irien Dombur had left on his own, but others undoubtedly did not. Cailet began to think it might be a good thing to have someone like Tarise around.

Collan greeted Lusira with a kiss on the cheek, a liberty she allowed only him. "As lusciously lovely as ever. Elo, your work is right over there—" He pointed at Sarra. "—and tell her if she doesn't take it easier I'll take her over my knee." The world ordered to his satisfaction, he favored them all with a sunny smile. "Brandy, anyone?"

3

CAILET entered Anniyas's rooms alone. The Ward set at the main door had faded almost to nothingness. Considering that Anniyas's imposture was of thirty and more years' duration, Cailet marveled that she had risked Wards at all. There was also an odd feel to the remnants, as if they'd been set in haste and not intended to last. This puzzled Cailet until she realized that on the last night of her life, the First Councillor had gone to the Octagon Court fully expecting to begin the process whereby the Malerrisi would come out into the open, with herself as acknowledged First Lord. She must have taken a few moments to Ward her suite, as she had not dared to do all during her tenure here in case her status as a Mageborn was discovered.

First was a Keep Out. Beneath it muttered a suggestion that Guards Are Coming. Both were so dim by now that Cailet could have simply walked through the door without bothering to unWork them. But unWork them she did, just for the practice.

The reception chamber was appropriately opulent—much gold leaf and ornamental plasterwork and finely carved wood—though most of the artwork had long since been removed. Truly told, everything that wasn't nailed down had been claimed by someone else. A week or so ago, the antiquated Councillor and Rising partisan Flera Firennos had shown her a little bronze statue of St. Miryenne, patron of Mage Guardians. "There was a charming St. Flerna I took for myself, but I thought you might like this one, child." Without a fragment of magic to her Name, Councillor Firennos had not felt what Cailet had on taking the St. Miryenne into her hand: a spiteful little spell that gave a Mageborn a needlelike shock, like a spark from a wool rug on a dry day. Cailet canceled the spell instantly, thanked the old lady for the gift, and packed the lovely little statue in a trunk that would eventually make its way to the new Mage Academy—wherever and whenever that might be.

The implications of the spelled artwork hadn't occurred to her until later. What had Anniyas been doing with an image, no matter how fine, of the patron Saint of Mage Guardians? Cailet had concluded that it had been a marker: anyone Mageborn who touched it would have reacted, if only with a start of surprise. Now she was positive that, as Collan suggested, Anniyas *had* been amusing herself.

Cailet paced slowly around the reception room, soft leather shoes making no sound on the dusty marble underfoot. Over there was the corner Ward Irien Dombur had mentioned. It practically laughed at her. Light from the window on the next wall limned a fresco of a handsome young man, several sheep, and a basket of wool. Captal Lusath Adennos had been a renowned Scholar all his life, and from his vast store of arcane knowledge came an image that Cailet matched from her own experience to the immense painting that covered half of Firrense. Shaking her head, she moved on to inspect the other two Wards.

Likewise in the dressing room was a stained-glass window—and on the closet door, a painted carving—of an obscure but identifiable Saint. Cailet stared in honest amazement. Anniyas could not have signaled her loyalties more clearly if she'd posted placards. How it must have amused her. Col was right, and these Wards were nothing more than her parting joke at an unwary Mage Guardian's expense. A good thing it had been Viko Garvedian who'd explored this place; his mother Tiomarin had taught him thoroughly and well how to protect himself and others.

Cailet decided to deal with the Ward near the wall fresco first. As she expanded her concentration, she recognized the sensations Dombur had described. Pathetic, really, compared to some of the Wards Gorsha remembered. She was about to begin the sequence of spells that would cancel the Ward when she heard voices in the antechamber.

"What do you think," Collan snarled, "she'll find lost millions from the Treasury and tuck them away in her pocket?"

"It's the opinion of the Council that there ought to be witnesses." Irien Dombur. Of course. "Lady Sarra and I will perform that function. There's no need for you to—"

"Where I go, he goes," Sarra interrupted. "Now, is there anyone else you'd like to invite to this, Dombur, or are three witnesses enough?"

Cailet went out to meet them. "Invite all Ryka Court if you like. There's not much to be seen—except for someone with eyes to see it. Come on, I'll show you." She led them through, pointing out the Saints depicted in paint, stained glass, and carved wood. "I realize that not one person in a thousand has ever heard of them, but how obvious did she have to be?"

"I don't understand," said Sarra. "Who are they?"

"The young man is Bleisios the Curly, patron of wool-combers. He's as unknown as they come, except in upland sheep country. The lady in stained glass is Avingery Lacemaker—see her spools and pins, and the lace she's just made, lying across her lap? And the carving is Dantian Circle-Spinner, seated at her seven-ringed spinning wheel. What they have in common, besides being in Anniyas's chambers, is that their patronages— wool-combers, lacemakers, and spinners—were assumed by another Saint when the Calendar was revised."

"Chevasto the Weaver," Sarra said, and Cailet nodded.

Dombur had the grace to look abashed. "Patron Saint of the Malerrisi. Captal, there must have been a Ward that kept everyone from seeing these things. Something that blinded us to the reality of this." He was practically pleading for this to be so, unwilling to acknowledge that the signs and sigils of Anniyas's reality had been right there all along.

"People see what they're comfortable seeing," Cailet misquoted Collan, whose mouth twitched at one corner. Then, to ease Dombur's obvious distress, "There might very well have been something to prevent true sight. If there was, it's gone now."

Sarra was gazing at her with admiration and perplexity. "Though I'm no Scholar, I have a fairly good education—and I've never heard of these Saints."

"You may have, without knowing it," Collan mused. "Every so often a variation will show up as a given name. Usually people think it's just a strange version of some other Saint."

Cailet nodded agreement. "Such names run in families for Generations, used again and again without anyone knowing where they really come from."

"Fascinating, I'm sure," Dombur said, suddenly nervous, "but should we be here, Captal?"

"There's no danger, if that's what you mean. The Wards appear to be straightforward—to keep people from prying—but they're rather weak by now. They weren't all that threatening to begin with, presumably in case a Mage Guardian showed up here and sensed them."

"And the spaces they Ward?"

"I was just about to have a look."

Cailet returned to the wall fresco, her three witnesses trailing her. She looked up at the innocuous portrait of the curly-headed youth with his sheep and his wool basket, admiring it impersonally for a moment before calling on her magic. Thinking herself prepared—for another and stronger Ward, for a triggered spell, or for simple nothingness if the Malerrisi magic had faded—she was shocked nearly senseless by the vision that blossomed from an exploding invisible Globe.

> *A handful of silvery sand sifted from work-roughened fingers. A similar handful of rich dark loam, another of reddish-brown clay, yet another of gritty ash sparkling with bits of obsidian. Fifteen handfuls from all the Shirs of Lenfell trickled down from stained, submissive hands into a tight-woven basket, bringing the flesh of a whole world to its ruler: Anniyas.*
>
> *Five white cloaks swirled in the breeze through the open window as the four lesser Malerrisi Lords watched and the First Lord nodded and smiled. Fifteen people, carefully bespelled, bowed their heads low in homage. And in silence, without a struggle, fifteen throats were slit to moisten the soil with the blood of a whole world, while five white cloaks spread like scavengers' wings in the breeze and Anniyas dug her beringed fingers into the blood and dirt and laughed.*

Cailet stumbled back, sickened. But the vision did not release her mind. The soaked earth seemed to separate for her, showing the stony dead sand of The Waste, the rich soil of Ambrai, the alluvial silt of the Kenroke marshes, the volcanic ash of Brogdenguard, all the different rocks and gravels and dust of which Lenfell was made. She could feel the victims' terror muted by magic, hear their liquid dying—and see Anniyas and her fellow Lords, smiling.

Strong hands gripped her shoulders. She recognized them, the support and comfort they gave, and bent her head so she wouldn't have to meet Collan's eyes.

"Cai? You all right? What happened?" His palm under her chin brought her head up. "What did you see?"

"Anniyas," she managed. And then, because he was worried and she had to tell someone, she found words enough. "They brought the land to her—here, in the room beyond this wall—she had their throats slit to blood it—

fifteen people, one from each Shir, bringing all Lenfell to her—and they watched, the Malerrisi, they watched and smiled and—" Her gaze was drawn to the placid pastoral scene of the youth and the sheep and the basket of wool, and sudden involuntary magic shattered the plaster fresco.

"Captal!" exclaimed Irien Dombur.

"She slaughtered people here and nobody ever knew it!" Cailet pulled away from Collan and spun on her heel. "Nobody ever felt any of it! I don't know how to deal with that kind of magic!"

"You must." The Councillor for Domburronshir came forward, all elegant clothes and studied mannerisms and Blood arrogance. "We need to know what Anniyas left behind. Who's to say there aren't other visions waiting for the unwary? At any time anyone in this room could be assaulted by magic—persons not as strong as you, who would be permanently damaged."

"Instead of only temporarily damaged, like her?" Sarra asked bitingly. "Captal, I'm a Councillor, too, and I hereby cancel the request to—"

"As *senior* Councillor here," Dombur interrupted, "I must insist that she continue."

He was right, damn him. Cailet turned again, concentrating on the place where St. Bleisios had been, and cast a spell that came to her without having to think about it. She'd given up trying to figure out who provided what she needed; all she knew was that unless a Ladder was involved, the spell didn't come from Alin Ostin.

The wall abruptly separated horizontally just below the ruined fresco. She heard the grind and crack of the mechanism that she broke asunder with magic—no matter, it would have taken hours to locate the trigger and use the device. Now no one could use it again. Just as well. A passage was revealed, glowing white as if the stone was lit from within. Another spell, of course, harmless but effectively eerie.

"There's your first architectural anomaly," she said over her shoulder to Dombur. "Have it investigated by whomever you like. I've unWorked the Wards so it's safe to enter, but I have no personal interest in anything Anniyas may have left behind."

The Councillor drew breath to object. One glance from Collan made him reconsider.

Cailet strode to the closet in the bedchamber, wondering what horrors were concealed by guileless Dantian Circle-Spinner. Sarra's worried call of her name behind her made her flinch, but she confronted the carving before they could follow her into the room.

Swords sang, wielded by two superbly skilled warriors. One was tall and broad-shouldered, with gray-green eyes that blazed in the ruined moonlit beauty of the Octagon Court. The other was slight, blonde, and possessed of a prowess not truly hers as she attacked with a sword not truly her own. The powerful man and the swift young girl battled under the laughing gaze of the First Lord of Malerris, and when the girl had won and her enemy lay prostrate before her, she plunged her sword into her father's throat. Tossing lank fair hair from her eyes, she approached the old woman standing where Generations of Ambrais had stood. "He was of no further use to me," Anniyas said. "It's time you took his place."

Cailet choked on horror. It hadn't happened that way, it never could have happened that way—

But St. Dantian's Wheels within Wheels were not through spinning.

The old woman lay murdered on the dais. The girl with the new-blooded sword stepped around the corpse to take her rightful place—as an Ambrai, as a Mageborn, as new First Lord of Malerris—and waited.

They came, as she knew they would. A beautiful young woman with long golden hair; a tall, handsome man with intensely blue eyes. They approached, mingled fear and defiance and pain in their faces. The girl lifted one hand. A blood-red Mage Globe appeared, called up from the vast

*store of arcane knowledge taken from the dead
woman who had dared to stand where none but
Ambrais ever stood. The golden-haired woman
cried out softly, crumpled to the floor, and died.
As for the man—he mounted the first step at her
spell-bound insistence and knelt at her feet.*

"No," she whimpered. "No—"
"Cailet!"
Her sister's voice was very far away, and the Wheels
had turned again.

*The girl was older now, her hair longer and
streaked with white. Long years of easy power
showed in the thickened body, the complacent
eyes. Expensive clothing of Malerrisi white and
a selection of rare jewels glowed in the sunlit
hall as she acknowledged with pleasure the ac-
colades due the First Lord. The sword at her side
was more of an ornament now than a weapon;
she let others take charge of the difficult physical
training, while she spent her days discoursing on
matters political and philosophical to adoring
students who lived for her every word. As they
should; as they certainly should.*
*All at once a sword lean with purpose sliced
toward her, and the First Lord fell bleeding to
the white tiled floor, murdered by one of her own.*

And again the Wheels circled, tightening the possibilities and the probabilities around her heart.

*She was the youngest, so she was the last. One
by one the others had died, leaving only her.
There might have been others to follow after, to
continue the long tradition, but the time to plan
and prepare for it had passed many years ago.
She wondered sometimes why the First Lord had
let them live. Of a certainty there was nothing of
sentiment in the order that she and her pathetic
remnant of Mage Guardians be permitted to sur-*

vive. She knew that many must have argued for their final obliteration, but for some reason her nephew had let them live. They were no threat; most likely they were an amusement to him. And now she was dying. There was no one to become Captal after her; no one to do the Making. She was the last of her kind, and with her passing the Bequest would be lost. All the Magelore, all the learning, all the Generations of Captals would die with her.

Fittingly. Fittingly. She had been unworthy. Daughter of a traitor to the Mage Guardians, sister of one First Lord and aunt of the next— how could they be expected to follow her, trust her, believe in her?

Killing her father hadn't been enough to prove herself. She was who she was, and that had condemned her even before she was born.

Hands held her up or she would have fallen. Voices called her name, begged for response. She had none to give. All she could do was gasp for air, her struggle to breathe spasming every muscle in her body.

The Saint's Wheels spun a fifth time.

The endless, trackless expanse of The Waste was met at the horizon by a searing blue sky. Through this pale and arid landscape a lone figure walked. Ancient, weathered, painfully gaunt, only the eyes were alive in that hollowed and haunted face. Ragged black clothes were clutched around the body by thin hands as the woman walked without goal or purpose, black eyes misted and other-seeing and not quite sane.

She didn't want to know. The years ahead stretched as empty and withered as the woman she'd just seen herself become. Better to have died at Ambrai with her father. At least that would have been a meaningful death, a fitting end for a Captal defending the ways of the Mage Guardians. What good was she now? She'd seen pasts that could have been, and now a future that might very well be. The visions scraped at her as if her mind was a raw wound, spinning round and round and round—

> *Again she walked through an assembly, this time dressed in plain proud black with her swordbelt tight around her waist. Her students bowed their reverence, her fellow Mages bent their heads in homage. As they should; as they most certainly should. She was the Capal, the one who had saved the Mage Guardians from oblivion, and they were right to humble themselves before her. Yet someone had dared challenge her authority, someone had questioned her right. She would answer in the ancient manner, the way of the past that she had reestablished because it had been her only guide.*
> *She reached the testing ground and raised her sword in ironic salute to the girl who faced her. Fair-haired and black-eyed, like her; the stamp of Ambrai and Feiran clear on her face, the passionate Rosvenir mouth curling with contempt. Her own niece, her sister's First Daughter—who was about to be taught a perilous lesson in the true powers of magic.*

Another voice spoke now, low and sickly-sweet: Anniyas's voice. As if she had anticipated everything, set these Wards and spells because she had knowledge of what might or could or would happen that night in the Octagon Court.

Who do you hate more? Me, for showing you the possibilities? Or yourself, for believing them?

People believe what they're comfortable believing— how wrong Collan was! Those pasts had been probable, given certain small twists in circumstances. And the futures, too. Quite likely—

But this was all wrong.

Where was Glenin? It was *Glenin* who had attacked her, well after Anniyas was dead—*Glenin* who had tormented her with searing visions and maimed her in body and spirit—*Glenin* who had nearly killed her—

Anniyas couldn't have known what would occur that night. She hadn't even known who Cailet was! Collan had been asked again and again to reveal the name, and even under the most vicious torture had kept silent. When Anniyas set these Wards and spells, when she finalized these snares, she had known *nothing*.

Anniyas had not known the future—*any* future. No one did. This was another trick, a trap waiting for any Mageborn who triggered the spell. It played on fears, used weaknesses, toyed with uncertainties. Malicious variations on the past, sadistic predictions for the future—

Yet she would be a fool indeed if she didn't understand the warning inherent in these horrors. Such things *were* possible. A lurch of the turning Wheels, and . . .

It was her responsibility—to the Mages, to her family, to herself—to make sure the *possible* did not become *probable*.

She struggled away from those who held her, standing on her own. Dantian's delicate fingers were still poised to spin, and Cailet stared at the Wheel made of seven concentric circles, like no real spinning wheel in the world. Applying another spell—this one with the flavor of Tamos Wolvar—with magic she gouged away the inner circles, leaving only the outer one. The last possibility. She faced it with clenched jaw and trembling heart. But it wasn't what she expected.

> *From the sunlit balcony of her private chambers she gazed down on the new arrivals. The girl and boy stood awkwardly in the central courtyard beneath the great spreading oak, waiting for someone to notice them. It was a new sensation for these two, who had been instantly noticed all their young lives.*
> *They couldn't know that orders had specifically been given* not *to notice them until she herself greeted them. She watched them for a time, wondering what they were like now. She hadn't seen them in several years. They'd grown tall and*

*straight and strong. The girl was as sunnily
blonde as ever, but the boy's hair had darkened
to brick-red. Other than that, she could tell nothing about the changes adolescence had worked
on them. At last they sensed her above them, and
looked up. The girl's eyes were the color of new
spring leaves. Her brother's were bluer than the
lake nearby. Fine eyes, clear and shining; fine
faces, too, proud of bone and pleasing to look
on, with strong portents of their maturity.
This would be her work: to shape them into the
woman, the man, the Mage Guardians her sister's twin children were meant to be.*

When Cailet woke to the world around her, she found
herself sprawled on the tiled floor, supported by Collan's
strong arms, with Sarra kneeling beside her. The wooden
carving of St. Dantian lay in splinters all around, as if it
had exploded like a Warrior Mage's Battle Globe.

"Caisha?" Sarra's voice was strained and anxious.

"Talk to us," urged Col.

She smiled. If they knew what she now knew—ah,
but she mustn't tell them. It would ruin the surprise. "It's
all right now. Everything's going to be all right."

Sarra smoothed Cailet's sweat-damp hair. "What did
you see this time?"

"It doesn't matter. I've made it all right." Glancing
around for Councillor Dombur, she said, "There's a very
small room behind this closet, but nothing much in it except books. I'd appreciate it if I could have first look at
them."

"Of course, Captal."

Something occurred to her then. "Did any of you
sense anything? Feel afraid, or apprehensive, or—?"

All three shook their heads. Well, she might have expected it. Sarra, though Mageborn, was deeply Warded.
Collan's Wards were even stronger. Dombur was about as
magically gifted as any given lump of coal.

"All right, then. The dressing room."

The stained glass of Avingery Lacemaker was the
finest of the Warded artworks. Cailet would very much

regret destroying it. But perhaps that wouldn't be necessary. The dressing room itself was large and airy, filled with light from the clear window rising six feet above the stained glass that provided privacy. More closets, most of them mirrored, were decorated only with gold door handles shaped like various flowers. Completely innocuous. But then, so had the fresco and the carving been.

Cailet opened the closets one by one. All were empty of what Sarra had told her was an extensive, if tasteless, wardrobe. "Who got the clothes?"

Dombur cleared his throat. "Actually, they were burned. Some few of the better jewels were taken off before, of course—"

· *Of course,* Cailet thought, amused.

"—and a Mage skilled in detecting Wards and spells—the very Mage who found these, in fact—certified the gems free of taint. Viko Garvedian."

"Viko has a special talent for sensing magic. It kept him and his mother Tiomarin safe for many years."

He didn't seem to notice the dig. But surely he understood her meaning: that thanks to the Council of which he'd been a part, Viko and his mother and hundreds of other Mages had been reviled and hunted all those many years. Still, Cailet was learning about the social nicety of on occasion pretending to be conveniently obtuse.

"And we all thank the Saints for his cleverness," Dombur was saying, "or we might not have known about these frightful Wards so quickly."

"I'm glad he was wise enough not to confront them himself." Cailet regarded the portrait of St. Avingery for a few moments more. Then, wondering what sinister spell would be called forth by spools and fine silk and fragile pins and the wealth of patterned lace spreading across the Saint's lap, she called on her magic once again.

The picture in the glass exploded at the touch of a Mage Guardian's magic. Every shard blasted like a needle into her mind, weaving a fine network of pain. The floor beneath her gave a convulsive shudder. Walls shifted, wooden doors groaned and cracked. Dust spewed from the agonized grinding stones of the outer wall. Cailet heard a distant scream and knew it was Sarra and could do nothing. The pain was excruciating, splinters of colored glass carving up the magic in her brain as a butcher carves a carcass.

She was going to die. All colors were gone, all life, everything was as white and dead as the trees of the Dead White Forest, as the cloak of a Malerrisi, as—as—

—as the white-hot heart of a Candleflame. As the silvery-white wings of a Sparrow. As the brightest Star in all the sky.

Miryenne and Rilla—the Candle and the Sparrow—but to which forgotten Saint belonged the Star?

Through the white horror came Lusath Adennos's chiding: *Oh, come now. You've seen the walls of Firrense. All three hundred and eighty-six Saints, painted over and over again in exactly the same fashion as they've been painted for centuries.*

The late Captal's pedantries infuriated her. She was in agony that neither he nor the Others felt; it was *her* mind being hacked to pieces, *her* magic being riven from her—

Sweet Saints, child, not even the First Sword could take your magic from you—and it would have been better so, when you were born, to be given back when you were ready for it. This silly spell is only trying to make you believe it's stealing your magic.

But magic *could* be stolen. She'd almost thieved an unborn Mageborn's power. And what of the things she had taken from him and Alin and Gorsha and Tamos Wolvar?

Oh, my dear child, that wasn't magic. That was knowledge. Surely you've discovered the difference by now?

Magic was power; knowledge was how to use it.

Just so. But while you're trying to argue me out of saving your sanity, others are in danger of losing that and much else besides.

No spell or Ward then, but a vision: Candle, Sparrow, Star. They arose in her mind outlined in white fire, and she felt the slivers of glass vanish as if they had never been. How silly of her to think she was going to die. She couldn't die now. There was too much work to be done,

fe to be lived. All those candles to be lit in
...ng Mageborns—all that magic to be set free on silvery
wings—all those stars to be wondered at in the night-
black sky. . . .

4

"CAILET? What did you just say?"

"Hmm?" She blinked, and to her surprise saw the
worried face of Elomar Adennos above her. "What are
you doing here?"

"Repeat what you said," he insisted.

"I can't. I don't know what it was. Where is everybody?"

Elo's lips thinned in disgust. "The next stupid question is, 'Where am I?' Lie quiet, and I might tell you."

"I feel perfectly all right." But she stayed flat on her
back, liking the softness of the pillow beneath her head.
She would've expected a colossal headache, but instead
she had the sensation of being light and free and clean.

"*I'll* tell you how you feel," the Healer grumbled. A
tiny Mage Globe hovered over Cailet's toes, and slowly
moved up her body at his direction. When it reached her
chest, its green-gold glow intensified. Elomar cast a stern
eye at her. "You know the reason for that."

The Ward disguising her maimed breast. She stared
him down. After a moment he let the little Globe continue
on its path. Softly luminous, gently pulsing to the easy
rhythm of her heartbeats, it completed its task without
changing again in warning, and then winked out.

"You're all right," Elomar said.

"Told you so."

"You've lied to me before, Captal. Now, do you remember what you said as you woke?"

"I was asleep?"

Breath hissed from between gritted teeth. "You were

unconscious—grinning like a madwoman and completely insensible when Councillor Dombur carried you in here."

"*Dombur*?"

"He has his uses as a mute pack animal. Tell me what you said just now."

She thought for a minute, then couldn't help a little laugh. "I remember. You'll never believe it, Elo—I'm not sure *I* do!—but I found out who the Star is."

"I'm assuming you're going to explain that."

"I can always tell when you're really upset—you talk a lot more than usual. The Star that goes with the Saint, although that's not his sigil. St. Mikellan. Startoucher."

"Never heard of him."

"Nobody has in centuries. But he's another patron of Mage Guardians—and he was there on the wall all the time!"

"What wall?"

"In Firrense, of course. St. Mikellan, climbing a Ladder to touch all the stars in the sky! And you know what the really crazy part is? He looks just like Alin!"

"Delirious," said Lusira Garvedian. She came forward from the doorway and perched on the edge of Cailet's bed. "Or maybe just demented—though she looks sane enough. Or as sane as anyone can be after destroying all those hideous Wards."

"I vouch for physical health," Elo growled. "Not mental."

"If Cailet's all right, you should go look in on Sarra," Lusira said quietly.

Cailet's heart suddenly went cold. "What's wrong?"

Lusira exchanged glances with her husband. When he nodded solemnly, she murmured, "She miscarried of the child."

Cailet couldn't see them anymore. Another image white-shrouded her eyes: a blonde girl, challenging her right to be Captal—

From a long way off she heard Lusira's voice say, "She wasn't having an easy time, and it would've gotten worse. Elomar says she would have lost the baby anyway. Another week, maybe two—it's so terrible, having carried this long, only to lose the child now."

—her own niece, a threat to her power—

"There's no reason she can't have another baby. Elo will be with her the whole time, keeping careful watch. I've already informed the Council that we're turning down their offer of the Public Health Ministry. Truly told, I don't much like Ryka Court anyway."

—Sarra's First Daughter, Ambrai-proud and Feiran-powerful, with the clear-eyed pragmatic honor of a Rosvenir—

"Cailet, it wasn't your fault. If that's what you're thinking behind that black stare, then put it out of your head right now. This would have happened no matter what."

—pride rebelling, power despising, honor loathing what Cailet had allowed the Mage Guardians to become. A First Daughter who would have challenged her and possibly—probably—won, and become Captal, and set the Guardians straight again.

A First Daughter who would never be born. Had *Cailet* been responsible for killing Sarra's daughter before she could become a threat? Before she could even be born?

She'd tried once—unwittingly, unknowingly—to steal an unborn child's magic. This time, had she killed? Her own sister's daughter—

"Have you heard a word I've said?"

She nodded in blind response to Lusira's voice.

"Then listen to this as well. When Collan brought Sarra to us here, Elo and I both sensed something about the baby as we were trying to help her. Just before it died, we felt—Cailet, there was something strange about the magic. Neither of us know what it was, exactly, but we don't think it was quite normal."

"N–normal?"

Flatly, Elomar said, "The sensations match some clinical descriptions of Wild Magic."

And all at once another vision came to her—a postulation, rather, conjured up by those within her who were wiser than she. A lovely golden-haired infant, precocious and perfect in every way—except for the peculiar gleam in her watchful black eyes. A gleam familiar to Cailet from somewhere . . . someone. . . .

"Anniyas," she whispered. "Her magic. Inside the baby. A taint left behind, like a disease to infect anyone not strong enough to fight it off—"

"Cailet!" Lusira took one of her hands. "That can't be so. There's no evidence anywhere of such a thing ever happening—"

"Not in Mage records, maybe. But what of the Maler-risi? And don't you think that as First Lord, Anniyas was powerful enough and innovative enough to devise this on her own?"

"Impossible," Elomar stated, but something haunted his eyes all the same.

"Maybe so, but there was enough of Anniyas left behind in those Wards to taint any Mageborn who couldn't defend herself. I don't know what happened, and I don't care. It *did* happen, and—" Her voice caught suddenly. *—and Sarra's First Daughter died because of it.*

Cailet sat up and swung her legs over the side of the cot. "Lusira, you and Elomar are Mages, and Mages obey the Captal. This is my order: you're going to watch over her until she births her twins, and—"

"Twins?" The Healer Mage took a step back.

"Twins," Cailet said again, firmly. "A girl and a boy. And when they're born, I'm going to set Wards around them so strong that no one can get past them except me. And Wards around Roseguard, too, and—damn you, Elo-mar, *no!*" she blurted as a spell washed over her, weakening her limbs and fogging her thoughts. "You son of a Fifth—"

"Fourth, actually," he said. "Shut up, Captal, and go to sleep."

5

SHE had to go see Sarra. She knew that. Anybody with
the courage to face down Malerrisi ought to be able to go
visit her own sister.

She took the long way through the Council's private
gardens, telling herself she'd pick some flowers for Sarra's bedside. A stupid offering: *"I'm sorry I caused the
death of your child, here's some flowers to make you feel
better."* Elomar had told her that so many bouquets had
been sent that the room looked like a hothouse and
smelled like a whorehouse. Not his words; Sarra's, before
she ordered the flowers sent to the maternity quarters of
St. Feleris's Hospital.

Cailet wandered the winter-bare grounds, stubbornly
determined to find something pretty to give her sister. If
it took her long enough, perhaps Sarra would be napping
after lunch and Cailet would have to come back later.

Sheltered beneath an evergreen bush she found a few
white flowers on long, slender stems. She had the usual
Waster's knowledge of botany—which plants stored fresh
water, which didn't—so these flowers were unknown to
her. They were pretty, though, so she crouched down with
hands extended to pinch off a few stems.

Her fingers were an inch from the flowers when she
heard someone say her sister's name. She froze. The
voice was a woman's, low and casual, not expecting to be
overheard here in the Council's private sylvan sanctuary.

"That Lady Sarra lost her baby is a great pity. Motherhood might have kept her busy and away from Ryka
Court for a while."

"I suppose it proves why there are so few Liwellans,"
a second woman said with obnoxious Blood smugness.
"Too many Thirds and Fourths taken to husband will do
that to a family. And who knows who this Rosvenir man
is, anyway? But the person who worries me most is the
new Captal. It's a shame she suffered no damage."

Concealed behind the shrubbery with thin winter

sunlight dappling her back, hardly daring to breathe, Cailet tried to identify the voices. Nothing came to her, not from her own memory or anyone else's. She wished fervently that she had Collan's ear for sounds.

"One would've thought Anniyas's magic more powerful, even after the passage of time."

"What if it *was* still potent, and the Captal's powers are simply greater? A prospect few view with delight."

"Truly told. The girl is a liability, you know."

There was a brief pause, and during it Cailet tried to make herself as small as possible beneath the overhanging shrubbery.

"Shall we sit down?" said the lighter voice, with a trace of an accent Cailet couldn't quite place. "I love how the gardens smell after a rain. Not those chairs, Granlia, they're still wet. The sun has dried these. How wonderful to be outside again! I can't recall a more dismal winter."

Cailet connected the melodious given name with the powerful Family Name, and with a very ordinary face. Granlia Feleson, elected last year for a third time to the Assembly for Gierkenshir, was a close cousin of the Jereth Feleson who had not been reelected to the Council. A back-bencher whose voice Cailet couldn't recall ever hearing in debate, her politics and personality were a cipher. To say such things so freely, she must be in company with someone completely trusted.

"The weather has matched the political climate," said Granlia Feleson. "These adherents of the Rising are bad enough. But Cailet Rille worries me. She's dangerously gifted. It was one thing to have sluggish old Lusath Adennos as Captal. This girl, though. . . . Magic is an unknown quantity in her very young hands. We have no idea what to expect from her. It would have been much better if she'd died."

"Tragically martyred," agreed the second woman, whose voice Cailet still did not recognize. "Useful as a rallying point, reassuring to a populace still wary of magic."

"Her death by magic would prove that not even a Captal is all-powerful."

"Exactly what I've been thinking. We still need

magic—but we also need to control it. If she'd died using it in the people's defense, what spells and Wards the government now deems useful would be accepted—suspect in some ways, perhaps, but accepted."

Cailet hunkered down, fists clenched on her knees. Branches dripped onto her shoulders and back, soaking her light shirt until she shivered. *Please,* she thought, *don't let them get chilled and leave before I hear it all. And don't let anyone else walk by and see me!*

"Trying to control Mage Guardians is what started everything twenty years ago." Granlia Feleson gave an impatient sigh. "We might have a chance while she's still young, but once she trains up more Mages and sends them out the way it used to be—"

"Do you think she could? It's the oddest thing, but I believe I actually feel sorry for her. What good is her life now? The Mage Academy is gone. And what's left? A hundred Mages from the old days, some badly trained Prentices, and whatever ragged group of Mageborns she scrapes together. It's not as it was before. Ambrai back then positively hummed with magic."

"Establishing a new school for Mage Guardians is the last thing she should be allowed to do," said Granlia Feleson in a vigorous tone. "Magic is dangerous. If she spreads Guardians across Lenfell the way it used to be, with no Lords of Malerrisi to counter their power—"

"They'd have no one to oppose them but the government!" the other woman interrupted. "And Mageborns don't enter government, so we'd have none on our side to check them if it became necessary. Sweet Saints, Granlia, I never imagined!"

She was lying. Cailet heard it in her voice. This was exactly where the conversation had been headed, and this woman had guided it there every step of the way.

Granlia Feleson said, "The renewed ban on governmental service is at the Captal's order, contrary to Lady Sarra's hopes. I'm told they had quite a spat about it."

"The Captal would do better to cultivate her only real ally on the Council. She must be stupid as well as naive. I mean, what sort of education can she have had in The Waste? Even if she does set up a school, half the Mageborns on Lenfell would lose respect for her the instant she opened her mouth and revealed her ignorance."

"And those who are Bloods wouldn't bother with her at all," Granlia Feleson agreed with all the lofty disdain Cailet loathed in old-line Bloods. "She *must* be a fool even to think of it."

"Yes, it would have been much better for all of us if she'd died. Even for her, poor thing. She'd have everlasting acclaim without having to work for it at all."

They were quiet for a few moments. Then the second woman said, "We need a dead martyr more than a living Captal. Granlia . . . could something be done to provide us with one?"

"It would have to be very subtle, very clever."

"Or very public and very obvious. A malcontent's vicious attack—"

"An assassination?" Granlia sounded intrigued.

"With the killer instantly apprehended, tried, and executed for the crime, and all Lenfell in mourning at the young Captal's tragic death."

"Whom could we find to do it?"

"Shake Ryka Court a little, and see what rattles."

"Do you know, I've always admired your ability to find the heart of the matter. An inheritance from your dear mother?"

"You forget, I knew Glenin Feiran rather well. Saints, it's getting cold even in the sunshine. Shall we go in?"

And they departed the Council's private garden, oblivious to the huddled presence of the girl they were planning to kill.

Cailet heard their footsteps crunch the gravel path back to the gates. When all was silent but for the whisper of a breeze, she let the shivering rule her. Her leg muscles cramped; she fell onto one hip in the dirt; her hands tore at the bush and the flowers in a vain attempt to keep her balance. Several stems ripped apart, oozing milky pinkish fluid onto her shaking fingers. But it was several minutes before she felt the acid sting on her skin, and when she did it was a good excuse for the tears in her eyes.

6

"I gotta get outta here," Cailet repeated, reverting to the accents of her childhood, the erudite vocabulary of three Mage Guardians obliterated by raw panic. She was eighteen years old, and somebody wanted to kill her.

Elomar finished smearing salve onto her hands. "Milkfire flowers were Anniyas's favorite," he said, relevant to nothing that she could tell.

"I can't be biding here." She could barely sit still long enough for him to finish his work. "You gotta find me a ship, Elo—they're gonna kill me!"

"I'm surprised no one uprooted those plantings before now," he went on, wrapping Cailet's fingers in gauze.

"Why won't you listen to me?" she cried, as furious now as she was frightened. "I'm no use to nobody, but I don't wanna die!"

"Milkfire won't kill you."

"Granlia Feleson will!" She slapped him away from her, wishing it was the Feleson woman she struck at.

Unperturbed, Elomar stepped back from her bed, brushing aside the silk hangings. "I'll change the dressing tomorrow. The swelling will be gone by then."

"I *have* to leave! Now! Damn it, haven't you heard anything I said?"

Elomar arched a brow. "I've heard a great deal of disgraceful grammar in a Waster accent thick enough to spread on toast. What I haven't heard are the words of a rational woman, let alone a Mage Captal."

Cailet gazed down at her white-swathed hands. She was beginning to hate that color. *White* meant *Malerris* to her. " 'S all I am to anybody," she muttered. "Mage Captal. You want me alive, they want me dead—am I s'posed to be grateful for the attention? If I wasn't Captal, nobody'd give a sandrat's ass about me!"

"Stop whining," Elomar ordered. "And lower that bastion of Wards, it's giving me a headache."

"Get out, then!"

"Gladly. I'm late for my nightly battle with Sarra over minor details like eating, sleeping, and taking her medicine. You Ambrais. Impossible women. Thank St. Miramili I married a Garvedian."

"You got one minute to get out," she snarled. "Walk quick."

He glared down at her for a moment, his gaunt, narrow, unhandsome face stiff with disgust. She did not have the satisfaction of seeing him hurry; his legs were so long that only a few of his usual strides carried him out of her rooms.

Cailet punched a pillow with her fist. Its yielding softness only increased her frustration. She got up from the bed and tried to pack her few items of clothing, but the bandages made her hands too awkward. At last she sat in a chair by the window and stared out at the rainy night, and after a time perversely lowered all the additional Wards she'd cast this afternoon. If they wanted to kill her, they were welcome. She didn't care anymore.

She was a good half hour into a fine sulk, ghoulishly considering the methods she herself might use to murder a Mage Captal, when someone entered her rooms.

"Cailet? Whatever are you doing in here in the dark?"

Splendid. Somebody else she was just longing to see: Lusira Garvedian, close cousin of the last truly great Captal of Mage Guardians. All Cailet lacked in life was another lecture.

"I brought dinner," said Lusira, casually lighting a few lamps with her magic as she entered the bedchamber. "There's enough for two, if you don't mind company. I'm starving."

Cailet didn't look around from the rainy window. "That's normal. You're pregnant."

Crockery rattled.

Cailet glanced over her shoulder. Lusira's exquisite dark eyes were rounded with shock and her hands shook so much she was in danger of dropping the tray she carried.

"Don't tell me you didn't know."

Lusira shook her head.

"Past thirty's old for a first baby," Cailet went on tactlessly. "But you're healthy, and your husband's a physician." She paused. "You really didn't know?"

"I'd hoped—there was a chance—but—" She steadied herself. "Cailet, are you *sure*?"

"Of course I'm sure. I'm the Mage Captal."

Stunned as she was, still Lusira reacted to the bitterness in Cailet's voice. "Elo said you were feeling sorry for yourself. I think he was wrong. I think you're angry—and frightened."

"You're damned right I'm frightened!" She made an effort; it had been unspeakably thoughtless of her to break the news so bluntly. "But don't you be. You'll have a fine, healthy baby, I'm sure of it." She wasn't, but forgave herself the necessary lie. Then she told another one to pay back the earlier rudeness. "If you can stand being around me, I'd be glad of some company."

Lusira set the tray down on a low table between chairs. She arranged plates, poured wine, doled out knives and spoons and forks, served lamb and mint sauce—all with the simple, silent grace of a truly great lady. Not even Sarra was so instinctively elegant; for one thing, Sarra rarely shut up.

When dinner was laid out, Lusira finally spoke again. "You never asked to be Captal."

Cailet blinked, a forkful of glazed carrots halfway to her mouth.

"No obligation ensues," she went on—an odd thing for a Garvedian to say. Her cousin Leninor had died defending those obligations. "It was forced onto you and no Mage living or dead would blame you if you chose someone else to carry the burden."

Not be Captal anymore?

"Elomar helped Gorsha in the Making. He can help in an unMaking, if you so desire."

Cailet very carefully set down her fork, bandaged fingers not just clumsy but trembling. Frightened? Terrified. Being Captal was the only thing she had—

"Cailet, you're so young. I know you hear that in a derogatory way from others. I mean it with compassion."

Lusira picked up her wineglass, looked at it in surprise, then set it down. She was pregnant; she shouldn't be drinking anything stronger than cider. "I was just a bit older than you when Ambrai was destroyed. I had so many plans for my life—and suddenly all were impossible. My mother saw trouble coming years before it actually arrived. Hers was a very rare gift, and people used to say she ought to've been named after Elinar Longsight instead of Falinsen Crystal-Hand. She decided when I was still a child to pretend I wasn't Mageborn. It saved my life—the way Gorsha's Warding saved yours. I lived at the Academy with her and learned magic in secret. But no one knew I was Mageborn except my immediate family—and Gorsha, of course."

Of course. Gorsha knew everything about everybody.

"I understand what it is to be trapped in a life you didn't choose. You have a chance to escape it, if you wish. Believe me when I say that no one would think less of you for it. No one who matters, I mean." Lusira reached across the table to touch Cailet's white-wrapped hand. "Consider it, my dear. You have your whole life ahead of you. If you want to live it without the weight of the Bequest on your shoulders, then do so."

And there was the crux of it. The Bequest. She couldn't give it to anybody else because she didn't really have it.

The Ladder knowledge of Alin Ostin, the Mage Globes of Tamos Wolvar—and bits of their personalities as well, because everyone learned in ways unique to their characters—these she possessed. She could still see the gleaming spheres of light and learning that contained their gifts to her. But the entirety of the Bequest, that quintessence of Magelore every Captal before her had possessed—this she lacked. And through her own fault, because she'd tried to steal an unborn Mageborn's magic.

She could not pass on the Bequest she didn't have. And even if she could, on whom could she shove this awesome responsibility? Who would be willing to shoulder it for her? Whom could she trust to do it?

Through the welter of feeling and speculation she tried to discover if she was tempted. With genuine surprise she found she was not. It wasn't only that the Bequest could not be passed on complete. Or that if she tried, they'd discover that she was unfinished, lacking the true depth and breadth of knowledge a Captal must have. It wasn't even that she couldn't think of anyone she could trust more than she trusted herself to carry out the obligation.

She *felt* no obligation. Truly. She was the Mage Captal. As Sarra had said, the only one they had. Gorynel Desse had Warded her at birth and twice more during her childhood to keep her safe, to prevent magic from tearing her apart before he could guide her into its uses. He'd done his best for her—they all had, done their best and given their best. It was her fault the Bequest wasn't complete.

It occurred to her that she would have to do something about that.

The thought tucked itself in a corner of her mind as something else came clear: she couldn't imagine *not* being Captal. Less than a year since the Making, and she couldn't imagine herself as anything else. She was eighteen years old, and her enemies were her enemies because of what she was, not who she was. What she was had been thrust upon her without her knowledge or her permission. And people wanted to kill her for it.

Even though she wasn't really what they thought she was. But even if, as Captal, she wasn't whole—well, the Cailet Rille who had grown up in The Waste had not been a whole person, either. How could she be, lacking her magic? It was part of her, so strongly that it had struggled to break free of the Wards, so powerful that Gorynel Desse had reWorked her Wards twice. Collan had only had his memories blocked; an essential component of Cailet's very life had been denied her. And when it had been returned, its power was such that in conjunction with the gifts of four other Mageborns, she had become Captal.

That was what she was. *Who* she was had yet to be fully discovered. But without the magic, without being Captal, she would never find out.

The magic and the position were hers. Both belonged to her now, and she could not give up either. For she could allow no one else in the world to face Glenin and her son when the time came. *That* was her obligation—not only to the Mage Guardians and Lenfell, but to herself. And to the father who had died saving her, and the mother who had died birthing her.

Try to kill *her*, would they?

She turned her fingers in Lusira's palm, pressing lightly, then let go. Smiling, she said, "You're all stuck with me, Saints help you. And no matter how well this technique worked to make me stop whining, the next time you have something to say, just say it, all right?"

Lusira laughed softly and shrugged. "As you wish, Captal. But it *did* work. Just as Sarra said it would." Laughing again at Cailet's outraged stare, she added, "With help from Collan, and my husband's small contributions. We know you, my dear. And whereas you have good reason to be afraid, you're not the type either to live in fear or give in to it."

"Maybe," she conceded. "But eventually somebody *will* try to give the government a dead martyr in place of a live Mage Captal."

"They'll have to get past all of us to do it."

Cailet shook her head. "I can't put any of you at risk. I have to leave—not because I'm scared for me, but because someone might try to get to me through any of you." The way Anniyas's vicious magic might have reached her through Sarra's First Daughter. "I have to find a place for myself, Lusira. For a new Academy, where I can teach in safety, out of their reach. I have to leave because I can't protect all of you."

Wrong. And now that you're no longer so frightened and can think rationally, after you finish your dinner, Caisha, I'll explain why.

7

THE Wraithenday dawned bright with sunshine and chill
with the wind off the lake. Cailet stayed late abed, watching rainbows cast by the faceted windows drift across the
walls. Finally she got up, ate an apple from the bowl in
her sitting room, and began to pack.

She bungled it, of course, awkward hands wrinkling
everything. She was about to give up and summon Tarise
to do it for her when Collan strode into the bedchamber.
He paid as little attention as Sarra did to the permanent
Wards, and in the long night of discussion and eventual
reluctant acquiescence to Gorsha's plans, she'd forgotten
to recast the new ones.

Collan spared a glance for the tangle of clothes on
her bed, sprawled into a chair, and said, "You haven't
been to see Sarra."

"No." She tried once again to fold a shirt, and failed
miserably.

"Look at me."

"I can't."

"Coward." He said it the way he would have said,
It's raining.

"She doesn't want to see me," Cailet muttered. "Neither do you. Why are you here?"

"Y'know, Cai, you have the most amazing capacity
for getting everything unequivocally wrong. The truth is
that *you* don't want to see *us.* Now, you want to tell me
what's rolling around that brain of yours that I'm the only
one here with sense enough to set straight?"

Cailet folded a shirt, unfolded it, crumpled it in her
bandaged hands.

"The baby," Collan said. "You feel guilty. Elomar
says Sarra would've miscarried anyway. It's why she was
sick long past the usual time for pregnant women."

So he hadn't told them about the other. About the
Wild Magic.

"He also says," Col went on slowly, "next time she'll have twins. A girl and a boy."

Cailet bit her lip and nodded. "Yes."

"You told him that."

"Yes. But he shouldn't have said anything to you and Sarra."

"She doesn't know." He paused, then remarked pleasantly, "But I bet *you* even know their names."

"No, I—"

"Don't lie to me." All the easy drawl had left his voice now.

"I'm not, I—"

"Shut up." His eyes were like the sigil of his Name: cold and cruel as steel knives. "I don't care what you know or don't know. I don't care if you go hide someplace where you never see Sarra again. But as of right now, this minute, you're going to go see her, and you're going to let her yell at you if she feels like it, or pretend she's fine if she feels like it, or cry over the baby if she feels like doing *that*, or any other damned thing she wants."

"I *can't*—"

"It's either that, Captal, or I'm going to wipe up the floor with you. She's hurting because of you, and you're not allowed to do that to her."

"I never meant—Collan, you don't understand what happened. I can't explain it fully, but things aren't the way you think they are."

He silenced her with a look. "You think whatever you want. I don't care about that, either. Not when Sarra's blaming herself." He brooded for a moment. "You know what she said? She wanted to know why it didn't hurt more. *More!* She said losing the baby should've hurt her more, because it was her fault."

"Oh, Collan, no," Cailet breathed.

"Falundir came in yesterday to sit with her. You know what she said to him? He told me after, using his List. She said the baby should've been safe inside her. Instead, she felt her daughter die, fighting to get out of the one place she should've been safe."

Cailet's throat closed over a moan.

"She wants to see you. And you're going to go in there and—"

"Your daughter died because I walked up to those Wards playing Mage Captal as if I knew what I was doing—"

"You *are* Mage Captal," he said flatly. "And don't give me any shit about being incomplete either. You *are* Mage Captal. You have to be, or everything that's happened is for nothing." Rising from the chair, he finished, "Now, are you coming with me to see Sarra, or do I break your arm?"

Cailet gave up. "I don't know what to say to her, Col."

"You'll think of something. Minstrels and Mages always do."

He escorted her down the corridors—not by physical force, but she sensed his hand ready to grab and quick march her if she showed any signs of flight. There were none. She had to go see Sarra.

Collan, as excellent a wall as he could be, was sometimes an even better window.

8

SARRA, confined to bed and not liking it one bit, did not yell, or cry, or evidence any emotion other than annoyance. "Elomar Adennos is a tyrant," she stated.

"You noticed," Cailet replied. Seating herself at the foot of the bed, she went on, "I thought I'd bring you some flowers, but I'm told you heard what happened the last time. So I brought you this instead."

She handed Sarra something wrapped in a scrap of silk scarf, something that had been in her pocket since sunup. She'd Worked it the night before at Gorsha's direction and with Tamos Wolvar's expert guidance.

"A Mage Globe?" Sarra almost touched it where it nestled in a scrap of silk, then drew back. "It looks like glass." Plucking up the long, thin gold chain, she let the inch-round crystal sphere swing back and forth. "What does it do?"

"Nothing—unless someone around you has nasty intentions. Then *it* gets nasty. It's a Ward that'll warn you if there's danger from magic nearby. Nobody else will feel it but you. Promise me you'll wear it."

Sarra gathered her unbound hair to one side, slipped the chain over her neck, and blinked when the little orb, milk-white flecked with gold, touched the skin between her breasts. It rested right near the birthmark over her heart. "It's warm! Is that the magic inside?"

Cailet nodded, and took back the box.

"I hope you've made one of these for yourself," Sarra said.

"I won't need one."

Frowning: "I don't agree. Elomar told me—"

"Elomar talks too much." Cailet smiled as her sister arched a brow. "Well, sometimes, anyway. I don't want you to worry about me, Sarra. I'll be very well protected, I promise."

"But you won't tell me how, will you?"

"If I understood it, I would. But I don't, so, truly told, I can't. But you know I have to leave here."

To her surprise there was no argument. "Where will you go?"

"The Waste. You can see people coming from a long way off."

Frowning, Sarra pushed herself higher against the pillows. "You can't be thinking of building your school there."

"No. I just want to spend some time thinking. The way I would've done at Falundir's cottage. I need that, Sarra. I'll be perfectly safe."

And you aren't the least bit ashamed of yourself for lying to her, are you?

If it keeps her *safe, no. Not the least little bit.*

"Caisha. . . ." Sarra hesitated. "About the baby . . ."

"It wasn't your fault," she said quickly. "It was mine, for letting you be where the Wards could hurt you. I'm sorry, Sarra. I'm so sorry."

"Stop that this instant," Sarra retorted. "Elomar gave me an oration—for him—on the subject. What I wanted to talk to you about was how it could have happened in the first place. It concerns you, too, and your future children."

Cailet had no idea what she was talking about, and said so. Sarra shifted in bed, curling her legs to one side beneath the covers, and fixed her with an intensely troubled gaze.

"It's safe to talk here, isn't it?" When Cailet nodded, she went on succinctly, as if two words explained it all: "We're Bloods."

Cailet waited, but that was the extent of it. "So?" she asked blankly.

"This isn't supposed to happen to people like us," Sarra insisted. "Losing a baby because it's not growing right. That's what Elo said happened. But it shouldn't have. Not to a Blood."

Cailet thought about it for a while. "Well, we Ambrais don't produce a lot of children, you know. If I remember it right, Great-grandmother had two, Grandmother had one, and Mother—" —*died giving birth to me*. She said, "Mother had three, maybe because she was half Ostin. Of course, compared to the Ostins, the Ambrais are pretty pathetic."

"But no miscarriages—none I know about, anyway. Why did it happen to me?"

Cailet's turn to frown. "Sarra, are you implying that there's something wrong with us?"

"Maybe. It could be why we don't have many children. I was sick all the time with this baby. Elo says it wasn't formed right, it couldn't have been born. So I have to think that there's something inside *me* that's not right, either. And it may be the same with you." She fidgeted with the fringed blanket across her knees. "It isn't supposed to *happen* to Bloods."

"Don't hear this wrong, but it might not be you. It might be Collan."

"I thought of that, too. It's a possibility, of course." She spoke coolly, as if analyzing a piece of legislation. Cailet understood; Sarra had done her weeping. Now she was investigating likely reasons and potential solutions. "We know nothing about his family. We have no idea what Tier he really comes from. What if it's something to do with him, and—"

It's not. You may trust me on this, Cailet. It's nothing to do with Collan.

And you're not going to tell me how you know. Damn you, Gorsha—

You'll know what you need to know when you need to know it. For now, I ask you to believe there is no fault in Collan—nor in Sarra or you. This child was never meant to be born.

Aware that Sarra was looking at her strangely, Cailet said, "Sometimes these things just happen. Even to Bloods. I don't think we can ever be sure."

"Perhaps. There's another factor here, though. Magic."

Cailet forced a shrug, swearing to dose Elomar with his foulest purging syrup if he'd let anything slip about what he and Lusira had sensed about the child. "I've never heard of a woman having a miscarriage because of—"

"What about Wild Magic? Is that what kind of child I would've had?"

Cursing Sarra's intuitive leaps, Cailet replied, "No. Mageborn, of course. But not—"

"How do you *know*?" Sarra cried. "Did it happen because of physical reasons? Is there something wrong with the Ambrai women? Is it something about me, or me making a baby with Collan? Is it the kind of magic I inherited? Or is it that I was Warded for so long *against* my magic—and still am?"

Helplessly, Cailet said, "I don't *know*. Sarra, your daughter is gone. There's nothing anybody can do about it, and no explanation except the one Elomar gave you. Let her go. Please. There'll be more children, I promise—"

"She was my First Daughter."

"I'm sorry," she said stupidly, not knowing what else to say.

After a time, Sarra spoke again. "I just want to know

why. That's all. If there's something tainted about me, or us—our Blood—"

"Then the whole structure of Bloods and Tiers was a lie from the start." Cailet stared down at the white gauze binding her hands. "Maybe it was. Maybe the Bloods are overbred, or inbred, or maybe it *does* have something to do with our heritage of magic. Maybe Glenin is right, and we *should* breed for it."

"*She* miscarried, too," Sarra said suddenly. "I'd forgotten that. I think I heard that it was a little girl."

And now Glenin had a son. All at once Cailet's insides twisted with sick knowing. Glenin's son, Sarra's daughter. . . .

Deep within her mind she sensed Gorsha's horrified realization that she must be right.

Gorsha, it's too horrible! Not even Glenin—

And what would she not dare, in the service of the Weaver?

"Caisha? What's wrong?"

"N-nothing," she managed. Glenin's son and Sarra's daughter. . . .

Only now that daughter would never be born.

To Sarra she said, "I'll ask Elo about—about maybe something being wrong with us physically. I can't tell about the magic. One thing I do know, Sarra, as surely as I know how much I love you: you *will* have healthy children. I swear it on the Captal's Bequest." Sworn on her hope of its eventual completion. On her determination to know it whole within her.

Sarra relaxed and smiled. "I believe you, Caisha. You'd never tell me such a thing if it weren't true."

From outside the closed door—and the Warding— came a familiar voice. "There's a rumor that not just one but two surpassingly beautiful ladies are to be found within this room, and I decided I simply had to come and see for myself!"

Cailet hastily canceled the magic that protected them before Telomir Renne could slam smack into it. A moment later Gorynel Desse's son, the oldest living Prentice Mage, strode through the door, bearing an enormous bouquet of silvery-blue roses that he proffered to Sarra with a bow and a flourish.

"For you, from Lady Lilen's own greenhouse—you remember, the one with the cactus—with the loving good wishes of however many Ostins there are in residence this week. And I must say that if there get to be many more of them, they'll own this whole planet."

"Thank you, they're beautiful. But what are you doing here? I thought you were visiting at Longriding until Ilsevet's." Sarra buried her nose in the flowers and inhaled. "How does she get them to smell like blueberries? And how did you know about—?"

"Mage Guardians are by and large admirable people, but they're also the most prolific gossips on Lenfell." He dragged a chair over to the bed, sat down, and said, "Now, since you're looking perfectly well and lovelier than ever, what do you have planned for tomorrow?"

"Tomorrow?"

"Don't tell me you forgot!"

"Forgot what?"

"Your adoring husband's Birthingday, of course." Telomir shook his head sadly. "Women are such unsentimental creatures. It's always up to men to remember important occasions. If it weren't for us, you'd forget your *own* Birthingdays."

"Especially when we reach an age where we don't wish to be reminded," Sarra retorted. "At which point, a man's so-called thoughtfulness becomes suspect. I don't have anything planned, and Collan doesn't expect—"

"Sweet Saints, of *course* he does! But don't worry about a thing, I've got it all planned."

And as much as they begged, bullied, and finally commanded him to tell, he said not a word more about it. Instead, he rattled on about the weather, the Ostins, the Maurgens, and any number of other chatty topics, proving the truth about gossipy Mages. Sarra kept up the conversation instinctively, adept in the social nothings required of high position. Cailet veered between envy of her skills and gratitude for the chance to observe them. She kept hoping that maybe one day she'd learn how to do this herself.

Half an hour later, Elomar came in, declared Sarra to be tired, and evicted her visitors. Outside in the corridor, Telomir dropped his cheery demeanor and addressed Cailet seriously.

"Will she be all right?"

"Yes. Get the details from Elo, I don't want to talk about it anymore."

"I understand. Come, I'll walk you back to your rooms and we can have a private talk."

"Will it take long? I have a lot of things to do before I leave—"

"Learn to be gracious, Captal," he murmured. "Especially when there are others around who might hear—like those people over there. Besides, we should be seen talking in public."

"A minute ago it was privacy you wanted. Make up your mind, Telo."

"Very well. The truth of the matter is that we must speak in private about something public, but must be *seen* talking in public, although what I have to say is strictly private."

And to think she'd recently accused Sarra of talking in circles. "Shall I look curious, worried, amused, or bored?"

"That's the spirit. Interested but not concerned."

Cailet assumed what she hoped was an appropriate expression. They walked through the corridors conversing in quiet tones about exactly nothing, while those they passed nodded greetings. Reaching the official quarters of the Council, their progress slowed as the hallways grew more populous. Bureaucrats hurried from one appointment to the next; couriers moved even faster across slick marble or wood floors, adroitly dodging any and all obstacles to the swift delivery of messages. Few took their time getting where they were bound, and these were all Important, at least in their own estimations. Councillors, several members of the Assembly, a Minister or two—they strolled and dawdled, admiring artworks and tapestries and the views out the windows, chatted with each other or the aides accompanying them. But of all the people moving through Ryka Court, not one failed to nod or bow to the Mage Captal. Neither did anyone say a single word to her. If Telomir's advice about her expression was responsible, she'd have to perfect this extremely useful face by practicing in front of a mirror.

At last they reached her private chambers. Lunch was laid out on the low table between chairs; Cailet warmed up the soup and bread with a casual spell. As steam wafted from the bowls, Telomir laughed.

"Exhibitionist."

"I can make yours stone cold again if you like," Cailet offered sweetly.

"Your pardon, Captal. What I meant to say was 'Thank you for your thoughtfulness.'" As they sat down, he added, "Though I know we have Tarise to thank for the meal. She's right, you know. You really ought to have somebody in your service to do all the everyday things."

"Complained to you already about my recalcitrance, has she? Well, truly told, I'm beginning to think it wouldn't be such a bad idea after all."

"It's an excellent idea. Once you start the school, you'll need someone to organize you, keep track of appointments—and order the meals, because you never eat unless something's shoved in front of your face."

Cailet sighed. "Oh, very well. I'll make Tarise's day happy by telling her to keep an eye out for someone. But *not* a Mageborn."

Telo looked surprised. "Of course not. Your privacy must be inviolable. Now, would you like to eat in peace, or shall I tell you why I'm here?"

"Your choice. If the news would sour the soup, then you'd better wait."

"Your school, then. Have you decided on a location yet?"

"I thought I had, until we ran into some local resistance. Anniyas still has loyalists out there, mainly in remote areas. But of course I *want* someplace remote, so . . ." She shrugged.

"You'd think they'd've gotten the idea by now. It's, what, thirty weeks since she died?"

"I wish somebody'd remind the people in upper Cantrashir and around Tillin Lake."

"Takes time, I think, in rural communities." He paused to savor the soup. "They're always more conservative—and more independent—not wanting any change in government that might mean attempts to interfere in the way they've always done things."

"I grew up in The Waste," she reminded him, amused. "I know all about resentment of Ryka Court's meddling in local affairs."

"Well, then, don't be too hard on the good folk of Cantrashir and Tillinshir. Have you tried Sheve? Most of the people who own most of it are friends of ours."

"You can talk in here, you know," she said, tearing off another piece of bread. "It's Warded six ways to the Endless Mountains. What you mean is my sister and her husband will soon be running the whole Shir. No, I can't ask them to sell me any of their land, and I can't be tied in any way economically or politically to a place owned or governed by people I know. That's why I've been looking in Tillinshir and Cantrashir. I'll find a place, Telo. Don't worry."

"At the risk of curdling the butter, I *am* worried. What's all this about a plot to kill you?"

She shrugged. "It's being taken care of."

"This is serious, Cailet. Their reasoning is politically sound."

"For the good of Lenfell, I have to die? What kind of sound politics is that?"

"The kind that sounds good to people who don't like Mageborns. They'll find plenty to agree with them, and give them all the help they need."

"I can protect myself."

"Do you know who's behind it?"

"More or less."

He sat back in his chair and regarded her narrowly. "And that's all you'll say about it." When she only nodded, he tried one last time. "I trust my father not to leave you undefended, but you know these people will never give up. You also know who's really behind the plot."

Relenting, Cailet said, "Glenin will keep trying to kill me as long as both of us are alive. It's her duty as First Lord—oh, don't look so surprised, Telo. You know and I know that if she isn't yet, she will be soon enough. She's powerful, clever, and far too ambitious to settle for anything less. And if I outlive her, she's got a son to try his hand at getting rid of me. But I can't live my life behind a bastion of Wards." She smiled a little as she used Elomar's phrase. "Lusath Adennos did, because he was ordered to by Gorsha—and by *you,* if you'll recall."

"It was necessary. He understood that."

"Yes, but he didn't much like it. Not that he was the same type as Leninor Garvedian, with more energy than sense."

"You judge your Captals harshly—Captal."

"Not *judge,* Telo. *Understand.* And not yet as thoroughly as I'd like, but more and more as time goes by. I have so much work to do, I can't possibly cower inside my Wards, flinching at every sound, waiting to be assassinated." Precisely what she'd done for almost a whole day—not something she cared to admit.

Telomir gave a long sigh. "You *will* be careful, won't you?"

"Of course. Now, tell me your news."

"What?" He blinked, taking a moment to reorganize his thoughts. "At least it may get you out of Ryka Court for a while. But the decision about what to do is yours, naturally."

"What to do about *what?* Out with it, Telo."

"There's something strange going on up north. Aside from Falundir's old place burning down in Sheve Dark, there've been reports of Wraithenbeasts across half the Wraithen Mountains." He waited for a reaction; when she offered none, he continued, "It had to come up sooner or later. Fear of Wraithenbeasts, I mean. The last of the old mountain Wards are finally gone—I'm astonished any lasted as long as they did, with no one to renew them—and it might be that the wolves and kyyos are free now to hunt the herds anytime they like. But one report has it that a twenty-foot grizzel got its throat torn out. No pack of wolves is stupid enough to attack a grizzel. A hundred miles from that sighting, a silverback was found with its legs ripped off. There've been at least five decapitated kyyos—"

"—all completely unnatural occurrences," Cailet finished. "Predators would have eaten the prey. These were meant to be found. How reliable are the witnesses?"

"In most cases, very. One of the kyyos was found by Fiella Mikleine, and you know she's the last person to succumb to hallucinations or hysteria. A wheatfield has more imagination than Fiella."

"So I'm to go up there and see what's what." It was all so simple. The Captal would stroll on in and solve any problem with a wave of her hand. She would call magic on command and at their convenience, the Council's very own tame Mage who performed on request, no applause or gratuities necessary.

She kicked herself mentally. It wasn't their fault they saw the old Mage Guardians in her, a tradition of Captals centuries ago. The new young Captal was a living symbol of the old days, when Wards and spells protected Lenfell. And if these Wraithenbeast reports were true—

Telo was saying, "I spoke with Fiella myself about the dead kyyo. She said when she found it, there was a strange feeling all around—as if she were being watched by something in a darkness she couldn't see, only feel. Something waiting to get her."

"She felt it as a Mage?"

"Not exactly. You know her, not a scrap of whimsy, doesn't even have nightmares like the rest of us."

"Do you?" Cailet asked, intrigued.

"Don't *you?*" he countered.

Not if there was a light left burning in her bedroom. The legacy of Gorsha's Wards: the Mage Captal was afraid of the dark.

"Forgive me," Telomir said at once. "That was unconscionably rude."

"What did Fiella sense?" Cailet asked quietly.

After a moment's hesitation, he said, "She compared it to the way she felt when she was ten years old, and went with her mother to Ryka Court when the Scholars were pleading Leninor's case. She saw Auvry Feiran halfway down a corridor—and wanted to run like hell."

Cailet gave a shrug to indicate that the reference didn't disturb her. It did—*Why is he so horrifying to everyone?* Anniyas *was the monster!*—but she was damned if she'd own up to it. "I'd like you to come back to The Waste with me, Telo, if you would."

"That's what I like about you, Captal. You don't *tell,* you *ask,* just as if I weren't a man."

"Oh, it's easy enough to do when I know for a fact you'd come with me whether I wanted you to or not. Is there anything else I should know about this?"

"I've told you everything I'm aware of. And now that *you* know, you can think about it for exactly one day. Because tomorrow night we're all going out to give Collan the finest Birthingday dinner he ever had."

"And you're not even going to hint at where, are you?"

"I love surprises." He grinned, and suddenly—though they were very little alike to look at—he reminded Cailet of his father.

She couldn't help grinning back. "I *hate* surprises."

"In the Captal business, you'd best get used to them."

9

CAILET entered the hospital room just as Tarise was brushing out Sarra's long golden hair. Any worries she'd had about her sister's health were soothed away by the excitement in Sarra's eyes and the color in her cheeks. She wore a richly subtle outfit that blended four shades of silvery-blue: shirt, tunic, loose trousers, and fringed shawl.

"Sarra, you look beautiful."

"Nice try, but we all know better." She plucked at the folds of her tunic. "I used to look pregnant. Now I just look fat."

"You look *beautiful,*" Tarise said firmly, adding, "Shut up," when Sarra opened her mouth to disagree. "And so does Cailet. And so, truly told, do I."

"And so will Lusira," Cailet remarked wryly. "But don't tell me you actually approve of my hair, Tarise."

"It's getting long enough to curl a bit. If you let it grow to Sarra's length, it'd be—" She broke off, and for just a moment, imagining Cailet with Sarra's wealth of blonde hair, Tarise came close to the truth. A puzzled frown shadowed hazel eyes, and tension thinned her lips. But as soon as it was there, the expression was gone. Cailet hid a smile for Wards that Gorsha had constructed around herself and Sarra long ago. No one would ever see past those Wards who did not already know the truth—or, as in Collan's case, a version of it.

"Long hair?" Cailet shook her head. "I don't have the right face. Too many angles."

Tarise considered critically, then sighed. "Well, maybe. But at least you might try it one of these days." As the hour chimed somewhere in the distance, she added, "Hurry, we'll be late. Here's your wrap, Sarra, and don't you dare take it off until we're indoors."

"I didn't know we were going *out*doors," Cailet remarked. "What's Telo got planned, anyway? A dinner cruise on the lake? That would be fun, I've never done that before."

It turned out to be nothing so mundane. In fact, it turned out not even to be on Ryka.

They assembled in Telomir's suite as requested. Lusira and Elomar—in matching velvets of Healer's green—were already there. So was Rillan Veliaz, Tarise's husband, wearing formal clothes with an elegance that belied his grumbles about how uncomfortable they were. When the ladies' beauty and the men's distinction had been given their due, they all sat around drinking wine, nibbling cheese and crackers, speculating on Telomir's plans for the evening (he grinned and shook his head at all suggestions), and waiting for Collan.

Last to arrive, the guest of honor was well and truly surprised. "You said dinner in your rooms with Falundir," he complained.

"I lied," said Telomir. "Come on, we're already late, thanks to you."

Two carriages were waiting in a courtyard. These

took them to a bookbindery in the city. Cailet, seated beside Telo and opposite Sarra and Collan, gave a start when she recognized the shop. "Telo, you can't be serious."

"Never more so. Come along, children," he urged, shooing them through the shop doors. "Gorynel's Griddle awaits!"

"Gorynel's Griddle," indeed!

Gorsha, darling, I hope the food and wines are so wonderful that you really, truly, sincerely regret being dead.

You're a cruel woman, Cailet Ambrai.

Within the bookbindery—now owned by the Ostin Web, Telomir informed them—was a Ladder to St. Eskanto's Shrine at Wyte Lynn Castle. The shrine, too, had been taken over by the Ostins; the ancient Votary turned out to be the great-uncle of Tiva Senison, Lady Lilen's first husband. He ushered them through the silent shrine, which was in infinitely better condition than the first time Cailet had seen it, and out to the street. Another pair of carriages transported them to a lovely old residential block right next to the main keep. As they assembled once again outside a porticoed entry, Collan regarded Telomir with real admiration.

"You've got style, Telo, I'll give you that. Not many people will travel two thousand miles for dinner."

Humph. My son the connoisseur. He probably couldn't get reservations in Firrense.

Cailet giggled, earning a baffled glance from the man whose father had just maligned him. As she accepted Telo's arm and escort into the restaurant, her amusement turned to awe.

The exterior of Gorynel's Griddle—venerable gray stone and a tasteful trio of columns—gave no indication of the opulence of the interior. A quick count of tables (only fifteen in a large room) and calculation of the cost of the decor told Cailet that the prices here would be atrocious. The walls were hung with crimson velvet draperies. The chairs were upholstered in pewter-gray silk. Crystal so dazzling it hurt the eyes competed for lamplight with gilt flatware and the finest Rine porcelain plates, all arranged atop snowy linens embroidered with a pattern of

St. Gorynel's Thorn Tree on the tablecloths and the Desse
Blood's Scroll on the napkins.

*Cailet, my darling, when it's discovered who's re-
sponsible for this travesty, will you please do me the favor
of casting on them a little spell I know? Nothing taxing,
just the occasional disfiguring genital warts and a suppurating sore or two. . . .*

That's disgusting. Where's your sense of humor? She
sat in the chair Telo held out for her and unfurled a crimson linen napkin across her lap.

*I am—or was—First Sword of the Mage Guardians,
not a theme idea for a dinner dump!*

I bet your son is part-owner, she teased. *A tribute
to you, dear. Now hush up so I can pay attention to the
conversation.*

As it happened, the Griddle was yet another Ostin
venture, the shared inspiration of Lady Lilen and her new
husband. Telo explained the circumstances after ordering
their meal.

"They really will end up owning most of Lenfell,
especially now that Lilen has the canniest of minds to
bounce ideas off." He chuckled. "Who'd suspect that a
fusty old Scholar like Kanto Solingirt would have a knack
for business? Anyway, this used to be an Assembly residence. It came up for sale last autumn when the Council
got rid of a lot of property—"

"We didn't make as much as we hoped on any of it
either," Sarra put in. "A lot of people practically stole
some of the best houses and farms on Lenfell."

"But the Treasury won't have to pay for upkeep anymore," Col reminded her. "That's a few million saved
right there. And it warms my soul to know that several
thousand flunkies won't be living like Grand Duchesses
off the rest of us from now on."

Cailet pretended horror. "You mean they'll have to
get honest work and pay for their own food and lodging?
Collan, you're heartless."

"And you adore me that way," he responded, grinning. "And *I* adore Lady Lilen. This whole venture was
designed to annoy First Daughter, wasn't it?"

Not to mention me. *And here all these years I thought Lilen had at least a few tender feelings for me—*

If she knew you were still rattling around inside my skull, I shudder to think of the scold I'd have to listen to! I'll bet she has plenty to say to you, even now.

Telomir was laughing. "Geria's fit to be tied. One of the Agrenir nieces officially owns it, but it can be traced, rather tortuously, back to the Ostin Web."

Lusira sipped wine and looked amused. "Lady Lilen is *still* cautious about revealing all her holdings?"

"Lady Lilen is perhaps the most cautious woman in the world."

Not to mention the most annoying. I wish Kanto joy of her.

As the various courses began to arrive, Cailet relaxed in the presence of friends—and the absence of Ryka Court. Only twice did the conversation grow awkward, and Cailet herself was responsible both times.

They were between courses when a group of Importances entered the restaurant. Recognizing so many famous faces from woodcuts in the broadsheets, they came over at once. After introductions were performed—the Mayor of Domburron, two local Justices, and their husbands—and fulsome greetings given, Cailet assumed that would be that. But the Mayor was a Dombur Blood, and because of the "shocking recent events" shared by her relative, she felt entitled to discuss Sarra's loss. The others had the sensitivity to be embarrassed, which deterred Vellerin Dombur not one whit. Collan, thank all the Saints, had five minutes ago descended to the cellar with Elomar, Rillan, and the wine steward to view the vintages.

"Such a tragedy, Lady Sarra, so disheartening—but you're young and strong, I'm sure you'll have a dozen children." Her sapphire-blue eyes radiated sympathy. "Still, nothing can replace a First Daughter."

Tarise turned so stiff with outrage that she visibly trembled. Lusira's hands clenched around the tablecloth, endangering dishes and crystal as the material bunched and stretched. Telomir looked ready to shove his fist down the Mayor's skinny throat if that was what it took to shut her up. Cailet was simply stunned that anyone could be so tactless. Sarra sent them all a brief, silencing glance, and said quietly, "Thank you for your concern."

"We're *all* concerned for you, my dear—your presence on the Council is a breath of fresh air. My cousin Irien often writes to me, and he says that very thing, a breath of fresh air. I hope you're recovering quickly and that you're not too terribly devastated."

Their young waiter was practically weeping with mortification. He tried and tried to catch Mayor Dombur's eye, but could not. Not yet experienced enough at his craft to have learned the art of graceful extraction from an awkwardness, good manners prohibited him from being direct. Cailet, already furious for Sarra's sake, began to be terrified that Collan would return in the middle of some further relentless rudeness. He'd take the woman apart piece by piece and put her together again inside out. A satisfying exercise, certainly, but scarcely politic.

So, with the privileges of Mage Captal, Cailet interrupted the next intrusive commiseration with, "We mustn't keep you from your dinner. The food is wonderful—Lady Lilen Ostin's own favorite recipes, I'm told."

It was not a happy choice of subject. Vellerin Dombur's narrow shoulders stiffened. "*Lilen Ostin* is responsible for this establishment?" She glanced around, extravagantly arched brows hiking up another inch on her forehead, nearly to the brim of her plumed velvet hat. "No wonder it's so common. Good evening, Captal, Lady Sarra."

The Justices attempted apologetic smiles before scurrying off with the Mayor—out of the restaurant, rather than to a table for dinner.

"Wonderful," Cailet muttered. "I've done it again."

Telo poured himself a glass of wine and gulped a good half of it before saying, "Lilen outbid the Domburs for some Council property near the Kenrokeshir border."

Shaking her head, she replied, "No, it's not the land, Telo—or at least not completely. I clean forgot about the Feud."

"The what?" Sarra asked.

Telo was nodding. "That's right. Her aunt, Lilen's uncle, no dower. No children either."

"How'd they manage that?" Tarise asked, distracted from fury by the ever-fascinating permutations of Ostin Web.

Telomir grinned. "Amazing, isn't it? A childless Ostin!"

"No, not that! The part about no dowry."

"She was a First Daughter, wanted to be an Advocate, live her own life, all that sort of thing. The Domburs had other plans for her. She worked her way through school because the family wouldn't pay for it and then set up practice in Renig—"

"Combel," Cailet corrected.

"Combel," Telomir acknowledged. "Anyway, she met a handsome young Ostin, they fell in love, and she refused his share of the Dower Fund—which for any Ostin male is fairly substantial. Said she could provide for him and their children without stealing from his family. When *her* family took the Ostins to court for nonpayment of dower, she defended the suit—successfully, I might add."

"And besides all *that*," Cailet added, "before she died two years ago she gave Alin Ostin all the right papers for unchallenged passage through both Domburr Castle and Domburron."

"Ladders," Sarra said succinctly.

Cailet lifted her wineglass to her sister. "Exactly. The upshot of the whole Feud is that no Dombur has willingly spoken to an Ostin in sixty years."

"Let alone spoken *well* of one," Telo finished.

Sarra gave a shrug. "Whatever the reason, you got rid of her, and that's all I care about. There must be more pleasant things to discuss. Somebody think of something quick, I see a certain redheaded Minstrel with a vicious temper coming back from the wine cellar."

Tarise took up the conversational gauntlet. "I meant to compliment you earlier, *Domni* Telomir, on how very dashing you look in that cloak."

He preened the lavish folds of velvet draped over the back of his chair—so dark a purple it was almost black.

"Like it?" he asked complacently. "I almost hate for spring to come, when it'll be too warm to wear it."

"Never pass up a really well-cut cloak," Collan said, resuming his seat beside Sarra. "Women love 'em."

"Another woman is all you lack," Lusira teased.

"Didn't say I *wanted* one. I just like it when they regret that Sarra snagged and bagged me first."

Rillan Veliaz choked slightly on his wine. Even after nearly a year's association with Collan he was sometimes shocked when Sarra didn't even bat an eyelash at the freedom of his manners. Cailet sent Tarise's husband a wry smile.

Telomir, grinning his appreciation, asked Sarra, "He's always like this, I take it?"

She gave a shrug. "Only in front of people he wants to impress. Otherwise he's as meek as a lamb. Am I right, dearest?" she cooed.

"You're *always* right, O Font of Wisdom," he answered in the same tone.

"That's a new one," Lusira remarked, and glanced at Elomar. "Husband, make a note."

"That's cheating," Collan reproved. "Think up your own."

Sarra gave a long sigh. "Refresh my memory. Why, exactly, did I marry you?"

He turned wide, shocked blue eyes on her. "You really want me to say? Right here in public?"

The arrival of the main course spared her the necessity of a reply. Wrapping herself in sublime silence, she applied herself to roast lamb with minted applesauce and fried strips of spiced potato.

The food was well worth attending to. Cailet happily plied fork and knife as the conversation danced merrily around her. Telomir, who had attended Lady Lilen's recent wedding to Kanto Solingirt, gave them a full description of the outdoor ceremony and its accompanying feast for six hundred, revealing his personal suspicions that Lilen had decided to marry again only because she needed a million new things for the rebuilding of Ostinhold, and wedding presents were the easiest and cheapest way to get them.

Cailet glanced up from her decimated plate. "Speaking of which, I should bring a gift of some kind. What does a Captal usually give a Mage when he gets married?"

"You're going to Ostinhold?" Lusira asked. "I thought you'd spend some time at Roseguard with the rest of us."

Sarra's whole expression changed, brows knotting over black eyes and lips thinning dangerously. Cailet wanted to draw back as her sister pounced. "The Wraithenbeasts. Cailet, have you lost your mind?"

Thus an innocent question about what to give the newlyweds became Cailet's second mistake of the evening. Someday, she told herself, she'd learn that Sarra's instincts were as inevitable—and as perilous—as an angry Warrior Mage's Battle Globe. "Sarra," she began.

Collan interrupted her blundering attempt at an explanation. "Have you ever even been near the Wraithenwood, Cai? Ever listened to the wind blow through the Dead White Forest like a million trapped Wraiths screaming for freedom?"

"I have," Rillan said suddenly, and Tarise regarded her husband with surprise. "A long time ago. I was up north of Longriding buying a stud for the Roseguard stables. A few ranch hands and I went sightseeing—young studs ourselves, tough and fearless—until we heard that wind. Fifty miles away, still the howling was as loud as if we stood in the middle of the Forest. All I knew was I had to get out of there. I rode that poor horse near to foundering."

Tarise's eyes were wide. "You never said anything—"

"It's not something I enjoy remembering. Even the water feels dead there. You put your hand into it, and—" He shrugged. "It's not just cold. There's no *life* to it. No fish, no insects, no moss on the rocks, no smell of the snow it melted from. . . ."

"I'll be going with her," Telo said.

Col ignored him. "You're not setting foot near that place, Cai. Rillan's got the right of it—and he was fifty miles away from the worst."

For a wonder, Gorsha was silent inside Cailet's head; so were Alin and Tamos Wolvar. But Lusath Adennos—or the portion of her mind she labeled as such; he wasn't the sheer Presence that Gorsha was—spoke with diffident concern. *I was never there, but I heard of it from a dozen or more who went to take a look for themselves—my dear, I comprehend your need to help, but I think this exceedingly foolhardy of you.*

Cailet politely acknowledged the warning and said aloud, "I know more about the place and the Wraithen-beasts than any of you—even you, Col." It was true, in a way. Lingering somewhere in her acquired memories was enough information about the Dead White Forest to choke a Scholar. The same was true of Mage Globes, Ladders, swordskill, Wraiths generally and the Wraithenwood spe-cifically, and a host of other topics. She was a walking library. But there were also odd gaps, silences, omissions, hazy rifts of ignorance. Her own fault; had she not at-tempted to steal an unborn child's magic, she would have been a true Captal.

But, as Sarra had reminded her, she was the only Captal they had.

"Bequest or no Bequest—" Col began.

"She must go."

This from Elomar; volumes in three words. Cailet didn't know whether to be grateful for his support or an-noyed at what amounted to a decree.

Though Collan liked and respected the Healer, his answer was strained with the effort not to snarl. "You probably have some perfectly logical Mage Guardian rea-son, but that doesn't change that fact that it's dangerous up there even for somebody like me. For a Mageborn—"

"She must go," Elomar repeated.

"Absolutely not."

As the men argued over what she would or wouldn't do, she began to wonder when they'd remember that she was sitting at the same table. She also wondered why she seemed destined to be surrounded by men who thought they knew what she knew better than she did. Saints, she *lived* with four of them inside her skull—she didn't need more of them nattering away right in front of her face.

And whatever happened to manners, anyway, and decent deference, and respectful submission?

"I'll be going with her," Telomir repeated testily.

"You're a *Prentice* Mage," Col retorted.

"Who's been Working magic longer than you've been alive and knows more spells than you do songs."

A scowl angrily conceded the point, but Collan wasn't through yet. "You don't know what it's like up there. I do."

"Fine," Telo said pleasantly. "Come with us." Fully expecting, of course, that Sarra would either forbid it or that Collan himself would decline, wishing to be with Sarra while she recovered her full strength.

Telo didn't understand the ins and outs of their marriage any more than Rillan did. Col didn't even glance at Sarra; Sarra said nothing to her husband.

"Fine," Collan replied, deliberately using Telomir's word and tone of voice. "I'll be there."

Telo looked so stunned it was almost funny. Cailet was forced to admire how quickly he rallied, and the accuracy of his next arrow. "You have Sarra to consider."

"Oh, shut up, the pair of you!" Tarise snapped. "Collan Rosvenir, I never heard anything so silly. Go to The Waste, when you've got a whole city full of responsibilities waiting for you at Roseguard? And that's not even considering the duty you owe Sarra!"

"He knows his duties to me very well, thank you," Sarra felt constrained to respond in her husband's defense.

But Tarise was on a tear, and not listening. "And as for you, Telomir Renne—why should rural gossip make you chase off into the back of the beyond—"

"It's not gossip."

"But what could you possibly do against Wraithenbeasts?"

"He can't," Cailet said. By their startled expressions, they *had* forgotten she was present. Making a mental note to work on creating a more definite impression—a Captal ought not be overlooked, after all—she gave them all a deliberately sunny smile and finished, "But *I* can."

"You won't get the chance," Col said through his

teeth. "You're not going. With us or without us, you are *not* going."

Elomar opened his mouth, presumably to reiterate his simple statement for a third time—which would start everything all over again. Lusira shot him a quelling look and said firmly, "Discuss it later. This is supposed to be a celebration, not a debate."

"Thank you," Sarra said. "We are now going to change the subject. Any suggestions?"

Only the determination of all parties—and liberal application of vintage wines—gradually converted the evening back to a pleasant one. But when they'd returned to Ryka Court by carriage and Ladder and carriage again, Sarra took Cailet aside in the hall outside her quarters.

"You don't understand," she murmured. "I've lost so many people I loved—Agatine, Orlin, Elom, Alin and Val, Taig, so many others—I couldn't control the risks they took."

Cailet, repressing annoyance that Sarra thought she could control *her,* said reasonably, "But I have to do this. You know I do—just as I had to do something about Anniyas's Wards."

"That's just it! I practically forced you to investigate—I could have stopped it, but I let you take the risk. I lost my First Daughter because of it. I could have lost you, too. If I let you do this—" Her voice thickened with tears. "If anything happened to you—"

To the Mage Captal, you mean, Cailet thought, ashamed but thinking it anyway.

"You're the only sister I have," Sarra whispered.

"Oh, Sasha—" She regretted the rare endearment the instant she spoke it; its very infrequency made it all the more powerful. Sarra trembled, her breath catching on a sob. "Listen to me, my dearest," Cailet said, suddenly feeling that she was the elder sister and Sarra the younger. "I learned from what happened with those Wards. I learned not to be so arrogant. Not to think I know everything. I'll be careful. But I have to look into this—because if Glenin's found a way to summon the Wraithenbeasts, then you were right about what the Malerrisi want. She can ask what she likes of the Council in exchange for

the freedom to come out of their castle and defeat the
Wraithenbeasts—and then do exactly as they please."

Not that she believed this. It was too soon. Glenin
would wait until her son was old enough for a prominent
role that would set him up as the next First Lord—not just
of the Malerrisi but of all Lenfell. She knew it with instincts as strong and sure as Sarra's—which she earnestly
hoped were clouded by emotion, or she'd realize Cailet
wasn't telling the whole truth.

"I'll be careful," she repeated. "And I won't let Collan come along. I'll spell him into a stupor if I must."
When this promise produced no difference in Sarra's
shivering, she added gently, "Do you think I'd take him
away from you, when he needs you so much?"

It was just unexpected enough to astonish. "*He*
needs—?"

"Of course. Oh, Sasha, didn't you know?" Cailet
smiled. "Most women *never* see in a man's eyes what's
always in his when he looks at you." She put a bracing
arm around her sister. "Now, go wash your face and don't
worry. The only place he's going is Roseguard."

Gratitude quivered over Sarra's lamplit face, but then
she shook her head. "You make sure he's safe, while you
go off to do Saints know what—"

"I'll have Telo," Cailet reminded her. "He'll come
with me. He may be 'just' a Prentice, but remember who
his father was."

"Don't risk yourself," Sarra pleaded one last time,
wiping her eyes. "I couldn't bear it if anything happened
to you."

"I'll be fine." As she gave Sarra a nudge down the
hallway, she hoped she was telling the truth.

10

THERE was yet one thing Cailet had to do before she left Ryka Court. It was not the construction of a spell to keep Collan from following her, or yet another Ward to add to his collection set by Gorynel Desse. But it did have to do with him, her belated Birthingday gift to him in a way, and an apology that she would not be taking him with her to the Wraithenwood.

Anniyas's leftover Wards were gone, and at terrible cost. But Cailet had told Sarra the fact of it: she *had* learned from what had happened. And now she was ready to face the last Malerrisi taint at Ryka Court.

So, at just past Fourth on the second morning of the new year 970, she threaded her way through a combination of simply physical and distinctly magical mechanisms to the white box of a room where Collan had suffered for nine long days. Upon reaching it, she unWorked every scrap of magic that permeated the walls and floor and pain stake. It took all Tamos Wolvar knew about Mage Globes, and all Gorynel Desse knew about spells and Wards and even Folding, and all Cailet had learned about caution, but she did it. Almost, she was fascinated by the complex arrangement of Globes within Globes, conjurations that triggered secondary and even tertiary magic—*almost.* She knew what had been done here, to Collan and to others. She could not help but know: their agony echoed in the magic. The perversion of power that fed off pain sickened her, but she had learned from unWorking Anniyas's Wards something she should have learned at the Octagon Court nearly a year ago. Her emotions were prey, and she could not give in to them and hope to face down Malerrisi magic.

It was weak now, hungry; its last meal, the glut of Collan's anguish, had faded, insufficient sustenance for all the elaborate workings woven through its walls. Each one gnawed at her. Some arcane spell that feasted on physical pain discovered the wound at her breast, and for a few moments she experienced the force of Glenin's magic all over again. But she knew she must not give in to it, and so drew on the strength of the Others within her. Denied the nourishment of remembered suffering, the spell died. So did all the rest, one by one, as Cailet forbade herself to respond even to the most hideously insistent of them. If she did not feel, they could not harm her.

At last the stark white walls were drained of magic, revealing nothing more sinister than a cold, leaky, unlit cellar. Cailet pulled the pain stake from its anchoring hole in the gray cobbled floor—only a wooden stick now, splintered and dry. Wearily climbing back upstairs, she fed the thing to her fireplace and watched it burn.

"Well, Gorsha?" she murmured as the last flames died to embers in the hearth. "Will I be a fit Captal one day after all?"

I never doubted it. But don't forget those books Dombur promised to have delivered. It's a long time since I had a look at the Code of Malerris. *And you and Telo will need something to read on board ship.*

She sat up abruptly. "What? We'll go by Ladder! Ryka Court to Ambrai, Bard Hall to the Ostin house in Longriding—"

No. The Code *is so made that taking it through a Ladder wipes all its pages clean. I learned that the hard way, a long time ago.*

"Oh," she said, inadequately. "By ship, then. But I hate being out of reach on a—" Suddenly she smiled, and shook her head. "You're determined that I'll have some quiet time, aren't you? Someplace where nobody can get at me, no Ladders and no Council and not even any other Mages except Telo."

Lacking Falundir's cottage, the next best thing is a sea voyage. Enjoy it, my dear.

"I'll try. The first few days I always lose my balance and knock into things—and for half a week after landing, I rock back and forth as if there was still a deck underfoot! Well, at least I don't get seasick."

A little gift I gave you and Sarra when you were born.

"Among others that you don't care to mention just yet?" Rising from her chair, she went into the bedroom and dragged her traveling case from the closet. While folding clothes, she continued, "How about the fact that I knew Lusira's pregnant when she didn't even know it herself? And Sarra's twins? What about *that?*"

The former was a talent your father possessed— which was why it was essential to keep him far from your mother once you were conceived. Before she could demand further explanation, he went on, *As for the twins— they are a possibility, not a promise.*

"But I *saw* them."

You saw many other things, too.

Soberly, she nodded. "I could have become all those things. But what scares me most is that I'd do *nothing* with my life. Could that really happen?"

All things are possible, Caisha. Discerning the prob-able *and working either to achieve it or avoid it—that's the real trick.*

"How can anyone tell? How do you know that if you do one thing, it won't lead to the very result you want to avoid? Or that if you do something else that you think might be wrong, it's the exact thing that will get you where you want to be?"

He responded with a wry chuckle. *That, my dearest, is called "living." All you can do is the best you* can *do, and hope it turns out all right in the end.*

"You're not very comforting. Or helpful," she complained.

Probably not, he replied blithely.

Cailet deliberately turned to the dressing-table mirror and made a face at her reflection. "'Probably.' Very funny."

11

A week later, Cailet was on the deck of the cargo ship *Amity,* watching Renig grow from child's toy to townscape on the horizon. The captain hoped to make the stop as brief as possible; Cailet admired his ambition. In the hold, treated with more care than the human passengers, were fifteen fractious Tillinshir grays—seven mares, five fillies, one stallion, and two colts—destined for Maurgen Hundred. Lady Sefana, having perfected her Dapple-backs, was expanding her business. She had successfully bid on the best horses in the disbanded Ryka Legion's stables, animals bred for military purposes that would, she hoped, add extra fire and strength to her own breed. Fire these grays possessed, truly told; Cailet estimated it would take two hours to coax just the stud down the gang-plank. Maybe the *Amity* would sail for Roseguard with tomorrow's tide as scheduled, and maybe not.

Cailet hoped Sarra wouldn't fret too much if the ship was late getting to Roseguard. Filling half the hold was her new furniture—in a manner of speaking. Timber from Shellinkroth, bolts of cloth from Bleynbradden, and crates of brass hardware from Tillinshir would be used by crafters in Sheve to make everything from beds to desks to butcher blocks for the kitchen. By purchasing the raw materials from other Shirs, the Slegin Web established new and lucrative trade partnerships. But by hiring local artisans to do the actual work, Sheve itself would benefit. It had all been Collan's suggestion—and who would have suspected that the footloose Minstrel would be so canny about commerce? Let alone that he'd throw himself so wholeheartedly into the masculine role of making a home for his Lady and her children?

Cailet intended to do some shopping in Renig for a few additions to the Roseguard shipment, and thus was glad of the extra time the *Amity* would be in port unload-ing the irritable grays. Instead of dashing around in frantic haste, she had time to saunter through town and browse for just the right items. Some local pottery, perhaps—nothing could challenge the elegance of Rine porcelain, of course, but she'd always thought the swirling iridescent glazes on Combel vases and bowls were more interesting, each one unique. She hoped to find some good sandjade carvings, too—and at this thought she smiled, for no one had equaled the skill of that strange old man who'd once lived in Crackwall Canyon.

She missed him. It was the most peculiar thing. Of all the friends and familiarities of her old life, what she longed for most was a cozy chat with a man who'd never been real. The substance of Gorynel Desse—Warrior Mage, First Sword, and Maker of two Captals—was in large part within her. But the one she missed was Rinnel, the wry old man who carved sandjade and told long, involved stories and taught her all sorts of fascinating things. From the burning of Ostinhold Lady Lilen had somehow rescued the pendant he'd carved for Cailet, and she wore it on special occasions as proudly as if it had been made of diamonds. For Gorynel Desse, she had great admiration and respect, even compassion; Rinnel, she loved.

But there was yet another aspect to him: the powerful, vigorous young Mage he had been in those last moments within the landscape of black glass, when he'd kissed her.

Gorsha had been conspicuously silent during the voyage. While she and Telomir worked on the books Irien Dombur had been reminded to relinquish, any difficulties of spelling or archaic phraseology were smoothly solved by Lusath Adennos. (Telo was initially astounded by her facility with language; she pretended it was part of the Bequest. For all she knew, it might very well be.) Not even the *Code of Malerris* woke Gorsha up—at least, not so Cailet noticed. Perhaps she was just too busy being alternately repelled and fascinated to register any reactions other than her own.

The *Code* amounted to an encyclopedia for ruling everything and everyone on Lenfell. From the begetting of children to their raising, from the testing of Mageborns to their education, from the simple spell that Warmed a teapot to the convoluted construction of a Net—all were laid out with bloodless precision. The orderly codification of magic was appealing; the unfeeling ruthlessness of its recommended applications was appalling.

They hadn't come anywhere near to reading it all, of course; there was too much of it, and too much that sickened. A few hours each day were all either of them could stand before turning with relief to other books. These included the never-finished *True History of The Waste War* by none other than Shen Escovor, Fourth Lord of Malerris from 767 to 779, and lover of Mage Captal Caitirin Bekke.

"Did they write it together?" Telo mused one evening. "It certainly spares neither side."

"I think they were working to find the truth," Cailet replied thoughtfully. "Once they had it, they'd tell everyone on Lenfell. The Mages and the Malerrisi would have to take their share of responsibility. It would all be out in the open. There'd probably be some persecution of Mageborns as heirs to the magic that destroyed so much, but when that was all over—"

"—it would end up pretty much as it is now," he finished, "with people realizing they *do* need magic. But, you know, I think they were after something even bigger. Reunification of the two Traditions."

"Dreamers," she shrugged.

"Is there anything in the Bequest that would give you any hints?" When she shook her head, he leaned back in his chair with a regretful sigh. "Pity."

"How can you say that?" Cailet demanded. "We haven't been through all the *Code* yet, but what we've read only confirms that everything they stand for is everything we hate most! What they admire, we loathe—what we hold sacred, they shit on!"

Telomir blinked in surprise. "I realize you have all the Generations of Captals' experience to draw on, which includes all their struggles against the Malerrisi. But a Mageborn is a Mageborn. Magic is magic. There's nothing inherently evil—"

"I know all that," she said impatiently. Springing to her feet, balance having adjusted days ago to the roll and pitch of the deck, she paced angrily about the tiny cabin. "In this theory, if you raise a Mageborn our way, she turns out 'good'—but if you raise her Malerrisi, she turns out 'bad.' It's all a matter of philosophy and education and instillation of belief."

"I'd agree with that," Telo said cautiously.

"So how do you account for Shen Escovor? Was he so much in love with Caitirin Bekke that he rejected the Malerrisi version of The Waste War?"

"They executed him because they thought he'd become one of us," Telo said slowly. Then, as low-voiced as if there were no Wards protecting them from listeners: "But that's not what this is about for you. What you really mean is how could a Mageborn trained in *our* ways turn to the Malerrisi."

She stumbled—telling herself it was due to a particularly vigorous lurch of the ship, and that only—grabbing for the back of a chair. "All right, you've got me," she said grimly. "If it happened to a Malerrisi like Escovor, it can happen to a Mage Guardian like Auvry Feiran. And if it happened once, it can happen again."

Dark eyes widened in shock. "Cailet—you can't possibly think that *Glenin* would forsake her training, her beliefs, the very thing that gives her the power she craves—"

"Holy Saints, you're as bad as Sarra! All you can see is that Glenin is wicked, selfish, ambitious, she could never in a million Generations understand the first thing about using magic to benefit anyone but herself!"

"So you believe that it's character and not education that determines how a Mageborn uses magic? If that's so, Captal, then you can trust no Guardian you don't personally know."

"I'm aware of that," she said steadily. "What I'm trying to discover is a way *to* know them all. And I'm very much afraid that I'll find it in *that*." She pointed to the *Code* lying on the table between them.

Telomir was silent a while before saying, "We must on occasion use the methods of our enemies. It's not admirable, or noble, but it *is* sometimes the only practical thing to do. Sometimes we can't choose."

"You're telling *me* that?" She almost laughed at him. "When did I choose to become Captal? Oh, don't look at me that way. I wouldn't give it up. But how do I know that I would've taken it in the first place, if anyone had offered me a choice?"

"It was necessary. *No one* had any choice. You can blame the Malerrisi for that. But not my father."

"As if all of this began last spring in Ambrai? Look at reality, Telo! Look what he did to me when I was born!

What he did to Sarra so she'd know nothing about me! As for Collan—who knows what's buried beneath those stacks of Wards? I offered to find out, you know. I asked him if he wanted me to get rid of them."

Was there the scantiest flare of panic in his eyes? "He didn't, of course."

"No. He is what he is, he's comfortable with it, and he figures Gorsha had good reason to do what he did. But you know what I think? I think this placid acceptance is another Ward. When Sarra miscarried, she worried that it might be some fault in her—or in Collan. I spoke with him about it in a general sort of way, and it never even occurred to him it might be something wrong with *him* instead of Sarra."

"It's not."

"I *know* that," she said impatiently. "The point is, Collan doesn't even wonder who his real family is. Whenever he does, he shrugs it off. Gorsha did that to him, I'm sure of it. To make sure nobody ever gets inside Col's head and finds out who and what he *really* is."

"Or what he might know? Do you think my father so dictatorial? So convinced of his own power and righteousness that he'd—"

This time she did laugh at his indignant defense of Gorsha. "You've just described him down to the way he tied his coif! And I tell you this, son-of-your-father—" She planted her fists on the table and leaned over, glaring at him without a trace of humor. "What *I* make of the Mage Guardians will be what *I* make of them. You've been pushing his program just now, haven't you? Don't think I didn't hear the wistfulness when you spoke of reunifying Mages and Malerrisi. It's not going to happen, Telo. Not while I'm Captal."

Unflinchingly, he responded, "Yet you have your own notions of 'rescuing' your sister from them. Hasn't it gotten through to you yet that she *is* the Malerrisi now? That she won't stop until she's Warden of the Loom?"

"What makes you think she isn't that already?"

Telomir looked shaken. "Do you know this?"

"Can you doubt it?" Cailet shrugged. "She's an Ambrai, a Feiran, and she has Anniyas's grandson. Of course she's First Lord by now."

"But she's not the real issue here. Don't you understand that the one you truly want to redeem is your father?"

"I understand why you'd think so. But you're wrong." Cailet sat down wearily and poured herself a cup of hot spiced lemonade. "He's the one who asked me to bring Glenin back. He doesn't need 'redemption.' He may have lived as a Malerrisi for twenty years, but he died a Mage Guardian."

"He *asked*—?"

"His Wraith did. I saw him. Talked with him. He loved me, and kept Glenin from killing me. That's how he died—saving me from her." She sipped at the lukewarm drink. "I have to try, I have to take every opportunity—this wasn't what she was meant to be, Telo, I *know* it!"

"And yet you say that character and not training determines the choice of how magic is used. Does it have to be one or the other? Truly told, Cailet, isn't it both?" He rose, looking down at her with pity in his eyes. "If so, I fear you're dooming yourself to a lifetime of disappointment—and foolish attempts to change everything Glenin is by heritage and training."

"It's *my* heritage, too."

Now he understood—and all at once he looked as if he would weep. "Cailet—oh, Cailet, is *that* what this is all about? Is it *yourself* you're afraid of? What have we done to you, child?"

"What had to be done, to hear everyone tell it." She ran both hands back through her hair, shook her head, and didn't bother wondering why Gorsha was silent within. "Don't worry so much, Telo. I just need the experience of doing things on my own—not the memories of what other people have done. In a way, I owe Anniyas for adding to my education with those Wards and visions. Everything I learn about magic teaches me something new about myself. It'll be all right. I just have a lot of learning yet to do."

The learning she had not done when she'd been Made

the Capital. Knowledge she had aplenty; the act of acquiring knowledge was her goal now. And one of the things she must learn was how to test the Mages she would teach, how to probe for power-greed. What could tempt them. If she found it in the *Code,* she'd use it. The only thing was, how far would such a technique—Malerrisi as it would be—tempt *her?*

Telomir placed a hand on her shoulder. Shock and pity had given way to compassion: the virtue of his father's Name Saint. "Cailet . . . forgive me. I didn't understand."

"It'll be all right," she repeated. "Why don't you go topside for a while? You could use some fresh air, and I could use a nap."

He nodded, pressing her shoulder gently, then left her. She lay down in the narrow bunk, closing her eyes. But it wasn't long before she turned her head to stare in mingled hunger and revulsion at the leather-bound bulk of the *Code of Malerris.*

12

BIRON Maurgen had come to Renig with four ranch hands to escort his mother's new horses to the Hundred. When he discovered Cailet on board the *Amity,* he instantly offered her the pick of whichever Tillinshir gray she wanted on the ride north. While he supervised the unloading of the animals—which took not two hours but four—Cailet tended to various errands in town. First she secured the *Code* and the rest of the books with Lenna Ostin in the strongbox of her law office, after Warding the volumes in eight layers ranging from the distracting to the gruesome. Then she bought a big rainbow-glazed bowl for Sarra and Collan, a stuffed velvet grizzel-bear for Lusira's and Elomar's baby, and sandjade mosaics of St. Alilen and St. Eskanto for the newlyweds at Ostinhold.

How she paid for all this brought up a sore point. The

Rille Name—all two hundred thirty-one of them—proudly acknowledged her as one of their own, as arranged long ago by Gorynel Desse. They'd produced a few Mageborns in the past, so it was remarkable but not incredible that one of them should become Captal. In their excitement at having such a notable in the family, they were all ready to share the income from their minuscule Web. Cailet spent two days composing a delicately worded letter of refusal to the First Daughter. She couldn't take their money. She wasn't truly one of them.

But neither could she agree to Sarra's plan that she take whatever she needed from the Slegin fortune. It felt like stealing from Riddon and Maugir and Jeymi, not to mention Sarra, Lady Agatine's designated heir. Had it been possible, she could have accepted what was rightfully hers: the inheritance of Ambrai. But she had no more access to it than Sarra did.

Elin Alvassy was now sole owner of everything the Ambrais had ever possessed. A goodly portion of it had been snapped up at bargain prices after the obliteration of the Ambrai Name. Recovery of these holdings was impossible; years in the law courts would result only in colossal fees for the Advocates and not a square inch of property or a cutpiece in compensation. Ambrai itself lay in ruins. The outlying farms would begin to produce income with this year's harvest, but all would go into rebuilding the city. Sarra had wanted to offer Elin free run of the Slegin Web—seized just a year ago by the Council and never dismantled—but that would have meant awkward explanations. Sisterhood in the Rising could not account for such extravagant generosity, and their Blood kinship could never be acknowledged.

Which was precisely Cailet's point when Sarra tried to give *her* access to whatever money she needed. They could never reveal their true Name or relationship. And how would it look if a Councillor was the sole support of the Mage Captal?

In the end, it turned out that Gorsha had anticipated the financial problem. When Allynis Ambrai's will was dug up in the Ryka Court Archives, the complexities of the Ambrai inheritance were detailed in all possible permutations. Even though nothing connected Gorynel Desse to it, his fingers were all over it. The date told the whole story: St. Gelenis's Day of 951, three days after Maichen Ambrai divorced Auvry Feiran. The will excised Glenin from the Ambrai line; even though by changing her Name to Feiran she relinquished all inheritance rights, still Allynis wanted to make official her expulsion from the family. Failing the survival of Maichen and Sarra, everything went to the Alvassys.

After the destruction of Ambrai, Elinar Alvassy and her husband Piergan Rille took their orphaned grandchildren to an obscure holding in Domburronshir. There, in 952, Elinar had written her own will, in her own hand, witnessed by four Advocates and three Votaries sympathetic to the Rising. This document assigned to Cailet Rille ownership of an iron foundry in Brogdenguard. Part of Piergan's dower—he who had lent Cailet his family's Name—it had become Elinar's property, and she was free to dispose of it as she wished. That it pleased her to deed it to some obscure relation of her husband's—a child she had never even seen, who had grown up a fosterling at Ostinhold—was explained in her own words: *"It is my desire that this girl, who is practically an orphan, attain upon her majority the financial independence that will allow her to pursue her own path in life, beholden to no one, not even her Name."*

Not the Name of Ambrai, nor the Name of Rille. Yes, Gorsha's fine manipulative hand had guided both documents. Cailet hadn't shared Sarra's surprise when the foundry's provenance revealed a Desse connection. Four Generations ago, scandals of unfair trading practices among some of the Webs had resulted in regulations demanding full disclosure of all holdings. (It also resulted in diversification of the Ostin ventures; now, a century later, only Lady Lilen and her chief steward knew exactly what the Web owned under what Names.) The Rennes owned the iron mine that supplied the foundry; because Gorsha's mother married a Renne, the Desses had to sell the foundry. Desse to Rille to Alvassy—and now finally to Cailet.

The upshot was that she had a tidy income from the

foundry, still stoked by ore from the same Renne mine—which, having been Orlin's dower when Agatine married him, now belonged to the Slegin Web, and Sarra. In these more liberal economic times, Cailet was free to sell the foundry to Sarra, which she intended to do for funds to build her school. And sell at a fair price, she was determined, not the inflated one her sister would doubtless try to sneak past her. For now, however, she had a healthy balance in the Renig branch of the St. Nialos Mercantile Bank—another Ostin venture, of course.

"Sure you don't want to invest in my firm?" Lenna teased as she escorted Cailet from her new law offices near the Council House.

"You're just feeling poverty-stricken after buying all this," Cailet retorted with a grin, waving a hand to indicate the fine oak-paneled foyer.

"Never more truly told! I had to outbid First Daughter for it." She paused to tell a clerk to inform her next client that she was on her way. "Geria wanted this place because she knew *I* wanted it. I can't even bring myself to hint at how much I had to borrow from Mother to pay for it. But once I'm firmly established as Renig's leading Advocate—with appropriately outrageous fees for my brilliant services!—I'll be all right."

"That'll take about six weeks," Cailet remarked. "I had a look at your secretary's appointment book—you'll be lucky to find time to eat dinner."

They stopped short of the front door, an extravagance in cedar and stained glass, that was being removed so a dignified oaken replacement could be hung. Cailet squinted at the bright window with its Council sigil, and gave a start at reading the rhyme along the bottom.

> *The Sky, the Stars, the Moons, the Sun—*
> *Before them all: the Name of Lunne.*

"Modest, don't you think?" Lenna asked.

That aspect had gone right past her. For the rest—no, it would be too much to ask. But she had to find out. "Not *Inara* Lunne? 'Tried by Seventh, convicted by Eighth, and executed by Ninth' Justice Lunne?"

"Former Justice—" Lenna laughed at Cailet's broad grin, and because she'd heard the tale she added, "—whom last you saw slumped over in blissful if unwilling slumber!"

At last all was attended to, and Cailet met Biron and Telomir for the ride north. Though the Tillinshir grays were a bit more spirited than any of them were used to, nobody fell off, and Telo even began thinking about purchasing the mare he rode.

They were eight days getting to Maurgen Hundred, through the most hospitable terrain The Waste had to offer. Cailet and Telo alone could have done it in two by Folding the road, and as they traveled through mile after mile of prickly scrub jooper trees, she wished they had. The scenery wasn't exactly inspiring, and the horses shied at every spindly windblown skeleton of sage. Stupid name for a plant—she could see no wisdom in making one's home where the sun shriveled new leaves as soon as they unfolded and the wind shoveled up roots.

The sagebrush didn't have much choice. The people did. So why did they live here? She knew her homeshir's history: devastated by a war between rival Mageborns, once The Waste was confirmed habitable again thousands left kinder climes to establish farms and ranches here. Some came for the challenge of it—and challenge there had been aplenty. Some came because their families had flourished here before The Waste War—though first sight of the ancestral lands must have been a shock. Some came because there was money to be made from the rebuilding. But Cailet couldn't imagine anyone coming for love of the land.

Still, the Ostins and Maurgens and Obrcics and Senisons and all their breed did love the place. Even those who left for one reason or another, professing to loathe it here—she was thinking of Alin and Val now, and Taig—never called anywhere else *home*. There was pride in being a Waster, in not only surviving but thriving in a harsh and ugly land.

Look at Biron over there—inhaling the dry, dusty air as if it were the sweetest of perfumes, commenting enthusiastically on a hilltop vista or the formation of sandstone pillars carved by wind and acid storms. Cailet had been born here, too, but whereas she had a Waster's disdain for those who had it easy elsewhere, she found nothing to love about this ravaged Shir but the people who lived in it.

She felt this even more strongly when they reached Maurgen Hundred. The hospitality she received had nothing to do with being Mage Captal. She was welcomed for herself by friends who had known her forever. She spent a relaxing evening catching up on all the latest gossip and slept more soundly than she ever did at Ryka Court. Moreover, she slept without Wards—but, as always, with a lamp burning at her bedside, to guard her from the depths of the dark.

She rose early. Refreshed by a morning bath—the Maurgen water-filtration system was the best available, rendering even acid-storm rain fit for washing and drinking—she wandered down to the kitchen. The cook exclaimed with pleasure on seeing her and insisted on serving her a huge breakfast. She gossiped with him over the meal, learning the latest about everyone in the district—the really scandalous things Lady Sefana pretended not to know.

Replete with scrambled eggs and fresh muffins and coffee, Cailet ambled across the yard to the stables long before Telomir was even reported to be awake. She saddled up a mare familiar to her from childhood—a year ago?—then chose a gelding for Telo. The ranch hands soon forgot her new position and they entered into a spirited discussion of just which Dapplebacks should be bred to the new Tillinshir grays, with what possible results. This led to a tour of the new foals and her promise to come back to the Hundred when she had time to choose one for herself; Lady Sefana still owed her the promised Birthingday gift. She returned to the main stable in time to see Jennis Maurgen crossing the yard with Telomir.

"That's the silliest thing I ever heard! What is *wrong* with men?"

"Women," Telo shot back.

"Imili, Feleris, and Alliz!" Jennis exclaimed, black eyes flashing. Cailet was distracted from wondering who the last-named Saint was when she continued, "My mother was on horseback two days before she delivered Riena and me—and she practically went into labor in the saddle with Biron and Val!"

Ah, of course: Alliz the Watchful, patron of mothers of twins. Cailet grinned to herself and prepared to enjoy the rest of the argument. Jennis was certainly having a good time; Val's departure from Maurgen Hundred years ago had emptied the place of the only man who'd ever contended with her or Riena. Biron wasn't exactly afraid of his sisters, but after watching them beat up on Val, he had long ago decided that placid avoidance was the wiser course.

"Having you go into premature labor in the saddle is all we lack!" Telomir broke off at sighting Cailet. "You're a woman, talk some sense into her! She wants to ride with us all the way over to Ostinhold!"

Because they were not, in fact, going to Ostinhold, Cailet suddenly understood his unmannerly tones: lacking any other good excuse, he'd used Jennis's pregnancy as reason to discourage her from joining them, hoping to annoy her enough to prevent awkward questions.

Cailet could have changed Jennis's mind. But one didn't do that to friends. Truly told, a Mage Guardian didn't do it at all; it was something from the *Code* that a few very powerful Malerrisi were capable of using on those not Mageborn. During those long hours of study on board ship, she'd concluded that whereas magic itself was inherently neither good nor evil, there *were* applications of it that—for lack of a better word—stank. She'd take what she found beneficial and adapt certain other things to the Mage Guardian ethic, but some Workings she would never touch.

She walked over to her childhood friend, put a light hand on her arm, and used the best argument she knew—which, though grossly unfair, at least had the advantage of being true.

"Jen, I just watched one friend lose a baby. Don't make me go through it again."

"Nonsense," Jennis replied briskly. "No Maurgen has miscarried since Fielto was a filly."

"I don't doubt it. But I can't help feeling that way. Please, Jen."

Telomir put in smoothly, "It isn't as if either of us needs directions to find Ostinhold."

Jennis rounded on him. "If you were a Senison hound, you couldn't find the end of a leash!"

Cailet, seeing that Telo had overdone it, intervened. "Indulge me, Jen. Just this once."

With an annoyed shrug, Jennis capitulated—but not without a last scathing glance for Telomir. "*This* is why I won't take a husband!"

Scowling right back at her, he retorted, "And why I never *became* one!"

Cailet thought this over as they rode out of the yard. Telo would have been a fine catch; no one knew he was Gorsha's son, but everyone knew he was Jeymian Renne's. Born a Blood with connections to many important families, rich, clever, good-looking, personable, and with an excellent career in government, thirty years ago half the women of Lenfell should have been after him. Perhaps they had been. Cailet didn't know. But he had never married.

Jennis's reasons for not taking a husband were obvious to anyone who knew her: she enjoyed men, but preferred women. She didn't need any man's dower; all she needed was an hour or so of his time on a day she was fertile. Tamaso Obreic, a comely green-eyed fourth son of a third daughter, had obliged; Jennis would be a mother by late spring. Lady Sefana had told Cailet the whole story last night, wryly amused at her daughter's cheerful plan to have children by any man who struck her fancy as a desirable sire.

Telomir presumably hadn't wanted to marry; Jennis didn't need to. So why did anyone get married at all? One could have babies without taking or becoming a husband; as long as the children were loved and provided for, what was the difference? She heard someone inside her head tag the word *provided,* and nodded to herself. But how depressing to think that money was the only real reason to marry, even though it seemed to be true. Well-dowered men were sought by women who needed money, and rich women by men whose families could not provide for them.

Ah, but then there was the case of Sarra and Collan. Sometimes it seemed to Cailet that they'd married for the sole purpose of having each other around to snipe at. Well, and to make love with. A voice clearly identifiable as Gorsha's laughed.

Dearest, they married for love. *So did your parents. So do millions of other couples. It's not* all *about money, you know. You'll find out, one of these years—see if you don't.*

That was just it, though. She *wouldn't* find out. There lurked in her things as fearsome as the Wraithenbeasts she was riding to investigate, things that would destroy the mind and heart of any man she bedded.

For the first time in a long time she deliberately thought of Taig Ostin. Almost a year since he'd died. The last thing he'd said to her was about loving another man. *"Find him, Caisha. Love him even more than you loved me."* She'd known with Taig's death that no one could ever replace—let alone surpass—him in her heart, that she could never want any man the way she'd wanted him. A few days later, Glenin had made certain of it.

There would be no children for her. Sarra's twins would have to suffice. One day they would come to her to be educated in their gifts. Her life until then must be spent preparing to teach them. And that meant a new Academy.

And just where she was going to establish it was a total mystery. Part of her purpose in her travels last year had been to scout possible locations. She'd thought she'd found a nice piece of land near Wolfprint Springs in Cantrashir—until the locals expressed their reluctance to have Mages living next door. It had been the same in five other places, though not everyone had been so honest in their rejection. That farmland near Maslach Gorge in Tillinshir, for instance, its only structure a burned-out farmhouse—the area residents had told her with absolute solemnity that the place was prone to bizarre winds and reliably reported to be haunted. In other places, property she would have bought and built on was either not for sale or the owners could not be traced; merchants she talked to regarding possible supply contracts were unable to furnish her needs. No one wanted a resurgent Mage Academy anywhere near them.

Well, could anyone blame them? Look what had happened to Ambrai.

The Mayor of Isodir had offered quarters in that city. But its wrought-iron banisters and balconies and gates would have made Working any magic problematic at best. The only Ladder she knew of there—one that led to Malerris Castle—was in one of the few buildings that *wasn't* laced and decorated with iron.

Still, iron could be an advantage. Sarra's instinct had been correct: the new Academy must be in Sheve or Cantrashir or Tillinshir, with the iron in Caitiri's Hearth on Brogdenguard a bulwark between the Mage Guardians and the Malerrisi. Cailet had tested out Sarra's theory while in Dinn last year, and was appalled at how easy it was to sense Malerris Castle, even at such a distance with Wards rendering it invisible to the eye. North of Brogdenguard, she could not feel the Castle, and therefore those within it could not feel her. She would have no idea what Glenin was up to—but neither would Glenin be able to spy on her. It was an equitable trade—but it limited her options in selecting a place for the Academy.

She supposed she could have built someplace in South Lenfell, but then she would have had to Ward the place as thoroughly as the Malerrisi had Warded their Castle. This she would not do. She would not hide or conceal her school. Too many people had suffered and died for the Mage Guardians' right to live and work in the open again.

Surely there was a place that met her requirements. And she must find it soon. Last year's journeys had yielded many young Mageborns ready and willing to be trained. For the present they stayed with their families, visited frequently by those able to set protective Wards if their magic became difficult to contain. But Cailet had to put them somewhere, all together, where they could learn how to set that magic free.

The one place she could not and would not bring them was The Waste. Magic was a living thing. The Waste was dead, or as close to it as made no difference. She supposed an argument could be made that such a place, where creatures must be clever and resourceful in order to survive, would be an excellent example. But she could counter with an equally valid point: that in this land eviscerated *by* magic, the oppression of living daily with its grim reminders would smother the most resilient Mageborn. And besides, the last thing the locals wanted was a swarm of magicians-in-training.

And besides all *that*, she hated the place.

Though Cailet wasn't one for cities, The Waste was a little *too* desolate; a mile outside any town, wilderness took over. Something in her blood that had known Generations of rich greens and blues in Ambraishir found no comfort in the washed-out hues of this land. Even where grass grew and trees clustered around shallow creeks, the grass was bleached to straw with barely substance enough to hold the soil together, and the trees were spindly, roots exposed when exhausted earth finally gave up and collapsed into ravines carved out by torrents of acid rain. In such places, pale clay was revealed in horizontal strips of rose and lilac, peach and melon—all delicate colors of flowers and fruit that belonged in thick greenery, not in this stark and pallid landscape.

No, she would not even begin to consider The Waste as a site. But she knew the question of location had an answer. Eventually she would find a place. What she would find at the end of this journey—and what she could do about it—were wholly unknown.

"Isn't it about time you told Kanto we'll be late?"

Startled from her thoughts, she glanced over at Telomir. "They won't expect us until afternoon. If I wait until then, it'll be too late for anyone to ride out after us."

He nodded. "They'll know at once where we're going and what we're up to." All at once he grinned. "Good thinking, Captal. Is it due to the Bequest, or your own instinctive wiles? After all, you spent your childhood sneaking your naughty way around Lady Lilen."

Sometimes Telo was a bit like Collan: he knew when she needed to laugh, and provided as good a reason as he could find on short notice. She obligingly grinned back.

"I was a very obedient little girl. I never sneaked, and I was *never* naughty."

"And St. Geridon was a gelding," he retorted, "St. Ilsevet can't swim, and St. Velenne is tone-deaf!"

At midafternoon she constructed a Mage Globe that would trigger Kanto Solingirt's. A select number of Guardians now possessed hand-sized Globes encased in blown glass, ready for just this purpose. Cailet needed a means of keeping in touch with them that fell far short of the absolute command of a Summoning; this was her best solution. At the beginning it had been awkward, though; wanting to inform Granon Bekke of a change in travel plans last year, she'd contacted his cousin Rennon instead. After some adjustments, the system now worked— more or less.

One problem was that the Globes were difficult to make, and Cailet alone could make them. Most of the senior Mages had them now, but soon she would have to spend several weeks creating enough for all of the rest. Another difficulty was that she alone could use them; Mages could not communicate with each other through them, only receive what messages she sent. And she could say what she wanted only by writing it down and then encasing the words in the Globe. Tamos Wolvar had taught her how to construct the kind of magical notebook all Scholars and most Healers used, but for some unknown reason words written in light did not transfer through the Globes.

Worst of all, she could never be certain when a message would be received. The other Globe could be tucked in baggage or resting on a shelf, for they were too large to carry around. Perhaps she could fine them down as small as the one given Sarra, small enough to be pocketed or worn on a chain and hidden in one's shirt. But Sarra's was a single, specific, protective Ward encased in glass; the Globes used for communication were much more complex.

Well, one day she'd figure it out. For now, she sat on a rock while Telomir watered the horses, scribbled a few lines on a scrap of paper, and spelled a Globe into being around it. Then, calling up Kanto's magical "signature" in her mind, she closed her eyes and thought in Ostin-hold's general direction. When she opened her eyes, the blue-white sphere had vanished and the paper had become a wafting of ashes in the breeze. Message successfully sent.

Telomir led the horses back to where she sat. "All done?"

"I told him we're going sightseeing."

He snorted. "You're lucky he can't send a reply."

"I'm luckier that *Lilen* can't. She'd scorch my ears even at this distance." Getting to her feet, she slapped dust from her trousers and finished, "Come on. I want to make the line shack before dark."

13

ALL ranchers in the northern reaches of The Waste contributed to the maintenance and supply of line shacks: stone huts, spaced roughly a day's ride apart, that had saved many a life. Stocked with water jugs, food, blankets, cookpots, and coal for small iron braziers, every spring and autumn the major owners took turns assigning ranch hands to ride the line shacks, packhorses laden with fresh foodstuffs to replenish whatever had been used up or spoiled, and to clear out any local opportunists of a furry nature.

But this winter and spring, animals and humans stayed close to home for fear of Wraithenbeasts. Lady Sefana told Cailet it was costing everyone a small fortune in feed to keep the herds and flocks in fenced fields, and an unvaried diet wasn't as good for them as the wild fodder they usually ate every summer. Cailet saw another problem as she rode north: without galazhi and sheep and goats to crop it, vegetation was sprouting unchecked. Summer heat would fry the overgrown grasslands and brushfires would be inevitable.

More immediately for her own comfort, without riders coming through to replace supplies in the line shacks, the water was brackish, the blankets moth-eaten, and the dried food had become positively desiccated. Quite a comedown, she thought with a smile, after the luxuries of Ryka Court.

Curiously, she felt almost at peace despite the unappetizing food and musty blankets. Ambraian by Blood, Waster by birth and upbringing, she couldn't pretend that she loved this land (truly told, she often hated it) but at least the deaths waiting here for the unwary were deaths she understood.

The fifth night out, they stayed in a line shack below a gigantic cliff. Sunset limned ragged rocks in gilded flames before the sky turned swiftly, deeply black. Cailet heard Telomir gasp at the suddenness of it, and smiled.

"Magnificent, isn't it?"

"I think I've worked indoors much too long. I'd forgotten there were so many stars." He didn't take his eyes from the gorgeous display. "Like the lights going out in an opera house at the end of the third act, and then the curtain falls—black velvet, embroidered in stars."

"Mmm. Collan's having an influence on you—you're getting positively poetic."

"I was hoping I could influence you into coming inside for some dinner. It's cold."

Cailet shrugged. "In a little while. Cold doesn't bother me that much."

"I suppose you soaked up so much sun in childhood that it heats you from the inside out." He tugged his own woolen jacket closer around his chest.

"Nothing so elaborate, just a Warming spell for my feet. Go on, I'll be there in a while."

Alone, Cailet hunkered down on her heels, staring at the sky. She had never been this far north in her life, but others had. This time it was Alin's memories that advised her to wait for something wonderful.

Ten minutes later, it happened. Sheets of light advanced across the sky, shimmering curtains made of rainbows.

Wraiths.

It took several minutes and a few dark specks in her

eyes before she remembered to breathe. She had seen something like this once before, when Anniyas died at the Octagon Court. There might have been hundreds of Wraiths then; no way to tell. But using that night as a measure, there were millions here.

General belief held that at death every person became a Wraith. After judgment by St. Venkelos, the soul or spirit or life-energy—or whatever one was comfortable calling the essence of a human being—assumed this strange and glorious form she saw in the sky now. Only those who had been despicable in life were condemned to the Dead White Forest. Warded in by other Wraiths, prevented from gliding through the night sky in this fantastic flourish of light.

That was the religious explanation, anyway. But if all persons became Wraiths, why did so much of Gorynel Desse, Alin Ostin, Tamos Wolvar, and Lusath Adennos linger within Cailet? Had they not become Wraiths? Or were their souls here with the others in shining splendor while their knowledge resided in her?

She could believe this of Alin (whose spirit would never part from Val's), of Scholar Tamos, and of Captal Adennos—but not of Gorsha. He was too real and vital within her—and too vocal, usually at the most inconvenient times. She could sense not only what he had known but what he had been—and Saints knew he spoke to her as clearly and idiosyncratically as when he'd been alive. That very word *idiosyncratically* was his; she winced slightly, remembering that after her Making, Taig had beseeched her to talk like herself again.

She watched the many-colored curtains undulate across the star-strewn blackness, washing the horizon in light, and wondered as countless thousands had wondered before her what the Wraiths really were. Wondered if Taig was among this group—for surely there were others, hundreds and perhaps thousands of shimmering rainbows floating above the Wraithen Mountains . . . night after night . . . for all time. . . .

She shook herself. It was not the spirits of the dead who concerned her now, but the monstrosities created by the combatants of The Waste War.

And in any case, the show was over for the night. She was on her way inside when distant hoofbeats and a warning whicker from her hobbled mare turned her around. A polite but purposeful dart of magic struck the walls Gorsha had long ago taught her to build. Her brows arched. A Mage Guardian, way out here?

Telomir emerged from the line shack. "Somebody's coming."

Cailet nodded. He seemed to be waiting for her to tell him who it was. As Captal, she should have known. At her Making, the identity of every single living Mage should have been given as part of the Bequest. She knew enough to know that, but not how to put a name to the approaching magic. Had she not been so impatient, Captal Adennos could have given her this knowledge—and so much else—before he died.

Telomir answered his own question a moment later. "Geridon's Golden Stones, I don't believe it! What's Fiella doing here?"

Fiella Mikleine it proved to be. Tall, lean, vigorous— and dark like all her Name that had produced Generations of formidable Mages—she galloped up on a Tillinshir gelding and jumped from the saddle as spry as if she'd just risen from a good night's sleep. She had a high-boned, handsome face, was as muscular in her magic as Imilial Gorrst, and Cailet had never been able to decide if her total lack of anything resembling an imagination was a liability or an asset.

"Good to see you again, Captal! How're you keeping yourself, Telo? I hear you're going hunting."

"After a fashion," Cailet replied. "We're just about to have dinner. Join us?"

"Delighted. As I recall, Telo's a middling good cook."

The meal consisted of dry bread, hard cheese, and a stew of dried galazhi meat softened in wine and thickened with lentils. If there was a slight taste of magic from the spells Telomir used to speed up the cooking, Cailet didn't notice. When coffee had been brewed potent enough for Fiella ("The color of *my* face, Telo, not yours!"), she said what she'd come to say.

"I've been seeking undiscovered Mageborns, Captal, and we Mikleines seem to breed a lot of 'em, so I've been visiting every cousin in the Census records." She grinned suddenly, an expression that made her look fourteen instead of nearly forty. "Rilla's Feathers, it's good to travel! Since Ambrai, those of us who moved around did so because we had to, usually at a dead run, and those of us who stayed in one place didn't dare leave it. Anyway, I'm riding along when up ahead about five miles I see a white mist. And my magic starts screaming at me. I follow this misty stuff, and where it had passed were dead things—a gutted kyyo, a stag, one of those big four-horned rams. All of 'em untouched, as if the scavengers didn't dare come near."

"I told her what you told me at Ostinhold," Telomir put in. "But you didn't tell me about the mist."

"I saw it just last week—there's a Mikleine small-hold this side of the mountains from Maidil's Mirror. Anyway, I ride faster to catch up with this haze—not a mist, seen close to, more like very fine white silk with a few rents in it. I'm riding along, concentrating on it, when I realize where I am."

"Fairly close to the Dead White Forest, I'd say," Telo remarked.

Fiella looked annoyed at being anticipated. "Heading smack for it, along a river with no fish, no plants, not even a shred of Mittru's Hair mossing the rocks. No trees, either, and fields so barren I started to worry about my horse's dinner."

Cailet nodded. "Like all the life and color had been drained out of it."

"You've been there?"

"No, but I'm told it's like that for fifty miles in all directions from the Dead White Forest."

Telomir said, "Personally, I'm surprised you're still alive, Fiella. Not everybody's smart enough not to drink the water."

She arched a thick brow at him and asked, "Have you ever known me to be a total fool? The mist turned on me then, and I tried to outrun it. Couldn't, of course." She took a long swig of coffee and ran one hand back through a mass of tangled black curls. "Spent my poor horse. I dismounted to walk him a bit, and the mist stopped about ten feet from me. I tried a little magic—nothing fancy, just a probe like the one I sent here tonight, Captal. Nothing. I know a bit about Mage Globes, though I'm not very good at them, and tried one. That got through it—or into it, I'm not sure which. And that was the last I saw of the thing."

"What happened to *you*, Fiella?" Telo asked.

She looked puzzled. "Nothing."

"It didn't hurt to lose the Mage Globe? You didn't feel anything at all?"

"Was I supposed to?"

"Not even around the dead animals?" he persisted. "Some kind of dread or fear?"

The Mage snorted. "I saw Ambrai burn. I lost my husband and most of my family and friends there—and damned near lost my son with his being born too soon because of what I'd seen. I lived like a mole in a hole for fifteen years in the muggiest village in Dindenshir, and begged St. Miryenne every night to restore the Mages to their proper place before Granon got old enough to come into his magic. Truly told, Captal, I don't scare anymore, and the only thing I dread is not being to hand if you're ever in danger."

Ah, there it was—the age-old stricture on all Mage Guardians that whatever else might happen, whoever else was imperiled, The Captal Must Survive. Whole cities could perish, entire Shirs be slaughtered, but The Captal Must Survive. Every time she thought about it, Cailet shivered.

"The cloud kept you away from the Dead White Forest," Telo mused. "But it didn't threaten you. That fits. No people have been attacked."

"But why were the animals killed without being eaten—not even as carrion?"

All at once, in a leap worthy of her sister's instincts, Cailet heard herself say, "Is the cloud responsible, or is it a screen for something else?"

Telomir stared. "I thought we were hunting Wraithenbeasts."

"Maybe we are. Maybe something else entirely. Something that can create this cloud as a screen while it kills." She hesitated, then finished, "Some*thing* . . . or some*one* Mageborn."

I would never have thought of it, but you may be right.

For the first time in two weeks she heard Gorsha's voice, surprising her so much that she completely failed to hear what Telo and Fiella were saying.

I would say it's quite possible, he went on. *We won't know until we get within range of it. But I don't like this, Cailet. It's outside my experience and I don't like it at all.*

Are you doing the impossible—becoming cautious in your dotage?

He didn't find the teasing at all funny. *Cautious? Not in the least. After all, I have nothing to lose—except your life.*

"Captal? Your pardon, but—"

"Mmm? Oh, I'm sorry, Fiella. Just thinking. What is it?"

"I can't say I was afraid, but I did feel tired, especially when the Globe disappeared. It isn't easy for me to make one, but I don't remember ever feeling that drained before."

"Drained of energy, or drained of magic?"

Fiella looked startled. "Magic," she said, as if just realizing it. "Like after Folding forty miles of bad road. What the hell *is* going on here?" When Cailet shrugged— all the answer she had—Fiella's jaw hardened. "Captal, I'd like to ride along with you and Telo, if that's all right. I want to find out what this thing is."

"As do we all. Why don't we talk more about it in the morning? By daylight it might not look as dire as by night." She smiled, knowing Fiella wouldn't recognize "dire" if it bit her in the foot. What this Mage Guardian wanted was to confirm that there was indeed a logical, practical, concrete explanation.

Telomir took the hint. "It's getting late and we should make an early start tomorrow. Fiella, my dear, I would be honored if you would accept an invitation to share my blankets tonight. It's damned cold in here."

She laughed heartily. "The only man I know who can proposition a woman by making it sound as if it's in her own best interests!"

"Family talent," he replied with perfect seriousness belied by a twinkle in his dark eyes.

Cailet lay down in her bedroll alone. It seemed only an hour later that sunlight stabbed in through a chink in the door onto her face, waking her from a formless dream of white mist that concealed dark threats.

They were another three days on the road before they saw the first of the rotting carcasses. Cailet nearly gagged at the sight of the wolf, its throat laid bare and its belly torn open, with not even a fly buzzing about the dried blood and spilled guts.

"I'm all right," she said when they looked worried, but her fingers were shaking as she uncapped her waterskin. A long drink later she had control of herself, and walked forward to examine the animal. "Are you feeling what I'm feeling?" she asked the others.

"No, Captal," Fiella reported. "Not a twinge of anything. But I've seen this before."

"I didn't mean queasy," she said impatiently. "I meant *feelings.*"

Telomir nodded. "I think I know what you're talking about." He prodded the wolf with a boot toe. "Two days dead, maybe three. And nothing's touched it."

"Would you, with *this* all around it?" She waved a hand to indicate the eerie heaviness in the air. "It must've been horrific when it first happened, to be this strong still. I'd say that wolf died of fright before he was gutted."

Fiella snorted. "What could terrify a wolf?"

Telomir circled the carcass, biting his lip. At last he said, "This was done for the pleasure of killing. Not for food, or even as a warning, but for the *joy* of ripping this animal to shreds."

"Not joy," Cailet corrected. "Anger. Killing anything that lives simply because it *does* live. For vengeance."

Fiella was bewildered. "I don't understand. What is it? What're you talking about?"

"Be glad you don't feel it." Cailet wondered how in

St. Miryenne's Name anyone could work magic and yet
be so utterly pragmatic in her outlook.

Telo was frowning. "I sense blood-lust, and exhilara-
tion in killing, but—"

"Nothing else? There's fury and vindictiveness all
over this place." She tried to shake herself free of it. "The
feelings didn't last long. To feel again, it'll have to kill
again. Like an addiction, needing more of it, more often.
We're going to find a lot more of these, Telo."

"I think so, too. We ought to bury this poor thing."

They piled rocks atop the wolf using muscles, not
magic. Afterward they rode on, finding another kill before
dusk: a golden-brown kyyo, her three pups lying dead of
starvation fifty feet away.

They rode up to the last of the stone line shacks just
before dark. Again Cailet lingered outside long after
nightfall, watching for Wraiths. They flowed in star-shot
silk curtains toward the east—exactly in the opposite direction the animal carcasses were leading Cailet, away
from the Dead White Forest.

"So," she murmured. "No help from you. This isn't
Wraithenbeasts, I'm sure of that much, anyway. But if it's
the Wraiths you banished to the Dead White Forest, I'd
expect you to do *something*. After all, you came for Anniyas before she actually died. In fact, I think you frightened her to death, the way the wolf died. But this white
mist scares even you, doesn't it?"

If there were Wraiths within that gathering that might
have answered, they were silent.

"Is it Glenin? Is she behind this? I don't think so—
but what do *I* know? I'm learning from everything that
happens, but what kind of substitute is that for what I
should've had from the other Captals?"

She knotted her fingers together, trying not to become angry. Just as swiftly she decided she had every
right to get as furious as she pleased; it was *her* emotion,
after all, something *she* felt, not forced on her by Wards
and spells and white mists that killed for the hot bitter
vengeance of it.

"Do I just educate myself at random? Saints, I can't
even choose how I learn! Am I supposed to be grateful

for all these wonderful opportunities everyone's giving me to experience wonderful things like fear and pain and dread of the future? Do *this* for the people, *that* for the Council—and there's my sister and her husband and my friends, and you four lecturing me inside my skull—and of course Glenin provides so much by way of enlightenment! I can't wait until my nephew's old enough to teach me *his* version!"

Well then, you'd better learn all you can now, hadn't you? And from whatever source presents itself.

Damn it, Gorsha, can't I even get mad in peace?

Your pardon, Captal. Shutting up now, Captal.

Of all the peculiar sensations associated with her Others, the most peculiar surely had to be when Gorsha took himself off in a huff.

The Wraiths were gone, vanished over the mountains. Cailet sat in the cold for a long time, not bothering to Warm her feet and hands. She had other things to do with her magic.

When at last she went inside, she saw what she knew she'd see: Fiella and Telomir, nested together in blankets on the floor, deeply asleep. She knew that tomorrow they'd feel too exhausted to get out of bed, let alone sit a horse for the last day's riding to the Dead White Forest. And she knew how furious they'd be that Cailet had gone off on her own.

She even knew what Gorsha would say, if he'd taken the trouble to say it: Apart from the folly of doing this on your own, you should be ashamed of yourself for doing this to them.

Ashamed of herself? Not very. A Captal did what was necessary.

14

THERE was no white mist such as Fiella Mikleine had described. There was only a stand of bare, blanched trees surrounded by fifty miles of fields bled dry of life and color. Cailet, not even tired after a morning's Folding of the blighted land underfoot, held back to observe from a few hundred feet away. The Forest was smaller than she'd thought—perhaps half a square mile, no more than two hundred trees. They had once been redwoods, as majestic as those growing tall and evergreen on the heights above. Some said the Dead White Forest had been the exact place where Mages and Malerrisi had met in the final battle of the long ago war. Cailet had grown up in The Waste and was familiar with its most forbidding landscapes, but this evidence of what the land had suffered was a desecration more horrible than any she had ever seen.

She walked forward, each step slow and deliberate, knowing now what Collan had meant about being watched. But she didn't feel eyes; she felt magic. Whether the mist had shrouded Wraiths or was in fact the Wraiths themselves mattered not at all. They had somehow escaped the Wards that kept them pent and were killing for the vile pleasure of it, leaving the carcasses behind, the spoor of their vengeful feast. Cailet must force them back into captivity. She knew they were here, as surely as she knew Wraithenbeasts were not.

And of which are you more frightened, little girl?

Cailet whirled, but there was nothing to see. Only the boundary of the land's most atrocious maiming, only the withered white trees.

Silly child, aren't you? Trying to see me with your eyes!

Cailet was surprised that the Others were surprised. It was obvious, wasn't it? When everything was put together, there could be only one explanation. She felt a quiver of pride that she knew something her constant companions did not. Maybe she wasn't hopeless as Captal after all.

"Why are you killing animals when what you really want to kill is people? Or is being a Wraith somewhat limiting, Anniyas?"

That's "First Lord" to you, child.

"There's someone hiding in Malerris Castle who'd disagree."

You refer to your eldest sister, of course. Shrewd girl, Glenin. She may yet make something of herself—or of my grandson. I would have done much better with him. But that's one of the points of this little exercise.

"I'll deal with my nephew some other time," Cailet said. "Right now I want to know why you lured me here. I'm assuming you have something to say, so say it and I'll be going. Unlike you, I have concerns among the living."

How wonderfully simpleminded of you! It's a real pity we didn't get to know one another. Whatever was that old fool thinking, Making an infant like you Mage Captal? I thought him mad when he chose Adennos—but then, he was only a box to hide the Bequest in, keeping it safe for you! What could Desse have meant, giving it to a child?

"I don't have time for this."

Whereas I have nothing but time. It's interesting, you know, being a Wraith. Even restricted as I was until I worked out a few things, one gains a certain perspective. My companions here proved occasionally fascinating. Information spanning centuries . . . but nothing from before The Waste War. Do you know why that is, child?

"I'm sure you're about to tell me."

Not only did the last battle destroy the living, it also destroyed the dead! Can you imagine *the power?*

"I grew up in The Waste," she replied.

Did you? Poor thing.

"I'm touched by your compassion. Is there anything of interest to me somewhere in the immediate future? If not—"

How disappointing. One does long so for intelligent conversation—which obviously isn't among your talents.

Very well. You're here because I wish to add to your education.

And as suddenly as Anniyas's dead voice had come to her out of nowhere, a gout of magic slammed against her. Cailet caught her breath, strengthened instinctive walls, and waited.

Anyone else would've responded by now. Well? Aren't you going to attack me?

"Why should I?"

Retaliation for the Wards at Ryka Court, if nothing else.

"I survived," she said coldly, refusing to think of the child who had not.

I could never be sure what Mage would find my little entertainments—I always hoped for Desse, or his deplorable son, but I'm glad it was you. Especially when I think about the Circle-Spinner. I'd love to know what she showed you. Setting that Ward was some of my finest Work—all the possibilities and permutations—what futures are you unable now to forget? Come, child, build me a Mage Globe and show me what awaits you!

"This is getting boring, Anniyas." It was nothing of the sort, but she was damned if she'd admit that. So Anniyas had set those Wards without knowing who would trigger them—considering the fine details of what Cailet had seen, she was impressed. Somehow, her own fears, even the hidden ones, had been used to create those visions. Remarkable crafting.

Did you see Glenin and my grandson? Show me him, at least. He's my Blood, I've a right to look on him as he will be—

"You have the right to *nothing*. And don't bother to threaten me. What harm can you do to me—or to anyone, or anything—as you are now?"

The wolves and grizzels and kyyos prove otherwise.

"But you killed no people. You haven't enough power. You're a Wraith, Anniyas. Not a Malerrisi with magic at her command."

Perhaps I simply didn't use it.

"I don't know how you got past the Wards that used

to be here, but if you have anything to say before I recast them, say it fast."

Ward this place all you like, little girl. I got out once, I'll do it again. The only way to keep me from killing whatever and whomever I please is to destroy me here and now. What are you waiting for?

She reached for the knowledge that would make Anniyas's Wraith visible to her—only to find the Magelore closed up like a walnut in a fist.

Don't look at her! Don't attack! That's what she wants you to do!

"Gorsha?" she whispered. "What—?"

A sudden magical assault reeking of rage and frustration staggered her both physically and mentally. She wanted desperately to defend herself, but she had been warned not to attack—

Fight me, damn you! I'll kill you with a single thought, and then where will they find another Capital to stand against Glenin and my grandson? Fight me!

She didn't. She couldn't. If Anniyas desired it, she must not do it. That was all the reason she needed.

Set the first Ward, Caisha, a voice urged. *She can't get at you—not unless you weaken and attempt to destroy her. Set the Ward, and be quick about it.*

It was hard, not knowing where exactly Anniyas was. Cailet risked just enough searching magic to sense her general position but not enough to see her. She dared expand the seeking to include the other Wraiths, those much less powerful but just as angry and desperate for freedom—but where were they?

Sweet Saints—that was how Anniyas had done it! Cailet nearly lost control of the opening sequence of the Ward as she realized where the power to escape and kill had come from. Pent with all those banished by their fellow Wraiths for having been too vile in life to tolerate in death, Anniyas had stolen their strength, their souls, their spirits. They no longer existed. There was only Avira Anniyas, First Lord of Malerris and First Councillor of Lenfell, now sole inhabitant of the Dead White Forest. In her was the energy of thousands, perhaps millions, of Wraiths—some of whom could rival her for power-hunger, some for sheer malevolence. That she had absorbed them all was incredible enough; that she dominated and used them was beyond anything any Mageborn had ever done.

But was it? Were there not other presences in Cailet's own mind? Was she not just as ghoulish as Anniyas, feeding off the dead?

If you persist in this nonsense, you'll never leave here sane, said Gorsha. *It's not the same at all. What we gave, we gave willingly. You didn't steal it, and you certainly didn't devour our souls! Now stop dithering and get on with it!*

Cailet gulped and did as told.

The storm of furious magic continued. But she could not fight Anniyas—because any spell of hers would be just that much more power for Anniyas to steal. Create a Mage Globe as Fiella Mikleine had done and it would be devoured as Fiella's had been, draining her of magic to the enhancement of Anniyas's stolen strength.

The Ward took shape more easily now that she knew it was only the single presence she must capture. She still didn't know how the magic worked, or why. She possessed it, but had never learned it. She only knew that Anniyas howled as the Ward collapsed in on her. Cailet Folded it like a square of cloth, smaller and smaller until within it was a screaming nub of a thing. This she wadded even smaller and, choosing a tree in the midst of the forest, set it into lifeless white wood.

Then she got busy with the real work.

It took all day to walk the perimeter, casting Wards onto rocks at regular intervals. Sunset brought with it completion, exhaustion, and Telomir Renne with a tiny Mage Globe to light his way through the dusk. Prentice though he was, he sensed at once what she had done. "Captal," was all he said, bowing to her most profoundly.

The homage embarrassed her. She didn't deserve it. She had damned near fallen into Anniyas's trap. For as she worked, she had reasoned out the rest of it with no help from Gorynel Desse. Anniyas, having seized the energy of others, had used it to escape the Dead White Forest. But she required more power still—and who better to steal it from than the Mage Captal? By flinging magic at her—Globe, spell, whatever arcane technique she dredged up—Cailet would have glutted Anniyas with magic. It would not have given her back a body, but it would have allowed her to go wherever she chose and kill whomever she pleased.

After drinking from the waterskin Telomir offered, she asked, "Where's Fiella?"

"Still asleep. I woke up early and thought it best to reinforce the spell. My compliments, by the way."

"Sorry." She shrugged.

"No, you're not. But you owe us neither apology nor explanation."

"That's right," she said with weary bitterness. "I'm the Captal."

"Yes," he said quietly. "You are."

As if her stupidity proved it. With another shrug, she asked, "Telo, would you please go around and check what I've done? And I'd appreciate it if you'd add a little something of your own here and there."

"I'm sorry, Captal, I'm very little use at Warding." She blinked; he made a little gesture of regret. "My esteemed father didn't pass along that particular gift."

"Oh. Well, go see if I've done it right, will you? I think I'll just sit here and rest a while."

To her utter humiliation, when he returned from his circuit of the Wards, he had to wake her from sodden sleep. It took several minutes to clear her thoughts enough to set the web of magic linking all the Wards. When Telomir tested it, he nodded.

"Gorsha couldn't have done it any better."

She accepted the praise without comment, but she was thinking that through her, his father *had* done it.

"And now?" Telomir asked.

"What? Oh. We'll head for Ostinhold tomorrow. It's over, here. I'll tell you all of it later. But remind me to have somebody ride up yearly to make sure of the Wards."

Telo cleared his throat. "In secret. The Captal has reset the Wards around the Dead White Forest. That's all anyone needs to know. If you indicated through open sur-

vey of the Wards on a regular basis that you were unsure
of your work—"

"I'm only trying to be cautious!"

"An admirable trait." He called up a brighter Mage
Globe to light them back to the line shack, while she
tiredly Folded the path. "But there's something you ought
to know about being Captal. About you *specifically* as
Captal. Leninor Garvedian was one type. Gorsha chose
Lusath Adennos on purpose to be as unlike her as possible."

"Passive instead of active. Yes, I know."

"You must be both. Careful but confident, assertive
yet understated. You must show yourself a powerful and
decisive leader for the Mage Guardians, but not so strong
as to threaten the Council and the people. They've lived
without us almost twenty years. They must grow used to
us again. You must show no weakness, but neither can
you be too strong."

It was nothing she hadn't already considered. She
spent a long time listening to the crunch of her boots in
dry stony soil—the same sound every time, the same nag-
ging prod of rocks into her soles. Right foot action, left
foot caution; right foot self-effacement, left foot leadership—it all felt the same. Every step she took was on the
same rough footing. She could stumble at any time. If
she dug one heel in too deep, the other must compensate.
Somehow she must keep her balance.

"I thought the idea was for Mage Guardians to live
and work in the open again," she said at last.

"Within the limitations imposed by the times. This
was always so—as you know from the Bequest."

That was just it. She *didn't* know. There were no
Generations of insight and wisdom. But even if there had
been, would she have made better use of them than Lusath
Adennos? What had Anniyas called him—*"a box to hide
the Bequest in"*? Was that all *she* was? A caretaker, waiting for a Captal worthy of the title to come along?

"All right, Telo. The Wards here will be checked in
secret." What did one more secret matter, anyway? There
were others far more dangerous. "But I won't cripple the

Guardians by making them mysterious. That's why the Malerrisi are feared, and I won't have that for us."

"And this is what will make you the Captal we need."

She shot him a sharp look, trying to read his eyes by the bloody glow of sunset and the silver-gold of his Mage Globe. "Maybe so. But I won't paralyze myself wondering constantly which foot to lead with—the careful or the bold. I'd go crazy second-guessing myself. I can't weigh everything in terms of a middle path between what Captal Garvedian and Captal Adennos would've done. I can't be anyone but myself."

. . . and Gorsha, and Alin, and Tamos Wolvar, and Captal Adennos himself—does it all balance out, Gorsha? Does it give me enough options? Would it be different if I had the full Bequest with all *the Captals' knowledge and experience?*

Yes, came the reluctant answer. *But I didn't choose you at random, you know. It wasn't because you were all I had to work with. You were born for this. Trust yourself, Caisha. What we were, what we knew, is here for your use. But the decisions are* yours. *I swear, dearest, the decisions will always be your own.*

Once, she might have let it end there, taking grateful comfort in the reassurances of someone older and more experienced than she. But now she knew that what she had been called on to do, he could never have done. His knowledge had made it possible—his, and the Others—but *she* had been the one to do it.

As she would have to do all else in the years ahead. Her life would never be her own; there were too many duties and responsibilities to shoulder. Yet by choosing to shoulder them, by deciding what must be done or not done, and how, and why, she would live that life the way she felt she must.

And wasn't that how it worked for everyone? Each person was born with certain gifts bequeathed by her ancestors; her life was in many ways determined by those inheritances. Whatever the world brought to bear upon her, the shaping of her life consisted in how she chose to use those gifts in response.

Cailet knew all at once that she was no different from anyone else. Not in that respect. What set her apart was the sheer abundance and power of her gifts—both inherited and bestowed. And if the world threw more at her than at other people, did she not have more with which to answer?

She knew Gorynel Desse was following the thoughts in her mind. So her answer to him was a wry one: *Did it really take me almost a* year *to figure that out?*

15

THE next morning Cailet sent another message to Kanto Solingirt, telling him to expect her and Telomir and Fiella at Ostinhold in a few days. The parts of her that were still eighteen years old chafed at the prospect of Lady Lilen's scolding her like a child; something even younger simply cringed.

Fifteen miles out of Ostinhold they were intercepted by Miram, accompanied by Riddon Slegin. Once greetings and introductions were over, Cailet grimaced and asked, "How furious *is* she?"

"Not very, now that you mention it. Oh, she was to start off, of course. But then Kanto explained a few things." Miram smiled her lovely, serene smile. "I think she's beginning to understand that you're the Captal now. As for being grown up—well, that may take a little longer for her to accept."

Riddon laughed. "Not surprising, Mirri—she's still having trouble believing that *you're* grown up enough to take a husband!"

"I know," Miram sighed. "And at nearly twenty-four!"

"What's this?" Telo demanded. "Another wedding at Ostinhold? Why wasn't I invited?"

"You will be, when we decide on a date that suits everyone."

"Sarra's the main problem," Riddon said. "Do you think we can pry her away from Ryka Court, Captal?"

"Cailet," she corrected. "Sarra's at Roseguard by now. But I'm positive she wouldn't miss your wedding for anything. Neither would I."

Miram made a face at her. "If that was a hint, you're about as subtle as Telomir! Of course you're invited. How could I get married without my favorite little sister being there?"

Though Cailet could never acknowledge who her Blood sisters were, she was more than willing to keep her honorary membership in the Ostin clan. That she was considered one of them was amply demonstrated by the welcome she received at Ostinhold. Only Kanto Solingirt and his daughter Imilial held back a little, still regarding her as Mage Captal—and, truly told, their eyes popped at the way Lenna and Tevis and Terrill and Lady Lilen and a score of Ostin cousins hugged her, teased her, and heaped affectionate abuse on her for staying away so long.

Yet as she sat down to dinner at the long, crowded table, she could not help but think of those who would never again share the warmth and laughter of an Ostinhold homecoming. Margit, Lilen's only Mageborn daughter, killed in an "accident" nine years ago. Alin—well, perhaps he *was* here, in a way; perhaps he *had* come home. But Taig never would. Nor would First Daughter Geria, not until her mother was dead and burned.

Cailet suddenly realized that her own mother had sat at this table. In the weeks before Ambrai's destruction and Cailet's birth, Maichen and Sarra had found refuge here. Which chair had been her mother's? What had she talked about over dinner? Had she laughed and joked with the rest of this boisterous family? Had anyone but Lilen known that their beautiful visitor was Lilen's first cousin?

Well, it hadn't been this table or these chairs in any case. Ostinhold had burned last year, thanks to Geria and the Ryka Legion, leaving only the stone walls and foundations. Perhaps that was why Cailet sensed not a thing from Alin; this wasn't the home he'd known. Nor was it Cailet's. Not Ostinhold, or The Waste, or even Ambrai—she'd felt twinges there last year, now that she thought about it, but nothing that meant *home* in any way she could feel in her soul.

That night, after Cailet had finally delivered her wedding present of two Saints' portraits in mosaic, Lilen herself escorted her abovestairs. "I can't give you your old room," she said ruefully. "There's nothing left of it. But this one is yours whenever you care to come visit."

Looking around, Cailet saw at once that the room was meant for no one but her. Its colors were pewter-gray and grass-green—for her assumed Name—with accents of the black and turquoise that meant Ambrai. And the pattern of the handmade quilt was of tiny flameflowers—St. Caitiri's sigil—inside interlocking octagons. She smiled, saying, "It's beautiful. Thank you."

Lilen had watched her note the references. "Miram and I were looking through quilt-pattern books in Combel and just happened to see this one. We'll pack it away when you're not here, of course, and no one will come in without your invitation, so I thought the lack of subtlety would be safe enough." Going to the double windows, she opened the green curtains to the view of nearby hills. "The outer walls are half again as thick as they were, so the window embrasures are very deep indeed! But I tried to make up for it with bigger windows to bring more light in. And Kanto designed shutters that fold in when they're not needed, but unfold and lock in no time when a storm comes."

"Scholar Mage, financial genius, now architect—I was thinking that all this activity was agreeing with you, but now I think it's ten weeks of your fascinating new husband that's made you look younger by ten years," Cailet teased.

"Wretched child!" Lilen actually blushed.

"Did you really have to fight off Sefana for him? Or maybe Mitra Senison? Everyone knows she's had her eye open for a fourth husband—"

"Cailet!"

"But that reminds me," she continued with playful sternness. "He may be *your* husband, but he's still *my* Scholar Mage, and if you don't treat him right, I'll—"

"If *you* don't hush up this instant, so help me I'll take you over my knee!"

Laughing, Cailet threw her arms around the only mother she'd ever known. "I'm happy that you're happy—and if he doesn't behave himself, I'll spell warts onto his nose!"

Lilen hugged back. "Don't you dare! It's a very nice nose, and I like it just the way it is, thank you very much!"

Cailet slept well that night. Even if this wasn't the Ostinhold of her childhood, it was still filled with people who cared for her. Ostinhold—in whatever incarnation—was filled with people, period. Cailet had never bothered to count how many had lived here while she was growing up. More had come when Scraller Pelleris, at Anniyas's bidding, had attempted the Ostin Web's financial ruin. Although the refugees from economic disaster had been sent away when the Ryka Legion threatened and then burned the place, many had returned. Whereas Cailet didn't know them, they certainly knew her; she was *Captal*-ed at every turn. Yet here she didn't mind. There was pride and even affection mixed in with the awe—for did they not live in the very place that had sheltered and nurtured her, and did that not make her in some ways one of their own?

She was, and in ways that could never be revealed. Sometimes when she went for solitary walks in the nearby hills and canyons, she liked to think that her grandfather, Gerrin Ostin, had hiked these same paths through tangled sage and willow washes. She wondered what he'd been like in childhood and youth, whether he'd regretted leaving The Waste behind for the wealth and glory of marriage to Allynis Ambrai and life at the Octagon Court. Of all the family tales traded around the Ostin table, that of the Ambraian marriage had never been told in Cailet's hearing.

Sarra's memories of Ambrai, shared with Cailet this past year, were the memories of a child who didn't know why the grown-ups suddenly became so grim. But she'd been old enough to know that her grandparents had a certain look and a certain smile they gave only to each other.

Later experience of watching Agatine and Orlin taught Sarra that such looks and smiles meant "love." And living with Collan completed her education in that particular emotion, especially as it happened between a woman and her husband.

Through Sarra, Cailet knew her grandparents had loved each other deeply. But there was so much more she wanted to know about them. How did they meet? Did Allynis come to Ostinhold to woo and win Gerrin? Did she dine at the very table their daughter would sit at years later? Did they take long walks atop the cliffs? Ride over to Maurgen Hundred and pretend to get lost so they'd have to spend the night in a line shack—as Miram and Riddon often did? Cailet couldn't quite feature her grandmother, the most elegant and comfort-loving of women to judge by all she'd heard, bedding down in blankets on a stone floor—even with the man she loved. But, truly told, Cailet simply didn't *know*.

She had known nothing about her ancestors while growing up. Being an orphaned fosterling had left her free to be herself. Now she knew from whom she had come: the richest, proudest, and most powerful Name on Lenfell. Until now she hadn't thought about that very much, too overwhelmed by becoming Captal and what she owed to the Mage Guardians to consider in depth what she might owe to her forebears. What would Allynis Ambrai think of her? Would she be pleased, gratified, appalled, infuriated, triumphant that her granddaughter was Mage Captal? Or would she be mortified that it was owed to magic inherited not from the Ambrais but from Auvry Feiran, whom she despised?

These were things Cailet had thought about before, of course. But now she had time to ponder them and explore their resonances in her mind and heart. She had time now, and the safety of Ostinhold in which to think about all this and more. To imagine, to dream, to plot out possibilities and plan likely pathways to her goals.

There was one absolute: she must build a new school for Mage Guardians, and both learn there and teach there until Sarra's children came to her. But prowling like a silverback cat caged in the cellar was another absolute.

Glenin would make some sort of move, but when? Her son would have to grow up first; Cailet surmised she had at least fifteen years, but not more than twenty, to prepare. But for what?

For every eventuality, of course; for the possible *and* the probable. All while serving Lenfell as best she knew, without seeming either too weak or too powerful, and simultaneously adhering to both Guardian ethic and her personal integrity.

Simple. Easy as getting drunk on St. Kiy's.

16

MIDWEEK of Spring Moon, Lady Sefana rode over from Maurgen Hundred with her daughters Riena and Jennis, her son Biron, and her only grandchild, Aidan. Val's son by Rina Firennos was nearly six years old and lacked only Val's rakish gold earring to be his father's very image. (Collan, who had somehow ended up with the earring, had promised it to the boy on his eighteenth Birthingday.) The influence of two powerful Councillors—Sarra Liwellan and Flera Firennos, who cordially detested Aidan's mother—and a tidy sum of money had not only changed the boy's residence but his Name as well. A Maurgen he looked, a Maurgen he was, and a Maurgen he would remain all his days.

He proved it by fearlessly marching up to her in the courtyard and saying with devastating directness: "You're the Captal. My papa died to keep you safe."

"Yes, he did," she managed beyond the ache of Alin's memories inside her.

"He wasn't a Mage Guardian."

"No, but he should have been. He was a very good man, and very brave, and he saved my life. And he was my friend."

"I'd rather be a Mage Guardian," Aidan said, and

Cailet almost asked if he thought the two were mutually exclusive.

In the next instant, though, she had an insight into an unanticipated quandary. No Maurgen had ever been Mageborn. Perhaps there was magic on the Firennos side—but even if so, it wouldn't manifest for years. There was no way to tell. But his determined little face was suddenly representative of hundreds of other children. Those who set their hearts on magic at so very young an age risked terrible disappointment. Cailet remembered her own dreams—not of magic, for she'd never dared, but of adventure and excitement anywhere but The Waste—and hoped that somewhere in the Firennos line there had been magic enough for Aidan to inherit.

But right now she had to say something. All she could come up with was, "Can we start out as friends first?"

Aidan thought it over, and nodded. "Mama said I shouldn't even talk to Mageborn people, but I like Scholar Kanto and Warrior Imilial. That's what I want to be is a Warrior Mage. My papa was almost one, wasn't he?"

"As close as you can get without being Listed. Do you know what the List is?"

"All the Mages who ever lived," he answered promptly. "Was Alin on it?"

"No," she said softly. "But he should have been."

"You're the Captal. Can't you fix it? Aunt Jen says you can fix anything." He hesitated, then added, "But she talks like that, doesn't she?"

"She certainly does. I can't fix *anything,* but I can certainly fix the part about your papa's and Alin's names being on the List. That was a long ride from the Hundred, are you thirsty?"

She learned then and there that she was no good at distracting children. Aidan gave her a disgusted look and said proudly, "I'm a Waster now."

Wasters didn't *get* thirsty, and even if they did, they never admitted to it. Suitably chastised by a six-year-old, Cailet was rescued from further idiocies by Lady Sefana, who called Aidan over to pay his respects to Lady Lilen.

A little later, as they were touring the latest com-

pleted section of Ostinhold, Cailet found herself beside
Jennis. "I can fix anything, can I? What've you been telling Aidan about me?"

Her old friend was uncharacteristically solemn. "Cai,
he knows how Val died. His mother made sure he knew
it—the filthy Fifth-spawn. Told him his father was
killed—senselessly, if you please, her exact word—
protecting the Capital, who's a dangerous person with sinister powers, also a direct quote. She made you out to be
some kind of monster. We had to guide him into thinking
well of you. If he gets to like you, so much the better."
Jennis made an impatient gesture. "What does it matter
what we told him, as long as he now knows that his father
died for a reason?"

Cailet nodded mutely. After a moment she asked,
"And—Alin?"

"Rina Firennos never knew about him. She knew
there was *someone,* but she didn't have a name to poison
in Aidan's mind. We told him about Alin—tailored to his
understanding, of course. And now that he's getting to
know the rest of the Ostins—" She finished with a shrug.
"He thinks of Alin as another uncle, like Biron." Jennis
gave her a crooked little smile of understanding and
linked her arm with Cailet's.

Left arm—she kept herself from tensing up at the
proximity to her maimed breast and the Ward disguising
it. Jennis never noticed a thing, and in fact said, "I lean
on everybody these days—Saints, if I'm this big this
early, can you imagine what I'll look like at full term?"
She laughed and patted her stomach. "It'll take three people to get me out of a chair!"

Cailet grinned. "Maybe by then Lilen will be finished
using that hoist over there, and you can borrow— No
fair!" she cried as Jennis jabbed a playful fist at her shoulder. "You're pregnant, and I can't hit back!"

The tour of the new building was completed with appropriate compliments on swift progress—but no congratulations on design, for this new Ostinhold was just as
much of an architectural mangle as the old and no one
could possibly think it beautiful. Praise would have had
Lilen laughing herself silly and calling the speaker a liar.

She and Kanto ushered their guests into the vastness of the Colonnade, finished only a few weeks ago and the one alteration Lilen had insisted on. She wanted a sitting room large enough to hold all her children, present and future grandchildren, and whatever guests happened by. The grand name had come from the six concrete pillars holding up the ceiling. No two were alike. The demands of keeping the eccentric roof aloft dictated a staggered placement that if looked at from the wrong angle made one dizzy. But nobody expected elegance in a house that had always sprawled where it would. The massive fireplaces at either end of the long chamber didn't match any more than the pillars did, one being moss-green marble and the other gray granite. But whatever the Colonnade lacked in design was more than made up for in its easy embrace of those welcomed within.

Although the room was not formally divided by screens and groupings of chairs and couches (which were dragged all over, to the detriment of the new rugs), people made their own small boundaries. Ostinhold as it was had never featured a room this size; everyone crowded into the old sitting room however they could. Miram or Terrill played their harps right next to clerks giving reports to Lilen, courting couples jammed in beside political arguments, and children laughed and squabbled everywhere. But the Colonnade was different. There was space enough to talk quietly with a friend or play chess or simply sit and read. The quiet would change, though, for as the Ostin daughters began to bring husbands home, children would soon follow. It was in happy anticipation that Lilen had ordered this huge room built.

For the time being, however, Lilen considered the Colonnade a little too peaceful when guests weren't present. Today, with the Maurgens here, Cailet had a glimpse of what it would be like when Miram and Lenna and Tevis and Lindren were married and breeding yet more Ostins. She also knew, quite abruptly, that this room was Lilen's way of defying her First Daughter. Mircia, Gerian, and Lile—Lilen's only grandchildren until Miram and Riddon got busy—would never set foot here while she lived, so she had created this place for her other daughters to fill.

Glancing at Miram, Cailet bit back a smile; to judge by the earnest conversation she was having with Jennis about pregnancy, it wouldn't be long before the Colonnade was as chaotic as even Lilen could wish. But for now there was only Aidan, who was squirming with the tedium of being polite and obviously wanted to escape all these adults and go find more congenial company. Cailet sympathized, remembering all the times she'd been bored witless by the irrelevant chatter of her elders. With a sudden grin she realized that except for Aidan, she was the youngest person in the room. And except for Lady Lilen—First Daughter of the Name with the biggest Web on Lenfell—she also had the grandest title at Ostinhold.

Kanto Solingirt approached with a glass of cordial that he claimed to have concocted himself. Cailet sniffed suspiciously at the pinkish liquid.

"What's in it?"

"Cactus juice. What else is there to make wine out of around here?"

"Send a few bottles to Collan," she suggested. "He's always looking for a new way to get drunk."

"Husbandhood doesn't agree with him?"

"Most of the time. But not at Ryka Court."

"Not the most ideal place to begin a marriage," the old man agreed.

Cailet eyed him quizzically. "And Ostinhold is?"

The Scholar laughed and stroked his mustache complacently. "If you're wed to the Lady, it can be! You've been here long enough to have noticed the rule. When our door is shut, it's shut."

"I'll have to suggest that to Sarra."

"Go on, try the cordial. It's a little sweet, but I'm working on that."

She was about to take a cautious sip when Jonna, Lilen's maid, came up to her and murmured, "Captal, an urgent message for you. The courier's outside. He looks worried."

"From Lady Sarra? Ryka Court?"

"He wouldn't say."

"Thank you, Jonna." She excused herself to Kanto and left the room, pausing just beyond the door to glance up and down the empty hall. Perhaps "outside" had meant literally that; she threaded her way through a jumble of corridors to a side exit into the courtyard, opened the door, and paused.

Three things happened then. And, as it occasionally did, time slowed to sluggishness that allowed her to view each as a separate action.

Fifty feet away from her, watering his weary horse at a trough, a small, brown, nondescript young man in Assembly livery caught sight of her and turned to rummage in his saddlebags.

Kanto Solingirt and his daughter Imilial Gorrst emerged from the main entry to Ostinhold and began to descend the steps.

Aidan Maurgen shot past Cailet at an all-out run, having followed her to freedom from the boredom of strictly minded manners.

Something inside her—inside *her,* not the Others—howled danger. She made a grab for Aidan, but in the slow expansion of time she watched her fingers miss the trailing ties of his coif by inches. She opened her mouth to call out a warning to the Mages, but her tongue had thickened within her mouth and she managed only a wordless cry.

The young man at the horse trough faced her now, with something wrapped in white cloth cradled in both hands. The cloth fell away. From a circle of crystal burst a shatter of silver lightning. With exquisite deliberation, so unhurried that she could watch it quest and then correct its course, the sword blade of magic sliced through the air toward her.

Aidan was running directly into its path.

The instant her gaze focused on him, time became real again, and too swift. She could never hope to reach the boy physically. There was no instantaneous spell ready for her use. She didn't even have time to curse Gorynel Desse as she dredged up a Mage Globe and filled its angry red depths with magic and hurled it at the lightning.

Something else got there first. An explosion of magic intercepted the gush of silvery fire. It split into a million sparks ten feet from Aidan, who was knocked sideways and fell into a breathless tangle of limbs. Cailet's own Globe absorbed some of the glittering fragments, hovered, then dissolved to nothingness, its target gone.

At least, she thought inanely, she'd had the sense to direct it at the magic and not the messenger. Him, she wanted whole. She swathed him in a Ward that froze him where he stood, the crystal in shards within the sleek white cloth draped over his hands.

"Captal!"

She spun around, heart lurching when her eyes lit on the toppled figure near the steps. She sprinted for him, shouting for help as she ran.

Imilial knelt beside her father, fingers at his throat to feel for a pulse. She looked up, wild-eyed, when Cailet stammered her name. "He pushed me back and conjured up that Globe—I didn't know he *knew* how to make a Battle Globe, an old Scholar like him—"

Cailet crouched down to cradle the lolling head in one hand. She unlaced his coif to let him breathe more freely, told Imi to straighten out his legs from their awkward sprawl, yelled over her shoulder for someone to see to Aidan. Kanto didn't move.

It seemed forever before she heard Telomir's voice at her shoulder. "I felt magic—the Malerrisi's, then his, then yours."

"He saved my life, didn't he," Cailet heard herself say.

"Yes." After watching Kanto's still face for a moment, he murmured, "Lilen must hurry."

Imilial moaned. "Papa—oh, St. Miryenne, *no*—"

Cailet glared at Telo. "I won't let this happen. I won't!"

"There's nothing we can do." He sat back on his heels, hands clasped white-knuckled between his knees and fury in his eyes. "It was over the moment Glenin finished her little gift to you. It was intended to kill whoever brought magic to bear against it. Mere Prentice I may be, but I sensed it. We can only thank the Saints that it wasn't specific to *you*."

"Kanto—?" Lilen fell to her knees beside her husband, groping for one of his hands. "Caisha, what happened?"

"Lilen—I'm so sorry—" Imilial's breath caught on a sob. "I wasn't fast enough—*I'm* the Warrior, not him! It should've been *me!*"

Bleakly, Cailet looked up at Telomir. They both knew it should have been *her.*

She relinquished her place to Lilen, who drew Kanto into her arms and rocked him as if he were a child. Halfway across the courtyard Lady Sefana was rocking Aidan, too, and for a moment Cailet thought she'd scream with the fear and the fury and the grief.

Telo murmured, "The boy will recover. He probably got the wind knocked out of him, and there may be a few burns. He's not Mageborn. If he were, he'd be dying, too."

She could only stare at him with the question in her eyes.

"You're safe. Kanto's magic took the killing force. But I felt the backlash, and once the shock wears off, so will you."

"I don't have time for that." She almost looked over her shoulder at the dying Scholar, but could not bring herself to do it. "I'm going to Longriding. Today. Now. And then to Bard Hall and then to Ryka Court, and then to Malerris Castle—"

"Cailet, don't be a fool!"

As fierce as her determination was, the trauma to her magic was the greater. She swayed against Telomir, felt him swing her up into his arms, and as her vision hazed he looked just enough like Gorsha for her to murmur, "Don't you dare say 'I told you so,' because you didn't."

17

DESPITE a brisk spring breeze, Ryka Court was celebrating St. Alilen's Day outdoors by the lake. Hordes of children hurtled across the lawns on Seekings, clutching paper lists of items they must find to win prizes. Women wore feathered headpieces; more feathers dangled from men's coif-ties. Group after group of amateur singers took the festooned stage to compete for the Saint's honors, while others strolled the fairground performing for cutpieces. It was rumored that Sevy Vasharron and several other operatic luminaries roamed the fair in heavy disguise, and the coins they collected would help refurbish Dinn's Opera House, damaged during the Rising. Adding to the happy confusion were Alilen's Dafties: mummers who capered about, teasing, juggling, declaiming nonsense poetry, adept at the sleight-of-hand that was all most people ever saw of "magic." All were dressed as birds—white doves, black ravens, red-combed banties, waddling blue geese—with the Daftie Master gorgeously costumed as one of the gorgeous rainbow-fantail birds strutting loose on the lawn.

All very pretty, all very festive. Cailet walked into the middle of it wearing solid black Mage Guardian regimentals—the ones given her on her eighteenth Birthingday by her sister, complete with flowing cloak and silver sash. The Candle pinned to her left collar point had belonged to her father, Auvry Feiran. The blade at her thigh had belonged to Gorynel Desse, one of the Fifty Swords said to have been forged by St. Caitiri Herself.

Everyone exclaimed on seeing her. Several people blanched. These she collected with her gaze and an inexorable spell—one from the *Code of Malerris,* which she considered fitting. When the three who were her quarry had come to her, she looked each in the eyes in turn. They fumed helplessly at her pilfering of their wills and their voices, but anger did not cover shock that she still lived—or fear of the knowing in her glittering black eyes.

Softly, she said, "You see before you a living Captal—not a dead martyr."

Granlia Feleson caught her breath. Irien Dombur's jaw tightened so severely that a muscle jumped and bunched in his cheek. And Elsvet Doyannis, biting both the pale lips between her teeth, began to tremble.

Cailet decided on Elsvet as the most likely to spew out everything she knew—if properly motivated. Fixing Glenin's childhood friend with her gaze, Cailet freed her. After a racking cough—the spell had not been gently cast—she began to sputter with incoherent outrage.

"Save it," Cailet advised, "for your trial."

"Trial? On what charge?" she demanded.

"Murder."

"What nonsense! You look healthy enough to me!"

Someone gasped. Dombur turned crimson; Granlia simply squeezed her eyes shut. Elsvet didn't realize what she'd done until Cailet arched a sardonic brow.

"I don't recall saying *whose* murder." Glancing around at the rapt crowd, pushing windblown hair from her face, she asked ingenuously, "Dear me—*did* I say whose murder? I'm quite sure I didn't."

"No, Captal, indeed you did not." This from the antiquated Tirri Mettyn, former Councillor for Kenrokeshir and lifelong enemy of Anniyas. Her gray eyes, sharp as whetted knives, flashed with glee as she shuffled closer across the new spring grass, clinging to handsome Granon Isidir's strong arm. "Keep going, this is getting interesting."

Nodding politely, Cailet turned to the threesome. "The charges are assault on Aidan Maurgen and murder of Kanto Solingirt, husband of Lady Lilen Ostin."

Elsvet had regained her bluster. "What drivel! I haven't the least idea what you're talking about! Are you sure you haven't taken the day to heart, Captal? St. Alilen is, after all, the patron of crazy persons."

"What I took to heart was the sight of a six-year-old boy lying unconscious, his face cut by glass and burned by magic." She kept a stranglehold on her temper as she went on, still in a quiet, lethal voice, "And the sight of my foster mother weeping over her husband of twelve weeks, a kind and loving old Scholar Mage who sacrificed his life to save the boy—and me."

"I've heard nothing of these matters," Elsvet claimed, and Cailet saw in her flat, cold eyes that technically she spoke the truth. "I'm sorry Lady Lilen's husband is dead, but it's nothing to do with me." And this time Cailet knew she lied.

"A young man currently in custody swears differently. He will testify that you knew all about it." Releasing Granlia Feleson, she went on, "And you as well."

She cleared her throat furiously. "How dare you use magic on a member of the Assembly of Lenfell? I'll have *you* up on charges, and with all these witnesses—"

"Oh, that's right," Cailet said, as if she'd just remembered. "You're part of the Assembly. Then that confirms the messenger's story of who gave him the Assembly livery he wore. You also provided money to purchase his passage to Renig and a horse from there to Ostinhold."

"Lies, all of it lies. I give money to no one but my husband and children and worthy causes. If this person had a uniform, he stole it."

"Which is a punishable crime," Elsvet put in. "Give us his name so he can be brought to trial for theft of government property."

Neither woman lacked for stubbornness, but it was no substitute for true courage. Cailet curved her mouth in a smile she knew to be frightening. She'd seen Jennis and Miram react to it when they asked what she planned to do on this rash solitary journey to Ryka Court.

"It's all lies," Granlia repeated, but she could no longer meet Cailet's eyes.

Granon Isidir cocked a brow. "If I were you, I'd keep practicing those denials. You'll need to be much more convincing before a Justice."

Cailet finally unWorked the magic holding Dombur. He stumbled, spat on the grass, and exclaimed, "What am *I* supposed to have done? Robbed the Treasury?"

"Yours was the responsibility for a certain item crafted in secret by a glassmaker at Domburr Castle, whose youngest son is a footman in your household. I'm sure you recall the item—round, quite warm to the touch, filled with Malerrisi magic?"

Another gasp, this time from dozens of throats.

"Malerrisi?" Elsvet manufactured a laugh. "They're either all dead or locked up in their castle in Seinshir, afraid to come out! What insane persecution fantasy is this, Mage Captal?"

You really must work on your judgment of character, Gorsha observed thoughtfully. *She made the initial mistake, yes, but now she's defending herself rather spiritedly. Though I must say that I also thought she'd be the one to break first.*

Cailet tilted her head slightly to one side, regarding the woman, seeing the truth of Gorsha's words. Elsvet hadn't broken, and might not—unless Cailet kicked her much harder. "Is it fantasy that this messenger sailed on a Doyannis ship? Or that even though the Port Authority records state that it was bound for Pinderon with no stops, it called in at Renig?"

"What proof—" Irien Dombur began.

Cailet ignored him, staring at Elsvet's stricken eyes with increasing satisfaction. "None but a Doyannis Blood could order such a thing. Still, this alone does not condemn you. But there's the note authorizing your groom to supply one of your own horses for the journey to Ryka Portside. A note this man showed to me when he told me the entire filthy tale."

Granlia Feleson shook with impotent rage and glared at Elsvet, but she was too smart to speak what was in her eyes: *You put something on paper? You fool!* Now Elsvet Doyannis was scared. Yet as Cailet waited for her to damn herself, she realized that it wasn't the Mage Captal that Elsvet feared.

And so, to finish her off, the Mage Captal murmured, "Sweet Saints, what *will* Glenin Feiran say when she finds out you've failed her?"

If Dombur had known the Malerrisi were involved, he gave a very good show of hiding it. "Are you mad? Glenin Feiran? A Malerrisi?"

"*The* Malerrisi," Cailet said blandly, again running one casual hand through her hair. "The First Lord. Or have you any doubts about either her abilities or her ambitions?" With a sidelong look for Elsvet: "*She* doesn't."

"I didn't know—" Elsvet's voice was a shrill gush of dread. "I swear I didn't know it would kill!"

"Shut up, you idiot!" Granlia Feleson snapped.

"It was at Shepherds Moon—she was there in my bedchamber one night and told me what she wanted, and it fit what had to be done—"

"Get your horrid magic off her!" Granlia shouted. "She's saying what you're telling her to say!"

Dombur seized on this in desperation. "Evidence gained by magical means is inadmissible in a court of law. You can't prove anything—"

"I didn't *know* it would kill!"

Cailet lifted a hand and all three of them were choked off in mid-cry. She could feel Gorsha's sword almost quivering at her side, and didn't dare touch it. Responsive to its wielder's truest emotions, not her conscious will, the blade would have hacked through all three conspirators while singing with the savor of their blood.

To Elsvet, Cailet said, "You knew very well it would kill. You just thought it would kill *me*. A dead martyr is better than a living Mage Captal. I heard you say it—you and Granlia Feleson—when you sat in the gardens pretending to feel sorry for Lady Sarra Liwellan after she lost her baby."

She fell silent, not wanting anyone to hear her voice shudder with the memory of hearing her death planned. In the quiet, she became aware of the stunned horror crowding around her. Some people were awestruck at the ruthless daring of those who would murder a Captal. But Cailet realized with a shock that the majority were furious. They did not value her because they knew Cailet herself, but they knew full well the value of a Mage Captal and her unique magic. She had more allies than she knew.

Tirri Mettyn, casting a baleful eye at the accused, placed a hand on Cailet's arm. "Unfortunately, the part about magic is correct," she wheezed. "Even if you didn't use magic on them, they'll swear uphill and down dale that you did, and none can prove them wrong. Further, the Doyannis whelp can claim that Glenin Feiran spelled her so she didn't know what she was doing. This can go to the law courts if you insist, Captal, but I guarantee you'll lose—if not at trial, then on appeal."

Cailet nodded. "I know. But what can be done?"

"I suggest resignations for Dombur and Feleson." Then she smiled with cheerful ferocity, for she despised Elsvet's mother, Councillor Doyannis, almost as much as she'd hated Anniyas. "As for the other one . . . do as you like with her. No one will object, not even her disgusting mother. I'll see to it."

"My thanks, Lady Tirri. But what I'd like and what I intend are different things."

"Too bad," she said with real regret.

Granon Isidir, with his customary exquisite politeness—and a positively feral gleam in his eyes—asked, "May I hope, Captal, that you have plans for the Malerrisi as well?"

"Plans," Cailet agreed, and matched the elegant Councillor's smile with that frightening one of her own.

The day after St. Alilen's, Irien Dombur resigned from the Council and Granlia Feleson from the Assembly. The official reason was "family responsibilities." Truly told, this was not far wrong; their families were now responsible for their good behavior. The First Daughters of both Names—Jaymia Feleson mortified, Eiras Dombur infuriated—soon sent letters to the Council and to Cailet avowing that their errant progeny would make no more trouble.

Elsvet Doyannis was another matter, and Cailet dealt with her personally.

On the third day of Seeker's Moon, the Captal ordered Elsvet brought to her. From Ryka Court they went by Ladder to Bard Hall. Elin Alvassy, Mage Guardian and Lady of Ambrai, posted guards to await their arrival—though Cailet didn't even have to set Wards on Elsvet. The woman was terrified, and so overcome at having traveled by Ladder that she was no more capable of escaping than if she'd been bound in chains. Cailet had no illusions about the true focus of Elsvet's dread.

From Bard Hall they were escorted through the

cleared streets and bustling reconstruction of Ambrai to the ruins of the Academy. Granon Bekke, the Warrior Mage assigned to secure all known Ladders, welcomed Cailet to the wreckage with as much aplomb as if vaulted halls and velvet chairs lay within.

"I'm glad to see you, Granon," Cailet told him as they picked their way along an aisle between shoveled rubble. "But I thought you were in Tillinshir."

"I was. The Ladder there is now Garvedian property—which is to say it's ours. When I got back to Ambrai this afternoon, I stopped by to pay my respects to Lady Elin, and her brother Pier told me something was up, so I thought I'd come help if needed."

"Your help is always welcome," Cailet replied warmly, for she liked this craggy-faced man who had just won his Warrior's sword and crimson sash when Ambrai was destroyed. Not yet forty, restored to his Mage-Right in the prime of his life, he was her idea of what a Warrior Mage ought to be: proud, strong, self-reliant, and utterly dependable.

I believe I'm jealous, said Gorynel Desse. *Though I must admit, the Bekkes always did turn out highly personable Warriors.*

Then you won't object if I make him Master of my Warders.

You couldn't have made a better choice.

Smiling at Granon, Cailet went on, "I don't anticipate any trouble, though. For one thing, they don't know we're coming—and for another, Glenin wouldn't dare."

"Glenin—?" Elsvet flinched at her own involuntary squeal.

No one made any reply.

A little while later, having reached their destination, Granon said, "So this was great-great-great-and-so-on Aunt Caitirin's love nest." He ran battle-scarred fingers over the obsidian hearth, then turned slowly to admire the frescoes of Brogdenguard on the walls.

"Haven't you been up the Captal's Tower before?" Cailet asked.

"There are a lot of Ladders on Lenfell," he responded laconically.

"There are indeed," she nodded, taking his point: that he had no time to visit those already owned by the Mage Guardians, there being so many that were as yet unsecured.

Elin Alvassy smiled a sweet, fierce smile that reminded Cailet of Sarra at her worst. "And our guest is about to go through this one."

As Elin, Granon, and the guards looked on with grim satisfaction, Cailet turned to Elsvet, whose eyes were fairly popping out of her head. "Here, take this," she said, handing over the foot-square wooden box she'd carried from Ryka Court. "Glenin Feiran used you to send a message to me, it's only fair that I use you the same way. I'm sending you on a trip, Elsvet. How—and if—you return is your problem."

If she could have turned any paler, she would have. "But—but my daughters—my husband—what will happen to them?"

"Lady Lilen had a husband, too," Elin reminded her coldly.

"And Kanto Solingirt had a daughter," Cailet added.

"A Warrior Mage daughter," Granon Bekke said. "*Domna* Doyannis, sing praises to your Name Saint that the Captal doesn't let Imilial Gorrst loose on you for five minutes."

"Do you really think it would take her that long?" Elin asked curiously.

"You're right, Lady. I do her an injustice."

Cailet sincerely enjoyed the effect of this on Elsvet. Typical Blood. she'd believed all her life that her Name would protect her from any unpleasantness more dire than a hangnail. "Don't drop that box," Cailet warned. "It's a very important gift for Glenin Feiran."

"You—you're going to k–kill her—"

"It's a thought," Cailet said, just to see how Elsvet would react; she was not disappointed. "But Mage Guardians don't work that way. This contains nothing more than a message. And there's something I want you to say to her face. It's quite simple, you won't have any problem remembering it."

Elsvet gulped and nodded.

"Tell her this: 'If you think you can succeed where Anniyas's Wards and Anniyas's Wraith failed, you're welcome to try.'"

The guards looked startled; Granon looked intrigued; Elin looked perplexed.

Elsvet looked thunderstruck. "Wraith?" she croaked.

Cailet smiled sweetly. "You *will* remember the exact words, now, won't you?"

Before she could begin to respond, Cailet took her arm and pulled her toward the obsidian hearth. A spell and a moment later the roar and chill spray of a waterfall battered at them. Elsvet shrieked, coughing on a faceful of water.

Cailet gave her a push out of the Ladder circle, shouting, "And do be sure to give Glenin regards from the Captal and Lady Sarra!"

"Wait—where am I?"

Pointing, Cailet yelled, "Malerris Castle!"

And then she was gone, back to the room where Caitirin Bekke had trysted in secret with Fourth Lord Shen Escovor, her Malerrisi lover.

Elin and Granon were waiting for her, as tense as the guards. Cailet collapsed the Blanking Ward and shook her head. "Don't look so worried. There was no trouble."

"You got back here awfully fast," Elin ventured.

"Only because I was getting drenched by that damned waterfall." She brushed drops off her black tunic before they could soak into the material.

"All the same," Granon said, "I think I'll wait here a while, Captal."

"As you like. Elin, may I impose on your hospitality for the night?"

Acquiescence was immediate—although Elin warned her that the accommodations were still so primitive that her brother Pier was asking how long she intended to camp out in her own city. Cailet didn't even feel strange asking for permission to stay in what should have been *her* city. Sarra would have; but Sarra had been born here.

All at once Cailet wondered how deeply Glenin hated Elin for being in her place. The Lady of Ambrai was an

Alvassy now. Glenin's city, Glenin's power, Glenin's rights and titles and privileges—

But that loathing would be as dust underfoot once Cailet's message had been received and understood.

And as she entered the plain wood-framed house Elin was calling home these days, assuring her cousin that a bed of blankets by the hearth would do her just fine, she thought of Glenin's rage and frustration, and smiled.

18

SHE was writing a letter to a Malerrisi sympathizer in Pinderon—a difficult, arrogant woman, but a Blooded First Daughter and excellently placed—when her aide burst into her sitting room.

"Lady—the Captal lives—"

The pen in Glenin's fingers snapped in two and she cursed bitterly.

"—and the Doyannis woman is here—"

"Here?" was all she could say, but when she motioned with one hand, Chava Allard took it as permission to admit the visitor.

Elsvet Doyannis—sopping wet, shivering with cold—collapsed into a chair, hands twisting around each other, and looked a piteous appeal at Glenin.

She gestured Chava out. "Well?"

"She—she didn't die," Elsvet stammered. "Some old man did—Glenin, you didn't tell me it would kill anyone but the Captal! You didn't tell me!"

"Why should I?"

"But—don't you care?"

"Why should I?" Glenin repeated impatiently. "Except that the wrong person is dead. How exactly did you bungle it?"

"I?"

"You, or that shit-witted Granlia Feleson. I suppose

it doesn't matter how or who—though it would have been nice to succeed on the first try."

"Glenin, you don't dare try again!"

She rose from her desk, consciously using her height as she'd seen her father do. "*You* are giving *me* advice?"

"No—I just—the Captal said that you—she sent something for you—a box—they took it away from me when they brought me to the castle—"

Glenin ignored the rest of her babble. "Chava!"

An instant later the young man presented himself at attention in the doorway. "Lady?"

"It seems Lady Elsvet brought me a little present from the Captal. Bring it here."

"It's not yet been fully investi—"

"Bring it!"

Hazel eyes went wide. "Yes, Lady."

Seating herself again, Glenin surveyed her childhood companion. "What other news? And do try to be coherent, Elsvet."

Loathing had not yet become stronger than fear; it would, once Elsvet warmed up and calmed down. Therefore, no blanket, no fire in the hearth, and no mulled wine.

"Glenin—it was horrible, you can't imagine. Irien Dombur and Granlia had to resign in disgrace—my mother is hanging onto her Council seat, but there's certain to be a recall election later this year."

"Dombur?" How could she have been so stupid? Dombur had been a secret, if halfhearted at times, member of the Rising. "Why did you use Dombur?"

"*He* came to *us!* After he watched the Captal unWork Anniyas's Wards he agreed that she's too dangerous to—"

Chava entered, gingerly carrying Cailet's doubtlessly unsisterly gift in both hands.

"She said it wouldn't kill you," Elsvet offered.

"How comforting." Taking the wooden box from Chava, she unlatched the brass fastening and raised the lid. "Of course," she murmured, knowing by the shape beneath thick black velvet that a Mage Globe lay within. Removing it, aware of the others' trepidation, she playfully tossed it in the air several times, catching it in one hand.

"Glenin—" came one half-strangled voice; "Lady," said the other; she threw them both a smile that faded when she caught sight of what was within the crystal sphere.

Four kinds of flowers were magically suspended within the Globe, a pretty arrangement unless one understood the symbolism. A sprig of yellow rue; a cutting of blue rosemary; a stem bearing three black-and-turquoise flameflowers; one purple thistle. Disdain she understood instantly; the combination of Remembrance and a symbol of St. Caitiri and the Mage Guardians in Ambrai's colors—*three* flameflowers, no less—was as absurd as it was insulting. But the thistle angered her, for it meant Cailet had somehow learned Glenin had a son.

For this alone, she flung the crystal onto the flagstones between carpets, for the fleeting satisfaction of watching it shatter.

But Cailet had wrought her spells shrewdly and well. And though the escaping magic could not affect Elsvet, Chava staggered and Glenin gasped, and from the nursery the baby whimpered. She heard her youngest sister's voice —pitched to her ears alone, with the particular tingle and taste of a magic learned from the *Code of Malerris.* The Mage Captal, with a copy of the *Code*—? She clenched her fists in fury as her son began to cry.

I knew you'd break it, Glenin. You'll try to break everything you can from now on. But you will never break the Mage Guardians, and you will never break me. Do what you must in your castle, but know that I am out in the world, waiting for you and for your son.

"What is it? Why do you look that way, Glenin?"

"Shut up!" she snarled. "Chava, have this swept up and thrown into the sea!" Stalking into the next room, she bent over the cradle to soothe her fretful son.

"Glenin, what was in the—" Elsvet had followed her, and now stopped at sight of the baby in her arms. "Oh!"

"Get out." She walked the Cloister rug, stroking the child's downy black hair.

"He's beautiful!" Elsvet exclaimed—sincerely,

Glenin was certain, for everyone had the same reaction to her child.

Turning her head, Glenin repeated slowly and distinctly, "Get. Out."

Elsvet actually looked hurt, and Glenin spared an instant to be amazed. Were they still ten years old, attending classes together with all the other little Blooded Daughters? Had Elsvet thought that the childhood association would produce lasting fondness in Glenin?

"You fool," she murmured, keeping her voice soft so as not to startle the baby further. "The one use you could have been to me, and you failed. Get out of my sight."

And with that, hatred finally triumphed. Rejected and reviled, Elsvet gave in to the satisfaction of having seen Glenin shaken by Cailet's magic. Her words were so smug that Glenin wanted to slay her where she stood. "She told me to tell you something, face-to-face."

"Say it and be gone."

"She said this, her exact words—'If you think you can succeed where Anniyas's Wards and Anniyas's Wraith failed, you're welcome to try.'"

Glenin's fingers clenched around the baby's blanket. When it became obvious that she intended no response, Elsvet turned and left, wet shoes squelching on the carpet.

The baby settled, blinking up at her. She touched his cheek, stroking the soft roundness, eager for the day when that cheek would be lean and bristly with a grown man's beard.

"So your grandmother failed, did she?" Glenin whispered to her dark-haired, gray-eyed son, her beautiful Mageborn boy. "When you're of an age, my darling, you and I will succeed. *A'verro,* we will."

TWINS

1

" . . . AND so you see, my Lord, the relinquished income from Sleginhold can be counterbalanced by an infusion of capital into the land-recovery scheme in Rokemarsh, which will in five years generate a tenfold return on the original investment. The initial outlay may leave some other enterprises with a cash deficiency, but this can be redressed by temporary diminution in production personnel at the mines, which will not only conserve remuneration but accommodate the concomitant advantage of a scarcity of ore, engendering an elevation in valuation and thus revenue. The figures are here, you can see for yourself—"

"Now, wait a minute," Collan said, stopping the factor in mid-oration, having heard exactly one thing that made any sense to him. "Turn people out of their jobs?"

The factor blinked rapidly a few times, pale lashes quivering over watery gray eyes, heightening his unfortunate natural resemblance to a rabbit. "Why, yes."

Col shuffled signed papers on his desk and gave the man his sweetest smile. "If it's salaries we want to save on, why don't we start with *yours?*"

"My Lord Rosvenir?" More blinks, and a hint of real water this time as tears threatened.

Though Collan had massive respect for the factor's organizational dexterity, he felt absolutely no sympathy for him as a human being; this was the third time in as many years that he'd proposed cuts in the Slegin Web's work force. "So the obscenity level of our profits goes down for a while. So what?"

"Profits must *always* increase, or—"

"Horse shit," Collan said amiably. Then, deliberately losing his smile, he went on, "As Lady Sarra has on occasion rather indelicately stated, we're rolling in it. Find the money somewhere else. Nobody loses work—*nobody*. Understand?"

"But—"

"Understand?"

A quivering sigh of regret. "Yes, my Lord."

"I thought you would." He stacked portfolios and reports and balance sheets with meaningful finality. "That's all for today. Thanks for your time, it's been fascinating."

Col made a quick escape from his office, leaving the factor muttering polysyllabically behind him. Had there been a guild for financial officers, this young man would be elected its master by acclamation. Collan flatly refused to spend more than an hour each day cooped up with him and his incomprehensibilities. Why, he grumped to himself, couldn't the factor's genius have come in a pretty little female package, like Sarra's legislative aide?

He knew very well why. Sarra had one very simple but very definite idea about the people who worked closely with her husband at Roseguard: they were invariably male. Liberal and enlightened as she was in her marital concerns, her attitude regarding her husband's proximity to pretty women—especially during her absences—was positively primitive. As if, Collan reflected on his way to the twins' rooms, even a beauty as spectacular as Lusira Garvedian could tempt him, even when Sarra had been gone for weeks.

Which she had. And thoughts of her were producing a reaction not at all convenient for a man who would be sleeping alone until she returned from Ryka Court.

"Damned conferences," he muttered. "Damned meetings, damned Council, damned government—"

Sarra would have told him that separation was the price they paid for the pleasure of the rest of their lives. She worked so much—even when they were officially on holiday—that he doubted she really believed this. But he'd taught her (slowly, it was true) that when the papers and portfolios and petitions were packed away in the office at the end of the business day, it was perfectly acceptable to apply her attention just as devotedly to him and the children. In fact, he demanded it. He hadn't spent the last thirteen years playing Traditional Husband—tending the Slegin Web, establishing and running a home, and raising the children—to spend his married life all by himself.

Roseguard had been quite a while in the rebuilding, but he'd finally gotten it the way he wanted it. Not having any personal experience of a home, but having seen plenty of examples in his travels, he knew more about what he didn't want than what he did. Roseguard was of necessity a combination of family home, public showcase, business office, and governing center. But the four did not overlap. He would never have raised children in a museum, an accounting agency, a bureaucratic maze, or a palace. On the other hand, he was equally thankful he didn't have to live in the chaos that was Ostinhold.

Truly told, Col was happy with his life at Roseguard—even though at times his life as Lady Sarra Liwellan's husband was not exactly what he'd had in mind.

Some of it was fun. The performer in him liked being the center of attention. And he received lots of attention—as manager of the Web, husband of the most important woman in the Shir, and a famous personage in his own right. The Minstrel in him loved to invite fellow musicians for evenings of song-swapping; Roseguard had become known throughout Lenfell as a pivotal Bardic and operatic center.

But having a lot of money and being able to spend it just as he pleased was the most fun of all. Surprised by the total of his own savings stashed away in various banks through the years, once he'd acquired a home to invest it all in, he found he had a real talent for buying things. Sarra's taste in interior decor rivaled her taste in dress: left to herself, she would be surrounded by and wear all sorts of faddish frippery. (She was not left to herself in the matter of clothing; he supervised all her trips to the dressmaker's.) Collan let her have her way in her private office, which was to him a nightmare of tapestries, carpets, statuary, and stained-glass windows. But he claimed the rest of the Residence for his own. Public rooms meant to impress did so—subtly. Guest rooms meant to be comfortable were—elegantly. Everything was airy and pleasant and warmly welcoming. And it had taken cartloads of money to make it that way.

Representatives from the biweekly *Hearth and Home Review* sent him letters five times a year beseeching an interview and access for a sketch artist, with the purpose of rendering Roseguard in prose and woodcuts for the edification of husbands with less innate elegance than Collan Rosvenir. He'd said "No" as many ways as he knew how without offending the publisher too much, but suspected that one of these days he'd have to get nasty about it. Sarra, naturally, found the whole notion vastly entertaining. "Well, it's your own fault for doing such a good job. I did my best by telling everyone you were *more* than just decorative, but—"

The thing that surprised him most about life as a husband was that life as a husband was quite enjoyable. It wasn't just that he was *Sarra's* husband, though this had much to do with it. He genuinely liked his position, his duties, his responsibilities, and all that lovely money.

He refused to dabble in politics, an attitude that earned him much credit with conservatives who avowed that a man's place was in the bedchamber, not the Council chamber. This interpretation of the geography of his marriage annoyed him. The old fossils couldn't seem to get it through their heads that if he'd *wanted* to participate in Sarra's public life, he would have. He got enough of politics and intrigue whenever Sarra felt it necessary to throw a pay-back-all-the-invitations-at-once entertainment. Collan was known as the most accomplished host in all fifteen Shirs—mainly because he refused to be bored at his own parties.

In addition to running the household, he kept the Web's books. This he found to be rewarding exercise for his mathematical quirk. And by managing the Slegin fortune that Sarra had inherited, he felt he was of some real use to her—even though the initial organization of the ledgers had taken a ream of paper for calculations, gallons of strong black coffee, and a week of lurid cursing. By now everyone knew he'd catch the slightest variance in figures; "mistakes" were rare, and so was the fun of calling the culprit into Lord Rosvenir's Awesome Presence.

Aside from his prowess with the balance sheets, Sarra also relied on his ability to tell a swindle from a sweet deal. Although the scope of the Slegin investments at first gave him pause, after thirteen years he was used to juggling fifty different ventures in nine different Shirs. From the start he was able to smell a mile off whether a new investment proposal was a cozening, a connivance, or a flat-out cheat. Thus dubious commercial propositions had become as rare as "mistakes" in the ledgers, depriving him of another source of amusement.

Midsummer of 971, something had happened that made up for the loss of such entertainment and provided two infinite sources of occupation—not to mention headaches, laughter, frustration, exasperation, and sheer unadulterated joy. What he loved best and found most satisfying about this life he never would have dreamed he'd live was a thing he'd scrupulously avoided all his life: fatherhood.

Motherhood had bewildered Sarra for the first several years of her children's lives. She was one of those women who became comfortable with their offspring only when they were of an age to make rational conversation. Collan *adored* babbling with the twins, bathing them and playing with them and watching them sleep and taking them to the park where total strangers exclaimed how beautiful they were. Sarra distrusted such compliments, believing that the bestowers always wanted something from powerful Lady Liwellan. Collan knew they were only speaking the Saints' honest truth. His children were utterly gorgeous. Precociously brilliant. Adorably witty. Truly told, they were perfect—and anyone who failed to see this was obviously demented.

It was a fine emotional and societal line most husbands walked when it came to children. A woman's babies belonged to her as surely as her husband did—more so, for they bore her Name and he did not. But he was the one who took charge of their upbringing and education; he changed their linen, taught them to read and count, soothed their hurt feelings, bandaged their scraped knees, and made sure they were clean and acceptably civilized during their daily hours with their mother. This responsibility inevitably produced feelings of possessiveness that were just as inevitably frowned upon. Any husband who said "My children"—as if he'd carried them and birthed them and nursed them—was reproached, publicly if need be. Circumstances varied within each Name, but by and large a husband's role was to supervise the children of the marriage exactly the same way he did the household: with diligence, exactitude, and constant consciousness that ultimate ownership was not his.

Collan found this imbecilic. How could he look at Taigan's funny little curling mouth or Mikel's bright blue eyes and not be struck in the gut that these children were *his?* Anyone whose eyebrows so much as twitched when he referred to his daughter and son as *his* daughter and son didn't understand the first thing about being a father.

And whenever he thought of what Rina Firennos had done to Val Maurgen—never acknowledging him as Aidan's father, never allowing him to see the boy—Col got sick to his stomach. Not raising his own children was inconceivable to him. Yet legally his claim on them was damned near nonexistent. That was the law.

Councillor Liwellan (as susceptible as any woman to pillow-talk) was in the long, slow process of changing the law. That was one advantage to husbanding a powerful woman.

One disadvantage was that too often she wasn't around to be a husband to.

His duty with the factor over for the day, he was climbing the stairs to the twins' rooms when he saw Tarise on the next landing. Dedicated as he was to his children, he could never have survived sane if not for Tarise. She loved Taigan and Mikel as much as if she'd birthed them herself. She was unable to have children of her own—which saddened her but didn't bother her husband in the least, for Rillan Veliaz, Roseguard's Master of Horse, considered every foal born in his stables to be his very own child.

"Well, what's the crisis today?" Collan asked cheerfully. "Broken crockery, smashed thumbs, or *I will not contradict my tutor* five hundred times on the slate board?"

"The nerve of you!" she grinned. "Maligning your own sweet, charming, obedient children! Especially when they're not here to defend themselves!"

"Where are they?"

"Treyze and Goryn Senison's." Tarise smoothed the violet silk of her skirts, adding, "I'm taking advantage of it by taking my husband out to a lavish, expensive dinner and the opera. They're doing *Ayidda* at All Saints'—cramped but magnificent, I'm told. And I'd better hurry before one of his damned horses casts a shoe or gets the colic or something equally tedious and unromantic."

"Barns can be very romantic—or did you forget where you and Rillan spent your first night of married life?" Collan teased.

"Don't remind me!" Passing him on the stairs, she paused to give him a playful thwack with her fan—lace stretched over carved wooden struts, the latest in fashionable accessories, highly practical in the summer heat, and Collan's most recent contribution to feminine adornments. Sarra thought them silly, but Taigan looked adorable fluttering one in front of her face with her mischievous green eyes sparkling above.

"You looked happy enough about it the next morning."

"Some wedding night! Two hours wed, the feasting not yet over, and his favorite mare chooses that exact moment to go into labor!"

"Complaints, complaints. You *could've* come back inside, you know, after the foal was born, instead of staying up in the hayloft until dawn."

"Well, no hayloft for me tonight!" She descended the last few steps, calling back over her shoulder, "The twins should be back home tomorrow morning after breakfast. Remember to send the carriage for them."

"Have fun," he answered, then sighed. No children to play with, no friends to dine with, not even a ticket to the opera—and no Sarra. It was going to be another dull evening.

2

"LADY Glenin? May I come in?"

Closing the *Code* on her desk, Glenin rose and smiled a greeting. Saris Allard was one of the few women she'd ever really liked, and a nice evening chat was just what she needed. She had spent a long day teaching her son the basics of Warming spells. His power was gratifying, but before she'd shown him how to restrain it, he'd set fire to a blanket, a cheese casserole, and a pewter tankard. Tangling with her son's formidable magic was ever an exhausting day's work; Glenin required some relaxation.

"Come in, Saris, please. Why don't we go out to the balcony where it's cool? I can't recall a hotter summer."

When they were seated outside with cups of iced wine, the Third Lady of Malerris, Threadkeeper, sighed and stretched out long legs in loose cotton trousers. "One would think that being pent up here all day every day, we'd run out of things to do by noon! Instead, there are never enough hours in the day."

"Anything I should know about?" Glenin asked idly, watching the starlight play on the waterfall far below the castle.

"Nothing serious. A few restless spirits wanting to get away for a while." She laughed softly. "And one who wants to come home! My son," she explained when Glenin looked sidelong at her.

"Chava? But I thought he enjoyed being out in the world."

"It seems the excitement of being a blacksmith in some Tillinshir village northeast of nowhere is beginning to pall. He'd rather be back here, working for you again."

Glenin sipped wine and considered. Chava had been an excellent aide, but she hadn't bade him stay. When he turned eighteen, nine years ago, he'd asked to do what many of the younger Malerrisi were doing: finding places for themselves in various Shirs. He'd felt caged here, as many people did. Those Glenin trusted were sent out to build lives and identities—and relay information. Those Glenin did not trust were closely watched at Malerris Castle.

"He's more use to us where he is," she said at last. "If you want to go visit him—"

Saris gave a little shrug of slender shoulders. "He's a grown man—twenty-seven this year. I shaped his life, but now he must live it according to my teachings."

"He never struck me as being restive."

"You didn't know him when he was little! The trouble I had getting that boy to sleep—! Mama, I want a drink of water, a story, a different toy, the sun to come up—"

"The trouble is the magic, you know," Glenin said. "It keeps them awake until they can learn to block it out. Someone's always doing some sort of Working at night, and even if it's relatively quiet, there are the Wards."

"Yes, you're right. Even though there weren't that many while Chava was growing up, he used to say that the one outside his bedroom sang to him sometimes."

"You Warded his bedroom?"

"Of course. The Most Noble Lady Ria was alive back then, you remember." She gave the name sarcastic capitals, and Glenin's mouth twitched with amusement. No love had ever been lost between Ria Shakard and any other woman at Malerris Castle. "And she didn't half like it that my son was the son of the Fifth Lord—may Vassa's Wraith personally trap hers in the Dead White Forest."

"Considering Ria's ambitions for her own children, it was wise of you to Ward Chava's room," Glenin remarked.

"Wiser still of you to send her and her repellent First Daughter to Dombur Castle."

"Nothing of wisdom about it." Glenin made wide, innocent eyes. "How could I have known that a Warrior Mage would discover them, let alone that Ria would botch a spell meant to protect her and her daughter?"

"How, indeed," Saris replied, lips twitching in a smile. Then, more seriously. "The Warden of the Loom arranges matters so that the Weaver may work without hindrance. That was Anniyas's mistake—she tried to twist the threads to her own designs and do the work herself."

"I sometimes understand why she succumbed to temptation," Glenin admitted—something she would never have told anyone else. "It's hard, compelled to remain here and 'arrange' things, as you put it, without actually having my own hand in it. What happened to Ria only confirmed the prudence of trusting to the Weaver. But what you said about Chava interests me. Surely he didn't feel the Wards on his room until his magic came to him?"

"You know, I think they *do* feel it, even when they're babies." Saris stretched again and poured more wine for them both. "*Yours* was ready to cast his first spell before he left your womb! And I understand we nearly had a conflagration this morning."

Smiling again, proud of her son, Glenin replied, "Better all the trials of teaching a child with strong magic than to birth some lumpen little thing with no magic at all."

"I quite agree. Speaking of which, the girl in Kenrokeshir has been dealt with."

"Ah. Excellent, Threadkeeper."

"Compliment the Fifth Lord, not me. I only pointed out the problem. He solved it." She sipped wine, then shook her head. "*A'verro,* Glenin, sometimes it *is* necessary to pull the thread with one's own hand."

Glenin nodded. A Malerrisi youth, sent out two years ago at twenty to establish himself in Rokemarsh, had fathered a child by a woman not Mageborn. Glenin had only learned of the baby's birth at Thieves Moon—appropriately enough, for the woman had stolen Malerrisi seed. She was now dead. The young man had been brought back to Malerris Castle. Glenin had several alternatives open to her, and must decide by tomorrow what punishment he would receive. As for the child—a physicker, secretly Malerrisi, had concocted a fever for the newborn girl, taken her to his hospice, and in due course reported her death. Now she was with a Malerrisi couple at Roke Castle. They would raise her as their own, and watch as she grew for signs of magic.

As Glenin brooded over this defiance of her authority as Warden of the Loom, she wished for the thousandth time that she could master the Mage Globe trick Cailet used to keep in contact with her Guardians. Based on spells in the *Code,* it should have been simplicity itself for Glenin to set up the same communication network. But some esoteric Guardian magic had been added, and in the dozen years since Cailet's little message had come by Elsvet Doyannis's hand, no one at the Castle had been able to figure it out.

Elsvet's failure had been Glenin's first and most painful lesson in keeping her fingers out of Chevasto the Weaver's way. The Fifth Lord excised errant threads from the tapestry. The Fourth Lord educated young Malerrisi to take their proper places in the great fabric. The Third Lord monitored each strand for strength. The Second Lord kept the Loom itself—the structure of Malerrisi across all Lenfell—intact and growing. Only Glenin could order any of them to make changes, but she was the Warden of the Loom, not the Weaver. The debacle of Elsvet had taught her that she must not contort threads of her own choosing to fit a pattern *she* wished to create. When opportunity arose, she would take it—as she had done with Elsvet herself. The woman had flatly refused to be taken anywhere by Ladder again, and had left Malerris Castle by ship—which had never reached Ryka. The Weaver had obviously finished with Elsvet, and dealt with her accordingly. Glenin schooled herself thereafter to surrender her will to St. Chevasto's—but sometimes it was hard. Very hard.

Her duty was not to create, but to take advantage of opportunities. The trick to being Warden of the Loom was to recognize signs that the Weaver was preparing something to Malerrisi benefit. Thus the young man and his unauthorized offspring had been retrieved; it remained to be seen whether either one would contribute to the tapestry.

The sordid little tale prompted another thought. "Saris, does Chava want to come home because he feels he's in danger? With some girl not Mageborn, I mean.

He's long past the age when a man begins to think of marriage and children."

Saris blinked several times. "Chava? Married? A father? I never knew anyone who wanted such things less! No, I think he's just homesick and wants to conjure a few spells without having to worry about getting caught."

"I know how difficult it is," Glenin mused. "Being the only Mageborn, unable to use magic, unable to talk about it with someone who understands. . . ."

"Not one of them out in the world can even be suspected of possessing magic—can you imagine what would happen if the Captal found out? She'd try to make them into Mage Guardians!"

Glenin forgot what she'd been about to say as a wholly new idea occurred to her. "How much chance would she have? Oh, not with Chava, I know he's loyal. But with others?"

Saris looked thoughtful. "I could begin some inquiries. Nothing obvious, just a visit here and there to ascertain loyalty."

"Do that. No matter how well-trained and dedicated they are, they must interact with all sorts of corrupting influences and make thousands of choices without disciplined supervision."

After a few moments, Saris said, "It's a terrible responsibility, Glenin. We must teach them how to choose, but those choices must always fit into the greater pattern of the Loom. We can instruct and demonstrate and give examples—and I'm not talking just about our students, but about our sons—while in the end we can only trust that we've done our jobs well, and beg St. Chevasto to guide them when we cannot."

"I wonder sometimes how anyone can raise a child with the idea of letting her become what *she* wants to be. How can a child make such decisions?"

"It should always be left to a mother. We're older, wiser, we know the world—"

"Some of us are wiser," Glenin said, thinking of Sarra and her twins.

"Some," Saris agreed. "The day can't come too soon when the unwise ones are kept from making all the wrong choices for their children—or letting the children themselves choose."

"Chava decided on blacksmithing himself, didn't he?"

"Yes, he did!" Once more Saris's sparkling laugh rang out. "What Mage could sense his magic if he's surrounded by all that iron?"

"You taught him well, Saris. I hope I do as well with my son—" She chuckled. "—if he doesn't burn down the castle first!"

3

A dull week of work and Web later, guests arrived at Roseguard unannounced. Collan was rounding a corner on his way to the kitchens for a snack when he nearly collided with a tall, sturdy, swarthy youth who'd beaten him to it. The young man sidestepped nimbly, balancing a large tray on the flat of one hand like an expert waiter. The fingers of his other hand were woven around the necks of three unopened wine bottles.

Collan surveyed the laden tray: bread, two halfrounds of cheese, sliced roast, two kinds of grapes, and a pyramid of chocolates. "I gather," he said dryly, "that having eaten your grandmother out of shelf and sideboard, you're here to do the same to us."

Aidan Maurgen grinned. "I'm a growing boy."

"And couldn't wait for the servants to bring you some lunch. At least you've grown up—this is more civilized than what Taigan and Mikel are eating this week." Collan snagged an apple from the tray and bit into it as they walked to the guest quarters.

"I thought they got over the pumpkin mush with cheese sauce stage years ago."

Col snorted. "If only. I'm just glad I don't have to feed 'em personally anymore. Their first year cost me a fortune in shirts."

"The way I heard it, you set a new fashion—no man dared to be seen without pulped carrots decorating his clothes."

"Spinach," Collan corrected. "Orange isn't a color redheads wear well. Don't think you're not welcome, but why are you here?"

"Just tagging along while Aunt Lindren finds a house for Miram and Riddon."

"Please tell me she didn't bring the twins. One set around here is all I can manage."

Aidan laughed, his father's wink twinkling in his eyes even as his father's gold earring shone at his left earlobe. Collan had sent it to Maurgen Hundred earlier this year to be one of the eighteen presents traditional on the eighteenth Birthingday. Now a man grown, Aidan was more than ever Val's handsome image; all he seemed to have taken from his mother's family were longer legs and lighter brown eyes than the Maurgens. "My adorable little cousins yelled and screamed for an hour when they heard we were going to visit Roseguard, but Lindren told 'em if they didn't shut up they'd be staying at their Aunt Geria's for the duration, instead of with Granna Seffie at the Hundred."

"Vicious enough," Collan allowed, "but an empty threat. None of the other Ostins has spoken to First Daughter in years. How is Lady Sefana?"

"Ready to knock Biron upside the head for dumping Val and Margit on her. Can't blame her—they bring the total pairs of twins living with her up to four."

"Four?"

"Riena's Sefana and Jeymian, Jennis's Solla and Valiri and Aliz and Lilen," Aidan chortled. "And Jen talks about having more! Granna Seffie swears by St. Alliz that after two sets of twins, if *she'd* gotten pregnant again she would've slit her own throat."

"Wise woman." Crossing the central hall to the reception room doors, he added. "Of course, your tagging along here has nothing to do with the fact that Marra Gorrst is enrolled in my class at the conservatory until Candleweek."

"Nothing at all," Aidan said blithely, not changing color and not fooling Collan a bit.

Not just Lindren Ostin and her husband Biron Maurgen, but his sister Riena and her husband Jeymi Slegin were waiting in the salon. Almost a full table tonight for dinner, Collan reminded himself to remind the cook. Taigan and Mikel would be thrilled at their inclusion in the grown-up ritual. Candles, gleaming crystal, a special arrangement of flowers, and the Roseguard dinner service of beautiful white Rine porcelain painted with the Slegin Rose Crown—all he lacked was Sarra to preside over the table. But thought of the dishes also reminded Collan to tell Mikel that if one of those plates was so much as chipped, his loving father would chip out one of his teeth to mend it with.

Lindren was the youngest of the six Ostin daughters, and Collan had always found her to be the most like her mother. Lady Lilen had once confided that each inherited something completely different from the Ostin agglomeration of traits. Margit, dead these twenty years, had received the magic; Lenna, the ingenuity; Tevis, the stubbornness; Miram, the looks; Lindren, the energy. First Daughter Geria had been gifted with nothing more agreeable than an ability to make money—which, with their mother's blessing, Lindren and Lenna had spent the last dozen years thwarting at every turn. Collan, loathing First Daughter almost as much as the other Ostins did, helped now and again. Thus, after greeting his guests, he asked Lindren how much of Lilen's money she wanted to spend this time.

"A lot!" she replied, grinning. "The less that's left, the less Geria will inherit."

"Lilen will spend everything she can without endangering the Web," said Riena Maurgen. "And then leave what she bought during her lifetime to the other children. I always knew I should've married an Ostin!"

"So should I," retorted her husband, a Slegin whose dower included swaths of Sheve and a mountain of gold coins in the Roseguard branch of the St. Tirreiz Bank. To Collan, Jeymi added, "I'm working on getting her to divorce me while Lenna and Tevis are still unmarried."

"They've both got far too much sense to follow Miram's example—or mine," Riena said serenely. "Slegin men are dangerous. It's the Renne Blood in them, you know."

If the Ostin daughters divvied up the family traits, the two sets of Maurgen twins split everything down the middle. Riena and Jennis and Biron and Valirion all looked pretty much alike, but the elder of each pair were twinned in unruffled temperament while the younger were more volatile. Jennis and Val had received all the fiery sparks, leaving Riena and Biron with the steady warmth of the hearth. Collan, applying the principle to his own children, told himself that the best of him and the best of Sarra were to be found in both Taigan and Mikel. He marveled again at the vagaries of heredity—which he had never in his life applied to himself.

All he remembered of his mother was her armband of blue onyx set in silver, and her beautiful voice as she sang by the fire. Of her looks, character, and other talents, he knew nothing. Of his father, he knew less than nothing. Gorynel Desse had given him the Name "Rosvenir," but Collan could have been anything from a Mikleine to a Garvedian. Hell, he could be an Ostin for all anyone knew—and considering their numbers, it was more than likely.

None of it interested him, truly told. He was what he was, what he had made of himself. And together he and Sarra had created two more lives. There was a satisfying freedom in that, in not being fastened to the past.

Talk turned back to the cheerful spending of vast sums of Lady Lilen's money, and Collan made suggestions about various properties in the hills around Roseguard. Biron made a list, with directions, and gave it to his sister.

"We'll go out looking after lunch," said Lindren. "Just Riena and me. I know what men are like when they walk through a house."

Jeymi rolled his eyes. "And I know what *women* are like. A single minute spent in the kitchen to make sure it has an oven, and even less time to count the bathrooms, without a thought to them other than whether the plumbing works."

"Snug roof, solid foundation, and dry cellar, that's all women ask about," Biron nodded. "Not a word about whether the garden's large enough to feed the household, or where to put a horde of visiting relatives, or how much it costs to heat the place in winter—"

"That," Riena serenely informed her brother, "is why we have husbands."

After luncheon, Collan offered a carriage to the women for their drive around to various properties. Jeymi went to visit old friends in the city, and Aidan expressed—of all things—a desire to go swimming.

"Could we?" Biron asked wistfully.

"You Wasters!" Collan grinned. "All right, then, come on. I know a great bower."

"Let's go!" Aidan leaped to his feet.

"A *what?*" Biron cast an alarmed glance at his nephew.

"Relax," Col advised. "Nobody's going to outrage your modesty or infuriate your women by bidding on you."

Someone in the Wytte Web had had the bright idea of buying up one of the nicer bowers and converting it into an exclusively masculine retreat. Most of the men in Roseguard had memberships. Sarra had given Collan one for his Birthingday last year, mostly because she thought he'd enjoy it and partly because she saw a chance to annoy the Wittes—not a one of whom she could tolerate for more than five minutes. The Wyttes were a (formerly) Fourth-Tier offshoot of the (formerly) Blooded Wittes, who never admitted that the only difference between the families was a vowel.

The Maiden's Prayer, choicest bower in Sheve, had provided only the finest young men in the most elegant settings, with prices to match. Now the young men were gone and the settings were book rooms instead of bedrooms, but the price of an afternoon at Wytte's was still extravagant. The Members' Entrance was through a sedate front door into a reception area that would not have been out of place in the most conservative household in the Shir. Within, all was very proper, dignified, and comfortable. There were three libraries for quiet afternoons with a good book; a card room for friendly games (no wagers allowed); a restaurant; a rooftop arboretum with fine views of the city and sea; a training room supervised by a massively muscular Wytte who'd spent fifteen years as a drill instructor for the Ryka Legion; and a bar.

"Fruit juice and coffee, no liquor—though I'm working on getting the city ordinance changed," Collan said as they rounded a corner and approached the building. "It's just a place to escape the women and children for a couple of hours. You'll find out what a relief that can be, Aidan, once Marra Gorrst opens her eyes and—"

"Marra Gorrst?" Biron asked, bewildered

Aidan wrapped his arms around his head and moaned.

"Have I said something amiss?" Col inquired innocently.

"Marra Gorrst?" Biron said again, more pointedly, then shook his head. "I *told* Mother that sending you to Mage Hall for six weeks was a mistake."

"No, it wasn't," Aidan said stoutly, emerging from his protective shell. "I had a great time and the Captal said that if I want to come back and work for her, I'm more than welcome. And now that I've turned eighteen, I can do as I please, with Granna's permission, of course, and—"

Biron sighed. "And you came along on this trip to get you more than halfway there before you broke the news. You say Lady Sefana agreed to this?"

"Of course she did! I'm not like Terrill Ostin, running off to join the Dinn Opera without even leaving a letter!"

Collan remembered the incident; Lady Lilen only discovered her only surviving son's destination when, eight weeks later, he sent her a playbill with his name listed as second assistant stage manager for a new production of *Regallata*. In the years since, he'd married Felera Irresh (a leading soprano), risen to Director, and staged Falundir's *Ruins of Ambrai* to worldwide acclaim. So much for Lilen's plan to make her youngest son manager of the Ostin Web. *"Not that I wouldn't have let him do whatever he pleased,"* she'd written to Sarra, *"and he knows it, but I suspect he didn't want a lifetime of the inevitable arguments with Geria. Who is, of course, livid. A brother in the theater is almost as bad as two brothers in the Rising."*

The Maurgens, uncle and nephew, were still glowering at each other. Col swung open the door of Wytte's, saying, "Come on, you can drown each other in the pool."

The young man on duty at the front desk directed them to sign the guest ledger and pointed to the changing room. As they were undressing, a brace of bower lads came in after their daily workout. At the sight of them, Biron and Aidan blushed all the way to their belts.

Collan sighed at this evidence of a provincial upbringing, but had to admit that if one hadn't spent much time around such youths, one could easily be intimidated. The pair were stark naked, without even the codpocket most men wore during a swim or workout, and built like sculptor's models. The blond one had skin like polished gold; the dark one seemed carved of walnut. Col guessed their ages to be about twenty-two. Their brief, dismissive glances indicated that Biron, thirty-six, was an old man— and forty-four-year-old Collan was positively decrepit. Aidan, however, received a glance of pure venom.

Guiding his guests from the changing room, Collan said, "They're paid to look that good. And they have to work at it, too. Not like us—we're just naturally gorgeous."

Aidan was looking thoughtful. "I've never seen any close-to. Do all girls hire one?"

Col smothered a grin, recalling another bower where Sarra had attempted to hire *him.* "Not all. Some mothers don't think much of that particular rite of feminine passage, and I know for a fact that Geria Ostin had to buy her own."

Biron snorted. "I hope he held out for a small fortune—it'd take that, to spend a night with her."

"Pinchpiece that she is, she probably hired somebody off the street," Aidan said.

Grinning, Collan opened the door to the pool enclosure, then froze as he realized that one day Sarra would have to make a decision about Taigan's education in such matters. His little girl, his bright golden darling, with some primped and pampered and polished bower lad? Over his dead body—

"I'm surprised," Biron was saying, "that they let such men in here."

Provincial was one thing; prejudiced was another. "Why?" Col asked. "Their bowers pay their way in."

"But they're—"

"Whores?" he interrupted smoothly.

"I didn't mean it like that." After a moment Biron smiled ruefully. "I guess if anybody needs an escape from women, it's bower lads."

"Never more truly told. Well, there's your water. Dive in."

They needed no further urging. Col shook his head. Enough clean water to swim in seemed to be the culmination of every Waster's wildest fantasies—he could swear Cailet had chosen the site for Mage Hall only because the property had its own little lake to splash around in. Otherwise the acreage in Tillinshir was a total loss as far as he could tell, which was why she'd gotten it so cheap. Ten miles from the nearest town—if the fifty-six houses at Heathering could be so termed. Spring consisted of high winds and flooding; summer gave new and graphic meaning to the weeks of Drygrass and Wildfire; autumn could only be described as scorching; and winter's only advantage was that even at that latitude there wasn't much snow. He'd never yet met a Waster who could even hear the word "snow" without a horrified flinch. And Collan knew why; unless you went out bundled to the eyes in six layers of clothing (especially socks), the acid in all that pretty white stuff corroded your skin until it scarred. He remembered snow from Scraller's Fief, and didn't blame any Waster for her dread of it.

Now that he compared Mage Hall to The Waste, he decided Cailet had chosen well. There were some good trees around the property—redwoods and incense cedars up the mountainsides, oaks in the valley, willows around the lake and creeks. Trees and water: either could excite rapture in a Waster, but both together were ecstasy.

Aidan called out an invitation to join them in the pool. Col replied that he intended to be lazy, and ambled over to a row of padded lounge chairs by the corner soak pool. Choosing a spot directly under a skylight, he asked the attendant for a stack of the latest broadsheets. He never used the pool except for cooling off, and had never even set foot in the workout room. *Other* men came here to preserve or reclaim their figures, but not Collan Rosvenir.

The broadsheets were the usual collection of current events, features, and gossip. After a mere five minutes, he despaired of finding something even mildly interesting to read.

ASSEMBLY DEBATES NEW TAXES

So what else was new.

BARDS CAPTIVATE THOUSANDS
The All-Lenfell Bardic Games, underwritten by the Geillen Name and judged by Bard Falundir, will soon be underway at Wyte Lynn Castle. Preliminary competition attracted more than four hundred contestants, and ticket sales for the finals at the new Bleynbradden Theater have topped five thousand. Half the proceeds from the event will go to rebuilding Bard Hall in Ambrai.

Finally somebody was doing something about the shortfall in funds. Elin Alvassy did what she could, but her priority was making Ambrai a working and livable city again; she couldn't be expected to finance the restacking of every stone and the renailing of every rafter.

ROKEMARSH FLOODS MAY BE WORST EVER
Experts surveying the Endless Mountains snowpack fear that the annual flooding in the Rokemarsh Delta of the River Bluehair could be the

worst in three Generations, threatening the region's picturesque stilt-houses.

He recognized Sarra's dainty, meddling little hand in this article, which went on to describe the disasters of flooding—not only to the people of Rokemarsh but to Lenfell's supply of certain fish, spices, and other products. The "picturesque" wasn't a bad touch, either— plenty of people holidayed in the Rokemarsh area, though why anyone would want to spend two weeks in a swamp was beyond his understanding. It had been his idea to use the broadsheets, of course: publicly link whatever project she favored for humane reasons to personal inconvenience for the general populace.

Is Your Daughter Mageborn?
Ten Telltale Signs

Ha! So Cailet had taken his advice, too. He'd told her years ago to use the broadsheets instead of racing all over the world. About time; she was wearing herself out trying to find new Mageborns and teach the ones already at Mage Hall.

St. Imili's Chronicles
The Lenfell Weekly Record *congratulates the following newlyweds. . . .*

Nobody he knew had gotten married last week. Of course, most of the men he knew were either already married or too smart to become so. Not every man was lucky enough to husband a woman like Sarra.

Sunfall from the skylight was moving slowly down his chest and he was trying to work up the energy to shift position when two voices he didn't know drifted toward him from the soak pool. Though the men spoke quietly, some quirk of tile and water and vaulted ceiling let him hear as clearly as if they shouted.

". . . diamond earring she gave me last Birthingday? I wore it to bed. She damned near chipped a tooth—but it cured her of biting!"

"When you find a way to cure a woman of scratching like a silverback sharpening her claws, let me know."

Collan repressed a self-pitying sigh. What he wouldn't give to have Sarra here to sink her teeth into his shoulder and rake his back with her nails. . . . He tried to interest himself in a review of a new play at the Ryka Theater (*Road companies soon to appear all over Lenfell!*) but the nearby conversation caught his attention again.

". . . at the Opera last week? She's not much to look at above the neck, but—oh, to be a bar of soap in her bathtub!"

"Then you don't know."

"Know what?"

"Ellus isn't here today, and it's his regular afternoon."

"So?"

"Bruises. And not the kind you get between the sheets. Oh, she never hits him where it shows—he teaches six days a week. But whenever he misses his day here, you can bet she's been at him again."

"Why doesn't he do something? There are laws now."

"What would—" The man broke off, and in a totally different voice said, "Yes, more drinks would be fine, Jaysom. Thanks. And a couple of fresh towels, please."

Collan waited, grinding his teeth, for the conversation to continue.

"If she divorced him—and she would if he even whispered a complaint against her—he'd have nothing."

"No dower?"

"His branch is out of the Web. Something about the grandmother marrying someone the First Daughter of the Name didn't approve."

"Great-grandmother. My great-aunt was the family's Advocate in the case. The whole branch was cut off—all they have is some little break-back farm outside Pinderon, and everybody knows the Web never pays the promised dowry. Ellus was lucky to marry at all, even with *his* looks. Though I suppose looks are why she married him."

"Only one brain in that marriage, and it's not between *her* ears."

"Well, if she divorces him, he could get work in any of the colleges. Our Alilia's in his Bardic Tales class, and he's got her reading and actually liking it."

"No money in teaching. Besides, he worships the children. Losing them would kill him."

"Have you talked to him about it?"

"The one time I said something, he told me he tripped down some stairs and it was his own fault. Now, the stairs were a lie, and he knew I knew it—but I really think he believes that when she knocks him around it *is* his fault."

There was a brief silence before the other man said thoughtfully, "I may *ask* Deika to scratch me tonight, out of sheer gratitude."

Drinks came, and talk turned to other gossip. Collan got up, adjusted the fit of his black silk codpocket, and dove into the pool for a few anger-quenching laps. He'd learned long ago to make cups of his hands to pull him more swiftly through the water, but he couldn't seem to make his fingers unclench from tight fists. When he was finally tired enough, he boosted himself out of the water to find Biron and Aidan staring at him.

"If that's what you call 'lazy,' " the boy said, "I'd hate to see your definition of 'energetic.' "

Col forced a grin, snagged a towel to dry off with, and made small talk as they went back to the changing room. But all the while he was considering the circumstances of a teacher named Ellus from a farm outside Pinderon who was regularly beaten by a woman who'd married him for his looks. There *were* laws, but if a man feared being divorced for even objecting to physical abuse, there evidently weren't laws enough.

4

OVER the next four days, the deans of six different schools were startled and flattered that Lord Collan Rosvenir deigned to visit their establishments. "Very wise of you to plan the education of Lady Sarra's children," they all said. Collan smiled and nodded and pocketed their brochures. He asked a few general questions, then moved into discussion of their literature programs. As a famous Minstrel, his interest in the subject was perfectly understandable, and his questions were pertinent. Finally, at St. Jeyrom's Academy, he got the right answer.

"Ellus Penteon directs our Literature Department, and I think you'll find the curriculum an excellent one. I wish we had a dozen more teachers like him—he's a young man with a fine future as a scholar."

"Married?"

"Of course! We don't hire unmarried men." The dean so far forgot the importance of her visitor that she allowed a look of outrage to cross her sour-apple face—an expression swiftly smoothed away when she recalled Who Collan Was. "Marriage is a necessity, especially when the man is as attractive Ellus Penteon. Our older girls are sometimes . . . impressionable. Not through any fault of his," she hastened to add. "Ellus Penteon is a modest young man, quite oblivious to the effect he produces in some of our adolescent girls. And of course he's devoted to Lady Mirya." At Collan's carefully blank look, she clarified. "He's married to Lady Mirya Witte. She's on our board of directors."

"Witte? I thought they all lived in Pinderon."

"Lady Mirya prefers the climate here in Roseguard."

Her bland tone and lack of facial expression told Col that "climate" had nothing to do with the weather in Roseguard and everything to do with the atmosphere in Pinderon. It was a good bet that her mother had not been happy that she'd chosen a gorgeous but dowerless man as her husband. Maybe she took it out on him.

"May I arrange a meeting, Lord Collan? He can give you all the specifics of the literature program. His special expertise is the Bardic Canon."

"Thanks, perhaps another time." He gave her a mild version of his *Too bad I'm married, beautiful, but maybe we can work around it* smile. It still worked, more or less; she didn't succumb to the usual blush, but she did reach up a hand to smooth her hair. "I'm just doing some preliminary research. Lady Sarra hasn't yet decided which school to send the twins to next year. Thanks for your time."

He stopped at a tavern for a cold one on his way home. Over his second tankard he tried to picture himself in Ellus Penteon's place. A Minstrel was supposed to bring from his own heart the characters in the songs he sang—*become* the young man pining for his beloved, the old woman reminiscing about her riotous youth, the child discovering the wonder of the starry night sky, the pious votary or the innkeeper's daughter or the dying soldier. But Collan's failure as a Minstrel was his failure now. Carlon the Lutenist back at Scraller's Fief had complained of it in lengthy exhortations to *feel* the songs; Falundir had been as adamant, though in silence. But Collan sang words, not feelings. Whatever emotion he stirred in his listeners was due to masterful lyrics and his own mastery of vocal inflection and fingering on the lute strings. The passion was in the words and music, not in him. He could fake it very nicely, using every Minstrel's trick ever invented, but the truly discerning ear always knew it was indeed faked.

Except when he sang love songs while thinking of Sarra. *Those* he felt, even when the depth of his own emotion discomposed him; *those* were real to him, because Sarra was real.

Thus it was that he couldn't even begin to identify with Ellus Penteon. He could understand how a dowerless young man could sell himself in marriage to a woman who desired him for his beauty. Happened all the time. Ellus Penteon had gained a home, children, work he evidently enjoyed, all the security that a man looked for in marriage.

But no man looked to be regularly battered by the woman he husbanded.

Sarra had once told him that while she was growing up, Agatine Slegin and Orlin Renne had helped her develop an intellectual understanding of social problems. But until she began to relate knowledge to experience, such problems had been mere abstracts, lacking human faces. Her outrage had been political, not personal. Ellus Penteon as yet lacked a face, so Collan couldn't grasp why his anger was so personal. Masculine solidarity in the face of feminine domination wasn't the answer. He'd never felt a twinge of it in his life. He couldn't find anything in him that could comprehend why a man would stay in such a marriage.

Ah, but what would *he* put up with in order to stay with Taigan and Mikel?

There it was. Ellus was a father. That was the point of contact between him and Collan. Nothing else in their lives might match, but that single similarity was a thing of such power that at last Collan understood.

And the idea of Sarra's ever lifting a hand to him was suddenly so funny that he nearly choked on his beer. Well, he could afford to laugh. Ellus Penteon couldn't.

Col finished his drink and started home. Having identified the parties involved, he had two choices. He could present the case to Sarra, who would see to it that the laws were changed—which he knew from experience would take half of forever.

Or he could do something now, himself, and wait for the laws to catch up.

No choice at all, truly told.

5

GLENIN smiled at the sight of her son playing with the dog: two strong, dark, gray-eyed young animals, growling as they rolled together on the carpet. It was play, and yet it was not. Each wanted mastery over the other. She knew which would win, and it had nothing to do with their relative sizes.

Silverclaw was three-quarters wolf. In a litter of seven, five turned out disappointing; they looked and behaved like Senison hounds, taking after their stupid, spotted sire. Silverclaw, like his brother Frenzy, was definitely a wolf. Like his mother. Glenin was not insensible to the comparisons.

Every child should have a pet, though this was not the whole purpose of the dog's presence in her son's life. Companionship was secondary to teaching him not to fear anything, not human or animal or magical.

"Come along, darling," she said. "Leave him to his dinner. I have something to show you."

The boy came willingly, holding her hand. Thirteen this coming autumn, he was taller than any other child his age—and most children a year or two older. He would have his grandfather's height, she knew it, just as she was certain that when he reached manhood he would have Auvry Feiran's powerful build. Power of another kind would come to him very soon now. The shocks given him while still in the womb, of Ladders and potent magic, had made him precocious, and she had taught him much during his childhood. But he was no longer a little boy, and his magic would fully flower within the year.

"Have you sent Frenzy back to The Waste yet?" he asked as they walked.

Glenin nodded. "Just the other day."

The boy laughed. "What a good joke! He looks enough like a Sennie to breed with them—and his get will come out wolf, and bite everybody!"

"Yes," said Glenin as they reached the courtyard, "but that isn't the only reason I did it. I want everyone to be reminded of how important it is to make sure bloodlines are kept pure."

"Like ours for magic."

"Very much like that." She smiled down at him. "Of course, if one of Frenzy's cubs happens to bite Lady Lilen, I won't mind too much!"

"*I* hope they bite the Captal when she visits Ostinhold, and she has to have lots of stitches that *hurt*."

"We can hope."

He held open a gate for her, with an elegant courtesy that would have satisfied Lady Allynis at the Octagon Court. "Lady Saris says you're leaving the Castle for a few days."

"Yes, I am."

"Can I come with you? Please, Mother?"

"Not this time."

"But I'm nearly thirteen, and I've learned so much magic—and it's not as if anyone would recognize me," he added shrewdly. "I've never been off this island."

So much for his manners. She stopped beneath an oak tree, frowning down at him. "Do you argue with me, child?"

"N-no, Mother," he replied; but then, because he was never cowed for long, burst out, "I want to *do* things, I want to *help!* Whatever it is you do, I want to be there with you!"

"You will do what I tell you, when I tell you to do it—like every other Malerrisi." Then, because she could never stay stern with him for long, she relented and ruffled his curling black hair. "Perhaps I'll take you with me. We'll talk about it tonight at dinner—to which I expect you to show up with your clothes and yourself decently cleaned up. Honestly, I don't know where you find mud when it hasn't rained for three weeks!" She tweaked his sleeve, and a dried splotch flaked off onto the cobbles.

"That was from Silverclaw."

Glenin snorted her opinion of this transparent lie as they crossed an inner court to the kennels. "Here, this is what I wanted to show you." She nodded to the kennel keeper, and they were admitted to the dog run. "The new litter is old enough to be weaned."

"Oh, Mother, just look! Aren't they beautiful? *All* wolves!"

She let him admire the cubs for a few minutes, then said, "Go in and pet them."

He showed not the slightest fear. She shut the gate

behind him and waited for the bitch to notice the interloper. A growl and a baring of teeth stopped the boy in his tracks.

"Remember what I told you," Glenin said.

He stood tall and stared the wolf down. "Can I have one of the cubs? To play with Silverclaw?"

"Yes, if you can master one. Why don't you try it?"

He studied the litter, then fixed on the largest one, a female. Not for him the runt of the litter. Boldly striding to the box, he reached down.

Establish your status from the start. She repeated the lesson to herself, watching her son. The cub snarled at him, thinking he challenged her for space and food. He grabbed her by the scruff and thumped her roughly on the back.

"Mine!" he declared, seizing the wolf's glittering gray gaze with his own. Nearly silver sometimes, his eyes were now the color of iron and just as unyielding. "You are *mine* now, and when *I* decide you're old enough I'll take you from your mother and you'll do exactly as I say."

The bitch growled again, gathering herself. Glenin held her breath. Her son, still holding the cub by the neck, stood taller and glared at the wolf. *If she leaps*— But Glenin didn't have time to finish the thought, even in her own head. The wolf surged up, teeth flashing inches from the boy's face. He didn't even flinch. He looked through the wolf, beyond her, wearing a bored expression. Glenin exhaled slowly. By trivializing the challenge, he had humiliated the animal and maintained his own superiority.

The bitch tried again, with the same result. She turned her head when the rest of the litter began to whine. Glenin could almost follow the animal's thoughts: she was too proud to admit defeat, and her unhappy offspring were excuse to abandon the challenge. Glenin smiled at her son, who grinned back and set the squirming female cub down.

"Excellent, darling," Glenin said. "What will you name the new one?"

"I'm not sure. She's pretty, isn't she? All gray and

black, not a Senison spot on her." He bent down again to scratch her ears.

That was his mistake. The freed cub had gotten an old rag in her mouth, and when a hand touched her head she whirled and snapped. Her teeth sank into the boy's thumb, and he cried out in surprise—and anger.

"Slap her!" Glenin ordered, but even as she spoke the boy had dealt the cub a clout to the head. He picked her up again by the scruff, shook her, and once again stared her down.

"Mine!" he repeated fiercely, a growl in his voice that brought a whimper from the cub. "Don't you *ever* bite me again!"

Glenin waited until he released the animal, letting her drop three feet to sprawl on the straw-strewn kennel floor, before opening the cage. "Come out of there and let me see your hand. How could you have been so foolish? I told you never to challenge a wolf for something already in its mouth!"

"I did it on purpose," he insisted as he locked the gate behind him. He did not proffer his hand for inspection. "She has to learn that she belongs to me, and nothing belongs to her unless I give it to her."

"Let me see your hand," Glenin commanded, and after a moment he yielded. He yielded to no one but her. "Not too bad—the skin's barely broken. Go have it washed and salved."

"You understand, don't you, Mama? I had to show her."

"Yes, I understand. But be more careful. Your hands—and your life!—may depend on it one day. And you have more important work to do than taming a wolf cub to your will."

"It was just practice," he replied, grinning up at her.

Wondering if the grin wasn't just as effective as the snarl, Glenin could not but relent and laugh.

6

"HOW'RE we going to find one opal earring in all this junk?"

Mikel gave his sister a look of dismay. Taigan was frowning at the jumble of boxes, cases, and coffers on their mother's dressing table. They had been detailed to find a certain earring in support of their father's efforts not to be late. Ten minutes ago, Fa had come into the music room and told Aidan to get dressed. The program at All Saints' had been changed at the last minute from *Son of the Ryka Legion* to a solo concert by Sevy Vasharron of Falundir's compositions. Thus it was that while Aidan and Fa hurriedly changed to formal longvests, the twins were supposed to find their father's jewelry— "Somewhere in that mess in your mother's dressing room."

The task looked impossible. The "junk" Taigan mentioned consisted of a whole Shir's ransom worth of jewels, strewn with the carelessness of the colossally wealthy all across the wide table. In between the glittering array were the mysterious paraphernalia of the elegant First Daughter: soft-bristle brushes, tortoiseshell combs, gold hairpins, clear glass bottles, ceramic jars, crystal flacons, silver pots, glazed canisters, and only their mother knew what all else. Mikel assumed and Taigan knew that these had something to do with the fact that Sarra Liwellan was one of the most beautiful women on Lenfell, but at eleven years old they had already come to the correct conclusion that Fa had a lot to do with that as well.

Mikel stared in consternation at the chaos. "I guess we'll just have to poke around until we find it," he said, doubt of success wrinkling the pattern of freckles across his nose.

Throwing both long golden braids back over her shoulders, Taigan pursed her lips and got to work.

The first thing Mikel found was a box of loose gemstones that enchanted him. One large, dark ruby in particular caught his attention, and without knowing why he imagined it set in silver—but the necklace that took shape in his thoughts was draped around the slender throat of a young blonde woman who was definitely not his mother. Puzzled for a moment, disoriented by the strength of the image, he put the ruby down and glanced at his sister. "Any luck?"

"Well . . ." Taigan shrugged. "I found this, but there's nothing special in it. Take a look."

Mikel considered the contents of a large, plain wooden box. A single glove; a few dried flowers; gold hoop earrings (simple, not their mother's style at all); a battered old identification disk; a gold-and-amethyst pendant earring; and a man's wristlet of dark green jade flowers. The twins traded glances again, disappointed by the "treasure," then jumped as Fa yelled from the bedroom, "Did you find it yet?"

"We're working on it!" Taigan called back.

The twins foraged through the table and ransacked the drawers. The opal turned up at the same time Collan Rosvenir appeared, wearing a turquoise brocaded longvest over plain black trousers.

"What do you think, Mishka? Teggie? Will I pass inspection?"

"Perfect," said his daughter.

"I know," he grinned back. "Now, tell me you've found my opal or—"

"Here," Mikel said.

"You're astounding, both of you." Quick hugs, then a struggle with his thick curling hair on the way to the door as he fumbled with the earring's clasp. "And don't stay up too late!" was the last thing the twins heard before the outer door closed behind him.

Mikel was drawn inexorably back to the wooden box. Feeling a little guilty, he sat on the floor and dumped its contents on the thick-napped Cloister carpet.

Taigan plopped down beside him. "So what do you think she saved this stuff for?"

"How should I know?" Taking up the identity disk, he peered at the engraving. " 'Jescarin, Verald—' Didn't he used to be Master of Roseguard Grounds?"

"A long time ago. He was killed in the Rising."

Mikel closed his fingers around the almond-shaped disk—and gave a sudden start. "It's cold! I mean, I *feel* cold when I hold it—"

"Let me." She took the disk from him, green eyes squeezing shut in a comically intense expression of concentration. When her eyes opened again, Mikel made a face at her, knowing she was making fun of him. "I don't feel anything. You're crazy."

"No, I'm not." Mikel picked out a few pink roses, long since withered. Not quite knowing what he was about to say, he stared at the flowers. "Mother wore these in her hair—and she didn't much like them either."

"That's easy enough to figure," Taigan scoffed. "She *never* wears pink." Or peach, or apricot, or lilac, or daffodil, or any of the other insipid fruit-and-flower hues to which a girl of Taigan's age and coloring was condemned. "When I get older, I—"

Mikel wasn't interested in his sister's gripes. "Here—take these for a minute."

He gave her the gold earrings. She cradled them in her palm, sighing her impatience with this stupid game. Then—

"Mikel—I feel something."

"What?"

Slowly, exploring the evocations of the gold in her palm, she said, "Not exactly a feeling. Not like being sad or happy. It's more like—"

"—like a sense, tasting or smelling or touching."

"Yes! Or when you're not feeling well, and I know it even if you're in another room." All at once she dropped the earrings. "I don't like this."

Mikel was holding the jade wristlet. "I've never seen him wear it, but this is Fa's." He hesitated, rubbing a thumb across the tiny carvings of flowers. "No—not Fa. But somebody close to him, somebody he knew—"

"That's enough."

"What? We haven't even started looking—"

"We have homework," Taigan snapped. "And you know how Taguare is when we don't get our assignments done."

"You're scared. You just don't want to admit it."

"I'm *not* scared! This is just dumb, and I'm going to go do my homework." She grabbed the glove and the earrings and a fistful of withered flowers, shoving them back into the box. But the glove caught on the little turquoise ring Auntie Caisha had given her at her last Birthingday, and her fingers closed around the silk without her wanting them to, and she gasped.

"Teggie—!" Mikel gripped her shoulders, and together they were inundated in memories not their own.

"Hurry, Maicha! We haven't much time—"
A black-skinned man in sorry old threadbare clothes, his green eyes blazing with urgency. She trusted him implicitly—and hated him almost as much as she trusted him.
"I can't find Sarra's cloak—and I haven't told Mother—"
A wild glance around a sumptuous bedchamber, lingering for an instant on a little blonde girl with huge, frightened black eyes—it's such a long journey, damn you, Gorsha—
"I'll explain everything to Allynis and Gerrin when I return. There's no time, Maicha!"
—eyes flashing past the bed—oh, my husband my beloved my betrayer—
"Wrap Sarra in a blanket if you must, but we have to get out of here now. Anniyas's people are all over the city."
—arrested by the sight of a mirrored reflection, her own reflection, pale and tousled and frantic, beautiful even in fear, one delicate hand clutching a single black silk glove—

"Teggie!" Mikel shook her, snatched the glove from her hand, flung it away onto the carpet. Taigan's breath caught on a sob. "What *was* that?"

"I don't know! It was me, but it wasn't—" She pulled away from his steadying hands and knuckled her eyes. "Get rid of this stuff, Mikel. I don't like it. It hurts."

"But who was she?"

"No. I don't want to talk about it. Put it all away."

He did as told, careful to pick everything up with just his fingertips. After a time, with the closed box resting on the carpet, he murmured, "I wonder why she kept all this. If it hurts her the way it does you and me. . . ."

Taigan shivered, trying to disguise it with a casual shrug. "If you've got the nerve to ask her, go right ahead."

7

A week after first overhearing Ellus Penteon's situation, Collan was able to put a face to the name. Recalling what the two men had said about Penteon's "regular day" at Wytte's, Col spent most of the appropriate morning and all afternoon there, and was at length rewarded.

Ellus Penteon wasn't just good-looking. He was gorgeous. Tall, dusky-skinned, long of leg and broad of shoulder, his narrow waist encircled by an ornamental gold chain, he made the high-priced local bower lads look like gawky farmboys. His face was a marvel: wide mouth, big hazel eyes, square chin with the hint of a dimple, and skin an ant could slide on. The wonder of it was that he seemed to have no consciousness at all of his beauty. Collan thought that perhaps it was because he was not tremendously bright, but that couldn't be it; the man was a scholar, after all, a gifted teacher. It astounded Col that someone with looks this spectacular could be so utterly unaware of them.

Yet in talking with him—casually, in the soak pool— Col discovered that it wasn't lack of awareness but refusal to acknowledge. That made sense: Penteon's looks had gotten him much that mattered to him, but what really mattered to him had nothing to do with his looks.

They chatted about their children. They spoke of the difficulties of running a home while teaching—Collan at the Conservatory, Ellus at St. Jeyrom's. Because both were well-versed in Bardic Canon, they also talked of songs and poetry. Collan offered to come lecture at Penteon's class at St. Jeyrom's; Penteon offered to send along a variant manuscript of an old ballad cycle that he thought might interest Collan and Falundir. He also asked in an offhand way whether any of Col's students might benefit from additional tutelage—"Not on the lute, for I'm no hand at it, but in diction, memorization, that sort of thing." It struck Collan as strange that a man with a house to run, children to raise, and students to teach six days a week was looking for something else to do. Maybe he wanted the money; maybe he just wanted to fill up his time so he wouldn't have to spend as much of it with Mirya Witte. But there wasn't a mark on that dusky-brown skin, or a single hint that she ever touched her husband with anything but the tenderest of caresses.

A curious thing happened in the changing room. *Domni* Pierigo Wytte, son of the lady who ran the establishment, took Ellus Penteon apologetically aside for a private talk. Collan heard little of it, but the three words he did hear were enough: "membership fee" and "late."

Col stopped by a tavern on the way home, a boisterous place where one could hear the latest and most reliable gossip in all Sheve. What he learned there was that Mirya Witte was late with every bill she owed. Her mother was disinclined to contribute even a handful of cutpieces to her First Daughter's support. She could come back to Pinderon and live in the family home, or she could make do with a less extravagant style of living.

So, Col thought. It was money after all. Kind of pathetic, though, for Ellus to think that the paltry sums he might earn by tutoring music students would contribute anything truly helpful to Lady Mirya's coffers.

That night, Lindren announced that after a week of looking, she'd seen the perfect estate for Miram and Riddon. "Out on the peninsula—fresh sea air, wonderful views, a vineyard and wine press, a huge old house with lots of room—"

"But not for sale," Riena said glumly. "And nobody lives in it! A dozen workers' cottages filled to capacity, but nobody in the big house at all. It's criminal to let a property like that stand empty."

"I think I know the place you're talking about," Collan said slowly, and the beginnings of an idea twinkled in his mind. "Stone pillars at the main road, gate covered in ivy, overgrown rosebushes the size of small houses?"

"That's the one. Shore Hill. Isn't it wonderful? Do you know who owns it? Could they be persuaded to sell?"

He grinned. "Trust me."

Lindren arched a brow at him. "Cailet says that whenever you say that, trusting you is the very last thing anyone ought to do."

"I am wounded. I am shocked and betrayed. I am positive the owners will sell."

Aidan snorted with laughter. "And *I* am positive that the Captal is right!"

8

COLLAN had long since learned that one advantage of being Who He Was had to do with gaining entry anyplace he fancied to go and seeing anybody he had a notion to see. It was better than being a Minstrel—well, not *better,* because he owed his welcome to Sarra and not to his own brilliant talents and winning personality. But he shrugged off his annoyance and took blatant advantage of the advantage of being married to a powerful woman. When he presented himself at the Witte house and rapped on the door—garishly painted with yellow and red chevrons—he was immediately admitted, shown to a pretty little salon, offered refreshment, and had to wait only a handful of minutes before Mirya Witte hurried to greet him.

Sarra's aversion to her breed—and Mirya's increasing penury—meant that they did not move in the same circles. Collan had seen the woman at a distance, of course, at the Opera and various civic functions, but his main recollection of her dated to a certain night in Pinderon nearly twenty years ago. The years had, if anything, rendered her face even more horselike. She had a spectacular figure, almost the equal of Lusira Garvedian's, and she dressed to show it off, but the face on top of it. . . . Well, he supposed a man could always close his eyes.

As they exchanged social pleasantries, he wondered what she'd say if she knew he was the Minstrel for whom the Pinderon Watch had been so avidly searching. Anger stirred even at this late date over the false accusation of rape Sarra had made, and the mess she'd gotten him into, and how it had only come out all right because he'd had his wits about him. Although, truly told, kidnapping her had been fun. . . .

He pushed aside his memories of absurd adventure as Mirya Witte led him rather gracelessly around to the purpose of his visit. He let himself be guided, saying smoothly, "Actually, I'm here on behalf of some friends. And it ties in nicely with my plans for expanding Roseguard's tax base."

"Tax base?" she echoed blankly.

"You're aware that several of the old estates are empty. In some cases it's because no one can afford to live in them, but the properties are tied to various Webs and can't be sold. My Lady is working with her colleagues on the Council to free up a few laws in that regard. I know you'll agree that it's much better to have a family living in a working, profitable holding than to let it stand mostly idle."

"Yes, of course," she said, not having the vaguest notion of where he was going, though dimly aware that it was probably not a destination she wished to reach.

"Quite a few places would benefit from new ownership," he went on. "With a family that can afford to live in them and work them to their best advantage, the production will increase and the taxes paid by other Shirs for export of the goods will go up, thereby benefiting Sheve as a whole." Saints, he was starting to sound like his factor. What was it about economics that demanded complexified sentences and multiplied syllables? Consciously dragging his vocabulary back to reality, he said, "For instance, Shore Hill. Your mother bought it, so she can dispose of it as she pleases. You currently hold the deed, but you don't live in it or have any tenants. Lady Mirya, I know you'll be pleased to learn that I've heard of a buyer who wants Shore Hill."

The long jaw grew longer still as her mouth parted to let her tongue moisten her lips—for all the world as if talk of money was fresh-cut oats and she a hungry mare. "How much?"

Collan appreciated her bluntness. "That depends."

"On?"

"On how much it's worth to you not to become a test case in the law courts."

Wearing an amiable smile, he waited for her to make the connection. Only after a full minute of watching her puzzled frown did he realize that she had no idea that she'd done anything to merit the law's attention. Collan damned himself for an idiot. As far as she was concerned, knocking her husband across the room was a recreational activity of no more consequence than kicking a discarded bottle out of her way on the street.

His smile vanished. "One ought to keep marital matters private. I'm sure you agree."

Still not a hint of comprehension. There *was* only one brain in the family.

"Tell me," he said silkily, "how is it you can be angry enough to hit your husband, but calm enough to remember not to hit him in the face?"

She caught on then. He admired her spectacularly heaving bosom even while wondering if she required something stronger than iced coffee to settle her nerves. He was about to offer to summon a servant and a liquor bottle when she found her voice again.

"I don't know *what* you mean!"

He got to his feet, towering over her in her low chair. She reacted by shrinking back. Well-bred men did not use height to intimidate women; most women wouldn't recognize such intimidation if it was ever tried. Then again, Collan had no claims to being well-bred, and Mirya Witte wasn't so stupid that she didn't recognize the real threat in his stance.

Still, she made a good try. "How—how *dare* you—!"

His smile returned, a baring of teeth. "I'll expect your factor to contact my factor regarding a price. No, don't thank me, and don't bother to see me out. I can find my own way."

Three days later he went to Wytte's in the afternoon, very pleased with himself—until a chat with the barkeeper informed him that Ellus Penteon was not expected in today. He had just been discharged from the infirmary attached to the shrine of St. Feleris, and was recuperating at home from three cracked ribs and a broken jaw.

9

THAT night, seated in the darkest corner of Roseguard's newest tavern, Collan brooded over his third tankard of the evening. He was not enjoying his own company.

How could he have been such a fool? Why hadn't he known that Mirya Witte would vent her anger and reply to his threat by beating her husband simply because she *could*? What could Collan do about it, truly told? Now, if it had been *Sarra* who confronted her, things would have gone differently. Women had power. Men did not—even men who were married to powerful women.

He should stay out of it. Look what his interference had accomplished so far. If he kept on, she might kill the man. Who would question whatever explanation she gave? Ellus Penteon had told the healers that he'd tripped on a rug and fallen half onto a marble table, half onto a chair. No one believed him—Col had gone to the shrine to ask about the "accident"—but no one could do anything about it either.

There wasn't even anybody available to discuss it

with—not that any of them could have improved the situation. Jeymi had taken Riena, Biron, and Lindren on a pleasure cruise aboard the old Slegin yacht, the *Agate Rose*. Aidan had gone up to Sleginhold to visit a friend. Falundir was still at Wyte Lynn Castle judging the All-Lenfell Bardic Games. Cailet was due in Roseguard soon after yet another tour, this time of Kenrokeshir, in search of Mageborns (the broadsheet articles had yet to bear fruit). Sarra wasn't expected home from Ryka Court until the twins' Birthingday at Midsummer Moon.

Which brought him to another, unrelated problem: his children. They were growing up faster than he'd dreamed children could grow, and his visits to various academies had reminded him that next autumn they'd start at a regular day-school. How would he fill up his time then? What would he do with himself?

He'd endured a trying hour with their tutor before dinner, and frustration had driven him out of the Residence to this tavern. It hadn't helped that his sympathies were entirely with Taigan and Mikel, not the long-winded Scholar Mage who could make even the most exciting parts of the Rising as dull as a day in Dindenshir. Why couldn't she teach history in a way that would intrigue eleven-year-olds? Still, Col supposed it had been more of a thrill to live through than to read about—though he didn't recall being especially thrilled at the time. He and Sarra had instructed that their own parts in recent history be downplayed.

How appalling anyway that his own life was now considered "history." Could it really be eighteen years since he'd kidnapped Sarra from that bower in Pinderon? Time had a way of catching up with him when he least expected it. He wondered if the same happened to Sarra and Cailet: so many years since this or that had happened, seemed as if this or that child had been born only last week, surely that poplar or willow or peach tree couldn't be so tall so soon. Maybe time really did speed up as one got older. Or maybe there was just more to be done. The Rising had been easy compared to the tasks of passing new laws, building Mage Hall, managing Sheve—and raising two rambunctious children.

Yet as he started in on his fourth Bleyn's Brown Ale, he had to admit all flourished in their chosen labors. Cailet was sending Mage Guardians out into the world now—slowly, yes, but the girl fairly glowed with confidence whenever she had time to visit them in Roseguard. *Girl*, hell; Cai was coming up on her thirty-first Birthingday. Sarra was five years older, but still looked about twenty-two as far as Collan was concerned. She'd had the most public successes, doing work she loved, work she had been born and bred to do.

And himself? Capable master of Roseguard and the Slegin Web; sought-after teacher of music; husband to a woman he adored; father of two fine children. He hadn't done badly for a Nameless orphan sold as a slave. If only life wasn't so . . . *domestic*. It was one thing to play traditional husband at Ryka Court for the edification of the conservative faction Sarra chivvied into passing reforms. It was quite another to find that his life and talents were circumscribed by home, hearth, and holdings—just like every other dull and dutiful husband in the world.

Perhaps he was supposed to feel grateful that Sarra didn't knock him around whenever she felt like it.

Somehow the plight of Ellus Penteon, caged in marriage with a woman who did just that, had made him examine his own life. He could not but cherish much of what he saw—Sarra, Taigan, Mikel, the home he'd made, the work he did. Yet however he looked at it, it was still a cage. Husband, father, teacher, manager of a vast home and vaster holdings—what had happened to the carefree, footloose Minstrel who went where he pleased and did what he liked and answered to no one but himself?

"Evening, handsome," purred a voice of sultry suggestion. He glanced up at a young woman dressed in a mane of black hair and as little else as the law allowed. "You look lonely."

"Sorry, *Domna*. I'm took."

She peered at him more closely in the dimness, and flinched. "Lord Rosvenir! I—it's dark in here, I didn't see clearly—"

"Don't worry about it." He smiled as she backed away, because despite domestication, at least he hadn't lost it—even though he hadn't used it on any woman but Sarra in years. He toasted the retreating woman with his tankard. Maybe the dashing Minstrel hadn't entirely vanished after all.

He was certain of it when he caught sight of a man coming through the front door. Lifetime habit had made him choose a table with a clear view of—and a clear path to—all entries and exits. The same instinct made his fingers itch for his knives as he recognized the bulky form, garish longvest, and flash of cheap jewelry at ears and throat. Twenty years ago, Siral Warris had been a moderately successful bower lad in Pinderon. Five years and a hundred pounds later, he'd become an informant for the Council Guard. Col thought he remembered skewering Warris in a tavern brawl back in 968, but evidently not.

"Collan!" The fat face creased into a visual echo of the whining voice as Warris waddled over, chains clanking tinnily down his chest. "How long it's been, old friend!"

"Vanish, Fifth," Col said.

"Oh, now surely you don't hold that little mistake in Neele against me? It was business, just business. You know how it is. We all have to make a living. And I hear you're making a good one these days—husband of Lady Sarra Liwellan, master of her many holdings, father of her two beautiful children asleep at home in bed—you've done well for yourself, Col."

Pity he couldn't gut Warris right now and take care of unfinished business. But certain standards of behavior were incumbent upon Lord Collan Rosvenir that the Minstrel had never had to worry about. Being a pillar of the community was a real pain in the ass.

"And speaking of business, I've got a sweet deal out Cantratown way—a guaranteed return on your investment—an amount so insignificant to someone in your position that—"

It had been a long time since anyone had come to him with a shady proposal—and if Warris was proposing, "shady" was a given. If it were anyone else, he might have amused himself by listening to the tale being spun.

But not this man. It was a real shame that slime like this could visit itself on nice places like Roseguard.

"You heard me the first time, Warris," he said with a pleasant smile. "And I hate repeating myself."

The used-carriage salesman faded away, replaced by a desperate man. Sweat began to darken the edges of his yellow coif. "You can't turn me down, Col, I've only got ten cutpieces to my name. I really need—"

"You really need to get out of here before I have your guts stretched and dried for lute strings."

"Same old Collan!" Warris hissed, necklaces trembling with his anger. "Too bad the Council Guard didn't move fast enough when I sold you to them in Pinderon!"

Warris was responsible for nearly getting him and Taig Ostin arrested? Pillar of the community be damned. Taverns were meant for brawls, and he owed this son of a Fifth. Collan got to his feet and, disdaining to dirty his twin Rosvenir knives, planted his fist in the flesh over Warris's left lung. By stepping quickly to one side he avoided most of the gush of noxious breath that resulted. The man's face was well on the way to the tabletop; with scrupulous concern for the innkeeper's property, Col stuck his knee in the way of Warris's nose. The crunch-squelch of impact meant that one of them had to move out of the way before blood got all over Col's trousers. So he shoved with both hands. Warris toppled to the floor, groaning.

Col was trying to decide if scuffing his immaculate boots was worth the satisfaction of kicking the stuffing out of Warris when the innkeeper's husband ambled by. Lirenz Tigge—six feet six inches and two-hundred-eighty-five pounds of seven-time South Lenfell Wrestling Champion—picked Warris up by the scruff with one hand. The former bower lad dangled like a hooked fish, huffing and wheezing and bleeding.

"Botherin' y'Lairdship?" asked Tigge, accent still as thick as on the day he'd stopped grappling swamp-tuskers in Rokemarsh to join the wrestling circuit.

"Nothing serious." Collan reached into his longvest

pocket for some coins and tossed them on the table. "Sorry about the mess."

Tigge bowed his massive respects and carried Warris one-handed to the alley door. Col left by the front entrance, ignoring the stares of the other customers.

Terrific. Now it'll be all over Roseguard by breakfast that Lady Sarra's husband was seen fighting in public. Can't even have some good honest fun anymore without people gossiping. Not that she'll *mind, but it does make her look bad. Damn it, I* liked *being anonymous—or nearly, anyhow, until people got a look at my hair. Used to be able to go anywhere and do anything, and now—*

But the sour taste in his mouth was not due altogether to renewed sulks. He'd been in Warris's position—by Pierga Cleverhand, he'd lost count of the times his pockets had been empty of all but a set of fingerpicks. There but for the grace of Sarra. . . .

No. He'd never sold another human being, not to the Council Guard or anyone else. He'd rather have starved and died.

The streets of Roseguard were quieter than usual after a rollicking St. Pierga's that left half the city with three-day hangovers. Collan nodded to a team of the Watch patrol. Yes, life was placid and orderly these days, and he was rich and secure, and a real icon for all conscientious husbands to emulate, and he was bored witless.

It was Fourteenth when he got home—appallingly early to return from a night's drinking. But Tarise had gone to a lecture tonight, and thus it was up to Collan to get the twins to bed on time—or as close to it as he could manage. Taigan and Mikel took after him in keeping late hours whenever they could connive it. Usually Col sat back and grinned while they tried to argue Tarise into letting them stay up just a *little* longer, until she threatened to have a Mage come and set Wards over them unless they went to bed *now* and stayed there.

The sitting room—which, with toys strewn about, more closely resembled an obstacle course—was empty. Tarise hadn't yet returned from the lecture—or maybe she had, and the twins had locked her in the closet again. It was definitely too early for them to be asleep without

fussing. He went down the hall to their bedchamber an
began, "All right, you two—"

And stopped.

All was silence. They were both curled up in bed,
sound asleep.

They're sick! was his first panicky thought. But Taigan's forehead was cool, and so was Mikel's. They
looked innocent as lambs, harmless as Senison pups, and
guileless as any children plotting the destruction of their
father's peace. But as he scrutinized the two faces, he
found not the slightest sign of impending raised hell.
They really were asleep.

As he turned the corridor for the music room, he
asked himself if perhaps they weren't starting to turn into
meek little mice. The idea brought an instant snort of
laughter. Meek? Sarra's children? They were probably
just tired out. They'd spent most of the day in the saddle,
circling the training ring, getting to know their new
horses—early Birthingday gifts from Falundir, of all people. When Col left this evening, they'd been engrossed in
Cailet's presents, guaranteed to keep them enthralled for
hours at a stretch. In fact, Collan had trouble understanding how Cai had brought herself to part with such marvelous toys.

Tangle puzzles were an invention of the redoubtable
Tamosin Wolvar. Nephew of the Scholar Mage whose
mastery of Mage Globes was unequaled in Guardian history, Tamosin had devised something entirely new to be
master of. Made of odd-shaped wooden pieces painted
white, the puzzle fit together only one way. But depending on which piece was chosen first, on completion the
white surfaces became a different picture every time.
These two—Cailet's first major effort—stayed blank until
ten of the hundred pieces were correctly put together.
Then part of the scene appeared and ten more pieces
began to glow around the edges. The players had one
minute to fit these, whereupon ten more pieces glowed,
and so on. In the week since the twins had unwrapped the
puzzles, Collan had seen renderings of a sailing ship,
Roke Castle, Tillin Lake, a galazhi in mid-leap, the St.
Tamas Temple at Pinderon, Roseguard, Mage Hall, and a

alloping herd of Maurgen Dapplebacks. In her Birthing-day greeting, Cai had told the children to start with the pieces tied with ribbons, and when they finally solved the puzzles they turned out to be notes informing them that there was one scene for every piece, depending on which piece they picked out first. One hundred pieces, one hundred pictures; the Mage Captal was definitely showing off.

Not to mention spoiling them, as usual. Everyone did. "Meek" would never describe Taigan or Mikel, but "scandalously indulged" occasionally came to mind. Col himself was hardly guiltless. His own gifts, not to be opened until the great day itself, were twin Rosvenir knives for his daughter (with emeralds in the hilts, to match her eyes) and a new rosewood lute for his son (inlaid with pearl fret-markers). Well, he argued with himself as he poured a glass of brandy, what father didn't want to give his children the best of everything? What they asked for, they ought to get—within reason, of course. Trouble was, Taigan and Mikel could think up such *persuasive* reasons. . . .

Chuckling, he sprawled in an overstuffed chair by the empty hearth and took up pen and notebook. In the absence of Sarra as inspiration to more enjoyable activities, he used his highly inspirational memories to prompt the only song he'd ever tried to write. He'd finished exactly four six-line verses in twelve years. His struggles proved what he'd known all along: a gifted Minstrel, he would never be a real Bard. Still, he kept at the writing when Sarra was away and he couldn't sleep. His excuse for meager output was that she was a difficult subject.

The lyric came one couplet at a time. Often he rearranged previous lines to accommodate new ones, and several times he'd thrown out every word and started over. The right words were hard enough. The melody had given him fits. Neither sweet nor somber, neither light nor pompous; playful in places, tender in others; hinting at her great dignity and even greater power; teasing and magical and a dozen other things besides—he'd set himself an impossible task, just with the music. But Falundir had nodded approval when Collan played it for him this

spring, so it must have at least a little merit to it. Legend
had it that some Bards wrote a thousand songs in a lifetime, others only a few, but each must be perfect. If Collan could get just this one song right before he died, he'd
go to his Name Saint a happy Wraith.

But Colynna Silverstring wasn't much help tonight.
He'd learned not to let lack of progress frustrate him—
fatherhood had taught him a modicum of patience, if
nothing else. Eventually he'd finish the song, and sing it
for Sarra, and the look in her eyes would reward all the
years of effort. He reviewed what he'd already written,
finding it as good as a mere Minstrel could manage, then
made a long arm for Falundir's lute on its stand. He
played the tune without singing the words; superstitious,
he would not put the words to the music until he sang it
for Sarra for the first time. She didn't even know he was
writing it.

Bushes rustled below the open balcony window at
the same time a Ward chittered a warning in Collan's
head. His fingers froze in mid-run. Leaping to his feet, he
cradled the lute on the chair and lunged for the balcony.

The Ladymoon was full; there was plenty of light to
see by. And what he saw, ten feet below him in the middle
of the Rose Tree Walk that had been Verald Jescarin's
pride, was a slight and utterly innocuous figure in dark
pants and shirt.

Col vaulted the balustrade as if he were still twenty
years old, surprised when his left knee nearly collapsed
under him. The one he'd broken Warris's nose with—no
wonder it hurt. Before the intruder knew what was happening, Col had hold of an arm and pulled her around so
he could see her face by moonlight.

His face: about thirteen years old (old enough to wear
a coif, anyway) and startlingly beautiful, even when terrified. The boy's huge gray eyes were framed by absurdly
long lashes and a green coif from which a few silky black
curls escaped. For a moment Col simply gaped—as surely
everyone did at first sight of him. Or hundredth sight, for
that matter. Compared to this boy, even the gorgeous
Ellus Penteon looked like a rough draft.

Finally recovering his voice, Collan demanded, "What the hell are you doing?"

"I was just looking—I didn't touch anything—"

The Ward was triggered not by touch but by presence. Set by Cailet and regularly renewed by her Mages, it was keyed to Sarra and even to Collan's unMageborn mind by some obscure and difficult spell. Something had set it off, and this boy was his only candidate.

"I didn't ask what you did, I asked what you're doing."

"I *swear* I didn't touch anything! I'm sorry, I just wanted to see the roses before we go back tomorrow— and then I heard somebody playing a lute, and it was so beautiful—"

The misery in his eyes embarrassed Collan. He wasn't in the habit of causing stark terror in children. "All right, don't worry about it. Where are you going back to?"

"Sleginhold."

"And you don't much want to," Col said.

Slight shoulders lifted and fell in a resigned shrug. "It's all the same to me. It pretty much has to be. I'm an orphan." He looked up at Collan as if to challenge a reaction from him.

"Me, too," Col said. The boy stared, then narrowed his eyes in a quick inspection of clothes and lack of coif. "I guess you pretty much have to do as you're told, huh?"

A sigh, a nod. Col figured he knew the problem. Like Ellus Penteon, this boy would be highly sought in marriage. By next year, brawls would break out when he walked down the street; women would forget what the word *dowry* meant when they looked into those eyes.

But something nagged at him, canceling any words of sympathy he might have spoken. Once this Ward was triggered, catching whoever tripped it would silence it until the next time. Col had hold of the boy's arm, but the Ward still chattered in his head.

"By the way," the boy was saying, calmer now, "your fountain needs work. Something's wrong with the machinery."

Collan blinked. "Huh?"

"Everybody knows that all the Roseguard waters play the same tune."

" 'Rose of Sheve Dark,' " Col said automatically. "By Lady Agatine's order, years and years ago."

A long finger pointed to the dancing moonlit droplets nearby. "That one sounds more like 'Broke My Spoke in Cantratown.' "

Holy Saints! How would a child his age know the bawdiest whorehouse ballad in five Shirs? Collan conveniently forgot that when *he* was a child this age, he'd already spent half a year earning his own living on the streets.

"It'd only take a couple of adjustments—I could probably fix it in an hour. Fountain machinery's delicate and needs tuning every so often—they're just like stringed instruments, truly told."

"Thanks for the offer, but it'll have to wait until morning."

"I'll be *gone* in the morning," he muttered.

Maybe it was his beauty, or something about his eyes that reminded Collan of someone, or—more likely—the suspicions still lurking at the back of his head with the nattering of the Ward. But he was strangely interested in this rather unusual boy. "So you like machinery as well as flowers, huh?"

"Yes, Lord Rosvenir." He gulped and suddenly seemed to find his hands quite fascinating. "It's—it's how I got in. I picked the lock on the gate."

That explained it, then. Not only did the intruder have to be caught, but the lock—if opened—had to be relocked before the Ward shut up.

"I'm sorry, truly," the boy went nervously on. "But it was so easy to open—"

Collan almost laughed. This youngster must be the darling of three Saints: Joselet Green-eyes for the gardener in him, Maurget Quickfingers for the mechanic, and Pierga Cleverhand for the lockpick. Perhaps Maidil the Betrayer, too, for the havoc that face would surely cause.

"You opened it, you go close it on your way out," Collan said.

Wide gray eyes went wider. "You mean—you're not going to—" The boy gulped. "—have me arrested?"

"Geridon's Stones, no—what for? But you'd better fix my lock and get back to bed before somebody misses you. Looks to me like you're not too old for a good spanking."

"I'm not a baby!"

"Then stop whining like one."

A moment of rebellious resentment; then the boy nodded.

"Relax. Anybody with ears good enough to know when a fountain's out of tune—let alone somebody who can fix it—is all right by me. Go on, fix the lock and get out of here."

In reply he received a dazzling smile. As the boy ran headlong for the garden gate, Col whistled softly between his teeth, a long descending note of amazement. He knew his own face wasn't painful to women's gazes, but he was very glad he hadn't been born *that* beautiful.

He returned to the music room—by the steps, not back over the balcony railing—and waited for the Ward to quiet down. Culprit apprehended, lock surely secured by now . . . but the warning still babbled in his head. He poured another drink, counting minutes. Maybe the thing was working about as well as the fountain, and Cai needed to reset it. Maybe it was his imagination that made it echo like this. He sipped brandy, gnawed his lip, and got up to pace, annoyed by the incessant Ward and the feeling that he'd forgotten something. . . .

And then he remembered what Warris said about the twins, asleep in their beds at home.

Whirling, he ran to their room. "Teggie? Mishka?"

Their beds were empty, the covers strewn on the floor.

10

WITHIN ten minutes, as the clock in Collan's office chimed Fifteenth, every member of the Watch had been alerted and the four Mage Guardians in residence had gathered at the Warded gate. Their opinion, after Collan's recital of events, was that the timing was wrong.

Biren Halvos, whose tawny good looks were such that Jennis Maurgen had let him father her second set of twins, shook his head. "I know this type of Working—fiendish clever, our Captal—and it targets only persons with malevolent intent. Otherwise the gardeners couldn't come in to mow the grass."

"But to the grass, the gardeners *are* malevolent, don't you think?" mused Tia Krestos, and neither her reputation as a Scholar Mage nor her eighty-five years could spare her Collan's venomous glare.

"As I said," Biren went on, "our Captal is clever. The Ward is quite specialized, and fixes on those persons entering with intent to harm those who live at Roseguard."

Cailet had neglected to mention that aspect of the Ward; typical.

Another Mage nodded her sleep-tousled head. Trelin Halvos, Biren's older sister, rubbed the side of her formidable nose and told Collan, "The boy wouldn't matter to the Ward because all he wanted to do was look at the roses. Or so he said."

"I never really suspected him anyhow," Col said impatiently.

"Suspect everyone," Tia Krestos muttered. "I always have. Kept me alive during Anniyas's Purge."

"Yes, of course," agreed Trelin, taking the elderly woman's arm. "But perhaps you ought to return to bed, Tia. It's very late."

"Nonsense, child. Stop fussing. My mind's no more mushy at Fifteenth than it is at Fifth." She eyed Collan, squinting upward a good foot and a half, a strand of white hair falling over her brow. "Timing. That's the thing."

"She's right," Biren said. "You heard the Ward, went immediately to the gardens, and saw the boy. He couldn't have come so far so fast—therefore he wasn't the one who tripped the Ward."

"But he opened the gate—he said so. Picked the lock," Col reminded the Mage.

"Timing—and intent." Tia Krestos nodded to herself. "A smart boy, to have concealed all his true purpose inside a desire to see your roses."

"That's not proved," Trelin objected.

"Whatever!" Collan snapped. "It's Siral Warris I suspect of stealing my children. The Watch is searching for him. What are *you* doing to find Taigan and Mikel?"

Trelin's long face drew into even deeper lines of unhappiness. "If we knew them to be Mageborns, as the Captal suspects they are, there might be a chance. But I'm afraid that unless magic is very strong indeed, it can't be traced in children under the age of twelve or thirteen."

"I've been searching," the fourth Mage said suddenly. "There's nothing."

"Are you sure, Maivis?" asked Biren. "Try again." When the older woman closed her eyes to concentrate, he murmured to Col, "She's the most sensitive of us, and has found more Mageborns than anyone but the Captal herself."

But Collan knew that Maivis Maklyn could have ten times the sensitivity of every Captal ever born and still would find nothing. Cailet had done her work too well on the twins, establishing Wards to protect them from what had happened to Alin Ostin. It had seemed a good idea at the time: gently but completely blocking their magic until they matured and Cailet could guide them without trauma into their powers.

Damn Cailet for her caution.

He didn't wait for Maivis Maklyn to report failure. Saying, "Let me know," to Biren, he left the Residence and strode through the public gardens toward town.

Roseguard had nearly thirty thousand inhabitants. Thousands more came through on business or pleasure.

A percentage of them would be amenable to sharing a ransom with Siral Warris. Lady Sarra Liwellan was a rich woman. But she was also a powerful woman, and the penalty for stealing her children would deter a sizable percentage of that percentage. Col did the mathematics quite coolly, and came up with a probable five thousand individuals, give or take a hundred, who would help Warris just for the money's sake.

Warris couldn't possibly know five thousand people in Roseguard.

All he needed was one.

Think! He won't risk staying in the city because he knows I'll search every square inch of it personally. He's a lousy rider, he almost certainly doesn't know the countryside around here, and it'd be hard to control two children on horseback anyway—unless he's got a carriage, or unless they were unconscious or dead—

No!

Taigan and Mikel were his own flesh and blood. He'd *know* if they were gone—

He crammed terror into a corner of his mind and shut a stone door on it.

No general alarm had been raised in the city; the Watch had been told to search thoroughly but quietly. Roseguard's streets were nearly empty, all good citizens at home by their own hearths. If Warris didn't have a hiding place, he'd be racing from shadow to shadow—but how could he do that with two children in tow? Unless they were unconscious, or—

Collan heard his heart's rhythm match and then outpace the clatter of his bootheels on cobblestones, and took in deeper breaths of chill night air to calm himself down. *Think!*

Warris needed money. His kind always did. He wouldn't kill the twins; he wanted the ransom.

He *wouldn't* kill them.

Memory supplied the fact that Warris had stolen aboard ships before—their second meeting had been dockside at Domburr Castle, Collan leaving rather hastily for Firrense just as Warris was being hauled off to the

Port Authority by an infuriated captain. But now he had two children to smuggle on board ship. . . .

Idiot. He won't try to steal them onto a boat. He'll steal the boat instead.

There were plenty to choose from. A short sail to a fishing village down the coast, a note sent to Roseguard—

But how could he be sure of finding someone to take him in—broken-nosed, swollen-faced, and with two children he'd have to keep quiet somehow?

Not even the most desperate man would be so stupid. Venal and vindictive he might be, but Warris wasn't fool enough to steal Collan's children without a workable plan for success. He wasn't smart enough to come up with such a scheme on his own.

Someone was helping him.

That gray-eyed boy, that future heartbreaker, had kept Collan out of the Residence for a good ten minutes.

It occurred to him then that the boy had known his name. Called him "Lord Rosvenir." Col hadn't been to Sleginhold in years—it was Miram's and Riddon's now—for the boy to recognize him. Yet he'd used his name.

Should he find the Watch and tell them to look for a black-haired boy in a green coif—a boy they couldn't miss for his staggering beauty?

The boy had come in first, leaving the way clear for Warris. Collan had heard the bushes rustle at the same time the Ward had been set off in his head. The distance between the gate and the fountain was too great to be run so fast, even by a swift-legged child.

But the boy didn't matter. Whether he was involved or not, his was not the mind that had conceived this. Neither had Warris. He was neither smart enough to steal the twins on his own, nor stupid enough to believe he could get away with it.

Someone else. Who?

Someone to whom Taigan and Mikel had great value. A *unique* value, not measured in ransom money.

His left knee was throbbing with new pain before he even realized he was running. Past dockside warehouses, past the boardwalk, past wooden gangways that mazed through skiffs and sloops, he ran with the air salted and cold in his lungs. Heading for the main wharf, boots pounding on planks five times his age, he cursed as his knee began to slow him down. No one about, not even the Watch; he'd expected that, now that he knew what he was looking for. He expected anything and everything, except that he wouldn't find Taigan and Mikel.

Taigan—fine-boned and sunny-haired, mischief and fire in equal measure shining in her green eyes, looking more like Cailet every day (and thereby hung another Ward, to keep people from seeing how much she resembled her mother's sister). Mikel—impossible, incorrigible, redheaded Mikel, who was Collan's own image right down to his blue eyes and swift quirking smile. Flesh of his flesh, born of his beloved, sharing his and Sarra's gifts between them, a rich heritage of brains and passion and swordskill and music and magic.

To whom would they be valuable except other Mageborns?

Col swore foully as he began to limp. Why hadn't he listened more carefully to Sarra's tale about leaving Roseguard with Alin and Val? Where on the damned wharf was the stupid misbegotten Ladder?

Here. He swung over the rails and grabbed a rope ladder, letting himself down to the catwalk just below the wharf planks. He'd never been taken through this Ladder, but he knew it was here—

—and that he was already too late. They'd be at the old mill in Kenrokeshir by now. And from there to Malerris Castle—

Why in Miryenne's Holy Name hadn't he gone back for one of the Mages to take him through? Why hadn't he thought that far ahead, planned for it—damnfool moron, hadn't even snatched up a torch from the rows lining the boardwalk—

But he didn't need a torch to see the bulky form that lay on the planks. Moonlight glinted from dozens of cheap necklaces. Siral Warris, strangled with a short rope, was well and truly dead at last.

There was no sign of Taigan and Mikel.

It wasn't possible that they were gone. He wouldn't

allow it to be possible. They were clever and resourceful—they'd find a way to escape—they were perfectly capable of outsmarting even a Malerrisi—

They were only eleven years old.

Collan clung to the rope ladder, balancing precariously on the catwalk above the tide. He squeezed his eyes shut and prayed—not to any Saint, but for the intervention of a strange and powerful woman young in years but ancient in Magelore.

"Cai—whatever it is you and Sarra have—lend me some of it now. Help me find them. I won't let them be dead—I won't let anyone take them and make them into—damn you, Cailet, answer me! Help me! They're your Blood, too!"

He heard nothing but the weak whisper of waves again pylons and shore. Felt nothing but the sick ache around his heart, the hot prickle of tears in his eyes.

And a quiet, almost imperceptible quiver deep in his brain.

He willed the small tingling awareness to grow, expand, seek its match in two Mageborn children. All those Wards, all those years of having magic in his head to protect him—surely something of it must linger, something that would lead him to his children. Forcing himself to move slowly, he turned his head and looked out to sea— due south, to Malerris Castle.

No. Not there. Westerly, then, imagining a map with the island of Bleynbradden riding the vastness of Great Viranka between here and Kenrokeshir. The tremor strengthened and his hold on the rope went lax, his knees buckling, his chin sinking to his chest.

Stars exploded in his skull.

His eyes stung as his gaze raked the docks for small boats riding low in the water. Dozens, hundreds—but only one outlined in spectral fire.

He didn't bother with the rope ladder. He jumped fifteen feet into waist-high water, staggered as his knee gave, caught balance and breath, slogged through feeble surf. Sopped to the shoulders, boots full of seawater, he ran across the dark sand to the planking and pounded through a maze of bobbing hulls and naked masts.

The little sailboat floated only out of habit. Barnacles held together its elderly Domburr oak. The filthy yellow sail was bunched in the stern, the mast was splintered in a hundred places, and the hull hadn't been painted since Anniyas became First Councillor. To Collan it was more beautiful than the Slegins' beloved *Agate Rose*.

He heard something that sounded very far away, something that could have been the night wind—or a quiet sigh. Cailet? No—he knew without knowing how he knew that it was not a woman but a man, infinitely relieved and infinitely weary.

He forgot all about it as the fiery outlines of the sailboat faded. Pulling in a shaky breath, Col crouched down and pulled aside a corner of the patched and stinking tarp.

Taigan and Mikel huddled on the deck: dirty, barefoot, and alive. He watched the moonlight on their sleeping faces for a moment, then scrubbed the moisture from his eyes and cleared his throat.

Taigan frowned in her sleep, then stirred and opened her eyes. "Fa?"

"Yes," Collan said, or tried to. His second attempt at speech was more successful. "I'm here. Looks like you two had an adventure, huh?"

She nodded solemnly. Nudging Mikel, always slower to waken, she said, "Fa's here."

Mikel shifted, jerked awake, and blinked wide blue eyes. Collan held out his arms and the pair flung themselves against his chest, nearly toppling him.

"Fa, it was awful—this lady came in—we tried to fight, but she did something to us and it made everything so *slow*—"

"—and we couldn't yell, we tried, but she pushed us out the window and we fell, but it didn't hurt—"

"—and then she took us outside the walls and—"

"Shut up and let me tell it, Mikel! She got mad and did something else and everything disappeared until—"

"—we got away! I kicked her and used all those tricks you taught me—"

"—we ran and ran—Mikel was really smart, Fa, he shoved barrels in the water so they'd think we fell in—"

"—but Teggie was the one who found the boat, and we hid—"

"—and they gave up and went away, didn't they, Fa?"

"Yes," Collan said. "They gave up and went away."

After a moment they pulled back from him. He brushed dirt from Mikel's cheek and picked dried seaweed from Taigan's hair. He'd been worried that this would frighten them half to death; he'd been wrong. They weren't scared. They were *mad*. He smiled, thinking how furious Sarra had been when he'd abducted her: the outrage of one who has never even dreamed that anybody could think of laying rough hands on her precious carcass. Yes, these two were her children, all right.

"Who were those people, Fa?" Taigan asked.

"Why did they do it?" said Mikel.

Typical questions. Taigan identified and categorized; Mikel's favorite word had been *why* since the day he'd learned it.

"They were our enemies, your mother's and mine."

"But *why?*" the boy insisted.

"Because they wanted money and we're very rich," he said, opting for the truth—just not all of it.

"We are?" Taigan blinked.

"Of course we are," Mikel scoffed. "Why else do Mama and Fa have to talk to so many boring people?"

Collan bit back a smile. Taigan would be the matrimonial prize of her Generation, yet she had no idea she was rich. He and Sarra must be doing *something* right.

"Come on," he said. "Let's get you back home and into a hot bath."

"But Tarise already made us take a bath today," Mikel wailed.

"Fine," Col said. "If you want to wake up reeking of fish, go right ahead."

Mikel subsided, seeing—or rather smelling—the point.

"How did you find us?" Taigan asked as she was set on her feet. "We were ever so quiet, and we didn't move for *hours*."

Col took his time about answering. The pair really

were a mess: nightshirts ripped and filthy, faces smudged, hair tangled with anything from pillow feathers to desiccated fish fins. As Taigan took a few steps favoring her right foot, Col realized their wild run had put splinters into bare feet. Sighing, he hoisted a child onto each hip.

"Oof. This was a lot easier when you were little."

"How did you know where to look for us, Fa?" Taigan asked again.

"We can walk," Mikel protested, wriggling.

"Shut up, Mishka. How'd I find you?" He hesitated, then grinned. "Well, it's my experience that every adventure ends with something special. So how about this: a Mage Guardian lent me some magic, and I sent it out to find you, and this stinky old scow lit up like a hundred Mage Globes."

"Oh, sure," said Mikel.

"Come on, Fa," chided Taigan.

Hitching the pair more securely into his arms as he walked, he shook his head sadly. "This is the respect I get? I give you a perfectly plausible explanation and all you do is make fun of me."

"What's *plausible* mean?"

Taigan said, "Something that sounds true but usually isn't. Like what Fa just said." She considered for a moment. "Like most of what he says."

"This younger Generation, I don't know," Collan mourned, thinking with an inner grin that Cailet was going to have the time of her life teaching magic to these two skeptics. "You tell them what they want to know, and they don't believe you."

The conversation continued in this vein all the way back home, with the twins scorning his every explanation. Rightly so; each was as absurd as the first. Except that the first, the most absurd of all, was the truth as far as Collan understood it.

"Well, two birds appeared right over the boat, one dark and one pale, to show me where you were."

"Try another one, Fa!"

"I followed a trail of cookie crumbs from Mikel's shirt pocket."

"Tarise didn't let me have any cookies tonight!"

"Well, how about this one—as a Minstrel, my hearing is far beyond the ordinary, and I followed the echoes of your footsteps on the planks."

"Next you'll say you have a nose like a Senison hound, and eyes like an eagle, and—"

"—and two children who seem to have forgotten their duty to believe their esteemed father in all things!"

Mikel peered at Taigan around Col's chin. "Is he being *plausible* again?"

"No. Just silly."

By that time they were home, and Tarise took charge of them. She scolded and hugged and exclaimed over their injured feet. Collan laughed and waved good night as she swept them off, chagrined, for another bath.

Only then did he collapse into a chair and squeeze his eyes shut and begin to shake.

Some while later, he heard Tarise come in and pour two large drinks. "You know who it was, don't you?" Her voice was thick with loathing.

"Glenin Feiran." He accepted a glass and drank deeply before meeting her hazel eyes. She was angry and frightened, and liquor had put a flush into her pale cheeks. "Are you all right?"

"I *saw* her." She sank into another chair, hands wrapped around the glass. "I'd just returned from the lecture—I should never have gone, it's stupid to leave them unguarded for an instant, even with the Wards—"

"Don't blame yourself. The Wards are the best Cailet ever cast. We all trust them. If it's anybody's fault, it's mine."

She shrugged. "We'll share responsibility—along with every other person in the Roseguard Residence, and don't think I won't have something to say to every single one of them tomorrow morning!"

"Tell me about Glenin."

Tarise shuddered and gulped more brandy. "She was there, in my room. Rillan's been gone for two days at the ranch tending a colicky mare—she probably arranged that. I wouldn't put anything past her. She looked at me and suddenly I was down on the floor and couldn't move!

Why didn't you come looking for me when you saw the twins were gone?"

"I didn't think," he said honestly. "I'm sorry. All I knew was they were missing—I guess I wasn't playing with all strings strung."

"You can't imagine what it was like for me, lying there fully conscious and unable to move a finger." She downed her brandy in three large gulps. "The Captal will have to strengthen the Wards."

"Until she can, does that husband of yours have any friends as big or bigger than he is?"

"Several."

"Good. I'll want to meet them tomorrow. Why don't you go get some sleep?"

"Why don't *you?*" she countered.

He smiled to concede the point.

Tarise finished her drink in a gulp and set down the glass. "Why did Glenin want them?"

That was an easy one. "To kill them, or turn them into Malerrisi. The former, she could've done right there in their bedchamber. But she didn't, so it has to be the latter."

"There's a third reason. She could have wanted to find out if they're Mageborn."

Collan shook his head. "That won't show up for another couple of years. But that brings up something I hadn't thought about. Why take them now, when they're still magically blind? It would've made more sense to wait, or to have taken them when they were babies and she could raise them to hate us from the first."

Tarise knotted a ribbon around the end of her braid and stood up. "Something else, Collan. She worked a spell so I couldn't move, but not one to hide her identity."

He nodded, understanding what she was getting at. "She *wanted* us to know. Whatever she did with them later, right now she wanted to use the twins to hurt Sarra. Personally. Just knowing her children were in the hands of that woman—"

"Yes, but politically, too," she interrupted. "After ten years of negotiations, the Mage Charter is due for a vote next week." When he looked blank, she made an impatient face and explained, "The Captal has been operating more or less illegally all this time. Nobody ever rescinded Anniyas's Purge. When Sarra tried after the new Council was elected, people started wrangling over just what the Guardians ought to be allowed to do. Their duties and responsibilities to Lenfell, when they should be called on, the whole scope of their activities. They've been debating it on and off ever since, and nothing's been done."

He remembered some sort of discussion years ago between Sarra and Cailet about the advantages and disadvantages of a legal Charter, but the twins had been teething at the time and he'd had no time to pay attention. Still, he knew who would be on which side. Sarra, with her passion for law, would want an established Charter; Cailet, adamantly opposed to governmental interference in Guardian affairs, would want no such thing.

"You really ought to pay more attention to what goes on," Tarise was saying.

"Probably. So now the Charter's up for a vote? What's that to do with the twins?"

"It's something Sarra fought to put into the document. Mage Guardians are the only legal practitioners of magic. Anyone Working magic without official Guardian status as determined by the Captal will be considered Malerrisi, and an enemy of the people of Lenfell."

He stared at her. "You're joking."

"Not at all. I think it's a very wise provision—"

"It's insane!"

"It's exactly like the Charters for all the guilds and professions," she replied heatedly. "What if a person who knew a little about herbs advertised herself as a healer—and somebody died because she had no idea how to treat a concussion? Or what about some fool with an ax setting himself up as a forester without knowing the first thing about land management? Every craft has standards of education and knowledge, Collan, for everyone's protection."

"And what happens when somebody really talented but lacking the official sigil of approval comes along?"

"She gets herself trained in her profession and—"

"What you mean is the guilds control who's allowed

to work and who isn't—and what they're supposed to know. Doesn't that feel a little like the Great Loom to you?"

"All it does is provide certain standards of knowledge and competence—"

"With no room for innovation."

Tarise flung the long braid over her shoulder. "Now I know why Sarra's got gray hairs at the age of thirty-six! You're impossible. And I'm going to bed."

11

GLENIN held tight to her son as the ship lurched and wallowed. She had hated traveling by sea ever since that dreadful voyage when Anniyas had ordered her to rid herself of her unborn First Daughter. Now she clutched Anniyas's grandson in her arms, bracing her back and legs against the wooden supports of her bunk, beseeching St. Chevasto to weave calm upon the waters before this scow went down, taking her and the hope of the Malerrisi with it.

Had things gone as planned, she would now be safe and warm and dry in her own bedchamber, her son sleeping peacefully nearby, her niece and nephew lying senseless and bespelled in a locked and Warded room. Instead, there was a nightmare of lashing wind and crashing water, cramped quarters, and food so foul her poor darling boy hadn't been able to keep down more than a few crusts of bread.

Damn Collan Rosvenir. Damn her sister's twin whelps. Thrice damn that whining fool Warris for daring to challenge her will. And, truly told, damn Glenin herself ten times over for taking her precious son with her to Roseguard.

Ah, but how was she to know that Warris was so accomplished a votary of St. Pierga Cleverhand? She hadn't known the velvet Ladder was gone from its leather satchel until she had the twins outside the garden walls, ready to meet her son and leave for Malerris Castle. During her frantic search for the Ladder, Sarra's children began to stir. She'd been rough in reWorking the spell. Cailet's Wardings were tricky—it took much more effort than Glenin had anticipated to seize the children, which boded ill for the future. When her son arrived, they were so glazed with magic they didn't even see him.

There was only one quick way out of Roseguard. Warris was waiting for them out on the pier, grinning as he flourished a knife in one hand and the white velvet in the other.

> *"You think I'm too stupid to know why I was supposed to stand lookout while you stole Collan's litter? There's not a constable of the Watch anywhere near the docks—and you think I don't know why? I knew you'd use me and be rid of me even before I heard my Name from the shadows—not because of the fight in the bar, but because some First Daughter said I stole her purse!" He laughed, and wiped his bloodied broken nose on the embroidered cloth. "I stole better than that, Lady!"*
>
> *"You don't even know what you hold! It's useless to you—"*
>
> *"To me, truly told. But to the Captal? Take me with you wherever you're bound, or I'll put it in her hands myself."*
>
> *She nearly killed him where he stood—and was grateful that she'd restrained her temper when he flapped the Ladder over the railings. If he let go, it would be lost in the dark waters below.*
>
> *"You think I'm too stupid to know all these little markings and signs mean magic?"*
>
> *"I think," said her son from behind him, "that you're too stupid to live."*
>
> *"No—!" Glenin cried, too late. Without using any magic at all, nothing but his strength and his height—and not even full-grown yet—he flung a*

loop of stout rope around Warris's neck and throttled him.

And during the struggle—for the rolls of fat at Warris's throat made it a long, difficult death— the white velvet Ladder was torn in two.

The twins were fighting her even as Warris fought her son. There was no question who was most important. She went to help him, and lost her grip on Taigan and Mikel. When Warris finally lay still, she heard pounding feet on the wooden docks, and they barely made it to the pylon Ladder in time.

So now they were on a cargo ship bound from Kenroke to Seinshir, lacking the twins and the irreplaceable Ladder. A disaster that had nearly cost her her son. He was too miserably sick now for her to have the heart to reprimand him. Once they were back home, however. . . .

Still, she thought as she cuddled him closer, protecting him from the battering storm outside, he had said something in Kenroke this morning that marked him as a true Malerrisi.

"He had a knife. He was going to kill you and me both, and ransom the twins. But he did worse than that. He disobeyed you, Mother. You! He deserved to die."

He understood. Her beautiful, brilliant, supremely gifted son understood what it was to be a Malerrisi. Let the Mage Guardians consider it a sin to use magic for personal gain; a Malerrisi knew that the only real sin was defying the Warden of the Great Loom.

12

"I think Tarise was wrong about the politics," Sarra said some two weeks later.

She and Collan were sitting up late on the balcony after celebrating the twins' Birthingday. A bottle of wine cooled on the low table between them, and the night air was rich with roses, and the Ladymoon glinted silvery on the gardens. Taigan and Mikel had been packed off to bed an hour ago, which meant it was finally quiet enough to listen to the fountain. The pipes through which the water passed had been rebored and the gears realigned and retimed so that "Rose of Sheve Dark" sang softly with the dance of fat droplets shining like earth-fallen stars. Collan could not have designed a better setting for his first night alone with his Lady in nine weeks, but he knew better than to think she'd be finished analyzing and discussing things before Fifteenth at the earliest.

So he indulged her passion for dissection, certain that in an hour or two she'd be ready for more interesting passions. "I think she's wrong, too, but tell me how you figure it."

"Hoping to change my vote by stealing my children is a foolish ploy unworthy of Glenin. What interest could she have in legalities? She sits in her Castle as she has for over ten years, training up good little Malerrisi for future mischief. Personally, I don't think she intended to take the twins anywhere. She just wanted me to know that she can if she wants to."

"I think you're mistaken there, but we won't quibble. What's important is that they're safe, and Cailet sent her best Scholar to renew the old Wards and set up new ones—and *you're* finally home again."

She smiled at him, lifting her glass in a toast. "For the rest of the year, Minstrel mine. No meetings, no special sessions, no convocations. I don't know how it happened, but I'm not going to argue with it." She sipped wine from a long-stemmed bubble of rainbow crystal. "By the way, Granon Isidir sends his warmest regards." When he growled an inarticulate reply, she grinned. "I just wanted to see if you were still jealous after all these years."

"Jealous? Me? Of that overbearing, underwhelming—"

Sarra was laughing. "Of course not—not after *all* these years. He's still a good dancer, though."

The image of Sarra, whirling past a bonfire clasped far too closely in Granon Isidir's arms on the night the

Rising won, was calculated to annoy him even further. He ground his teeth, pasted a sweet smile on his face, and said, "You'll pay for that, Lady."

"I'm counting on it!" She refilled their wineglasses and asked, "Did Miram ever find that boy? The one in the gardens that night."

After much interior debate, Collan had decided to mention the boy but tell no one—except Cailet—his suspicions. The timing was still wrong for his involvement in the kidnapping; Taigan and Mikel hadn't mentioned any boy being with Glenin at any time; and would Glenin have risked her precious son in such a venture? Col doubted it.

"No, Miram and Riddon haven't been at Sleginhold much the last few years to keep track of everyone there, what with the babies coming one after another." He grinned. "I think they're trying to outdo Lady Lilen in sheer numbers of Ostins."

"I would have liked another child," Sarra said wistfully.

"We've got our hands full with these two," he replied at once, not wanting her to dwell on the daughter they'd lost and the daughters and sons they would never have. "Me, I can't wait to send them off to Cai, so we can get a little peace around here."

"Liar," she accused. "You'll miss them terribly, and the last thing you ever wanted in your life was peace and quiet!"

He shrugged and sipped wine. "I just hope they don't change too much, you know?"

"If Glenin had taken them, by this winter we wouldn't have known them for ours," she said grimly. "When I think of what she must be doing to her own son—I wonder what he looks like?" she interrupted herself with seeming irrelevancy.

"If there's any justice, he'll be short and dumpy like Anniyas."

"No, Glenin's tall, and so was her father." She was silent for a moment, staring at the fountain. "When he turns up—and he will—I want to know him for who and what he is." She turned her glass around in her fingers. "All right, Collan. You can tell me the rest of it now."

She'd done it to him again—switched subjects so swiftly that he felt his brain lurch to keep up with her. "The rest of what?"

"Something's bothering you that has nothing to do with what happened to the children. Out with it, Minstrel."

"Nothing's bothering—"

"Then why, by your own admission, were you in a disreputable tavern drinking the night away?"

"With you gone, there's not much to do at night. And it's not disreputable."

"Not with that great bull Lirenz Tigge keeping watch, I suppose. But that's not the point. If I had to guess, and it seems I must, I'd say you were bored."

Collan leaned back in his chair, propping his booted feet on the balcony railing. "I think maybe I am," he said slowly.

Even though she was right, and he'd admitted it, she was in the mood for an argument. "Truly told, I don't see how. You have at least as much work as I do. One would think that you'd scarcely have time to breathe, what with the children, the Residence, the holdings—"

"It's too much. And it's not enough."

That stopped her for a moment. "Why don't you take on some more students? You love music and teaching—"

"I *hate* teaching!" This startled even him; Sarra almost flinched. "Sorry," he muttered. "But you don't know what it's like, trying to find just one student—"

"—worthy of your priceless instruction?"

Collan hung onto his temper. "Falundir wasted his time on *me*. I have an obligation to share what I know. But there's a political aspect to it as well. Some of my students are important Names. No matter how inept they may be, I can't afford to offend them."

"For my sake," she murmured in a completely different tone. "I'm sorry, Col, I hadn't realized."

He shrugged and drained the wine down his throat. "It's not that I hate it. I just don't feel as if I'm accomplishing much."

"With the music?"

"With any of it."

Now she sounded bewildered. "The children are healthy, happy, doing very well in their lessons, and haven't destroyed anything significant in the last few weeks. I'd say that's an accomplishment. And *I'm* happy, which is entirely your doing. Does that count?"

"Of course it does. Never said it didn't."

Sarra sat up straighter, like a child coming to attention in the schoolroom. "Any man I can think of would look at you and think how lucky you are. You're essential to so many people—not just me and the children, but all those who depend on your management of the Slegin Web. I don't see the problem. Tell me what's wrong."

"There's nothing *wrong.* Just not everything's right."

She said nothing for a long time. Then, very softly, "I miss the old days, too, you know. I can't count the times I've wished I could be doing *anything* other than listen to those idiots drone on and on in Council. But our lives have changed, and we're responsible for making those changes, and if the price we pay for it is a little boredom, then. . . ."

He rose, paced the balcony for a few moments, then turned to look down at her. The luster of moonlight created of her unbound hair a cascade of silver-gilt silk. But her face was in shadow, and he was glad; it was easier to say what he had to when he couldn't see her eyes.

"Sarra, I love you and the twins more than my life. These have been good years, and I've been happy—but it's not enough anymore. I'm surprised it hasn't happened before now."

In a small voice she asked, "Are you bored with *me?*"

"Holy Saints, *no!* How could you ever think that?"

"I knew what kind of man you were when I took you to husband. They say it's a husband's job to make sure a woman doesn't get bored in the marriage, but I knew from the start that I'd have to work hard to keep you interested in *me.* There've been so many other women. . . ." She sighed. "I haven't been trying very hard lately, Col, and I'm sorry."

"Sarra—" This was one of those situations where a hundred well-crafted lyrics came to mind, and not one of them could say what simple honesty could. "Sarra, there *are* no other women. Ever. Not for me."

She didn't seem to hear him. "Maybe I keep busy so I won't have to think about losing you." She looked up at him, moonlight radiant on her beautiful face.

"*Losing* me—?" Sometimes he could anticipate the directions her mind would jump, sometimes he was a little slow to follow—and sometimes he got completely lost.

"Collan . . . are you truly *un*happy, or just not as happy as you ought to be?"

"Both," he replied helplessly.

"I can spend more time at home," she offered. "We could take a holiday—we haven't visited Cai since the twins were little, and then we could go up to Tillin Lake for a few weeks—"

"I'm not talking about a few weeks. I'm talking about what the hell I'm going to do with the rest of my life." He heard himself talking and didn't even know what he was about to say. "Teggie and Mishka don't need me the way they used to. They already spend more time with their tutors than with me. And they got away from Glenin all by themselves. I'm proud of them for that, but I also know what it means. They're growing up, growing away from us. It'll happen more and more, and—"

"Collan! They're only eleven years old!"

"At that age, you were bullying the Slegin boys, Cailet was running wild in The Waste, and I was a lute-playing slave at Scraller's Fief. *Our* eleven-year-olds escaped Glenin Feiran! They don't need us, Sarra. Not like they used to. And it won't be too long before they'll be gone, and Cailet will have the making of them as Mageborns."

"But—it'll be several years before they come into their magic—she said so, she doesn't want them to go through it too young—"

"What she meant was that she wanted them to be just ours as long as possible. The day we have to give them up isn't here yet, love, but it'll come faster than we think."

"And it's worse for you, isn't it?" she whispered. "Your life will be more empty of them than mine."

"It already is," he confessed. "I can't sit around practicing the lute, or giving lessons, or supervising every twig in the orchards and every cog in the clock towers. There has to be something for me to *do*."

"What do you *want* to do?"

How many men ever heard that question from the women who all but owned them?

"If I knew, I'd go out and do it."

"Do you have to decide right this moment?"

He forced the tension from his shoulders and made his lips curve in a smile. "No. And I'm not going to decide it all myself either. This will affect both of us—*all* of us. Whatever it is I end up doing."

She smiled back, a bit hesitantly. "You know what *I* want to do?"

Collan grinned down at her. "What you always want to do."

"Then can you pretend to be a properly dutiful husband for just a little while longer, and indulge me?"

"Lady, I may be on the wrong side of forty, but I'll be ten years a Wraith before I take 'just a little while' about it!"

13

FOUR days after Sarra came home, Cailet arrived in Roseguard—overland, Folding the road all the way from Mage Hall in Tillinshir. Accompanied only by Granon Bekke, she walked through the city gates at Half-Twelfth of a warm, dusky evening. Tired and thirsty, she spent a few minutes relaxing in her own house, catching up on local news with the Scholar Mage who lived there as caretaker with his family. After a brief wash and a change of clothes, she left Granon to the bath she'd been promising him for three hundred miles, and walked to the Liwellan Residence.

"I regret that Lady Sarra is unavailable, Captal," said the legislative aide, a Vekke fifth daughter connected somehow to the Ostins—as almost everyone seemed to be. Though only two years older than Cailet, Dellian Vekke had cut her teeth on politics; her mother had been mayor of Neele for thirty years. Their branch of the Vekkes, secretly in the Rising, had been instrumental in securing the city in 969.

"Holed up in her office again," Cailet interpreted. "Since lunch?"

"Since breakfast." Dellian smiled, an expression that turned her high-boned face into that of a mischievous water sprite straight out of *St. Mittru's Book of River Feys.* "Truly told, it's time she was interrupted. Sorry about what I said before—it's my stock phrase for visitors. I could set it to music by now."

"I'll bet. She probably hasn't had any dinner—how about some coffee and something to nibble on? I'll take it in."

"Not that she'll notice it's you and not a servant." Dellian shook her head, bright silvery hair swirling, as she rang for someone to take the order down to the kitchen. "If not for your Wards, a Malerrisi could walk in anytime and Sarra wouldn't even hear the door open."

The First Lady of Malerris had done just that two weeks ago. Cailet hid a wince and said, "I'll see what I can do about getting them to yell at her louder. How've you been, Dell?"

They chatted until the food arrived. The Mage Captal then played servant, opening the office door with one hand while balancing the tray in the other. Sarra didn't even glance up from the folio on her desk.

"Put it anywhere. Thank you."

So much for Mageborn instincts. Cailet decided a lecture on the advantages of observance was in order—plus a really shrill Ward.

"I do so know it's you, Cailet."

Laughing, she set the tray on a nearby table. "What gave me away?"

Black eyes met hers briefly, a tired smile in them. "After that first shock of recognizing you in Pinderon all those years ago, do you honestly think I don't know the instant you enter a room? Sit down, I'll be with you in a minute."

"A lie if ever I heard one," she remarked, surveying Sarra's desk. It fascinated Cailet, whose own organizational skills did not extend to vast quantities of paper. Sarra had made a science of it, all through the simple expedient of five painted wooden trays. Blue was for *Immediately*, red meant *Next Week*, orange indicated *Soon*, green denoted *Pretend It's Lost Unless Somebody Asks*, and yellow signified *Not My Problem*. The contents of each eventually ended up in the sixth, much larger, tray behind her on a windowsill shelf: black, for *Get This Out Of My Office NOW*.

Sarra was plowing through the red tray, having emptied the blue, when Cailet considered that a reminder of her presence—and the cooling coffee—might be useful. She cleared her throat.

Sarra gave a shrug of one shoulder. "If you have any suggestions about flood control along the River Rine, I'm all yours for the next ten minutes. Otherwise—"

"—file me in the black tray," Cailet finished, grinning. "Shall I have Dell schedule me in your appointment calendar?"

"I'd love to spend some time with you, but a courier's due by Fourteenth and I really have to get this done." She scribbled her name on the bottom of a page, closed the folder, and tossed it—without looking—into the black tray behind her. "Try the sunroom," she said, opening a new folder. "The twins will be playing with their favorite toy—Collan." She spared Cailet a glance and a grin. "I don't have two children, I have three. Go join them, if you dare."

It so happened that Cailet was too late for the fun. Col was deep in a massive overstuffed chair by the window, one eleven-year-old sleeping on each shoulder. He smiled when Cailet came in. She sank into the matching blue-striped chair, noting that the stain still hadn't come out where Mikel had emphatically disagreed with some strained carrots—Saints, how long ago now? Eight years? Nine?

"They've grown," she murmured.

Col nodded. "They do that. From one minute to the next, sometimes. Magic them a little deeper asleep, will you, so we can talk without waking them?"

She did, and struggled not to show her reaction on her face. The Wards she had set on them at birth—and renewed every so often and ever so subtly—were more worn around the edges than she'd anticipated. Strong magic, indeed, to begin pushing through when they hadn't even reached their twelfth year.

You were the same, Gorsha told her. *Only worse.*

I'll Ward them while I'm here—but will it hold?

I'll show you the tricks I used on you. *Powerful little beasties, aren't they? I don't envy you the teaching of this pair.*

Thanks for the encouragement.

Don't mention it.

Taigan started snoring a moment later. Col adjusted her gently on his shoulder; she sighed, and her breathing was quiet again.

"We won't be able to fit in this chair much longer," Collan said. "Will you look at the legs on these two?"

Cailet nodded, thinking that she wouldn't be able to fit their magic tightly into Wards much longer either. She didn't say so, preferring that Collan and Sarra think their children gifted Mageborns, but not as strong as they truly were. Where had it come from? The Ambrai gift was negligible; the Feiran potential great; but what was there in Collan Rosvenir that had merged with Ambrai and Feiran to produce Taigan and Mikel?

Gorsha didn't even stir within her. Which meant that he probably knew, but wouldn't tell her if she begged until the day she died.

"They *smell* so good," Col said suddenly, rubbing his cheek to his son's blazing red hair. "Other children smell funny, or downright stink, especially when they're babies. But these two—ever since they were born—" He chuckled. "And it's not because they're cleaner than other children, because I know damned well they're not!"

Cailet wondered when she'd ever get used to the sight of the independent, free-spirited Minstrel as a besotted father.

"I think it's because they're mine, you know?" he mused. "Everything about them, their scent and the sound of their voices—it just goes right to my gut, Cai. It all says protect them, take care of them, love them—"

She smiled to hide the pain his words brought her. These were things she'd never know: the smell of her babies, the sound of their voices calling out for her, the feel of their arms encircling her neck, the sweet weight of their heads on her breast. . . . She could share a little in the twins' young lives, but Taigan and Mikel had never fit into her arms they way they did into Collan's and Sarra's. No child ever would, because no child would ever be *hers.*

She forced the hollow ache back where it belonged, in the secret part of her that not even her sister suspected: the place where she kept bitter longing for a husband and children and a normal life. She would never wound Collan by revealing how he had unintentionally wounded her.

But even concentrating on his children, he was more sensitive to her than she'd thought. "You'll find out what I mean one of these days, Cai. There's nothing like it. Nothing."

I'll have children of my mind and heart, if not my body, she told herself—the usual palliative for this emptiness inside her. *For the next fifty years, children will come to me to become their truest selves. These two will, in time. None of them will ever be my own, but—but almost any woman can make bubies. I can make Mage Guardians. And that's—*

—more important?

Let me be, Gorsha. Let me enjoy what I can of them without wanting what I can never have.

Your capacity for self-delusion—

I said let me be!

"Cai?"

"What? Oh, sorry. I wasn't listening. What did you say?"

"How's Taguare doing?"

She was glad of the chance to smile. "He's only been

at Mage Hall for three weeks, but he's organized our library within an inch of its life, and now our little school system is getting the same treatment. He'll submit a report to the Council late this year on the education we're giving the village children. It'll be a help, Col—show everyone that we don't just sit in Mage Hall conjuring up Warming spells for our coffee."

"So," Collan said with satisfaction. "From a treatise on early private education—using my children as his experimental subjects!—he's now forming policy on public schools. Quite a change from being Bookmaster for Scraller Pelleris!"

"Oh, I'd say his first experiments were on *you!*" she laughed. "And then on the Slegin boys. Teggie and Mikel got the refined version."

"They miss him."

"He sent letters for them, and for you. And there are a couple of old manuscripts in my luggage as well that he thought you might find interesting."

He arched a brow. "Bardic manuscripts from the old Mage Academy library? He's been promising me something special."

"Copies, actually, by someone called Elseveth Garvedian. Taguare thinks she was like Falundir—a Bard as well as a Mageborn. It's a rare combination. You wouldn't think it would be, because there's a lot of magic in music. But to have both talents so strongly, as this Elseveth seemed to, and to become both, as not even Falundir has done—"

"Too bad the Mage Lists were lost at Ambrai. You might be able to identify her. It'd be nice for Mikel to have somebody to emulate." He smiled into his son's riotous curls. "I have the feeling he'll be Minstrel *and* Mage."

"You take care of one, and I'll see to the other. Oh, and Taguare says to tell Taigan he expects her to emulate *you,* and at the very least learn how to add!"

"If and when she does, I'll set her to work on the Web accounts!" He paused, shaking his head. "After hearing how they got away from Glenin, I wouldn't put anything past them."

Cailet had heard the whole tale, and knew what he was coming around to. "What happened wasn't your fault."

He didn't appear to have heard her. "I didn't do such a good job of protecting them. Truly told, I'm not good for much. Men aren't, you know. There's no power in being a man."

Confused, she waited for him to continue, to explain himself.

Instead, he asked, "What would you do about a woman who hits her husband?"

"What?"

"Not just a slap now and then. I mean she beats the shit out of him. And don't quote the law at me—he can't file a complaint because he's got no dower for her to return, and she'd divorce him, and he loves his children too much—"

"Collan, what in the world are you talking about?"

"Power," he said succinctly.

Still floundering, she said, "Are you asking my reaction as a woman, or as Mage Captal?"

"I'm asking as a *person*. And why should there be a difference? As a woman, do you have a vested interest in retaining the right to—"

"What goes on in somebody's home isn't the government's business." But it sounded feeble even to her.

"So a husband ends up with about as much legal recourse as a slave."

Cailet nearly fell out of her chair. "Collan—are you equating marriage with slavery?"

"It amounts to that for some men," he said sullenly.

For Collan? Impossible.

"Marriage is great for a woman," he said. "She gets somebody to take care of the house, raise the children, work the farm—while *she* controls the money. If she gets tired of him, he's gone—back to his own family, not young enough anymore for another marriage. Geridon's Balls, you should see some of the pathetic fools in Wytte's—trying any asinine remedy for baldness, running around and around the track like turnspits in a kitchen treadmill, trying to keep their waistlines—when a good-looking young stud comes in, they all want to kill him."

"Col—"

But he was well into his tirade by now, and would not be stopped. "There's no place in society for a single man. What choice has he got, even if he's married to a woman who knocks him around? And you know what? She makes him believe it's his fault! He had it coming—to put him back in his place. She's out of control and it's his fault he made her angry, so he has to be punished for it." Mikel stirred, and Collan stroked his son's curling red hair. "It's got to change," he said fiercely. "I won't have my son grow up into that kind of world."

There was nothing Cailet could say. Her woman's instincts rebelled against his words—which, taken to their logical conclusion, could only lead to men's legal and social and economic parity with women. And that was contrary to everything Lenfell was. No one knew for certain what the world had been like before The Waste War, but in its aftermath a woman's power to bear a healthy child had quite rightly given her power in all else as well.

Cailet considered herself enlightened—she taught both women and men on an equal footing at Mage Hall, didn't she? But when she looked at it from the perspective Collan demanded, she felt her deepest instincts conflict with her humanity.

Suddenly impatient, she wanted to ask what the hell Collan thought she could do. She was Mage Captal in a time when the Mage Guardians were few and weak, and the task before her was quite enough for one lifetime. The law was Sarra's work. If the laws changed, society would change with them.

But because she loved and respected Collan—as a man and a person—she said quietly, "You know of such a man. And you want me to help him."

"If you want to, fine. But that doesn't cure the larger problem."

She laughed uneasily. "I never thought I'd see you become political!"

"Is it politics when a woman can break her husband's

jaw without being called to account for anything but the medical bills?"

Power. I have it. So does Glenin. But this is about Sarra's kind of power, not mine.

She was about to say so when Collan went on, "You probably could take care of this one case. But how many others are there? If there were no magic, problems would still have to be solved. That's how the Mageborns—*all* Mageborns—caused The Waste War. They thought magic runs the world. It doesn't. Magic is a tool, not a living thing."

"I might disagree with you there." Glenin certainly would.

"Well, don't," Col said bluntly. "That's where you Mageborns went wrong. The world is *people*, not magic. And if there weren't any magic at all, we'd have to find other ways of curing the world's ills. Harder ways, maybe, but more human."

Cailet flinched. " 'More human'?"

"I didn't mean it like that." He shrugged impatiently, and Mikel murmured a protest in his sleep. "Magic is like—like a bandage over a wound. It hides the injury, maybe helps with the pain and the healing. But the damage is still there and won't heal completely until the body does the work itself. The real, nonmagical, human body. Magic destroyed The Waste. Did anyone ever try using magic to heal it?"

She shook her head.

"You see, Cai? If they could've, they would've. So if you want to bandage this particular marriage, go ahead. But there're thousands just like this man who don't have a Mage Captal conveniently hanging around."

"Changing laws is Sarra's work."

"She's not doing it fast enough."

Recalling the sight of her sister working her conscientious way through piles of folios and folders, Cailet bit back a sharp retort.

Collan shifted Taigan in his arms. "It all comes down to power. Men don't have much."

And Collan, she suddenly realized, was feeling its lack.

Wishing she'd thought of it sooner, she deliberately woke the twins. Their spirited welcome provided the perfect distraction—and warmed her heart besides. She forgot everything else in the delight of playing honorary Auntie Caisha to children she could never acknowledge were her kin. If they knew, they would know their grandfather's Name—and their other aunt, and the boy-cousin living at Malerris Castle, whose magic must be just as strong as theirs.

14

THE next afternoon Falundir finally returned from the Bardic Games, and Sarra ordered a gala dinner to celebrate. Thirteen people crowded around the octagonal table for dinner, and for the first time in a long time she found herself presiding over a meal the way Grandmother Allynis used to. Dishes, flatware, crystal, candles, flowers—all had been arranged by servants, and she felt a little guilty that she had not done it herself. She really must pay more attention to her family life, she told herself, and find more time to be with Col and Teggie and Mishka.

But time was not *found*. It was *taken*. You had to grab it by the throat and wrestle it to the ground. Otherwise it got away from you.

The way her children's childhood had escaped her. She could point to a new legal code as her major accomplishment of the last eleven years—yet she had not been the one to teach her daughter or son to read. Thousands of people's lives had changed for the better due to her work and her hard-won wisdom—yet her children's lives *as* children were nearly over, and she had missed most of it.

Taigan, seated next to her by First Daughter's right, was lovely and golden in the candlelight—still a little girl, but with the promise of exquisite womanhood already showing in her face. Mikel, seated at the other end of the table next to his father just as a son should, was excited and not-quite-resigned to decorum—still a little boy, but with the strong bones of manhood already showing in his face. When had this happened? When had they grown so close to adulthood? Why had she allowed it to happen without her?

She paused before lighting the candles to survey the family and friends gathered around her table: Collan, Taigan and Mikel, Cailet, Aidan, Falundir, Riena and Jeymi, Lindren and Biron, Tarise and Rillan. Sarra struck a match to the rose-scented candles and murmured a brief prayer to the Saints for the health and happiness and safety of everyone seated at her table. How long had it been since she'd done this? What sort of an example had she been to Taigan, who would preside over her own table one day?

And how could Collan be restless, bored, discontented? He shared the lives of these two miraculous children. He'd steadied their steps, soothed their hurts, taught them books and music and right from wrong—he had raised them while she was off doing other things. Important things, she reminded herself. Vital things, that only she could do. She'd spent her years in making for her children a world better and more just than the one she'd been born into. But she'd never had time to show them how to live in this new world she would give them.

They were only eleven years old. Cailet had said their magic would not begin for another few years at least. Sarra would not have to give them up to her sister until then. And she vowed that these years would be filled with her children, not with the files and folios and endless busywork of her official position.

She'd start tomorrow. She'd send back all the work that was unfinished—well, no, she couldn't do that. But she'd complete everything tomorrow or the next day and refuse delivery of anything else. She'd send Dellian Vekke to Ryka Court to look after her offices there—well, no, she'd have to go with Dellian and help her, but only for a week or two. She'd make it known that emissaries, ambassadors, and petitioners were not welcome at Roseguard—well, no, she couldn't do that, but she'd limit their time with her to no more than half an hour. As for the next session of the Council . . . she had to attend, she had no choice. But that wasn't until early next year, and she'd go by Ladder from now on, much as she disliked that mode of travel.

After dinner, the men left the women alone at the table, repairing to the sitting room to discuss whatever it was men discussed when women weren't present. Servants removed the dishes and Cloister-woven lace table-cloth, leaving the great black glass octagon bare of all but various brandy bottles and squat bell-shaped glasses. Taigan casually reached for one, earning a sternly raised brow from Tarise. Sarra gritted her teeth as Taigan sighed and subsided into her chair. Her own daughter, obeying someone other than herself! Her own fault.

When Taigan had been provided with iced coffee and the other women with flavored brandies as their tastes dictated, Riena Maurgen fixed Cailet with worried dark eyes, obviously continuing an earlier conversation. "It's a wonderful opportunity for Aidan, of course, and I don't object any more than my mother does—but is a Hall filled with Mageborns truly the place for one who has no magic?"

Cailet shrugged. "Aidan's of an age to do as he likes, with Lady Sefana's permission. I share your concern, though he did all right during his visit a few years ago."

Sarra blinked. She could have recited the positions and dispositions of every single member of Council and Assembly, but she had no idea what her own family was talking about.

Lindren Ostin circled the lip of her brandy glass with one finger, staring at it as she said, "Ever since he was little, he's wanted to become a Warrior Mage. When he turned fourteen and it was obvious he had no magic, he was crushed."

"That's why I invited him to Mage Hall the next year," Cailet said. "Lady Sefana and I discussed it at length. She felt, and I agreed with her, that he ought to see how Mages live and work and are educated—and that he could be just as useful in a community of them even if he wasn't Mageborn."

"It appears," said Tarise, "that you accomplished it.

We talked when he got back from Sleginhold, and he seems to think he'll be of greater use to you *because* he's not Mageborn."

"How come?" Taigan piped up. "I mean, I'd feel pretty stupid being in music class if I didn't know anything about playing a lute."

Cailet sipped brandy and smiled at her. "But there's more to music than playing an instrument. Even if you're like I am, with no talent whatsoever, you can still listen. Perhaps in such a class you'd be the one to tell them how they sound."

Taigan had a habit—picked up Saints knew where—of shifting her lower jaw to the right and tapping the misaligned teeth together when she was thinking very hard about something. Sarra was almost pathetically grateful that she recognized her daughter's facial quirk.

"You mean Aidan will keep them honest?" Taigan said at last.

"In a way," Cailet smiled.

"As long as he's not looked on as a token," Riena said. "I know you'd never intend that, Cai, but I'd imagine some of your students are fairly arrogant when they arrive."

"It takes a while to cure some of them of it," the Captal admitted. "And yes, Aidan will be good for them in that respect. But I'm thinking mainly of myself, you know."

"You need somebody around you who's not Mageborn," Sarra said.

Her sister eyed her thoughtfully. "You must annoy your fellow Councillors no end when you do that."

"Do what?" asked Taigan.

"Know what you're thinking practically before you think it. Surely you've been subjected to that little trick of your mother's."

Taigan shrugged, and Sarra hid a flinch. To Cailet, she went on, "He can't be for show—just to demonstrate to everyone outside of Mage Hall that you don't discriminate against those who aren't Mageborn."

"But that will be one result," Lindren said. "A good

one, just as his presence will be good for your magic-proud students."

"Yes," said Cailet. "But he wants to do this, Lindren, and I need someone I can trust without even thinking about it. Oh, I have no qualms about the others, don't mistake me. But when most of them look at me, they see the Mage Captal. They give their loyalty to her."

Sarra frowned as the black eyes in the thin, angular face focused on the brandy bottles. Suddenly she remembered how, that first year Cailet had been Captal, she'd numbed her fears and griefs with liquor. Far too much liquor.

"The Captal must survive," Sarra heard herself say.

The Captal nodded, saying softly, "Can you imagine what it's like to have a hundred people around you who have freely sworn that your life is more important than theirs—than anyone else's in the world?"

"But it *is*," said Taigan. "You're the Captal. Do you need Aidan because he thinks that way even though he's not a Mage Guardian?"

"I need him because just about the first thing he ever said to me was that his father died to keep me safe." She shook her head and looked at Riena. "In serving me, Aidan's doing what his father did. Of his own will, of his own needs. And of *my* needs, I'm going to keep *him* safe. For his father."

Tarise cleared her throat. "Well, for all these noble sentiments and motivations, Marra Gorrst may have something to do with it, too."

Cailet's head turned so fast Sarra could almost hear her neck crack. "Marra Gorrst?"

The tension was broken by Riena's delighted laughter. "Now, here's history! We know something the Mage Captal doesn't!"

A little while later they joined the men in the music room, where Collan was playing idle runs on Falundir's lute while its true owner sat nearby with eyes closed and a dreaming smile on his lips. Rillan Veliaz, as fascinated by Cailet's tangle puzzle as the twins, was on the floor with the pieces spread out all around while Mikel searched for the one that would bring up the view of

Mage Hall. Taigan, weary of serious discussion, joined them eagerly. Tarise consulted with a servant about coffee and card tables. Riena and Lindren sat with their husbands; Cailet drew Aidan aside by the empty hearth, a puzzled look on her face that changed to amusement when he blushed at something she said. Sarra remained in the doorway for a few moments, telling herself she'd been a fool to let so many years go by with so few of these evenings in them.

Collan smiled when he saw her. He always did, whenever she came into a room—as if every sight of her was exactly like the moment when his memory had come back that night at the Octagon Court. She was hardly that girl anymore, nor he that young man. They were both older; he was a little grayer; she was a little plumper. Yet whenever he looked at her like this, and smiled, she was twenty-three again.

Ridiculous. And how much more a fool she'd been to stay away from him and that look and that smile for so long. She went to his side, drawn by that awareness of him that had been in her from the very first—yes, even when he'd thrown her over his shoulder like a sack of beans and carted her off as a hostage. She dimpled on recalling it, and he grinned back at her.

"I'm about to give you something else to laugh about," he told her, resting the lute on its stand beside his chair. Rising, he rapped his knuckles on the wooden table to gain everyone's attention. Falundir opened his eyes with a start; Collan shrugged a rueful apology and then bowed to Riena and Lindren.

"Ladies," he said, "I confidently and happily report that the estate of Shore Hill is yours whenever you want to write out the payment voucher."

"What?" Lindren gasped.

"When did this happen?" Riena demanded.

"I thought the owners wouldn't sell?" said Jeymi.

"Did I," Collan asked severely, "or did I not tell you to trust me?"

Cailet gave a sardonic snort of laughter. Col glared at her, then grinned again.

"Shore Hill?" Sarra asked. "The Wittes will never

sell it. Mirya still has grandiose notions about setting herself up in style—"

"Now she'll be able to," Collan said, "just not as a
landed lady at Shore Hill."

"How'd you manage it?" Lindren asked.

"She changed her mind about wanting to live in the
country," he replied blandly.

"How much is it going to cost my mother?"

"Several thousand less than you offered. I drive a
hard bargain."

Sarra eyed him suspiciously. But it wasn't until they
were alone in their bedchamber that she got the truth out
of him.

"I blackmailed the miserable bitch," he said bluntly.

"You what?" Naked, she picked up her nightdress
from the bed.

"When she broke her husband's jaw, I finally had
medical evidence against her."

Sarra sat down hard on the bed, her nightdress sliding
to the Cloister carpet in a puddle of white silk and lace.
"Collan," she breathed, "what have you done?"

"It's what she *won't* be doing anymore that's important." He shrugged out of longvest and shirt, and sat to
take off his boots.

"Medical evidence?"

"The healers weren't eager to swear out statements,
but I finally convinced 'em. With those in hand, plus the
offer for the estate, plus the fact that Mirya needs
money—" He glanced over at her. "Plus a threat to bring
her up on charges and make her a test case in the Council
regarding the laws—"

"Oh, no," she whispered.

"I went about it wrong at first," he continued, oblivious to her shock. "And it cost Ellus Penteon. But with
the healers saying there was no way his injuries could
have come from anything but a beating—" He shrugged.
"I also told her that if she divorces him for any reason
but his own consent, or if I ever hear of the slightest mark
on him again, the deal is off and I'll have her up on
charges."

"Before the Council."

"Damned right, before the Council. Her Web's too tight with most of the members of the High Court, they'd never even hear the case. But you can take it to the top, and she knows it."

Sarra got to her feet and put on her nightdress and went into the bathroom to wash her face. When she returned, she was reasonably certain that her temper was under control.

She was wrong.

"You used the power of my office to threaten a citizen of Lenfell?"

He nodded. "You bet I did, First Daughter." He slid a silver-and-onyx earring from one lobe and went to work on the silver-and-moonstone in the other. "You've done it plenty of times. You used your power to get Aidan away from his mother and change his Name from Firennos to Maurgen. You rewrote the laws to give fathers more rights to see their children, even if they're divorced or unacknowledged. What's so different about this?"

"*My* office, Collan—not yours!"

He slapped both earrings onto his dressing table and whirled around, more enraged than she'd ever seen him. And even though she was just as angry, it smote her that she had no idea why he was so furious.

"*Your* office!" he snarled. "*Your* power! *You,* who never see anything until I shove it under your nose! Well, this time you weren't here to see it even if I *had* performed my usual humble function! What'd you expect me to do—wait until she killed the poor idiot?"

"That's not the point!"

"It's exactly the point! I find out something, I come to you with it, you get it changed. Well, this time I did the changing myself—and you're lucky I did it the way I did! What I *really* wanted was to give Mirya Witte a taste of what broken ribs feel like!"

"You wouldn't dare!"

"No man would, is that it? Saints forbid that he should even defend himself if the woman who owns him wants to break his jaw! Look at it, First Daughter! I'm showing it to you now, this nasty little secret society lets them keep—what goes on in a woman's home is her busi-

ness, and what happens between her and her husband is
no concern of the law!"

Sarra glared at him. "You used who and what I am to
blackmail Mirya Witte into selling her property—don't
you see how wrong you were?"

"No," he snapped. "I used your power because I
don't have any of my own. That's what life is like for
men. I happen to be a man married to a woman with a lot
of power. So I used it. So what? Lindren got Shore Hill,
Mirya Witte got the money she needs, Ellus Penteon gets
to live without fear of getting beaten to a pulp—"

"And what did *you* get?"

"The satisfaction of *doing* something!"

Sarra consciously unclenched her fists. "I think," she
said slowly, "that you had better find someplace else to
sleep tonight."

"This is my bed just as much as it is yours. *You* go
find another one."

Thirty-nine Generations of Ambraian ice stiffened
her spine. Knowing from her experience in Council that
if she said another word, she'd say something too lethal
to forgive, she stalked past him out the door.

15

"CAPTAL?"

Cailet looked up from the desk, where she was writing a letter to Lady Sefana about Aidan. "Mikel. Come
in. But why so formal? I've always been 'Aunt Caisha'
before."

The boy closed the door behind him and smiled
shyly. "I guess I need to ask you something *as* the
Captal."

Setting down her pen, she turned in her chair and
regarded him thoughtfully. "Something to do with
magic."

Mikel nodded. "Is it possible—I mean, does it hap-

pen to other people—" He sighed and started over.
"When you touch something, can you *feel* things?"

Cailet blinked. "Feel what, exactly?"

He came closer, gaze fixed on the gleaming hard-
wood floor. "There was this glove."

"Whose glove?"

"I don't know. It's in Mother's room—you won't tell
her we looked, will you?"

Confused, she said, "Looked where?"

"She had a box—it's got dried flowers and some
other stuff in it, some gold earrings, and the glove. *Please*
don't tell her we saw it."

Sarra had a treasure chest? If Mikel hadn't been so
worried, Cailet would have smiled. "I won't tell. What
was so special about the glove?"

He told her.

Cailet sighed softly, all impulse to amusement gone.
*Gorsha, what is this? I've never heard of a Mageborn
who can feel and see other people that way.*

*I told you they were powerful. It's rare, but not com-
pletely unknown.*

The glove . . . it belonged to my mother, didn't it?

*Yes, dearest. Though I'm a trifle put-out at Mikel's
description of me as "an old man." I wasn't even sixty!*

She did smile then, at his vanity, and her smile was a
good thing—Mikel was starting to get even more nervous. "You know what I think?" she asked her nephew.
"I think someone spelled the glove with some pretty powerful magic."

"Then it wasn't *us?* Teggie and I aren't Mageborn?"

"I don't know," she lied. "I won't know for another
few years."

He bit his lip and scrubbed his fingers through his
curls. "I had to ask."

"I understand." *And I also understand that I'll have
to block that memory when I reWork their Wards tomorrow.*

*A wise precaution. Let them be normal children as
long as they can, without even a suspicion of what they
truly are.*

"Normal?" You're beginning to sound like Collan with that insulting "human" remark.

There's more truth in what he said than you're willing to admit.

What she wasn't willing to do at the moment was argue it with him—not when Mikel was standing there waiting for her to say something. "Very strong magic is sometimes used to identify an item—magic so powerful that even those not Mageborn sense it."

"Like Wards to keep people out."

"Exactly."

This is a new theory. I'm intrigued, Captal.

I had to think up something to tell him!

"So Taigan and I might be Mageborn, and we might not." He made a wry face, shrugged and finished, "I guess we have to wait for that, just like for everything else."

"Such as?" She smiled.

"Just—you know, to grow up, that stuff."

"You've probably heard this a million times, but believe me, it's true. 'That stuff' will happen soon enough, and last for the rest of your life."

"Three million," he grinned. "One each from Mother and Fa and Tarise. And she'll be coming after me in a minute to put me to bed as if I was still four years old. I better go."

"If you want to stay and talk a while, you're welcome," she offered.

He shook his head. "Teggie and I have early riding practice tomorrow."

Cailet decided to open the doorway a bit more. "I'd like to hear what happened that night."

The freckles suddenly looked darker against the pallor of his skin. He didn't want to talk about it. He kept his expression calm, though, which impressed Cailet. This one was deep.

"But I should probably hear it from both you and Taigan," she went on smoothly.

Mikel nodded, showing no sign of his relief. "I better get to bed. Good night, Captal." After a slight pause, he amended that to, "Aunt Caisha."

"Sleep well." She watched him leave, then got ready for bed—already planning the configuration of Wards that would make remembrance of the glove and its accompanying sensations impossible. A pity she couldn't unWork all the protections yet, and explore this odd talent the twins seemed to share.

One day you'll have to unWork every Ward you ever placed on them, Gorsha reminded her. *And Saints help you when you do.*

16

"**IS** Collan right?" Sarra had gone to Cailet's room. In her own house, her own home, she had nowhere else to go.

Cailet, sitting up in bed, hugged her knees to her chest and rocked slowly back and forth. "Yes. But there are worse things than being right, Sasha. If he doesn't find something to do with himself, he's going to be miserable."

"Even more than he is now? But what can I do?"

"Change the laws he hates so much, for a start. It's the purpose he serves in your public life, you know. He's absolutely right about that."

"I know, I've always known." Sarra thought back to a conversation in a lightless cell in Renig Jail. Collan had always been able to make political theory personal, give principle a face and a name and a set of tragic circumstances. "He keeps me real by showing me reality."

"But you're the one with the power to do something about it. Consider what kind of man he is, Sarra. Truly told, I'm surprised this hasn't happened long before now."

"*What* hasn't happened?" she cried forlornly.

"You know that, too."

Sarra got up from the bed to pace. She *did* know, and it frightened her. "I can't lose him. I can't. I've spent so much time away from him and the children—just now, tonight, I decided that I have to put them first, and stop working so hard—"

"About time," Cailet observed.

"I'll resign from the Council."

"Now, let's not go too far! I'll grant you a river of regret, but don't drown in it. How happy would *you* be if all you did from now on was wander around Roseguard, harassing the gardeners? I know you, Sasha. You and Col are just alike. You both need to *do* something."

She spun on her bare heel to face her sister—who was maddeningly calm and almost smiling. "Anything I suggest to him, he shrugs it away!"

"Depends on the suggestion." Cailet unwound her arms from her knees and sank into a snowbank of pillows. "What does he do best? How can that be used so he feels necessary?"

Sarra regarded her with narrowed eyes. "You have something in mind," she accused.

"I might."

"What?"

"You think about it for a while." She patted the coverlet beside her. "Come lie down. Let him stay awake all night in that gigantic bed, remembering just how gigantic it is without you in it—"

Sarra slid into bed and drew up the quilt. "What makes you think he'll notice? He spends more time in it without me than with me, anyway."

"Oh, stop feeling sorry for yourself!" Suddenly Cailet laughed. "Do you know how good it feels to *finally* throw those words back at you, big sister?"

"When did I ever—"

"Too many times to count. Here, have a pillow."

"Cai?"

"Mmm."

"You haven't said anything about—"

"Glenin. What is there to be said?"

"Shall I write up a list?"

"All that counts is keeping the twins safe from her. Can I go to sleep now?"

"No. Why do you think she tried to take them?"

"She sees patterns you and I don't. And if we did, we'd do everything we could to rip them to shreds."

"She wanted to make Malerrisi of them."

"Sasha, she's not that deluded."

"Then why—?"

"She's trying out her power just the way I am—and you, too. These past years we've all been testing ourselves, finding our limits. When her son's old enough, she'll know the extent of what she can and can't do, and weave her plans accordingly."

"Cai . . . she won't try again, will she?"

"No."

"Are you sure?"

"Yes."

"Why?"

"If you always chatter like this late at night, it's a wonder Col hasn't kicked you out of bed long since. She won't try again because she tried once, failed, and learned from it. Besides that, she knows I've taken precautions now against this and several other eventualities—and no, I'm not going into details. All you need to know is that you don't need to worry about Taigan and Mikel. They'll be protected here. And then when they're sixteen or so, you'll send them to me, and I'll protect them personally. Now, go to sleep."

"I can't. And don't you dare spell me into it either! I can't stop worrying about her son. Our nephew. I still can't quite believe that."

"I know what you mean. It's as hard to think of him that way as it is to think of Glenin as our sister."

"He's thirteen, isn't he?"

"Almost. At the Autumn Equinox, or thereabouts. Sarra, *please* go to sleep. Or at least shut up so *I* can. I don't get much, and every minute is precious."

"One more question, and then I'll shut up, I promise."

"All right."

"You said to consider what Collan does best. Traveling Minstrel was his occupation before I married him."

"And?"

"There are Mage Guardians enough now to begin

working the way they used to—going from Shir to Shir, helping where they were needed. But you're sending them out alone, not in groups of three, of Warrior, Scholar, and Healer, the way it was before. Do you have it in mind to use Minstrels the same way? With Collan organizing, and meeting with them around the world, the way you do with the Mages?"

"That's more than one question."

"Just answer me."

"Yes. It's exactly what I had in mind. I need this, Sarra. Minstrels go everywhere and hear everything. People talk to them more openly than they do to Mage Guardians."

"If I were a vindictive woman, I'd be shouting right now that when *I* wanted to use the Mage Guardians to support the government, you turned me down flat. But now *you* want to use the husband of a Councillor—"

"No, I want to give Minstrel Collan Rosvenir something constructive to do. I trust you heard the difference in that."

"There's nothing wrong with my hearing, thank you very much. I still say you're a hypocrite—or I would, if I were a vindictive woman."

"And if you weren't so worried about Col."

"Stop *knowing* me so well, damn it! My point is that he *is* my husband, and that's too close to the Council. It'd all have to be done in total secrecy. He can't be known to be connected to this."

"Truly told. But every Minstrel will have to be personally selected by him. That means he'd be gone a lot."

"He's miserable here, Cailet. If he has to travel, home may start looking better to him."

"What about the twins?"

"Oh, Caisha—I found out something awful tonight—"

"What have they done *now?*"

"Not them, idiot—me. I found out that I'm a mother with two children whose childhood I missed."

"You did what you had to. We all do. I'm sure they don't blame you for it."

"But I haven't been what Lady Lilen was to you, or

Agatine was to me. Learn from my example, Cailet. When you have children, stay home with them as much as you possibly can. Don't miss the things I did."

"You love them. They know that."

"I'm going to spend a lot more time proving it from now on. But this group of Minstrels you want Collan to put together—he'll have to think it was his idea, you know."

"You've been on the Council nearly thirteen years. From what I hear, you've learned how to be slightly more subtle than a shipwreck."

"I do wish you'd stop laughing at me. Do you honestly think I can use the same techniques on my husband?"

"Well . . . I'm sure you'll think of something. Is it dawn yet?"

"All right, all right, I'll go back to my own bed."

"I was wondering when you'd take the hint. But if I know your husband, I very much doubt that once you get there, you'll be any better able to sleep."

"If only."

"Sasha! Never tell me *that's* a problem between you two!"

"No, of course not. It's just— Cai, do you think he's still angry?"

"Yes. But that won't prevent him from doing the other thing he does best."

"Cailet!"

"I'll tell the servants to let you sleep in tomorrow morning."

"Do that. Good night, Caisha."

"Good night, Sasha—no, leave the lamp on— please—"

And it was only then, hearing the note of panic beneath the words, that Sarra learned her sister the Mage Captal was afraid of the dark.

17

FALUNDIR'S List, once compiled and copied in Sarra's fine, neat hand, stayed with the Bard only when he was at Roseguard. He never took it with him on his travels, for he had long since communicated to Collan, Sarra, and the twins that there was no one else on Lenfell he cared to communicate with.

Just prior to St. Mittru's Day, Col returned from an afternoon at Wytte's to find the List on his desk. This was remarkable enough; that the page had ink marks on it was unprecedented. The sight of short, wavering lines beside four words surprised him less, though, than the words they emphasized:

Know   Minstrel   Secret   Travel

Two verbs, two nouns, none of which made any sense to him. Know what? Whose secrets? Travel where?

Minstrel?

"You found Falundir's solution, I see."

He turned at the sound of Sarra's voice. She was sunburned from her tour of the new warehouse facilities, and looked inordinately pleased with herself.

"What's he trying to say?"

"Think about it for a while," she advised, stripping off shirt and scarf on her way to the bedchamber. "I'll even give you a hint: you're the key."

Col followed her, page in hand. "To what?"

Boots and trousers were tossed onto the floor. Naked, her every delectable curve caressed by golden lamplight, she rummaged in a closet for a silken robe. "I'll be in the bath when you finally figure it out."

He snatched the robe from her fingers. "You'll stand there and stink until you tell me what this means, First Daughter."

She made no move to reclaim the garment. "Isn't it obvious? Considering what he wanted to tell me, he was very clever in his choice of words. Then again, a Bard always is. Add it all up, Collan."

"To *what?*" he repeated.

"And here I always thought you were so clever!" She grinned over her shoulder.

Col ground his teeth. *Travel* and *Minstrel* described him in his misspent youth. That left *Secret* and *Know*— obviously related, but how they matched the other two words was—

All at once he gasped. "You're both out of your minds!"

"Not really."

"You want me to traipse all over Lenfell—?"

"If you like. But there are plenty of energetic young Minstrels eager to do the traipsing for you. Falundir would supervise them himself, I think, if he had the time. As I recall, you were complaining not long ago about having too *much* time."

"Was this your idea?" he asked suspiciously.

"No."

"Huh!" he snorted.

She twined her arms about his neck and smiled up at him. "I'd rather have you home, as you well know." And she proceeded to prove it so thoroughly that two more hours passed before she got to her bathtub, and when she did, he joined her.

Thus was the Minstrelsy born. Collan spent the next twelve weeks selecting young musicians who were gifted, self-reliant, itchy-footed, and most especially unmarried. He started with sixteen Minstrels, but within the year expanded the cadre to nearly thirty. They were assigned to whichever Shir took their fancy, with orders to keep their eyes and ears open—and to report only to him.

In the spring of 983 Collan left Roseguard for a twenty-week tour of Lenfell, ostensibly to assist Falundir in finding new young talent and supervising productions of his opera. Along the way he set up a system of information transferral formulated by Sarra and Tarise—the very system, in fact, that Sarra had diagrammed with hair ribbons years ago. On Collan's return to Roseguard, the Minstrelsy was so well-organized that all he really had to do was sit back and wait for the reports to come in. Instead, he went traveling whenever the urge hit him. Itinerant Minstrels naturally went out of their way to meet with the renowned Collan Rosvenir—who, truly told, was their exemplar in all things.

So it was that in 984, well in advance of an election in Dindenshir held to replace an Assembly member who had died, the Captal knew that the leading candidate was in fact a Malerrisi. On St. Rilla's Day, a week before the polling, the candidate inexplicably withdrew and disappeared. It was rumored that she had been seen taking ship for Seinshir.

So it also was that in 985, a grain merchant at Roke Castle was beset with a plague of mice that ate up all his stores before he could load his ship, the *Sea Spinner*. The manifest read "Domburr Castle" but the captain had been ordered to sail for Seinshir—and didn't. The grain merchant was financially ruined when her family's Web refused to make good the loss.

A soprano at the Havenport Opera; a votary at a shrine to St. Gelenis in Kenrokeshir; a tailor in Longriding; a sheep farmer and her husband and two children in Firrense; a glasscrafter in Shainkroth—these and a dozen more were found, indisputably identified as either Malerrisi or their agents, and told the departure time of the next ship to Seinshir.

In early 987, a blacksmith working in Heathering, Tillinshir, was quietly escorted out of town by a Minstrel and three Mages from the nearby Hall. A local resident for fourteen years, an honest tradesman and taxpaying citizen, he loudly protested his innocence all the way to Pinderon. But once away from the iron bastion of his calling, the Mages knew him for what he truly was. They put him on a cargo ship bound for Dinn by way of Seinshir, and gave him a personal message from the Captal for Glenin Feiran. A simple note, not even sealed in an envelope, it read:

I look forward to meeting your son.

PRENTICES

1

"WHERE is he? He's late."

"You worry too much, Mikel. Relax. He'll be here."

Mikel eyed his sister. "If we're not back by the time Mother gets home—"

"She'll have us skinned alive and our hides nailed to All Saints' as a reminder to other presumptuous infants." Taigan shifted uncomfortably in the saddle. "Damn! I forgot to fix the stirrup length again."

"If only your feet didn't grow every time your legs do," her brother said snidely.

"*You* talk of big feet, with those size fourteen boots at the end of your shins?"

"Size twelve," Mikel corrected loftily. "Perfectly in proportion to my height."

"They'll get bigger," she predicted confidently. "You're only fifteen."

"Sixteen in seven more days, just like you!" he pointed out. "And if Mother finds out what we're up to, we'll get her dainty little size fours right in our backsides. I hope you know what you're doing, Teggie."

"They won't even know we're gone until after we're back. Besides, I'm sick of being treated like a baby. I thought you were, too."

"You know I am. But—"

"Here he comes!" Taigan broke in, and they both snapped to attention, dragging their mares' heads up from succulent spring grass.

Taigan scraped wisps of long blonde hair from her forehead, gaze intent on the cloud of dust in the distance, while Mikel scanned the horizon for indications of other company. He was at first glance as unlike his sister as it was possible for siblings to be. He had their father's blue eyes and curling coppery hair; she was as golden-fair as their mother, though with leaf-green eyes. Resemblance came in the freckles that danced across their noses, the long-legged grace of movement now that they had shed adolescent awkwardness—and the growing need, grown ever stronger in these weeks before their sixteenth Birthingday, to prove themselves as adults.

The lone rider galloped closer, reined in for a moment, then approached more sedately. Mikel held up his right hand, clenched it in a fist, then straightened his fingers, palm outward. The man hesitated, then replied with the same gesture. He was tall and lean, with a week's worth of stubble darkening his wide jaw, and wore a dun-colored coif that concealed his hair. Even at shouting distance he seemed only a little older than they.

"Your pardon for the rudeness," he called, "but who the hell are you?"

"We're here to take the relay," Taigan replied.

"I guessed that, thanks." He kneed his exhausted horse a little closer. "Didn't expect an official Roseguard reception, though."

"How'd you—"

"Those are Lady Sarra's horses."

"Shit," Taigan muttered. "Forgot about that, too."

The mares ridden by the twins were unmistakable to anyone who knew horseflesh. Maurgen Dapplebacks were now as famous as Tillinshir grays—and of all their many patterns, the Moonstreak variety was possessed only by the Roseguard stables. Slate-colored horses with jagged white flashes on foreheads and rumps, they were Rillan Veliaz's pride and joy. Tarise had only last week threatened to dye her hair black and silver, for her husband certainly never spent as much time combing and braiding *her* mane. To which he replied that he was Master of the Roseguard Horse, not a lady's maid, and she had neither the complexion for black hair nor the years for silver. Though the twins, he remarked in their hearing, were capable of aging everyone around them five years for every one spent in their company.

"So the Lady sent you herself," the young man went on, regarding them with cool gray eyes that, if there had been a little more amusement in them, would have been insulting. "I can scarce believe my luck!"

"Uh, well," Mikel began.

Taigan interrupted smoothly, "Whatever you're carrying can be trusted to us for safe delivery."

The man dismounted. In courtesy, so did the twins, and wrapped their reins around a fence post. They walked forward, immediately and instinctively in step with each other—despite Mikel's four-inch advantage in height, for he automatically shortened his strides a little to accommodate his sister, just as she lengthened hers to keep up with him.

All at once the man conjured a Mage Globe fully three feet in diameter and sent it wafting gently toward the twins. "Stay put," he ordered. And as the bluish-green Globe neared, they found they had no choice but to obey.

There was nothing inside the sphere. It hovered before them, glimmering and opalescent, sparking something inside both young minds that was familiar and desired and thus far denied them. After a moment the Globe vanished. The Mage was nodding as if he'd seen something within it that answered all questions and settled all doubts.

"Well, it seems you're telling the truth. You can be trusted. But I'll tell you right now you were stupid times ten for so quickly trusting me."

Though all magic was gone from the air, the twins continued to imitate statuary.

"My name isn't important. But this is. For Lord Collan, with my compliments." From a pocket he produced a wrapped parcel eight inches square. He slipped it inside Taigan's saddlebags, a grin showing whitely in his dark, bristled face as he grinned over his shoulder. "I wish I could be there to hear you explain how you happened to be the ones to receive it! Truly told, I do wish that very much!"

Blue eyes met green eyes; both faces winced.

"Nice to have met you at last. One hears a lot about Taigan and Mikel Liwellan."

The twins exchanged glances of dismay. The Mage laughed to himself as he swung back up onto his horse.

Rallying, Mikel said, "Don't believe all of it."

"Just most of it," Taigan added.

The Mage grinned once more. "So the Captal says."

Mikel said politely, "I hope she was well when you saw her last."

"You must've learned your manners from Lady Sarra—Saints know Collan Rosvenir hasn't any. I'd love to stay and chat, but I think this road is becoming a little too populous." He nodded at the four riders cresting a hill from the coast road.

"Tourists," Taigan said with a shrug, preparing to mount her horse.

"I don't think so," Mikel murmured. "Look."

The young Mage narrowed his eyes at the approaching riders. "Shit! Get in your saddles and ride like hell!"

"Too late," Mikel gasped. "Here they come!"

The four big Tillinshir grays had jumped a fence and were racing at a full gallop across a sloping field, trampling the tall green grain. No swords flashed in the sunlight, and the men were wearing no distinctive colors or sigils—but threat thundered toward them and the young Mage drew his sword to stand between the horsemen and the twins.

Taigan moved almost as quickly. Her belt-knives were in her hands, poised to fly straight and true when the riders were within range. In her cool response to danger she was unlike nearly every other female on Lenfell; the attempted kidnapping years ago had taught her that though she was the Blooded First Daughter to a powerful woman of great wealth and high position, her precious person was not sacrosanct. Fa had taught her to use her twin Rosvenir knives. The only flaw—and only Mikel knew it was a flaw—was that ever since Glenin Feiran had tried to steal her and Mikel for the Malerrisi, Taigan had been itching to show just how good she was with those knives in protecting herself and her brother.

"What do you think you're doing?" exclaimed the Mage.

Taigan didn't even bother answering. Mikel—weaponless, cursing the fact, and knowing his sister would never relinquish one of her knives to him—sought shelter between the two Maurgen Dapplebacks. All he could think as the grays galloped down on them was that if one single scratch slashed their beautiful hides, Rillan Veliaz was going to kill him.

Four against two. *Not* terrific odds. But one of the two was a Mage Guardian who called up a Globe the size of a garden shed, all crimson shot with silver and gold. Mikel stared, wishing passionately that he and Taigan had been Mageborn. To command such power, to so confidently Work magic—

The four riders split into pairs, leaping the roadside fence, evading the massive Mage Globe. It followed one set, and when one horse plowed into it a shower of sparks exploded. Both grays reared, screaming, and their riders tumbled into the dirt and lay still.

That left two more. The Mage had barely turned his head, his eyes dazed with the backlash of power, when first one man and then the other jerked in his saddle. A knife sprouted like silvery spring wheat, one in each belly. A second huge Globe appeared, encasing one rider and then collapsing in on itself. The horse bellowed and bucked, and a third man hit the ground. The gray snorted, shook his head so that his slate-colored mane flew like a million separate wings, and galloped down the road back to Roseguard.

The fourth man, after yanking the knife from his right side and flinging it to the ground, spurred his horse around and fled the way he'd come.

Mikel whooped with triumph and ran for Taigan. The Mage seized his arm and spun him around.

"Get out of here! Now! I'll take care of these three!"

"I need my knives back first," Taigan said calmly.

"I'll get them." Mikel shook himself free. A few moments later he kicked Taigan's victim over onto his back, extracted the knife, and wiped the blade on the man's longvest. Fingers suddenly closed around his ankle. Yelping, he kicked again and jumped back. The man subsided with a groan, eyes shut, the wound in his stomach bleeding profusely.

"He's still alive," Mikel called back over his shoulder, hoping his voice didn't shake too much.

"Find the other knife and get out of here," the Mage ordered. "I told you, I'll take care of them."

By which he meant, *I'll kill them.* Mikel heard it in his tone, and everything in him rebelled. Mage Guardians didn't kill people—not unless the Captal was directly threatened. Magic wasn't a weapon, it was a tool. He scanned the dirt road swiftly for a glint of silver, turmoil thudding in his heart. At last he found Taigan's second knife, and this one he cleaned on his own shirt.

Then he saw what he'd done. And it felt appropriate that there was blood on him. And disturbing, that the shirt was dark brown and the blood didn't even show.

He gave the blades back to his sister, who quietly sheathed them at her belt. The Mage, eyes blazing with anger, pointed wordlessly to their horses before striding off to check on the other two men.

"*Now* we can leave," Taigan said. "And *not* because he told us to."

Mikel took his sister's arm and pulled her toward their mounts. "Come on, Teggie."

"Maybe we should stay and help."

"In case you hadn't noticed, those men were trying to kill us! This isn't an afternoon tea social!"

"Mikel!" she exclaimed. "We're supposed to be at Treyze Senison's by Ninth!"

"Of all the ridiculous things to think about at a time like this—" He scrambled into the saddle. "I *knew* we were going to get into trouble! Come *on!*"

"Oh, shut up! I'm coming, I'm coming!"

After that, they were riding too fast to squabble. Half-Eighth passed, and they were only halfway back to Rose-guard. There would never be time enough to see to the horses, get cleaned up, and get to the Senisons' party without being scandalously late. Tarise would already be looking for them. Their father would be enlisted in the search soon thereafter. And Saints only knew what their mother would say when she learned they were nowhere to be found. That they were on a mission for Fa's Minstrelsy would hold about as much water as a sieve. Strange, though, that a Mage Guardian had delivered the package, and not a Minstrel. Mikel said as much when they finally neared the Roseguard gates. Taigan shrugged a reply.

"It's not as if we know everybody who works for

Fa," she said. "This Mage probably offered to take the package for the Minstrel, save her a trip."

"Then why—"

"Because," she said impatiently, "it's probably more important than usual, and a Mage could keep it safer. Come on, we're already almost too late!"

"We were too late half an hour ago. But I guess we have to play it out. What d'you think it could be, anyway?"

Taigan thought for a minute. "One of those Globes the Captal uses to keep in touch with her Mages? It's about the right size to hold a small one. And that new Scholar here—what's his name, something-or-other Irresh?—he doesn't have one yet like Trelin and Biren Halvos do. I'll bet that's it, Mishka—it's supposed to be delivered to him, and the Malerrisi found out and tried to take it so they can figure out how they work, and we stopped 'em!"

Mikel turned his head to stare at her. "I know you can usually gut-jump just about as well as Mother, but isn't that pushing it a little? Malerrisi?"

"Who else?"

After another half mile, he said, "You enjoyed that, didn't you? It didn't bother you at all that you had to—"

She looked quickly around, as if fearing to be seen or heard. Then, holding out one hand flat, she said, "Don't you believe it, little brother. I was scared out of my mind."

And Mikel was oddly comforted to see how her fingers trembled. It seemed to go with the blood on his shirt somehow. He wasn't clear on why this should be so—and in the next moment forgot all about it in concern for his sister. "Are you all right?"

"Mostly."

He decided not to tell her what he suspected the Mage would do to the three attackers.

They passed through the Roseguard gates. Mikel heeled his mare into a faster walk through the streets. "Where do you want to hide it until we can give it to Fa? Tarise found the hole in your bathroom ceiling weeks ago."

"Then she won't be looking there, will she?"

Somehow they avoided Tarise. It was just after Half-Ninth when they emerged from their rooms, hastily washed and dressed in the latest young fashion. A little too young, as far as they were concerned: Taigan hated her loose, low-waisted, high-collared pink dress as much as Mikel loathed his pastel blue longvest.

"We look like ten-year-olds," he muttered.

"At least you get to wear a coif," she retorted as they slipped out a back entrance and walked swiftly toward the Senison townhouse.

"What an honor. I get to swelter and sweat just like a grown-up."

"This Birthingday I'm going to demand new wardrobes," Taigan vowed, "We can't go on dressing like children."

"We won't get it unless we set fire to all the old stuff."

"Fa's a walking fashion broadsheet—he'll be glad if we show some interest—"

"Fa still thinks you don't have tits," Mikel replied. "Not that anybody'd notice, in that dress. Do something about your hair before we get to the front door, will you?"

She eyed him sideways. "You're picky all of a sudden."

Swaggering a little, mainly because he knew it would annoy her, he said, "A *man* likes his sister to look pretty and do him credit—with tits or without."

Taigan punched him a good one in the arm.

The social life of youthful Roseguard was beginning to revolve around its two most important members—and Taigan and Mikel knew it. Soon they'd be attending parties and balls and dinners in their honor, and dressing (they devoutly hoped) in the elegant style of their parents. For now, they were condemned to make their appearances in "cute" clothes at "fun" morning musicales and "festive" afternoon tea socials. And appearances they must make, or risk insulting those who invited them. They had yet to give their own first big party, which would occur on their sixteenth Birthingday at Midsummer Moon. But because every mother in Roseguard wished her daughters and sons to attend this grand occasion, invitations had been coming thick and fast all spring. Tarise decided which they would accept, after careful inquiry into who else was on the guest list. Tarise was, in fact, turning out to be something of a snob—not regarding ancestry or wealth, but politics. She saw the twins' social life as useful for signaling Sarra's displeasure at the attitudes of certain Roseguard families. For themselves, Taigan and Mikel longed for the day they could wear clothes of their own choosing to parties of their own choosing, and Tarise's political opinions be damned.

Treyze and Goryn Senison weren't high on their list, not since the day Taigan had caught Treyze trying to kiss an unwilling Mikel and defended her brother's honor by giving the girl a black eye. (They'd all been twelve at the time.) But the Senisons at least provided a tasty meal, and after the morning's long ride and no lunch the twins were hungry enough to be courteous to their hosts. They were discourteously late, but their guilt over it lasted only as long as it took them to realize that it only mattered that they had arrived at last.

The other guests were the usual group who had Tarise's approval. They bore the Names Rikkard and Irresh, Girre and Raninis, Maklyn and Berekard—and if any had once been Bloods, no one would know it. For, as Collan pointed out in disgust, "They're *all* arrogant little shits."

Taigan and Mikel ate and chatted and effortlessly charmed in the light social way their mother had long since perfected. By Tenth they were actually beginning to have a good time. The food was plentiful and excellent; the three comely Irresh girls were proving susceptible to the grin Mikel had inherited from his father; Taigan won her bet over which of Mili Berekard's five older brothers would be first to marry; and the gossip was flowing thick and fast.

"Did you hear," said Mili in a hushed voice, "about Lady Mirya's new boy?"

"*Another* one?" Taigan allowed herself to be drawn aside to a secluded window seat. "What's this one like? Besides young and gorgeous, I mean."

" 'Young'? He's not even eighteen! And 'gorgeous'

isn't the word, if what Nialla Kylades says is true." Mili shrugged plump, pretty shoulders nicely displayed by a cool, thin-strapped summer dress—the kind Taigan wished her father would let her wear. "Her brother Jaysom works at Wytte's—"

"Jaysom? Oh—flat forehead, big nose, no shoulders?"

Mili grinned. "That's why he switched from stacking towels and serving drinks to helping that man-mountain who supervises the exercise room! Anyway, the new boy just arrived at Wytte's, and Jaysom told Nialla that he's absolutely unutterably *perfect*. But this one's different— she's not being seen with him, he's not just her newest toy. She's *paying* for him to stay at Wytte's!"

"To pretty him up and improve his manners before she takes him out in public?"

"Before she takes him into her household, more likely."

"She's never done *that* before. It's disgusting. She's even older than my mother!"

"Age has nothing to do with lechery," Mili said sagely, and dipped into a pocket for a flat tin of lip-paste—another grown-up privilege denied Taigan. As pink was applied with a fingertip, she continued, "There's almost thirty years between him and Lady Mirya!"

"Well, who's going to complain? Her husband's been teaching at St. Caitiri's on Brogdenguard almost three years, and he's got the daughters with him, so she's on her own. She has as much right as any woman to amuse herself. It's her taste in who she does it with that's degenerate."

"Teggie, don't tell me you actually believed all that squirm about her husband's taking the job so he could oversee their education? She just wanted them all out of the way so she could do as she pleased without her mother getting angry that she was setting a bad example for her daughters. Which she's been doing with a new boy practically every season."

"But you say this one's special. . . ." Taigan frowned, then caught her breath. "Mili, she's going to divorce her husband and marry this new boy!"

The little tin of pink gloss snapped shut. Shrewd blue eyes narrowed. "New boy here, husband and children finally away—it makes sense. But she can't marry him until he's eighteen and can legally sign a contract."

"And it'll cost her," Taigan remarked. "She's the reason my mother got the divorce laws changed, you know. But don't tell anybody—I'm not supposed to know that."

"The things you must hear!" Mili said admiringly.

Taigan smiled like a cat. The things they'd *done* were even better. But she said nothing about the morning.

"I've told you my best of the week," her friend continued. "Now it's your turn. You never tell me any good political gossip, but what's being planned for your Birthingday? Is it going to be as spectacular as your father's other parties?"

"Better—or so he says," Taigan laughed. "But he won't tell us anything!"

"Typical male. Well, then, what about that luscious new tenor? They say he'll rival Sevy Vasharron one of these years."

If she knew anything about the tenor, Taigan didn't get the chance to share it. In the arched doorway of the salon appeared the tall figure and grimly scowling face of Rillan Veliaz. Two minutes later the twins had perforce made their excuses and were being hustled down the front steps of the Senison townhouse.

"Not a word," snapped Rillan.

"But—"

"You heard me, Taigan!"

Ten minutes later they were hearing their father, and it did not make pleasant listening.

"Of all the stupid, crazy, damnfool stunts you ever pulled, this one's the limit! You're lucky I don't knock your heads together just to hear 'em crack! Who the hell d'you two think you are?"

Taigan looked her raging parent straight in the eye and replied, "First Daughter and only son of the two smartest leaders of the Rising."

That actually stopped him in mid-tirade, and he shot her a suspicious glance. "Smartest?"

"You lived through it."

He snorted. "Nice try. We weren't smart enough to stay childless! And don't you try to sweet-talk me, girl," he warned, pointing a long, lean finger at her. "So you wanted some excitement, did you? All the usual crap you pull isn't enough for you anymore, is that it? You had to steal the horses—"

"We didn't steal them, Fa," Mikel put in. "We just arranged to meet the courier and—"

"Shut up! Did you ever think he might've been followed? Or that he wasn't who he said he was? Did you think of that? Do you ever think at all?" Collan stalked over to a chair and flung himself into it. Hooking one knee over the chair arm, he swung the leg back and forth for some minutes, glowering. The twins looked at each other from the corners of their eyes. He was *really* mad this time.

And he had reasons he didn't even know about yet. But neither Taigan nor Mikel was about to tell him.

"Well," came a new voice, cool and biting, which made the pair flinch as all their father's shouting could not. Lady Sarra Liwellan strode through the sitting room, rustling crisply in an ivory silk trouser suit, the lacy tunic picked out in black thread—the kind of clothes Taigan dreamed of wearing. Turquoises glowed from her ears and from the clasp holding her golden hair at the nape. She was elegant and straight-backed and beautiful, and as always the twins were filled with pride that this remarkable woman was their mother.

The sting of her voice was anything but beautiful, however. "Congratulations. I hear you've surpassed yourselves. I didn't think it was possible for any exploit of yours to surprise me, but it seems I was wrong. My compliments."

This was worse than the time they'd restrung Fa's second-best lute backwards just before unexpected guests arrived. Or the time they'd replaced sweet green peppers with hot green peppers in the condiments dish at the St. Velireon's Day feast. Or the time they'd sneaked into Wytte's and switched all the clothes around in the changing room. Or the time—well, this was worse than *anything*.

Mikel shifted nervously, and Taigan's defiant gaze finally lowered to contemplation of the flowered Cloister rug. This morning, everything had been so easy and daring. (Well, mostly easy.) They'd been sure that once their part in the courier's hand-off was revealed, they'd be hailed as full adults with all rights and privileges pertaining thereto.

This was obviously the last thing either of their parents had in mind. Their father had stopped yelling at them, but his eyes still smoldered. Yet there was something else, something they'd seen only once or twice: fear. It was in their mother's eyes, too.

Mikel cleared his throat. "We're sorry. Really." He nudged Taigan with an elbow.

"Truly told," she said. "But we—"

"Be quiet," Sarra said, and for all the coldness of her eyes, her voice trembled. "You have no idea what you're talking about!" Pacing away from them, she went to the windows, her small pale figure framed by the spring garden outside.

"Sarra," her husband said softly, "they're home safe."

Taigan thought it might be time to point out the obvious. "And we made the transfer just fine, Mother."

Mikel gulped and stared at the carpet.

"Oh, so *that* makes it all right?" She spun around and glared at them.

"What is it?" Collan asked. "And where?"

"Just a box," said Taigan. "We didn't look inside."

Mikel added, "It's in Teggie's bathroom ceiling." This earned him an annoyed glance now that promised another fist in the shoulder later.

Their father sighed. "I thought I told somebody to have that fixed."

"I'll go get it," Mikel went on, seeing an escape route.

"You'll stay right where you are," commanded his mother. "What sort of box?"

"Plain wood," Taigan answered. "Walnut, I think. No lock or anything."

"But you didn't try to open it?" Black eyes narrowed at them.

"No, Mother." Taigan glanced at Mikel again, sharing the thought: how strange that they hadn't even considered taking a look inside.

Their mother turned to their father. "Why would it be Warded?"

"Warded!" Taigan exclaimed.

Mikel nodded sagely, as if he'd known it all along. "The courier *was* a Mage Guardian."

Collan swore under his breath. "Name? Age? Looks?" he snapped.

"Uh—he didn't tell us his name. And he kind of looked like. . . ." Mikel trailed off and frowned at Taigan. "Was he as tall as I am?"

"I don't know. Maybe. I think he had dark hair—and maybe a beard?"

"I don't really remember. And he could've been about twenty-five, or a little older, or—" He blinked. "He didn't just Ward the box—he Warded *us!*"

"No," Sarra said grimly, "himself, so you couldn't describe or recognize him later." She started for the door, her husband right behind her, pausing only long enough to fling back over her shoulder, "Stay put. I'll deal with you later—and I guarantee you're not going to like it."

Left alone in their parents' chambers, the twins stood silent and immobile for a full minute. At last Mikel ventured, "If the courier wasn't supposed to be a Mage, who was he?"

"And if the box isn't just a box, what is it? And how come those men wanted it so bad?" Taigan gulped. "Come on, let's go."

"Where?"

"Anywhere. If we're lucky, the box will keep them so busy they won't even remember we exist until tomorrow."

"If they can't find us, they'll only get madder," Mikel warned.

"What could be worse than the way Mother looked

just now?" Cool as Taigan had been most of the day, now she was fidgety. Sarra could have that effect on people.

"How about the tree house?" Mikel suggested.

"Perfect."

But they discovered from the footman waiting in the hallway that orders had been given to confine them—not just to the Residence, but to their rooms.

Taigan maintained her composure until they'd turned their backs on their grim-faced escort and were halfway up the stairs. "Damn it!" she muttered.

Mikel heroically refrained from saying *I told you so.* Instead, he mused aloud, "For just a little while there I felt kind of grown up, y'know?"

2

COL was about to step up onto the porcelain commode to get at the hiding place in the ceiling when Sarra came into the bathroom.

"Holy Saints! Let me do it, you'll break the fixtures and we'll have water all over everything!"

He moved aside, bowing with a flourish of one hand. She shrugged out of her jacket, tossing it onto the small velvet-covered stool before Taigan's dressing table. Steadying herself with a hand on Collan's shoulder, she hopped up onto the commode lid, strained on tiptoe, and groped around in the hole where a bit of plaster had come down.

"I could kill those two," she said.

"Stand in line," he advised.

"Where—oh, here it is." She extracted the small, square box and jumped down onto the tiled floor. "Who was the courier supposed to be?"

"Savachel Maklyn."

"The one with a second cousin at Mage Hall?"

"The very same. And Sava's got about as much magic as your average fish." He tilted his head and regarded her curiously. "How do you keep all this information in your head?"

"You know a million songs," she retorted. "How do *you* do it?"

"My job."

"Exactly. Besides, Savachel's the favorite grandson of Councillor Vasha Maklyn—first Minstrel in three Generations of the family, and she loves music."

"He *is* pretty good," Col allowed. "Who do you think took a whack at him?"

Sarra turned the box over and over in her hands. "How would I know? Other than a Malerrisi, that is. Those *idiot* children! Look at this, Col—Glenin practically advertised!" She pointed to the crafter's mark on the underside: a spool with a threaded needle stuck into it. "How did they get away with their lives?"

"Dumb luck. We'd better call in Trelin Halvos—unless you think you can get past the Ward and open that thing."

Going past him into Taigan's bedroom, she said, "We don't need her. This is meant for me, from Glenin Feiran."

"I'll send for her anyway—and don't you dare open that until he arrives."

But it was too late. Sarra did nothing to the box's lid, but her presence, her voice, her hands upon it—whatever the identification, it was enough to trigger the Ward. Heat radiated from it until she could no longer hold it. With a sudden cry she dropped it onto the carpet. The joining came apart, the hinge dropped off, and it separated into six equal pieces: four sides, the bottom, and the lid.

Collan hauled her toward the door as six translucent Mage Globes, each as large as the box had been and flashing all the colors of the rainbow, coalesced five feet above the floor. They hovered, rearranged themselves into a circle, and chimed the same note in six octaves, the highest almost painfully shrill. But the voice that issued from each in turn was Glenin Feiran's.

"*Greetings, Sarra!*"

"*Lovely weather this spring, don't you think?*"

"How are your charming children and handsome husband?"

"I remember them all very well and look forward to seeing them again!"

"My regards to the Capital!"

"And here's a little gift for you!"

Collan grabbed Sarra to his chest and flung them both out of the bedroom. He got them out of Taigan's chambers and two steps down the hall before a blast of sound and heat struck their backs and knocked them sprawling to the floor. Sarra, half underneath her husband, caught her breath, squirmed free and got to her feet. Collan rolled over and stared up at her.

"You all right?" he asked at last.

"Fine. I think, however," she said coolly, "that we'd better call the architects. Taigan's room will need redecorating."

3

IT was very late, or very early, depending on whether or not one had slept. Sarra, dressed in a filmy silver nightrobe, sat at her bedchamber windows and gazed out at the gardens. Collan was asleep. From time to time she glanced over at him, a smile touching her lips. She'd grown up knowing that somewhere a Blooded son, suitably wealthy and advantageously connected, would be found for her to marry; that her choice had fallen on an all-but-Nameless Minstrel still amused her.

"Stop thinking so loud," he said.

She rose from the window seat. "It's just that the gears are stuck."

He was propped on his elbows, head tilted slightly to one side. The years—or maybe raising their impossible children—had added gray to his coppery curls and a few lines to the corners of his very blue eyes, but also a certain unexpected sweetness to his smile. "What is it? Teggie and Mishka?"

"Partly." She sat on the bed, watching his face by moonlight. "It may be time they went to Cailet."

His frown was everything she'd expected. "Another year."

She hated to ask it, but she had to. "Col, can we keep them safe?"

"Yes." When her brows arched at his vehemence, he shrugged and went on, "I know, I know—either they learn to use this magic of yours and Cai's, or they'll get killed doing something even more stupid than they did today."

After the explosion, the twins had confessed. Sarra had been struck dumb—though whether terror or fury predominated, she had no idea. The combination had rendered her mute. Not so Collan, though he hadn't so much as raised his voice. In a quiet, lethal tone, he'd told the twins never to do anything like this again. Period. End of conversation.

But not end of speculation. The young Mage had not been a Mage but a Malerrisi; far from defending their lives, he had arranged the attack himself to bolster his credentials with whoever had arrived for the transfer. How he had managed to find out that a transfer was indeed scheduled for that day and place and time was accountable by the fact that the Minstrelsy courier had limped into Roseguard early this evening with an egg-sized lump on his head, a swordslice to his thigh, and a message for Collan from an agent in Sheve. How the Malerrisi must have exulted when the couriers turned out to be Taigan and Mikel Liwellan.

"They need to learn how to protect themselves from things like what happened today," Collan went on. "But they haven't learned everything you and I can teach them yet."

"Sometimes I wonder. They're growing up— growing restless."

"Like you and me."

She nodded. "I'm just not sure how much longer we can keep their wings clipped."

All at once he grinned. "Did you get a look at them today? Especially Taigan?"

Sarra made a face. "Reckless, arrogant, defiant—exactly like you!"

"I humbly contradict you, First Daughter—the arrogance they get from *you!*"

"I'm never—"

"Well, we won't quibble." He picked up the trailing end of her braid and toyed with it. "I want them with us just a little longer, Sarra. They may *think* they're all grown up, but—"

"—but they're *not.*" She paused. "Even so, they're older than most of Cai's Prentices."

He said nothing for a moment, then pulled an annoyed face. "I guess I still don't quite believe that children of mine are going to become Mage Guardians."

"Does it bother you?"

"Some," he admitted. "But I'm proud of 'em. It's just strange to think that something I made turns out to be Mageborn."

"I had something to do with it, too, you know."

"Did you? I don't remember. Remind me."

And he pulled her down into his arms. While kissing her, his fingers undid the braid and spread her hair all around them like a curtain of gold. She barely felt it: he had a magic all his own, and when he let her up for air, she told him so.

"Think that's something?" he scoffed. "How about *this?*"

Much later, as they lay side by side with a silk sheet draped over them as shelter from the soft night breeze, Sarra felt his arms tighten around her again. "What is it?" she asked sleepily.

"Cai."

"What about her?"

"Been a long time."

Sarra thought that over. Her sister had last visited Roseguard just after Glenin tried to kidnap the twins—five years ago—when without their knowledge she'd Warded them yet again. She'd said then that this was the last time; and now that Sarra thought about it, she knew

Cailet meant that at their next meeting, the Wards would be taken away forever. Cailet had spent years waiting for the twins, just as Gorynel Desse had waited for her. But neither Taigan nor Mikel would go through what Cailet had in coming into her magic. She'd made sure of it.

Sarra and Collan tried to get up to Tillinshir to visit Cailet every year or so. The Council didn't have as much of Sarra as it used to, but Collan's Minstrelsy had much more of him. Their time with each other and their children was more precious than ever. In retrospect, Sarra felt a little guilty at having neglected Cailet.

"I'm not sure I know her all that well anymore," Collan said.

"I know her," Sarra replied quietly. She could always feel her sister's living presence, ever since that shocked moment in Pinderon so many years ago. But lately it seemed Cailet had withdrawn a little, putting measures of mind as well as of distance between them. "I know her," Sarra said again, to reassure herself. "She hasn't changed. Just gotten older, like all of us."

"Not you," Col said. "Any girl who can do what you just did—"

"Collan!"

He laughed and tugged at a lock of her hair. "I love you, First Daughter."

"Oh, and now I'm supposed to tell you how much I worship and adore you, what a wonderful husband you are to me, what a marvelous life we have together—"

"Oh, I know all that," he replied blandly.

"Then why did you say what you just said?"

"Because it's true. I love you."

A rare and simple statement; it brought sudden tears to her eyes. She rested her forehead on his chest and whispered, "I love you, too."

4

THE card table's marble top—dark blue with a gold grain, highly polished—made a fair mirror at the correct angle. Thus even with her gaze lowered, Taigan could still judge her father's expression as he leaned over the six pieces of the Malerrisi box. The wood had survived yesterday's blast of heat and wind; Taigan's room had not. She had moved into one of the guest chambers. Her wardrobe had also been a casualty, which was why she had refused to accompany her mother and brother to that morning's meeting of the Sheve Justiciary. She had no intention of being seen in public wearing the same dress she'd worn yesterday—now the only dress she had. Naturally, the disaster was to her eyes the perfect opportunity to replace her little-girl wardrobe with clothes of elegance and sophistication. Equally naturally, her parents didn't see it that way. But Taigan was, if nothing else, her father's daughter.

"I could make an appointment with Ela Agrenir this afternoon, and have something to wear by tomorrow."

"Mmm," her father responded.

"After all," she continued as Collan continued to inspect the six interlocking squares of wood, "I'm sixteen, and that's quite old enough to be dressed by Mother's designer."

"Uh huh."

"Besides that, I have to learn what looks best on me, so that when I make public appearances I create a good impression." She smothered a grin of triumph as, reflected in the tabletop, one corner of his mouth twitched with involuntary amusement. This was definitely the line to take with him: an appeal to his pride. His long musician's fingers turned a piece over and over, testing weight and smoothness, and she went on, "It's part of my position as your daughter to be at the forefront of fashion. How does it look when I'm wearing some tacky old thing meant for a little girl? We have a reputation to uphold."

"That so?" He exchanged one piece for another seemingly identical one.

"Everybody else is wearing—"

His head lifted and his blue eyes regarded her, brows arched above them. "Mistake," he said. "Don't tell me you want to be a trendsetter and then talk about what all the other girls are wearing. What you *should've* said was, 'You should see the awful stuff some of my friends had on at the party yesterday—it's my civic duty to show them how to dress.' "

Taigan slammed the flat of her hand on the table. The pieces of the box rattled. "I'm tired of looking like a twelve-year-old!"

"When you stop whining like one, then maybe I'll consider making an appointment for you with *Domna* Timarrin to replace your wardrobe."

Her breath caught. Timarrin Allard was the most exclusive designer in North Lenfell. Though Mother preferred to patronize the local Roseguard designers, she ordered one special gown each year for the reception following the opening of the Council. And Fa was offering whole closetfuls of Timarrin Allard clothes—!

"You mean—*everything*?" she asked her father in hushed tones. "Dresses and ball gowns and shirts and trousers and suits and—and *everything?*"

"It would mean a trip to Ambrai. She doesn't go to her clients, they go to her. And we can't get anything from her before your Birthingday party—sorry, pixie."

That didn't matter to Taigan. It was only one party. There'd be hundreds more, all of them with her in the splendor of a Timarrin Allard Original. "How do you know she'll see me?"

"Because she owes me a favor for letting her dress *me*. And because there's nothing she'd love more than to show off her work on the prettiest girl on Lenfell." With a few deft movements he fitted the pieces of the box back together and set it onto the table. "Y'know, if the Malerrisi were really smart, they'd make this like those puzzles the Captal used to send you. So that whichever way it was put together, it'd do something different."

Taigan was distracted from the entrancing vision of

herself in one of those scrumptious gowns like Mother wore. "Oh, that's all we need—another explosion, or a spell to knock us all blind and deaf. It won't do anything else, Fa. The magic's all gone."

"Is it?" He cocked his head and eyed her strangely.

"Well, yes," she said, not quite knowing how she knew. Her mother knew things—*gut-jumping,* she called it—and Taigan had in some measure inherited that gift. It was how she'd known that Lady Mirya Witte was going to divorce her husband and marry her new boy. It bothered her that she'd been so wrong yesterday about the Malerrisi and what he carried; maybe the excitement and danger had clouded her ability. And maybe not. But gut-jumping had nothing to do with being Mageborn.

Or did it?

"Fa," she said slowly, "Mikel and I are too old now, aren't we? To become Mage Guardians. If we had magic, it would've shown up years ago."

"Possibly. You mind much?"

"I don't know. It doesn't matter much if I do, does it? I can't do anything about it."

He gave a quiet sigh. "Have we reached the what-do-I-do-when-I-grow-up stage?"

She didn't say that thank you very much, she *was* grown up. "I've been thinking about it some, yes."

"Thought about what? Business? Medicine? Politics, like your mother?"

She couldn't repress a grin. "Spend my life the way you used to, with a ledger book and a long-winded factor droning in my ears? Not a chance! And not medicine either—I hate the sight of blood."

"My delicate little flower," he grinned back.

"As I proved yesterday! Knives for me, Fa, not scalpels!"

"Well, what *about* politics? Your mother carves people up on a regular basis in Council."

"Every word Mother says when she's wearing her Councillor Face bores me to death. And I'm pretty useless at everything else—" She sighed. "Just like every other rich girl my age."

"That's not true, Teggie. You just haven't found what it is you want to be."

"Well, becoming a Mage isn't an option."

"But you wish it was?"

"Sometimes." She shrugged uncomfortably.

Collan smiled, turning the box around in his hands. "I think you're kind of like this—locked up tight, waiting for the right thing to trigger what's inside you. And knowing you, there's definitely going to be an explosion!"

5

"ARE you certain you wouldn't recognize him again?"

Mikel chewed a mouthful of salad greens, swallowed, and shook his head. "All I can say for sure is he had light-colored eyes—pale blue, maybe gray. I guess he's pretty good at Warding, huh?"

His mother shrugged. "It's all right. An identification would have been useful, but. . . ."

"Are there lots of them wandering around?" He didn't bother to lower his voice; wherever Lady Sarra Liwellan went, people listened to her conversations. The lunchtime patrons of Velireon's Kettle, Mikel's favorite restaurant, were no exception, neglecting their own chatter in an attempt to overhear what was being said at Lady Sarra's table. At least the waiters, just as eager to catch a word, provided attentive service.

Mikel had spent the morning listening to three Justices blather on about the shocking assault on him and Taigan—who, his mother blithely lied to the officials, had merely been out for a pleasure ride. As a reward for sitting still and keeping his mouth shut, she was treating him to lunch. They sat outside at a table with a little striped canvas roof and a view of everything. Mikel preferred the tables next to the wrought-iron trellises where vines screened diners from curious passersby, but the vines were blooming and his mother refused to spend lunch picking purple flowers out of her meal. They'd gone through the usual appetizers and were waiting for lemon-lamb stew to appear from the kitchen. Mikel sopped up spicy salad dressing with a chunk of bread and waited for his mother to answer his question about the Malerrisi.

" 'Wandering around'? Nothing so random. I'd guess there are probably about as many young ones as the Capital has sent out from Mage Hall. As for the older ones . . . well, nobody really knows how many survived the so-called destruction of Malerris Castle in 960."

"Twenty-seven years is enough time to train up half an army. Is that why the Captal tries so hard to find Mage-borns before the Malerrisi can get to them?"

Sarra nodded. A waiter arrived, burdened with a tray bearing two bowls of stew, another basket of bread, a fresh pitcher of iced mint tea, and a glass of white wine. "I didn't order this," Sarra said as the wine was placed before her.

"With the respectful compliments of *Domni* Witte." The waiter nodded to an outdoor table fifteen feet away.

Mikel and his mother turned to look—he with intense curiosity about any man who would dare such a liberty, she with a carefully neutral expression on her face. The table was occupied by a middle-aged man Mikel had never seen before. But the woman who entered just then was familiar to him—and of great interest, as he recalled Taigan's gossip. Lady Mirya Witte appeared not to notice anyone in the whole restaurant as she sailed by, trailing flags of green silk from tiny sleeves and half bared shoulders. *Domni* Witte rose and bowed, half-turning to include Mikel's mother in the salute.

Mikel, knowing that his reaction would be common chat by the end of the hour, said, "What a beautiful dress—if it was on somebody Teggie's age."

The waiter was present, so Sarra was compelled to frown at the impertinence, but her black eyes were dancing. To the waiter, she said, "Please thank *Domni* Witte for the kindness, but this is not a vintage I prefer."

Mikel applied himself to his stew. Then, when he and his mother were as alone as they would get in a public place, he said, "If she were a man, she'd look like an overage bower lad."

"And what would *you* know about such persons?"

"Not much. I guess Teggie's right, and she's trying to look twenty years younger for her next husband."

"What?"

Mikel related what Taigan had told him last night. Sarra's frown was genuine this time.

"Divorced and remarried? We'll see about that!"

"Who's *Domni* Witte?" He poured more tea for her, then himself.

"Mirya's brother. A miserable excuse for a Blood," she sniffed, "who once was deluded enough to think he might have a chance to marry me."

"Long before Fa was around," Mikel said confidently, and grinned. "He would've taken him apart and put him together again backward!"

"Mmm—your father's a little more creative than that," Sarra chuckled. "Let's just say that once he got finished, *Domni* Dalion's face would've wanted to sit down."

He joined in her laughter, but the next moment turned serious. "Mother, did you and Fa know right away? I mean, all the songs and stories talk about love at first sight and all that, but the ones about *you* always say—"

"—that we spent most of our time shouting at each other?" She gave him a merry wink that made her look nowhere near the forty-one years they'd celebrated at her last Birthingday. "Truly told, that was how we knew!"

Confused, Mikel asked, "Because you were always mad at him?"

"Because everything he said and did annoyed me so thoroughly that it was either fall in love with him or kill him." She paused. "Something slow and lingering, involving a roomful of lutes played off-key. . . ." Suddenly she eyed him. "Why do you ask? Is there a young lady of your acquaintance that you'd like to murder?"

"No," he said, without even the hint of a blush. "I was just wondering how to recognize her when I find her."

"You'll know," she assured him—and not with the amused condescension of most adults either. She said it because she believed it from personal experience, and she expected him to believe it, too. She smiled at him again, his favorite smile that warmed and teased and loved him not just because he was her son, but because he was Mikel. It was fashionable among his friends to denigrate one's parents, to consider them fusty and foolish; Mikel would rather have died than admit it to his peers, but he had never looked on his powerful, beautiful mother and handsome, talented father with anything less than pride, admiration, and gratitude that he was their son. He was about to say something unfashionable to that effect when a commotion at the entrance caught his eye.

Two more people had come into Velireon's Kettle: a plump, badly dressed woman of about sixty, and a young man who, even judging by Taigan's fourth-hand description, could only be the new boy.

In a word, gorgeous.

He was tall—he had at least two inches on Mikel's father, possibly more—and not even the modesty of a loosely fitted longvest could disguise the lithe power of his body. His chest was deeply muscled, with correspondingly developed shoulders, arms, and thighs, but the overall effect was one of physical perfection, not massive or aggressive physical strength. Mikel—not quite sixteen and not quite full-grown, despite the size of his feet—felt scrawny just looking at him.

And then there was his face.

Large, deep-set gray eyes. Thick black brows saved from severity by a whimsical arch. Wide, full-lipped mouth. Straight nose, square jaw, angular chin—strong-boned without heaviness, finely made without delicacy. An errant black curl escaped his plain dark coif to grace a high, broad forehead. Two things spared the young man's face from monumental and overpowering perfection. The first was a fractionally off-center cleft in his chin. The second was a fractionally crooked front tooth revealed by the uneasy smile he gave Mirya Witte.

Looking at this quintessence of feminine dreams, Mikel—who already had eligible girls swarming around him (one anonymous young lady even sent him bad poetry every Saint's Day)—felt about as attractive as a kyyo with mange.

Mikel sneaked a glance at his mother and struggled against a grin. Her jaw hung just a little unhinged, and her eyes were just a little wider than usual, and her cheeks were just a little flushed. For her, this was the equivalent of flopping to the floor in a faint.

He leaned across the table, whispering, "You look like you want a divorce so *you* can marry him!"

Startled from her stunned stare—in which she was joined by every other woman in the restaurant—Sarra cleared her throat. "Don't be ridiculous."

"Don't worry," he soothed. "I won't tell Fa."

"Nothing to tell," she said firmly.

"Uh-huh. First a former prospective husband sends you a drink, and now you have to pick your eyes up from the table when some handsome young stud walks by—"

"Mikel," she cautioned, and when he grinned again, she told him, "I may have your father take *you* apart and put you back together again, and with some manners this time!"

The young man was now seated opposite Mirya Witte. Mikel would've thought she'd have him right next to her, the better to get her hands on him, but he supposed this positioning allowed her to look her fill. "Wonder who the other woman is."

"What? Oh—well, if Taigan's right about Mirya's wedding plans, Dalion is there to represent the Wittes in the negotiations. So the other lady must be representing the boy—as well as making sure Mirya doesn't paw the clothes off him in public. Disgusting, at her age!"

"He must be incredibly poor. I mean, with his looks, he could get anybody!"

"It's one of the worst aspects of society that a dowerless man must trade on his looks—"

"—and a rich one can be as ugly as a grizzel," Mikel said.

"I've done what I can, but almost forty Generations of custom are difficult to overcome." She caught and held his gaze with her own. "Thank Imili and Maidil and every other Saint in the Calendar that you won't have to go through any of it. Marry the girl you love, Mikel."

He shrugged. "I've got lots of money and a face that doesn't scare horses. But it's finding the girl that's the real trick, isn't it?"

"You will. And when you do, you'll know."

6

"AND of course," Sarra said at dawn the next morning, voice rich with amusement, "it never even occurred to him that even when he finds the girl, *she* might not like *him!*"

"For shame!" Col grinned. "Thinking such a thing about your own son!"

"In this, my immodest Minstrel, he is distinctly *your* son!" She finished buckling her sandals and stood up from the bed—dragging all the sheets off him in the process. When he blurted a protest, she smacked him on a naked thigh. "Time you were out of bed, lazy. You're off to Wytte's today, remember, to look into the boy's situation."

"Exactly. I'm resting up."

"For what?" she scoffed. "Lying around the pool?"

"Lady dear, if this infant is indeed being primped and primed for the voracious Mirya Witte, then the very last thing he'll be doing is lying around the pool."

This proved to be the case, to Collan's everlasting regret.

There was another recent arrival at Wytte's besides Mirya's new boy. In the foyer was a statue. Not a particularly good statue—the pose was awkward, and several fingers had broken off and been inexpertly welded back on—but Col assumed its technical quality was secondary to its visceral impact. The bronze was seven feet tall, impossibly muscular, and hung like a Tillinshir gray. *That* was the only part of him that wasn't green with rust.

Collan took one astonished look and burst out laughing.

"I must say," remarked *Domni* Pierigo Wytte, "that's the first time he's gotten *that* reaction."

"Well, just look at him. You could give the rest of him a polish, you know."

Pierigo grinned and flicked a finger against the statue's outsized member, shining gold against the tarnished rest of him. "We bought him from a bower in Neele. The customers used to rub it for luck."

"This was on display in a bower? Bad for business. Nothing in anyone's stable could measure up."

"You'd be surprised. Here for a swim?"

"Actually, I thought I'd visit the torture chamber. Strained a shoulder the other day, maybe I can work the kinks out."

"Hauling Lady Sarra away from the little Malerrisi gift? Yes, we all heard about that. Shocking. But she doesn't weigh enough to wrench a muscle. You're out of condition, lad."

"And you're a natural blond," Collan replied sweetly.

Domni Pierigo laughed heartily and escorted him down the hallway. As they turned in the opposite direction from the pool room, he began to hear the grunts and groans of men in serious pain. Collan held open the double oak doors so the other man could precede him—but mainly because he didn't want Pierigo to see him wince.

The room was approximately the size of the Malachite Hall at Ryka Court, but the activities conducted within were considerably less stately. Reeking with sweat, echoing with the bellows of the Master Torturer and the whines and whimpers of the torturees, the place was packed with men straining at weights or pounding around the bordering track oval or contorting themselves into various impossible positions. All were naked but for codpockets, and most of them looked utterly miserable.

They were also, every single one of them, in perfect shape. Not a paunch, not a bulge, not an untoned muscle, not a hint of excess flesh. Collan found them absolutely nauseating.

Pierigo Wytte cast an amused glance at him. "Change in policy since you were here last. They're all bower lads. We now reserve Seventh through Eighth exclusively for them, to keep them separate from the other patrons. They found it too depressing."

"I can't imagine why," he muttered.

"*This* is why," he grinned, slapping Col's belly. And then he realized whose depression Pierigo was talking about. "We'll start you off easy," he went on as they hurried across the track between runners. "It's not wise to rush it with men your age."

His age. Wonderful. Not yet fifty, and he was classed with the great-grandfathers.

"Where do I start?" he began to say, but the words never left his mouth. Coming around the outer curve of the track, running as smoothly as if those long legs could run forever without breaking a sweat, was unquestionably the most dazzling young man Collan had ever seen. Sarra's description—suspiciously lyrical as it had been—hadn't done him justice.

Pierigo watched him go by, frowning. "He needs a little more work," he said critically.

"*Where?*" Collan asked in a strangled voice.

Pierigo patted his arm consolingly as they continued toward the scales in the center of the hall. "We were given specifics by our cousin Mirya," he said, grinning as he claimed kinship with the formerly Blooded Wittes—a connection they venomously refused to own. "Why do you think Ellus Penteon spent so much time here, and wore that chain around his waist? She had it welded on him the day she married him." Pierigo shrugged. "She's just as fanatical about her own figure, of course, so it's not as if she's one of those women who puffs up like a ripe melon and then screams if her husband gains half a pound."

Collan shook his head. "Women," he intoned, "are horrifying creatures."

"Hah! *You're* complaining? You husband the best one in Sheve!"

"In all fifteen Shirs," Col grinned.

Pierigo bowed his apologies, and waved at his cousin

Deiken—Master Torturer, former drill instructor for the Ryka Legion, six years Collan's senior, and still looking as if he could break a horse's jaw with one finger. Deiken left off bawling insults at a sweating torturee, ran his gaze down Collan's fully clothed body, and gave a broad grin.

Col thought of Sarra. He thought about the difficulties Sarra was going through to ascertain who had legal guardianship of the boy, and whether marriage negotiations had begun, and whether or not Ellus Penteon wanted Mirya Witte to divorce him. He thought about the strain she was enduring, putting pen to paper to write letters to the Census Bureau, the Justiciary, and the Dean of St. Caitiri's that would accomplish these objectives.

He thought about poisoning Sarra's soup.

Gritting his teeth, he told Deiken Wytte that he didn't mind being here at the same time as the bower lads. Yes, sight of them would provide ample motivation for whipping his sorry old carcass back into shape. Of course he was looking forward to it.

Poisoning Sarra's soup was too merciful.

Forty gruesome minutes later, he limped to the pool enclosure and collapsed into the huge soak-tub, newly tiled in soothing deep blue. What little was left of his strength after the workout was drained away by steaming water stinking of supposedly healthful minerals. With his head cushioned by a rolled towel on the pool's edge, he floated insensate for an unknown length of time until the entry of another body washed a tinny-tasting wave onto his lower lip.

"Sorry," said a deep, musical voice. "Didn't mean to splash."

Col grunted and cracked one eye open. Blue was definitely this boy's color. So, Col suspected, were green, red, yellow, purple, orange, and any other damned shade in the rainbow.

"You look like you can still lift an arm—call the boy over and order me the biggest, coldest apple juice they ever served, will you?"

A tentative smile from that glorious face, a nod of that damp curly head, and it was done. When Col had drink in hand, he shut his eyes again and waited for the boy to talk.

The boy said exactly nothing.

It would be at least two weeks before the Dean of St. Caitiri's got Sarra's letter, another two before a reply returned. But Mirya the Mare's plans for this boy did not depend on her husband's willingness to be divorced—although the process required at least a show of consent on the husband's part, and if it had been Collan, he would have taken the children and vanished long ago. But the three Witte daughters were with Ellus in Brogdenguard, and wouldn't finish their education for several years yet. Col doubted their mother would want them to come home while she disported herself with a new young husband. Still, she didn't have to marry him—she might not even intend to, although Col had learned to trust Taigan's instincts almost as much as he trusted Sarra's. What he was supposed to find out was if the boy was willing, whether to be husbanded or kept.

He could be subtle about it. He could slowly get to know the young man, sound him out with casual, disconnected questions over the course of a few weeks at Wytte's. He could then invite him to lunch or dinner at the Residence with his guardian, let Sarra and the twins form opinions, and wait for the word to come back from St. Caitiri's about Ellus.

"So," he said, not opening his eyes, "you're Mirya Witte's new boy."

7

"IT was pathetic," he told Sarra that night as they lay in bed.

"Your performance in the Torture Chamber?"

"I could've gone another hour and still run fifty laps—" Then he stopped, a sore back muscle twingeing rebuke for the lie. "Who am I trying to fool? I'm not thirty anymore. I'm not even *forty* anymore."

"Couldn't prove it by me," she murmured, stroking his ribs.

"Stop that."

"Why?"

"It does things to me that make me want to do things to you that right now could be the death of me."

Sarra laughed softly and kissed his ear. "Tell me about the boy."

"He's called Josselin Mikleine. But it's not his real Name."

"He has no idea who he really is?"

"None. Truly told, Sarra, it *is* a pathetic story—what little there is of it. His mother died birthing him. Some Mikleines took him in, gave him their Name, then *they* died when he was about three, and he got passed around for years, family to family. He doesn't remember half the places he's lived in—doesn't even know his own Birthingday. Sometime in 969, but that's all."

"How did Mirya latch onto him?"

"He's been with a family up in Sleginhold for about a year—they took him in when the last family's daughter wanted to marry him, and of course he's got less than nothing. They were in Pinderon this winter to arrange a marriage for one of the sons. Mirya was on one of her begging visits to her mother." He snorted. "When I think what the Ostins paid for Shore Hill only four years ago, and she's already out of money! Anyway, she sees him on the street and falls over weak-kneed. I bet most women do."

"Not all. Of course, it helped that I was already sitting down. . . ."

"I'd make you pay for that one, but I'm not up to the effort just now."

"I'll make sure to repeat it when you're feeling stronger. I think I can finish the story from here. Mirya found no financial joy at her mother's, so when she got back to Roseguard she sold her furniture store over on St. Oseth's Lane."

"And bought Josselin with it."

"How does he feel about it?"

"I get the impression he doesn't talk much to other people, but he sure didn't shut up once he got going today. He knew my name, so I think he also knows I can help him."

"Then he wants help."

"Sounded that way. Not that he said a word against her—just how lucky *he* is, how generous *she* is, and such-like drivel. As if somebody'd told him so many times he memorized it."

"But you think he doesn't want to marry her."

"I'm sure of it." He paused a moment, remembering the young man's face as he spoke about his good fortune. "A lot of men would brag about all the money and being called a Lord and so on. He doesn't seem to care. But he'll marry her because he can't see any way out of it."

"He can't until he's eighteen," Sarra mused. "If he's not sure of his Birthingday. . . ."

"He thinks it's one of the Equinoxes. He's not sure which."

"Well, the autumn one isn't for another eleven weeks." She was quiet for a moment, then said, "I saw the preliminary contract in Mirya's Advocate's office this evening."

He snorted. "Leaving aside the question of how you got into a private office after hours, let alone got a look at private documents, are you saying she's providing the dower?"

"No, I'm saying she's buying his Mikleine guardian's cooperation."

Collan snorted. "Bet the former guardians are furious at missing the money."

"They would be—if they weren't *all* Mikleines. First time a man's dower is going *into* his family Web instead of out of it."

"You can't blame any of them, really. Look at the advantages." After years of experience, he could sense when Sarra's rescue instinct was blossoming. He shifted to ease a sore shoulder, settling Sarra's head more comfortably on his chest. But she was out of his arms and sitting up in bed, clad only in her long golden hair that had not even a hint of silver.

"Advantages?" she echoed incredulously.

"Mirya's a Blood—your pardon, Lady—*former* Blood. He'll husband a First Daughter and be called a Lord. When her mother dies, she'll have shiploads of money. Land, title, wealth, prestige, a big house and a Web to run—"

"And no children."

"Maybe he doesn't want any. Even if he does, her three daughters will eventually marry and he can help raise the grandchildren. Besides that, the Mikleines will be comfortably settled. He must feel some kind of obligation to them—"

"They're pushing him into it for the money," she protested.

"Reconciling him to the inevitable," he corrected. "After all, if not Mirya Witte, then some other woman. So they'll sing sweet songs about what an honor it is, that his future's made, that he'll have the kind of life he deserves, that he couldn't have been born so beautiful for nothing. Getting him to think of it that way, it's only a kindness."

"It's barbaric!"

Collan swallowed laughter: full bloom. "Lenfell is full of savages. Happens all the time, one way or another. This is just a little more blatant than usual."

"Col—doesn't it bother you?"

"It's not as if we have to choose that path for Mikel."

"But it's one step removed from slavery!" She fumed for a couple of minutes, then burst out, "I still say it's barbaric! And I don't care how many boys it happens to, it won't happen to this one—or any others when I'm through with the Council next session." Black eyes narrowing, she snapped, "And stop looking so smug. You didn't have to rub my face in it, I was going to do something. I'm not as blind as I used to be, and I don't need things written in letters twelve feet high and shoved under my nose."

"But you're so adorable when you're mad," he teased. "So it'll go to trial?"

"On charges of conspiracy to enslave? I might make that stick." She grinned a purely, sweetly, deliciously evil grin. "I want this to be an open warning to other women not to try the same thing. And this time I want to gore her in public, not in private the way we did last time."

He forbore to point out that *he* had done the goring, and she'd been furious with him for it. "I wonder if Josselin knows she's got a habit of bruising pretty faces."

She settled back down again, curling at his side beneath the silk sheets. "Remember Maivis Doriaz's letter?"

He did. Shortly after Ellus Penteon and the three Witte girls had arrived at St. Caitiri's, the Dean—who was also a Scholar Mage—wrote to apologize for her reluctance to hire the man based on Sarra's asking Cailet to ask Maivis for the favor. Penteon was a brilliant teacher and an asset to the Academy, the girls were delightful, and she was very glad to have gotten them all away from Mirya Witte.

> But it will be a long time—if ever—before he stops feeling guilty at having escaped a situation that I now firmly believe did put his life in danger. He says little about it, but what he does say tells me more than he realizes. Lady Sarra, I thank you for this chance to rescue a fine mind and a man who, with years and distance, may someday come to know that none of this was his fault.

"I doubt Josselin would put up with being knocked around," Col said slowly.

"Then he has a temper?"

"Lady love, I suspect he has something much worse—a *spine.*"

8

JUST how stiff a spine, Collan learned five days later.

It was two mornings after the twins' Birthingday. Col had drunk quite a bit even before the guests arrived, while Taigan and Mikel opened presents from the family. (Cailet's were particularly admired—enameled cloak pins of Heathering manufacture depicting the black Liwellan Hawk clutching a silver Rosvenir Knife in each set of gold talons.) Proud of his exquisite daughter and elegant son, Collan toasted them, the day, the gifts, and anything else that struck his fancy. Later, as everyone who was anyone in Roseguard danced the night away in the ballroom, he drank not quite enough brandy to dull the poignant ache of seeing his little girl and little boy so grown up so fast.

The next morning he hadn't even been human. Neither had Sarra. Or Tarise. Or Rillan. Falundir had simply locked his door. Only the twins, who had sneakily imbibed several glasses of sparkling wine through the course of the evening, had risen clear-eyed and hearty. Youth was wasted on the young.

But Mirya's money had not been wasted on Josselin Mikleine. Collan dragged himself from the Residence to Wytte's, hoping to sweat away his hangover, just in time to overhear Josselin pronounced flawless by Deiken Wytte. His body was honed to perfection; his stamina was that of a racehorse; his skin from head to toes was immaculate (though if a blemish ever had the temerity to appear on that face, it would die aborning for shame); his teeth and hair and even his fingernails were faultless.

"Now, don't ruin all my work," Deiken growled. "Don't stuff your face, don't slack off on your exercise, don't even cut yourself shaving."

Collan, passing by and overhearing the remark, saw Josselin's carefully mild expression tense and his quiet gray eyes flash. For the first time, he looked like a seventeen-year-old boy who really, really wanted to do something really, really bad, like gorge himself on chocolates that would ruin both his waistline and his complexion.

In this mood of rebellion he floated beside Col in the blue depths of the hot pool a little while later, a frown pulling his brows down over his long nose. Col judged the expression in stormy gray eyes to be exactly what he'd been waiting for.

"Shame you have to waste it on Mirya Witte."

Josselin shrugged, sending ripples through the calm water.

"Unless you want her, that is."

"Of course I want to be married. I'm very lucky. Lady Mirya is generous, and kind, and—" He stopped, swallowed hard, and said, "May I ask you something?"

"Sure."

"What's it like?"

"What's what like?"

"Being with a woman you care about."

Collan felt sorry for him. He was probably the only man on Lenfell who would. Given a choice, what male *wouldn't* want to be young, strong, spectacularly good-looking, and have as his only duty in life the expert pleasuring of a woman with an admittedly spectacular body? Truly told, when Col had been Josselin's age, he would've given anything but his lute for the chance. But at Josselin's age, Collan had been a virgin. He'd made up for lost time since—but he knew what the boy meant, because it had never been real and true for him until Sarra.

"The first time," he said slowly, "it's like she's this amazing new song you're going to learn, or an incredible lute you've been given the chance to play. Then in the middle of it you find out that you're *both* music. The same music, the same instrument. You're inside the same skin—you know how she wants to be touched and what her reaction will do to you both. But at the same time there's always something new about it. No matter how often you make love to her, it's always different. Place, mood, time of day, even the color of the sheets—" He spared a reminiscent chuckle for a particular bed draped in black silk that did breathtaking things to Sarra's golden skin. "Point is, with some women you have to work at making it new. When you *love* her, it's easy. There's always something about her to learn or explore, or just go back over what's familiar that you've learned to love exploring."

Josselin looked politely skeptical.

"Don't worry," Col smiled. "You'll find out."

"If my face doesn't get in the way."

"And if you ever get the chance to make love to a woman who isn't old enough to be your grandmother," Collan finished. "I didn't ask if you wanted to be married, I asked if you wanted *her.* Stop repeating what everybody's told you and think for yourself."

"And just exactly how much good would *that* do me?" Josselin asked acidly.

"A lot, if you can get past the money and the chance to be called Lord Josselin and the so-called honor of it."

"What else does my situation have to recommend it? What choice do I have?"

Col repressed the urge to snarl at him to stop whining. The boy was still only a boy, after all: seventeen, an orphan dependent on charity all his life, with only his beauty to trade on for advancement in the world.

"Not until I can say I'm eighteen, anyway," Josselin finished. "I can't legally sign a marriage contract until then—but I can't legally refuse to sign anything either."

The glass of fruit juice nearly slid from Collan's fingers. Gray eyes glanced at him sidelong. Their flicker of amusement took him aback—and it shouldn't have. This boy had been secretly giving people this look all his life when they underestimated him.

"Shocked?" Josselin asked blandly.

"Relieved." He grinned. "I told Lady Sarra you might possibly be in possession of a spine. Glad to find out I'm not a liar."

"*I* am, though." He shook his head. "I'm letting them all believe I'll go through with it."

"If I told you there's a way to keep your word *without* having to go through with it, what would you say?"

A wry smile curved the corners of the perfect mouth. "I'd say you and Lady Sarra have been plotting, as you are famously rumored to do."

"Only rumors?" Col asked, disappointed.

"Mirya warned me against you both, you know," Josselin went on. "Some bilge about your trying to interfere in our happiness once we're married."

"And are you aware," Col asked grimly, "that her idea of happiness includes breaking your ribs?"

"Oh, she already raised her hand to me," the boy said quietly. "Once." *And only once,* hung unspoken between them. After a moment Josselin went on, "I reminded her that I couldn't allow her to damage the goods before she took legal possession of them."

Having a new measure of the young man—a measure that had nothing to do with the size of his biceps—Collan asked casually, "How'd you like to come to dinner tonight?"

Three hours later, the persuasions of being Who He Was having liberated Josselin from Wytte's without his guardian's permission, Collan stood in the garden doors of the family sitting room and watched his blithely self possessed daughter get her first look at Josselin Mikleine. Newly turned sixteen, wearing an elegant off-the-shoulder dress, and well aware that the apple-green linen turned her eyes to emeralds, Taigan strolled in late with a casual apology on her lips. It died after three words when Josselin got to his feet, bowed, and shyly expressed belated happy Birthingday wishes.

Mikel openly laughed at his sister. She threw him a furious look and, wrapping the rags of her dignity around her, permitted the young man to be made known to her. Tarise took pity on Josselin with nothing resembling altruism; explaining that they were all waiting on Sarra, as usual, she offered to show him the gardens. Rillan—who didn't know a poppy from a pine tree and didn't care—announced himself curious about the new flower beds, and went with them.

Taigan turned her back on their exit, studiously examining a tapestry familiar to her since birth. "He's not properly dressed for a dinner at the Residence."

"Like that matters!" Mikel chortled.

"We came straight here from Wytte's," Collan said blandly.

"Yes," Taigan said in acid tones, "he has that pampered and polished look."

Her brother grinned merrily. "Are you in love, or just in lust? Thinking of giving Lady Mirya some competition?"

"I'm thinking of giving you a black eye!"

"I gather," Sarra said from the doorway, "that our guest has been introduced." She walked across the Cloister rug, followed by Falundir, who took one look around and began to laugh silently. Sarra settled into a large upholstered chair. "So what do you think of him, besides the obvious?"

Mikel shrugged. "He seems nice enough. Doesn't talk much, though."

"Compared to *you*," Taigan remarked, "the whole world has taken a vow of silence."

"Now, now," Col admonished. "Be nice. And be observant, all right? Your mother and I really want to know what you think of him."

"Are you going to rescue him from Lady Mirya?" Mikel asked.

"I think he's got plans of his own in that direction," Col said. At Sarra's look of surprise, he went on, "Don't ask him about it. He can't do other than deny everything at this point. But don't scare him by gawping all through dinner, ladies. *Either* of you," he added, just to see identical expressions of outrage appear on both faces. Trading grins with his son and Falundir, he finished, "I'll go call them in to dinner."

"I'll help," Mikel said.

Watching their backs, Sarra observed crossly, "I see he's learned one of his father's primary lessons. Always have an escape route!"

This time the elderly Bard laughed right out loud.

Dinner was polite without being overly stiff, mostly due to Sarra's charm in drawing Josselin from his shyness. He was awed and amazed by the company he kept tonight, especially by the presence of Falundir. Though he answered questions readily enough, he volunteered little. A few details about his current guardian's farm outside Sleginhold, a reference to places he'd lived before (a

remote smallhold on the edge of Sheve Dark, a small village in Tillinshir). But he only shrugged when asked who
had fostered him prior to that. Though he wasn't exactly
evasive, it was clear that his past was not a pretty topic
for him. Col could understand that. His own memories as
an orphan weren't precisely fond.

After dinner they repaired to the music room. Mikel
threatened to bring out the harp Cailet had sent for his
last Birthingday; Tarise told him he could only if he
promised that the Captal had Warded the thing to sound
good even though he didn't yet know how to play it. He
settled in behind the hammered dulcimer he *did* know
how to play, and ran through a two-stick song to check
the tuning. When he slid two more felt-tipped sticks between his knuckles, Taigan called him a show-off. But he
had inherited his father's music, and Col watched with
pride as the boy's supple hands brought ringing chords
from the forty-six strings as easily as he struck pristine
single notes. The dulcimer was a difficult instrument, one
Collan had never quite mastered. It took young, clever
fingers and total concentration. Mikel played with the casual ease of one born to it. He was similarly adept on lute,
mandolin, guitar, and a variety of flutes and pipes. Collan
was a fair Minstrel, but Mikel bid fair to become a master.

Father and son then sang a duet that became a trio
after the second verse—for Falundir began to hum the
high harmony. Since Mikel's talents had been discovered,
the Bard had taken to making music more and more often,
pleasure gleaming in his bright blue eyes.

> *Look: the stars are trembling*
> *Shaking the sky apart*
> *Listen: they weep just like you*
> *With the longing in their hearts*

Josselin was so stunned that he was actually hearing
the most revered Bard in Generations that he didn't even
join in the applause.

Mikel played on while the others chatted. Rillan had
heard of the upcoming trip to Ambrai for Taigan's new
wardrobe, and proposed to extend it to The Waste for a

look at Maurgen Hundred's new crop of foals. He and
Collan were discussing the logistics of the journey with
Tarise while Sarra talked to Josselin and Taigan rummaged through stacks of music folios for a song that
would really challenge her brother's talents.

All at once Mikel faltered in his playing, the felt-
tipped hammers striking any whichway on the dulcimer
strings. Taigan jerked upright from examining sheet
music. Josselin was on his feet, backing away from Sarra
in a panic.

"No—I can't, please don't—"

"It's all right, if you feel you can't—" Sarra spoke
soothingly, as if to a small child.

"You don't understand, I—" He took a deep breath
and calmed down, but his gray eyes were still skittish.
"I'm sorry. It's just—I don't want to be called into court,
or have my name spread all over the broadsheets—I just
want to be ordinary."

Not with that face, my lad, Collan thought, annoyed
with Sarra for being so unsubtle about proposing his circumstances as a test case. Rising, he asked loudly if anyone wanted brandy. Serving Sarra first, he gave Josselin a
glass at the same time—earning himself betrayed looks
from his offspring when he failed to include them.

The atmosphere in the room settled. Mikel went back
to his music with Falundir at his side, Taigan joined Col
on the sofa near Tarise and Rillan, and Sarra spent the
next few minutes reassuring Josselin. But Taigan glanced
at the young man rather more often than even his looks
could account for, and Mikel was frowning over his dulcimer.

St. Miramili's rang out Half-Thirteenth, and Josselin
again got to his feet, saying he was honored by their attention and had enjoyed the evening more than anything
since his arrival in Roseguard, but he really ought to return to Wytte's. Tarise and Rillan escorted him.

"Too dark to find the way back by himself?" Taigan
muttered after they left. "Or too drunk?" This with a resentful glare at Collan.

"Too expensive," Mikel told her. "Lady Mirya

would have us in the law courts if he even stubbed his perfect toe."

"All right, you two, that's enough," Sarra warned. "He can't help the way he looks."

Falundir arched both brows at her and brought out his List. With the slim silver pointer he told her something that made her frown, then collected his nightly tribute of kisses on the cheek from her and Taigan, and departed.

"Don't ask what he said, because I'm not going to tell," Sarra informed her family. "Now, Collan, what did you find out today?"

The four of them gathered at the blue-marble card table, the twins trying to hide excitement at inclusion in parental counsels. Noting it with an amused glance for Sarra, Col repeated the afternoon's conversation. He ended with, "So what the hell happened tonight?"

Mikel blinked. "You didn't feel it?"

"Feel what?" Sarra asked.

The twins looked at each other across the table, and at the same time said, "He's Mageborn."

"What?" Collan exclaimed.

"That's what Falundir told me," Sarra said with another frown. "I didn't believe him. And how would *you* know, anyway?"

Taigan shrugged. "I just know, that's all."

"Oh, come on, Teggie," Mikel said. "Don't try to make a mystery of it. You felt just what I did, or you wouldn't've reared up like a startled horse. Whatever Mother said to him, he reacted really strong to it. And we reacted to him. It was kind of like with the Malerrisi who wasn't part of the Minstrelsy—something inside my head felt all tingly and strange—"

"And like when Glenin Feiran tried to kidnap us," Taigan added, nodding. "I hadn't thought about it before, but that's what magic feels like."

"And Josselin. . . ?" Sarra couldn't seem to finish.

"Same thing."

"No, it was different," Mikel said. "I mean, it was the same but different, you know?"

"No, I *don't* know," Col said pointedly. "Explain yourself."

He started to rake his fingers back through his hair, a habit of childhood; when thwarted by the coif all men wore after the age of fourteen (all but Collan Rosvenir, anyway), he grimaced and yanked the blue silk off his head. A scrape of long fingers through unruly red curls, and he finally said, "The other two felt like they were trying to get inside our minds. I guess they ran up against the Captal's Wards, huh?"

Taigan said, "It was like he was trying to put up his own Wards, and didn't know how, and the magic was just bouncing around with nothing to do. But it was definitely magic."

Collan exhaled a long breath. "Mageborn. I'll be damned."

After a time, Sarra shook her head. "Well, this settles the question of marriage, truly told. Josselin will be more use to Cailet as a Mage than he'll be to me as a legal precedent—or Mirya as a plaything." She smiled, that same wicked little grin that always appeared when she was smugly satisfied. "She'll just have to find herself another boy."

Taigan and Mikel traded looks again. Collan waited for the cutpiece to drop in both minds; not surprising it had taken so long, considering the Wards Cailet had set up in them. Finally, Taigan said for both of them: "Then—we're both Mageborn. We have magic, too."

Quite calmly, Sarra said, "Yes. The Captal thought it wisest to protect you from it until I judged you old enough to be trained at Mage Hall."

"So we're Warded," said Mikel. "Not just against people who'd try to spell us, but—"

"—but against our own magic!" Taigan exclaimed.

"Yes," Sarra repeated. "Taigan, if you'll remove that expression of betrayal from your face, you may come upstairs with me and help write the letter to the Captal explaining about Josselin Mikleine."

"Are you going to explain a few things to *me?*" Taigan asked resentfully.

"Perhaps," Sarra conceded.

The pair of them left, not entirely in charity with each other. Collan helped Mikel put away the folios and the dulcimer, silently waiting to find out how the boy would react.

At last Mikel asked, "Why did Teggie and I feel it, and not you and Mother?"

"We're Warded even stiffer than you two—and by a real master. Gorynel Desse." Knowing this was inadequate—and regretting the slur to Cailet—he went on, "You were right about Josselin's magic running up against your Wards. That's the way I understand it, anyway." He closed the cabinet doors on tidied folios and leaned his shoulder to carved wood, arms folded as he regarded his son. No resentment there, no rebellion against not being told the truth before now. Ah, but that was Mikel: easygoing, accepting, pragmatic. Col wondered where the boy had gotten such qualities—for they certainly hadn't come from himself or Sarra.

"So what'd you think of Josselin, anyway?"

"He's all right. Do you think he really wants to become a Mage Guardian? I mean, escaping Mirya Witte isn't the noblest motivation in the world."

Collan laughed. "Nobility is for fey tales at bedtime, Mishka. I'd say Josselin Mikleine's motives are about the most honest I've ever run into—always supposing, as you say, that he agrees to go to Mage Hall."

"How'd the Captal miss him? I thought she could sense a Mageborn at a hundred miles."

"A hundred paces, maybe. I've heard that some people Ward themselves on instinct alone. Maybe Josselin's one of 'em."

"Oh." Mikel hesitated, fingers caressing the wooden case of his dulcimer. "Fa, something's bothering me about him. Ever since I first saw him, it's been driving me crazy—who he reminds me of, I mean."

"You've met him before?"

Mikel frowned. "That's just it—I can't be sure. I don't really recall what he looked like—"

"Who?"

"I know he had pale eyes and dark skin, and I'm

pretty sure he had a beard, but the rest of his face is all unclear."

"Who?" Col asked again, though he knew what Mikel would say.

"The Malerrisi. The one who gave us the box."

9

IN the tumult over the danger to the twins, the Mage who was a Malerrisi, the attack that wasn't really an attack, the box that wrecked Taigan's rooms, and the discovery of Josselin Mikleine as a Mageborn, everyone had forgotten the message Savachel Maklyn had been bringing to Collan.

Everyone *except* Collan.

By the time the poor young man straggled into the Residence, still headsore from a thunk on the skull and limping from his leg wound, the handful of flowers in his satchel was crushed almost beyond recognition. But Col—who supervised Roseguard Grounds less from real interest than from loyalty to Verald Jescarin, who had been their Master—knew the shape of those leaves.

Rue, the Wraithen Ward.

The other part of the message was a piece of paper with an apparently meaningless shape drawn on it and an *M* in the middle. A piece of a puzzle, indeed. Col spent a frustrating hour at the card table before he finally found the piece that, when placed correctly, called up a certain image on Mikel's gift from Cailet.

Accordingly, a few days after the twins' Birthing-day—once Mirya Witte had been informed that her boy was going to become a Mage Guardian—he packed his saddlebags, took the best horse in Rillan's stable, and told Sarra he was setting off with Falundir for Sleginhold.

The Bard was seventy-six years old, with the whitened hair to prove it, though he looked much younger as eunuchs sometimes did. Falundir's brilliant first career

had ended at the age of forty, when First Councillor Anniyas cut out his tongue and sliced the tendons of every
finger. Never again would he sing, never again play the
fabled lute that was more beloved than any woman could
have been, even had he been whole. Gorynel Desse had
settled him in a cottage in Sheve Dark, and provided an
antidote to bitterness in a young musician recently a
slave: Collan. For more than four years they'd lived simply, though not silently. Somehow, despite being crippled, the great Bard had taught Collan the craft. They
both knew he would never rise beyond the level of Minstrel. He had an excellent voice and clever fingers, but
missing in him was the spark of true genius that made a
Bard.

On St. Lirance's, the first day of 956, Falundir and
Desse gave Collan the Name Rosvenir and the eighteen
gifts—including the lute—that marked his Birthingday.
Then they took from him all memory of his time with the
Bard. The next time Collan saw him was the worst trauma
of his life—images roiling up, stunning him, negating everything he'd believed about his childhood for the thirteen years of his manhood.

What Falundir had done during those years was yet a
mystery. Col assumed that Desse had found him a new
home somewhere safe, where he waited as Desse had
waited for the Rising to oust Anniyas from power. Now,
eighteen years after the First Councillor's fall, with three
operas finished and two more in the works, Falundir's
status as the greatest Bard in ten Generations was assured.
He lived accordingly: celebrated wherever he went, avidly
sought to judge musical contests, presiding over the
Bardic Games every year, commissioned to write com-
memorative pieces for events of all kinds. He accepted
few of these requests, though he had composed an entire
song-cycle for his friend Sevy Vasharron's fiftieth Birthingday concert last year. Falundir was, in short, at the
height of his powers, unmatched in prestige and wealthy
into the bargain.

And he was as bored as Collan had been a few years
ago, when he'd started the Minstrelsy, and for much the
same reason: Taigan and Mikel were growing up. Collan

had steadied Taigan's first steps, but Falundir had shown her how to dance. Collan had guided Mikel's fingers in his first attempts at playing the lute, but Falundir had taught him how to sing and bought him all manner of other instruments to experiment with. The twins adored him and thought nothing of his inability to speak; from babyhood they held long conversations with him, understanding his language of brief gesture and sparkling green eyes and eloquent dark face. Neither did they regard his hands as crippled; he could hug them, and let them climb all over him when they were little, and when they went someplace together each held onto his useless fingers the same way they took their father's strong hands.

But the time had passed when Taigan and Mikel needed to cling to anyone's hand. Falundir knew it as well as Collan did. The Bard had become increasingly involved in the Minstrelsy—cursing his renown and his disabilities that made him too conspicuous for secrecy. This journey to Sleginhold was only his third foray into the field with Collan—who was just about as visible as he. But it was a perfect mission for them to undertake together, for Collan could say he was going to check on the Web's holdings with Falundir along for the ride.

Accomplished horsemen, they made good time, with Collan talking as incessantly as he used to in Sheve Dark long ago. He told the whole tale of Josselin Mikleine again, murky start to what he hoped would be a satisfactory finish at Mage Hall. He talked about his worries and expectations and plans for his children when they finally went to Cailet. He discussed Sarra's political aims, Taguare's tasks as Minister of Education, new ballads by aspiring Bards in Ambrai and old ones Falundir and others had rediscovered in the archives. He spoke about anything, in fact, but his worries about the warning of rue.

He knew Falundir would notice. But as day after sunny day passed, the Bard made no indication of his curiosity. They rode farther north into rich cropland and stayed in comfortable inns, occasionally singing for the awed patrons—Collan giving them the words while Falundir hummed high harmony. The landscape changed to rolling hills and orchards, and then on the horizon there appeared the vast thick redwood forest of Sheve Dark.

Collan reined in a few miles from Sleginhold, pausing to drink from his waterskin and remember. There, in the village, on St. Sirrala's Day, he had met Sarra for the first time. A vile little gap-toothed brat she'd been, insulting him with the impunity of a Blooded lady for all that she was only nine years old. He'd met Verald that day as well. And Sela Trayos, just ten and adorable in a green dress with a pink sash, had given Collan his first kiss.

He smiled, still tasting the candied violets on his lips. He remembered all the things he'd been Warded not to remember about his years with the Bard. Glancing over his shoulder, he knew Falundir was remembering, too.

"What a long, strange trip it's been," he said.

Falundir grinned and whistled a few bars of the very old song he'd stolen the line from. Then they rode down the hill to Sleginhold village, and up the rise to the mansion.

Halfway to the gates, a slim blonde girl of fifteen dodged merchants and farmers and horses and carts to skid to a halt before Collan and Falundir. "We saw you from the windows!" she reported excitedly. "Well, Cailie saw you first, but she's too little to come greet you in all this." She waved to the bustle around them. "Welcome to Sleginhold!"

"Many thanks, Lady Tevis," Col responded formally, then reached a hand down to swing her up in front of him in the saddle. "So tell me—when did you get beautiful?"

"Last week," she laughed over her shoulder as they rode. "It's been threatening for over a year, but it finally happened!"

"Truly told, it did," he informed her with a smile. "From now on, the word will go forth wherever Tevis Ostin is bound: Ladies, lock up your sons!"

Tevis wrinkled her freckled nose at him. With beauty had come humor and poise; a shy child, scarcely daring to say two words, she had bloomed delightfully. Collan was always a favorite, but not even he had ever been treated before to this smiling, confident young woman.

They grew up so fast, he told himself, thinking of

Taigan and Mikel. The point was emphasized when Alyn and Cailie met them at the family's entrance. Alyn had lengthened from chubby child of eight to tall, slender girl of eleven on the verge of adolescence. Cailie, just six, seemed six inches taller than when Col had last seen her. Soon he had to readjust his mental image of their four-year-old brother, Renne, as well. Miram, a true Ostin, had added to her family last year: Kantia, named for her mother's second husband.

Miram and Riddon, happier together now than on the day she'd told him she would marry him whether he liked it or not (he had, and she did), eventually shooed the children out of the sunroom and settled down to discuss Collan's visit. He told them about the sprigs of rue and the puzzle piece that yielded Sleginhold as a direction, then asked what they'd heard.

"Not a thing," Riddon said. "We lent the Maklyn boy a horse, as we always do for the Minstrelsy, and sent him on his way."

"Did he have any idea what it all meant?" asked Miram.

Collan shook his head. "I don't even know which of my people originated the message. But I'm sure someone will contact me, now that I'm here."

It happened the day after Col arrived. He was in the village with Tevis, shopping for gifts, amused by the furtive glances young men directed at Miram's pretty daughter. He asked her whether she'd noticed—teasing her; *every* woman noticed when she was being admired.

"Oh, it's not *me* they're interested in—not today, at any rate. It's you. You're famous, you know. All the women are staring, envying me my handsome escort!"

"You, Lady," he said severely, "are a flirt."

"I'm a *shameless* flirt, Grannie Lilen says. And she's right!"

He laughed with her, and they entered a bakery to buy pine-nut brittle. He was munching a sample when another customer came in. Short, dark, compact, about Collan's age, with the ruddy complexion and worn boots that proclaimed a life on the road, the woman made straight for the cream cakes and bought half a dozen.

While the baker's apprentice wrapped her order, she devoured a chocolate tart and inspected first Tevis and then Collan head to toe.

"Aren't you the one who calls himself Rosvenir?"

"An honorable Name," he responded warily.

"And *mine*," she retorted.

He blinked. "Truly told?"

"Just once in all these years did you ever come to pay your respects?" she went on severely. "Or apologize for the trouble you caused? In the years before the Rising, every official in a hundred miles came to the Farms all hours of the day and night to interrogate us—"

"For that, I'm sorry," he replied, trying to mollify her. "It was never my intention—"

"Huh! We Rosvenirs are good honest folk, and your wild ways nearly ruined us!"

Collan had no idea how to respond. It was true that he'd never made much effort to contact the Rosvenir kindred, who were no kindred of his. They kept to themselves at the Farms along the Dindenshir side of the River Rine, and for Generations had been invisible in the greater world. Fine with him; at least he never saw "Rosvenir" on petitions for investment.

"Now, *Domna* Amilie," the baker began, "he's more than made up for his wildness since."

"The only good thing to say for him," the Rosvenir went on, "is he isn't Mageborn, like my great-great-grandmother's great-nephew Viko. But a Minstrel's damned near as bad."

Tevis, who'd been listening wide-eyed, now frowned in a way reminiscent of both her grandmothers. Those were Lady Agatine Slegin's gold-flecked brown eyes kindling with anger, and Lady Lilen Ostin's strong jawline turning rigid. But the arrogant lift of the chin was all Tevis's own.

"Lord Collan saved my father's life in the Rising— and plenty of other lives, too. He's a brilliant Minstrel and a substantial man of affairs in his own right, he husbands a Councillor for Sheve, and—"

"Who might *you* be?"

"Tevis, First Daughter of Miram Ostin and her husband Riddon Slegin."

Amilie Rosvenir sniffed. "Your shoes squelch in the mud just like everybody else's."

"That will do," Collan said rudely. Scorning him was one thing; one could say she had the right, being a real Rosvenir. But insulting Tevis was quite another. "I believe your purchase is ready, *Domna.*"

"Time for me to leave, that it? Let me tell you something, *Lord* Collan—you may wear our two knives and our gray and turquoise, and sign documents and even spell it right, but if I had my way you'd be as Nameless as the slave you used to be!" And with that she grabbed her bag of cream cakes and huffed out of the shop.

Collan smiled a rueful smile and rubbed the back of his neck. "Well. *That* was pleasant."

A moment later the door slammed open again. Amilie Rosvenir was back, holding a folded scrap of paper she thrust at Collan. "Our First Daughter of the Name lives at this address. The least you could do is send flowers on her Birthingday. You can afford it."

"I did—once," he snapped back. "There was no reply." And now he knew the reason: they all hated him.

"Try again," she retorted. "She's ninety-four this Candleweek. And don't think this means the rest of us are softening—she ordered all of us to be looking for you. Pure chance that I saw you first." She looked him down and up again, derisively. "Grandmother's getting addled in her old age."

Once more she stormed out, this time for good. Collan sighed, pocketing the paper unread. Tevis was still fuming.

"Two brass cheeks, that what she's got!" exclaimed the baker.

"Four," Tevis corrected. "And blows foul air out of both sets!"

Collan choked on laughter. The baker whooped until she wheezed. "Saints, child, if your father ever heard you talk that way—!"

"Where do you think I learned how?" Tevis grinned, humor restored.

Four kinds of brittle bagged and ribboned, they returned to the mansion. At dinner that evening, Tevis regaled the family with a spirited retelling of the incident—though she didn't include her own remarks. Collan chuckled to himself; Riddon might employ a few pungent phrases now and again, but knowing his daughter had repeated them in public would mortify him. Kind of Tevis to spare her father's sensibilities. Saints knew Taigan rarely spared Collan.

He didn't read the note until he returned to his room late that night. It was lying on his bed, still folded. The longvest it had been in was gone, taken away to be laundered by efficient servants. Expecting an address in Dindenshir, he was startled to find six words that abruptly turned this journey from interesting to urgent: *Falundir's Cottage, Sheve Dark—Velenne's Vow.*

Oh, shit. Amilie Rosvenir was his contact.

Col shook his head to clear it. He'd picked every member of the Minstrelsy himself, and he was its only Rosvenir. How had she known? The burned-out shell of Falundir's old place was one of a few havens in each Shir; nobody knew their location but the Minstrelsy, Cailet, and a few Mage Guardians. (He'd thought about using that peculiar house he and Sarra had stumbled upon in The Waste years ago, but the price of leaving it was a Truth—and he didn't want his people forced to confess their personal secrets just to get out the door.) Even more telling than knowledge of Falundir's Cottage, however, were the last two words. "Velenne's Vow" went back to a song about the Bards' Saint, found by Falundir in the Bard Hall archives.

> *In the darkest week of all*
> *Neversun, when spirits fail*
> *Through blackest nights and grimmest days*
> *While winds that wreck and wail*
> *Blow bitter cold into your soul*
> *I beg you, sing this tale*
> *Of Velenne's Sacrifice and Vow—*
> *Bard, sing sweet in Her praise.*

The odd rhyming scheme marked it as very old indeed. There was only the one version, which was unusual for something that ancient. Songs that had been around more than a hundred years developed ten or twelve variations. Not this one. It told how St. Velenne sang the sun back into the sky over the eleven days of Neversun. By the time the sun finally reappeared, she could barely whisper her songs and the lute itself was bleeding. Velenne turned her face to the sun's warmth, vowed that thenceforth all Bards would sing during that bleak dark week each year, and then died. The lyric ended with a charge to all those who could make music: use the gift, for music challenged the dark so light could triumph.

Collan and Falundir agreed that "Velenne's Vow" would signal only the grimmest of messages. He'd seen or heard it eight times in the five years of the Minstrelsy, each time to report a Malerrisi discovered.

He'd taken his time leaving Roseguard for Sleginhold. He couldn't miss his children's Birthingday, and there'd been the problem of Josselin Mikleine. But now he had to do something, and right away. Rue was the Wraithen Ward. And "Velenne's Vow" signaled the duty of all musicians to sing back the darkness.

But a Minstrel had no hope against Wraithenbeasts.

10

THE morning after he received Amilie Rosvenir's note, Collan mounted his Maurgen Dappleback and rode to the site of Falundir's old cottage. He didn't ask the Bard to come along; the memories of those first years of his maiming would be too painful. Or perhaps, he thought as he entered Sheve Dark, perhaps recollection might be kinder than that, of the years he and Col had spent together in peace and quiet.

Certainly nostalgia was one of Collan's emotions when he came upon the charred ruin. Tethering his horse to a log, he walked slowly to the chimney, thinking of all the times he'd sat before it with music folios in front of him and Falundir's lute cradled in his arms, practicing. Always practicing. Kicking fallen roof timbers out of his way, he stood on the stones where he'd sat so long ago. His mind rebuilt the cottage. Door there, windows here and here, sink and kitchen counter behind him, table and benches in the middle, sagging comfortable armchairs on either side of the hearth. Outside, the vegetable garden and woodpile, and a cauldron of rocks where the cauldron of mead rested over the fire.

All of it a wreck now. Blackened timbers, ashes, and weeds. It reminded him of another cottage near Maslach Gorge in Tillinshir. He'd been there in 968, poking around to see if there was anything left of his real family, anyone who'd known them. No luck. Well, it had been twenty-five years, after all.

Two scorched houses, and a pallet in the slave quarters of Scraller's Fief. That was what remained of his childhood and youth. Now he lived in what was almost a palace. Sarra had asked him once if he wasn't curious about his past, if he didn't want to find out who he truly was. Looking around at the remains of more than four years of his life, he repeated to himself what he'd told her then.

"You can say the past made me who I am, but the making wasn't all that enjoyable. The past is gone, and can't be changed. What I have right now is what's important."

It was true, and he believed it—yet now, as then, he couldn't help but wonder if the Wards set by Gorynel Desse had included a strong antipathy to wondering about his past.

Well, it didn't matter anyway. For one thing, it truly *didn't* matter. For another, he couldn't live his life second-guessing his own instincts, wondering if they were really his or something left him by Desse. For a third, he was too damned busy to worry about it.

Like now. Impatiently he waited for whoever had been following him for half an hour to arrive at the cottage. If stealth was a goal, this person had failed miserably. Seating himself on what had once been the front step, Collan let his forearms rest loosely on his drawn-up knees, hands in swift reach of his boot knives, and decided once and for all that the present and the future were infinitely more interesting than the past—whatever that past might have been.

When his follower finally arrived, he wasn't surprised to see it was Amilie Rosvenir. She swung down off her horse, slapped dust from her trousers, and said, "You're early."

"You didn't specify a time." He didn't get to his feet.

"I've heard you're always late."

"No, that's Lady Sarra."

Amilie snorted, kicked a rock, and sighed. "Not *all* Rosvenirs loathe you."

"Nice to hear," he drawled. "If I cared one way or another, that is."

"Grandmother's threatening to visit you. She hasn't left the Farms in fifty years."

"She's always welcome at Roseguard. Or maybe one of these days I'll go see her in Dindenshir." He stretched out his legs and leaned back on his hands. "All right, what's the problem so serious it merits a 'Velenne's Vow'?"

"I can't tell you. I have to show you."

"You'll tell me or I'm going back to Sleginhold."

A corner of her upper lip lifted in a sneer. "Manners like that are one reason you could never pass for one of us with anyone who knows us."

Collan smiled pleasantly. "I wouldn't even have to open my mouth. I'm much too tall to be one of you. Now, are you going to tell me, or am I riding out of here?"

Amilie gave in with poor grace. Seating herself on a boulder that had once marked the boundary of the herb garden, she seized his gaze with her dark brown eyes and said, "There's a child. Not one of our Name." She didn't include him in the *our*.

In a village of foresters near the Wraithen Mountains lived a little boy, six years old, named Toman. Though there were many others his age to play with, he preferred his imaginary friends. Nobody thought anything of it, and indeed indulged him more than other children because of his sad history.

He was born three weeks after his father died in an accident, and was named for St. Tomanis, patron of widows. In the spring of 982, when he was a year old, his mother took him along on a picnic with his older sisters and three other children. The baby lay in a blanket-padded basket at his mother's side in the wagon. Clouds came up over the mountains and a thunderstorm broke in the high country. As the wagon crossed a gully, the water rose in a flash flood. The terrified horse strained against the traces, snapping them. The wagon overturned, and Toman's mother, sisters, and three other children drowned. The baby in his basket was swept downstream. He was found that afternoon, washed up on a sandbar, as snug and dry as if in his own cradle at home. Identified by the blanket his mother had woven, he was taken to his grieving grandmother.

Because of this infant trauma, he was treated very tenderly. No one ever talked to him about the tragedy, even when he was old enough to understand. He was always considered a little fey—he stared into the distance for an hour at a time, babbled to people who weren't there, and was slow to talk with his grandmother and others.

One day this spring a relative came to visit. This cousin asked his name—and he gave the name of one of his dead sisters.

Amilie broke off her tale and took a swig from her waterskin. "His grandmother and this cousin questioned Toman—gently—and discovered that he had five imaginary playmates. All had names: Jennia, Felena, Imilan, Imbra, Deik—the children who died that day. Not only that, he knew their Birthingdays, the names of their mothers, sisters, brothers. *And* he could read and do sums as well as a child of ten or eleven—though he hadn't yet started school." She paused for another long swallow of water. "He and his grandmother are waiting at a farm near town."

Collan chewed his lower lip and stared at his boots. Cailet. This child must go to Cailet. Nodding, he found his voice somewhere in the shocked hollowness of his chest and said, "I'll take them to the Mage Captal. She might be able to help."

Amilie Rosvenir sighed deeply, but didn't thank him. "You're wondering how I fit in."

"Not really," he said, surprising her. "I thought over what I know of the Rosvenirs last night. Your grand-mother is First Daughter of the Name. Two of her brothers married sisters of a foresting family near the Wraithen Mountains. One had a grandson who was Savachel Maklyn's roommate at St. Sesilla's in Firrense. The other died when a tree fell on him. He fathered two daughters and a son, didn't he?"

She nodded.

"You're the cousin who asked Toman his name. You got word to the boy who knows Sava, and he sent me a message, and here we are." When she blinked, he added, "I interview all Minstrelsy prospects. And after that, I have their lives turned inside out by those already working for me." He didn't tell her that Miram Ostin, who should've been at Census, regularly researched families for suspicious connections to the old government, espe-cially to Anniyas and the Malerrisi. "I have a question, though. Why not send directly to the Captal?"

"Because I meant what I said about Viko Rosvenir," she said bluntly. "He's the only Mageborn we ever pro-duced—and we've been trying to live it down ever since. You don't understand how it is in South Lenfell. The less contact we have with Mages, the better."

"Anniyas made you suffer, those years of the Purge?"

"Not entirely because of your involvement in the Ris-ing," she allowed grudgingly. "We're a small Name, but with rich lands. There's plenty who want them—Anniyas's allies back then, the Domburs now, for all that their holdings are two Shirs away."

Collan shrugged and got to his feet. Politics bored him, and he had enough troubles protecting his own Web to worry about the Rosvenirs'. "Let's go see the child."

"Will the Captal help?"

"She'll try. No promises, except that she'll try." He

smiled. "Her trying is usually more effective than any-body else's doing."

11

THANKS to Taguare Veliaz's incisive report to the government, by 985 the school system run from Mage Hall had become a model for rural education. It began modestly enough in the summer of 971, when Cailet made the rounds of nearby Tillinshir villages to introduce herself and acquaint her new neighbors with her plans to build Mage Hall.

"Welcome, Captal, and more'n welcome!"

"Mages, y'say? For why?"

"No Mages hereabouts for twenty year'n more. We learnt to take care of our own."

"Well, long as you bide quiet and don't cause no trouble and pay your taxes—"

"Well, the Wardings back like in the old days would come in handy—up t'the backland, wolves and kyyos been at the herds somethin' fierce."

"Healers, too. Physicker comes by once a year 'n' never does much good when she does. Regular Healer'd come in handy, 'specially for spring calving."

If Cailet had thought that the proximity of a hundred Mageborns would be universally cheered, she was quickly educated otherwise. Oddly enough, the thing she'd thought would win them over proved to be the thing they were most wary of: a school.

In rural communities, girls learned reading from the local votaries (the texts were *Lives of the Saints* and other morally edifying works) and the family trade from their mothers and aunts. They needed nothing else. When Cailet proposed more—much more—the villagers smiled pityingly. When Cailet mentioned that the school would be for sons as well as daughters, they howled with laughter.

Sons worked. From birth until age six they were supervised by males of the family too old to work the fields. Then boys were assigned simple household chores or helped with the animals. As they grew older, their responsibilities increased. This was their training for marriage. As husbands, they were sought for specific skills needed by other families; the best workers married young. They worked until old age, and spent their last years tending grandchildren and great-grandchildren. What need had boys for reading and writing? Why spoil a boy's mind and sully his natural simplicity of character with superfluous nonsense?

But in each gathering of villagers, Cailet saw a few women whose eyes gleamed with interest before they joined the general chorus of jeering disapproval. She remembered their faces and their Names, and on returning to the Mage Hall site conferred with her Senior Mages and the few among the survivors of Ambrai who came from Tillinshir.

For the most part, Cailet had followed the old organization of the Mage Guardians. She had a First Sword in Imilial Gorrst, a Master Healer in Elomar Adennos, an Archivist in Imi's cousin Lirenza, and a Master of Warders in Granon Bekke. Other positions—Novice Master, Prentice Master, and a full complement of Captal's Warders—would be filled as Mage Hall became established. But before she could begin the education of young Mageborns from all over Lenfell, she had to persuade the local populace that having so many Mage Guardians around wasn't such a bad idea.

That summer of 971, Mage Hall existed only in architectural drawings. Seated around an arrangement of planks atop four logs (called the "conference table" only through courtesy), lively breezes ruffling pages of notes, the Captal, First Sword, Master Healer, Archivist, and four Tillinshir-born Mage Guardians began the campaign to win back all Lenfell.

"We start small," Cailet said. "We have to. First, regular rounds from the Healers." She eyed Elomar. "And no turning up your noses at treating a dry cow or a colicky horse, either."

Elo gave her one of his vastly tolerant looks and said nothing. But Trez Shelan returned her grin. He was forty-one, a Healer Mage who barely survived the destruction of Ambrai and had walked with a limp ever since. "If they think like my great-grandmother," he remarked, "they'll sooner let us work on them than their animals."

"Fine," Cailet said. "Humans, cows, horses, or pet cats, I don't care. Treat whatever's sick, and be sure to tell them how to prevent future occurrences of the ailment if that's applicable. Only tell them *tactfully*. Now, as for the Warriors—" She turned her gaze to Imilial Gorrst. "I don't want any of you setting foot outside the Hall. I saw several locals itching to try their strength against you, just for the fun of it. The last thing I need is a challenge over swordskill."

"Truly told, Captal." Another of the Tillinshir Mages, hardly older than Cailet and only last week entered into the new Mage Lists as a Warrior, grabbed for a page about to be blown off the planks. "Truly told," Maidia Keviron repeated, plunking a rock on the errant papers, "considering the size of some of these farmgirls and boys, *we'd* be the ones needing Healers."

"Anytime, Maisha," said Trez, with a refined leer Cailet could have sworn he'd learned from Collan. "My examining room is over there someplace," he added, waving vaguely to a bare patch of ground outlined by the surveyor in green ropes.

"Settle down, children," growled Lirenza Gorrst. "Elomar, Imi, control your Mages."

Her cousin pretended offense. "We know how to behave. We've had lessons."

Maidia Keviron tried to smooth her dark hair as she said, "Trouble is, the locals will want to lesson *us*. Captal, the Warrior Mages will have to participate in St. Caitiri's and St. Delilah's. They celebrate the holidays a little differently around here." She went on to describe all-day festivals that included blacksmithing contests, nail-driving competitions, swordfights, and wrestling matches. "And there's a special hour of Delilah's devoted to Steen Swordsworn, when only men can compete."

"Oh, wonderful," Cailet groaned. "I can hardly wait."

"We'll go easy on 'em," Imilial assured her.

"A dozen strapping farmboys who practice with scythes? Better pray to St. Delilah that *they* go easy on *you.* Well, at least we don't have to worry about it until later this summer. But that reminds me—Snow Sparrow and Candleweek should be celebrated *here.* Rilla and Miryenne are both our Saints, after all. Make a list of all the local traditions, introduce a few from elsewhere, and let's make that whole week between full moons an open party—something fun or interesting happening every day, with feasts on the Saints' days. I want everyone in the area to see what we're building here, and that we're just people like them. Next order of business is the Scholars. Either of you three born close by?"

Agava Maklyn said hesitantly, "My mother's great-uncle married into the Wentrins up near Tillin Lake."

"I can do better than that," Kembial Adennos said. "My father was a Wytte from Wretched Wreck."

Cailet stared. "I beg your pardon? From *where?*"

Kembial—Mageborn like the majority of the Adennos Name, but completely uninterested in the medicine that so fascinated most of her cousins—grinned broadly. "You'd know it by its real name—Rikkard's Rest. Mother rode in one afternoon for dinner and an overnight—and stayed for six weeks, trying to persuade First Daughter that she didn't care about Fa's pathetic dowry. Finally she got pregnant and demanded him as her husband so there'd be somebody to take care of the baby. That's the way a lot of marriages happen around here. Families don't want to part with the dower or a good strong farmhand until they absolutely have to, for one thing. And for another, the Wyttes were ashamed to marry off a son with so little to a real live Adennos."

Agava stared at her. "But you were born during the Purge. Did your mother actually admit what she was? Adennos screams 'Mage Guardian' almost as loudly as Desse."

"Ah, but our family is mostly Healers. Not Mother! Besides, why do you think she called me Kembial?"

Cailet silently thanked Lusath Adennos—also not a Healer in a line famous for them—for identifying the Saint: Kembial the Veiled, patron of fugitives.

"As for the dower," the girl went on, "they finally settled on the best Clydie in the stables and two of her foals. Rent money used to come in every St. Jeymian's, even when we were in hiding." Suddenly Kembial looked surprised. "If they're still alive, I own them now."

Cailet nodded. "Then you've got a connection here. Good. You and Agava will be our first teachers. They'll trust you with their daughters—and eventually with their sons."

Agava Maklyn rubbed her forehead—deeply lined though she was only thirty-six; Anniyas's Purge had been hard on her family. "Pardon my asking, Captal, but how do you plan to get around that? They're not likely to want their boys educated."

"We'll see about that," Imilial smiled.

The Scholars soon reestablished contact with their relations. In the process, they mentioned the advantages of educating daughters in more than the usual. A family of smiths, for instance, could do better if their girls knew the latest methods of assaying metal for impurities; farmers could keep up with the latest in soil replenishment techniques, pest control, and higher-yield crops if their daughters read the agricultural journals. There were dozens of reasons to educate a daughter beyond the bare basics, and in the course of their visits Kembial Adennos and Agava Maklyn casually mentioned them all. Change was looked on askance, of course—too many changes had happened since the Rising two years ago. But Cailet knew rural folk, and how tough life could be on them. If she offered music and dancing and poetry, she'd lose. So she offered improvements in their lives and incomes instead.

The villagers, advised by the Wyttes and Wentrins related to Mages, eventually agreed that schooling would be a good thing. Cailet, understanding the difficulties of distance, decided that one school would be impossible. She couldn't ask young children to walk miles each way; wasting the family horse (assuming the family owned one) was out of the question. So Scholars would ride the circuit a day apart, and teach for one day in each village before moving on. This way, every girl would be in school two days a week. All Cailet asked from each village was a classroom. Barn, storeroom, shrine—anyplace out of the sun and wind and rain, with tables and chairs. She would supply books, paper, pencil, maps, and all else needed.

It worked.

Cailet longed to ride the circuit of nine villages herself to see how things progressed, but wisely kept out of the way. As Captal, she was intimidating at best. The reports Kembial and Agava brought back were enough to tell her the plan was a success. She added another two teachers; the girls were now in school four days of every ten.

After half a year, Cailet sent yet another Mage out on the circuit to establish a fifth teaching day—for boys. Women who seemed interested in having their sons learn were quietly contacted, and after a week or two of public outrage and empty classes, boys began to shuffle in—a few at first, then a few more, finally most of the area's sons. Derision gave way to a demand: why only one day a week for boys, but four for girls? Cailet grinned and added a sixth teacher. On the afternoon he returned from his weekly circuit with the news that two villages were taking up a special collection to build a shared permanent schoolhouse, Cailet so far forgot her dignity as Captal to dance him around the room.

The curriculum expanded to geography, astronomy, history, literature, and music. The students learned botany by planting and caring for trees and flowers around local shrines. One boy, showing a hitherto unsuspected talent for drawing and architecture, designed the new schoolhouse in Heathering. On St. Alilen's Day of 972, proud mothers from all nine villages saw their children line up for a choral performance in the Saint's honor. Each class wrote letters to children their own ages in Roseguard, Neele, and Havenport, and the days when letters and drawings and samples of leaves and flowers came back were the best days of all.

Every other week Elomar Adennos came by to talk

about medicine and conduct a clinic, and as the years wore on the number of cases of everything from malnutrition to colds declined as his lessons sank in. He discovered three girls and a boy with the talent and dedication to become Healers, though not Healer Mages, and eventually persuaded their mothers to send them to Ambrai, where Elin Alvassy had established a new Healers Ward, with scholarships for needy students.

Kembial Adennos found several teenagers who demonstrated a gift for teaching the littler ones. By 976 each village had its own schoolhouse and locals were teaching two days a week. A year later, delegations from outlying areas visited the nearly completed Mage Hall and asked how they could set up a school system.

"And not just the girls, and not just a few days a week either," Kembial reported excitedly to Cailet. "They want six days out of ten!"

Classes at Mage Hall were conducted every day of the week except the Saints' Days. From five buildings scattered on the south shore of the little lake—one each for Scholars, Healers, and Warriors, a central refectory, and a small house for Cailet—the complex expanded to include infirmary, classrooms, workshops, lodgings for Prentices and teachers and visiting Mage Guardians, a fine suite of rooms for Cailet and her staff, a gatehouse, stables, barns, and various outbuildings that supported the home farm.

But the very first thing Cailet had had built—and by the Prentices, not the construction crews—was a wall.

It wasn't a very high wall—only about four feet tall, more of a boundary marker than an obstacle. It started at the gatehouse a quarter of a mile from the main site, and the first thing each Prentice did on arrival was pile bricks and mortar into yet another section.

It wasn't a very consistent wall, either—parts of it leaned off-kilter, and in some places the mortar was thicker than in others, and the top surface dipped and rose eccentrically, and in no ten places was it the same number of bricks high.

And it wasn't a very pretty wall—the bricks were of all different colors: rusty red, sandy gold, dusty green, smoky blue, coffee-brown, eggshell white, depending on what could be bought cheap and shipped from Cantrashir or Sheve and sometimes even The Waste.

It was, in fact, a ridiculous wall—not high enough to keep out a lame galazhi, listing this way and that, uneven, wildly colored. But every Prentice Mage who came to Tillinshir could point to her or his section of that wall and proclaim, "I built that as my first lesson in magic."

Just as, years ago, building a wall at Rinnel's shack had been Cailet's first lesson in magic.

One late-summer day in 987 the wall changed forever when a new Prentice came to Mage Hall with more luggage than could be explained by the few clothes and personal items he stashed away in his closet.

Cailet always watched the new students arrive—a small personal ritual in anticipation of Taigan and Mikel. Her original quarters, built on a rise above a hollow where a gigantic oak grew, had been expanded and subsumed into a larger building. The tree was now the center of a sunken courtyard, with a wooden-railed stone balcony running three-quarters of the way around, crossing over breezeways that led to the other buildings. At the top of brick steps opposite Cailet's suite, an arched gate led down into the enclosure, and more steps ascended to the broad and lofty room that was Mage Hall itself. Cailet lived in four rooms overlooking the courtyard on one side and the lake on the other, and from the balcony she observed without words or magic each new arrival.

But that day in 987, the tenth of Drygrass, she was expecting no new Prentices, and went walking in the hills. She lazed with a book on the moss beside a forest pool most of the day, smiling whenever she recalled the unsubtle urgings of Aidan Maurgen and Marra Gorrst to take some time for herself. Fresh air, cool stillness, away from all the work and worries of being Captal—oh, they'd wanted her out of the way, all right. It had been a tricky thing, to resist just enough so they'd think she knew nothing about the surprise celebrations planned for the day after tomorrow—St. Caitiri's, her thirty-sixth Birthingday.

Thirty-six. She'd now spent half her life as Mage

Captal. And, all things considered, she hadn't done too badly at it.

When she judged that she'd given Aidan and Marra enough time to plot, she started back to Mage Hall—with some reluctance, for, truly told, she'd enjoyed the peace and quiet.

The first she saw of the new Prentice was his back as he knelt beside the wall. Approaching silently, she paused ten feet from him and wondered what in the world he was doing. She took a few steps to the side, and nearly laughed: he was planting roses.

"I hope they're hardy," she said. "And I hope you're prepared to water them morning and night. Roses don't do very well here."

The young man fell back on his heels, then on his rear end. As he scooted around in the dirt so he could see who had startled him, it was Cailet who was startled.

Saints and Wraiths!

She would have said it aloud if she'd had air enough in her lungs. The boy's looks were literally breathtaking.

All the Saints in the Saintly Calendar and every Wraith in the Wraithen Mountains!

"I—I'm sorry, Captal," he stammered, "these had to be planted at once—I brought them all the way from Roseguard and—is it all right to put them here? They like walls to grow on, and this wall could certainly use. . . ." He trailed off, a crimson blush staining coffee-and-cream skin.

"What you mean is it's the ugliest wall in fifteen Shirs," she heard herself say. Amazing; she could actually form words, and moreover ones that made sense. "What kind of roses?"

He scrambled to his feet—awkward, though she knew that this tall, long-legged boy would be supple in any other circumstances. It was her fault he was falling all over himself, she thought; he knew by her black clothes and the pins on her collar that he was in the presence of the Mage Captal, and his limbs would not obey their instinct to grace. He was older than most of the Prentices who came to her, maybe eighteen or nineteen. And

belatedly she remembered the message from Roseguard.
This must be Mirya Witte's would-be boy.

But as he brushed off soil-stained trousers and tried
to tuck glossy black curls more securely beneath his coif,
she could not for the life of her remember his name.

"That one," he said, pointing to a leafless stick that
looked like all the other leafless sticks planted and un-
planted along the wall, "is Ambrai Pride. It's as close to
turquoise as a rose gets. The one next to it is Wraith-
shadow, and then Magefire, Sheve Flame, Ryka Miniature—"

Cailet began counting as he recited the names.
"Thirty-six rose bushes? You must've come here in a hay
wagon!"

"No, Captal, one of Lady Sarra's carriages. She had
a lot of things she wanted to send you. The roses are a
Birthingday present from her and Lord Collan and their
children."

"I see. Thank you for bringing them along." Not
knowing what else to say, and still infuriatingly unable to
recall his name, she started for the gatehouse.

"Captal?"

She turned, and once again was stunned by the young
man's beauty. She wondered if she—or anyone else at
Mage Hall or on Lenfell—would ever get used to it. No
wonder Mirya had been willing to sell her most lucrative
enterprise in order to marry him.

"It *is* all right, isn't it? The roses."

"It's fine."

He smiled, to devastating effect on her respiration—a
slightly crooked front tooth notwithstanding. "I'm glad.
It really is an ugly wall."

She felt herself smile back, and forced herself to start
walking.

A little while later, when she was waiting for the
bathtub to fill, Marra came in with an armful of clean
sheets and towels. After one look at her face, the young
woman grimaced.

"I see you've met him."

"Him?"

"Nice try, Captal, but not quite innocent enough. *Him* him. Josselin Mikleine."

Of course. *That* was his name. "Yes, out by the wall, improving the scenery."

Marra laughed. "Yes, I'd say he's extremely scenic!"

"That's not what I meant! He's planting roses."

"Uh-huh."

"Marra—!"

But she only laughed, and left the towels on the counter, and as Cailet soaked in her bath, she wondered just how much trouble this extremely scenic young man was going to be.

12

" . . . AND thus the sword is used *before* magic, because the sword is something people comprehend." Cailet laid both hands on the sheathed sword across her knees, watching the new group of Prentices to see which would be brave enough—or skeptical enough—to let show doubt about what The Mage Captal Herself had just said.

"No objections?" she asked, deigning to smile. "Not one of you will tell me that if a Mage Guardian uses magic right off, people will do as they're supposed to without the danger of bringing out a sword? Shouldn't magic be our first resort instead of our last?"

It was an interesting harvest this autumn of 987, most of them rather older than was usual. Shy, reticent Jioret Canzallis—distant cousin of Steen, and nothing like the handsome, volatile Warrior-in-training—was just sixteen. He'd learned he was Mageborn only four weeks ago when he left Isodir for the first time in his life to visit a newly married brother in Dindenshir. Jioret, astonished by revelation of what he was (the Iron City dampened magic unless it was very strong indeed) would eventually become comfortable with it—but from past experience of his type, Cailet knew he would be one of the quiet, unobtrusive Mage Guardians whose gifts are rarely used. She envied such Mageborns the gentleness of their power.

There was the usual addition of Adennos cousins to Mage Hall—two girls, Halla and Hallan. Fourteen years old, they'd been born three days and five thousand miles apart, and before coming to Tillinshir hadn't even known the other existed. But the pair were so alike in their long-legged builds, long-jawed faces, and long-lasting silences (Elomar all over again, Cailet told herself with a grin) that they might as well have been twins.

If the Adennos mold had struck true, so had the Maklyn, in the form of two dark-haired, green-eyed boys from Wyte Lynn Castle. Cailet reminded herself that she really must find out one day if something in Bleynbradden's water bred up Maklyn Mageborns. In 969 she'd discovered a round dozen of them—Alizia, Elina, Fiellan, Ketri, Lenn, Lila, Piergal, Rinna, Rolin, Truan, Venka, and Viranon—all between the ages of twelve and fifteen, none of them closer than second cousins, and with no discernible relation to the known Maklyn line of Mageborns. Of the two new ones, Trys was sixteen and Tirin was the baby of this class at just thirteen.

And then there was Josselin Mikleine. Utterly incapable of being invisible, he'd somehow managed to be unobtrusive, escaping Mage Hall as often as possible to lavish time and care on the roses Sarra had sent. Though Cailet was compelled to admire his ambition, she was convinced that nothing could improve the dreadful wall. Josselin was the oldest of the first-year Prentices, a man grown—for whichever of the Equinoxes was his Birthingday, the autumn one had passed four days ago and he was officially eighteen, and of age. One would have thought being stuck in class with five children would grate his manly pride. No such thing—not yet, anyway. Cailet wondered when it would hit him that by now he could have been Lord Josselin, husband of the Witte First Daughter, instead of sitting here under the courtyard oak listening to the Mage Captal blather on.

When no one ventured a comment, Cailet said, "So you're just going to take my word for it, are you, that magic should be used only if all other means of persuasion fail?"

With the simplicity of his gifts and his person, Jioret Canzallis said, "You're the Captal."

"So I am. And if I told you that the sun will rise in the west tomorrow morning, would you also take my word for that?"

Tirin Maklyn grinned. "Everybody knows it won't! Besides, not even the Captal has that much power."

"What if I did?" Cailet persisted, turning to the Adennos cousins. "Halla?"

"You wouldn't," the girl said succinctly. Then, with an unexpected flash of humor, she added, "Just think how it would confuse the roosters."

Her cousin Hallan frowned at the levity; every lesson in being a Mage Guardian was a matter of supreme seriousness to her, the more so when the teacher was the Captal. Cailet hoped the girl would follow the example of other Prentices and develop a sense of humor one of these days.

"So what you're saying," Jioret offered, frowning, "is that just because a Mage Guardian *can* use magic, it doesn't mean she *should*."

"Perhaps," said Josselin in his low, sonorous voice, "the best solution is to avoid situations where magic or the sword must be used at all."

"Certainly," Cailet agreed. "A wise constable of the Watch knows how to subdue a surly street drunk with his cudgel, but chooses to put him in an armlock instead."

"Wouldn't it be easier to knock him out cold?" Tirin asked.

"The First Rule of Magic is to harm nothing. The Second, according to Gorynel Desse, is to be subtle. The Third, according to *me*, is that the easiest way is usually the worst."

That's the silliest thing I've ever heard, muttered a voice in her head.

You say that every time I give this lecture. Hush up and let me finish, will you please?

Yes, Captal. I hear and obey, Captal. By Geridon's Golden Stones, that boy is exquisite!

We all know that, Gorsha.

And are we going to do something about it?

This startled her so much that she shifted in her chair. *I'm* twice *his age!*

So? A mere technicality. That boy would sire beautiful children—he reminds me of somebody, I can't think who—and his get would be Mageborn as well—

Gorsha, shut up!

Distracted by the interior conversation, she'd missed whatever it was Hallan Adennos had just said. But the girl was looking upward, where someone had just flung open the gates at the top of the steps. Rather than descend to the courtyard, a thin, dark boy of about six raced around the balcony overhead, yelling at the top of his lungs. Several adults pushed through the gates behind him, shouting.

A moment later Granon Bekke shoved past them and pounded after the boy. Cailet stood, her sword in her hand—still sheathed—and told the Prentices to go indoors at once. They scattered at her command, but hid within the breezeway to see what would happen next.

The boy smashed upstairs windows with bare fists, howling with rage but not with pain. Poking his head between broken glass, careless of shards that scraped his face and scalp, he screamed frustration before moving on to the next window.

"Captal!" bellowed Granon as he caught up with the boy and grabbed his collar.

"Cailet!" roared another voice, just as familiar but stupefyingly out of place at Mage Hall.

Collan? What's he doing here?

"Toman!" shrieked a woman from the top of the stairs. "Toman, please! Somebody help my grandson!"

"Captal! Get out of here!" Granon yelled.

The boy's magic has gone Wild. Don't question me, Cailet, I know the scent of it! Do as Granon says and get to safety!

But she stood there, fingers wrapped around the hilt of her sword that had once been Gorsha's, watching in frozen horror as Granon lost his grip on Toman and the boy flung himself over the balcony railing. Collan was racing down the stairs toward her, sweating as if he'd already run at least a mile.

Damn it, Cailet, move! *He knows you're the Captal, he saw Granon call down to you—*

Toman fell twenty feet to the paving stones, landing in a heap that should have meant stunned unconsciousness if not broken bones. But he was on his feet at once—a lanky, wild-eyed child, laughing hysterically as he rushed directly at Cailet.

Josselin Mikleine snagged part of a sleeve that ripped with the force of the boy's charge. As the young man grappled with the frenzied child, dirty fingernails clawed that oh-so-perfect face and left trails of blood. Toman squirmed free and came for Cailet again, dark eyes red-rimmed and completely insane.

A Mage Globe appeared in the air ten feet in front of Cailet. It swelled, Warrior crimson, and shattered as Toman crashed into it, his Wild Magic breaking through Granon's. The boy faltered for one or two steps, then gathered himself for the final lunge at Cailet.

Collan got in his way, pounding across the flagstones to intercept him. "Cailet! Get the hell out of here!" he shouted, making a grab for Toman. The child eluded him with insane speed, a blur of skinny limbs and tangled dark hair and torn clothes that evidenced more than one try to restrain him. Col lost his balance, crashed into a flowering trellis, and staggered backward before it fell on him.

All at once she felt the sword wrenched from her hand. She saw it wielded in bloodied fingers—the blade still sheathed, swung as inelegantly as a tree branch, its flat striking Toman's shoulders and back. Over and over the sword slammed down onto the boy, and at last his body's injuries were too much for his mind's Wild Magic to counter. He went down in a tangle of scrawny legs and blood.

Josselin stood over him, not even breathing hard. He turned to look at Cailet, and for several moments said nothing. Then, gravely handing back her sword: "First resort. And for me, until you teach me, the only one."

13

THAT evening, an hour after Cailet and Collan had dined in private, Granon came to Cailet's chambers to make his report.

"Elomar sedated him until you can Ward him," he said wearily. "Had to give him enough to send an ox into a stupor, truly told."

Cailet nodded, remembering how Josselin—five times the boy's size and ten times as strong—had been forced to hack at him. "Injuries?"

"Bruises, sprains, cuts from the glass—nothing that won't heal. His grandmother's with him." Granon shook his head. "I've heard about Wild Magic, but I've never seen it before. My apologies, Captal. I should have—"

"Don't be ridiculous," Collan told him, making a long arm to pour Granon a large mug of cinnamon-flavored coffee, then laced it with brandy. "Sit down, Master Bekke, and we'll tell you the whole story."

Granon accepted the mug with thanks and lowered himself into a chair opposite Cailet, his craggy face drawn into grim lines. He blamed himself, she saw—which, as Collan had said, was absurd. Not even Gorsha had guessed what was truly wrong with the child until Collan told Cailet about the drownings five years ago.

As Col went over Toman's history for the second time that evening, Cailet conducted an interior conversation with the most vocal of her Others.

All right, Gorsha, let's hear it.

You're working from theory, not fact, he argued.

I'm working from stories that go back five hundred years or more, she retorted. *This is incredibly rare, but it has happened before.* Effortlessly she recited the information, taken from what she'd received of the Bequest. If her mental voice took on some of his pedantic vocabulary, there was no one but Gorsha to remark it.

The most reliably reported case occurred in 598, during the Kenroke Fever Epidemic. A child survived all her family—who all died within a day of each other. Seven of them. Twenty years later, after a life lived almost entirely alone, with everyone thinking her strange because of what she'd witnessed at the age of three, a Healer Mage came to the village for the first time. The young woman fascinated her, and after a week or two she found out pretty much what Toman's grandmother and cousin did. There was nothing to be done, however. The girl wasn't Mageborn. She lived to be ninety, all the while with seven other people inside her mind.

And you think that because Toman is Mageborn, you can help him?

I think it's likely.

We don't risk a Captal's life and sanity on a likelihood.

What else can I do? she cried. *Ward him to total insensibility? Kill him?*

"—so I brought him here, hoping the Captal could help," Collan finished.

Cailet sighed quietly. "Merciful St. Miryenne, I hope I can."

"Any idea what set him off?" Granon poured himself another coffee, this time without brandy, and stirred sugar into the cup. After one sip he grimaced and reached for the cream. "Saints, Marra brews it strong! What would've triggered such a display from the child, Captal?"

"Proximity of magic." This she had learned from Gorsha in a stern lecture this afternoon. "I take it his village is isolated, and a Guardian visits only once or twice a year?"

"If that." He paused, then bit his lip before saying, "What I did with the Battle Globe—it only made things worse, didn't it?"

"Probably not. You saw him." She nodded thanks as he refilled her cup. "It wasn't your fault, Gransha."

He shrugged this away. "I'm surprised the rest of us weren't writhing on the ground, with that much magic gone crazy."

"Its direction was me. It happens that way sometimes—focusing on the strongest magic in the vicinity to the exclusion of everything else." Something else she'd learned from Gorsha. "I'm just glad it was a boy and not a girl."

Collan snorted. "Do you think a little thing like that would've stopped Joss Mikleine? It could've been a girl, a grown woman, or his own mother, and he would've done the same."

"I agree," Granon said. "If he turns out to have a talent for the Warrior side of things, I'd be pleased to have him as a Captal's Warder. He's got the right instincts."

"The Captal must survive." Josselin hasn't been here thirty days, and he's already shown himself a Mage Guardian.

Yes, said Gorsha. *And a powerful one.*

Mmm. But how much did your sword have to do with it?

"We could use a few more Mages who know what to do with a sword besides not trip over it," Granon was saying, and for an instant Cailet was lost between two conversations about weaponry. "Most of the Scholars don't even wear one, nor the Healers either. Those sent out as itinerants know how to defend themselves— Rennon and I make sure of it!—but there're few among them who want to become Warrior Mages."

It was part of a larger problem: the scarcity of Mageborns. Cailet sat in silence while Col and Granon discussed it. During the years from the destruction of Ambrai in 951 to Anniyas's death in 969—the years of the Purge—hundreds of Mageborn children had been lost. The few lucky ones had been found by a Mage and Warded so strongly that their powers were locked up forever. The many unlucky ones were killed by frightened neighbors, just like in the terrible days after The Waste War.

And then there were the tragic ones: the ones who went mad.

Most of the Mage Guardians had died at Ambrai. Their children had died with them—or never been born. Some Mages had escaped, lived in hiding, married, and either feared to bear daughters and sons or bore them in fear of the future, when their children might or might not have access to training that would control and nourish their magic.

Hundreds dead, hundreds unborn. In the seventeen years since establishing Mage Hall, Cailet had on average added only five names each year to the Lists. Fewer than ninety new Mage Guardians—while those who had survived Ambrai gradually died, their memories of the old ways dying with them.

"It'll take Generations to rebuild your strength," Col said. "It's not surprising that the Warrior lines were hit so hard—you Bekkes, the Garvedians, the Gorrsts—all of you were at Ambrai, defending the city."

"Good thing we didn't lose the Adennos line of Healers," Granon said. "Or the Scholarly Escovors."

Collan rose. "Marra brews it strong, but also potent. Cailet, does your exalted Captalship possess anything so mundane as a commode?"

She grinned and pointed. When he went through to the bedroom and the bathroom beyond, she looked at Granon again. "What is it?"

He hesitated. "I tell you truly, Captal, if it came to it, we wouldn't have enough Warriors to defend Mage Hall. The Wardings you have from The Bequest must be bulwark enough."

"If we're attacked, Gransha," she said with a thin smile, "it won't be from the outside, with swords and magic."

He winced, suddenly showing the wrinkles of his fifty-four years. "Like today, you mean? I don't even want to think about it—but now I have to. Would it be possible for me to observe while you Ward the boy? I'd like to learn how, in case I ever need to."

"Tomorrow morning first thing," she said. "But I don't think it's something you can learn."

"At least let me help—if I can."

She smiled at him, and nodded. *Dear Gransha. Could I have chosen anyone better as Master of Warders?*

He protects you as I would have, came the acknowledgment.

Granon stood and stretched his Warrior's muscles.

"I'll be there. I wish you a good night, Captal. Please give my respects to Lord Collan."

"I will." Cailet sipped coffee for a while, staring at nothing. At last Collan returned.

"No, I didn't fall in," he said. "Marra's in your bedroom tidying up, and we had a little talk. Aidan's happy here. All Lady Sefana's fears about his not fitting in were unfounded."

"Thanks be to St. Miryenne for it," she agreed.

"Wish Val Maurgen could be around to see him." Collan sprawled in a chair and sighed. "So what're you going to do for Toman?"

"I'm not sure yet. I'll have to think about it tonight."

"Is that an unsubtle hint that it's late and I should be going?"

"Not at all. I don't usually go to bed until First, sometimes later."

"And you look it, too," Collan observed ungraciously.

Cailet only smiled.

"Whatever your worries now," he went on, "just wait till the twins get here."

"I have been waiting," she replied. "For sixteen years. But I can wait a while more. They're not finished learning what you and Sarra can teach them."

"That's what I keep telling her." He shifted in his chair, hooking a knee over the arm. "Cai—will they do all right here?"

"Yes."

"Don't go easy on 'em. They're mine, and I love them, but Taigan can be an arrogant brat and Mikel can talk his way out of almost anything." He paused for a moment. "The Mikleine boy—Mikel thinks he's seen him before. So do I."

"You have? Where?" She tried to sound casual about it.

Cailet—what are you thinking?

"I like the boy—he's pleasant enough and he's got a brain between his ears. I like him," Col said again, unnecessarily.

"But—?"

"But he might've been the one who delivered that box." Collan looked her straight in the eye. "And I'm pretty sure he's the boy I saw in Roseguard Grounds the night the twins were kidnapped."

" 'Pretty sure,' 'might've been'—what are you trying to tell me, Col?"

"Don't try that song, Cailet, you never could sing in the key of Stupid. He could be a Malerrisi."

Geridon's Balls! Cailet, tell him he's wrong!

"So could any of them be." *I can't.*

"And you're not going to try and find out?" Collan chewed his upper lip, shaking his head. "Risky. What if—"

"What if *what?* Life is one long 'what if,' Col. What if I died in the middle of the night, all alone, without Elomar and Granon here to have the Making of another Captal in my place?"

A cheery thought, growled Gorynel Desse.

You'll like this one even better. "What if Glenin Feiran arrives one morning with an army of Malerrisi to attack Mage Hall? I can't deal in 'what if' and stay sane. All I can do is work with what I have, and keep a close eye on Josselin Mikleine—as close as I keep on all the other Prentices. You don't have to be raised at Malerris Castle to use magic the wrong way."

"Like Auvry Feiran," he said, and she hid a flinch.

"Frankly, if Josselin *is* Malerrisi, I'd rather have him here where I *can* watch him than planted in Heathering like that blacksmith your Minstrelsy rooted out earlier this year."

"Sorry we didn't find him sooner. And how did we get started on this depressing conversation, anyhow?"

"Late hour, too much brandy. And that poor boy." She shrugged. "I'll do what I can for him. But I can't promise anything. I can Ward the Wild Magic, though it might take a while."

He rose and stretched as Granon had done, saying, "And you've not only got to plan it out, you need rest in order to get it done tomorrow." Unlike Granon, who would never have dared even think it, Collan came to her and ruffled her hair. "G'night, kitten."

"Good night, Col. Sleep well."

Later, after Aidan had consulted her about the next day's schedule of classes and Marra had brought in a late-night snack that Cailet left untouched, she slid between cool sheets and stared at the little lamp burning in the corner of her bedchamber.

"What about the sword, Gorsha?" she asked aloud.

It seizes on magic, and the intent of the user, he said. *You know that. Josselin's intent could not therefore have been to kill the boy.*

"Or he'd be dead. Yes, I can accept that. But he didn't *need* to kill him, did he?"

What are you thinking?

You have no idea what a relief it is that it's impossible for you to read my mind. Of course, it's equally impossible for me to read yours. . . .

What are you thinking?

She did not reply, watching firethrown shadows dance on the ceiling as a soft breeze sneaked under the lamp's clear glass.

Cailet!

Oh, very well. Just this—it was a splendid opportunity for him to distinguish himself, not just from those in his class, but from every Prentice who has ever come to Mage Hall. Saving the Captal's life isn't something most Listed Mage Guardians get to do in a lifetime.

And you suspect him because of it? Suspect him of what?

Sarra sent me an interesting letter with Josselin and the roses. You were off somewhere thinking deep thoughts while I read it. Where do *you go when you're not talking to me, anyhow?*

My memories. When all the other Mages who remember Ambrai have died, Lusath and Tamos and I will still be here to remind you. What did Sarra have to say?

What Col repeated tonight—that Mikel thinks Josselin might have a few physical characteristics in common with that Malerrisi neither he nor Taigan can quite remember.

He gave a complex snort. *Believe me, those who see that boy even once will remember it until their dying day!*

Collan does. Cailet turned over in bed and curled around a pillow. *He remembers a beautiful dark boy with gray eyes. You heard what he said tonight. Think of it, Gorsha—what better place to hide a Malerrisi than in a Hall full of Mages? What do we know about Josselin, anyway? An orphan, born in 969 at one of the Equinoxes—*

Glenin wouldn't dare. She wouldn't risk—

He's the right age, she mused. *And we have no idea where he was living until a year or so ago.*

This is insane.

Taigan and Mikel trusted the Malerrisi after he "saved" them from an attack. Perhaps I'm meant to trust Josselin for the same reason. She felt his shocked denial, and decided to confront him. *You knew my father. Does Josselin look like Auvry Feiran did at that age?*

Cailet—!

I didn't think you'd tell me. Go back to your memories, Wraith. I'm going to sleep.

You're turning nasty in your isolation, Captal.

Don't start that again!

But he was gone, and it was a long while before she slept. When she did sleep, she dreamed of Auvry Feiran—whose face changed to that of Josselin Mikleine.

14

GORYNEL Desse was the only Mage in history to have the honor and responsibility of the Making of two Captals—Lusath Adennos and Cailet Rille. The second time, it had killed him.

Elomar knew from Cailet's Making that there was a place where such things occurred, but understood no more than she did about the process of getting there. Lusira monitored their physical bodies—Elo's work when Gorsha had supervised The Bequest. Gorsha, wearing full regimentals on a lean, strong body no older than Cailet's, guided them to the featureless grayness she had inhabited once before, half her life ago. She could feel Elomar's presence in the background, and even hear his footsteps on the black-glass surface, but when she turned to look for him, she couldn't find him.

But she did see three other men: hazy, indistinct, each shining in his own way. A Candle and a Sparrow just like her own glinted from one man's collar; a pure white Mage Globe hovered between the hands of another; a shock of golden hair glowed in the dimness.

"Alin—" she breathed, and though she could not see his face clearly, it seemed to her that he smiled.

Gorsha took her elbow and turned her gently around. "They'll be here if you need them," he said as they walked, "just like always. We must find the child."

As if conjured by his words, another haze coalesced before them. It became not one child but six, all between the ages of four and seven, huddled protectively around the slight form of Toman.

"The same ages they were when they died," Cailet murmured. "They haven't aged—"

"They still see themselves as they were in life," Gorsha agreed.

"Like you do, my vain First Sword?" She glanced at him quizzically, and he winked. She touched his arm, feeling the solidity of him; looked up into brilliant green eyes; saw his lips part with a suddenly caught breath. He loved her. She knew that, depended on it. But the abrupt reality of him—in a completely unreal place—young and vital and compelling—

She recoiled, her cheeks burning. His head bent, and he sighed, and said, "There's work to do, Captal."

Nodding mutely, she turned and walked with slow, careful steps toward the children. A close look at their faces told her how startled they were at being separate again.

"Is this what it's like for you and Alin and Tamos and Lusath?"

"Not in the slightest. We were adults, and we deliberately chose. These are children, who had no idea what they were doing."

"But how did it happen?"

"Find out. Ask them."

She stopped walking when one of the girls flinched back. This was far enough. "Hello, Toman. Do you know who I am?"

"Captal," the girl said, eyeing her with wary blue-green eyes. Toman bit both lips and said nothing. But his eyes knew her better than the Others' did.

"You can call me Cailet. You're Jennia, aren't you?" she said to a girl who had Toman's dark eyes. "And that's Felena, your little sister." The girls nodded. They stood on either side of their brother, holding his hands. Cailet smiled with what she hoped was reassurance, and looked at the other children. "Imilan, and Deik, and Imbra, right?"

More nods. Cailet had to keep reminding herself where she was, what was going on here. They were just six children: blonde Imbra, rusty-haired Deik, tall Imilan, the three dark Lille siblings. All of them were clean and neat in bright sweaters, pants, and boots; Toman's sisters wore matching green ribbons in their hair.

They looked just as their families would have sent them out on a spring picnic—five years ago.

Imbra, who at seven was the eldest, took a step forward. "Where are we?"

Cailet hedged a little. "This is probably a scary place for you, but I promise it's all right. You're safe. Nothing will hurt you."

"Magic?" When Cailet nodded, Imbra asked, "Who's he?"

He—Gorsha. Tall, broad-shouldered, impressive in black regimentals—intimidating despite the mildness of his expression. "He's a friend of mine," Cailet said. "He's here to help us."

"Help us do what?"

Cailet stuck her hands in her pockets, keeping her body loose and casual. "I think maybe you know. You have magic, too, after all."

The girl looked at the Others, then at Toman, who was practically cowering. Turning back to Cailet, she burst out, "But magic hurts! He hurt us! With the sword!"

"I'm sorry for that," Cailet began.

Deik spoke up. "It felt like the thing we put in the box."

"The—?"

Behind her, Gorsha whispered, "Wards."

Oh. "That was your magic."

"But it *hurt!*" Imbra insisted. "The sword hurt all of us, Toman worst of all—and before that we felt all those people—"

"I'm sorry," she repeated. "Nobody wanted to hurt you. But the man who had the sword promised to protect me, and—"

All at once her frightened defiance melted away, and she shuddered. So did the Others, and Toman. "We didn't want to—it just *happened*—"

"It's all right. I understand."

"We couldn't stop it! We kept it all boxed up for a long time, but then it got out—" Tears trembled in her blue eyes.

"How did you put it in a box?"

Jennia let go her brother's hand and came to stand with Imbra, stroking her blonde hair to soothe her. "We did it at the very start. When we came together."

"I see. You must be very strong to have done that." All six children nodded. They had responded to their own names and could speak as individuals, but they always used *we*. Cailet tilted her head, pursing her lips as if mildly curious. "I'd like to know how you did it. Maybe I could help you do it again. Do you remember?"

And all at once she was drowning.

—water—can't breathe—help me—
—swim swim catch Deik's hand—cold so cold—
—rocks—head hurts—can't see—
—let go my arm let go let go LET GO—
—Papa, help—please, Papa—cold and dark—
—can't breathe—
—hungry scared up-down-side-side stop want Mama scared hungry—

THERE!
And what had been six became one. That was all
any of them remembered. How it came to be,
what deliberate process or random chance led
them to Toman, none knew. They had been sepa-
rate, and now were joined.
And they wanted to take her with them—

"Cailet!"

She gasped, shaking as violently as the children. Leaning against Gorsha's strength, she raked the hair from her eyes and saw that they were huddled together again, hanging onto each other. All at once Tamos Wolvar strode toward them, followed by Alin, and Captal Aden-nos—and even Elomar. Each man knelt, embracing frightened children, murmuring that it was all over, they were safe, nothing would hurt them.

Cailet stood straighter. "I'm all right," she managed. "Did you find out how it happened?"

She nodded, and kept her voice low as she explained.

It had been an accident. They hadn't meant to do this, whatever it was. But they had, and the infant personality was not strong enough to reject them. Indeed, it never considered rejecting them—for it only knew itself abandoned, and in need. The Others were suddenly *there*, and in this there was comfort.

Four-year-old Felena, a sister. Six-year-old Jennia, the other sister. Both familiar, and loved in the way a baby loves anyone who cuddles and coos and feeds it. Imilan and Deik, also six, were unknown, but Jennia wanted them there, felt comfortable with them, and so it was all right. But the last, Imbra, was strange. Something burned in her, something her friend Jennia hadn't known about before but had watched with the Others in a paralyzing jumble of fascination and fear. The thing crouched within her like a stalking silverback cat, bright and patient. Imbra was scared of it, but all it did was curl up tight to wait. They surrounded it with their fear of it, and fear had been vigilant in protecting them.

When Cailet finished, Gorsha shook his head. "It's the most remarkable example of spontaneous instinctive self-Warding I've ever heard of. Makes you wonder how many other children do it this way, and so effectively that no magic ever escapes."

"It took six of them to do this. Could one child accomplish it on her own?"

"I suppose it would depend on the magic's strength. But this case is surely unique. It's not the host child who's Mageborn, it's Imbra."

"And with her magic crushed like that, Warded up with their terror of it, no wonder it turned Wild." Cailet thrust her hands into her pockets again.

"But why now?" Gorsha stared hard at the children, who were calmer now and responding to the four men who comforted them.

Cailet shrugged. "She was seven when it happened. She's twelve now."

"She's inside a six-year-old! There's no possible way that the onset of puberty could trigger her magic!"

"You know that. I know that. Imbra doesn't know that, so why should it affect her?"

"What she doesn't know can't influence her?" He snorted.

"Do you have a better explanation?" she challenged. "You're assuming that magic is a thing of the body. Of blood and bone and brain—not mind. You should know better. You're no longer in your own body, but you can still Work through me."

Grimacing, he replied, "I may not have a physical brain anymore, but this is definitely giving me a headache. What do you plan to do?"

"Toman's like me, in a way. He has Others living inside his head. But they're children who don't understand that he has a right to live his own life."

"There's a rebuke in there somewhere."

"No, not really." She paused, then admitted, "If on some level I hadn't *wanted* what all of you gave me, I don't think you could've forced me."

"Thank you for that," he said stiffly. "But what about them? Tragedy deprived them of their own lives, so they took Toman's. How do you propose to convince them it wasn't right?"

"Imbra's old enough. She'll understand."

"You hope."

"That's what I love about you, Gorsha," she snapped. "I can always count on you for optimism when I need it." She paced away from him, wanting to hear what her Others were saying to Toman's Others.

Alin patted Imilan's shoulder, ruffled Deik's russet hair. "You understand, don't you? It wasn't your fault."

"It'd be nice to be the way I was before," Deik mused. "Just me. It happened so fast—"

"Poor Toman," whispered Imilan. "I never meant to do this."

Cailet wished she knew what exactly it was they'd done.

Tamos Wolvar held both of little Felena's hands. "But you know what's the matter now."

She nodded. "I'm sorry. It's just—they were so *young. . . .*"

"They"? she thought, perplexed. *Who is "they"?*

Elomar was wiping Imbra's tears away. "It'll be all right."

"But I'll be different from them, won't I?" She dragged a sleeve across her face. "Because of the magic."

Cailet realized then that they were speaking in the singular. Not *we; I.*

Lusath Adennos sat cross-legged on the glossy black glass, Toman on one knee and Jennia on the other. "So you know what must be done. Is it all right with you, Toman?"

The boy's oldest sister reached across to touch his lank hair. "It'll be better this way," she said gently. "Really it will. I promise."

Toman spoke for the first time. "But I won't have any magic!" After a whimper and a hiccup, he added, "And I'll be all alone."

Surely it ought to be the other way around. He would be abandoned yet again, by himself for the first time since babyhood—yet he was more concerned with losing the magic.

"The need can be powerful," Gorsha said softly. "I had to Ward you three separate times. And when you were coming to 'Rinnel' in The Waste, it was all I could do to keep filling in the chinks where your magic was trying to hack its way out."

"Can I Ward this boy?" she asked.

"Yes. I'll show you how—it'll be different than it was for Taigan and Mikel. But first the Others must leave."

"I don't know how they did it, but that won't be a problem." She gestured. Imilan and Deik were hugging Toman. They stepped back, shepherded by Alin's hands on their shoulders. He saw Cailet, and smiled to break her heart. She'd forgotten what it was like to feel those blue eyes soften when they looked at her: beloved little sister and cherished friend, not the Captal.

Alin bent and whispered something to the two children. They turned, and said "I'm sorry," and faded into gray mist.

Tamos held Felena's hand while she said farewell to her brother. With a respectful nod for Cailet, he led the little girl a little ways across the shining black glass, then let her go. She, too, vanished. Jennia followed after thanking Lusath Adennos and kissing Toman's cheek.

That left Imbra. The Mageborn. Cailet's heart twisted as she drew herself up and apologized to Toman and told him good-bye.

"You would have been a good Mage Guardian," she said when Imbra looked at her. It was all she could give the child.

"I'm sorry for what happened," Imbra replied with poignant dignity. "Will you tell that to the man with the sword?"

"I will."

Toman cried out wordlessly as Imbra disappeared. Lusath had firm hold of him, or he would have run after her. *The magic,* Cailet thought sadly. *Always the damned magic—*

Damned or blessed, Gorsha told her silently, *you must use it now to Ward him.*

In a minute.

She went to Tamos Wolvar first, taking his hands. "I

never did thank you, did I? Not then, or in all the years since."

"You've Worked well, Captal," he replied. "It is an honor." He pressed her hands, smiled, and drew away. "Continue to be wise, Cailet Ambrai. Fare well."

She turned to her predecessor then, but before she could speak, he held up a silencing hand. "It was my fault as much as yours, for dying too quickly. Believe me when I say that if I could have held on, I would have."

"I know. But you're not to blame."

"You have what you'll need," he told her. "Have faith in that." All at once he grinned, and she blinked; she hadn't known the old Scholar-Captal could so much as smile. "And stop worrying so much!"

She had to grin back.

Someone tapped her on the shoulder, and she swung around to be caught in Alin's arms. "He's right," her foster brother whispered in her ear. "You worry much too much. You didn't used to, when we were children together."

"Alin—" But her throat closed up, and she couldn't speak. It had been so long since he'd been as distinct within as Gorsha always was—longer still since she'd been able to look at him.

"It's all right. I know." He released her, and raked a hand back through his shining hair. A gesture she'd picked up from him—but in childhood, not because he was a Presence within. "How could I *not* know? And you're wrong about what just happened. It wasn't us, really—not *as* us. It was *you* as us."

"I don't understand."

"We're you, Caisha. Just like when you read one of those awful adventure stories you love so much—" He grinned. "You see yourself as the heroine. Well, you see parts of you as us sometimes, too. It's not us telling you what to do, it's *you* telling you with our voices."

"Maybe," she allowed. "But it's not the same with Gorsha."

"No. He's different. And he's waiting. So are Elomar and poor Toman."

She kissed Alin's cheeks. "One for you, one for Val."

"You know what he'd say? He'd tell you to laugh more."

"Is that you telling me or me telling me?"

"It's Val telling me to tell you to tell yourself!"

"Cailet," Gorsha interrupted.

She went to him where he stood with Elo and the boy. The Healer Mage was looking a little ragged around the edges. She'd better Work fast.

15

IT took ten minutes to assure Lusira that her husband was only sleeping off the strain. "He'll wake up just fine, I promise," Cailet kept saying, but Lusira kept directing a Healer's Globe up and down Elomar's lanky body, alert to the tiniest flicker of black or gold across its green surface. Finally Cailet just shrugged and left the infirmary for her own chambers. She was in need of some rest, too.

Collan escorted her, and once or twice on the stairs she was glad of his strong arm to lean on. Aidan had brought lunch, then dinner, and taken both away again while Cailet worked. Spread on a table now was a copious selection of foods, one of which really should have tempted her appetite. But she hadn't the energy left to do so much as Warm the soup.

Collan poured her a stiff brandy, then bustled for a while, slicing bread and slathering cheese. She sipped her drink, watching him. Sarra was lucky, to have this man to take such good care of her. Gorsha would have done the same for her, she told herself. She'd just been born two Generations too late.

"So, kitten," Col said at last, his first words since leaving the infirmary. "What the hell happened?"

The brandy had warmed and revived her a little, enough to tell him the basics, anyway.

"The souls of those children didn't want to die," she finished. "They were self-centered and strong-willed, the way young things always are. They have to be, in order to survive."

He snorted. "You haven't seen self-centered *or* strong-willed until you try dealing with Taigan. Will the boy be all right?"

"I've Warded him six ways to the Wraithenwood. They're set to fade very slowly as he grows up and grows into his own personality." She hesitated, taking another swallow of liquor. "But it's very likely he'll be seen as strange all his life, and never be completely normal."

"He didn't develop the way other children do," Collan said. "I think it's just that he's got some catching up to do. But I'll tell you one thing—from what I saw on the way here, if loving kindness can heal him, his grandmother's the one to do it." He leaned forward in his chair to snag a peach from the fruit bowl. "I'll take them into Heathering when they're ready to leave—they can catch a post coach from there back home. I'm off to Neele next. I can probably get back to Roseguard by St. Delilah's. When you write Sarra, let her know, would you?"

"Of course. But what's going on in Neele?"

"Some fancy financial dancing in every branch of the Homestead Hearth Bank. A Renne cousin of the Slegin boys—" They were still called that in the family circle, even though Jeymi, the youngest, was almost thirty. "—is the director, and at a meeting of her regional managers she noticed a lot of new accounts. Every Shir."

"Why is that odd?" she asked, trying to appear interested.

"There're Web accounts—usually in four or five different banks. Then there're business accounts, usually in one bank that has branches all over, with smaller accounts for each shop or factory or whatever in the chain. Payroll in the big account, everyday operating expenses in the small ones. And then there're individual personal accounts." Noting her blank look, he laughed. "I bet you don't even know how much money you have in the bank! Anyway, what alerted Falin Renne was a lot of every kind of account being opened in all their branches."

"I still don't see—"

"It wouldn't be so weird if it was just the Homestead Hearth. Falin had a chat with a couple of other bankers, casual stuff, and found out all their banks are opening lots of new accounts, too. Some of 'em for pretty big sums."

"I haven't the slightest idea what you're talking about," Cailet declared, "and what's more, I don't care! Breakfast on the balcony tomorrow, if the weather holds. Good night."

"Good night, kitten," he replied, with a satisfied smile. And then she knew he had done it all on purpose: taking her mind away from the Working of this day and night, and boring her silly just for good measure. She made a face at him and went to bed.

16

EVERY St. Agvir's, Cailet observed her own private memorial to Alin Ostin. On that day in 961, when she was ten, she'd broken her arm in a fall from Ostinhold's St. Agvir's Wood. Her Warded magic, responding to Alin's suffering as an inept Scholar Mage botched the job of teaching him, had distracted her during the climb. She could still remember the world spinning dizzily, and hearing Alin cry out, and being unable to help him, and tumbling to the ground. That day had tragically defined him: crippling his magic so that he would never become a Mage Guardian, hurting him in ways not even Gorynel Desse could heal. Alin was just fourteen. At sixteen, he left The Waste with Val Maurgen. At twenty-two, he was dead.

But what had survived in him of magic—an uncanny ability with Ladders—survived still within Cailet. She remembered her Others, too, each year, not on their Birthingdays or the date of their deaths—the day she'd become Captal—but on occasions that had defined them as Mage Guardians. These scenes she had from their memories, joyous occasions for each: Tamos Wolvar on the third day of First Frost, when he'd spontaneously conjured his first Mage Globe at the age of thirteen; Lusath Adennos on St. Deiket's, when he'd received his Scholar's gray sash and pins; Gorsha on St. Miryenne's, when he'd been promoted to First Sword.

Of the four special dates in Cailet's personal calendar, only Alin's was bitter. Alin was a warning. The others had given her their knowledge and wisdom of experience. But Alin's legacy was more than information; he was brother, friend, and grim example of a Mageborn mind injured beyond repair. On St. Agvir's Day, Cailet locked her doors and lit a single candle, and spent a solitary evening remembering Alin and renewing her own resolve that what had happened to him would never happen to another Mageborn.

This year—eighteenth since Alin's death, twenty-sixth since that day at Ostinhold—she would not be alone in remembering him. His sister Miram was visiting Mage Hall with her three daughters. With them had come Jennis Maurgen, pregnant with her third twins. She'd brought along the first two sets—seventeen-year-old Solla and Valiri, eleven-year-old Aliz and Birana. The latter girls, fathered by Biren Halvos, had inherited his tawny coloring; Jennis worried that they might have inherited Biren's magic as well.

"I know you can't tell at this age," Jen said to Cailet the afternoon of their arrival, as Mage Hall prepared to celebrate St. Agvir's. "But if you can let me know what to watch for—"

In the thirty years they'd known each other, Cailet had never seen Jen nervous. She smiled reassurance, a corner of her mouth quirking as she imagined teaching Prentice Mages who had Jennis's prickly temper.

"There's never been a Mageborn Maurgen—" Jen went on.

Miram interrupted with laughter. "For which we thank Miryenne, Rilla, Mikellan, and any other Saint who takes an interest in magic!" She sat in one of the chairs Aidan had brought out onto the balcony. It was a glorious day, the late-summer warmth tempered by cool autumn breezes that rustled the leaves of the great oak tree. "Can you imagine what Val would've been like with a few spells to hand?"

"Besides the natural Maurgen magic, you mean?" drawled Aidan, handing around goblets of iced wine. His aunt Jennis took a playful swipe at his rear end as he passed—he evaded her easily, grinning.

"Speak when you're spoken to, boy," she told him. "Cai, you're too lenient with him."

"Me?" Cailet, leaning a hip against the balcony rail, made big, innocent eyes.

"Don't blame Cailet for my manners," Aidan said. "They're your fault, Aunt Jen."

"Not anymore," she retorted. "You're Marra's responsibility now."

With a smile reminiscent of Val at his most complacent, Aidan replied, "Oh, but she finds me charming—don't you, light of my eyes and joy of my heart?"

With a cloyingly sweet smile, Marra cooed, "Devastatingly charming, my own true love."

Miram rolled her eyes. "Enough! Run along and play, children, while we . . . discuss. . . ."

What Miram intended to discuss would never be known. A young man suddenly appeared from the arched corridor at the end of the balcony, stopped on seeing the group gathered outside Cailet's quarters, smiled a shy apology, and returned the way he'd come.

Cailet exchanged amused glances with Marra and Aidan, and all three waited for it. Sure enough, it was Jennis who broke the silence with a short, explosive sigh.

"Cailet, tell me this instant or I'll rearrange those Globes on your shelves so you'll never be able to contact another Mage Guardian as long as you live. Who was that *revoltingly* beautiful young man?"

The Captal managed to hide most of her smile. "Prentice Josselin Mikleine. I thought you might notice him. Most people do." A grin escaped as Aidan snorted at the understatement. "But I have to ask, Jen—why 'revolting'?"

"Because I'm too pregnant to take him to bed, damn it," Jennis sighed. "Maybe after I've delivered. . . ."

Miram burst out laughing. "You're incorrigible!"

"No, frustrated! Oh, don't worry, Cailet—I didn't travel all this way to poach Prentices—male *or* female!"

"If you tried, you faithless flirt," Cailet teased, "I'd have to tell Maidilin Canzallis."

"Now, how did you—" Jen interrupted herself with another sigh. "My sister. It was my sister, wasn't it? Riena is the worst gossip in The Waste."

"It was *not* Riena, and you have a nerve complaining about Aidan's manners when you're sitting here maligning your own sister!"

"So how did you know about me and Maisha?"

Cailet looked pointedly at the ring on Jennis's right hand—the Canzallis sigil of an eagle holding a snake in its talons. "Besides, I remember Maidilin from school, and she used to lope along behind you older girls like a Senny pup."

She regretted the reference as soon as it left her lips; a Senison hound had turned unexpectedly wild earlier this year, savaging Lady Sefana's right arm to the shoulder. All the skills of a Healer Mage brought from Renig had been insufficient to prevent loss to infection of hand, then arm, and then life. Sefana had died two weeks after the attack, and Riena ruled at Maurgen Hundred now, years before she had expected it.

Jennis saved the awkward moment by smiling. "I assure you, if Maisha were here, she'd be positively panting after this Mikleine boy! How much trouble *does* he cause whenever he walks into a room?"

Aidan tugged on his father's gold earring as he answered, "Well, not trouble, exactly—more like the silence usually reserved for a holy shrine."

Marra laughed. "I thought you'd gotten over being jealous."

"I'm not jealous. I pity the boy."

Jennis gave a derisive chortle. "Pity the rest of us!"

"No, truly told," Aidan insisted. "Can you imagine what it'd be like to be *that* beautiful?"

"I'd rather imagine something that beautiful in circumstances that include any reasonably comfortable flat surface," his aunt retorted.

They all laughed, but that night at dinner in the refectory Cailet sneaked a few glances at Josselin, trying to see him again as Jennis had—with the shock of first encounter. Mage Hall had grown used to Josselin's looks—more or less. Most of the languishing glances had faded and sighs ceased to gust in his direction. This doubtless had to do with the fact that he had shown favor to no one. Josselin paid not the slightest attention to his looks—behaved, in fact, as if he were just passingly attractive—and his disarming manner melted resentment. But he encouraged no one's attentions, and in fact seemed to be genuinely shy.

He was the target of all the usual prejudices held by less-endowed brethren inclined to envy. Anyone that gorgeous must be stupid beyond belief, and/or in sexual pursuit of every rich/powerful/beautiful woman on Lenfell, and/or sexually pursued by every woman on the planet no matter what her age, station, or condition (short of comatose), and/or incapable of loving anything but his own beauty, upon which he lavished much time and care. If he was shy, it was only a pose calculated to earn him a reputation for sweetness. If he complimented another's clothing or hairstyle, it was only in amazement that anything could improve the appearance of lesser creatures. If he was friendly, it was only because the object of his efforts could be useful to him in some way—foil to his own looks, conduit to a woman he desired, or for reasons known only to his conniving little brain. And "little" his brain was guaranteed to be.

On reflection, Cailet decided she agreed with Aidan: she pitied the boy. Josselin was far from stupid—not only had Collan told her of his plan for delaying marriage to Mirya Witte long enough to come of legal age with the right *not* to marry, but his teachers reported him quick to learn in classes. He bathed and shaved just like every other man here, but otherwise did nothing special that anyone had been able to discover. Naturally, total gorgeousness with total lack of effort was even more infuriating.

Josselin *was* shy, as it happened. Recently, though, an acidic sense of humor had emerged—usually at his own expense. He was pleasant and friendly and determined not to take offense when others punished him in a thousand small social ways. The one demand he made was implied rather than specified: he wanted to be treated as just another Prentice Mage. He was willing to wait for others to get over his looks, but there was a limit to his patience.

It had been reached three days ago. Aidan brought Josselin and Sevy Banian, a twenty-year-old Prentice, to Cailet's office in disgrace; the two had interrupted their teacher's lecture with a fist fight. Sevy's bloody nose had its source in Josselin's bruised knuckles, and a slight limp proclaimed that Sevy'd gotten in a good kick at some point. Cailet ordered them to apologize to teacher and class at the next session. Both agreed—but Josselin added quite matter-of-factly that if anyone else called him a "walking whore-cock from the cheapest fuck-house in Sheve," he could not promise not to apply his fists to mend that person's manners.

Oddly, Cailet was pleased by evidence of temper—she had begun to think the youth perfect beyond belief. Even more oddly, Josselin and Sevy were showing signs of becoming friends, sitting at the same table for the last couple of meals, their issues with each other apparently resolved.

But that evening, just as Cailet and Miram were about to withdraw from the singing that celebrated St. Agvir's Day, a commotion delayed the private ritual for Alin. Sevy Banian's sharp Havenport accents rose in a shout of "You fucking son of a Fifth!" and all hell broke loose near the refectory door. Cailet shoved her way through the crowd to find Steen Canzallis on the floor tiles with one hand clapped to his left eye and Josselin slumped in a chair with both hands over his nose. Sevy's hands were behind his back—as were his arms and most of his shoulders, fixed there by the glowering Granon Bekke, Master of the Captal's Warders.

Cailet cast a scathing glance at the three young men and ordered them all outside. When the door was shut behind them—Granon's glare outblazing the torches that lit the hallway—Cailet enquired as to what precisely was the meaning of this outrage.

But she knew. Steen, two years a Mage Guardian and now in training to become a Warrior, had for most of his time at Mage Hall been voted Most Magnificent Creature on Lenfell in an informal poll of female students (and quite a few males). She need look no further than the young man's volatile temper for the source of Josselin's broken nose. There were no fresh marks on Josselin's knuckles, though. Sevy had done the damage to Steen's eye—and pride. The subsequent sullen explanations confirmed her surmise.

"It was my fault," Josselin said in conclusion.

Steen curled his lip; Granon gave him a look to fry ice and said, "Shut up. You, too, Sevy. As for you—" He eyed Josselin. "Don't play noble with me, boy. And none of you darken the Captal's eyes again for a week, hear me? Get to your rooms and if you're very, very lucky, I might send the Master Healer around sometime tomorrow morning. March!"

They departed. Cailet cocked an eyebrow at Granon, startled as he began to chuckle.

"Well, it *is* funny, truly told. Think of it, Captal—two of them at each other's throats only a few days ago, and now the one defending the other against a third."

"I'm surprised Josselin required defending."

"He just didn't move as fast as Sevy. I saw most of it. Didn't hear whatever ugly remark prompted it, though." He sobered, shaking his head. "Steen deliberately picked a fight—and I think Josselin was ready for it. Might even have encouraged him, just to get it over with."

"I don't understand."

"Schoolyard politics," Granon shrugged. "Or maybe I should say 'barnyard.' Steen has a lot invested in his looks and where they can take him. Josselin, on the other hand, has had women invest real money in that perfect face of his."

"Men!" she exclaimed, and he grinned.

As it happened, the perfect face healed a little less than perfectly. In the weeks that followed, it became clear that Josselin's nose would always take a very slight left turn at the bridge. He was remarkably cheerful about it, and Elomar reported that the boy regretted that there'd be no scar.

Cailet shook her head in amazement. But in an odd way, she understood. Not that she knew what it must be like to be a male version of Lusira Garvedian, but as Mage Captal she had long since learned that little imperfections in someone ostensibly perfect were soothing to others. It was a principle she applied to herself—not that she was so inherently perfect that she must pretend imperfections. Far from it. But others, through some need of their own, saw her as infallible; that same need made them resent their own self-imposed perception. So she usually shrugged off her mistakes as helpful to her image. It all went back to what Telomir Renne had said years ago about the path she must tread as Mage Captal. Powerful, but not too powerful; knowledgeable, but not omniscient; unique, but still human.

The final irony of the whole incident was that the minuscule bump in Josselin's nose only made his other perfections more perfect by contrast.

"Can't win for losin', as my Fa used to say," Granon remarked with a shrug when Cailet pointed this out with a smile. "By the way, I've talked it over with Imi and we've agreed that Steen Canzallis would benefit from a season or two in Ambrai."

"As punishment? That's more like a reward, isn't it?"

"My nephew Sirron is the most blithely malicious Warrior Mage in all fifteen Shirs—apart from our beloved First Sword, that is."

"And you!" Cailet grinned. "Just how malicious is it to send him to train under the only Mage Guardian who damned near broiled my brains at his Listing Ritual?"

"Sirron will teach Steen to discipline that temper of his or he isn't my sister's son." He laughed his deep, gravelly laugh. "And I deeply resent the characterization, Captal. I'm a perfect lamb at heart."

"Oh, yes," she agreed sententiously. "Just as sweet and harmless as Imi Gorrst. Well, do as you think best about Steen. But if there's any more trouble regarding Josselin, I may break Lady Sarra's nose for sending him here. Saints and Wraiths! Why does this one boy have to be so revoltingly beautiful?"

17

HEATHERING'S celebration of St. Delilah's Day was always as riotous as the Tillinshir Mages had promised back in 971. The residents of Mage Hall enthusiastically joined in commemoration of the Saint's many patronages. Morning saw sedate contests for best needlework and finest tailoring (from winter cloaks to festive gowns to farmhands' overalls). By Ninth, after everyone had feasted at trestle tables and imbibed tangy local wines, the celebratory games began. There were competitions with sword and stave, footraces, wrestling matches, nail driving, horseshoe making, hammer throwing, and the curious local sport of heaving a twenty-foot pine log that in less-than-expert hands imperiled everyone within shouting distance. When the sun went down, there was another meal and more wine before the dancers had their turn: clog-stepping, leaping over flashing swords, weaving intricate foot-patterns between crossed blades.

Cailet loved St. Delilah's in Tillinshir. It had been a relatively neglected holiday in The Waste—the week was not called "Wolfkill" for nothing, and at that time of year everyone was out collecting the herds into winter pasturage safe from the wolves and kyyos. But in this part of Tillinshir, St. Delilah's was the last festival when one could reasonably rely on clear skies; the following week was Water Moon, and then came First Frost, and by then rain and soft sleet kept everyone indoors. Snow was a once-in-a-Generation occurrence in these parts; the votaries attributed this to a ritual, unique to them, designed to distract Deiket Snowhair. The first strong wind from the south every autumn saw scores of kites flown aloft and then let loose—kites made from layers of broadsheets, so that the bookish Saint would forget about Heathering and its neighbors to chase the precious printed word north beyond Tillin Lake, and deposit the winter's snow on the Wraithen Mountains where it belonged.

This St. Delilah's, clouds billowed behind the hills and there was a taste of rain in the air, but the sky overhead stayed serenely blue. Cailet got everyone started early on the walk into town, and along the way consulted with Aidan about which of the Mages would enter which contests of strength, speed, and skill.

"It ought to be a fair contest again in the smithing," Aidan observed, "now that the Malerrisi is gone."

"Mmm," said Cailet. "Too bad about him. I never saw a man shoe a horse in less time and with less fuss. Four hooves, eight toes, twenty-four minutes flat."

"He spelled the poor creatures, that's why."

"Horses can't be persuaded to a Folding. There's no reason to think they'd take to any other kind of magic. Either they're very clever or very stupid, no Mage has ever been able to decide which."

"Well, good riddance to the blacksmith," Aidan insisted. "The thought of him so close to Mage Hall for so long—"

Cailet smiled. "He saw what everyone else sees. Nothing but a college community—"

"—with a very unusual curriculum," the young man finished for her, making a face. "Do you really think nobody notices us? Especially after—"

"Don't say it," Cailet warned, laughing now. "Every time anyone mentions that incident, we discuss nothing else for the rest of the day!"

"'Incident'?" Aidan echoed incredulously. "We nearly lost you, two Prentices, and the stables!"

"Not another word!"

He shrugged, and the topic of The Great Mage Globe Mishap was shelved. "You asked me to find out how Josselin Mikleine is settling in. Officially, just fine. Unofficially. . . ."

"Let me guess. Most of the females and a fair number of the males are still smitten."

"Make that *all* the females," he corrected glumly. "Not even Marra is immune, and Saints know I have more than my fair share of looks, charm, wit, talent, intelligence—"

"And modesty!" she laughed, with Alin grinning inside her head. "Your father's son, truly told! Don't worry, they'll all get used to him in a few more weeks."

"Only if he puts an end to it by choosing somebody to sleep with."

Cailet looked at him sidelong. "He reciprocates no one's attentions?"

"He's friendly enough, but makes no friends, if you know what I mean." Aidan shrugged once more. "It's the ones who aren't attracted to him that concern me. Several promising flirtations between other couples have dried up and blown away since he arrived, and a few of our younger men are smoldering a bit."

"I'm sure Josselin knows how to deal with it. He's had that face all his life, after all. Let's see what he does."

"That's just it!" Aidan exclaimed. "He doesn't have to do *anything!*"

"Whereas," she teased, "you lesser creatures must willfully exercise your looks, charm, wit, talent, and intelligence! Thanks be to all the Saints that I wasn't born a man!"

Cailet didn't mingle much with the Prentices except on holidays such as this. At Heathering, in the midst of general revelry and in the spirit of fun, she could escape the role of Mage Captal—and her own shyness. Yet she could not become overly familiar with any Prentices or even the Mage Guardians. That difficult walk balancing on a rocky path again. In the world outside Mage Hall, she trod cautiously between too much involvement and too little. In the world she had created for herself and her Mages, one step was authority, the other fellowship; one the Captal's power and the other Cailet's personal needs.

And what *did* she need? Someone to talk to sometimes—someone who wasn't Gorynel Desse, someone whose face she could see. Aidan and Marra helped fill most of that function; letters and visits to and from Sarra and Collan were her solace. But not even to her sister could she—or would she—confide her deepest doubts and musings and worries. These she kept to herself, hidden even from Gorsha.

What she lacked, and knew she lacked, was someone to share the everyday things with. Banal it might be, but she wanted someone at her side when she walked up to the lake of an evening, chattering about nothing or staying companionably silent. Someone who was there when she came in from the last class of the day, who'd listen and share all the little joys and annoyances and triumphs and problems of day-to-day living.

Aidan and Marra had that. So did the other couples among the Mages at the Hall. But Cailet didn't want what Sarra and Collan had—nothing that intense, that passionate, that contentious. What Cailet wanted was something quieter, simpler, easier . . .

. . . something she could never have.

She caught sight of Tirez Escovor, a wily old Mage who delighted in teaching overawed Prentices, showing a group how to perfect their Folding technique. They were all laughing as one of their number Folded himself right into the roadside ditch. Cailet smiled, wishing she could join the fun. Truly told, she envied her own students. They were learning their craft and their magic gradually, in orderly fashion, with time to enjoy the nuances. Skills were mastered, new skills followed, with wise teachers present to answer questions and provide guidance. The Prentices earned their knowledge—unlike Cailet, who only possessed it because it had been given to her. Because they'd worked hard for it, they had a confidence that she lacked.

And so she prized days like this one, when she didn't have to be Captal. A good time at a village Saint's Day was something she understood. And Heathering put on a wonderful St. Delilah's. Cailet enjoyed every moment of it, right up to the time the young man appeared.

If he wasn't as beautiful as Josselin Mikleine, it was a near thing. If he wasn't quite as tall, or quite as powerfully made, few noticed. Certainly Cailet did not, for the very first thing she noticed about him was his magic.

Raw, untrained, yet neither Wild nor Warded, it sang

from him like shrine bells at dawn. Copper bells, she thought distractedly, watching him in the sword dance; bells she could turn to gold. He was perhaps seventeen, gray-eyed, black-haired, darkly bronzed, and he moved on the torchlit dancing ground with the sudden supple grace of a silverback cat.

He won the competition, of course. And when Cailet had Aidan bring him to her afterward—gripping his prize of a single gold eagle in one hand and his discarded black coif in the other—he looked her straight in the eyes and said, "I didn't win by my magic, Captal."

"I know. What I'm wondering is how you escaped Mageborn notice."

He gave a shrug of lean, muscular shoulders, shifting a too-short, tattered cloak around his body. "It's just something I do. Anyone without a Name learns how, in order to survive."

"Ah. Orphaned, then?"

"In the Rising, as near as I can figure it."

"What do you call yourself, then?"

"Jored. I use the Name Karellos—there are a lot of them in The Waste where I grew up, and I didn't think they'd mind one more."

"Why not Ostin?" Aidan asked, arching a brow. "There's even more of them."

"Lady Lilen keeps close watch on the Name."

Cailet nodded. "And if she'd found another Ostin, of her Blood or not—"

Jored's fine lips tightened. "Everyone knows of her generosity, and I don't take charity. I've worked all my life, with help from nobody. If you accept me at Mage Hall, Captal, I'll work for my keep and my training."

"Oh, you'll work, all right," she said.

All at once he smiled, with happiness and humor and singular sweetness. "You'll have me, truly told? I can become a real Mage Guardian, and not have to fight what's in me anymore because I don't know how to use it?"

"I will, you can, you won't, and you'll learn," Cailet told him, returning his smile. "Come to Mage Hall tomorrow, Jored. You'll join our new group of Prentices."

To her surprise, he gave her a bow as elegant as a

Ryka Court Blood's. "Thank you, Captal. You won't regret it." Extending his open palm, the gold eagle coin gleaming in it, he said, "This is all I have. It's yours, as I am yours."

"What's this?" Aidan asked, amused. "Are you offering the Captal your dowry?"

Jored's long, sculpted jaw went rigid. Cailet shook her head; young men and their pride! "Save it," she advised him. "Or, better yet, go buy yourself a decent cloak. Until you earn a Guardian's, you'll have to keep yourself warm."

After he had gone, Aidan murmured, "He'll rival Josselin for the number of girls offering to keep him warm at night."

"*Two* young, exquisitely beautiful, orphaned Mageborns!" She gave an overdone sigh. "Which of the Saints blessed me with such riches?"

"You could always make them both wear *masked* coifs," Aidan suggested.

"But how would I tell them apart, with only those two sets of gray eyes to go by?"

Much later, back in her own chambers at Mage Hall, she felt a restive stirring from Gorsha. *Don't say it,* she warned.

Are you now reading my *mind?*

I don't have to. We're both thinking the same thing. Which of them is it? She shrugged out of her clothes and into the nightdress Marra had laid out for her.

Does it have to be either? My advice would be to rid yourself of both.

There aren't so many Mageborns in the world that I can afford to lose even one. And neither of them tastes like a Malerrisi in his magic, Gorsha. It may be neither of them.

But you'll keep them both here, and keep an eye on them, as you told Collan.

She turned over in bed so she could see the lamp in the corner. Aloud, as much to herself as to him, she asked, "Am I a fool to keep them both here?"

Not if you're doing it for the right reasons. If it is one *of them, she's had him for eighteen years. No one could undo her work.*

Anniyas undid your work, with my father.

Gorsha said nothing.

"Well?" she asked aloud. "Didn't she?"

You know nothing of Auvry as he was then. All you knew was the man he'd become.

The man the Malerrisi made him? No—I knew him as my father—who loved me.

He made no reply, and at length Cailet went to sleep. Over the years she had become adept at it, no matter what her worries—as long as there was a light burning in her room. And because the worry brought by Josselin Mikleine and Jored Karellos would not go away anytime soon, she figured she might as well get used to it.

18

THEY waited, the three of them, six days past the scheduled meeting. They were inconspicuous in Pinderon: two middle-aged women (though Glenin resisted the adjective; at forty-seven, she looked thirty) and a younger man, travelers on business staying at moderately priced lodgings in a pleasant but not fashionable part of town. When they were not at warehouses and factors' offices arranging accounts and purchasing supplies, they shopped or strolled the beach. They attended morning devotions at Pinderon's St. Tamas Temple on the feast of St. Pierga, three days after their arrival, and left a modest offering in the collection bowl. They were like any other visitors, drawing no attention to themselves and conducting their affairs with a minimum of fuss.

It wore on Glenin's nerves unbearably. At Ambrai, at Ryka Court, and especially at Malerris Castle, her position was the highest, her presence anywhere an honor, and her person deferred to at every turn. She loathed playing the part of an ordinary woman.

And it was no aid to her temper that her son did not keep the prearranged rendezvous.

On the seventh morning of their wait, a letter came to St. Sollian's Hostel. Glenin opened it eagerly while Saris Allard handed the messenger a few cutpieces for his trouble. Chava escorted him to the door, his handsome face managing to express both openness and reserve all at once; it was a trick he'd picked up from his mother, who as Threadkeeper could contemplate the most efficient form of slaughter while laughing at the imminent victim's jokes.

"He's not coming," Glenin said, not bothering to hide her disappointment as she scanned the few scribbled lines. "He can't get away."

"I feared as much," Saris murmured.

"I'm surprised he risked a letter," Chava remarked.

"Oh, he was very clever with it," Glenin told him. "No salutation, no signature but the initial *J,* and your name and that of the hostel for an address, Chava. Your *real* name, not the Tillinshir one."

"I wish I was still there," he fretted. "To keep an eye on him, carry messages, be close by if he needs me."

"He's not a child anymore." Saris smiled. "And I can't think of any circumstance in which his own resourcefulness wouldn't be enough. Besides, you wouldn't even recognize him! You left Malerris Castle while he was still a little boy, and returned after he was gone."

"I'd know him," Chava stated.

"Truly told?" His mother laughed outright. "Not after Glenin and I taught him to hide every single trace of his Malerrisi magic!"

"I wish I'd been able to," he sighed. "I'd still be in Heathering."

"We learned from your mistakes," she soothed. "Thanks to you, we could Ward him perfectly. Isn't that right, Glenin?"

"What? Oh, yes." Glenin paced to the window and looked down at the street. It was good to be back in the world again, even though Pinderon was shockingly crowded and noisy after nineteen placid, quiet years at Malerris Castle. Nineteen years—the length of her son's life plus the spring and summer spent waiting for him to be born. The boisterous street scene below her faded as she remembered those long weeks of pacing the balcony of the Sanctuary Tower, hating the imprisoning iron in its walls but blessing it, too, for the protection it afforded her from prying magic. Now iron had well and truly become her enemy, the bulk of it in Caitiri's Hearth preventing her from watching her son's progress at Mage Hall from Malerris Castle.

She missed him, her beautiful boy now grown to manhood. He'd been under Cailet's tutelage for many long weeks, but their last contact had been long before that. And now he was all alone out in the world, without even Chava nearby in his guise of blacksmith to turn to if he needed help. Damn that bastion of iron ore in the mountains of Brogdenguard, thwarting Glenin's vigilance.

Below her, a street vendor banished from her position outside a wineshop began a raucous diatribe, claiming the wine within was colored kyyo piss. The Watch was called for, but while they waited the locals gathered to listen to some really creative maledictions. Glenin shook her head in disgust. So many people, all dithering their way through their lives without the slightest direction or order—*her* direction, the Great Loom's order. Who knew what they were thinking or saying or doing, or to what purpose their thoughts and words and deeds were put? The horrifying chaos flayed her nerves more than the uproar of their voices. She missed the Castle, the comfort of her chambers, the beauty of the waterfall and the flame-colored roses growing wild on the hillsides, the Working of magic when and as she pleased.

What an appalling place the world was! But she calmed herself with the knowledge that all these gibbering people were unimportant. The worst any of them could do was fray the edges of the tapestry; the grand design was made up of more important threads. Hers; her son's; and, unfortunately, Sarra's and Cailet's.

And those twin children, her niece and nephew. They ought to have been with Cailet by now, learning to be good little Mage Guardians. What ailed Sarra, to keep them with her so long? Didn't she understand that magic had its own demands, and motherhood was the art of acknowledging those requirements for the good of the children—and, ultimately, of Lenfell?

Taigan and Mikel. She remembered them well from the scant time she'd had them in her grip six years ago. Pretty children, and too damned cunning. Their escape had been her own fault, for underestimating them. She ought to have known that the offspring of Sarra Ambrai and Collan Rosvenir would be resourceful little brats.

Glenin tasted that word in her thoughts: *resourceful.* Saris had used it and Glenin had repeated it to describe all three grandchildren of Auvry Feiran. But there was only one true son and grandson of Malerrisi First Lords, and his was the thread that must be protected as it wove itself into the pattern that was Lenfell's future.

She turned abruptly from the window. "Pack our things, Chava," she ordered. "We're going to Roseguard."

The journey was not as impulsive as Saris and Chava obviously thought it to be. Ever since the abortive attempt to seize the twins, Glenin had been postulating various methods of dealing with them. Their personal Wards were formidable; those set around their home and school were nearly as strong. Cailet's Workings were fiercely effective. Plans had been postulated to take advantage of any opportunity that arose, and none of them had any chance of success that would justify the risk. The abortive attempt on Cailet's life and the failed kidnapping proved the wisdom of not twisting the threads awry. Chevasto would provide; Glenin's task was to keep her eyes open for the Saint's intimations.

But the one thing Glenin was certain of was that if *she* could not have Taigan and Mikel, Cailet must not be allowed to have them either.

She had waited, musing and scheming, forced to grudging acknowledgment of one sister's magical skills and the other's maternal vigilance. And that father of theirs—the oddest of all in magical terms, lacking any trace of power but protected by vigorous Wards and his own unruly personality. By the Great Loom, she had reason to know that strength of will, having tried to break it nearly twenty years ago.

When the twins reached Mage Hall, they would be more shielded yet. And Glenin's son was alone, surrounded by the enemy. . . .

Taigan and Mikel must not become Mage Guardians. Negligent of her to leave it this long—but Sarra still showed no signs of giving them up to Cailet. That they were Mageborn was obvious, even Warded from their magic. But they were seventeen this year, and they must go to Cailet soon or the repressed power might wither inside them.

What made it difficult was that Glenin had no intention of killing either of them. Their Magelines were much too valuable. They were Auvry Feiran's grandchildren.

She used her contact in Pinderon—a woman of wealth and high position—to book passage for Roseguard. Her appearance changed: she cut her hair into the short Ambraian style she hadn't worn since childhood, and added a number of rings to her fingers as an obvious indication of status. For her disguise changed as well: instead of two women and a younger man on business for their own family, she became an important Web factor traveling with her assistant and her son.

Chava did not much resemble Glenin—they had height and fair hair in common, nothing more—but he did look quite a bit like his late uncle, Golonet Doriaz. And Chava's eyes were a shade of hazel not too far removed from Glenin's own gray-green. So, poignantly, Glenin pretended he was her own, the offspring of her first and best-loved tutor in magic. The son she might have borne, and would have, had Golonet lived.

The charade would be easier once Chava stopped stuttering over the word "Mother" each time he had to use it for her and not Saris.

They were an obscene amount of time getting to Roseguard. The shipboard accommodations—clean, relatively spacious—were no recompense for the dozen stops they made between Pinderon and Roseguard. All manner of goods were loaded and unloaded; Glenin would have been amazed at the variety of Lenfell's material wealth if she hadn't been so impatient to reach her destination.

Finally, on the last day of Healers Moon, they arrived. Their lodgings in Roseguard were much more agreeable than those in Pinderon—a beautiful old inn on the outskirts of town, with fine antique furnishings and magnificent views of hills to the north and ocean to the west. The innkeeper, a minor scion of the Elgirts, was deferential to start with and positively fawning when she learned who Glenin supposedly worked for. Recommendations about the best restaurants ("Just mention my name") and most stylish shops ("Quite the equal of Ryka Court, our good Lord Collan Rosvenir has seen to *that!*") were capped by an offer to secure tickets to the opening of the new theater.

"Of course, it's been sold out for weeks and weeks, and everyone who's anyone is going, but my cousin is Sevy Vasharron's dresser, and he could probably get you in."

Glenin presumed the name should impress her, and obligingly looked impressed. "'Everyone who's anyone'?" she echoed, wide-eyed, then glanced at Saris, who wore her blandest smile—belying the predatory gleam in her eyes. "It sounds exciting. I would be extremely grateful if your cousin could get tickets for us."

Domna Elgirt beamed with pleasure. "Tomorrow night, then—St. Mittru's Day. I know you'll enjoy it."

Chava tugged at his coif-ties in a show of masculine dismay. "But I don't have anything to wear!"

As it happened, all three of them required appropriate clothes. They had not expected to attend this kind of glittering social event. The afternoon was spent in the pleasurable pursuit of gowns for Glenin and Saris, and a new formal longvest for Chava.

That evening, exhausted and bemused, Glenin confessed to Saris that she hadn't realized how much she missed shopping. "I had my own dressmaker at Ryka Court, naturally, but I still scoured the stores for shoes and gloves and suchlike. I'd forgotten how much fun it could be."

"I'll be on my third bucket of hot water before my

feet forget," Saris observed wryly, wriggling her toes in a steaming basin. "*They* didn't think it was fun at all!"

"But the rest of it was delightful. And revealing," she added thoughtfully, sipping a glass of wine. "Although if I had to listen to that shopboy rattle on one more instant about how Taigan Liwellan searched all over town before finding the perfect color of stockings in *his* inventory, or that Mikel Liwellan will be wearing boots identical to those in *his* window—"

"Quite the little darlings of fashion, aren't they?" Saris drawled. "*Please* tell me I can make the girl spill something sticky down her dress, Glenin, please?"

"I had something much more entertaining in mind."

"Tell!"

Glenin laughed. "Patience, Threadkeeper. I promise you'll enjoy yourself thoroughly."

"I'll hold you to that, Lady Warden!" Then she grew serious. "I don't care what happens to the boy, but would it be possible for Chava to have the girl?"

Glenin took another swallow of wine before she replied coldly, "As his reward for being discovered in Heathering?"

"No," Saris replied forthrightly. "Because he is the last Malerrisi of the Allard line—and the Doriaz, come to it. Besides, it's time I had a granddaughter."

Glenin considered—*Would the child look like* my *Doriaz?*—then shrugged. "Perhaps—after *I* have a granddaughter."

19

THE intended mother of that granddaughter entered the theater on the arm of an adoring young puppy in a green-and-turquoise coif. It was the latest innovation to wear one's Name colors and sigil as prominently as possible. Even former Thirds and Fourths had the right to an emblem—a sundering of tradition enacted by the Assembly only last year. At least the young Halvos escorting Taigan Liwellan had an ancestral Blood claim to the two feathers featured in the embroidery of his longvest—unlike the army of Jaronians in yellow and blue, sporting matching pectoral necklaces of grinning sunburst faces. There were a dozen Agrenirs in various versions of purple and red, their newly minted sigil of crossed scythes a deliberate insult to their cousins, the Grenirians. So was the Wyttes' arrowhead, strongly reminiscent of the Wittes' chevron. The Vasharrons were in red and blue, men and women alike wearing huge gold earrings in the shape of stylized nightingales—a tribute to their most famous son, who was to dedicate the theater this very night with a recital.

Glenin, Saris, and Chava arrived unfashionably early, the better to reach their seats, which were not in any of the boxes but back under the first balcony. The theater was decorated in elegant ash-rose. Four gigantic silver chandeliers dripped crystal, as did sconces along the walls. Over a thousand seats upholstered in cream-colored velvet were arranged in five sections: seriously cheap (second balcony), cheap (first balcony), affordable (where Glenin sat), expensive (first twenty rows), and seriously expensive (the boxes). A velvet curtain like a waterfall of thick cream wove patterns of roses around silver sigils of various artistic Saints. Alilen the Seeker's feather, for singers; Delilah the Dancer's crossed swords; the trumpet flower of Capriel Leatherlungs, whose patronage was wind instruments; Colynna Silverstring's coiled strings; the five bees belonging to Sesilla Honeythroat, patron of choral singers; and Velenne the Bard's lute for actors, poets, and musicians in general.

The choice of St. Mittru's Day for the gala was puzzling, for that Saint had nothing to do with performing arts. Glenin learned from listening to the chatter around her that the original date, St. Alilen's, had been scrapped for two reasons. Sevy Vasharron had another commitment he couldn't break, and Collan Rosvenir had sent back the velvet meant to cover the seats as being closer to the color of curdled milk than sweet cream.

"Pretty," Saris murmured. She'd been conducting

her own inspection. "How much of the performance will we have the chance to enjoy?"

"Let's see." Glenin opened her program and ran a finger down the list of pieces. "Choral excerpts from Falundir's second opera, then a break, followed by Vasharron's recital, then a second break, and then the last act of *Regallata* featuring members of the Roseguard Opera. I think we'll wait for the encores."

Saris nodded agreement. "Standing ovations are nice and noisy. I wonder about the congestion caused by early departures, though." She glanced significantly at the shimmering crowd working its way into the theater, finding seats, apologizing for trodden-on toes.

"Unless things go wrong—and they won't—no one outside the Liwellan box will know anything has happened."

"Even if someone notices, we can depend on Chava to get us safely out."

Chava tapped the program against his knee and shrugged. "I've shouldered and elbowed my way through any number of unbridled herds." He smiled slightly, flexing a few muscles. "Of course, it helps to have enough shoulder and elbow to make it work. The aisles may be a little constricted, but that won't be a problem."

If it came to it, Glenin would use magic to push a path through to an exit and vanish into the streets of Roseguard. Still, she wished she was in one of the boxes. Named for the six Saints who were special patrons of theatrical arts, the boxes sat four in comfort, six with some cramming, ten if they used a crowbar.

The twins had the box named for Colynna Silverstring—purchased, she was sure, in honor of their detestable father. If she lived to be a hundred, she would never forget an instant of her time with Collan Rosvenir. The pair's arrival with their escorts created the polite stir that youth, wealth, position, and beauty always bring. Glenin remembered her own years at Ryka Court. Seated down here with the common ruck, wearing the humble black-and-gray of her assumed Name of Colvos, she lost her excitement at being out in the world again in the annoyance of her circumstances. She should have been in the best box, proudly displaying—ah, but which colors and sigil would she choose? Not Ambrai. She had discarded that long ago. The green and gray and Leaf Crown of the Feiran Name? Or the pure white clothes, gold baldric, and badge of the Great Loom that were her privilege as First Lady of Malerris?

Taigan and Mikel were wearing feathers just as false as her own tonight: Liwellan blue and turquoise. The latter was right for Ambrai, but should have been accented with black. Glenin lifted her rented opera lenses to scrutinize the pair, surprised to see reference to the Rosvenirs in the subtle brocade of the boy's longvest and the girl's full skirts, a silvery gray that cut the brightness of the two shades of blue. It was *not* the current trend to include one's father's Name in one's attire—but Glenin suspected it would be by tomorrow.

Neither was it considered stylish—yet—to wear one's longvest unbuttoned or one's hair down at a formal function. But the boy obviously knew he had a fine body and enjoyed showing it off; the girl knew just as well that her hair was an absolute glory of gold. Chava certainly thought so; he was staring almost slack-jawed upward as Taigan settled into her chair.

Saris poked her son with an elbow. "Compose yourself," she hissed. "In another minute, you'll be drooling."

Mikel displayed perfect manners as he squired a darkly handsome young lady to her seat, draped her shawl across the back of her chair, and perched just behind her to hang on her every word. Glenin sniffed, reminded of her late husband, Garon, in the months before his death, when a spell had been responsible for his fawnings. Mikel seemed in need of no magical urgings to hover around the pretty little Banderiz in her orange and crimson dress. Disgusting, to see a proud young man behave so, and to a former Fourth Tier. Certainly her father would not have been caught dead dancing attendance so on her mother, nor would her mother have wanted him to behave like a flunky. Just then she caught the arch of an eyebrow Taigan directed at her brother, and a barely repressed grin he gave her in reply. So. A game, a social convenience, a show for the watching multitudes. It fit. Glenin had always known that broadsheet reports of Collan Rosvenir's sterling husbandly virtues were greatly exaggerated.

She looked for her own parents in the twins. A hint of Maichen Ambrai's willfulness in the girl's chin, some of Auvry Feiran's arrogance in the set of the boy's shoulders. Glenin saw—vaguely at first, then more definitely as she concentrated—the strong resemblance between Taigan and Cailet, much more pronounced than between the girl and her mother, though Taigan was infinitely prettier. She set the lenses aside and nodded to herself. Wards disguised the likeness, of course. It suited Glenin that the Liwellan whelps went unrecognized for the Ambrais they were. She had her own ideas in that direction.

All at once the house lights dimmed and the stage lights began to glow as if by magic—and magic it was, teasing at Glenin's senses, provided by some cooperative opera enthusiast with a talent for Mage Globes. The audience found it nothing out of the ordinary, which annoyed Glenin even more. That one of her own kind should use her rare and precious gift to convenience the lighting director in a provincial theater—

No, she reminded herself as the curtain rose, *not* one of her own kind. One of *Cailet's* kind. And if ever she had needed a reason to obliterate the Mage Guardians, their own Captal had just provided her with one.

She sat through the first part of the program in frigid silence. She declined to join Saris and Chava in taking a stroll at the intermission. She didn't even look up to the box where her niece and nephew sat. She felt magic swelling, her body and brain scarcely able to contain it.

Patience. Soon. Don't tangle or fray or—Chavasto forfend—break this thread.

When Sevy Vasharron took the stage, she had calmed herself sufficiently to enjoy his performance. He was big, brawny, bearded, with a grin that lit the rafters. His voice had been called the best in five Generations; Glenin, even in her foul mood, had to agree with the critics that he was superb. Through passionate arias and poignant ballads she allowed him to move her spirit. Music was powerful magic. Anniyas had been correct to cripple Falundir. The old Bard was Mageborn, she would've staked Malerris

Castle on it. She'd been there, that St. Tamas's Day of his maiming, and remembered the spell his song had woven. She had learned since that her pity had been misguided. No one with a voice and words and music such as his, with real magic besides, could be allowed to retain their use. He still composed, but had not spoken, sung, or played any instrument in thirty-seven years.

Vasharron's magic was all vocal, but potent enough. Glenin actually felt tears sting her eyes several times during his recital and was very glad when he was done.

During this intermission she again declined to plow through the common hallways, to see and be seen, to overhear idle gossip and drink inferior wine. Instead she prepared herself, hoping that Vasharron, on his return in the final act of *Regallata*, would work his own spells on the audience again. Especially on the pair seated with their escorts in the best box in the theater. Where Glenin and her son ought to have been. Where, one day, they *would* be. Not because it was all that important to them as Malerrisi. Because it was *due* them *as* Malerrisi—and Feirans, and even as Ambrais.

Only let Vasharron do his work, and the other singers as well, and capture the souls of the audience. Whatever Cailet's Wards, Glenin had every confidence she could penetrate them and capture Taigan and Mikel.

For the third and final time the house lights dimmed, and the curtain went up—this time on a scene from Isodir. *Regallata* had no specified setting, and the director had chosen the Iron City to give her an elaborate backdrop of spiraling, curving wrought iron. Glenin supposed it was symbolic of the twisting plot, or something equally artistic and therefore meaningless. Her fears were alleviated when she found—with a little twisting magic of her own—that the "iron" was but painted wood.

The gist of the opera was this: Regallata, a woman whose Fifth-Tier origins are obvious in her hunchbacked ugliness, repays her Blooded patron's kindness with treachery. The Lady has a son whose hopes of marriage to a beautiful and accomplished First Daughter Regallata destroys with rumors in the first act. But the hunchback also has a son—a circumstance utterly against the law—

who, contrary to all logic, is supremely beautiful. This is attributed to his Blood father, whom Regallata drugged into soiling himself and his Name by siring the boy. In the second act, Regallata introduces young Geldar to the Lady, hoping she will fall deeply in love with him, planning to reveal his lowly origins once they are wed. All goes as planned until someone discovers Geldar's true identity as a Fifth. Regallata, seeing her vengeful plot foiled, hires an innkeeper, also a Fifth, to murder the Lady. On the night of the assignation, when the Lady will tell Geldar it is impossible for them to wed, the innkeeper—startled by the noble identity of his visitor—hears her sing of her devotion to Geldar and curse the cruel fact of his tainted heritage. The purity of her love moves him—but fear of reprisal by her Blood Name moves him even more. He decides to renege on the contract.

And so the last act began. Glenin watched the innkeeper—lame, black-toothed, and covered in suppurating pustules that were a triumph of the stagecrafter's art—escort the Blooded Lady to an upstairs room to recover her calm. The innkeeper then sang of how he would keep the Lady alive while collecting his fee from Regallata by giving the hunchback a body in a sack to throw into the river. He decides to kill the next woman who comes in and substitute her for the Lady.

Typical Fifth-Tier, Glenin thought, with the rest of the audience; nothing could compete against the possibility of profit, and to that end he had no qualms about murdering any innocent who happened to walk through the door.

Geldar—played by Vasharron—overhears the innkeeper's plan from just outside. He accosts a young First-Tier woman on the street, wrestles her cloak from her, and shouts at her to run away or lose her life. The audience—shockingly enough—applauded.

Saris whispered in Glenin's ear, "It's not what it seems. The program says the First-Tier is played by a local girl. They're applauding *her*, not what 'Geldar' has done."

While Vasharron silently donned the cloak and girded

himself for death, the innkeeper warbled of the Lady's undoubtedly swift recovery from her infatuation. For comic effect he whistled every sibilant through his teeth, but not even that could amuse Glenin enough to ignore the lyrics.

> *Women are capricious! Fickle and vicious!*
> *First she adores you—then she ignores you!*
> *Trust not a charming face or a fervent embrace!*
> *False tears and falser smiles—young men, beware*
>   *their wiles!*
> *Women are capricious! Volatile and vicious!*
> *First she adores—then she ignores!*

What came next was worse, unless one recalled from the first act that Geldar's Blooded father had been tricked into sleeping with Regallata. It was the only explanation for Geldar's bravery: paternal purity overcame maternal degeneracy. Vasharron entered the deserted taproom and let out a piercing wail when he met the point of the innkeeper's knife.

Regallata burst in, gloating over the body concealed in a canvas sack. The smirking innkeeper collected his money and vanished. Just as the hunchback was about to hoist the corpse over her shoulder for the walk to the river, the Lady began to sing upstairs, bemoaning again her hopeless love. Horrified that her intended victim still lived, Regallata tore at the sack. Beholding her son's dying face, she wept as with his last breath he berated her for breaking the law by bearing him and for breaking the noble Lady's heart.

The cream-colored curtain fell, silver sigils and embroidered roses glistening. The audience applauded until their hands stung. Glenin waited until all of them were on their feet before she summoned her magic and cast it upward.

And smashed into Wards the like of which she had never encountered. A howling engulfed her mind but she did not break off the attack. Mikel—where was he?

Yes—there—more, don't let him evade it—yes! Listen

to him scream, feel his magic begin to shatter—I'll take your mind and magic for my own, boy, and then take your sister to be my son's brood mare—try to fight me, *will you? Pathetic Mage Guardian Wardings—not even the Captal could protect you now, boy!*

But it wasn't the Captal she felt surging up between her and her prey. Every Mageborn in the audience shrieked with agony, yet defied her, battered at her power, deflected it if they could—back toward her—a killing blaze that would sear her very soul if it struck—

Glenin staggered and fell back into her seat. Saris collapsed onto the carpeted floor, writhing; beside her, Chava let out a scream to rival Geldar's, as if he, too, had received a death wound. Others were down—Mageborns, Mage Guardians. Glenin struggled to her feet. Her magic was bruised and lacerated and would not obey her, and she could not see beyond the crushing chaos of the crowd to Taigan and Mikel.

She pulled Saris up from the floor. They had to get out of here, vanish into the terrified throng before a Mage sorted them out from the others and identified their magic as Malerrisi. Chava pushed himself to his feet, wild-eyed. Glenin shook Saris. Her head lolled, her eyes wide open and sightless—as blind to the world as Glenin's injured magic had blinded her mind.

"Go," Chava rasped, picking up his mother's limp form. "We're not important! Go!"

With a final furious glance up at the box, Glenin fled.

20

TAIGAN and Mikel were rushed out of Roseguard that very night.

"As if *we* did something wrong!" Taigan complained—but in a whisper, for even though the streets were nearly deserted in the pre-dawn hours, their mother had ears like a silverback cat. And Sarra was not at present disposed to conversation—especially not her children's.

They'd been given time to change from their formal wear and collect any personal items that would fit into their pockets and small carry-sacks. As they packed, Taguare—visiting on Ministry of Education business from Sleginhold—assured them that the rest of their belongings would be sent later. The hurry was such that Taigan almost forgot her knives and Mikel his lute; their mother nodded curtly on seeing the former, but told Mikel to leave the instrument.

"You can borrow Marra Gorrst's at Mage Hall—*if* you ever have five minutes to spare for music. Come on." And she led them through a secret exit from Roseguard that they'd never dreamed existed, hidden in the old Have-A-Word Room and giving out onto an alley.

Was this what life had been like for their parents during the years before the Rising? Neither dared ask. No one spoke to Sarra Liwellan when she had that look in her eye.

They didn't even pause to sleep the next night. They snatched a few hours' rest during the worst heat of the summer day, which did nothing to assuage the twins' vicious headaches; they had another couple of hours that evening, when Sarra called a halt after Falundir stumbled with weariness on the road he was Folding for them. They hadn't even known he was doing it until dawn on the first day, when they realized that they were very much farther from Roseguard than five hours' walk would account for.

Falundir—*Mageborn?* Taigan's first reaction, whispered to Mikel, was that she'd always suspected something of the sort; he told her she was a rotten liar before it hit him that maybe, after he learned magic, he'd be able to learn music from Falundir *through* that magic.

"But why bring him?" Taigan murmured, casting an amazed glance ahead at the old man. "He's almost eighty, he belongs at home, not tramping across half Sheve!"

"And half Tillinshir," Mikel added. "Maybe Mother doesn't trust any of the other Mages as much as she trusts him."

"Or maybe he made it clear that he was coming along, and that was that."

It seemed likely; neither of their parents ever argued with Falundir, once he made his wishes known. But Taigan and Mikel didn't ask their mother for an explanation. Only their father was equal to asking her anything when this mood was upon her. And their father was away on Minstrelsy business.

Familiar landmarks gave way to country they'd seen only a few times, and then to unknown territory. They'd never traveled like this before in their sheltered young lives: on foot, a Mageborn speeding their way, avoiding all habitation. They felt like hunted animals. After what had happened at the theater, they knew that this was precisely what they were.

At dawn of the fourth day they reached the outskirts of Heathering. A few wagons rolled down the rutted road, bringing fresh produce in to market. Otherwise they saw no one, and Heathering itself—what little they saw of it after detouring by a side path—was uninviting. The summer landscape was just about as grim. Thick willows clustered by several small creeks, but the hillside grasses had gone yellow below the cool green of the pines.

"Pretty desolate," Taigan whispered to Mikel. "How long will we be stuck here?"

"As long as it takes, Taguare says."

"How long *does* it take to become a Mage Guardian?"

All of a sudden it was frightening. They knew they were Mageborns; they knew they would eventually learn how to use their magic. But *eventually* had become *now*.

The gathering sunlight promised a sweltering day. Sarra finally stopped beside a stream and told them to wash. "Taigan, straighten your collar. Mikel, either put your coif back on or comb your hair. I don't intend to present the Captal with a pair of ragged beggars trying to pass themselves off as Liwellans of Roseguard."

Her sharp tone betrayed a nervousness that made them both gulp. Taguare, who had at least talked to them along the way, now behaved as if they didn't exist; he splashed his face, filled his waterskin, and peered into the distance with one scholarly, ink-stained hand shading his eyes. Falundir ignored them even more thoroughly, sinking wearily onto a hummock of brown grass beneath a willow, looking terribly old.

All they knew about what happened was what Taguare had told them—and their own muddled memories of a storm of magic that left them with wrenching headaches. Every other Mageborn in the theater had felt it, Taguare said, and the Mage Guardians had known it for Malerrisi. The Wards they'd individually conjured to protect themselves and Taigan and Mikel had deflected the magic. And if the twins thought *their* heads hurt, they should consider what an assault of that kind had done to Mageborns not personally Warded by the Capital herself.

As for who was responsible—that was a given. One woman had died, identifiable only by the strange necklace she wore beneath her gown: a golden spool on a thin golden chain, marking her as Threadkeeper of the Malerrisi.

"She would've taken you both," their old tutor concluded grimly, "and wound you on her little spool to be woven into the Great Loom—and there's nothing you could do about it."

And so they were going to Mage Hall, to learn how to do something about it if it ever happened again.

But there had to be more to it. More than just self-protection through instruction in the intricacies of magic. They were to be Mage Guardians, weren't they? There must be a place ready for them—with their money and connections and Name, there had to be a special role reserved for them in the Capital's plans for the future.

And their mother's.

But that was the way *Malerrisi* thought. Everyone had a specific function, a prescribed pattern in the Great Loom, no individual choices allowed. You did as you were told: no more, no less. When you failed, your thread was cut from the tapestry. When you succeeded. . . .

What *did* happen when you succeeded?

Nothing. There was no reward for doing what you were supposed to do. All success meant was that the Warden of the Loom and the Master Weaver had done *their* work well. Failure meant that *you* were flawed, not they.

"So what was the point?" Taigan whispered to Mikel as they washed faces and hands. "If victory was taken for granted, and failure was your fault alone, then—"

"Survival, I guess," Mikel ventured. "You do your job, you get to live."

"And if you fail, you end up like the Threadkeeper." Taigan eyed her mother's straight, unyielding, untiring spine. "We're expected to succeed at *this,* you know."

"We're Mageborns. We can do it."

"Of course," she said quickly. "I just wish I knew what else Mother expects of us."

"And Fa," Mikel said moodily, kicking at a stone with a scuffed boot.

"I wonder what he'll think when he finds out what happened."

"Truly told, the Threadkeeper's lucky she died when she did."

"Before Fa got back from Roke Castle, you mean?" Taigan snorted. "What makes you think mother would've let her live that long?" She paused, another idea making her frown. "Do you suppose she really died, Mishka—or was she killed?"

He mulled that over. At length, sending another rock flying with the toe of his boot, he shrugged and said, "From what I know of the Malerrisi, if it was me, I'd kill myself before I let Glenin Feiran get hold of me."

"Why does she want *us?* I mean, we're Mother's children and all, not to mention Mageborn, but why are we so important that she'd try twice to take us?"

"Take us—or kill us?"

Taigan shivered as if the hot sun had vanished in a snowstorm.

Now, following their mother and Falundir and Tagu- are through a gate set in walls festooned with roses, they saw their new home. It was singularly unimpressive. Tai- gan, who'd been to Ambrai with her father and seen the ruins of the Mage Academy from across the river, almost gave voice to her disappointment. Almost.

As they neared, Mage Hall seemed even more bleak.

No roses climbed the brick buildings to soften their stark lines; only a few trees provided shade and greenery. There was an orchard about a quarter of a mile distant, a garden of vegetables and herbs, and a few big clay pots set here and there where some optimist encouraged vines to grow up wooden trellises, but to eyes accustomed to the verdant splendor of Roseguard Grounds, the place was about as dismal as The Waste.

They reached a red-brick archway and paused while Taguare opened the gate. Below, down a long flight of steps, was a courtyard in a natural hollow. Buildings rose on three sides, with breezeways leading from the court elsewhere. Doors and windows appeared at odd intervals; the upper story, really the ground floor, was set back to accommodate an encircling wooden-railed balcony. Sand-colored flagstones paved the whole but for a space around a matriarchal oak tree. A wooden bench circled the base of the trunk; someone had left shallow bowls of seed for the small flock of sparrows. The birds scarcely looked up from breakfast as the five new arrivals descended and walked across the courtyard.

"St. Alilen is with us," Mikel whispered.

"Good, because I *know* we must be crazy," Taigan responded.

"Be quiet," their mother snapped. "Wait here."

She and Falundir and Taguare climbed the side stair, leaving Taigan and Mikel alone. But for sparrow chirps, there wasn't a sound to be heard, not a stirring in the oak's branches. They stood awkwardly beneath the tree, waiting for someone to notice them. It was a new sensation, being ignored—they who had been the center of attention all their young lives.

At last they sensed someone looking at them. It had been several years since they'd last seen her, but the Mage Captal in solid black was unmistakable. She stood at the balcony rail, silent and still and staring down at them with a strange expression on her thin, wide-jawed face.

Taigan cleared her throat, about to speak. The Captal's head tilted slightly to one side; a smile hovered around her lips. She turned then, and went indoors.

It took a moment for Mikel to find his voice. "Teggie . . . do you get the feeling she's been expecting us?"

"How could she?"

He shrugged helplessly. "She's the Captal. Remember when we were little, and were convinced she knew everything?"

"She couldn't know something before it happens."

Recalling the little smile in those black eyes, Mikel wasn't so sure.

21

CAILET wore her habitual black, a choice Sarra deplored despite its traditional association with Mage Guardians. The color was too harsh for her, accenting her sunbleached hair and the depths of her eyes and the pallor beneath her bronzed skin. Moreover, the cut of trousers and shirt was too severe, emphasizing her thinness. Sarra frowned slightly as she accepted a chair just inside the balcony doors; Cailet, recognizing the expression as worry, made a face.

Down below, Prentices had begun to assemble in the shade of the old oak, attending with interest to the woman seated on the bench. She lectured animatedly, with broad gestures and much laughter. Odd; Sarra hadn't thought an education in magic would include humor. Certainly Cailet evidenced little of it, judging by the weary bitterness in her eyes.

Aidan Maurgen served iced fruit juice and set a tray of small cakes on the low table, then left after telling Cailet that the twins were just outside, waiting to be introduced. Sarra waited until the door had closed behind him, then stared her sister straight in the eye.

"Tell me."

"Tell you what?"

"Whatever's bothering you."

Cailet pulled in a long breath, sinking back in her

chair and crossing slim legs at the knees. Sarra sensed a struggle within her between the need to keep her troubles private and the need to share them. All at once Cailet looked directly at her, and looked so much like Taigan that Sarra's heart tore. The same bewilderment came into her daughter's eyes when she'd done everything she thought was right yet still fell short of her goals. Cailet's face was hurt, slightly angry, and deeply puzzled—and in a voice so young and lost that Sarra felt twenty years her senior, she said, "I'm afraid."

Her first impulse was to tell Cailet not to be ridiculous, she'd never been afraid in her life. But the look in black eyes stopped her. She *was* afraid.

"Tell me," she said again, very quietly. "Show me how to help."

"I don't think anybody can. It's—it's like a darkness, gathering around me and—"

"—and *in* you?" Now, that *was* ridiculous. "You're starting at shadows."

"The shadows in me." Cailet rose, walking over to the open balcony doors. Staring down at the lively lesson being taught below, she murmured, "I finally figured out why I'm scared of the dark. It's the echo of what's waiting inside me. It's as if—it's as if they ever meet, the darkness outside and the darkness within, I'll be swallowed up." She glanced over her shoulder and gave a rueful little shrug. "So—I'm afraid."

All at once Sarra wanted Collan, needed his clear-sighted, sardonic common sense. And thinking of the man who had fathered her children, she was less afraid for those children. They were hers—but they were also *his*.

She had Collan. Cailet had no one. *She is so alone,* Sarra told herself, not for the first time. And the loneliness was killing her gentle little sister, despite her magic and her knowledge and the strength of her purpose. Surrounded by the Hall she had built from nothing, working with Mages she had trained and teaching Prentices who reverenced her—still she was utterly alone. Sarra had never understood why—no, that was wrong. She was afraid she understood all too well. Cailet had sacrificed her personal needs to Lenfell's need for a symbol. They'd tried to make her into one years ago—a dead martyr instead of a living Captal. Cailet had escaped the one but embraced the other. What man would look at her and see just Cailet? Sarra had always been suspicious of men who approached her, certain they were interested in her wealth and position, not her. It had taken a long time for her to realize that Collan would have preferred it if she'd been like him: an orphan without a cutpiece to his name. Cailet needed someone like that. But where would she find him?

Perhaps, Sarra thought suddenly, *he* would have to find *her*. But until that happened. . . .

Ah, but now she wouldn't be so thoroughly alone. Taigan and Mikel were family, and Cailet clung very hard to her bonds with Sarra and Collan, with the Ostins and Maurgens. It had long ago been decided that the twins must come to her as students and not as kin, not even knowing what Collan did, that Sarra and Cailet were sisters. But Cailet knew and loved them as family. And Sarra's spirits rose at the thought of her two young, untrained, intuitive, powerful Mageborns—who'd keep Cailet too busy to worry about anything else.

But what would they do, how would they react, when they found out who *they* truly were? Grimly she cleared her mind of speculation. Once they were Mage Guardians, fully adult and able to judge their own hearts and minds, they could be told. Until then. . . .

"You know why I'm here," she said abruptly.

Cailet turned, smiling slightly. "Not exactly. I knew you were coming, but I'm not sure why you're here with them *now*. What happened?"

Sarra described the events at the theater. As she spoke, Cailet's smile vanished.

"I'm sorry, Sarra. I should have known this was coming. Taigan's of childbearing age."

She felt all the blood drain from her face. "Are you saying Glenin would—"

"She planned the same for us, didn't she? Why would she balk at mating your daughter and son to whomever she believes would make the most powerful Mageborn children?"

"Is *that* what you've been sensing?"

A shrug. "I don't know. Probably not."

"Then how did you know we were coming?"

"I *could* say that magic is responsible—but the plain unvarnished truth is that the sentry saw you up by the creek." Suddenly she grinned. "Sorry to disappoint you."

Sarra made a face at her. "Do you always give away your secrets?"

"Only to you. Well, do you think they're nervous enough yet to be properly subdued when they meet me?"

Rising from her chair, Sarra went to open the door into the next room. A few moments later she was watching her children make their bows. Subdued, yes; nervous, certainly; but at least they hadn't forgotten their manners. Further, they met Cailet as Mageborns to Mage Captal: not equals, never that, but like meeting like.

"They've grown a bit," Cailet said at last.

A ridiculous understatement. Mikel was at least a foot taller than when Cailet had last seen him; Taigan had added half as much height; both were young adults now, with manly muscles and womanly curves to prove it. But to Sarra they seemed too young still, far from ready to become Mage Guardians.

Taigan found her voice. "It's good to see you again, Aunt Cailet—"

The Mage Captal arched a brow; Taigan turned crimson and shut up. Sarra marveled, never having suspected anyone but herself capable of quelling Taigan with a single glance.

Mikel interposed smoothly, "We're very glad to be here, Captal."

"Tell me that in a few weeks. Marra will have found someone to show you to your quarters. You have until Eighth to get settled before you're given the grand tour."

Taigan was not accustomed to being summarily dismissed. Her green eyes narrowed fractionally and she opened her mouth to say something else—Sarra would never know what, because Mikel grabbed his sister's arm and hissed, "Teggie, come *on!*"

When the door shut behind them, Cailet burst out laughing. "Wonderful! She's even worse than *you!*"

Sarra grinned back at her. "Why else do we have

children, other than to pass along our most admirable qualities—and hope they surpass us at them?"

22

FOR the first time in all their lives, Taigan and Mikel were not in adjoining rooms. They weren't even in the same wing of the residence building.

Outside the Capital's quarters, Marra Gorrst led them down to the courtyard level and through one of the arched breezeways, where her husband, Aidan Maurgen, joined them. He took charge of Mikel; Taigan went with Marra; they didn't see each other again until lunch.

Not that Mikel didn't try to find his sister. He just got lost on the way.

Aidan didn't say much—unusual for him. He didn't even ask what had happened to bring the twins so precipitously to Mage Hall. Through a bewildering tangle of curving corridors, small courtyards, and spiraling staircases, he pointed out facilities, rattling off identifications Mikel was evidently expected to memorize on the instant. Workrooms, classrooms, kitchens, refectory, storage, library, greenhouse, offices, stables, gardening sheds, infirmary, chambers and offices belonging to the Archivist, Master Healer, First Sword, and Capital's Warders. The only thing Mikel swore he'd recall was the route to the refectory; he was starving.

His room turned out to be a cubicle on the second floor of the men's quarters. There was a bed without a headboard (let alone posts and hangings), a chair without a pillow, a desk without so much as a pen on it, and a window without a curtain. The bath was down the hall, shared with nine other students. Aidan helped him stow his few possessions in the wardrobe, gave him a schedule of Prentice classes, and told him someone would come by soon with sheets and blankets for the bed.

Responsibility to a new student done with, Aidan relaxed and grinned. "You ready for all this?"

If Mikel said *No,* he'd sound like a coward. If he said *Yes,* he'd sound like a fool. Either way, Aidan would probably laugh at him. He chose instead to say, "All *what?*"

Aidan laughed anyhow. "You'll find out."

"Any general rules I should know about?" he asked casually.

"Such as?"

"Whatever's not on this sheet." He gestured to the page on the desk.

"You'll get the feel of things soon enough."

"I just don't want to do anything glaringly offensive."

"You'll be all right."

Mikel decided he was really looking forward to the day when he was a Mage Guardian and could give evasive answers to frustrate the uninitiated. Immediately following this thought he was more confused than ever: Aidan was no more Mageborn than any other Maurgen. Mikel supposed, sourly, that it was something contagious in the water.

"I'll leave you to settle in. You had a long walk from Roseguard." Aidan patted his arm companionably. "Don't worry, Mikel. You'll do just fine here."

But when Aidan was gone, and Mikel sat on the unmade bed staring out the uncurtained window at the uninspiring view of yellow-brown grass, he wondered how well he'd do until the Wards protecting him from his own magic were unWorked. And by the Captal herself, who had set them in the first place. He'd tried to explore his own mind, prodding memories and things he supposed were at least partly magical, but he figured it might be like tone-deafness: if you didn't know what a note sounded like, how could you tell if it was on key or not? Which was a stupid analogy for someone with perfect pitch, but it was the best he could come up with.

Well, he'd find out soon enough, he supposed. As he waited for the bedclothes to arrive, he looked over the page he'd been given. Closely printed in the new, simplified typeface designed by Archivist Lirenza Gorrst, it listed all the teaching Mages in residence, the classes they taught, the rooms they taught them in, and their office hours. Aidan had said there were thirty-four Prentices at various levels of training, not counting Mikel and Taigan; counting, he found there were twenty-seven teachers, and whistled. That was an amazing ratio of Prentice to teacher. But further perusal showed him a little mark beside twelve names, and a sentence at the bottom of the page that said these people were themselves in training as teachers—presumably to take their knowledge (not just of magic, Mikel guessed) out into Lenfell at large.

He recalled having seen quite a few elderly Mage Guardians; these were listed below the teachers, with the notation that they were retired from active service. How did a Mage retire? he wondered. It wasn't like a singer, compelled to forsake the stage when the voice went. Magic was lifelong. But he supposed that the thirty or so antiques living here had no families to give them house room, or for one reason or another had chosen to live at Mage Hall instead.

The thought of families gave him pause—he'd seen no children, and no one who wasn't wearing the solid black of a Mage Guardian or the buff-colored shirt and black trousers of a Prentice. Another look at the page gave him the names of a cook (a Calorros from Tillinshir; there hadn't been a Mageborn Calorros since they'd nearly been wiped out in The Waste War), an art teacher (a Hathwy with a Certificate from the Firrense Institute— Mikel was impressed), and about twenty other women and men without duties attached to their names whom he assumed were married to Mages. And married couples inevitably meant children—he figured they were in schoolrooms someplace around here. Would all of them be Mageborn? He doubted it. And it occurred to him that Aidan wasn't completely alone here, remembering that Lady Sefana had expressed her worries about that to Mother years ago. Tone-deaf in a community full of accomplished musicians; Mikel shook his head, knowing he would never have been able to do it.

No sheets or blankets or Prentice's garb arrived by

the time Mikel had memorized the names and classes and
general guidelines for life at Mage Hall (he was assigned
bathroom clean-up every other day). Bored, he decided to
go find Taigan.

It felt peculiar, not being right next door to her. They
didn't have the kind of rapport identical twins were said
to have—knowing even at a thousand miles what the
other was thinking and feeling, that sort of thing—but
he'd always had a special awareness of her that seemed to
depend on proximity. At Roseguard he took it for granted;
Mage Hall was about the same size as the Residence, but
right now he couldn't sense her at all. Maybe it was all
the magic in the air—magic he couldn't yet feel as anything more than a vaguely annoying tickle somewhere
deep in his head.

Still, he ought to be able to find her. He always could
at home, even when she didn't want to be found. So he
wandered the corridors and courtyards and stairways, and
within five minutes was thoroughly lost.

In the time it had taken to meet the Captal, be shown
his room, and unpack, Mage Hall had woken and break-
fasted. Now the cleaning duties of the day had begun:
making beds, scrubbing bathrooms, sweeping flagstones.
Mikel was amazed that there were no servants—though
Aidan had said something about the new cook, a professional hired away from a minor college in Shainkroth in
the never-ending (and futile, as far as Mikel could tell)
attempt to put some flesh on the Captal's skinny bones.

Mikel roamed the maze, puzzled when he saw black-
clad Mages working at every imaginable task. He could
understand that students would be expected to take care
of their rooms and belongings—it was like that at all the
residential colleges he'd heard about. But that Mage
Guardians would be assigned to tend the kitchen garden,
mend a saddle, repair a wobbly table, rebind a book, put
up preserved fruits—

Then he realized that all these people had had trades
and crafts before they'd ever come to Mage Hall, and contributed their talents as needed.

And his own talents? He stood in a courtyard shadow
watching a young woman grind dried herbs into powder

for medicine, and writhed inwardly. Mikel Liwellan, pampered and protected son of a Councillor, could contribute nothing more useful than music.

He *really* needed to talk to Taigan. She was as new and useless here as he was. He meandered around, completely disoriented. Chances were Taigan had left her room, too, and was exploring. He hoped ruefully that she was doing better than he was.

The oddest part was that nobody said anything to him. Not a word. A few people smiled or nodded, and everyone seemed friendly enough, but nobody talked to him. He wasn't quite invisible, but near enough to set his teeth on edge.

He felt like an interloper. At least those who'd come here before him had *felt* their magic. His was locked away. Until it was released, he was on the same footing with Aidan Maurgen and the cook. And he didn't like it much.

"No need to stand there like a tourist," a woman's voice said from inside a dimly lighted room. "Come on in."

Mikel gave a start, then accepted the invitation and stepped inside the doorway. Manners asserted themselves, and he bowed to the middle-aged Mage Guardian. She was seated on a tall stool near a high table, one foot tucked casually under her, the other long leg dangling. Around her trim waist was a red sash that marked her as a Warrior Mage, and gleaming from her collar were two silver pins, Sword and Candle.

"You're Mikel Liwellan," she went on. "Want to know how I could tell?"

He sighed. "I look like a lost puppy?"

She laughed heartily. "Well, there is that. No, what really gave you away is that hair and that very elegant bow—both of which came from Collan Rosvenir. Sit down, Mikel. Soon you'll be in this very room, mangling your work like these two. This is Ollia, and that's Joss."

Now that his eyes had adjusted, Mikel saw the students—one an attractive young woman with startling turquoise eyes, the other a devastatingly handsome young man. Neither was past twenty, and one was familiar. The impossibly beautiful face was just the same, except for a slight irregularity in the bridge of his nose—barely noticeable, but bearing mute witness to a collision with something less yielding than itself.

"Josselin Mikleine?" Mikel asked with a tentative smile.

The young man nodded, pleased to be recognized—which was ridiculous, because who could ever forget that face? Or was it the face Mikel and Taigan had both forgotten, the face of the Malerrisi who'd brought them that box?

No; couldn't be. The Captal would never have taken him for training if he was anything other than what he appeared to be: a Mageborn who'd discovered it later than most, and was working hard to catch up.

Josselin said, "Nice to see you. Did Lady Sarra come with you? I'd like to thank her again for sending me here."

"*I'd* like to know why she ever thought it would do any good!" the Warrior grumbled. "Don't sit too close to him, Mikel, his Mage Globes have a tendency to explode."

Josselin sighed dismally. The other student nudged him with an elbow, her whimsical smile including Mikel as she said, "We all singe our fingers—but Joss's mistakes are truly spectacular!"

"This," said their teacher, "from the girl who's been working on the same Globe spell for six weeks!"

"Please, Imi, don't remind me!" she moaned, clutching distractedly at reddish-brown curls.

"Imi"? Holy St. Delilah—that's Imilial Gorrst—the First Sword! Mikel nearly made another bow, much deeper and more profound than the original, but caught himself in time. From all he'd heard of her, and from what she'd said when he came in, she'd only start teasing him again.

Then something else occurred to him: that neither student was the slightest bit awed by their teacher, even if she'd been a Warrior Mage for nearly forty years and First Sword for about as long as they'd been alive. He decided he liked that; nobody around Roseguard called his mother

"Lady Sarra" or his father "Lord Collan" unless a guest required impressing. Mikel, until his Wards were un-Worked, was a guest, but nobody was trying to impress him.

Then again, he thought as Ollia began conjuring another Mage Globe in the dimness of the workroom, he'd walked into the place pretty much overwhelmed from the start. They didn't *need* to impress him.

He was about to excuse himself to go get even more lost when Ollia's Mage Globe took on a crimson hue, minuscule bolts of silvery lightning dancing across its surface.

"I've got it," she breathed. "It's done."

Imilial Gorrst nodded. "You hear that? She *knows.*" Hopping off the stool, she strode to the center of the room and in an eyeblink conjured a red-fire Globe of her own. "All right, let's see what you've got."

Mikel stepped back a pace, then another. Josselin stayed where he was, watching in avid fascination as the two women faced off.

"What—?" was all Mikel could whisper.

"Watch," Josselin whispered back. "Ollie's going to be a Warrior Mage, like almost all the Bekkes. This is her first real Battle Globe, and—well, you'll see."

He did.

He saw the crimson spheres approach each other: slowly, warily, with a low humming that was magic in his mind, not music in his ears. Imilial Gorrst stood casually balanced, confidence in every line of her. Ollia Bekke poised tense and trembling, and with the first lick of blood-colored lightning from her Globe a slick of sweat shone on her brow. The other Globe caught the flare, absorbed it silently, pulsed—then shot a fist-sized yellow fireball in response. Ollia caught her breath and bit both lips together as the attack struck her Globe with a sound like a ringing bell, but she and her conjuring held firm. The miniature sun blazed briefly, then disintegrated into chiming tendrils of energy that enveloped Ollia's Battle Globe. She gasped again, sweat dripping in her eyes, and after a moment the golden sparks died.

"Conceded," said the First Sword. "Take it back."

Ollia held out both hands. The Globe drifted to hover between her cupped palms. She cradled the ruby glow, then slowly brought her hands together. The sphere vanished.

Imilial Gorrst did the same, a stately ritual that ended with the participants exchanging bows in the sudden gloom. "Very good, Ollia. Very good indeed. You're ready for the Captal."

Ollia Bekke straightened proudly. "I'll go tell her."

The Warrior Mage hooked her thumbs in her sash, dark eyes dancing. "She already knows, girl. She already knows."

Ollia faltered slightly, then gulped and nodded. Mikel stared at her, then at Imilial Gorrst, then at Josselin—who was smiling as if he'd known, too. Recovering herself, Ollia left the workshop, fingers curled at her sides as if the feel of the Battle Globe lingered within her palms.

During the short silence that followed, Mikel met the First Sword's eyes again, trying to find words enough to ask a question. Imilial Gorrst shook her head, smiling. "Someday," she murmured.

His cheeks grew hot at the gentle reminder of how young he was. But someday in the future there would be a moment like this for him, too. He'd been born to it.

Josselin gave him a sympathetic look. "I know how you feel."

"It was—" Mikel struggled with it. "It was beautiful—so much power—"

"And deadly," said Imilial Gorrst. "Never forget that. A beautiful glow against the darkness and violence—but it can swallow your soul if you use it unwisely. Remember that."

Mikel fought confusion. How could something so alive with beauty be a danger to him? How could that powerful song turn into a death-chant for a Mage Guardian's soul? It made no sense to him. All he knew was that he wanted to create light and magic and soundless music of his own. He curled his fingers into his empty palms.

And then he remembered the Malerrisi, and the box, and the attack that had been no attack—and the blood on his hands when he took Taigan's knife from a man's belly. That beautiful Rosvenir knife, shining and powerful and deadly.

The First Sword was nodding slowly, as if she knew every thought in his head. "Go on, go find your sister. You'll have a lot of talking to do." Then she turned to Josselin. "Meantime, you can explain to me why you can see what Ollie did, understand it, even *feel* it—and be completely incapable of duplicating her achievement."

Mikel tactfully departed as the First Sword renewed her affectionate abuse of Josselin's training, talents, and tenacity. He walked through the corridors in a daze, even more profoundly lost now and not caring a bit as his fists clenched around emptiness, and he swore that one day he *would* feel the magic glisten and sing between his hands.

23

TAIGAN'S room in the women's wing was spare and plain. The window faced north—always the most undesirable for lighting and warmth, which irked her mightily. The view was of a few dull trees across summer-dun hills and, beyond, the pointed green tip of St. Lirance's copper-clad belltower in the otherwise invisible town of Heathering. Marra Gorrst watched her like a hawk, obviously expecting disparaging remarks—especially when the shared-bathroom arrangement was described. Taigan simply nodded. She wasn't here on holiday, after all. She was here to become a Mage Guardian. And the sooner her Wards were unWorked and the process began, the happier she'd be.

When Marra left her alone to unpack (a task occupying three whole minutes), she took time only to change into a fresh shirt and brush the dust off her boots before leaving her tiny chamber to explore. Unlike Mikel, she didn't get lost. But she didn't learn anything interesting either—not until the early afternoon.

She joined her brother and the rest of the community

for lunch in the refectory. Neither her mother nor the Mage Captal attended, which surprised her not at all. They were old friends, and probably had a lot of talking to do—mainly about Taigan and Mikel. The twelve long trestle tables were packed with Mage Guardians and Prentices, chattering and laughing and teasing and discussing the morning's lessons and chores. But for the age of some of the senior Mages, it was like any other refectory at any other college on Lenfell (with the exception of St. Senasto's, where aspiring votaries were educated in almost total silence). There were even patron Saints painted on the walls—direct copies of the ones on the walls of Firrense, Taigan noted, and done very well, too. Miryenne with her lighted candle and Rilla with her white sparrow were obvious. She recognized Mikellan, of course, source of her brother's name: a blond young man climbing a ladder. Delilah was there, too—she who had been a Mage Guardian in life—and Caitiri at her forge, plainly in tribute to the Captal. But Gorynel? Oh, of course; a reference to the famous First Sword. That explained Elinar Longsight and Lusine as well, for the last two Captals, Leninor Garvedian and Lusath Adennos. Deiket was for the Scholar Mages, she supposed, just as Delilah was for the Warriors and Fielto for the Healers—and Steen Swordsworn must be for the Captal's Warders.

The Mage Guardians certainly laid claim to a lot of Saintly protection, she told herself as she sat beside Mikel and waited for the food to be served. A young man came to their table with huge platters of bread, cheese, and sliced beef; another with pitchers of water and lemonade; yet another with a bowl of sliced raw vegetables. Simple fare, simply served. Taigan wondered if the evening tradition of candles and flowers held here, and decided it couldn't. There were too many people, too many tables, and too much chance of hot food going cold.

A young woman with reddish-brown hair introduced herself to Taigan; Mikel had evidently met Ollia Bekke already, and plied her with questions about how one became a Warrior Mage. Taigan listened with half an ear, wondering if her brother really intended that specialization or whether he just found the girl pretty. Probably the latter; he wasn't the soldierly type. That led her to consider the ins and outs of personal attachments at Mage Hall. All these people living in a small community for years at a time—there had to be flirtations and love affairs and marriages. And babies; she saw several women in various stages of pregnancy.

Taigan was interested in children and marriage—most girls her age were, especially those as eligible as she. While making polite smalltalk with the others at the table, she considered again her musings of the past four days on the road. She would reach her majority next year and become a Mage Guardian thereafter (though just how soon thereafter was unclear), and she'd realized long before the long walk from Roseguard that her husband would have to come from the ranks of Mage Guardians.

She'd analyzed it all quite coolly. Not many families could rival hers in wealth, which narrowed her choice from the start. She had no intention of marrying a man who must needs be utterly subservient to her because he must utterly depend on her for his needs. Her father had his own money, spent as he liked; she had seen and liked the difference that made in her parents' marriage compared to those of her friends' parents. Mili Berekard's father, for instance, had brought the usual huge Krestos dowry from his family's paper mills, but hadn't a cutpiece to spend without permission. He hopped to whenever Mili's mother cleared her throat.

As for eligible Mageborns—that list was even shorter. But neither did she want a man who couldn't share magic with her. Finding someone rich, independent, *and* Mageborn would be difficult, but she also knew that two Mageborns had a better chance of producing Mageborn children—and whatever this thing was that had been Warded up inside her, however it expressed itself, she wanted her offspring to have it as well. It was like inherited wealth: if one had it, one had a duty to pass it along.

As for where love came into it—well, she'd grown up observing several passionate marriages in detail, and saw no reason why she shouldn't find the same emotional and physical satisfaction. Her parents; Tarise and Rillan; Riena and Jeymi; Miram and Riddon; Lindren and

Biron—oh yes, she'd seen it many times. She wanted the same thing for herself, and sooner or later she'd find a rich, handsome, intelligent, charming, well-mannered, kind, loving, witty, accomplished young Mageborn man to provide it. Granted, her list of desirable attributes was somewhat lengthy, but if she had exacting standards it was hardly her fault. All the husbands she knew were most of those things.

And she saw none of them in complete combination in either of the young male Prentices at her table. They were nice enough, but not to her taste. Glancing over at Ollia Bekke, she realized for the first time that what applied to herself must also apply to Mikel. He would husband a Mage Guardian. She eyed her brother critically, deciding that he had the looks, charm, and wit—St. Tirreiz knew he had the dowry!—to catch any woman he wanted. But all at once the thought of him as a father to Mageborn children (to *any* children, for that matter) made her giggle under her breath. Imagining Mikel as a husband was stretch enough; picturing him with three or four little carpet-crawlers throwing up on his boots was too funny.

The youth opposite her, believing he had scored with his latest joke, beamed in pleasure and enjoyed the chagrin of his companion. Taigan didn't even notice.

She did notice when a dessert of cookies and fresh fruit was brought around to the table. She had a sweettooth, inherited from her mother, but the chocolate triumph of the baker's art interested her not at all. The young man carrying the platter did.

He was a year or two older than she, tall and broadshouldered, the rest of his body hidden by a loose smock that kept his clothes clean of kitchen spills. His face was quietly handsome—not spectacular like Josselin Mikleine's, and all the more attractive for it to Taigan's way of thinking. (She had never forgiven Josselin—or herself—for her reaction at first sight of him in Roseguard.) The young man's nose was straight and proud, his eyes slate-gray with flashes of silver, his mouth finely made, his skin deeply tanned. Thick black hair waved smoothly back from his brow and curled over his collar.

(No coifs at Mage Hall; Mikel would appreciate that.) He set the platter at the head of the table, looked up, and met Taigan's eyes in a long, assessing look that came close to making her blush. The Prentice across from her said something; the young man nodded a greeting but did not speak, and after a sidelong glance at Taigan returned to the kitchen.

She felt as if a Clydie stallion had stomped on her chest. With all four split-toed hooves. Shod. Maybe in iron spikes. Not that it hurt, exactly; she just couldn't breathe very well. She wished she'd taken the time to brush her hair. She wished she'd worn the green shirt that set off her eyes. She wished she'd heard his name.

She wished she could start breathing again without this catch in her throat.

After the meal, she sought him out. She roamed Mage Hall looking for black hair and gray eyes. She thought she saw him once—but it was only Josselin Mikleine, too tall and too dark, with hair that curled too much.

He appeared from nowhere in the main courtyard as Taigan paused beneath the oak tree. The kitchen smock was gone. Abruptly confronted with the outlines of a lean, supple body, all she could think was that compared to him, Josselin was as crudely muscled as a blacksmith's overworked apprentice.

"Good day, Lady Taigan," the young man said, and his voice was velvet vowels and silken consonants. "Are you pleased with what you find here?"

She wanted to sink into the flagstoned walk, for though the words ostensibly referred to Mage Hall, she knew he was politely rebuking her for staring. She felt unbearably stupid and hideously young. But as she met those silver-shot eyes, she realized that he was as interested in her as she was in him. Confidence came back—enough, anyhow, for her to say, "I've been promised a tour. Would you care to show me around?"

"I have duties until sunset, but perhaps after dinner."

"I'll meet you here."

He nodded, and a lock of thick hair fell forward over his eyes. He swept it back with a careless hand—the fingers long and powerful and sensitive. "Your mother, Lady Sarra—she's very beautiful." A slight pause, and the gray eyes looked anywhere but at Taigan as he added, "You favor her."

The horse stomped on her chest again.

He paused, then shook his head as if he'd said too much. "Until later, Lady Taigan."

"Please—just my name." She didn't know she would say it until the words left her mouth.

Her reward was her first sight of his smile: a glory of generous lips and straight white teeth and bright eyes and a warmth that reached right into her vitals.

"Thank you. I'm honored." He bowed and vanished through one of the breezeway arches.

Taigan watched him go, and it was a full two minutes before she realized she still didn't know his name.

She and Mikel got the grand tour that afternoon. That evening they were privileged to dine with their mother, Falundir, Taguare, and the Captal in the latter's quarters. Taigan didn't eat much.

"Too excited to appreciate the cooking?" Taguare teased. "Well, it won't hurt you. But try to get some sleep tonight. You'll need it."

She met the young man in the courtyard after dinner, as arranged. His arrival was announced as much by the sudden lurch in Taigan's chest as by the whisper of his footsteps.

"Is there anything special you'd like to show me?" she managed. "I've seen everything now—all the rooms that weren't in use, I mean, where we'd disturb people at work." She was babbling—she, First Daughter of a Councillor, offspring of a Minstrel, both with a talent for words that suddenly seemed to be the very last thing Taigan had inherited.

"Special?" he echoed, then nodded and smiled. "This way."

The Ladymoon, five days past full, was the only illumination in the long, lofty chamber to which he took her. Upstairs from the Oak Court, cool white light spilled through a wall of open windows onto a glossy tiled floor, leaving the barrel-vaulted ceiling in shadow. There were no furnishings and no decorations—not even carving on the doors or chiseled patterns on the stone arching high overhead. The only adornment was the central design of the tiles, and Taigan walked forward to inspect it.

From the black floor all around, silver tiles outlined a square twenty feet on each side, with its corners at the cardinal points of the compass. Diagonals formed four equal triangles. Four more triangles, equal to each other but not to those in the center square, projected outward with their apexes at the compass midpoints. The whole formed an octagon in silver on black. As Taigan bent to touch the smoothly perfect ceramic, she noticed close-to what moonlight washed out at even a few steps' remove: a single tile in the very center of the square was black, painted with three interlocking octagons—green, gray, and red. *Healer, Scholar, and Warrior Mages,* she thought to herself, nodding. After the meager attention to architecture and decoration in the rest of the complex, at last she'd found a place worthy of Mage Guardians.

"Beautiful," she whispered, glancing over her shoulder as she stood upright. The room *and* the man—but he didn't seem to notice her double meaning.

"This is the place we enter as Prentices," he said softly, "and emerge as Mages."

"What happens?"

"No one ever says. It's just Prentice and Captal, for anywhere from a few minutes to several hours." He walked to the middle of the room, moonlight flooding his body. "After comes the Listing, with due ceremony before everyone. But that's only a formality, after this."

"Will it come soon for you?"

He shook his head, smiling again. "I'm a slow learner."

"I'm glad." Hearing how that sounded, she felt her cheeks burn. "I mean, I'm not *glad,* not that you won't become a Mage soon, but that you'll be here a while, so we can get to be friends, maybe." Saints, she was stammering like a fifteen-year-old at her first tea social.

"I'd like that," he replied. "But perhaps you need to know my name before we can start being friends."

She waited for him to offer his name, and when he

didn't immediately do so, she couldn't even think up words to ask him. This was insane. She was rich and important; the brains her parents had bequeathed her, she knew how to use; she was pretty and amusing and everyone said she was too clever by half; she was more than accustomed to roomfuls of good-looking young men competing for her attention.

So why couldn't she ask a simple question?

"I'm Jored Karellos."

"Jored," she repeated idiotically.

"It's from St. Jiorto Silverhelm."

"Patron of armorers," she supplied automatically, and he gave her a half-smile.

"I hope it's appropriate—I'd like to be a Warrior Mage someday. Though I've no idea what my mother meant by naming me that."

"Didn't she tell you?"

"I never knew her. I was orphaned shortly after my birth."

"Oh. I'm sorry."

"The Karellos Name took me in—I'm not really one of them, but Lady Lilen Ostin's example in adopting strays like me is widely admired in The Waste." He shrugged. "Everybody takes in at least one, just so they can say they did."

"You're from The Waste?"

"Probably. During the Rising there was a lot of confusion, a lot of refugees. I don't know where I was born. One of the Equinoxes of 969 is all I know about the date."

"Like Josselin."

"Yes. He and I have quite a bit in common." Jored smiled again, and her heart heeled over. "People around here sometimes refer to us as 'The Twins,' like the two Adennos girls."

"I met them this afternoon."

He nodded. "But now there's a *real* pair of twins here—you're the first, you know, you and your brother."

"Are we?"

"Mageborns are rare enough. But *twin* Mageborns—especially as powerful as you are—"

Taigan blinked. "Are we?" Saints and Wraiths, she was a scintillating conversationalist tonight.

"Oh, yes. I can sense it in you. And a little bit in your mother."

"She's the one we get it from. I kind of think it comes from my father, too, except that everybody says he isn't—but I don't know, music is a kind of magic, isn't it? And he was Warded a long time ago by Gorynel Desse, before the Rising when he and my mother and the Captal defeated Anniyas and Glenin Feiran together, and—" Aware that she was not only babbling but bragging, she shut up.

"Your parents are remarkable people," Jored said. Then he turned his head toward the door. "Someone's coming."

"I don't hear anything."

"I do." He escorted her to the door, closed it behind them, and bowed slightly. "Good night, Taigan. I enjoyed our talk. If it pleases you, I *would* like us to become friends."

She managed to nod. Jored melted into the darkness of the hallway, and Taigan went to her tiny chamber—and slept, incredibly enough, as soundly as a stone.

24

"STAY another day," Cailet urged.

She and Sarra had hiked up to a glade on the banks of Willowfall Creek, where she and Collan had gone the day after her exhausting work with Toman. Cailet was determined not to think about the boy, and how she'd almost botched the whole job. The day was too fine for thinking about anything but the grass, the sky, the cool water, and the lavish picnic lunch the cook had prepared.

The sisters had spent the morning discussing everything from current politics to what the twins would learn in the next several years. Then Aidan had flung open Cailet's office doors and banished them outside with a grin and a laden hamper of food. The sunlit climb had refreshed them both, clearing out thc tangle of concerns, but in the heat the cool shadows of the willows and oaks were more than welcome.

"I should go back," Sarra replied.

Cailet crouched beside the creek and scooped up a handful of water. Shc looked into it for a time, seeing the lines and sword-calluses of her palms through clear liquid. She'd been born with the creases; the calluses, she had earned. But though her hands were marked, they were never filled.

"You should stay."

"I need to be at Ryka Court."

"You need what's here."

Sarra paused, the basket half-unpacked around her on the grass. After a moment she said slowly, "You've never asked that of me before. Why now?"

"Just what I said. You need to learn—"

"It's too late for me, Cai. Let my children do it. Don't try to make a Mage Guardian of me, too."

"As you wish." She let the water trickle from her fingers.

"There's no time for it. You have to see that. There's never been enough time."

"I can't keep you here if you don't want to stay."

"You're the Mage, not I. It's not necessary for me to learn magic."

Cailet looked sidelong at her. Despite the words, the conflict was there in Sarra's black eyes: she knew enough to want to know more, yet she feared the knowledge. Cailet understood that only too well. But if Sarra had no access to her magic, if she had no idea how to use it, she would be helpless in the face of what Cailet knew was coming. If only she'd stay just a little while, learn just a little. . . .

Cailet could not compel her to stay. She couldn't shape her sister's destiny to her own will. That was one of the hardest lessons of being Mageborn, of being the Captal, and one of the most insidious darknesses inside her. Cailet knew she could have arranged Sarra's continued presence here; the *Code of Malerris* provided several methods. But she refused to exert that influence, even for Sarra's own good.

So I'm helpless to prepare Sarra for what Glenin will surely do soon—and Sarra will be helpless to defend herself. Ah, but when was "helpless" a word to be used about this woman? She has more strength than anyone I know. Whatever comes, whatever happens, Sarra will survive it—probably even thrive on it. Don't you think so, Gorsha?

But he remained silent.

"I didn't mean to hurt you," Sarra said softly. "I know you want to help, but there's no time, Caisha. And, truly told, no need. But I *would* like to see you at work, sit in on a class tomorrow, if that's all right."

"If you'd like, then tomorrow morning at first light you can watch something very special. I think you'll find it interesting."

"What?"

She grinned. "That's a secret I'll keep to myself for now." She scooted over on the grass to help unload the food—cold spicy chicken, marinated vegetables, bread, three kinds of cheese, and a salad of rice, nuts, and apples. There were bunches of crimson grapes and paper-wrapped chocolates for dessert, and to wash it all down the sweetest, coldest water in all Tillinshir right to hand. Sarra laughed when Cailet produced a pair of crystal goblets to drink from.

"Aidan takes very elegant care of you!"

"He and Marra try, anyway," she replied with a shrug. "I don't really have the right instincts. But we've made improvements over the years. We're not quite camping out, the way we used to." She gestured to the sprawling buildings below, barely visible through the trees.

"I was right about the roses. Was I right about Josselin Mikleine as well?"

"You know you were." *And I hope to all the Saints that I'm wrong about him, and about Jored, too—but I can't be wrong about both, if not one then the other—unless I'm completely wrong about all of it.*

Sarra tore off a hunk of bread, munched, swallowed,

and said, "How does he get the roses to grow so fast? I only sent them—what, last summer?"

"Magic," Cailet teased. "The oak in the courtyard grew two feet last week."

She made a face. "Very funny, little sister."

They ate every scrap of lunch, then sat licking chocolate from sticky fingers like a pair of six-year-olds. Afterward, both sat beside the stream, boots and stockings off, to dangle their feet in the cold, clear water. Cailet hated to bring the rest of the world back into their tiny corner of it, but eventually she had to ask.

"How's the Dombur situation shaping up in the Council?"

Sarra lay back flat on the grass, sighing. "Do you want the long version or the short?"

"I already know the latter. Vellerin Dombur is setting herself up to be the next Grand Duchess of Domburronshir."

Sarra squinted sideways at her. "Now, how did you figure *that* out? All she's done so far is decline to run for a Council seat."

"Why should she bother? Her close cousin is the leading candidate to replace poor old Isibet Omarra."

"Any word on whether that accident *was* an accident?"

"Nothing to indicate otherwise. After all, one does take a few risks when one insists on climbing mountains at the age of seventy-three."

"So how did you know about Vellerin's ambitions?"

"I have a contact at Census. She wasn't sure at first, so I only heard about it recently, but all winter she's been getting seemingly unrelated requests for official Dombur documents—none of them traceable back to the good Mayor of Domburron, of course. But you stack them all on top of each other in order, and you've got their family history back to Veller Ganfallin."

"It's absurd," Sarra declared. "As if someone who died over two hundred years ago has any bearing on what her descendants are today!"

"You can say that—you're a Blood," Cailet responded wryly.

"So are you."

"No, I'm Third Tier, and I know what it means to have people who lived *eight* hundred years ago determine your place in the social structure."

"Not anymore," Sarra said stubbornly.

Cailet let it go. Shrewd as her sister was, to some things she was blind.

"And anyway," Sarra went on, "all the children of the so-called Grand Duchess died or were executed." When Cailet made no reply, Sarra sat up abruptly. "Do you mean one of them survived? Is there *evidence* for that woman's descent from Veller Ganfallin?"

Cailet shrugged and wriggled her toes in the water. "More than there is for my being a Rille. I was going to tell the next Minstrelsy visitor about it, but since you're here. . . ."

"It's absurd," Sarra repeated. "What difference can it make?"

She sighed quietly, wishing for Collan's incisive bluntness; Sarra's eyes were best opened by her husband. "Since the rising, the Council has abolished slavery, Bloods and Tiers, and a lot of the worst marriage and inheritance laws. You've overhauled the electoral system, changed and expanded the Assembly and Council, reorganized most of the government from the village level on up, and—"

"And not done nearly enough," Sarra interrupted.

"On the contrary, you've done too much. And too fast. Everybody used to know exactly where they stood. What was expected of them—what *they* could expect from the world. I'm not saying that the changes aren't good and necessary. But there've been so *many* that a lot of people are nervous. They see the old society being torn down piece by piece, and they're not sure if what's been put in its place will work."

Sarra frowned down at her hands—those slim, delicate fingers that were responsible for dismantling much of Lenfell's traditional structure. Sarra said, "They want someone to come in and tell them what to do, based on hereditary right—just like the Bloods."

"Yes. And Vellerin Dombur knows it. Veller Ganfal-

lin didn't live so terribly long ago that what she did and
how she lived has no relevance to today's Lenfell. When
our would-be Grand Duchess of Domburronshir has adequate documentation, she'll let someone publish the news
that she's a direct descendant. It's been tried before, and
to rather telling effect."

The golden head snapped up, black eyes sparkling
with anger. "Anniyas was elevated to First Councillor because of that other putative Ganfallin. Her victory over
him was engineered by the Malerrisi."

"I wouldn't worry about that. Glenin has more imagination than to use the same ploy twice," Cailet said.

"*Is* it the same? Consider. Let's say Vellerin Dombur
gains control of Domburronshir. If Glenin is helping her
now so she can defeat her later—just the way Anniyas
did—she's a fool. The last claimant was a man, remember. He was an upstart not only because of his ambitions
but also because of his sex. It'd be much harder to topple
a woman in the same position."

"Yes, but—"

Sarra glared her to silence. "It's more logical to assume that Glenin intends to rule Domburronshir *through*
the Domburs. Vellerin would have no qualms about using
Malerrisi magic to her own ends, thinking that because
they're so far out of the public eye and political power
that she is indeed using *them,* not the other way around.
With Domburronshir as a base—economic, political, and
military—and Vellerin Dombur's craving to seize Veller
Ganfallin's kind of power, and at the absolute worst to
emulate her conquests—"

Cailet's emotions were primarily composed of horror
at the prospect and disgust that she hadn't seen it herself.
But she was also filled with admiration for Sarra's gut-
jumping. She wondered suddenly what it might have been
like, to hold the positions they'd been meant to in Ambrai: Sarra the Councillor, Cailet the Mage Guardian,
and—and Glenin, the Lady of Ambrai.

"That's what she'd take next," Cailet blurted out. "It
wouldn't end in South Lenfell. She'd attack Ambraishir.
She wants it, Sarra, she always has—she's First Daughter
in an unbroken line of First Daughters."

Sarra blinked, then nodded. "What can we do?"

There was no hopelessness in the question, nor help-lessness—nothing of what Cailet so often felt when con-fronting the future. Sarra had unlimited faith in her own ability to accomplish, to succeed; when had she ever con-fronted failure?

But she didn't know about Josselin Mikleine and Jored Karellos either. Cailet had lied about not knowing the source of the shadows.

"Let it play out," she heard herself say. It was what she was doing with the two young men. For—and she hardly dared think such a thing—for if *she* succeeded, and made a Mage Guardian of a Malerrisi's son, Glenin would be broken. The Malerrisi would survive—for a time anyway—but Glenin's arrogance and ambitions would be shattered.

"'Let it play out'? Not damned likely!"

"Do what you have to," Cailet said woodenly. "Polit-ical maneuvering isn't my area of expertise."

"No, it's *mine*," was the forthright reply. "Leave it to me, Caisha."

She would have to. She had enough to worry about within the rose-draped walls of Mage Hall.

25

IT was not quite dawn. Sarra sat alone on the single chair at the far end of the real Mage Hall, the large vaulted chamber where formal assemblies were held. She'd been to Mage Hall only twice before (Cailet usually visited them at Roseguard, or they met elsewhere when conve-nient to their travels), and had never been inside this room. Aidan had woken her early, waited in the corridor while she dressed, and escorted her here. Then he'd dis-appeared without a word, leaving her with no one to ask about the pattern of tiles in the floor.

She smiled when she saw it was an octagon. *Conve-*

nient, that it forms an eight-pointed compass! Collan forgot to mention that after his visit. Very clever, little sister, even better than my eight-petaled rose on all the official Sheve documents.

Yawning, she glanced at the windows again, unsure if it was any lighter outside than it had been five minutes ago. She had spent a restless, uneasy night, her dreams filled with images of Collan, Cailet, Taigan and Mikel, Warrior Mages who conjured Globe after crimson Battle Globe, and the tall broad-shouldered Wraith that was all her mind would ever allow of Auvry Feiran. It had been a relief when Aidan knocked on her door.

Cailet had promised something interesting. Sarra hoped she'd get on with it soon. She wanted to go home. Falundir would be staying at Mage Hall for a while, so she and Taguare would borrow horses for a *very* long ride south to Cantratown. From there, they'd take ship to Roseguard. And maybe by then Collan would be home from Roke Castle, and she'd tell him about Glenin's second attempt on the twins, and why they were now Prentice Mages. She'd be lucky if he didn't take ship himself—for Malerris Castle, to dismantle Glenin joint by joint.

Wondering with genuine curiosity how other women managed to control their husbands, Sarra gave a start as the double oak doors opened and a young woman strode into the hall. In the pre-dawn dimness Sarra could see no more than that she was tall and long-limbed in her formal black regimentals, and that her hair was cut short to curl around a dark-skinned face. Of her age, her looks, or her Name, Sarra knew nothing. But the stance she took in the center of the compass octagon was not that of a student preparing for a lesson.

Cailet appeared then, in the complete ceremonial ensemble of the Mage Captal: black silk trousers and shirt and hip-length vest, silver pins at her collar, silver sash around her waist, and Gorynel Desse's sword at her side. That sword—Sarra's eyes narrowed below a frown as scabbard and hilt caught every scrap of light in the chamber and reflected it back in an arrogant gleam. One of the legendary Fifty, supposedly crafted by Caitiri the Fiery-

Eyed, Delilah the Dancer, Jiorto Silverhelm, and Steen Swordsworn, this blade obeyed the intent of its wielder. To defend, to threaten, to chasten, or to kill—the sword *knew* the true purpose of the mind that commanded it— sometimes better than that mind itself knew.

No, she told herself, that wasn't quite right. Collan and Falundir had unearthed an archaic ballad cycle that detailed the making of the Fifty Swords—designed by Jiorto Silverhelm, forged by Caitiri the Fiery-Eyed, imbued with power by Steen Swordsworn and with their peculiar instinct for the wielder's true intent by the wily Delilah the Dancer.

> *The Fifty: forged in Magefire glow*
> > *For Warders' grip in strife*
> > > *For bold defense*
> > > *Of innocence*
> > *For the Captal's very life*
>
> *The Silverhelm on sheets of gold*
> > *Drew the Fifty o'er and o'er*
> > > *With silver pen*
> > > *Again, again*
> > *With all his swording lore*
>
> *Forgeflame shone in Fiery Eyes*
> > *She kindled, hammered, chilled*
> > > *With steady hold*
> > > *To shape and fold*
> > *With all her smithing skill*
>
> *But a sword is naught but lifeless steel*
> > *Until—unless—a Mageborn heart*
> > > *With truth and grace*
> > > *The sword embrace*
> > *With magic from the start*
>
> *So Swordsworn stood by Caitiri's side*
> > *His prowess Globed and glowing*
> > > *With will to right*
> > > *And all his might*
> > *With Warrior's secret knowing*

Drawn by the bright and fiery forge
The Dancer in graceful fingers
With sudden grasp
Each sword she clasped
And her fierce magic lingers

It was the heart, not the head, that ruled the sword. However the mind might protest, whatever the user might think her goals to be, the sword knew better—and acted on it. What would it be like, Sarra asked herself, to fight one's sword as well as one's enemy?

Without acknowledging Sarra's presence, Cailet approached the student who stood within the octagon. "Ollia Bekke," she said softly, her voice ringing from the plain stone arches high overhead, "would you become a Mage Guardian?"

"I would," the Prentice replied.

Bekke—ah, then she means to become a Warrior, like most of her Name. Sarra nodded to herself and sat a little forward in her chair, understanding what Cailet had meant her to see this morning. Not a lesson, but a ritual. There had been no formal recognition for Cailet of her status as Mage Captal; evidently she had decided that there was value in ceremony, even a private one between herself and a Prentice. Perhaps *more* value, Sarra thought, watching them face each other. It would be gratifying to stand before one's fellow Prentices and be recognized as a Mage Guardian, but there must be an even greater satisfaction to be so recognized by the Mage Captal—privately, as equals.

"Prove yourself," Cailet said, a simple challenge.

Ritual, yes—eventually. For now, a testing, to demonstrate that the Captal's acceptance had been earned. Sarra felt her hands clench as Ollia Bekke, standing within the compass octagon, lifted both hands waist-high and conjured a crimson sphere, a Battle Globe. By its eerie glow, she saw Cailet arch a brow.

"You choose to defend first? Not in keeping with what I know of you. But I'll admit it does take real courage to attack first. Very well."

Cailet's Mage Globe was pure white, veined in scarlet. Sarra hadn't seen her make so much as a gesture. Her hands were still at her sides. The milky sphere—barely fist-sized, not even a quarter the circumference of Ollia Bekke's—drifted around the perimeter of the octagon, casual, almost lazy. Ollia didn't turn to follow it with her eyes, instead holding Cailet's gaze with her own. The two orbs, red and white, lit the hall with bizarre radiance, and as the white suddenly shot toward the red, the light seemed to push back whatever dawn had seeped through the high windows. There was a small ringing sound, and then silent darkness.

Sarra blinked dazzled eyes, resisting the urge to knuckle them. Fragments of light spun in the gloom, then died away. Sarra's vision adjusted, and she saw that Cailet was nodding.

"Adequate."

Ollia Bekke stiffened visibly.

"You managed not to kill yourself in setting up a defense. Am I to understand you expect *praise* for that?"

Cailet was deliberately baiting the girl, reminding her who was the lowly Prentice and who the lofty Mage Capital. Sarra didn't have the vaguest notion why—but there was power here. Dangerous power. Magic.

This time it was Cailet who conjured a Globe, and this time it was dark crimson: livid, sparking, dark with intensity, much more of a threat than Ollia Bekke's had been. With a sigh that actually sounded bored, Cailet hooked her thumbs into her silver sash and cocked her head to one side.

"Well?"

Ollia Bekke appeared to be confused. Annoyed, her pride stinging, but also bewildered by this turn of events. Sarra knew just how she felt. What was Cailet doing?

"Leave the compass," Cailet ordered.

Ollia's body shifted automatically to obey.

"You don't deserve to stand there."

The girl went rigid and stayed where she was.

"I told you to—"

"I heard you, Captal."

"Well, then?"

"No. With respect."

"Why respect?"

"You're the Captal."

Cailet laughed. "Oh, I see. And because I'm the Captal, you respect me enough to disobey me?"

"I have a right to be here," Ollia said stubbornly.

"According to whom?"

And Cailet's flashing, bloody Globe heaved forward, met barely in time by Ollia's defensive sphere—which was almost its match in color if not power. There was another detonation of energy, and this time the clang of it made Sarra wince.

When it had dispersed, Cailet shrugged. "Again, adequate. You managed not to kill *me* in defending yourself. But the command remains. Move away from there."

"Again, with respect—no." She paused, as if gathering courage to say what her pride demanded. "Only when you acknowledge that I have a right to be here. That I'm a Mage Guardian."

Cailet took a step, then another, decreasing the distance between them to about fifteen feet. "Out. Now."

Ollia said nothing, and stood her ground.

"Do you know," Cailet said conversationally, "that as a Listed Mage, you'll be sworn to give your life for mine? That your duty above all things is to keep me safe?"

"I know."

"And?" Cailet gestured *go on* with her right hand.

"And?" the girl repeated, perplexity overcoming all other emotion once more.

"And will you? Look at me. Nothing much, am I? Just an arrogant woman with a few paltry tricks and a sword." She stroked the hilt gently. "As a Warrior Mage—I assume that's your ambition?"

Ollia nodded, and the first rays of sunlight glinted her curls in russet and copper.

"Wrong. A Mage Guardian has but one ambition: to die for me." She shrugged once more. "As I was saying, a Warrior eventually receives a sword. But no sword in the world is like this one."

Ollia tensed, and so did Sarra, assuming Cailet was about to attack with that sword. Instead, yet another Mage

Globe appeared to the Prentice's right, and she was so startled that she turned to face it. Barely countering it in time with an angry crimson sphere of her own, she spun once more when Cailet flung another, and another, and another at her.

"I could go on doing this all day," Cailet said through the bursts of light and sound and magic as Ollia frantically defended herself. "But I'm getting bored."

And then she *did* draw Gorynel Desse's blade. Ollia Bekke, lacking one of her own, backed up a pace, then two, then three—then realized she had almost obeyed Cailet's order to step out of the compass octagon. She stopped, and lifted shaking hands to Work the largest Globe yet—so darkly red as to be almost black, covered in pulsing veins like a living heart. Sarra had the wild thought that if Cailet punctured it with her sword, it would flood the floor with blood.

Cailet didn't just pierce it; she sliced it in two. Magic rippled halfway up the blade, flickered, and died.

"Can you do no better?" Cailet asked.

There was no haughtiness in the question, yet Sarra could feel Cailet's fierce pride in her own magic. Perhaps this was the darkness she feared, the temptation to use her power and The Bequest for the sake of her own pride. Sarra couldn't tell. She only knew it was wrong to humiliate the young Prentice this way.

At last Ollia seemed to notice Sarra's presence, as if her sympathy had reached out for attention. The girl's eyes were a brilliant turquoise, almost the Ambrai Blood color, and there was shame in them and in the flush on her dark cheeks that someone had witnessed this scene. She had entered expecting, perhaps, to be tested somehow, and to emerge as a Mage Guardian with all rights, honor, and pride attached thereto. Instead—

Cailet reached over and thwacked the girl on the shoulder with the flat of her blade.

Ollia suddenly snarled, and whirled around, and sent a throbbing Mage Globe directly at Cailet. The sword's easy parry was an insult. As the infuriated Prentice—twice the fighter now that mortification lashed at her—sent sphere after lightning-swathed crimson sphere at the

Captal, Sarra remembered whose skill was really at work here.

Not Cailet at all. Gorynel Desse. First Sword for fifty-one of his seventy-six years.

Pale lids drooped over coal-black eyes, as if Cailet hardly cared to see her opponent at all. Every movement, every flex of muscle and stretch of sinew, even to her very bones, seemed permeated with magic. It blazed along the sword now, not rising from the Mage Globes that shattered on the blade but coruscating downward from Cailet's hands on the hilt. Sweat pearled her brow, dampening her blonde hair, but instead of growing tired she was stronger and swifter with each clash of the sword against magic.

Yet Ollia Bekke's power was growing, too, the Mage Globes smaller and fiercer, wasting no fragment of magic, intense and compact and outglowing the sunlight now streaming through the windows. Sarra was inundated in power, battered between the strength and purpose that seethed along her sister's nerves and the dark fury that burst from every smashed and broken sphere. The two women, the sword, the recurring circles of bloody magic—all blurred in Sarra's gaze, light-and-shadow, blaze-and-blackness.

And then, very suddenly, she understood, and that knowledge brought the combatants into focus again. She knew what Cailet was doing and was able to follow—even to anticipate—every move Captal and Prentice made.

Cailet had taken away Ollia Bekke's arrogance, shamed her into anger, pushed her deliberately toward hate. Thus the girl was using magic against her Captal—the woman she would swear to protect at the cost of her own life. But Cailet had also been waiting, waiting, with a terrible and desperate patience, precisely aware of Ollia's emotions—and the explosion that now occurred was not of a Mage Globe cracked open by a sword, but of a Mageborn mind shocked into growth.

Ollia faltered, and the Mage Globe half-Worked in her right hand sputtered and faded and vanished. "C–Captal—"

Sarra watched the sword lower, point almost touching the black tiles. Cailet smiled—wry and apologetic and admiring and intensely proud of her Prentice who had just become a Mage Guardian.

"Cailet," she said. "To you, now, my name is Cailet."

Ollia stared.

Cailet sheathed Desse's sword and wiped the back of her hand across her forehead. She sent a brief glance in Sarra's direction, then started with surprise as Ollia began to take the last step out of the compass. "Don't you dare!" she exclaimed. "That's *exactly* where you belong!"

The new Mage Guardian hesitated, then walked *forward,* toward her Captal, with a rueful little smile on her face. Deliberately she stepped over the silver bordering tiles. Cailet grinned and gave her a swift, fond embrace.

"Go on—Marra will give you some breakfast in the anteroom. Then get some rest. If you put half as much into that as I had to, you'll need to lie down for a while!"

The easy acknowledgment of skill complimented Ollia as nothing else could have. Arrogance had died in her, replaced by precious confidence. It shone in her eyes as she bowed to Cailet—and to Sarra—and walked out of the Hall.

After a moment's silence, Sarra got to her feet—as exhausted, truly told, as Cailet. "Well," she said casually, "you certainly taught *her* a thing or two."

Cailet grinned tiredly. "There'd better be some breakfast waiting for *me,* or I'll have Aidan's head on the end of this sword. Come on."

They left the sunlit hall for Cailet's quarters. Aidan had indeed left a copious meal for them, and as they settled down on either side of a low table, Cailet said, "You knew what was going on, didn't you? What'd you think of it?"

Sarra went to the crux of it at once. "What if she hadn't accepted you?"

"What if her anger had turned to real hate, you mean? And she'd *really* tried to kill me?" She poured juice for them both and shrugged. "I don't know. It's never happened. They're all furious with me, of course, and try to sneak past my guard somehow—one of them went for my throat with his bare hands once." She laughed. "Damned near got me, too!"

"You begin to frighten me."

"I do?"

"I know where you took her, but I'm not sure how you got her there."

"Neither am I—exactly how she got there, I mean. It's different for all of them, I suppose." Cailet drank down the juice and selected a nut-filled pastry from her plate. Leaning back in the low chair, she crossed her legs and sighed.

"I thought Mage Globes were supposed to be difficult."

"Used to be." Cailet smiled. "I wouldn't be able to do this at all if it wasn't for that copy of the *Code of Malerris*. Gorsha got hold of one once—but before he could read it, he took it through a Ladder, and it disintegrated. The *Code* we have now, added to the Bequest's information about Mage Globes, lets me teach everyone how to Work them very well indeed. Some people still have some trouble until they get the knack of it, but it's a skill most Mages can use—and much more effectively than before."

"Ollia certainly seems proficient," Sarra observed dryly.

"She's already a Warrior, even though it'll take Imilial and Granon a few weeks to test her out in all the particulars. I don't envy them the job!" Sighing again, she rubbed the nape of her neck. "It takes more out of me than it used to. But there's one more Mage Guardian to do our work, Sarra. One more."

"They attack you, and—"

"And never forget it. Those moments of being power-drunk—I can always see it in their faces, even sense it in their magic. When they get over it, and open to me completely, the magic tangibly *changes*. Every person's magic feels different. You learn to recognize individuals, like a signature. A Mage Guardian's signature is completely different from a Malerrisi's."

Sarra lifted her teacup—a beautiful thing of black Rine porcelain rimmed in St. Caitiri's flameflowers—and sipped to ease her dry throat before replying. "Do you think it's fair to them, Caisha? The shock of what they try to do to you?"

"I don't enjoy it. It has to be done. They have to know where power can lead them. The warning's got to be there for them, the memory of being tempted—and to kill *me,* the one they've sworn to give their own lives for."

"I see."

Cailet looked up from shredding the pastry in her fingers. "If you're thinking about Taigan and Mikel—"

"No," she said, too quickly. Of course she was thinking of her children. How would Taigan react when Cailet deliberately humbled that high pride? Would Mikel have confidence enough in himself to fight back at all, or would he give in to despair and certainty that he *was* unworthy of standing within that silver octagon?

She drank again, burning her tongue.

"Sasha—"

"This is what you wanted me to see," she said.

"Yes. For the twins' sake, so you'll know—but even more for your own."

"You want me to stay."

"The Council doesn't need you right now as much as you need to be here—as much as you need your magic."

Sarra glared at her sister. "You've taken my children," she snapped. "Isn't that enough for you, Captal?"

Cailet flinched as if Sarra had struck her across the face. No—she wouldn't have reacted to any bodily hurt; the look in her black eyes was heart-pain, something very few could make her feel. But before Sarra could frame an apology, a mask slid over the thin, angular features, a calm and remote mask that Sarra suddenly feared.

"Did I *take* them?" the Captal asked quietly. "Did you and Collan *give* them to me? Or have they come because what's inside them is as undeniable as what Gorsha blocked for eighteen years in me? What you *insisted* he release, without my knowledge or my consent!"

"I can't go back and undo that—and I *wouldn't,* even

if I could. You were needed. It was necessary. I won't apologize."

"I don't want an apology. I only want you to understand. . . ." All at once Cailet sagged back in her chair, cheeks ashen, eyes sickly dull. "Please, Sasha," she whispered. "Don't be angry with me—don't let's fight. I'm tired. Saints, I'm so tired. . . ."

Sarra leaned over, sweeping the lank golden hair from her sister's face. "Caisha? I'm sorry. Are you all right?"

"Just . . . just so damned tired."

Guilt raged in her. Cailet had just undergone a great strain, physical and magical and emotional, to guide a young Prentice into becoming a Mage Guardian. And now here Sarra was, Cailet's own sister, pestering her with doubts and accusations and demands. She rose and set about loosening the collar of Cailet's shirt, checking the weary pulse in her wrist, dampening a linen napkin at the washstand basin to wipe the cold sweat from her face and neck.

"Thank you, Sasha."

"Who causes, should cure," she quoted, tenderness and worry obliterating all her anger.

"You didn't cause it, but thanks anyway." Cailet sat a little straighter, the luster returning to her eyes. "Keep a sharp watch on Vellerin Dombur. I'll do what I can through the Mages assigned to the Shir, but—"

It was tacit concession that Sarra would not be staying at Mage Hall. "I'll send one of the Minstrelsy soon to let you know what we know. For now, you stay here and get some rest. I'll come back after I've said good-bye to the twins—if someone's rousted Mikel out of bed yet, that is."

"Not even *he* could sleep through the magic that got loosed this morning." She smiled. "And not even *I* can Ward someone that well."

"Go easy on them when you do the unWorking."

Meekly, but with brightly laughing eyes, the Captal replied, "Yes, Lady Sarra. But considering the trouble I had setting and then resetting their Wards, you'd do better to worry about *me!*"

PART TWO

988–989

THE HUNT

1

TAIGAN collapsed onto her narrow bed, flushed and sweating after the morning's run. Mikel sank bonelessly down the wall nearby to sit on the floor looking numbed.

"If you survive me, make sure I get a nice funeral."

Mikel shut his eyes. "Sorry. I'm already dead. Tell Mother and Fa I gave it a good try, will you?"

Taigan rubbed at an abused thigh muscle. "How does she *do* it? She's twenty years older than us!" After running five miles, the Captal had looked as if she could do another fifty without breaking a sweat. It was humiliating. "Besides, I thought we were here to become Mage Guardians, not train for the All-Lenfell Games."

"If they have an event for corpses, I'll enter." Mikel sighed. "And *win*."

"Feeling sorry for yourselves, I see." Aidan Maurgen's sardonic comment made the twins look up. He stood in Taigan's doorway, arms folded across his chest, a smile on his face. Mikel thought briefly about getting to his feet as a mark of respect due his elder, then abandoned the idea as requiring too much precious energy.

"Is it like this for everybody?" Taigan asked.

"No." Aidan grinned. "Sometimes it's worse. The Captal wants to see you two. Come along, and stop imitating martyred Saints. It'll get easier."

"When?" Taigan muttered as she lurched to her feet.

Following Aidan along cool hallways, Mikel said, "It has to get easier. Doesn't it?"

His sister shook her head. "Dreamer."

Aidan heard them. He stopped, turned, and asked, "You know the old one that goes, 'Cheer up, things could get worse'?"

Taigan sighed tolerantly and finished it for him. " 'So we cheered up, and sure enough, things got worse.' "

"Heard it at Fa's knee." Mikel made a face and asked Taigan, "Do we deserve this kind of abuse?"

Aidan only laughed at them.

Climbing the stairs to the Captal's chambers was agony on Taigan's bruised muscle. Aidan bade them wait in the anteroom on an uncushioned bench, vanished into the private office, and came back a few moments later. "Come on. She doesn't bite, you know."

The Captal, looking cool and composed in her severely elegant black, welcomed them with an unsympathetic, "Recovered yet?"

They nodded without enthusiasm.

"Good." Gesturing to chairs on either side of a low table, she said, "Have a seat. Aidan, tell Jenira and Tirez they'll be along in a little while."

"She said last night they'll be ready for 'em." The grin he gave them this time was gleefully malicious. "Question is, are they ready for Jenira and Tirez?"

Ready for who *to do* what? flashed in a look between the twins, swiftly followed by a mutual, heartfelt: *I don't want to know!*

"I gather the last four days have been rather uncomfortable," said the Captal, perching on the windowsill near her desk. Late-morning sunlight cast a nimbus of gold above her silver-gilt head, bright contrast to her long shadow on the rug. "Believe me, you'll grow even less comfortable. But right now I have a question for you." She paused. "Why are you here?"

Taigan shifted in her chair. "We want to become Mage Guardians."

"Why?"

"Because—" She stopped, confused. All Mageborns wanted to become Guardians, didn't they? Except their mother, but she was a special case.

Mikel spoke for them both. "Because we want to learn how to use our magic."

"For what purpose?" The Captal held up a quelling hand. "Please, no noble mouthings about the good of Lenfell, the defense of the weak, and the protection of the downtrodden. I get enough of that from your mother— and I know your father much too well to believe that he raised you to be self-sacrificing altruists. Why do you want to learn the uses of magic?"

Taigan's green eyes darkened below a frown. "We'd be able to answer better if we *had* the use of our magic," she pointed out. "We've been here four days, and we're still Warded."

"Truly told," agreed the Captal. "Do you know why?"

Taigan shrugged. "We're dangerous."

The Captal snorted.

Mikel hastened to explain. "Because we've been Warded so long, and so powerfully, that when our magic is set loose, it might—"

An arched brow silenced him. "My thanks for the compliment on the Wards I set on you two in childhood, but pay me the further honor of believing that not only do I know my Work, I know how to unWork it. Believe me, you compliment yourselves. You're not dangerous— nothing a halfway competent Mage couldn't handle while in a coma. Now, for the third time, why is magic something you want to learn?"

Why seemed to be to the Captal's favorite word. Taigan suddenly boiled over. "Because I don't want to spend my life like Falundir!"

Shocked, Mikel stared at his sister. But the Captal was nodding slowly, as if the answer was not only understandable but pleasing.

"And you, Mikel?" she asked softly. "Do you also fear having your magic locked up inside you, as the Bard's music is locked inside him?"

"But it isn't," he heard himself say. "He can't sing anymore, or play a lute, but the music comes out of him just the same. He writes songs and operas and—"

"—and can't perform them," Taigan interrupted. "He knows how it should sound, but he can't make the sounds himself. That's how magic is for us, Mikel—we know it's there, we've felt it sometimes, but we can't *do* anything with it." She met the Captal's gaze squarely. "Yet."

Pale lids drooped slightly, seemingly weighted down by long, thick lashes—dark like her brows, but sun-

bleached at the tips as if brushed with gold dust to empha-
size the limitless blackness of her eyes. Taigan was
abruptly captured in the depths of those eyes and caught
her breath. In the next instant Mikel did the same.

*Too cold, too bright, too loud—freezing air in-
haled in protest escapes in a shriek of outrage,
and eyes squeeze shut against the painful blaze
of light, and fists batter helplessly at the onslaught of noise—*
"There's the first one. Perfect in every way.
Hand it over, Collan, before we all go deaf."
*Warmer now. Quieter. Cradling softness, a famil-
iar slow rocking/floating, a low rhythmic mur-
mur that soothes—*
"Now, Sarra—deep breath—push! Again!"
*But the light suddenly invades, and expands, and
reaches into every shadow—and it doesn't hurt
at all anymore—*
"Two fine, healthy babies. Excellent. You're all
done now, Lady. Beautiful work."
Oh, yes, beautiful—bright warm shining—
"Very funny, Elo. Your work, or mine?"
—MINE!
"Excuse me, but did I have something to do with
it?"
—MINE MINE MINE—
*Yes, but only for this moment, my dears. Forgive
me.*
*No! Don't take it away! MINE! Want it back,
give it back—*
*Hush now. You can have it back again one day, I
promise. For now, it's better so.*
NO! WANT IT NOW!
Hush.
*And for a long time the bright warm light is
masked.*
*But then it glimmers within, teasing and promis-
ing, rising up like a kindled hearthfire to shield
them from her—*

*SHE WANTS TO TAKE THE MAGIC! JUST
LIKE THE OTHER ONE DID!*
Hide it, disguise it, pretend it isn't there—
But it is *there, though it cannot be touched. And
it hides itself a moment later, drawing back be-
hind its mask, until something just as powerful
and much more knowing fashions a stronger dis-
guise.*
This was a lot easier when you were little.
*Fa said the same thing a few weeks ago, when
we got away from that woman—*
*Who was she? What had she looked like? We
can't remember anything about her anymore—*
No, and you won't *remember her, any more than
you'll remember this or your magic, until the
time is right.*
But it's mine, *it belongs to me—*
One day. Not yet.
WHEN?
One day.

Now.
They opened their eyes. Had the Captal spoken
aloud? Both looked at her where she still sat at the window, slender hands clasping one knee, face lit with a
whimsical smile.

"There. *Much* simpler than when I Worked your
Wards. By all the Guardian Saints, back then you two
fought me every inch of the way. Truly told, it's a relief
to've had your active cooperation."

The twins stared at each other. Their Wards were
gone?

"Even if it did take two hours to accomplish."

Two *hours?*

At least that long; the Captal's shadow on the Cloister
rug was much shorter than when they'd entered, pooling
now at her feet.

"Do you feel different?" Mikel blurted.

Taigan bit her upper lip. "I'm not sure."

"Give it some time," the Captal advised. "And take

it carefully. It hits everyone differently, and you may be a little off-balance for a while."

Taigan stood up and knew instantly the wisdom of the caution. She glanced at Mikel, who also swayed on his feet.

The Captal shook her head. "Sit down before you fall down. You can stay here until you feel able to walk down to the Oak Court."

"What happens there?" Taigan asked suspiciously.

"You meet Jenira Doriaz and Tirez Escovor."

"What do they teach?"

"Oh, this and that." And the Captal smiled.

Another glance flashed between the twins: *At last! We're going to learn some magic!*

2

WHAT they learned from Jenira Doriaz and Tirez Escovor—who between them had over a century's service as Mage Guardians—was how to lay bricks.

The two elderly Mages marched the twins from the main buildings out to the wall—all the way to an eighty-foot gap that led into the apple orchard. Waiting for them were two piles of rust-colored, smoke-blackened, woefully uneven clinker bricks, two pails of mortar, and appropriate tools.

"Get started," Escovor said. He set up folding chairs for himself and the other Mage, produced a flask from one pocket of his black longvest and a book from another, and settled back to bake his seventy-nine-year-old bones in the warm noonday sun.

"Started—?" Mikel echoed faintly.

Jenira Doriaz nodded, placing her chair beneath a poplar whose shade would protect her fragile fair skin. She, too, had a flask and a book. "Don't you take too long about it, neither," she said in an accent redolent of the Dindenshir farm she hadn't seen in sixty years. "I'm almost ended with this volume of the *Adventures of St. Delilah,* and I didn't bring the next one along from the library."

At first the incredulous Prentices thought they were meant to close the space completely, but Jenira Doriaz explained that the Captal required a wagon gate here, so all they had to do was extend the wall about thirty feet from either end.

"You, commence right here," she finished, pointing to Taigan and the wall that ended beneath the poplar.

"And you, over here," said Tirez Escovor, indicating the section near his chair.

With that, the two antiquated Mage Guardians settled down to sipping and reading.

Taigan stared. "We're *Mageborns,* not bricklayers!"

Mikel sighed. "For the rest of the afternoon, we're bricklayers. Come on."

He spent a few minutes inspecting two other lengths of the wall, presuming he'd find guidance. One part was made of mostly bluish bricks which despite their erratic sizes were set in a woven pattern that actually made a virtue of their irregularities. Somebody had known what she was doing—and Mikel hadn't a hope of emulating her. The second section was more what he could expect to produce: sulfur-yellow bricks, sooty from incompetent firing, were placed any-old-how and drooled dried mortar at every seam. Envisioning the pathetic results of his own performance with the rusty bricks he was supposed to use, he shuddered. The idea of anyone's coming here and pointing out the wall that Mikel Liwellan had built horrified him. He'd have to talk to Josselin Mikleine about planting enough roses to hide it.

He got to work, sorting bricks and trying not to slice his fingers on the sharp extrusions of black glass. He supposed Mage Hall had a contract with the locals to buy what they couldn't use. The Captal, he decided, was frugal. (Taigan would have said "cheap.")

Mikel stacked bricks at five-foot intervals so he wouldn't have to carry them all from the main pile. Mortar ready—or as ready as his inexperience could judge—he started the first layer. A narrow trench had already been dug for the anchoring row, and Mikel assiduously wielded trowel, bricks, and level. On his knees in the dirt, summer heat beating down on his back, careful to put the same amount of mortar between each brick, he was sweating and exhausted by the time he'd placed the bottom row.

He finished the second row, offsetting it from the first. If he was lucky, the thing would stand up when done. Then a third row, more or less even with the first. He was getting very thirsty, and he hadn't had anything to eat since last night—usually everyone ate breakfast after the morning run, but today they'd been summoned to the Captal's quarters and now it was long past lunch, and his stomach was growling.

Fourth row. This was insane. Teggie was right: they were Mageborns, they should be learning how to use their magic—not be hunched down in the broiling sun slapping bricks and mortar together for extensions to the ugliest wall in all fifteen Shirs.

Fifth row. The sun was in his eyes now, and he thought about switching sides of the wall, but he'd just have to reach over the set rows to get at more bricks, and it was too much added effort.

Sixth row. He'd given up on the level—it took too much time. He established a routine: spread mortar, set brick, carve off excess glop, reach for another brick while spreading more mortar. It was mind-numbing, but unfortunately his body was still complaining—not just his stomach and his dry mouth, but his shoulders and hands and knees.

Seventh row. The damned bricks were ten inches long and five inches wide and only three miserable inches high—which meant that allowing for the anchoring row in the ground, his ninth row would make the wall two whole impressive feet tall. The sun glared at him from the west. Another foot of bricks and it would be dinnertime; if Tirez Escovor wanted a four-foot wall to match the nearby section, Mikel would be here till Fifteenth.

Grimly he continued. He ordered himself to ignore the late-afternoon sun stabbing his eyes, and the freckles he could feel popping out on his nose and cheeks, and the cramps in his back and thighs, and the cuts on his fingers. He told himself there must be a reason for this. He was damned if he could figure out what it was, but there *must* be a reason.

If there wasn't, he'd have the Captal for dinner.

What did bricklaying have to do with becoming a Mage Guardian? The rhythm of the work became more and more automatic as he tried to figure out what possible purpose there might be to this imbecilic exercise, other than to extend this hideous wall. Maybe that was it— maybe Prentices did this so they could say they'd helped build Mage Hall. But that hawk didn't fly very far with Mikel. He finished the ninth row, and the tenth, still unconvinced that there really was a reason for this.

As a Mage Guardian, he'd have to know more than how to slather and slap and slice off gritty glop. He knew quite a few Mages, and they could do all sorts of marvelous things.

All at once he wondered if the idea was to frustrate him so much that he'd use *magic* to build the wall.

No, that couldn't be—because he'd reached his limit of exasperation at least an hour ago, and nothing flared up in him that told him how to set bricks with a spell.

He knew what magic felt like, though. How peculiar it had been, hearing what people had said at his birth. Remembering the light outside and the cold and the noise, and then the warmth and the incredible blaze *inside*—and being denied it. He *had* fought the Captal, he knew that now. He'd wanted his magic, even though he'd been only minutes old. And then, later, after Glenin Feiran had tried to kidnap him, the Captal had made sure his magic would stay locked up until she released it. He remembered how angry he'd been, how he'd struggled—and how foolish to do so, because she was *so* strong. And she'd meant him no harm. She'd given the magic back to him, just as she'd promised—the Wards were gone now, and he could touch the bright glowing core of power within him.

He just didn't know how to use it.

And making this stupid damned wall wasn't going to teach him.

Well, at least all the Wards were gone. That was something, anyway.

He looked at that thought, and wondered what might happen if Glenin Feiran tried for him yet again. That night at the theater opening—now, *there* was power to challenge even the Captal's. And it had been only the Captal's Wards that had kept Mikel's brains from being scorched.

What was there to protect him now?

Only himself—but he didn't know how to *use* his magic to guard himself. The bastion the Captal had built around him was gone, and he had nothing to take its place, and if a Malerrisi or *The* Malerrisi attacked him again—

He became aware that his groping hand had closed over nothing several times now. Blinking, he looked down at the place where a small pile of bricks ought to have been.

Then he looked at the wall. It was four feet high—and the last five rows of bricks had been set with masterly precision.

Tirez Escovor—collaterally related to the Fourth Lord of Malerris who had been Captal Caitirin Bekke's secret lover—got up from his chair. He slipped flask and book into his pockets, folded the chair, and smiled.

"Hungry?"

Right on cue, the deep distant bell of St. Lirance's in Heathering rang out Twelfth. The Ladymoon, a halved circle like St. Venkelos's sigil, shone silvery in the twilight. Mikel gaped at the elderly Mage.

"If you're not, *I* am. Come on. We'll be just in time for dinner."

Mikel glanced over to the other part of the wall.

"Oh, never mind them. They'll be a while yet."

Jenira Doriaz—collaterally related to the Fifth Lord of Malerris killed in the Rising at the Octagon Court— dozed in her chair below the poplar. Taigan was still working. Her movements were stiff with weariness and muscle strain, her expression jut-jawed and resentful. Mikel realized suddenly that in all his musings while building the wall, he'd thought of *himself*—not of the two of them together, not as "we" or "us"—just himself *as* himself, as if he'd been born before her or after her but not *with* her.

Shaken, he fumbled about inside his own head, wondering if the awareness of her was still there. Yes—but different now. What he'd assumed was a connection of instinct that came of sharing their mother's womb was now clearly revealed as a function of magic. He almost used it to "touch" her—then held back. She wouldn't welcome the intrusion, not by the look in her eyes. Still less would she like having it thrown in her face that he was finished and she was not.

Escovor extended his flask. "Care for a nip?"

Mikel was allowed watered wine with dinner. He hadn't tasted anything stronger since he and Taigan stole a bottle of Fa's brandy (and told Tarise when she found them with it—empty—that they were only honoring St. Kiy on her feast day, which of course got them nowhere with her).

"Thanks," he said, and took a swig.

3

SARRA had lied to Cailet. She wasn't particularly needed at Ryka Court; now that the twins were at Mage Hall, she wasn't needed at Roseguard either. Until she had hard evidence—*any* evidence—of Vellerin Dombur's intentions and/or Glenin's involvement with them, the Council wouldn't listen to her. And for so many years she'd had so little to do with the running of Roseguard and Sheve that none of the clerks, stewards, or factors ever listened to her anyway.

She asked Taguare if he had any pressing business, and got a cheerful "Nothing I can't postpone. Did you want to do some traveling?" in reply. Then she asked if he'd care to go to Ambrai with her.

He would. They did.

Rather than ride southwest to Cantratown, they

headed for the Sheve side of Tillin Lake. Tucked into forest that came right down to the water was the resort town of Peyres, whose indigenous population was exclusively composed of the Families Fenne, Ildefrons, Lille, and Sonne. The local Mage Guardians—a young Healer, a middle-aged Warrior, an elderly Scholar, and a young Mage with three daughters—were all Sonnes and lived together in two floors over a storefront. They supported themselves with the lending library run by the Scholar, the apothecary run by the Healer, and the brisk trade in souvenir pottery run by the Mage's husband (a Golebirze from Rinesteenshir, with cousinly connections to the ceramics trade). When Sarra presented herself at their shop—an improbably harmonious collation of books and folios, pots and plates, all overhung with pungent scents from the Healer's drying herbs—she was welcomed as warmly as if she, too, were a Sonne. Or a Mage Guardian.

Scholar Virrena took Taguare off into some dim corner to peruse literary oddities. Her grandson Kanelto, the Healer, brewed up a tea guaranteed to restore the energy of the weariest traveler. The Mage was named Dantia, and shooed her daughters upstairs before making herself and Sarra comfortable in the soft, ancient chairs provided by the hearth for book-browsers. During tea and talk, Sarra caught a glimpse every so often of awed young faces framed in silver-blonde curls, peering down from the banister rails at their august visitor.

As she sipped and chatted, one part of Sarra's mind mused on how nice it might have been to live this way: husband, children, family, a small business in a small town, and nothing more pressing to worry about than whose book was overdue and where to find febrifugal herbs and whether there'd be any shipping breakage in the latest consignment of ceramics.

Collan would have lost his mind in short order. So, truly told, would she. But it was nice to dream a little of a simpler life.

The Warrior Mage, Avin, was off on his weekly rounds of nearby villages; his role was more that of legal resource than constable. Dantia laughed when Sarra asked about crime, saying that her uncle's most spectacular case in the last seven years had been finding and apprehending a horse thief.

"We have the usual petty burglaries during the season, and he keeps a sharp eye on all the tourists, but I don't think he's unsheathed his sword in years except to practice with it. Every so often he gets enough locals together to hold a fencing class."

"A Warrior, but not the warring type?"

Dantia nodded, short golden curls bobbing. "His presence is enough. Makes good people feel safer, and bad people feel watched. Now, Lady Sarra, what can I do for you? Besides a bed for the night, that is. Most of the inns are packed full, and the ones that aren't I'd recommend only to a Malerrisi. If the bugs didn't get her, the food would."

"You're very gracious. I accept the offer for myself and *Domni* Taguare." And she'd leave a little something behind to compensate the Sonnes for their hospitality. They'd refuse direct payment, but not gifts for the daughters. Reminding herself to look through her saddlebags for something appropriate, she continued, "I was hoping that one of you Mages might take us through the Ladder tomorrow."

"No trouble at all. The opera house will be empty until the crew comes to set up around Eleventh." She smiled at Sarra's bewilderment. "That's where the Ladder is. And it's a lively place, for all that we're so far from anywhere. Off-season it's strictly local talent, but while the city-folk are here, we hire in some of the best voices on Lenfell. Sevy Vasharron himself comes every year for a week." Dantia tried to conceal pride, and failed. "This Allflower he told me my eldest has a real career ahead of her, and to come see him in another year or so."

"I'll expect to see her at the opera one day," Sarra said. "If she's not Mageborn, that is."

"Thirteen, and no sign of it," Dantia said with a sigh, and after some quick calculations Sarra decided that Dantia must've had her first child when barely out of childhood herself; she couldn't be much more than thirty now. "I'm hoping music will make up for magic."

"I'm sure it will," Sarra replied. "Music is a magic

unto itself—I've had Bard Falundir's example of it before me all these years, so I can attest to it."

The Mage winked slyly. "And that husband of yours has his own kind of magic as well, yes? We hear about him, even up here."

Sarra dimpled because it was expected of her, then asked, "But why is the Ladder in the opera house?"

Dantia grinned all over her round, snub-nosed face and quoted, " 'Under over, over under/Ladder rungs are made of thunder.' It's located in the special effects stall."

"Where they create the appropriate noise for the scene on the moors in *Lusina Delammeror,*" Sarra supplied, smiling back. Alin Ostin would have appreciated that one.

"I hear you figured out quite a few of those rhymes yourself."

"One or two. And not really my doing. So, Guardian Dantia, is there anything you'd like to bring to the attention of a Councillor?"

"Not a blessed thing, St. Miramili be praised. We lead a quiet life here, Lady Sarra. There's no trouble."

Sarra sighed happily and held out her cup for more tea. "Do you know what a relief it is to hear someone say that?"

That evening she took a solitary walk by the lake. The collection of inns—some grandiose, some modest, all with wonderful views—sprawled along the shore a mile from town, and she could just make out families and couples strolling or swimming or seated on the narrow beach sipping cool drinks. Sarra again wondered what it would be like to bring her husband and children here for a holiday—away from legislative aides and Web factors and all manner of petitioners. Nothing to do but eat, drink, sleep, read, paddle in the water, and make love with Collan. It sounded just about perfect.

Sarra found a convenient rock to sit on, and slipped off shoes and stockings to dangle her feet in the water. It wasn't too late for a calmer life. She could retire from the Council at the next election. Her first term, from 969 to 975, she had gotten quite a bit done. Her second term, a full one of eight years according to the new laws, had been highly satisfying. She had run unopposed in 983—though that had been only a year after Glenin had tried to kidnap the twins, and she'd thought seriously about retiring then. But whatever position she held, she and her children were a threat to the Malerrisi, so she concluded that she might as well be where she could do some good. She was up for reelection in 992 for the eight-year term that would take Lenfell to the next Census in the year 1000. Did she want to stick it out that long?

Ah, but who did she want to see in her place?

And who could do the work as well as she?

And who but a Councillor had enough power to change things?

Well, she'd deal with Vellerin Dombur (and possibly Glenin), then decide. If she waited until the Fortieth Census to retire, she'd be—Saints, fifty-four? And Collan in his sixties? She laughed a little at that, and kick-splashed the lake water with both feet. Truly told, Col *was* showing some gray hairs in that head of coppery curls, but he would *never* be old.

All at once she felt a shimmering in her mind, a strange unheard call—and a chill at her breastbone. Confused, it took her a minute to realize the tiny Globe Cailet had given her was the source of the cold. She drew it out of her shirt and looked at it: milky-white still, but with a subtle crimson pattern of sparks deep in its heart.

Danger. Danger from magic.

She grabbed her shoes and stockings and ran up the empty beach. The little protective Globe had never done this before—she usually forgot it was anything other than a unique piece of jewelry—and she had no intention of staying around to find out what its insistent warming chill meant. She needed Mages around her for protection.

As she hurried back up the darkening streets to the library-apothecary-pottery shop, she held the sphere in her fist. It slowly warmed to its usual temperature, just a little warmer than her body. By the time she got inside the shop, it was as if the Ward had never called to her.

She glanced around at the placid domestic scene and felt foolish. The three girls were eating their dinner by the hearth while their father cooked for the guests, the

Scholar was recording the day's lendings and returns in her ledger, the Healer ground mysterious things into a mortar, and Taguare sat with Dantia Sonne discussing her daughters' school. So normal, so serene. None of them had felt a thing. Perhaps she hadn't, either.

But as she slipped the Globe back into her shirt, she remembered Cailet's talk of shadows, and how her sister had tried to get her to stay and learn how to use her magic. If she had, she would know how to protect herself without running to the nearest Mage Guardians.

As she lay restless in bed that night, the round bit of crystal seemed to poke into her whichever way she turned. She should have given it to Taigan long ago—it might have given some warning of Glenin's presence at the theater that night. Cailet had never provided either of the twins with one of these—she'd trusted to her Wards, and in the end she'd been right. But Sarra had never let her sister set Wards over her. Whatever Gorynel Desse had done to her in the past was enough. Besides, *she* trusted more to Collan's protection than to magic.

And as she turned over yet again to face the empty half of the bed, she knew that the person she *really* wanted to run to was thousands of miles away.

4

"Taigan, honey, you keep lookin' at that glass ball as if it'd been a snake and bit you."

Taigan hated being called *honey*. She hated the silly glass ball she'd been ordered to treat as if it were a real Mage Globe. She hated Jenira Doriaz's Dindenshir drawl. She hated the Captal for assigning her education to this fossilized relic of a bygone era. And she most of all hated that in the six weeks since Mother had brought them here, Mikel was surpassing her at every turn. He could not only run the Morning Five without breathing hard, but also hold his own with Rennon Bekke in sword practice and construct a living, shining, power-born Mage Globe *and* defend himself with both.

She was beginning to hate Mikel, too.

Sullenly obedient to the lesson she'd been put through every day for a week, Taigan picked up the glass orb and cradled it in one palm. With the other hand she drew one of the twin Rosvenir knives from her belt. Not the sword lying ready for her on the workbench; knives had always been good enough for her father, who'd taught her how to use them.

Jenira Doriaz sighed. They'd been through that argument before, with the old Mage insisting on the sword and Taigan stubbornly adhering to her knives—*toad-stickers,* Jenira called them.

"Y'know, maybe you'd care for the notion that a sword's a man's weapon, not a woman's, on account of we're just too dainty in the wrists. But you know what *I* think? I think a man with a sword's a more dangerous thing, on account of they're more likely to use it once it's took up in their hands."

"What?" Taigan tried to picture Mikel as a blood-thirsty, blade-swinging maniac.

The Mage settled onto a chair, thin knotted fingers clasped around her knees. "In my young day, my cousin Maidi married a big strong boy, as good in the heart as he was in the fields with a plow. They lived in a ram-shackle about ten miles from us, and worked and sang and made lots of babies, happy as Dafties on St. Alilen's Day. But one summer's day, a no-Name drifter come through, and she saw how many babies Maidi had—eight by then—and decided she had so many she couldn't miss one of 'em. So the drifter woman took one of 'em—a girl, of course, to pass off as her own First Daughter."

Taigan shifted from one foot to the other, glass globe in one hand and knife in the other, wondering if there was a point to this long-winded lecture.

"Now, Maidi was up to town with her First Daughter and the two older boys, seeing to some buying and sell-ing, and her husband was out working their fields, and the other children were under the care of their hired man. The drifter knocked him upside the head and made off with the little girl, and nobody knew anything until the husband came back at noonday. He found the babies howling, and the hired man lyin' on the floor with an egg-lump at his ear, and the baby girl gone. His hand took up his reaping scythe and he set out after the drifter, and he tracked her down by the sound of the baby crying, and he came up on the drifter woman and sliced the head right off her shoulders. And then he took the baby girl back home."

"He *killed* the woman?" Taigan exclaimed.

"He did that. On the way back to home, he was thinking about what the hired man must've been thinking, to let a stranger into the house—and she was a pretty stranger, so he figured he knew why—he set the baby down with the other children and shut the door, and took the hired man outside, and lopped off his head, too." Jenira Doriaz rocked back and forth on her chair, hands gripping bony black-clad knees, shaking her head. "It was darkfall by then, and Maidi and the three older children come up the road, and he saw them and realized he was as good as dead for having killed a woman. He—"

"But if she was a drifter, and Nameless, then how would anybody find out?"

The old Mage cocked a brow. "Your father's daughter, right enough. Taigan, honey, people *always* find out. Don't you ever have yourself any secrets, because people *always* find out and use 'em to trap you. Anyway, he thought on what he'd done, and looked at the bloody scythe, and went out the back door down to the creek where nobody would see him in the gloom. And he propped the scythe just so between some rocks, and toppled over onto it like a great big tree. The blade sank into his heart and he died."

Taigan waited for more. There wasn't any. Knowing some sort of reaction was expected, she said, "It was wrong of him to kill the woman—I can understand why he did, but he didn't have to. He could've threatened her with the scythe and taken the baby safely away. But since he did kill her, he should've hidden her body and nobody would've known."

Jenira shrugged. "And the hired man?"

Taigan went on, "It was his fault the baby was stolen—more or less—but killing him wasn't justified. And it was stupid, because it couldn't be covered up. But it was *really* stupid to kill himself—he left your cousin with eight children and no husband to raise them."

"Is that what you get out of it, girl? That yes, he was wrong, but worse, he was stupid?"

"Well . . . yes."

"What about the scythe?"

"What about it?"

In answer, the elderly Mage stood and hefted the sword from the workbench. Without warning—and with speed and strength impossible in someone her age—she swung it at Taigan.

Yelping, Taigan dropped and rolled. Her knives were no defense against that shining length of steel—which, though blunt at the tip and lacking an edge, could bruise her badly if it connected. The glass globe shattered on the floor. Taigan scrambled away from the shards, but not quite fast enough, cutting the heel of her thumb.

"And you didn't even steal my little girl," said Jenira Doriaz, and set the sword down and walked out of the room.

Taigan sat on the floor and picked glass from her thumb. What had that crazy old woman tried to do? *"What about the scythe?"* What was *that* supposed to mean?

Ordinarily she would have gone to Mikel to talk it over. But Mikel was beyond this lesson, presumably, and it would be like the two of them had always been with music: he'd look at her with a kind of confused, pitying helplessness, and try to explain without condescension, but he'd never be able to make her understand.

There wasn't anyone she could talk to about this. Not Mikel, not the Mages, not the other Prentices—

Her thoughts leaped to Jored Karellos. But he'd long since learned whatever it was Jenira Doriaz had wanted to teach her today. He'd probably look at her the way Mikel would.

"Your father's daughter, right enough." And just what the hell was wrong with that? Taigan pushed herself

up off the floor and glared down at the slivers of glass. This was the ninth such globe she'd broken, one way or another, in the last week. As she found broom and dustpan to sweep up the remains, she felt a dejected certainty that it wouldn't be the last.

All right, she was supposed to learn something. The drifter was wrong to steal the child; the husband was even more wrong to kill her for it. And, Taigan maintained, foolish not to hide the body. Killing the hired man was also wrong, and even more foolish. Killing himself—

Glass tinkled into a waste bucket from the dustpan, and the sound startled her into another thought. She could see her father killing the woman and the hired man. She didn't doubt that had he caught up with Glenin Feiran she'd be as dead as the drifter and the hired man. That was how Fa was. But he would never have killed himself afterward. He was worth more to her and Mikel and Mother *alive,* and he knew it.

So was she supposed to glean from the story that the husband didn't know his own value to his family? She didn't think so.

And she couldn't fit the scythe into it.

Back to the beginning. The husband came home, found the baby gone, and went for the scythe. Taigan still thought he should have used it just to threaten. He didn't have to kill the woman, or the hired man, or himself—

And then she had it. If the scythe hadn't been there, three people wouldn't have died. The husband did the killing, but the scythe made killing possible. A necessary farming tool had become an instrument of murder.

Was a sword like that?

No—a sword was *meant* for killing. It was an instrument of murder from the instant of its forging. So were her knives. Fa had taught her how to use them to defend herself, which included techniques for killing an attacker if it came to it. She was the envy of her friends, whose parents couldn't envision their darling daughters ever needing to defend themselves against a world that could never be hostile.

But Taigan knew how to use her knives. They and the sword required hands to wield them, just as the scythe did. And what had the Mage said earlier, about the danger of a sword in a man's hands because he's more likely to use it? Was a sword *less* dangerous in the hands of a woman?

That made no sense. Had it been *her* daughter the Nameless drifter woman had stolen, Taigan would've killed her with her bare hands if necessary. She'd be dangerous, even without a sword.

Or was this not about swords at all, or knives, or scythes, or any bladed thing?

Was it about magic, and the weapon it could become?

Magic required a Mageborn to use it. Magic could be dangerous, no question about that. What if the husband had been Mageborn, and gone after the drifter with his magic?

"She'd be just as dead," Taigan said aloud, "and so would the hired man and even the husband, because killing was what he *wanted* to do. How he did it makes no difference—"

And suddenly the glowing thing inside her, still imperfectly sensed and unavailable for her full use, frightened her.

She fought that. She had never been frightened by anything in her life. She *was* her father's daughter—much more so than her mother's, a thing not to be admitted in a world where the brief spark of a father's seed was held to be much less important than the steady flame of a mother's nurturing. Mikel had Fa's music, his red hair, and his looks, but Taigan had his spirit.

Thus she repudiated fear. The magic in her was *her* magic, and she'd use it as she saw fit, and if at some point in her life she decided she must kill with it, then. . . .

But that wasn't what being a Mage Guardian was about, was it?

Mages had killed during the Rising. Warrior Mages were trained for it. Every Mage vowed to do anything necessary to protect the life of the Captal—Taigan had witnessed Ollia Bekke proudly swear that very thing at her Listing Ritual. "Necessary" could include killing; that was implicit. How did that fit an ethic of protection, defense, and beneficial use of magic?

Well, some people needed killing.

And who decided who those people were, and how they were to die?

Fa had killed. He'd made the decision that someone else's life wasn't as valuable as his own, that this specific person in front of him needed killing. He trusted his own judgment.

But he would gladly die for Taigan and Mikel, and Mother, and even the Captal. Hadn't he resisted Auvry Feiran's tortures for days and days rather than reveal Cailet Rille's identity?

"*. . . I know your father too well to believe that he raised you to be self-sacrificing altruists.*"

Taigan slumped in a chair. How did you know when it was time to sacrifice yourself for someone else? How did you decide who it would be? How did you figure out whether or not somebody needed killing? How did you know that you were worth more than somebody else?

That husband who had killed the drifter and the hired man and himself—his daughter was obviously worth more than the drifter's life. More than the hired man's. But his own life?

And what if the scythe hadn't been there?

What if Taigan didn't carry a sword or knives?

What if she didn't have magic glistening inside her—still just out of reach even though the Wards were gone?

She knew only one thing for certain: she'd never thought learning to be a Mage Guardian would *hurt* so much.

5

"ARE you sure this is a good idea?"

Mikel turned a fierce look on Taigan in the midnight dimness. "I got put through that blunt-sword-and-fake-Mage-Globe routine, too."

"You don't know what a relief it is to know you feel the same way I do about all this."

He shrugged and touched her arm. "If we can get this done, then they'll stop treating us like children. Come on."

They left the corridor outside her chamber and stole downstairs, heading for the stables. In the last few days, Taigan had managed not to break any more glass balls and Mikel had managed to Warm a huge kettle to boiling as well as Fold a quarter-mile of the road to Heathering. But the truth of it was that not only were they convinced they were being held back from learning *real* magic, they missed each other's company at lessons. Except for the wall, they'd been taught nothing together. They were so accustomed to sparking each other's thoughts and ideas while learning the same things at the same time that they felt off-balance.

But Mikel now had the basics of Mage Globes, and he'd offered to teach Taigan, and so they were headed out to the stables in the dead of night. Taigan intended to dazzle Jenira Doriaz by getting the Globe right; Mikel wanted Taigan to bounce ideas off for more advanced versions he'd so far only imagined. Her instincts were almost as good as their mother's.

They had chosen the stables primarily because at this hour it was populated only by horses, barn cats, and furry vermin. They had also heard the tale of the Great Mage Globe Mishap, and what better way to show everyone they were ready to learn serious magic than by succeeding where others had failed?

Some years earlier, two Prentices had decided to see if they could encase a living creature within a Mage Globe. Their first attempt used a cricket; it chirped, hopped, struck the glowing magic, and then refused to move. Releasing it, none the worse for the experience, they chose to try something bigger—a mouse, for preference. But catching mice was much harder than catching crickets, so one of them made friends with a barn cat. In due course, she was presented with a little brown bundle of fur—stunned but still living. The cat, having received due tribute, sat grooming herself while the Prentice conjured a Mage Globe around the mouse. All well and good—until the mouse, realizing it was in no immediate danger of becoming lunch, started to run.

Around and around the sphere it galloped, like a kitchen boy in a turnspit wheel—the Globe rolling right along with it. The Prentices chased frantically after it all over the stable. The cat, vastly intrigued by this glowing new toy, joined in—hunkering down in hunting mode, batting the sphere with a paw when it got within reach. Mouse-in-magic, fascinated feline, and horrified Prentices dashed about, bouncing off hay bales and seriously annoying the horses.

Then the second Prentice had the bright idea of putting a large Globe around the smaller one. But she was a little too enthusiastic: she caught both scurrying mouse *and* stalking cat within the sphere. The cat was more than seriously annoyed. Denied escape by the large glittering ball around her, denied as well the prey within the small glittering ball, she, too, began to run. And because a cat is bigger than a mouse, and the Globe around the cat was bigger than the Globe around the mouse, her speed across the stable floor was astonishing.

Now the first Prentice gave it another try. She caught sight of the Globe's glow behind a hay bale, and created the largest sphere yet to trap the two smaller ones. She did so without checking on the location of her friend—who happened to be kneeling beside the double orb that had just fetched up against a corner.

Ensphered with dazzling suddenness, she fell over—and the great Globe rolled every which way, the trapped mouse and the trapped cat and the trapped Prentice tumbling over and over inside their respective Globes, knocking into stalls and the door of the tack room and the appalled Prentice, who couldn't for the life of her remember how to cancel the spell.

Naturally, at this point the Captal showed up. Back from an afternoon ride into Heathering, she slid from her saddle laughing so hard she could barely stand up. Her mare, a Maurgen Dappleback of sixteen venerable years, was not at all disposed to such nonsense in *her* stable. Horses had no patience with magic. So the mare let fly both hooves into the Globe as it spun past. All the magic burst into a million sparks: the Prentice escaped, and then the cat, and then the mouse, but nobody noticed the latter two scurry away because the sparks had set the nearest hay bale on fire.

"They say," concluded Jored Karellos, telling the story at dinner one night, "that the Captal was still laughing as she helped put out the fire."

Everyone at the table chortled, but Josselin Mikleine raised a finger in warning, speaking in dire tones belied by dancing gray eyes. "The two Prentices were assigned to mucking out stalls for the next six weeks, and the cat was never more seen at Mage Hall."

"Smart cat," Jored grinned.

"Who were the Prentices?" Taigan asked.

"Nobody knows," said Josselin. "Or at least anybody who *does* know isn't telling."

"And the moral of the tale, my children?" Jored inquired sententiously.

Joss beat him to it. "If you build a better mousetrap, it'll find a path to the door!"

Taigan and Mikel thought the story as funny as everyone else did, but to them the moral of the tale was that the two Prentices just didn't try hard enough. Thus they entered the stables that midnight not to build a better mouse-trap, but to prove to themselves—and all concerned, especially the Captal—that they were powerful enough in their magic to ensphere a living thing and produce it tomorrow morning perfectly safe and sound.

They weren't after a mouse, or a cat—and they certainly weren't going to experiment on each other. No, the real challenge was the animal that didn't believe in spells.

They were going to present the Captal with her own horse, gift-wrapped in magic.

Worthy of their father at his most outrageous, it was, of course, Taigan's idea. It would amuse everyone at Mage Hall, and the Captal would get a good laugh out of it (she hadn't been seen to so much as smile for weeks), but it would also show everybody that they knew what they were doing when it came to magic.

The stables were dark and quiet but for the sleepy

snorting of the horses and skittering of mice and rats as they avoided hunting felines. Mikel lit a glass-shaded lamp beside the tack-room door, and sat on a hay bale, and began his lesson.

"All right, stand in front of me—not too close, if you louse this up I don't want you to singe my eyebrows off. Imagine you're holding one of the glass balls. Sort of feel it in your hands. Now find your magic inside your head. Get it?"

"I think so."

"You have to *know* so before you can do this, Teggie."

She paused a moment, then squeezed her eyes shut. "Got it."

"All right, now you send it down your arms, and form it around the glass in your hand—like shaping clay around a mold—"

"But there *isn't* any glass in my hands!"

"You have to *imagine* it, to give you something to shape the magic around," Mikel responded patiently.

"Magic," Taigan said, opening her eyes, "is *not* imaginary."

"Oh?" He leaned against a stall door, folding his arms. "What is it, then—solid rock?"

"You know what I mean. And stop sounding so superior, just because you can do this and I can't—yet." She paused. "You *can* do it, can't you?"

For answer, Mikel cupped his hands in front of his chest, frowning with concentration. A Mage Globe flickered into being. It was hazy around the edges, and more gray than white, and the usual lightning didn't flash across the surface but instead crawled in little snail-trails, but it *was* a Mage Globe.

"There. You see? Told you."

It was how they'd accomplished things all their lives—one of them learning how, and egging the other on with smug demonstration of the new skill. Taigan had been first to learn how to jump her pony over the garden hedge; Mikel, how to do fractions; her proficiency at dancing had spurred him to at least reasonable grace; he'd taken to the water like a fish and she'd followed him in because she was damned if she'd be left behind in anything. Only his music had eluded her. And she had nothing to match it with, unless you counted being good with her knives—but *he* was by all accounts getting very good with a sword, so he was still at least one up on her.

But this Mage Globe thing—this she could do. This she *would* do. It was all a matter of learning how to use the magic already inside her. And if Jenira Doriaz wasn't going to teach her, then she'd have to learn it from Mikel.

Accordingly, she again shut her eyes, and cupped her hands, and tried very hard to imagine the feel of the glass ball.

It took shape in her hands, the coolness of it, the smooth curves, the bubble-weight that suddenly grew heavier as her mind gave forth of its magic, and she opened her eyes to see a pale gray-gold glow shaped between her palms in a perfect sphere—

"I did it!" she gasped.

And it vanished.

"Don't worry," her brother soothed. "Same thing happened to me the first time."

"Did you see it? I *did* it! I *felt* it!" She clapped her hands together, grinning. "Now I'm going to make it come back, and this time without imagining any silly old piece of glass either!" She shut her eyes and felt the kindling along her arms, down wrists to palms. She felt as if she juggled stars in her hands, stars made of dazzling light and searing heat that could never hurt her because *she* controlled these stars—they were *hers,* created of *her* magic that tingled on her skin and danced off her fingertips.

She didn't hear the cats yowling, or the horses screaming, or her brother's single horrified shout of her name.

She did hear the Captal's stern command, and a gout of ice surging up her numb arms, following the path of her magic back into her skull.

STOP. NOW.

And all at once it was as it had been all her life—the magic was locked inside her. Warded. Shut away, boxed up, denied her—

No! she screamed inside her head. *You* can't—*not when I'm just learning to use it!*

She opened her eyes, blinking away tears of rage and frustration. The Captal stood before her, like a slim black candle with flaming golden hair. Taigan saw her through a crystalline sphere shot with yellow and crimson and deep blue lightning.

It wasn't a Ward that imprisoned her magic. It was a Mage Globe, imprisoning *her.*

She couldn't hear anything. She could see the Captal's lips move, and Mikel walk shakily to the Captal's side, one sleeve of his shirt blackened as if he'd fallen into a pile of soot. He said something, shook his head, and the Captal nodded.

The Mage Globe disappeared. Taigan pulled in a deep breath, wondering why the air smelled burned.

"How dare you?" the Captal demanded. "Is this how you repay the kindness and patience of your teachers?"

Mikel stood by in miserable silence. Taigan tried to meet the Captal's black gaze, and couldn't. She looked anywhere but at this woman who had once been their adored Aunt Caisha—and saw that the whole space before the tack room, hay bale and wooden walls and the halters hanging on nails, was . . . *singed.* As if flames had shot through the area, extinguished before they could catch fire and burn. She looked again at Mikel's shirt, and whimpered low in her throat at realizing what she had done.

"Is this how you repay your mother, for bringing you here before you were ready?" the Captal asked in a voice that charred the pride off Taigan's soul. "Is this how you repay *me?*"

"I—I didn't mean—"

"You didn't *mean* to. But you did. Until your training is equal to your power, you'd best be careful of what you do. Or you're liable to *kill* without meaning to." She conjured up a brilliantly glowing sphere from thin air. "You want your magic very badly, don't you, Taigan? And you, Mikel? To affirm your own magic by teaching her what a Mage with over fifty years' experience couldn't teach her? Well, here's more magic. Inside this is all the knowledge about Mage Globes you could possibly want. Take it. Either of you, both of you—I don't care. Take it. Will it make you a Mage Guardian?"

Mikel's blue eyes filled. "No," he whispered. "I'm sorry, Captal."

She glared at him for a moment longer, then turned on Taigan. "What about you? You seem to want magic even more than he does. Take this, why don't you? That way, you'll *know* how without ever having to go to the trouble of *learning* how. Take it!"

Taigan shook her head, unable to speak.

The Mage Globe dissolved in a glare of crimson light. "I think we can all agree that what you did tonight surpasses mere stupidity. I leave it to you to decide which of your actions were cowardly, and which were the barest beginnings of wisdom."

And with that, the Captal strode from the stables, leaving two frightened Prentice Mages behind her.

6

"So now they're scared of me—isn't that just perfect? I lost my temper and yelled at them and now they're terrified of me and what am I going to do about it?"

Falundir looked slightly amused, presumably at the notion of Sarra and Collan's children being terrified of anyone or anything.

The Captal had been pacing for a solid hour. The Bard had been watching for most of it, appearing at her door a few minutes after she returned from her face-off with the twins. At first she was silent; then she let loose a few of Gorynel Desse's choicest expletives; then she wore down the nap of a Cloister rug a while longer; finally she started talking.

Gorsha, having expressed mild shock at her appropriation of the vulgarisms, further observed that everything she said was a question. "Do you know what they did tonight?" and "How could they be so stupid?" and

"What if I hadn't felt their magic?" and "Don't they understand how dangerous it is?"

Falundir, of course, could not have answered even if he'd *had* answers.

"What am I going to tell Jenira and Tirez about how to take it from here?" and "How can I discipline them without making them fear me?" and "Should I have waited until they were older—or brought them here years ago?"

At last she heard a question she knew the answer to: "Should I take over their training myself?"

She sighed, shaking her head. "I can't. They're scared of me now."

Falundir shrugged.

"You're right," she said, whether to him or herself, she didn't know. She paused at a table to trim the wick of an old-fashioned lamp. "And I've got a hell of a nerve. Lecturing them on *learning* as opposed to *knowing*. I'm such a damned hypocrite. How did *I* get to be a Mage? The easiest way in the world—I had it all handed to me on a gilt plate."

In the thirty-seven years since First Councillor Anniyas had cut out his tongue and slit every tendon in his fingers, Falundir had never even attempted speech. He did not move his lips to form words for others to read; he did nothing more than arch a brow or cock his head or smile or frown—when he deigned to react to other people at all. But Cailet, Sarra, and Collan were not "other people." To them, when he wished to communicate and his List was not to hand, he hummed.

It worked best with Collan, who knew almost as many songs as the great Bard did. A few notes, a phrase, and Collan could identify not only the song but the lyric that said what Falundir meant. Sarra had scant ear for music, but nearly twenty years with a Minstrel husband had perforce taught her quite a few ballads, and Falundir was adept in his selection when he wanted to tell her something.

Cailet didn't have to rely on her own knowledge. She had Gorynel Desse, Alin Ostin, Lusath Adennos, and Tamos Wolvar to identify the tunes for her.

Falundir was humming now, and after a moment the song flitted through her mind. And though she'd worked herself into a fine sulk, she couldn't help but giggle.

" 'The world is a peach/And I am the pit/That the carelessly wealthy/Spew out with their spit'? Thanks!"

He grinned and kept humming, and the words of the next verse sang cockily in her head:

> *I am the pit*
> *In the succulent peach*
> *The wealthy bite into—*
> *And shatter their teeth!*

That brought a real laugh from her. "You're impossible!"

Falundir smiled modestly.

"So what *do* I do about the twins?" She fell into an overstuffed armchair by the window. It was still dark outside, not even halfway through the night yet. "Maybe being scared of me isn't so bad—if what you meant is that they've taken a big bite and cracked a tooth or two. But they really *do* have the strength to spit me out if they feel like it." Propping her feet on the footstool, she contemplated the scuffed toes of her boots for a moment before continuing. "You wouldn't believe what I saw when I unWorked those Wards. It was amazing enough when I set them in the first place—and it only got bigger by the time I Warded them again. Now. . . ."

It was a guilty pleasure to let loose this way, especially to someone who wouldn't try to reason with her or ask questions she couldn't answer. Falundir just listened. Not even Collan did that anymore. She kicked at the footstool, not so much because she wanted to as because she wanted to do it when someone could see her. She was the Captal, and she wasn't supposed to have petty impulses like that. She wasn't supposed to do or be a lot of things.

Especially scared. That was the trouble. And that made her angry. But she wasn't allowed to get angry. The instant she raised her voice, everyone shrank back as if about to be blasted to cinders with her magic.

But if she could indulge in the silliness of kicking the

inoffensive footstool, she could also indulge in admitting the truth to Falundir. He would never—could never—tell.

"They're frightening in their potential," she said quietly. "And now they're scared of me because I'm scared of them."

Falundir nodded patiently, blue eyes bright in an almost unlined face. One useless hand gestured gracefully for her to go on.

But she had nothing else to say. Anger's brief spark had died, leaving her exhausted. She spread her hands helplessly, let them drop to her lap.

"I don't know what to do."

The Bard was quiet for a time, then began to hum a slower, gentler song. It took Cailet a minute, but this one she identified herself, from a long time ago when she was a newly Made Captal and Collan had sung her to sleep.

> *Come and lie you down, little one,*
> *The golden sun's a-yawning,*
> *Ladymoon's quilt of silver stars*
> *Will wrap you 'round till morning. . . .*

And whether it was the beauty of his voice—the one thing Anniyas had been unable to take away from him—or that voice augmented by his magic, she felt her head drooping back against the soft comfort of the chair.

Sent to sleep like a child. . . .

To someone as old as he, you are *a child, Caisha.*

Mm . . . it'll be nice to be old. . . .

Age has little meaning. All you have to do to grow old is

live long enough.

Or fast enough.

Sleep, Caisha.

7

IF Elin Alvassy was surprised by a visit from Sarra, only her chief butler knew it. By the time Sarra and Taguare arrived in her private reception salon, she had had five minutes to collect herself, and rose to greet her guests with a warm smile.

Sarra, who had just been escorted through her own childhood home (and of course had not told the footman that she knew very well the way to the north wing), could not completely hide her astonishment at the changes Elin had made here. Not that she'd set foot in the Octagon Court since that horrible night in 969; Ambrai belonged to the last of the Alvassy daughters now, and Sarra would have it no other way. There were ghosts here for her. She'd never considered before that Elin must feel the same ghosts.

"Yes, we've made quite a few changes," Elin said in response to Sarra's stare. "It's not the way it was during my childhood, which is all for the better as far as I'm concerned. There are memories enough without everything looking just the same."

"I feel the same way about Roseguard," Sarra told her quickly. "I didn't mean to appear so shocked—it's just so different from the woodcuts done during Lady Allynis's time. This room was much bigger then, wasn't it?"

"It used to be the Tapestry Room—very famous, I'm not surprised you recognized it. We've had to put weight-bearing walls in quite a few of the old grand salons." Elin gestured her visitors to a pair of couches facing a broad bay window, where an efficient staff had already laid out cold drinks and nibble-food. "It was less expensive to do it this way than to shore it up from inside the remaining walls. There are dozens of rooms we still can't use. I don't know if we'll ever be able to put them to rights."

Sarra sat down. Taguare busied himself with pouring drinks for the ladies and selecting choice tidbits for their plates. She thanked him, sipped something strong and icy that tasted of citrus and just enough wine, and looked out onto the gardens. These, too, had changed. The elegant formal plantings her grandmother had favored had been replaced by an easygoing ramble of trees and shrubs and flowers; Lady Allynis's precisely geometrical pebbled walks had become meandering pathways or were overgrown with grass. Sarra was grateful that the little shrine where she had married Collan nearly twenty years ago was out of sight on the other side of the Court. She didn't want to know what changes had been made there.

She hadn't been sure what it would feel like to come back. She'd been even less sure why she wanted to. Now she knew: this life was dead for her. She'd known it the instant she walked up from the wharves and seen the vast expanse of the palace before her. What she had been, who she had been—the child who had scampered through these halls, built mud castles in the flower beds and massive forts of the furniture, and been beloved of parents and grandparents and all who knew her—that child no longer existed. And if the daughter of Maichen Ambrai did not exist, neither did the daughter of Auvry Feiran.

She was a visitor here, no more. A guest. A stranger. She had no claim on this place, and it had none on her, not even through memories. She'd always felt sorry for Cailet, having no experience at all of growing up at the Octagon Court; now, sitting in a room completely changed and looking out at gardens completely different, she realized that the lack of memories freed Cailet. She could be what and who she was because she had nothing to live up to but her own standards and ambitions. Sarra remembered the brilliance and vivacity of this place, knowing she could never achieve what Grandmother Allynis had so effortlessly accomplished every day of her life. The hard work, Sarra could do; the easy graciousness of her home, Collan had provided just as Grandfather Gerrin had done for Grandmother. But the Generations of elegance, of prosperity, of pride that an Ambrai inhaled here with every breath—these were not to be found at Roseguard. Sarra, suddenly and passionately glad of it, felt free for the first time in her life. Allynis's example had always been hell to live up to.

Taguare had been carrying the conversation much too long. Sarra attended to his next remark and Elin's reply, then joined in the casual talk with the smoothness of long practice. If either noted her previous silence, neither commented on it. Sarra steered the talk around to Elin's three daughters and then to what six years ago had been the scandal of two Shirs: the marriage of Pier Alvassy to Mircia Ostin.

Sarra, who loved gossip, asked with a grin, "Has Geria ever resigned herself?"

"On the days she recalls only that my brother is an Alvassy of Ambrai, he's perfect. When she remembers he's also a Mage Guardian, she schemes to divest herself of as many holdings as she can, so Mircia won't inherit as First Daughter of the Name—and so Mircia's children won't inherit as Alvassy kin."

"*That* must entertaining to watch," Sarra observed with a grin. "She's been remarkably acquisitive since the Rising, trying to rebuild what Lady Lilen diversified to the other children."

"It must be terribly confusing for poor Geria," Elin agreed, with a flash of the wicked humor that seemed to be an Ambrai legacy—though her elder sister Mai had shown none of it, Sarra remembered. All at once she wondered what, if anything, Glenin laughed at these days.

Elin went on, "One hand wants to fling away what the other hand grabs. Usually her husband can talk her out of the former. Mircian Karellos has an interest in seeing his namesake as First Daughter of the Ostin Name one day, after all. And it rankles Geria unbearably that Lady Lilen looks to live forever."

"Sweet Saints, how old is she now?"

"Nearly eighty, and thriving. Mircia and Pier spend as much time with her at Ostinhold as they can—and the new baby, if it's a girl, will be named for her."

"How many do they have now?"

"Only three so far—but Mircia's an Ostin!"

Sarra envied the Ostins their casual fecundity. But the Alvassys hadn't done too badly. Elin's three daughters—twelve-year-old Grania, nine-year-old Gorynna, and four-year-old Piera—meant the succession at Ambrai was assured. For a moment she wondered how Taigan might have taken to being Lady of Ambrai, and smiled. Taigan had enough to worry about in becoming a Mage Guardian.

Which reminded her of something. "Elin, has there been any trouble about your magic? Does anyone ever object to a Mage holding so important a position in Ambraishir?"

Elin shook her head. "I don't use magic much anymore. And I'm not Lady of Ambrai the way Allynis was. She ran every aspect of the whole Shir, not just the city. I'm on the Civic Council, but my vote doesn't count any more than anyone else's."

"So you have roughly the same status as, say, Scholar Mage Lisvet Senison does in the Kenroke Town Meeting."

"Just about. I'm a landowner and a businesswoman, so I automatically have a seat on the Civic Council, just as Lisvet does in the Meeting. The Captal is quite adamant about no Mage Guardians serving in official positions. We don't run for elected office, and we don't hold government appointments. She's never made an issue of it, but we all know her mind."

Sarra wondered then why Cailet had tried to persuade her to become a Mage. If she did, and it was known, she would have to give up being a Councillor. Perhaps Cailet was merely anticipating—with uncanny accuracy—Sarra's own leanings toward retirement.

"And I must say," Elin went on, "I'm just as glad that Mage Charter never went through."

Sarra blinked. "But it would have given legitimacy—"

"—to bigots," Elin finished forcibly. "That's something the rest of you never take into account, Sarra, if I may express it so bluntly. Mage Guardians can be ruled by no one but the Captal. Not our training, or how we find Mageborns, or their choice to be educated in magic or Warded against it, or how and when and where we serve Lenfell. The government has no more business in such matters than we have in government."

"I don't agree," Sarra replied with equal frankness, "but it's not a dead issue."

"It must be," insisted Elin.

Taguare, seeing that the ladies—each entirely accustomed to unquestioned rule—were about to begin arguing rather than discussing, interposed with, "I saw some activity at the old Mage Academy grounds, Lady Elin. Are the rumors true?"

"What rumors?" Sarra asked irritably.

"The Civic Council is thinking of turning it into a park," said Elin.

Sarra half-choked on her drink. "A *park?*"

"What else is there to do with it? We've been sorting through the rubble for years, shipping whatever looks interesting to Mage Hall—not that there was much left. But the view from Captal Bekke's Tower is spectacular. I can arrange a tour for you tomorrow, if you like."

"Don't the Mage Guardians still own the land?"

"I talked to Cailet a year or so ago about that. The land is held in trust with the Captal as administrator. She offered to deed it to Ambraishir, but I think we'll end up paying her for it."

Sarra couldn't get over her own reaction. Whatever Elin did to the Octagon Court was all right with her—she didn't want it, not for itself or its memories or its legacy. Why, then, should she feel such indignation that the age-old home of the Mage Guardians was about to be turned into a public garden?

Cailet's fault—reminding her that she was Mageborn also, that she could be trained to use her magic, that she had defenses (and weapons) beyond her wits and eloquence. "I think it's a fine idea," she made herself say, to spite her sister and her own response. Then, because she could not deny the magic that lived within her (unused, uneducated—*wasted?*), she added, "But wouldn't it be dangerous, opening up the Captal's Tower? The Ladder in it leads straight to Malerris Castle."

"Warded," Elin replied. "By five different Mages, myself included. Layer on layer, as strong as we can make them. And on top of *those* is Cailet's own Warding." Her expression turned grim. "My cousin Glenin will not be paying Ambrai a visit through that Ladder."

Elin's cousin, the Warden of the Loom—admitted, acknowledged, and unquestionably part of the reason Elin rarely used magic. But Elin's cousin was also Sarra's sister. Whatever magic was at work in the Ambrai Blood could take either direction. Maybe that was why Sarra had shifted her proprietary interest from the Octagon Court to the Mage Academy. It was a way of choosing sides.

But Elin's being Mageborn had nothing to do with her grandfather, Telo Ambrai—Lady Allynis's brother. It came from her grandmother, Gorynna Desse, Gorynel's sister. Sarra's magic came from Auvry Feiran, the man who had fathered a Mage Captal and a Lady of Malerris.

And a Councillor. Was it Sarra's part to mediate between the two?

She was still mulling it over when she went upstairs after dinner. The whole family, except for little Piera, who was deemed too young—gathered around the huge table Sarra remembered from her childhood. The chips and mars had been repaired so skillfully that one could almost think it undamaged. Everything else was new: gleaming flatware, shining plates and glistening crystal, linen and candle holders and vases for the spectacular arrangements of flowers that were Elin's specialty. If Sarra lowered her lashes to blur the proceedings, she could almost see Grandmother Allynis in Elin's place.

But it was Elin who had taken Allynis's place—and welcome to it, Sarra told herself firmly. Almost all those who had once sat at this table were dead: Allynis, her husband Gerrin Ostin, their daughter Maichen and her husband Auvry Feiran, Elinar Alvassy and her husband Piergan Rille, their daughter Tama and her husband Gerrin Desse. Only that third generation remained: Glenin and Sarra, Elin and Pier. Of the two other cousins, Mai Alvassy was long dead by Glenin's hand—and Cailet had never known the Octagon Court as it had been.

And of the next generation? Elin had three children, Pier was father to another three. Most of them would probably turn up Mageborn. Sarra's twins were at Mage Hall now learning their craft. And then there was Glenin's son, eldest of them all, with the Feiran gift and the magic inherited from Avira Anniyas.

Sarra stood on the balcony of her room, gazing out across the night-blackened river at Bard Hall. It had resumed its function in a small way, but the real pivot of Bardic activity these days was Roseguard—ostensibly because it was Falundir's residence, secretly because Collan directed his Minstrelsy from there.

In the old days, there had been two hubs of power on Lenfell: Ryka Court and Ambrai. One the center of government, one of magic, scholarship, and healing. The first still existed in its intended function; no matter what Elin accomplished, the second would never resume its eminence. Power now resided in two other places. If, Sarra mused, Cailet and Glenin were the living symbols of Mage Hall and Malerris Castle, then was she the embodiment of Ryka Court? Was she stronger for their opposition to each other? Or was she—and all Lenfell— fated to be crushed between them?

Glenin *was* using Vellerin Dombur as her political tool. Sarra knew that as surely as she knew she was an Ambrai. But was Cailet using Sarra the same way? No. Cailet stayed aloof from government—

—because she had Sarra to handle it for her.

Was that what Glenin was after? A balance of herself and the Domburs against Cailet and Sarra?

The balance of Ryka Court and Ambrai had ever been a precarious one. No central government—and the Malerrisi wanted nothing if not to become the central government—could easily tolerate the brilliance and independence of a state ruled by a clever, intelligent Name. Thus had Anniyas attempted to insinuate Auvry Feiran into Ambrai's power structure by forcing him down Allynis's throat as Chancellor. Grandmother hadn't known about the Malerrisi part of it, but she'd been as determined as her dear friend Captal Leninor Garvedian that no Mage would ever hold high political office.

Anniyas must have known that, Sarra told herself. Feiran would have told her it was hopeless. But that concerned Sarra less than why he had cast his lot with Anniyas to begin with. Had he wanted to be Chancellor so much that he would betray the Mage Guardians? Or had there been other reasons?

If there were, Sarra didn't know them. Neither did Cailet. Perhaps Glenin did.

Feiran's daughters had achieved every kind of power he'd ever dreamed of. Glenin had the Malerrisi, Cailet had the Mages—and Sarra had politics. Was that how it had been planned? Did it all come down to just the three of them? Arrogant folly to believe so—and yet. . . .

Long ago Sarra had told Cailet that if Ambrai had not fallen, Glenin would have eventually become Lady of Ambrai, with Sarra and Cailet free to choose what they'd do with their lives. Sarra tried to imagine what she would have done if politics had been closed to her—for of course the sister of Ambrai's ruler could never have been allowed onto the Council. She couldn't think of any task she would have excelled at as she did at the work she had done for the last twenty years. Nor could she imagine Cailet as anything other than Captal. And *that* would almost assuredly have been forbidden. One Ambrai sitting in the Octagon Court, another on the Council, and a third at the Mage Academy? Unthinkable.

And where would that have left Sarra?

Where did her life leave her now? Her elder sister ruled the Mallerisi, her younger sister ruled the Mage Guardians—and Sarra was in the middle.

No. She was with Cailet in all things, especially magic.

But she'd spent the first four years of her life with Glenin. Admiring her, infuriated by her, playing and quarreling and sitting every night at the great octagonal table while their family discussed art and science and gossip and the events of the day. She had loved Glenin. The child in her still did, still looked up to her big sister, still wanted to make them a family the way their family used to be.

But the little girl had not seen what the young woman had seen. Had not witnessed the results of Glenin's torture on the man deeply—if at first reluctantly—adored. Had not felt her heart turn to lead within her breast as she was told of Glenin's attacks on her children. Had not heard her beloved little sister confess terror of Glenin's lurking darkness.

The chime of a clock in the room behind her made her flinch. It had gone First, and she'd been standing here since Half-Fourteenth. Either she was slow of thought tonight or her usual gut-jumping quickness had gone to sleep. It didn't often take her this long to come to a conclusion about anything.

Her instincts might be slumbering, but her mind and body were wide awake. She moved to the far end of the balcony, shivering a little in the night breeze, but from here she couldn't make out the ruins of the Academy. She'd been there this morning, taken through the Ladder from the opera house at Peyres to the "snowy Ladder"—a belowstairs ice room that had served the main Academy kitchens. A few Mages lived in a few rooms near the old infirmary, but she hadn't visited them. She and Taguare hadn't explored at all.

Thousands had passed through the Academy as students of magic; now thousands would descend there for evening strolls and holiday picnics. What it had been, it would never be again.

But all at once, even though she could see nothing of the Academy with her eyes, it rose before her, a vision limned in moonthrown shadows—not as it had been in her childhood, but years before. The trees were different, the flowers, the paint on the lintel of the door to Captal Caitirin Bekke's Tower.

Two men emerged from the doorway, soberly dressed in dark clothes and coifs. One was tall, a black-skinned man in his prime; the other was taller still, though only a youth. She heard them as clearly as if she stood beside them.

"I'm sorry. You understand."
"Yes."
"It's simply too dangerous."
"Yes. Of course."
"Your magic is so strong—in a way, it's a compliment that the Captal can't have you living here."

"It's no compliment. She's scared of me. They all are."

"You can hardly blame them. Your magic came hard to you, I know. Learning to use it and control it will be no easier. But I promise I'll do all I can."

"It doesn't matter. I don't want to live here anyway." The young man turned to the older. *"The only promise I need from you is that you'll teach me. That I won't be completely alone."*

"You have my word. You know you do."

"And—and that if my magic really does turn Wild, you'll kill me."

"Auvry—"

"Swear it. Please. On the way here I came close to killing you without even knowing it—if I ever show signs, promise you'll—"

"It won't come to that."

"But if it should—"

"I'll swear no such thing, because it won't happen. You're strong, you're intelligent, you're more than capable of learning—"

"Gorsha—are you scared of me?"

She never heard the answer. The same voice, older but just as sad, spoke behind her.

"Sarra, are *you?*"

She whirled. He stood there, a tall, dignified Wraith in black Mage Guardian regimentals, gray-green eyes regretful and compassionate and loving.

"No," she whispered, meaning *No, I am not seeing you* and *No, I am not afraid of you.* Both, she knew, were lies. He *was* here, and she *was* afraid.

"Sarra," he said again.

"No!"

He was the darkness, *he* was the shadow Cailet feared. *Him,* inside Cailet's very blood and bones.

Inside Sarra's blood and bones and terrified mind.

"Daughter—"

"NO!"

She stumbled backward, colliding with the scrolled

iron balcony rail, bruising her hands as she groped for support. She could not look away from those sorrowing gray-green eyes.

Gray, like Josselin Mikleine's. Green, like her own Taigan's.

"Sarra—" he said for the third time, and she sobbed aloud as a fingernail snagged and split to the quick on the balcony rail. "I felt that you were thinking of me—please, listen—"

So he could make of her what he'd made of Glenin?

There was another door to the balcony, leading into the bedchamber. Locked. She struggled with the handle, then used her elbow to break the glass pane. She heard him catch his breath behind her—he'd come out into the night, he was following her, he'd hunt her down like an animal and she'd be forced to see him, be with him, listen to his lies—

Her fingers fumbled with the inside door latch. Unlocked it. Opened the door. She ran through the lamplit bedroom, disoriented, gasping. She saw her wild reflection in a tall mirror and cried out. He stood behind her in the mirror, massively tall and utterly black against the blackness of the night outside.

Somehow she found the door into the sitting room. Somehow she found the door into the hallway. She didn't stop running—not even when a footman dropped a tray of glassware at the sight of her—until she was outside in the gardens, the now-unfamiliar gardens that held only one place of refuge.

She fell onto her knees in the little shrine of St. Imili and St. Miramili, the place where she had married Collan Rosvenir amid friends and family and flowers and joy. She huddled there shivering until dawn, cold sweat drenching her, terrified of the shadows that waited for her outside this small sanctum.

That afternoon she boarded a ship for Roseguard. For home. For Collan.

8

SEVERAL holidays in the Saintly Calendar had gradually been shifted from Heathering to Mage Hall over the years. The two patrons of Mage Guardians, Rilla and Miryenne, were celebrated each autumn as the Capital had originally intended. The week-long festival between Saints' Days brought people from all the surrounding villages, who bedded down with relatives in Heathering or in empty classrooms at the Hall between desks and bookshelves. The Guide's Market midweek attracted itinerant swappers from three Shirs, who stayed in their brightly painted wagons out by the walls. It was the last great gathering before the winter set in, and everyone made the most of it.

Somehow the Hall had also become the location for the feast of Lusine and Lusir at Shepherds Moon, the second week of the year. Nobody knew exactly why this was so, but nobody questioned it much—they had too good a time abandoning lessons and duties for an afternoon of games and singing and dancing centered around children—whose patrons the Twin Saints were. There were at any given time at least a dozen daughters and sons of Mage Guardians making life interesting at the Hall, but on the first day of Shepherds Moon the whole place became a riot.

A tradition had grown up—again, no one knew quite how—that on this day all the babies born in Heathering since last Shepherds Moon were presented to the Captal. Never mind if she'd seen them at festivals, or visited their mothers at their homes or farms; this was the great day their families commemorated in their annals, the day little Tamasine or Miri or Velen officially met the Mage Captal. On the holiday in 989, Taigan was privileged to see the Captal introduced to seven infants who (respectively) cooed, shrieked, giggled, slept through it, kicked her in the ribs, yawned in her face, and spit up on her immaculate black regimentals.

Just before this disaster—which made the Captal grin and the mother turn crimson with mortification—Aidan told Taigan that all these babies' mothers had been among the first students in the school system established while Mage Hall was being built. "Almost as much of a shock to the Captal," he said with a grin, "as seeing you and Mikel all grown up."

From the perspective of her seventeen-and-a-half years, Taigan could only shrug. People grew up, got married, had babies; that was how life worked. Why should it be a shock?

Then again, the Captal was a woman about as far removed from the normal courses of life as if she lived at The Cloister. Maybe she didn't even notice time's passage until it was pointed out to her.

Taigan was like Sarra in that infants and toddlers bored her. Children were interesting only when they reached an age for semirational conversation—and in large numbers, as today, even a semblance of rationality was doubtful. She watched from a safe distance as balls were thrown at targets, eggs were carried in spoons, cut-out paper tails were pinned to drawings of sheep, and multi-layered mud pie masterpieces decorated with multi-colored pebbles were solemnly judged by the Hall's cook. It might not have been so bad if it had all occurred outdoors, but a sudden shower had chased everyone inside to the refectory around Tenth. Taigan, who had drawn mop duty this week, glumly surveyed the muddy wreck of the floor she'd have to help clean up.

She stayed long enough to witness her brother demonstrate a hitherto unsuspected fatherly streak by leading the older children in song. It was one Fa had often sung to them when they were little, about a kyyo who tricked a silverback cat into sharing her lair. Mikel used a light, breezy voice to portray the kyyo's blandishments about two being warmer than one, and keeping out unwanted guests while the silverback was hunting, and helping her teach her cubs about life. Taigan grinned to herself as her brother signaled the children to growl the silverback's reluctant agreement just before the first chorus. He kept on playing the lute, but suddenly paused in mid-verse to audition for the two cubs. Amid much giggling and an incredible amount of noise, he settled on a girl and a boy to play the parts, told them when to come in, and resumed the song. The cubs, alone with the kyyo while their mother hunted dinner and the kyyo prepared to make dinner out of them, yipped, yelped, and howled on cue as they made the kyyo's life a misery with impossible questions, playful bites that took out chunks of his fur, and demands to be fed and cuddled and licked clean from nose to tailtip. Just as the silverback returned, the kyyo ran from the lair—and every child clustered around Mikel's feet let out an ear-splitting howl.

A performance worthy of Fa at his best, Taigan thought proudly. But the subsequent uproar as everyone clamored for another song was absolutely the limit for Taigan. Dutifully applauding her twin's success—and glad that all those sticky, muddy little hands weren't touching the good lute he'd left at home in Roseguard— she sidled her way through the raucous crowd into the kitchen. She brewed a mug of spiced mint tea and took it out the back door of the refectory. Despite an increasing restlessness, she intended going up to her room to study—at Mage Hall, not all lessons were in magic, and she had a test on the Revised Statutes of Lenfell two days from now. It ought to have helped that her mother was responsible for much of the revising, but the table-talk of politics that her Roseguard friends so envied had always been more about personalities than law. The latter tended to bore her father.

She was passing the library on her way to the Prentices' Quarters when she saw movement by lamplight through a window. Pausing, she recognized Jored Karellos's dark head bent over a large sheet of paper, pen and ruler in hand. She was in the middle of a debate with herself about going in to talk to him now or returning to the kitchen for another mug when he glanced up, saw her, and smiled.

Taigan went in. "Escaping the mob?" she asked, while holding another interior debate about whether to sit beside him or opposite him at the table. He solved her dilemma by hooking a foot around the chair next to his and drawing it closer.

"I like children—but one or two at a time," he said. "So many of them, and I'm scared I'll step on one, or trip and fall on several, or—"

"—or go deaf with all the yelling," she finished. "I know exactly what you mean." She sipped tea and then offered it to him. "What're you working on?"

"Thank you—smells wonderful." He drank and politely handed the mug back. "It's a map of Mage Hall and environs. There isn't one, you know—just architectural drawings. Because nothing was built at the same time, there's no one comprehensive plan all on one page."

"For art class?" One of the Mages had earned a Firrense Institute Certificate, and when he wasn't teaching geography he taught drawing.

"No, just for the archives. I like to draw things, find out how they fit together—though one of my foster mothers used to say I liked even more taking things *apart!*"

"Machinery and such?"

"Sometimes." Jored leaned back in his chair and smiled. "I'll admit I was a bit destructive on occasion. But I mostly put things back together again afterward."

Taigan examined the drawing more carefully, liking the neat labeling, the precision of line. "These are the floor plans—are you going to do it in elevation as well?"

"Maybe. Now that you're here, can you check the Prentices' rooms for me? I think the women's side is a mirror of the men's, but I've never been there to find out for sure."

"Jored!" she laughed. "You've drawn every building here and haven't learned yet that nothing, absolutely *nothing,* about this place is symmetrical?"

He chuckled low in his throat. "Point taken. But at least it's not *all* as ugly as that wall!" He paused, eyeing her sidelong through heavy lashes. "I don't suppose you noticed my subtle way of saying that I've never accepted any invitations to that side of the building."

Taigan knew flirting when she saw and heard it. Males had been flirting with her since her cradle days, to hear Fa tell it. But the usual flippant replies all felt strange in her mouth—because this wasn't *just* flirting. She gave him one of her standard not-quite-encouraging replies, amusing and kind but designed to put a bold (if polite) man in his place. He grinned his appreciation, and they went to work.

Correcting the map took some time. Only when she sipped tea and found it stone cold did she realize how late it was. Mage Hall was silent now, the distant singing and laughter from the refectory long faded. She glanced to the windows, trying to judge the hour, and started at the image of herself and Jored and the lamp reflected in dark glass. The pair of them looked almost like Mother and Fa, up until all hours working on plans for the Minstrelsy or the Council or improvements to Roseguard.

Suddenly her restlessness had a source: she was homesick. All the children reminded her of her own childhood, when on holidays she and Mikel hosted riotous parties. The song he'd sung tonight as an adult had been one of their favorites when they were little. And now the reflection in the window had recalled her parents to mind, their work together, their partnership that was almost that of equals. It was what she wanted for herself—a thing rare in her parents' youth, but through their example becoming more and more the model for a marriage. She smiled a little to herself as she thought of her father's annoyance that he was no longer the only such husband on Lenfell, no more the only man who had his status and responsibilities and worth openly acknowledged by the woman who'd married him. Still, it ought to make him happy that he wasn't alone anymore; Fa always was one for setting a new fashion. . . .

"I'm no artist," Jored said, "but my trees and shrubs aren't *that* funny-looking, are they?"

Taigan became abruptly aware that she was chuckling. "No, it's not that at all. I was thinking of something else entirely."

He gave a quiet sigh. "Late at night, all alone with a beautiful girl, and she's thinking of something else. Hopeless."

"I like you better when you're not trying to flirt with me," she heard herself say.

He lowered his shining gaze to the drawing spread out before them. "I wasn't sure you liked me at all," he murmured. "But it's what a man does, isn't it? To get a woman's attention? Flirting, I mean."

"Some men. It's amusing, I suppose." She shrugged. "And it can be fun in the right setting. But I'd rather talk honestly, with a man whose opinions interest me."

He said nothing. She regarded him by lamplight, noting the incongruous gold highlights in hair she'd thought to be pure black—and startled by the sudden straight look she received from gray eyes she'd never noticed had tiny flecks of moss-green in them.

He drew a short breath between his lips, as if he'd seen something new about her, too. Still he was silent, and as the moment lengthened she told herself in despair that flirting was *much* easier than waiting through this unbearable, interminable, excitable quiet.

Then he smiled ruefully. "Would you scold me again if I tell you that right now, in spite of what you said about my opinions being interesting, I can't think of a single thing to say?"

Taigan was glad of the chance to laugh. "Something will occur to you eventually. Come on, it's late and I've got early clean-up duty tomorrow." Rising, she stretched deliberately in a way she'd seen her mother use on her father—not that the shapeless tan winter woolens Prentices wore had any of the fluid elegance of her mother's silk clothes. "Let me know if you need any more help with the map."

"I will. Thank you, Taigan."

She was still a little homesick as she scrunched into her blankets that night, but it was longing not only for the home she had known but the home she would one day make. With Jored, perhaps; perhaps with another man; but one day, when Roseguard was hers. . . . She reminded herself drowsily to have Mikel come and sing to her children often . . . a girl and a boy, she decided . . . her First Daughter would look like Mother, black-eyed and blonde . . . and her son would have Fa's coppery hair and beautiful gray eyes with hints of moss-green. . . .

9

IT was a long hike around the forest that huddled beside the river. Cailet had told Josselin to take the lead through the grasslands and up the slope of the hills, since he'd been through this before and knew the location Cailet wanted. She had asked Josselin along for the purpose of honing his skills—and on a kind of personal dare to herself. *Is he—? Isn't he—?* Until Josselin had faced her in the compass octagon, and his magical signature was fully known to her, he would remain a mystery.

And he'd been avoiding that test for a long time now.

For having spent only a year at Mage Hall, Josselin was remarkably advanced in his education. Lirenza Gorrst, the Archivist, gave him excellent marks at Scholarly pursuits, especially Mage Globes. Granon Bekke, Master of Captal's Warders, reported him a confident swordsman. Elomar said he wasn't half bad at basic medicine, which for Elomar was a high compliment. Josselin was adept at any number of spells, some of them quite complex.

She half-despised herself for her misgivings. But the lives of every Mage Guardian and Prentice depended on this risky little game she was playing. *Is he—? Isn't he—?*

And the same applied to Jored. He wasn't as precocious as Josselin in his work, and almost every lesson came hard to him. But there was something about him, too. . . .

Jored was also with them this morning. Following Josselin in single file through the bright autumn morning were Mikel and Taigan, eager for a new skill and to prove themselves worth Cailet's trouble after last week's transgression. Behind Taigan came Jored, silently ignoring the glances Taigan tried not to direct back over her shoulder at him. An interesting development there, Cailet told herself; happily, one's first infatuation usually played itself out with only temporary heartache. She'd seen it happen dozens of times here. But if Jored was Glenin's son—

No, she wouldn't concern herself with that today. This was one of her favorite lessons to teach young Prentices, one she always took upon herself, and she intended to enjoy it without shadows.

The last member of the group was Dessa Garvedian—First Daughter and only child of Lusira and Elomar. She was eighteen this year, as darkly beautiful as her mother, with her father's gift for medicine and few words. Following a fashion that had become popular after the Rising, her first name had been taken not from a Saint but from a Family in her ancestry. Lusira, as it happened, was the daughter of Falun Garvedian and Gorynel Dese.

For Lusira, hiding her father's identity had no longer been necessary after 969. Habit had made her continue it until her daughter was born the next year. When Cailet had heard the baby's name and the reason for it, her jaw simply dropped. She heard Gorsha's laughter in her head and demanded to know why he'd kept this from her.

Forgive me, dearest, but it was none of your business.

None of my—! Geridon's Balls, this makes Lusira part of my Family too, you know! First Telo, your son with Jeymian Renne, and now Lusira! Does Telo know he has a half sister?

Of course he does.

Nice of you. Just how many other offspring of yours are wandering around Lenfell?

That, too, is none of your business.

Dessa had her grandfather's dark skin and startlingly green eyes. When she and Josselin were in a room together, all hearts and every conversation came to a stuttering stop. Come to think of it, Cailet told herself whimsically as the group hiked up into the hills, the company this morning was visually daunting. Dessa and Josselin won the honors, but Jored wasn't exactly ugly and Mikel was ever his handsome father's son. Taigan gave Dessa real competition—she was the best of both her parents, a green-eyed and much improved version of Cailet herself. Which nobody ever saw; *that* Ward had not been unWorked.

On the twins' arrival, Cailet had done some earnest thinking about the Wards around her own chambers. Sarra's blithe entrance into any room Cailet bespelled for privacy told her that her powerful family could stroll right through whatever she created. This was not a good idea with the twins around. So she'd had Granon Bekke re-Work the protections around her rooms. She could get past them, and so could the Mage who had constructed them, but the trick had been to allow Aidan and Marra through to attend her when she wished it. Eventually they'd figured it out. But she told no one the real reason for the alteration, saying only that she had decided her Master of Warders ought to be the one to Ward her.

She should have done it last year, when Josselin and then Jored arrived. But she hadn't—because if one of them had tried to enter her chambers and succeeded, she would have known him for blood kin. Neither had ever tried. She wasn't sure if she was glad or sorry for it.

The hell of it was that she *liked* both of them. They were quiet around her—all the Prentices and a goodly number of the Mages were—but in the classes she taught they were diligent students, pleasant in their manners, thoughtfully spoken when she called on them. Neither was wildly popular, but each had friends. They fit seamlessly into life at Mage Hall. Cailet's suspicion would have shocked the entire community, had they known. They didn't know. No one did, except Gorsha.

He had always dominated the Presences in her mind. He lived within her more surely than the others ever had. They offered their learning and their wisdom when she needed it—though by now she had absorbed most of it into the regions of her mind that were truly her own. Perhaps Alin had been right after all when he'd told her *she* was the one who'd convinced the children to leave Toman—though she had no conscious memory of anything said to persuade them.

But Alin and Tamos and Captal Adennos—she heard their voices so rarely. Gorsha she could talk to, and he would answer—most of the time, anyway. As the group of Prentices reached the broad meadow that was the site for the lesson, Cailet reflected that if she ever told anyone that she held lengthy conversations in her head with the long-dead First Sword, she'd be declared a dangerous maniac and locked up for the rest of her days.

Of course, the gleeful enjoyment she anticipated from today's little exercise was probably indication enough of a thoroughly twisted mind. She preferred to think of it as a slightly twisted sense of humor.

At her signal, Josselin gathered the other Prentices around him. Cailet spent a moment concentrating, then strode uphill to the stepping stones she'd placed years ago in the creek in midmeadow. The land sloped downhill with the watercourse at a gentle angle between groves of tremendous pines, its grasses, flowers, and seeds sweet fodder for all manner of creatures. But those Cailet coaxed from the trees today with a soft spell were her special favorites.

A small herd of pakka—local for pakassos—ambled out into the meadow. Four feet tall at the shoulder, with mottled hides ranging from slate-blue to silver, they looked an unlikely cross between deer and pony. Short, delicate antlers spread over decidedly horsy faces with huge, liquid brown eyes. Though they had no manes to speak of, their tails were extravagant silken plumes that arched impudently before falling all the way to the ground. Their most singular feature was a pair of furry little wing-stumps. Alin had seen other pakassos herds in his travels with Val, and, as a Waster long familiar with the oddities that still turned up unexpectedly in that part of the world, considered them yet another example of the effects of The Waste War. But Lusath Adennos, the Scholar Captal, corrected his impression: the pakkas' winglets were vestiges of a time when they'd been smaller, and light enough to fly.

Cailet walked slowly toward the matriarch, a lovely creature who fluttered her wings to show off the silvery glisten of her hide. Pakkas were shy as a rule, but Cailet had been coming to visit this little herd of twenty or so for a very long time on their migrations to and from Tillin Lake. The current empress was the daughter of the one Cailet had first made friends with seventeen years ago. The Captal approached with all due respect and was allowed to scratch the tuft of black forelock between the slender antlers.

"Going a little gray, your ladyship?" she murmured. "Well, so am I! But not quite ready to give up pride of place to a youngling. Speaking of which, I see your First Daughter is getting to be almost as beautiful as you."

The pakka in question, paler than her mother, skipped over to demand attention. After a perfunctory baring of teeth and a switch of long black tail to let the youngling know who Cailet had really come to see, the empress sauntered off as if she'd grown bored. Her daughter butted Cailet's hip demandingly; Cailet obliged, rubbing her back at each wing-joint. This was some sort of signal to all the little ones, who galloped up, skidded to an untidy halt near Cailet, and made her wish she had a dozen hands to stroke and scratch and pet.

She could have brought them all to her with magic, of course. She'd done that with the empress's mother, the first time she'd come exploring. But it was much nicer to call them and wait to see if they wanted to be friendly. They usually did. Only a few times had they shied back from her, always in spring after a hard winter. She guessed that they remembered being hunted up north for food, and regretted mightily that she couldn't Ward them.

She glanced back over her shoulder. The Prentices were staring—pakkas were rare in other parts of North Lenfell, and never seen in the South at all. "Come on," she called softly. "They don't bite."

Josselin held back, said something to Mikel, and walked off into the nearest trees as if to relieve himself. Cailet hid a grin and watched the other four hop the stepping stones. The older pakkas eyed them thoughtfully, but when they made no threatening moves a few of the animals strolled over to be given their due: crooning admiration and wing massages.

Cailet gave the usual brief lecture on their habits, diet, and social organization, noting the pale kingly buck who immediately singled out Dessa for his regal notice. She'd lived all her life at Mage Hall but never seen a pakka close to, and by her blissful smile as she petted wings and tickled an upraised chin, she was as pleased with the reigning prince as he was with her.

Cailet droned on, the information not as important as the time her discourse was giving Josselin. She answered a few questions, mentioned Alin's speculation and Lusath's certainty about the pakkas' origins (though she did not give proper attribution, for which she silently begged their pardon), and finally got the Prentices round to talking about the magic of animals.

"Magic?" Taigan asked, looking up from where she knelt to cuddle a fuzzy-muzzled yearling with iron-gray dapples on his hide and white wings. "It's just instinct, isn't it? I mean, the temperature tells them when to migrate, and their own trails through the forest tell them how to get there."

"Truly told," Cailet agreed. "But think about this. About seventy years ago, a professor from Shainkroth College took a small pakka herd from Tillin Lake to Maidil's Mirror. She made sure the area was exactly like the place they'd left—same forage, same elevation, same predators, same timing of the seasons. The pakkas were happy as St. Kiy with a full winecup until spring—when the professor expected them to migrate south to the plains around Ambraishir. They didn't. They walked all the way across Sheve Dark to their old grounds at Tillin Lake. Now, is that instinct, or magic?"

"Maybe a little of both," Dessa smiled.

"Captal. . . ."

She half-turned. "Yes, Jored?"

"Aren't instinct and magic sort of the same thing?"

"When the first magic you ever did popped out of your head, did you have to think about it? My guess is that you didn't—any more than the pakkas had to think about where to go for the winter. It's something about the way our brains are put together as Mageborns—just as it's something about the pakkas' brains that tells them when and where to migrate."

Mikel was frowning as he sat in the grass and snuggled a sleepy pakka on his knees. "But we have to *learn* how to use magic. They don't have to learn how to walk from one place to another. They just know." He listened to himself, and flushed crimson beneath his freckles.

Cailet merely nodded, secretly glad he was still embarrassed about the incident in the stables. "It could be that 'use' is the wrong word. We learn to *control* the effects our magic produces. Those who cannot learn, or who never get the chance, or whose magic is too forceful to control, are the ones we say have Wild Magic. Point being," she finished as she saw Josselin leave the forest—from a completely different place than he'd entered by, "that if magic is an instinct with us, we have brains enough and will enough to control it. If we don't, our magic might just as well be Wild. Now, if you've all picked up enough fleas for one morning—"

"He does *not* have fleas!" Dessa objected indignantly, stroking her king's arching neck.

Cailet grinned. "He may not, but the grass does—this meadow also feeds quite a few other furry beasts who aren't as meticulous about bathing as the pakkas."

"They *bathe?*" Jored asked, blinking.

"Very modestly, after dark, and with the empress on alert the whole time. Then they all gather and turn their backs while she has her swim. It's quite a thing to see by moonlight." She walked over to give the matriarch her respects as a good guest should. Fondling the tufted black ears, she said to the Prentices, "While we're here, let's see if there are any late berries."

"So *that's* why we brought the sacks," Mikel said, standing to brush himself off. The dislodged pakka sneezed, gave him a look compounded of disgust and betrayal, and trotted off to his mother.

"Haven't you learned the Captal's Rule yet?" Dessa teased. "Never do only one thing when you can do two. Or three. Or better yet, six."

An hour of berry picking was an unexpected treat. Cailet saw what she'd expected to see: Taigan approaching Jored for some time alone in the woods, and Mikel trying to decide if he dared suggest the same to Dessa. Josselin strolled over, a cloud-dappled pakka with a luxuriant slate-blue tail cantering along behind him. He nodded at Cailet, a gesture that could have been a sign of respect or greeting or apology for his long absence. She knew better. It meant everything was ready.

Now all she had to do was relax beside the stream and watch.

Mikel, who hadn't quite worked up the gumption to get Dessa alone, was the first victim. Josselin grinned when the young man strode purposefully out of the trees, stopped, looked around in befuddlement, then shook his head and returned to the forest. After a few minutes, he repeated the performance, but this time chose another path into the trees.

"Forgot Something," Josselin said.

"Forgot what?" Cailet asked.

"Whatever," he said cheerfully.

"How vicious did you get?" She knelt by the stream to drink from cupped hands.

"Not very. Nothing like the ones Dessa's charming cousin Viko set for *my* group."

A loud sneeze issued from the place Taigan and Jored had disappeared. Then another. And another.

"I may have left a few more of those around than absolutely necessary," Josselin remarked as a fourth and fifth sneeze, both Taigan's, sounded. He settled in the middle of the creek on one of the stepping stones, drew up long legs, wrapped his arms around his knees, and gave Cailet an innocent smile.

Taigan sneezed again. Cailet shook her head. "She seems more susceptible than Jored."

"Or she hasn't figured out yet that all she has to do is move away from that big boulder." As Dessa came out into the meadow, heading straight for the stream, he said, "That was fast. I'm Thirsty shouldn't've lasted more than ten feet or so."

"She's like her father—once an idea gets into her head, it takes a team of Clydies to haul it out again." They watched her stoop to drink. Cailet waved brightly, hiding another smile. "What else is in there?"

"Oh, one or two things I've been saving up. But not many berries, truly told. We won't be having pie tonight." Josselin eyed her from his perch on a rock. "You set a few of your own, didn't you, Captal?"

"Whatever gives you that idea?" Her smile matched his for spurious innocence.

An inelegant snort emanated from an elegant (if slightly imperfect) nose. "Talk about vicious! I told Mikel I needed to find a convenient tree—and not five minutes later, I thought I really did need one!"

"Sorry."

"It was a bit frustrating, you know—that's a good location," he said, as if they were discussing the placement of shop wares on a display shelf. "I was all ready to use that log myself for a Stone in My Shoe." He paused as Jored let out a yelp. "That'll be the snake."

She narrowed her eyes at him.

"It's just a little one," he said defensively. "He must've stepped right up to the bush."

"Taigan will protect him," Cailet said, laughing. She stopped when she caught Josselin looking at her with an odd intensity. And when she caught him at it, he blushed. It wasn't easy to see beneath his dark skin, but he definitely blushed.

She leaned over for another scoop of water, then settled back on her heels again, boots sinking into the soft mud beside the creek, and tried to think of something to say. Suddenly Mikel came out of the woods for what was obviously the last time: he wore an expression as betrayed as the pakka that had gone to sleep in his lap, and he was scratching furiously at his rear end.

"*That* wasn't very nice," Cailet observed.

"It's not mine," he defended. "I Warded for an itch between the shoulder blades, over where Dessa is."

"Shoulder blades is even *less* nice—impossible to get at!"

Mikel marched down the slope, fire in his blue eyes that reminded Cailet powerfully of his father.

"All right," he snarled at Josselin, "fun's over!" To Cailet he continued, "Do you know there's a Ward in there that makes you think there's a whole pack of hungry kyyos staring at you from behind the trees?"

Cailet slanted a look at Josselin; the kyyos weren't one of hers, so they had to be his. He shook his head. She arched a skeptical brow and said to her nephew, "I gather you were so startled—" A more tactful term than *frightened*. "—that you fell into a bush?"

"With thorns," he replied angrily. "The kind that *sting!*"

"Console yourself with the thought that you're the very first to realize the truth," she said, smiling.

"So there's a purpose to this—other than keeping you amused for an afternoon?" Mikel aimed the question at Josselin, of course; not even ignition of his father's temper could make him yell directly at Cailet.

Joss tried to look innocent again—an effort ruined by the laughter glinting in his eyes. Cailet repressed a snort and answered her nephew with, "You know all the Wards at Mage Hall. You didn't know any would be out here."

"Or anyplace I might happen to find myself in the future." He began to look mollified. A little, anyway. "Oh, all right. I guess I understand." And, as natural good humor reasserted itself, he added, "At least it didn't take all day, like building that damned wall!"

Cailet counted one success in the exercise, and hoped that another was now storming out of the forest. "Josselin, whatever did Dessa run into that's made her this mad?"

He squinted, counting the trees behind her furiously approaching figure, and bit his lips against a smirk. "I'm Stark Naked in the Middle of the Forest With No Idea How I Got That Way." When Cailet arched a brow at him, he got defensive again. "It's practically time-honored by now—it's the same one Viko Worked and *I* fell for. Actually, I consider it very appropriate that his cousin—"

Cailet interrupted, shaking her head. "—was your victim with the same Ward? Josselin, I don't know if your sense of humor amuses or appalls me!"

"Vengeance," Mikel informed him haughtily, "does *not* become you."

Dessa was almost upon them, ready to chew Josselin up and spit him out—her explosive temper was definitely not taken from either of her parents, and Cailet suspected a certain First Sword was responsible. Gorsha protested at once: *You never knew her grandmother!* And Cailet recalled another hotheaded Garvedian: Leninor, Lusira's first cousin, Mage Captal for twenty-six tempestuous years.

But before Dessa could vent her fury, every pakka grazing in the meadow suddenly shrieked and bolted for the trees, winglets flapping madly in desperate instinct to fly. The empress stayed behind, tossing her deadly-sharp antlers until her charges were all hidden. Then, with an angry bellow that rang off the rocky hills, she galloped off and vanished.

Cailet was so startled she sat right back into the muddy creek bank. Josselin lost his balance completely and fell with a splash into the water. Mikel spared a glance from his own astonished alarm to indicate a soaking was the least amount of justice he expected for those tricks with the Wards. Taigan and Jored came running, slowing only when they saw that everyone was unharmed.

"What the hell—?" Dessa gasped.

Josselin had picked himself out of the water, soggy boots slipping on moss-covered rocks. "Captal—I didn't Work anything in the meadow, and nothing at all that would do this, I swear it!"

Cailet said nothing. She stood, casting about with her magic. It was difficult—because right at the moment the herd had screamed, shadows had fallen across the sunlit meadow. She'd felt them, and the answering shadows in her own heart.

Taigan and Jored had reached them now, asking anxious questions. Cailet only shook her head. She had no answers for them.

Jored, scowling his bewilderment, finally shrugged and said, "I guess something spooked them. After all, they can't control their instincts."

Cailet cast him a quick glance to see if he was being sly. He wasn't. Somehow, that made it worse.

10

"SO how *are* the miserable wretches doing? Cailet throttled 'em yet?"

Sarra looked up from her office desk, where two letters delivered to her that morning lay open for comparison. Taigan and Mikel had addressed their correspondence to their mother, as dutiful children should, but the words were meant for both parents. So she read Collan both letters and waited for his reaction.

He realized it at once, just as she had. "Mikel mentioned this Jored's name four or five times, but Teggie doesn't talk about him at all. *She* writes about Josselin Mikleine."

"And Cailet hasn't said a word about either in any letter I've had from her in the last year—except that the roses we sent with Josselin are growing miraculously." Sarra tapped the nub of her pen on the blotter, splotching it like a Maurgen Dappleback. "What do you think?"

"How handsome *is* Jored?" He grinned at her from his chair by the hearthfire.

Sarra gave an inelegant snort. "Meaning she's *your* daughter and will naturally go for the best-looking specimen around? Well, from what I recall, he's quite attractive, but Josselin's more to *my* taste."

"Sweet Sarra my own, Josselin's more to *everyone's* taste. If this Jored comes in second, then Taigan would set her sights on him. Less competition for her own looks. After all, that's why I husband you instead of Lusira Garvedian."

She laughed and looked around for something to throw. Nothing came to hand that wouldn't stain the carpet with ink, so she settled for launching herself at him. A brief tickling match later, they subsided into a comfortable snuggle, Sarra in Collan's lap with her legs dangling over the arm of the big, soft chair.

"So are you going to ask Cai about it?" he said, picking up the thread of the conversation.

"I don't know if she even notices things like that. Marra and Aidan were a total surprise to her, and so were Elin and Granon Mikleine."

"I see what you mean. Anybody else would've tripped right over either couple. We could always ask Mikel for the whole story."

"Mmm . . . I doubt it. His letter tells on Taigan as far as he's willing to go. They stick together, Col. They always did."

"But they sound different now. Which you'd expect—they've been with Cailet for a whole autumn and winter. But that part where Taigan was describing her lessons didn't match at all with Mikel's."

"They're learning at different rates, I guess. But that's not going to affect their solidarity." She chuckled. "Remember the time—"

And they were happily occupied with reminiscences about their errant offspring, and the trouble they'd caused—always together. But Sarra was aware that Collan was right: the twins' paths were diverging now, and she hoped their closeness did not suffer too much for it.

Her own closeness to her husband was becoming insufferable with all these clothes on.

"Why, First Daughter," he murmured as she got to work on the closings of his longvest—not buttons, but concealed hooks-and-eyes that would, as usual, shortly be the latest fashion. "This *is* a surprise. To what do I owe the honor of—"

"Oh, shut up and help," she muttered.

Being a good, dutiful, obedient husband, he shut up and helped.

Surely no other man kissed the way he did—his lips both cool and burning, yielding and demanding. She could have gone on kissing him all day and half the night, but he had other ideas. One moment she was still in his lap, struggling to push the longvest and shirt from his shoulders, and the next she was on the carpet, watching as he stood and stretched and let his clothes fall where they would. He grinned at her upturned face, perfectly aware of her rapt gaze, luxuriating in it. Saints, he was beautiful—as lean and muscular as he'd been twenty years ago, the lines of his body long and clean and hard. This man would never grow old. He stood framed by the garden window, knowing he was fine to look at, deliberately giving her time to think about how much finer he was to touch.

Conceited pig. She grabbed an ankle and yanked.

His arms windmilled wildly as his rear end struck the seat of the chair. He slid off and landed on the floor with a thud and a grunt. "Sarra!"

"Collan!" she mimicked.

He grumbled for a few minutes while she arranged things to her own satisfaction (and, not incidentally, his), then sighed and subsided with, "You're lucky I've got a soft spot for rich First Daughters."

"I'm not interested in your *soft* spots right now, Minstrel."

Except his skin—ridiculously smoothly silky, much darker than a redhead's should be, without a single freckle to mar its perfection. Incredible, how a body so hard could be sheathed in such softness beneath her fingertips. How a man so tough could melt with her caresses. How a throat so eloquent in song could produce no sound more coherent than low whimpers at the touch of her lips. Oh, yes—such lovely, loving softness when she made love to him. She laughed, and he woke slightly from his haze of sensation and frowned up at her.

"I know what it is you do to me," he growled, "but I've never figured out how the hell you do it so *fast!*"

"Did I tell you to shut up?" she asked, and before he could answer made sure that his only answer was a moan.

Much later, as they lazed love-spent and drowsy on the carpet, what was bound to happen *did* happen. The Slegin Web's chief factor and two representatives of the Shipmasters Guild entered after a perfunctory knock on the door—for who would suspect that Lady Sarra and Lord Collan would be doing such a thing in her office in the middle of the afternoon?

"Uh—excuse us—we didn't mean—so sorry—" babbled the factor, turning white.

"Beg pardon, Lady," blurted one of the shipmasters, blushing furiously.

The other one grinned and bowed her homage to Collan's nakedness—which her brown eyes swiftly, comprehensively, and expertly assessed—then snagged her male companions by the elbows and hauled them backward from the office.

As they left, Sarra heard the factor say, "In the middle of the day!"

"On the rug!" exclaimed the first shipmaster. "In her *office!*"

"And with her *husband!*" the woman laughed, mocking their outrage. "Put your eyes back in your heads—and if I ever hear that either of you have described Lady Sarra in detail, I'll call you the liars you are. All that hair—you couldn't've seen anything. Fortunately, all that hair was *not* covering her husband!"

The door slammed shut, propelled by a well-aimed bootheel. Sarra laid her forehead to Collan's shoulder and groaned. It would be all over Roseguard by dinnertime, and all over Lenfell by next week.

Collan, of course, was laughing. "What a scandal!"

"I don't see how," she said grumpily.

"You could be forgiven only if you'd been caught with a lover."

"A lover would be more discreet about it, truly told." She raised her head to glare down at him. "Why didn't you just stand up and take a bow?"

"They weren't here long enough."

"You might as well have—lying there flaunting everything you've got—"

"Getting a little possessive, aren't we?"

"You're *my* husband and *my* lover and what I do with you in my own house is *my* business—and you're *not* to be leered at by—"

"—by anyone except you?" he finished, laughing harder as he hugged her to his chest.

Annoyed, she pulled away with some difficulty and sat up. "I do *not* 'leer' at you. And you seem very happy to see me so possessive for a man who once yelled in my face that he couldn't be bought!"

"Not with money, First Daughter." He trailed a finger down the center of her chest to the birthmark over her heart. "Smooth your ruffled feathers, Sarra. Who cares if the whole world knows we make love on the rug in the afternoon? I'd do it on the floor of the Malachite Hall—"

Despite herself, she giggled. "No you wouldn't. The stone's too damned cold."

"I'd make sure *I* was on top." He propped himself on his elbows and grinned again. "Just think if they'd come in and found us in *that* position! Not just scandal, but perversion!"

"I'd blame it all on you," she replied serenely. "Besides, you're bigger than me."

"From the glint in our guest's eye, I'm bigger than every other man she's ever seen."

She could have accused him of being a conceited pig, a braggart, an egotistical son of a Fifth, and several other less polite characterizations. Instead, she closed one hand around the relevant portion of his anatomy, smiled sweetly, and said, "Oh, she only saw you like *this*." As he responded—with a start and a catching of breath and the inevitable—she purred, "*I* am the only one who sees you like *that*."

He rallied enough to manage, "With all privileges and—and rights p–pertaining thereto—Sarra, either stop doing that or do something with it!"

Precisely *what* she did with it would not only have shocked and scandalized the general populace, but cemented the certainty that Lady Sarra and Lord Collan were indeed hopelessly perverted.

11

"TAIGAN, Mikel—grab some mugs and come join us." Dessa Garvedian lifted one hand and the twins walked the length of the frescoed refectory hall to the window tables in the back, where a small group of Prentices sat up late over hot drinks.

"We're taking bets on how long the rain will last,"

said Akin Penteon as the pair took seats, and poured their mugs full of hot coffee laced with cinnamon and orange.

"No fair," Josselin accused with a smile. "Genetic conflict. The Rosvenir side gambles, but the Liwellan doesn't."

"Our virtuous natures were corrupted by Fa at a very early age," Mikel said solemnly, then grinned.

Taigan sipped coffee, then wrapped her hands around the mug to warm them. "Jored told me yesterday that winter rains last for weeks around here. The first few hours were nice, but—*weeks* of this downpour?"

"If you'd spent any time in The Waste," said Josselin, "you'd appreciate it more. Being able to walk outside in the rain is a rare treat."

"Ah, but having somebody to walk in the rain *with* is even better," sighed Jioret Canzallis, whose relationship with Eira Agrenir had fallen on its face a few days ago. Mikel, who had watched couples form and break up before, judged the wound painful but not fatal. Mage Hall was replete with pretty girls. He cast a sidelong glance at one of them. Lirenza Mettyn, great-granddaughter of the late Councillor Tirri Mettyn, was the first Mageborn of her Name in nearly two hundred years; magic ran in her father's line, but of all her siblings she alone had inherited it. She was eighteen this year, fun, fascinatingly dark, and besides that, she knew her way around every wind instrument in the orchestra. So far she and Mikel had played duets only in music, but. . . .

"I didn't know you'd lived in The Waste, Joss," Taigan said, interrupting Mikel's covert admiration of Lirenza's amber-flecked brown eyes.

Josselin shrugged broad shoulders. "I've been there, is all. When I was little."

"I thought you'd spent all your life in Sheve," she went on. But before he could frame a reply, she spotted a new arrival at the main doors and got to her feet with a mumbled excuse.

Mikel caught Akin and Dessa exchange knowing glances, and bit his lip. If the two senior Prentices—who didn't even spend much time around juniors like him and Taigan and Jored—had heard rumors, then everybody must know. He wondered what they expected to happen, and hoped it wasn't what *he* had tried harder and harder not to mention in his letters to Mother. Mikel wasn't sure she or Fa would approve of Jored; truly told, Mikel wasn't sure *he* approved of him. The young man was good-looking, no doubt of that, but there was something odd about him.

And about Joss, too, if it came to it. Taigan's remarks about The Waste had obviously made him uncomfortable, which struck Mikel as being a little weird.

Taigan returned with Jored at her side. Room was made on the benches, another mug was filled, and Jored gulped gratefully at the hot coffee. "Saints, that's good! My room is like an ice cave. Can somebody *please* teach me the Warming spell?" he asked, holding the mug near his face to inhale the steam. "I never did get the knack of it."

"Frugal of the Captal," Taigan observed, "not to provide fireplaces or even braziers in any of the rooms."

"Motivational," Akin corrected.

Lightning flashed outside, and Jored flinched, spilling coffee. "I'm sorry—I—"

"No damage done," Dessa said, plying a napkin.

"It's so stupid," he confessed. "My foster parents always said I must've been in the Rising, with Mage Globes exploding all over the place, to be so skittish in a storm." Thunder rolled through the refectory, and he stiffened for an instant before consciously relaxing. "It sounds like the sky's at war with itself."

"*Were* you caught up in the Rising?" Lirenza Mettyn asked.

"Who can tell?" He sighed and smiled. "I could've been born at about the right time, but . . . truly told, I know about as much about my background as Joss knows about his. For all either of us knows, *we* could be twins!"

Mikel snorted. "Separated at birth, lost to each other until your magic showed up and you were reunited at Mage Hall? Somebody hand me a hankie, I'm going to weep with the poignancy of it all!"

Taigan kicked him under the table, but she was laughing just the same. "It sounds like one of those sentimental ballads Tarise is always asking Fa to sing."

"Only to annoy him," Mikel explained to the others. "Tarise is about as sentimental as a hungry kyyo on the hunt!"

"And Fa wouldn't touch a story like that with a barge pole," Taigan went on.

"Pot's empty," Akin announced, holding up the pitcher. "Whose turn, Dessa?"

She pondered a moment. "Homeshirs, Names, or Name Saints?"

Mikel traded a puzzled look with his sister. Jored smiled and explained, "Ollia Bekke started us on a silly game—we delegate who has to make the coffee, but nobody can ever remember which letter we're on in all the categories."

"Joss and Jored are the worst," Akin complained. "No Homeshir, no idea of their real Names—the only way we can get either of 'em is on the Name Saints."

"And every time that category comes up," Josselin shot back, "*you* claim 'Akin' comes from 'Viranka' instead of 'Deiket'!"

Dessa folded her arms on the table, smiling serenely. "Name Saints it is."

Mikel made a face at her. "You don't *have* one!"

"Of course I do. It's implicitly understood that Gorynel is my Name Saint, for my grandfather. But I'm pretty sure we're on *M* tonight," she added wickedly.

"For Family Names," he retorted.

Lirenza Mettyn glared; Josselin Mikleine shook his head. "Not a chance."

"Nice try," Dessa added. "But *M* and Name Saint is the consensus, right?" She glanced around the table.

Taigan came to Mikel's rescue—and about time, too, he grumped to himself. "I don't think you want to do that," she said.

"Why not?"

"Well, Fa isn't exactly the most domesticated male on Lenfell."

"Meaning?"

"He couldn't teach Mikel the things he never learned himself."

Akin sighed. "Such as how to make decent coffee?"

"Such as how to make coffee, period."

"All right, all right!" Josselin said, climbing to his feet. "I give up. Family Names, adopted or not, *I'll* make the damned coffee!"

"Thank you," Lirenza said sweetly, and Mikel grinned at her—rewarded by a wink from one of those lovely, long-lashed eyes.

"*He's* not quite domesticated either," Akin commented. "But at least he was taught how to boil water in that fancy bower of his."

Although Mikel had grown up in a household where everyone spoke her mind, Akin's total lack of tact astonished him. But Joss only turned, giving Akin a slight smile and a long look from moonstone-lucent eyes. "And wouldn't you love to find out what *else* they taught me there!" Then he sauntered off to the kitchen, coffee pitcher in hand.

Mikel was even more astonished to see that Akin was blushing.

"Don't be so nasty," Dessa advised the young man in sharp tones. "He turned you down. So what? Joss turns *everybody* down."

"*I* was nasty—?"

"You deserved worse than what he said. Now shut up about it—and go lose your grudge somewhere, will you? It's boring."

"I'll go," Akin said with a shrug. "He makes lousy coffee anyway."

He left. Nobody said anything for a moment. Mikel was busy trying to picture Joss and Akin as a couple, and couldn't do it. Granted, he didn't know either of them well, and it wasn't as if they'd look ridiculous together (though somebody as dark as Joss paired with somebody as ashen-blond as Akin would certainly make for an interesting physical contrast), but he really couldn't see Joss with *anybody.* He was friendly enough, likable enough— yet he was close to no one. He held himself aloof somehow, maybe because of his spectacular beauty. Mikel was graced with looks enough of his own to know that a lot of people thought that looks were all he had. That there could be a brain behind a handsome face was not a thing some people wanted to acknowledge; it made them envious, angry that one man had received so many gifts, and anger could make people cruel.

Look at what Akin had said tonight. Joss's reply indicated that he knew how to defend himself—he'd been remarkably polite, to Mikel's way of thinking. But it also indicated that Akin wasn't the first to want something Josselin would not give. He'd been burned by other people's wants and expectations and prejudices, and he stood back a pace or two as a result. That was how Mikel read it, anyway.

All at once Josselin could be heard cursing in the kitchen at the recalcitrant coffee maker. Dessa drawled into the silence: "Jored, if you offer to teach Joss a few swear-words that don't involve anatomical impossibilities, he might tutor you in the Warming spell."

Jored made wide, innocent eyes at her. "I was hoping he'd teach *me* to swear! You've got to admit it's creative."

"It's disgusting. He'll corrupt young and innocent ears."

Mikel grinned at Taigan across the table. They'd heard worse from their mother—and *much* worse from their father.

Suddenly Jioret perked up from glum contemplation of his empty mug. "Captal!"

They all looked around; sure enough, the Captal had appeared in the doorway. The Prentices all got to their feet. She gestured for them to sit back down.

"I wish you wouldn't do that. It makes me think you're preparing to help some doddering old woman find a chair before she collapses." Seating herself next to Mikel, she went on, "What are all of you doing up so late?"

"I guess none of us could sleep," Taigan offered with a shrug. "The rain's loud on a slate roof."

Josselin returned and the cups were refilled—and the coffee was excellent, Mikel noted, flavored this time with hazelnuts. There was another brief silence as everybody tried to think up something to say, but the Captal spared them the effort.

"You were missed in Tamosin Wolvar's class this morning, Josselin. I assume the roses will survive, and you'll attend tomorrow?"

"Yes, Captal. I'll be there."

Jored said, "You must be really close to success with the Warrior's Globe, Joss."

"Close," the young man agreed. He finished his drink and rose. "But it's getting late. Good night."

The Captal's presence constrained conversation, and the group broke up as soon as it was polite to do so. Mikel was surprised when Taigan chose to walk with him rather than with Jored. He was also slightly annoyed, hoping to improve on his progress with Lirenza. But Taigan had something to say, and when they were alone in a hallway she said it.

"I know she can laugh, we heard her when we were children."

"Maybe she's forgotten. Or maybe she can't, among the students. Discipline and respect and all that."

"I don't understand her. Do you remember when we built the tree house, and next time she was in Roseguard we had lunch there?"

"We had a great time. So did she, I guess."

"Exactly," Taigan paused in the lamplit hallway leading to her room. "So why does she treat us like she treats everybody else?"

Mikel sighed. "Because here, we *are* like everybody else."

"You may be. I'm not. I'm a washout in almost everything, Mishka. I'm thinking of giving it up and going home."

"You can't!"

"You're so far ahead of me! I'm still in classes with Tavis Agrenir, and she's fourteen years old! Even she can do more than I can with magic."

"It just takes time. And it takes some people longer than others. Look at Akin—he's twenty, and nowhere close to being Listed. Or Joss—he's almost the same age, and—"

"And the Captal is pushing him—didn't you notice?"

"Of course I did. But that's not what we're talking about, Teggie. If you want to get *really* depressed and feel *really* sorry for yourself, how about comparing your progress to Kanen Mossen's? *He's* only sixteen, and everybody says he'll be Listed for sure this summer."

She scowled at him. "I'm not depressed, and I'm not feeling sorry for myself. I'm being realistic. I can feel the magic in me, Mishka, I just can't *do* anything with it! If the Captal would just show a little understanding and sympathy—"

He couldn't help it; he knew he shouldn't, but he said it anyway. "I thought you were getting plenty of that from Jored."

Taigan went rigid for an instant, then turned abruptly and strode toward her door.

"Teggie—I was just teasing!"

The door opened, then slammed shut.

Mikel sighed. "Nice work," he muttered to himself. He knew his sister; she wouldn't speak to him for at least a week.

12

ONE of the Assembly's first and finest achievements in the years after the Rising was reformation of the postal system. Formerly the responsibility of each Shir's Ministry of Internal Affairs in conjunction with its Departments of Commerce, Transportation, and Revenue (whose officials franked the envelopes both coming and going), relative efficiency ranged from the abysmal to the merely appalling. But timely mail delivery was now supervised by a special committee of the Assembly, with all postal employees answerable directly to it, and woe unto any worker who was discovered dawdling with a sack of letters. Transit time had been cut in half in most instances, and one could now confidently assume that missives sent from, say, Dinn to Neele would not go by way of Roke Castle, Renig, and Havenport.

Which was not to say that all mail was sent through the official postal service.

When Sarra had nothing more important than gossip to convey, she used the regular mail to Mage Hall. When she had real news, she sent it by the Minstrelsy. When her message was urgent, she went to Biren Halvos at Roseguard or one of the Mages at Ryka Court, who used the special Globes given them years ago by Cailet.

In the late winter of 989, all three types of communication reached Cailet in quick succession on the same day.

First came the regular post. The bearer was a young woman known as a Rimrunner, for her route took her all the way around Tillin Lake—and no Rimrunner had ever completed the circuit more swiftly than she. Her two big, powerful Tillinshir grays moved like the wind, one carrying her and the other carrying the mail bags. She was so quick at it, in fact, that in the year she'd been on the job Cailet had never set eyes on her or even learned her real name. She would arrive at the gatehouse, call out while loosing the bag containing Mage Hall's mail, and before the sentry Mage was out the door had already galloped off to her next delivery stop.

But the sixth day of Ilsevet's Moon that year was thick with snow, unheard-of just a week before the official beginning of spring. It had taken Cailet several winters to stop dreading the sight of snow; here, it was soft and clean and delightful, nothing like the searing acid-laced horror it was in The Waste. One still bundled up to go out in it, of course, but one never had to worry that exposed skin would end up scarred. Every Wraithenday she helped build Winter Wraiths with the children at Mage Hall, and secretly wished the sculptures were Malerrisi in their white cloaks, to melt away with the next sunshine.

Broadsheets reported that this winter had been a harsh one all over North Lenfell, with a storm sweeping down from the Wraithen Mountains nearly every week.

Ambrai's streets were impassible for the first time in twenty-five years, and sleet had fallen in Roseguard twice.

So when snow blew yet again around Mage Hall, Aidan left orders with the duty sentry to have hot coffee waiting for the Rimrunner—along with an invitation to come up to the Hall until the weather eased. For the first time in her career she hesitated in her routine, looked at the white sky, and nodded acceptance. Thus it was that Cailet received her sister's letter from the Rimrunner's own hand.

"My thanks for the shelter, Captal," the young woman said, shaking dark brown hair from darker brown eyes and unbuttoning her heavy wool jacket. "Deiket Snowhair must've gotten up on the wrong side of the mountain today."

"You're welcome to stay if you like," Cailet replied, setting aside a novel (she hadn't lost her taste for adventure stories). "It looks as if this won't stop all day."

"Again, thanks—but I'd better push on as soon as it slackens a little." Reaching into a pocket, she produced a second letter. "Though I'm glad to do you a service beyond the usual. This was given me by a girl used to live up in Peyres, who's singing with the Cantratown Choir these days—she's young for it, just fifteen, but she's a voice to make Sesilla Honeythroat weep for envy. Her mother's one of your Mage Guardians."

"You must mean Jiora Sonne, Sevy Vasharron's discovery," Cailet smiled, accepting the second letter and giving no sign that she knew it had come by way of the Minstrelsy. Jiora was its newest and all-time youngest member. "When you see her again, please give her my best wishes."

"I'll do that." She glanced out the windows at the swirling white landscape, fretful as a silverback cat trapped in a den not her own. "I think it's easing up, don't you?"

"If you're determined to ride on, then at least let me Warm your coat." The Rimrunner looked startled at being offered a spell from the Captal's own magic; Cailet smiled.

When the Rimrunner was Warmed and gone, Aidan

brought in a steaming pot of chocolate-flavored coffee to warm Cailet. She snuggled into the big green-velvet chair in her bedroom and opened the envelope franked ROSE-GUARD first.

> *Dearest Caisha—*
> *I hope this finds you well and not yet seriously disposed to eviscerating my children—who undoubtedly deserve it, but consider the mess it would make on the carpet. Collan and I are well, the more so for not having to restrain ourselves from similar justifiable mayhem. We both send our sympathies.*

Cailet snorted. Sympathy would do her a lot of good. She ought to give Sarra the particulars of the mischief in the stables.

> *Roseguard's quiet is not to be found elsewhere. Vellerin Dombur has turned acquisitive, as we guessed—but in a perfectly legal manner. She's spending a small fortune buying up parcels of Domburronshir. This came out when Elin Alvassy mentioned in a letter—quite irritably, too— that the smallhold where she and Mai and Pier took refuge as children with their grandparents was under economic siege by a woman known to be associated with Vellerin. It was originally Dombur land—from Enis, who married Aidil Alvassy, Elin's great-grandmother—and this is what started me looking into things. It turns out Vellerin is buying up all the old Dombur holdings. Dowries of Generations ago, farms sold off in the last two centuries, properties in cities and towns, tracts of forest, whole mountaintops that are no use to anyone—she wants it all, and she's willing to pay for it. Not directly, of course, but through those multiple accounts the Rennes were suspicious about. Many of them have been traced to her daughter and cousins and sisters.*
> *Especially her First Daughter, Linsel, who is*

currently resisting Vellerin's efforts to get her divorced from her husband—they have only the one child, a son named Rennon, and Vellerin wants an unbroken line of First Daughters to follow her. Evidently Linsel loves the man, and as they're both still young they have hopes of more children. But I'd like you to ask your Allard Mages about the husband—his name is Jaymer—I can't seem to find out anything other than that he's yet another Nameless adopted orphan. (Is it my imagination, or are we positively hip-deep in such persons? My husband, your two handsome Prentices—and you and I, now that I think about it!)

"Very conscientious of you to mention it, Sarra," Cailet murmured, "in case somebody happened to open this letter. But not very subtle of you, inquiring after my two handsome Prentices. What has Taigan been writing to you about Jored, I wonder?"

Ask your Allards if they can place Jaymer in the Family. The only Allard I know is the Timarrin in Ambrai who designs clothes—which reminds me. Taigan sent Domna Timarrin a letter asking her to make up two sets of Mage Guardian regimentals for her, one black velvet and one black silk, if you please! Anticipating the day a trifle, I'd say, if your hints about her progress—or lack of it—are any indication. But she is her father's daughter!
My love to you as always, dearest Caisha.
Sarra

Cailet paused for a swallow of coffee, and as she set the letter aside on the lampstand her eye was caught by the little bronze statue of St. Miryenne, gift from long-dead Councillor Flera Firennos. The Saint wore a gown of many delicate pleats, and in one hand held an unlighted candle. It was Cailet's occasional conceit to set a diminutive Mage Globe atop that candle to read by. Though today there was more than enough light from lamps lit early by Aidan against the stormy gloom outside, Cailet indulged herself and spent a few moments watching the Saint's mysterious smile by a tiny silver-white glow. Miryenne was a patron of Mage Guardians, and Cailet always felt a subtle release of tension when she gazed at the serene bronze face. How malicious it had been of Anniyas to spell this lovely work of art with a shock only Mageborns would feel; Cailet touched a fingertip to the Saint's outstretched hand, sensing only the gentle warmth of her own magic.

Smiling, she opened Sarra's second letter. It was almost as long, and while just as gossipy to casual inspection, was very much to an indignant point.

> Cailet—
> Vellerin Dombur's husband turns out to have an even stronger tie to Veller Ganfallin than she. The Census archives produced a direct line to Ganfallin's youngest son, who was only a baby when his mother died and somehow escaped the carnage at their fortress in the Endless Mountains—so you were right about one of the children having survived, more's the pity. The connection appears genuine, and the documents are not forgeries.
> His Exalted Lordship Stene Dombur is at Ryka Court these days, declaiming his frightful poetry to large audiences eager to find favor with Vellerin. He gives his recitals wearing white on white—the Dombur colors, but also very convenient in other ways. With this ensemble he wears a large, vulgar gold pendant (you should hear Collan on the subject of his taste!) in the shape of a banner hung from a crossbar on a pole, just like the pictures in the history books of the battle flags carried by Ganfallin's armies, only with the Dombur Ice Ax emblazoned on it. The impudence of the man!
> Linsel is divorcing Jaymer Allard—resentfully, at her mother's direct command—to marry one of

Stene's nephews (Chevaz, a name that will find favor in certain quarters). Though the elimination of the Fifths was supposed to have rid Lenfell of all possibility of such things, Rillan says (and I bow to his expertise as a breeder of horses) that the union of bloodlines so closely related for at least three Generations and probably more will result in exactly the kind of First Granddaughter Vellerin Dombur deserves: a drooling, lop-eared, knock-kneed, spindle-shanked, wall-eyed, broken-winded, slack-jawed, gabbling moron.

Cailet was whooping with laughter by the end of this tirade. For nineteen years, ever since that Birthingday dinner Telomir Renne had thrown for Collan at Wyte Lynn Castle, Sarra had ranked Vellerin Dombur lower in the scheme of things than the average rabid rodent.

You must be sure to tell her, chuckled Gorsha's voice, *not to be so shy, and tell you what she* really *thinks!*

As droll as her sister's letters were, they contained several points of more than passing interest. Cailet considered them on her way out of her quarters—and was interrupted in her considerations by Aidan, who demanded to know where she thought she was going with nothing but a shirt and shortvest on her shoulders. He produced a fur-lined black woolen cloak from the sitting-room closet and bundled it around her, ignoring her mild reminder that she was a Mage, she could spell herself Warm.

"Granon and the other Warders went to a lot of trouble to have this made for your Birthingday last year. The least you could do is wear it every so often."

She conceded to the tyrant who ran her life and wrapped herself in the cloak, pulling the hood around her head. It truly was a lovely thing, she had to admit—velvet-soft wool, black fur downy as a cloud, and so wonderfully warm that she felt none of the cold even when she ventured out into the snowstorm for a walk—even if the silvery tips of the fur tickled her nose.

Josselin's roses had long since been pruned and

mulched for protection against the winter, but she saw his tall form slogging through four-foot drifts around the wall, a hoe over one shoulder and the other hand holding an assortment of gardening tools. One of her two handsome, Nameless, orphaned Prentices. She shook her head and switched directions so she wouldn't have to meet up with him.

Sighing for her ineptitude at purely human things, she trudged through the snow toward the orchard. Taigan's section of the wall was a singular mess; Mikel's, on the other side of the new gate, was almost as bad for half its height. But she could tell precisely where his magic had awakened, and where it had merged with his consciousness, and where it had begun to thrive as it should. Cailet conceded in private that Mikel had always been her favorite of the twins, but perhaps only because his was the sweeter temper, the more genial disposition. He was, simply, easier to love. Cailet was no less fond of Taigan, but there had always been an edge to the girl's personality—whetted to a cutting blade by her frustrations here. That Taigan herself was the one most often hurt by it grieved Cailet. Sarra was just as headstrong and stubborn, and nobody but Collan had ever been able to tell Sarra anything. Whoever he might be, Jored was no Collan. That was what frightened Cailet—that, and who he might truly be.

She rested her ungloved hands on Taigan's wall, staring at the bare fruit trees without seeing them. After a time she realized the snowfall had stopped, and from very far away heard the muffled ringing of St. Lirance's in Heathering. Eighth already? She turned, squinting against the icy wind, and retraced her steps through the snow to Mage Hall.

The refectory was steamy and fragrant, almost stiflingly so after the outdoor chill. Soup thick with sausage and noodles was being devoured by hungry Prentices and Mages, who'd spent the morning shoveling snow and climbing roofs to clear possibly dangerous drifts. Mage Hall had not been built for such weather. Aidan stood at the serving counter, calling off names and handing out letters. Cailet stood in line—she insisted always on standing in line just like everyone else—for a bowl of soup and a hunk of bread and a mug of scalding tea, and found a seat with Granon and Rennon Bekke. The latter's given name reminded her of Sarra's words about young Rennon Dombur, and she mentioned to her Warders that she'd like to talk with Esken Allard—this afternoon if he was available.

Granon blinked. "Captal, Esken's been in Firrense since last Neversun, visiting his mother."

She felt herself blush—a reaction fortunately rendered invisible by the cold-red already suffusing her cheeks. "Oh," she said inadequately. Esken was the only Allard currently assigned to Mage Hall; she'd have to find out if anyone here had a father or uncle or whatever by that Name, or was in some other way allied to the Family, or—

Stop babbling, even to yourself, Gorsha ordered severely. *And don't beat yourself over the head either. You can't be expected to remember where every single one of your Mages is at all times. As if you don't have enough to concern you.*

Maybe you don't expect it, but I do. They're my *Mages, Gorsha.*

Rennon Bekke was obviously itching to know why she wanted to talk to Esken Allard, but a glance from Granon kept him silent. Cailet drew breath to explain, but at that moment she noticed two curious things happen at the refectory door—or perhaps it was only one thing in two versions.

Aidan and Marra were on their way out. He still had a handful of undelivered letters, which he nearly dropped as she swayed slightly against him. She was looking a little greensick; she was in the first weeks of her first pregnancy. But what snagged Cailet's notice was the entrance, within three steps of each other, of Josselin Mikleine and Jored Karellos. Aidan shoved the letters at the former so both hands could be free for Marra. Josselin stopped in his tracks with a frown and asked a worried question— probably about Marra's health. Jored, looking past Joss to scan the tables, bumped into the other Prentice. The letters scattered onto the floor. Both young men knelt to scoop them up while Marra hurried from the refectory, clinging to her husband's arm.

Jored got to his feet just as Josselin, still on one knee gathering strewn letters, handed him an envelope. Jored's face froze. Recovering swiftly, he sorted through the dozen or so envelopes in his own hands and gave one to Joss as the latter stood upright. An almost identical chill passed over the superbly beautiful face.

Cailet's brows arched in startled reaction. Neither Jored nor Josselin *ever* received mail. And now both had letters in hand—letters that went instantly into pockets when they read and, to Cailet's eye, recognized the handwriting on the envelopes.

How very singular, she thought to herself. Both young men were so dark-skinned that neither blush nor sudden pallor could ever give them away. But the furtive concealment of their letters, the manner in which two pairs of gray eyes avoided each other and everyone else, the haste with which they parted, and the grim faces they wore. . . .

Geridon's Balls! exclaimed Gorsha. *You're not on about* that *again!*

Cailet ignored him, caught by the sudden horrible notion that she'd been wrong all the time, and it wasn't one or the other who'd been sent here by Glenin—it was *both*.

Joss took his lunch out of the refectory, presumably back to the privacy of his room to read his mail. Jored, behaving as if he hadn't received a letter at all, sat beside Taigan at a corner table, beneath the fresco of St. Elinar Longsight with her owl on her wrist.

Cailet had lost her appetite. She returned to her quarters. The atmosphere within was nearly as thick as in the refectory; Aidan had built up the hearthfire into a substantial blaze. Cailet opened wide a window in her bedroom and sat down in front of it, staring at the snow.

Granon Bekke found her there an hour later. Hesitating to disturb her, but alarmed both by her empty-eyed expression and her convulsive shivering, he strode through, slammed the window shut, and draped the black fur cloak over her.

"Captal, if you insist on catching your death of cold,

please do it someplace where I'm not responsible for you."

She glanced up. "What? Oh—is it cold in here? I didn't notice."

With an exasperated sigh, he leaned a hip against the windowsill and continued, "There's a message for you from Telomir Renne."

Cailet roused herself with an effort and held out a hand. "What does *he* want?"

Rather than give her an envelope as she'd expected, he brought a fist-sized glass ball from his longvest pocket. The Mage Globe within it was stained an anxious violet.

Cailet stared at it for a few moments, then mentally shook herself and Worked the spell that would free the message. Within the crystal sphere and the Globe it contained there appeared ten words:

Glenin coming to Ryka with Domburs at Midsummer. Please advise.

There was a brief flare of silver magic before the Mage Globe resumed its clarity within the glass.

"Trouble?" asked the Master of the Captal's Warders, his shoulders already stiffening as if for battle.

Cailet nodded slowly, rolling the empty crystal between her palms. "But not just yet, Gransha. Not just yet." She was sure of it. The shadows weren't yet dark enough.

But that night she curled into the furred cloak in a chair before the fire, ignoring the half-read novel, moving only to pile on another log to keep the light burning brightly, brightly until dawn.

13

FOR eight weeks, a great deal was said but absolutely nothing happened.

Sarra sent Cailet another letter through the Minstrelsy, revealing her plan to go to Ryka Court for Glenin's appearance at Vellerin Dombur's side. Cailet sent Telomir Renne a message through his Mage Globe, advising him that at this time she had no advice to give him. The broadsheets doubled in size as distinguished guest columnists generously—and verbosely—shared their different and sometimes diametrically opposed opinions about What It All Meant. At Mage Hall, speculation was equally rife—as Cailet assumed it must be all over Lenfell.

Only Glenin was not heard from. And neither Jored nor Josselin ever said a word about the contents of their letters.

In any event, Cailet did catch a cold from her hours in front of an open window, and had to spend a week in bed at Elomar Adennos's glaring insistence. The first three days she was so miserable she didn't much care what, if anything, was going on. The next three days she spent fretting herself into a relapse. By the ninth day she was on the mend again, sniffling but no longer coughing. Elo then allowed various Mages to visit and make their reports—mainly because no one had much *to* report. Midweek of Spring Moon Cailet declared herself ready to get out of bed and resume her duties. In his eloquently succinct way, the Master Healer disagreed. Cailet demanded to be let out of jail for St. Alilen's Day. Elomar replied that celebrations at Heathering had been canceled; half the populace was down with fevers and sore throats, and a big gathering was the surest way to spread the illness to the other half.

By the time Cailet did enter the world again, she found spring had arrived with a flourish, as if to apologize for the hardships of winter. Josselin's roses were already blooming along the wall in a tumult of breathtaking color, the meadows were thick with wildflowers, and samples of all the blossoms began to appear in vast bouquets in Cailet's rooms. The pakkas returned from the north rather earlier than usual, already fat on sweet grass. The orchards were sprouting new leaves, and as Lovers Moon turned to Green Bells and then First Flowers, buds burst open with the promise of a massive harvest. The Mage in charge of the home farm warned the cook to start teaching more Prentices how to put up fruit for preserves.

As St. Maidil's Day approached, Cailet was forced to begin considering what would happen at Ryka Court this Midsummer Moon. With her Birthingday gift to Sarra at First Flowers—a slender book of pressed roses from the wall, matched to applicable verses from *Rose Rhymes*, the life's work of Mage Ilisa Neffe's grandmother—she included a letter suggesting they could simply ignore Glenin. Their sister would not have made her visit to Ryka Court so public so far in advance if she hadn't wanted them to plot and fret themselves into total confusion and nervous exhaustion. That this recommendation elicited a blistering reply was no surprise. But a few days later another letter came, in which Sarra showed unexpected sensitivity by asking if Cailet was really that frightened.

She was.

She could not afford to be.

She spent long hours over the next few weeks debating various plans with Gorsha, interrupted by Aidan or Marra bringing meals they insisted she eat.

Having been denied the music and revelry of St. Alilen's, Heathering planned to make up for it at St. Maidil's. Flirtations begun at First Flowers had had nearly three weeks to prosper in the profligate glory of this year's Tillinshir spring, and several betrothals had already been announced. Only the sourest skeptics muttered that while St. Maidil was the patron of new lovers, she wasn't called The Betrayer for nothing.

On the afternoon, as St. Lirance's rang out Twelfth, the majority of Mage Hall residents were walking the north road to Heathering. Everyone carried money in their pockets and a wrapped bundle of clothes for later on; the former was for purchasing masks, the latter to complete their disguises for the dancing. Cailet fell in with a farmer and her husband, chatting about crops and livestock and wonderfully ordinary things while six of their seven daughters scampered around and the baby clung to her father's neck, wide-eyed at all the people. The First Daughter gave the usual challenge: name all the sisters in order. Cailet responded (as always) by getting them all wrong, which (as always) sent the girls into gales of giggles.

"It's Tomia first, then Selia, and I'm Shonna—"

"—then Sollina, Savasha, Sattina, and Tiana!" finished the First Daughter.

Cailet moaned and clutched at her hair. "I'll *never* get it right! And don't you dare have any more daughters, Shonya, just to confuse me further," she warned their mother, who didn't look old enough to have borne one baby, let alone seven.

Jayan, proud father of the flock, grinned. "If we did, we'd have to call her 'Hey You'—we've flat run out of names!"

By then they'd reached the outskirts of Heathering, and the girls ran off to greet their friends. Cailet wished Shonya and Jayan a pleasant holiday, and wandered down the booth-lined street to outfit herself with a mask for the evening's dance. In Cantratown and Pinderon and other large cities they called it a Masked Ball, but here the old name was used: Maidil's Feign. And to pretend to be someone she was not—an impossibility unless she covered herself head to foot as well as wore a mask—Cailet required a disguise.

Plenty of people had already bought their choice of masks, and carried paper-wrapped packages. She saw Mikel playfully shoo off three of the local girls from a booth as he tried to keep his selection a secret, and down the street other Prentices and Mages picked through the offerings for exactly the right persona amid much merriment and teasing.

Cailet's favorite vendor, the one she always bought from, was the local blacksmith who also had a fine hand

for more delicate work: she made all the collar-pins for
Mage Hall—Sparrows, Candles, Herb Sprigs, Mage
Globes, and Swords. Her smithy featured two painted
signs: Caitiri the Fiery-eyed for her forge and Maurget
Quickfingers for her sideline in jewelry. But she was the
perfect picture of the Saint her mother had named her for:
Brisha Strong-arm, patron of their craft. Brishan greeted
Cailet with a smile and some choice bucolic gossip, then
brought out the special masks saved for special customers. She showed Cailet a cunning creation of scrolled
iron-shavings imitating a lion's mane; a silly and brilliantly made clown face with a garish two-foot nose; a
mirror-mask of polished tin pounded paper-thin and lined
with goosedown for comfort; mossy green velvet stitched
with tiny brass bells shaped like flowers; bird-masks
feathered with everything from gray doves to bronze ban-
tie roosters to gorgeous iridescent fantails.

"Here's one you might like," said Brishan, reaching
under her table to produce a plain foil mask decorated at
the brow with a single painted flameflower. "For our own
St. Caitiri."

"But everyone would know it was me behind it!"
Cailet smiled. "What about one of the birds? They're
beautiful."

"A new line, proposed and constructed by my grandson," the smith reported proudly. "The hawk is popular
this year, so you wouldn't be the only person wearing
one."

She was about to agree—as a tribute to Sarra's
adopted Liwellan Hawk sigil—but then her eye was
caught by another mask. "That one," she said definitely.
She took a quick glance around to make sure no one was
looking (silly of her, but the spirit of the day had infected
her), and accepted the invitation to try it on in privacy.
Slipping behind a short curtain, she eased it over her head
and turned to judge the effect in a small mirror. It was
more of a headdress in the old-fashioned style of twenty
years ago than a mask, made of wire covered in smooth
plumes that fit snugly from brow to nape. With her black
eyes ringed by snowy feathers, her fair hair hidden, and
her face concealed nearly to the chin, she felt reasonably

confident that it would take even those who knew her well at least a minute to grasp her identity.

You realize, of course, the irony: the mask one chooses is ultimately revealing.

What? I don't understand. She looked at herself in the mirror as if by looking at her own dark eyes she could see Gorsha's green ones.

Don't you want to know why you chose the owl?

Not really—but you're going to tell me anyway, aren't you?

It's St. Elinar's sigil—and you'd love to have a little of her Longsightedness about what's going to happen. Moreover, the owl hunts at night, she's not afraid of the dark—

Stop it! Don't spoil today for me please—

—and it cries out a single question: WHO.

Shut up! she ordered viciously, glaring at her own masked face in the mirror. *I'm not listening to any more of your rubbish, do you hear me? Let me be, you horrid old man! Leave me the hell alone!*

She composed her expression, carefully removed the mask, and pushed the curtain aside. "This one, absolutely," she said, more to Gorsha than to her friend.

"Excellent choice." As Brishan wrapped it in paper and string, she said, "Any news of that young man?"

"Which young man?" Cailet asked before she thought.

"The one who beat me five Delilah's Days out of six at the smithing," Brishan grumbled with a wry sidelong glance from eyes nearly as black as Cailet's own.

"Oh, him. No, not a word."

"Pity. He was a bit young for me, but I'd gladly've married him if only for the right to forbid him to compete!"

Cailet laughed. "Don't try to fool me, Brishan—you'd've married him and then cheered him on!"

"Well, at least he didn't leave until I got his secret for shoeing a Clydie in no time at all." She gave Cailet the wrapped mask. "Here you are. And I'd better see this out on the dancing circle tonight, my grand Lady Mage Captal!"

Cailet made a face at her, laughed, and departed. Despite Taig's long ago and Collan's more recent tutelage, dancing was not one of her accomplishments. She'd gotten over stepping on her partner's feet, or leading in the wrong direction, but anything more complex than a waltz utterly defeated her. So it was that when everyone—herself included—had changed in private to their party clothes, and gathered in the yard of St. Lirance's to dance, Cailet merely watched.

The early evening rituals of food and drink and sociability had concluded. All the familiar faces of Heathering, the surrounding smallholds, and Mage Hall were masked. By torchlight (and a few strategically placed Mage Globes) the real business of St. Maidil's Day commenced: the coaxing of flirtation into love, love into ardor, and ardor into the nearest secluded location.

Cailet watched, and smiled, and sipped wine, and didn't pay much attention to the order of the dances. Her mistake. There was a time-honored progression to the sequence—reel to jig to promenade to square to two-step—with just enough pause in between for the women to select new partners if they were so inclined. The selection of tunes was up to the musicians (local folk, every bit as good as the professional bands other communities hired), but the succession of dances never varied. So Cailet should not have been surprised when, at a gesture from their conductor, every musician suddenly yelled out, "Contrariwise!"

Gleeful whoops greeted this permission for the men to ask the women to dance. Every male above the age of fourteen—and a few bold boys even younger—went scrambling toward their chosen ladies. Impertinent behind Maidil's Day masks, which protected them from open discovery even if everyone in Heathering knew exactly whose face was concealed, the men began to swagger into the dancing circle escorting their laughing partners.

Cailet swore under her breath and looked for an escape. On any other night, few of the men here would have the presumption to ask her to dance. But the masks that licensed some occasionally outrageous behavior also sanctioned them to ignore the real identities of even the most important and unapproachable women. And so she found herself being bowed to by a tall, black-clad young man wearing the mask of a black-and-amber hawk.

She knew who it was, of course. There was no mistaking Josselin Mikleine's height and build, even if his face was completely covered and he wore gloves to hide the telltale darkness of his skin. She looked narrowly at him from behind her own feathers and saw moonstone-gray eyes twinkle merrily in response. She couldn't refuse; that wasn't allowed any more than acknowledgment of identities was allowed. She accepted his gloved hand with a nod.

Joining the other dancers, waiting while the musicians tuned up, all at once she wasn't so certain that it was indeed Josselin who had asked her to dance. There was another tall young man in black nearby, wearing an almost identical hawk mask—ah, but the girl he'd chosen sealed his identity. Taigan, despite a gold-painted sunburst mask nearly as concealing as Cailet's owl headdress, was easily recognizable by her long-waisted, lissome figure and the wayward tendrils of golden hair curling down her slender neck. Cailet assumed that Jored's mask was a deliberate tribute to the Liwellan Hawk sigil; she glanced briefly up at Joss, wondering if he had intended the same.

Cailet never had to think about the Ward that disguised her maimed breast anymore—but she found herself nervously reinforcing it as Josselin drew her into his arms and they began to dance. Naturally, it was a waltz.

> *The journey long, the perils many,*
> *The road a thousand thirsty miles,*
> *Still my steps shall never falter*
> *My faith and purpose never alter*
> *For you are by my side*

It was one of Collan's favorite songs to sing languishingly at Sarra, teasing her—yet she never complained, only blushed and laughed the special low, soft laugh given to her husband alone. Cailet wondered if Josselin was making fun of *her*.

> *You, and only you, dear love,*
> *You, with whom I am myself*
> *You, my courage and my solace*
> *You, whatever might befall us,*
> *You are by my side*

Josselin was holding her much too tightly. She couldn't upbraid him for it—she couldn't even show that she'd noticed. The night of St. Maidil's was for piquant pretense, and never could she indicate that she knew who clasped her so closely. Her position demanded that she behave as if she hadn't even been here. So Joss was free to embrace her as tightly as he pleased, and to slide his hand down her back to her waist, and whirl her around and around to the dizzying strains of the waltz—

> *The world may turn its face away,*
> *The Saints abandon, the Wraiths draw near,*
> *But no fear or grief can ever claim me*
> *No cruel words or looks can shame me*
> *For you are by my side*

Thanks be to all Saints that Josselin didn't try to engage her in conversation, disguising his voice or assuming an accent. But if he was who she suspected he might be, he could use magic to deceive—and, truly told, she felt a diminutive tingle of magic in the night air, possibly coming from him, possibly not.

> *You, and only you, dear love,*
> *You, for whom I'm more than me*
> *You, whose arms and lips I covet,*
> *You, my first and best beloved*
> *You are by my side*

At length the waltz was over. Tradition demanded that the woman ask her mysterious partner for another dance immediately thereafter, but Cailet smiled beneath her mask and gestured that she was tired, and thus escaped a second dance with Josselin. She slid between couples and jumped down from the circular platform, not bothering with the steps, and headed for a refreshment table. Sipping at a cup of wine, she caught sight of Joss's tall, hawk-masked form moving toward the side door of St. Lirance's. What business he could have inside the shrine was unknown; probably he didn't want people to see that his chosen partner had refused him that second dance. No, ridiculous; it couldn't possibly matter to him what people here thought. Doubtless Joss had asked her to dance as a subterfuge, and had now sneaked off to be with the real object of his intentions tonight. Yes, that must be it.

But she was rather annoyed, for the portion of the festivities for which Mage Hall was responsible had arrived, and Joss, who was very good with Mage Globes, had promised to help. Cailet, alert for the conductor's signal, collected Granon and Rennon Bekke, Imilial Gorrst, several other Warrior and Scholar Mages, and a few enthusiastic Prentices around her. Cymbals suddenly crashed, taking Cailet by surprise, but Imi was ready. She sent a Mage Globe soaring into the night sky, all flashing with green-gold sparks, and then exploded it in midair. The other Mages and Prentices followed suit, giving Heathering a "fireworks" show more spectacular (and much safer) than any other on Lenfell.

People gasped and applauded and marveled, especially at the set-piece Granon and Rennon had been working on for weeks: ten Battle Globes, each a different shade of red, that expanded from pinpricks to the size of small houses, circling each other for a full minute as they grew before slamming together in a brilliant collision. Cailet clapped her hands and laughed as the whole of Heathering was illuminated—and caught her breath when she saw, over by the corner of St. Lirance's, a slender, golden-haired girl tiptoeing to kiss a tall young man, their masks of sunburst and hawk lying forgotten at their feet.

Cailet turned away to prepare her own contribution to the display—a dazzling rush of silver-white light that would seem to stretch from the Ladymoon to her little companion and then all the way down to the tower of St. Lirance's. But in the last glow of the Bekkes' flourish, she also saw another tall young man striding southward across the fields, taking the short route home to Mage Hall.

And somehow what she had planned to do with her magic turned out very differently. What appeared, entirely without her volition, was a very good imitation of the Wraiths as she had last seen them, shimmering rainbow curtains drifting sublimely through the northern sky.

Someone blurted in startlement; a few children began to cry. Cailet damped down her magic and with guilt-spurred swiftness did what she'd intended to do in the first place. The ribbons of silver light swept across the black sky and white stars, flinging the Wraithlike veils from sight, and everyone was so caught up in the wonder of it that the bizarre presentation of a moment earlier was almost forgotten.

Granon and Imi stood on either side of her when it was over, frowning their concern. "Where the hell did *that* come from?" Imi demanded in a low voice.

"I don't know." Cailet shrugged them off. "I'm just tired, I suppose. I hope nobody was too upset."

"Actually," Granon said, "it was quite beautiful—if you didn't know what it was supposed to be."

Hiding a wince, Cailet nodded and walked away from them. She tugged off her owl mask and wiped the sweat from her face, cursing her carelessness and her magic that had not obeyed her.

Perhaps it wasn't your magic at all.

Not now, Gorsha, she said wearily.

I'm serious. What's going on here?

I don't know. I'm tired. Leave me alone.

I must rely on your senses, and if you don't test the wind for magic, then I can't interpret it for you. It's my duty as First Sword—

She ignored him. It wasn't easy, with him nattering away in her head like this about strange things occurring tonight and where had those Wraiths come from and had they been real or something dredged up from her own mind. But she eventually succeeded in bricking him up behind the wall he'd taught her to build so long ago, and heard his voice no more.

As Fourteenth approached and couples glided off into the night for private unmaskings, the dancing circle was populated now mostly by married couples stealing one last waltz before taking their sleepy children home to bed. Cailet saw Mikel, unmasked now, bow to a pair of local girls and turn for the road home, Taigan beside him and looking deeply thoughtful. Briefly she wondered where Jored had disappeared to, then shrugged. After paying her respects to the mayor and a few other dignitaries—none of whom dared ask about the weird vision preceding her silvery magic—she gathered energy to Fold the road back to Mage Hall.

She didn't enter through the main gate, but instead circled around to the east and climbed the wall, careful of the thorns on Josselin's roses. A long, slow hike took her up to the pakkas' meadow. Stars were flung out above her, shining with unrivaled brilliance now that the Lady-moon had set. She followed the stream uphill into the forest, and lit no Mage Globe to guide her through the darkness. She knew the way through the dense wood by the Wards she had placed here years ago. Knowing what to expect from her own spells, the Working usually made her smile: Itchy Ankle, Dropped My Knife, Thirsty, Look That Way, Somebody Watching. So many days spent here observing Prentices learn to recognize and resist Wards. . . . But she wasn't smiling tonight as she turned left at this Ward and right at another. She relaxed only when she reached the deepest forest, where the spring that was the creek's source bubbled from a rocky cairn into a small, moss-rimmed pool.

Starlight shone down from the break in the heavy trees, glinted off the water. Cailet sat on a broad, flat stone and propped her elbows on her knees, gazing at the deception in the pond. The stars overhead were fixed, absolute; the mirror-dance of their reflections was a lie. But a beautiful one—as beautiful as Josselin Mikleine's face, as the graceful curve of Jored Karellos's back as he bent to receive Taigan's kiss.

Which one? Which?

Her lips quirked in a bitter smile as she remembered the question of her owl-mask: *Who?*

Cailet had been waiting a long while now for Josselin to complete his training and come to her for the ritual that would make him a Mage Guardian. But the teachers reported that he could more often be found tending his roses or tinkering with various bits of machinery around Mage Hall. He was, truly told, dawdling. Cailet couldn't understand that. Time and again she'd witnessed—instigated—the supreme moment in a young life when everything, *everything,* came together in one radiant burst of comprehension. There had been no such moment for her, but she treasured each shared experience of it with her new-made Mages.

Josselin resisted. And when Cailet had approached him on the subject, he was evasive.

"I'm in no rush, Captal. Besides, if I needed a ceremony to feel myself a Mage Guardian, I'd be a pretty poor imitation of one, wouldn't I?"

"That's an excuse, not a reason. What are you afraid of?"

"I'm not afraid." But the moonstone-gray eyes had avoided her, and Cailet knew he was lying. "I know what happens, Captal—you may think nobody's ever talked about it, but there've been rumors. Ritual combat until the Prentice tries to use magic against you—*really* use it, in earnest, trying to win. I'm not *interested* in winning. It doesn't matter to me. If that makes me less than a Mage Guardian, then I'm sorry. But I won't fight you, and that's all there is to it."

Did the rumors also say that during this time, the essence of a Prentice's magic altered subtly, becoming its truest self, and in that profound instant this signature was imparted to Cailet for all time? Did Josselin fear he would not be able to keep his Malerrisi magic hidden from her any longer, and reveal himself as Glenin's son?

Now, Jored . . . he was a little slower than most Prentices, and had to work harder at the craft of magic, but so did Taigan. As for their budding relationship—Cailet's skin crawled as she considered Glenin's dynastic plans for the Ambrais. Was Jored nothing more than what he said he was, and therefore innocent in his attachment to Taigan? Or was he Glenin's son, and pretending to be slow so that he had more time to make his own cousin fall in love with him?

Cailet had looked into Jored's eyes, and into Josselin's, and never seen anything reminiscent of Glenin. Or Auvry Feiran. Or Avira Anniyas.

Which meant exactly nothing.

She was aware of Gorsha's angry, insistent voice calling to her from behind the bastion she'd raised. All she lacked at this point was an argument with him. She was perfectly capable of shredding her nerves herself, thank you very much, and had no need of him to—

Cailet!

Not Gorsha. One of the others—Alin?

Cailet, you're in danger!

Danger—? Alin, what—

Shut up and get out of here! Get back to Mage Hall NOW!

And all at once the darkness was more than that of the night around her. It was a thing of air thickening in her lungs and thoughts freezing in her brain and blood congealing in her heart and she was running before she even knew she was running. Her hands ached for her sword, Gorsha's sword, and she could feel the length of steel shuddering faraway in her chambers with the power of her need. She crashed through the forest, not hearing the birds cry out in fear, not hearing the pakkas flutter their wings and gallop from their sleeping dens to the meadow, not hearing her own ragged breathing or the pounding of her boots on grass and rocky soil.

What she heard was the repeated explosion of Mage Globes—almost like the ones she and the others had fashioned tonight as fireworks. Almost. These cracked with lethal magic, detonating with horrible regularity and, as she topped a rise and could see Mage Hall, with blasts of furious crimson light.

The refectory, the living quarters, the classrooms, the stables—all were collapsing in bursts of magical fire, orange and gold and scarlet and white, all the colors of real flames. Mages and Prentices stumbled from the buildings, ran for their lives, were flung forward with the force of more explosions that tore bricks from mortar and hurled the fragments into living bodies that lurched and fell and lived no more.

This is Malerrisi work, she heard Gorsha say.

And from Lusath Adennos, *This is how it must have been in The Waste War. Saints forgive us, this is how we must have fought back then.*

Alin was silent. But Tamos Wolvar, master of Mage Globes as no other before or since, quietly presented a range of spells and Wardings and other, more esoteric Workings for Cailet's use with a calm, *These may be of some use to you, child.*

It was a strange thing, really. She didn't want the magic. Part of her knew it was hopeless. Most of her simply and profoundly wanted that sword. It knew her, understood her. No person living did—and no one dead, either. The sword was an extension of herself, of her will, of her need to destroy those who were destroying her life's work. As she bolted down the hill and leaped the rose-strewn wall she wanted nothing more in this world than to kill.

But there was no one *to* kill.

No attackers. No invaders. No army of Malerrisi or even mere soldiers.

Just magic.

One man's magic. One tall, beautiful, gray-eyed young man's magic.

He appeared before her, both of him, cloaked in black and reeking of smoke. One of him was carrying Imilial Gorrst's ruined body. The other was supporting Mikel, who bled from a wounded shoulder. Behind them came Taigan, and half a dozen other Mages and Prentices, and behind them limped a few more. So few. So few.

Cailet exchanged a single glance with her sister's daughter, who nodded and began snapping orders as imperiously as Sarra ever had. Cailet ran on, making for the gate to the sunken courtyard. The stenches of death and smoke stung her eyes and nostrils. The cries of the dying were louder in her ears than the continuing explosions. The great oak tree was ablaze, its branches not a canopy of cooling shade but of fire that rained down on the flagstones. Beneath the tree sprawled Granon, a gaping hole in his chest. Cailet sprinted to him, falling to her knees as embers fell all around. Shielding him with her body, she began to work her hands under his powerful shoulders to haul him to safety. He frowned at sight of her.

"Shut up," she told him fiercely. She didn't want to hear any damned dutiful noises about protecting the Captal, giving his life for hers—

A smile tugged a corner of his mouth. "Dear fool," he whispered. Compassion and affection shone in his eyes, and, for just an instant, a sweetly tender love. And then he died.

She stared down at his burn-scarred face in disbelief. "Gransha?" And the name was so close to the name of another Warrior Mage who loved her that for a moment it was as if they were both dead beneath her hands.

No, dearest. I'm still here. And I believe his Wraith will see you safe before he leaves you. Come, love, you must go now. There's nothing you can do here.

He sounded so sad. So resigned.

She was resigned to nothing. She wanted that sword. His sword. *Her* sword.

There was a crash from the great Hall upstairs. She felt it deep in her guts, like her own death. All of it was gone, everything she'd spent her adult life creating, gone forever in a flood of fire. She took the stairs three at a time, glancing once toward the living quarters. The breezeway was a tunnel of flame. Those who had slept in the rooms beyond, believing themselves safe—how many were dead? Her Mages, teachers who'd given everything of themselves to educate young Mageborns, the elderly who had earned rest and ease; those not Mageborn, wed to magic, bearing and fathering children of magic—sweet Saints, the children—

She stumbled, and grasped for the railing with one hand to steady herself. She couldn't bear it. What he had done, he would pay for with his life. Slowly. One cut at a time from that sword, one thin ribbon of blood for every death he'd caused—

Cailet ran the length of the balcony, where vines

blossomed now with fire. She kicked open the door to her quarters, screaming for Marra and Aidan. Untouched, everything in the three rooms that were her only home was utterly untouched. Couches and sideboard in the sitting room—shelves of Mage Globes in her office—bed and wardrobe and the big green-velvet chair Sarra and Collan had sent last Birthingday—all of it untouched. But that would follow; the sword was here, and Glenin's son would not relinquish it to the fires.

Then she saw past the things, and saw Marra. She was on her knees beside Cailet's bed, and in her arms she cradled her husband's dark head, and when she looked up there were streaks of moisture gleaming on her soot-stained cheeks.

Aidan was dead.

For this, too, *he* would pay.

The sword. Where was the sword? Without it, she could not kill the one who had done this. Whichever one he was.

But how silly of her. She would simply kill *both* of him and have done with it once and for all. Should've done it long before now. Stupid not to. Where was that damned sword?

14

IN theory, Mikel knew what he was doing. His father had not neglected his basic education, and there'd been plenty of girls at Roseguard more than willing to further it if he so chose. He hadn't chosen, and at almost eighteen his knowledge was still theoretical—if thorough in all practical details.

What he *didn't* know was what Lirenza Mettyn was doing. Or why her mouth should taste sweeter and headier than the wine he'd drunk tonight. Or why the pressure of her body against his while they danced had driven every thought from his head except the urgent need to get her alone. Or why, now that they *were* alone, all he could think was that theory was all very well, but in practice he was too sadly lacking to deserve her attentions.

He sent up a silent prayer to St. Maidil, whose feast day this was, for he qualified in both her patronages; he hoped to become a new lover, and he was certainly a fool. If only Renza didn't laugh at him—

But she *was* laughing, low in her throat, as she coaxed him up the ladder to the hayloft. Barns and stables—if not overpopulated by their smelly rightful residents—came fondly recommended in Fa's reminiscences. So Mikel willingly went along with Lirenza's suggestion.

But now she was laughing. Mikel gulped, then relaxed as he saw the soft excitement in her eyes. He'd seen the same teasing sparkle when his mother looked at his father, and suddenly seemed to hear Fa's amused voice: *"Enjoy it, boy—and never make love without it!"*

So Mikel smiled, and enjoyed it, and when he and Lirenza were both naked in the silvery moonglow through the skylight, they spent a few moments admiring each other's strong young bodies. She was small and delicately curved, and her skin was as soft as a cloud beneath his fingertips. When she pushed him gently down onto the straw he simply couldn't lie there passively as a well-mannered man must, but reached for her because he couldn't stand not to touch her. Though she was only a year older than he, she knew what she wanted; but though neither of them had said a word about love, she also had tenderness enough for him to discover what he liked. Before long they were both laughing with the delight of what they discovered in each other.

They lay together, exploring with lips and hands, not yet joined, not so eager as to be foolishly swift. Mikel's father had impressed on him several important rules, primary being to make the lady take her time about it—which made it incumbent upon a man to restrain himself no matter what she might do. He found that in this, as in most other things, Fa had it right—though some of what Renza was doing made the counseled control damned near impossible. Still, every time she tried to hurry things along, Mikel grinned and evaded her. She growled at him, and swore, and her amber-flecked dark eyes laughed as she renewed her efforts.

At last he allowed her to guide him into her warmth, and gasped with the reality that was to theory as singing was to silently reading music on a folio page. He forgot all about Fa's advice, forgot everything but what was happening to his body.

Afterward, when he had drawn his cloak up to protect her sweat-sheened skin from the night's chill, he wondered which of a woman's usual phrases he might hear now. Fa had told him that when one was not a husband but only a bed-partner, the woman often felt some comment necessary. *"After she catches her breath, she'll say something like, 'That was wonderful,' or 'You were great,' or 'I didn't have to teach you very much!' Smile and be gracious when you compliment her in return, and above all look smug. For some unknown reason, they think smug is adorable in bed. But once you're married, it's different. When things are finished, like as not she'll remind you that the hedges need trimming, or to tell the cook there'll be twelve for dinner tomorrow night!"*

So he waited for Lirenza to catch her breath, hoping she'd say something flattering that wasn't *too* dreadful a cliché. He'd like to remember her words with pride and pleasure as being for him alone, not a standard phrase mothers taught their daughters for such situations.

She snuggled close to his side, burrowing her face into the curve of his neck. "Mmm," she sighed. "Nice."

After a few moments he realized with a wry grin that this was all the praise he was going to get. Well, if not exactly eloquent, at least it was sincere—

The explosion was too near and too loud for his ears to comprehend. What he heard, an instant later, was like the aftershock of thunder and the afterglow of lightning—and the jangle of glass on the wooden floor below. Then came the glow of fire from empty byres beneath the hayloft. And the smoke, blown upward by drafts through shattered windows toward the jagged remains of the skylight over his head.

He choked, and tried to sit up, but Lirenza's slight body was suddenly heavy and limp in his arms. She didn't cough with the thickening smoke. There was a second explosion, and a third farther away, and she didn't flinch. He spoke her name, then shouted it, struggling free of her embrace, and saw blood on his own bare shoulder where her head had been, and a six-inch shard of glass embedded in her nape like a dagger.

He staggered to his feet, bent, gathered her up in his arms. He carried her to the ladder and looked down through billowing smoke. It was twenty-five feet to the wooden floor. He would never be able to carry her down—not in time to save himself. He drew a shaky breath, coughed again, and placed her very gently onto the straw. Her head lolled back, eyes closed, a smile still on her face, and he wondered bitterly if he ought to be glad he'd been the one to put it there. If not for him, she'd be alive; if not for her, he'd be dead. Was that a fair balance, on St. Venkelos's scale of judgment?

Knuckling tears from his eyes, he drew her hands up, folding them between her breasts. The pose of a corpse reading for burning. Silver glinted from one delicate wrist. Hesitating only a moment, he unclasped the bracelet of gray agates and yellow topazes that were the colors of the Mettyn Blood, not knowing to whom he would give the token or even if he'd survive to do so. Coughing, half-blinded by smoke and tears, he stroked back her dark hair and murmured her name one last time.

Then, his clothes bundled in one arm, he descended the ladder into an inferno.

15

"WHAT the hell are you doing with *that?*"

Josselin gave Taigan a blank stare. "With what?"

She pointed accusingly at the sword at his hip. "The Captal's sword, that's what. Where did you—" She was distracted by a moan, and turned to where Elomar had set up a rough—very rough—field hospital at the gatehouse.

The patient sprawled on the wooden floor of the warming room was Prentice Nilos Doriaz. Glass slivers were embedded all along one side from his cheek to his ribs. Taigan surmised he'd been in bed when an explosion shattered his window. Nilos was barely fourteen years old.

Elomar, assisted by his daughter and lacking any medical instrumentation, was removing fragments with his fingertips. Taigan gulped as a large ragged shard was eased from the boy's neck. But no blood spurted out; the artery had not been cut. Elomar flung the piece into the capacious warming-room hearth—and barely missed hitting Timar Grenirian, who was stripping twigs for kindling. Taigan was inexplicably fascinated by the old man. There was a certain rhythm to the motions of his hands— pile kindling, reach for a new branch, wipe at his broken nose. When a spark at last caught and the wood flared, Taigan flinched. It took her a moment to realize that she'd been picturing him doing exactly the same thing thirty-eight years ago, the first time the Mages had been destroyed.

No, she told herself fiercely, *not destroyed, not then and not now!*

Taigan glanced around the warming room, where only last week she'd sat with her fellow Prentices to learn the responsibilities of sentry duty. All the chairs had been shoved to the walls, forming a kind of long, uncomfortable bed with the wounded lying head-to-heels. More people lay on the floor, or curled with arms wreathing knees by the huge brick hearth.

How had they gotten here? Without her help, that was certain. She'd been in her room, carefully wrapping her mask to preserve it as a souvenir of the night. Suddenly the explosions began. With everyone else who survived the initial onslaught, she'd run from the Hall to the gatehouse, escaping the flames. Now she was ashamed of her panic. There were things to be done—the wounded were being cared for, nothing she could do for them, but there must be others still alive back there. And where was the Captal? Josselin had the sword—where had he gotten it?

She looked around for him. But he had moved toward

the door, the cloak once more covering the length of the Captal's sword in its scabbard. Grimly, Taigan went after him, determined to find out how and why he had left Mage Hall with that sword.

Her brother waylaid her halfway to the door. She'd glimpsed his coppery curls earlier on the way to the gatehouse, but he'd been carrying someone and was slower than she, and in her terror she'd run right past him. Guilt smote her once more; Mikel had helped, she had only fled. He'd probably seen her. For a moment she couldn't bring herself to look at him, then decided she must brazen it out. If she'd been a coward before—well, that was over.

"Are you all right?" Mikel asked anxiously, drawing her aside.

"Fine." She surveyed him. Singed here and there, but unharmed that she could tell. "You look awful. Are you hurt?"

"Right shoulder," he replied. "Just a pinprick— falling glass. I still have one good arm."

"With which you are going to do exactly nothing. Mishka, don't argue with me! You got out of there once, Saints alone know how—I'm not letting you go back there again!"

"I have no intention of arguing with you. I'm not going to stick around long enough for you to argue *with*." So saying, he stalked out into the night, beyond the range of the crackling hearthfire and the Mage Globe Lusira had conjured for her husband to work by.

Taigan hissed between her teeth and went after him, with one look back over her shoulder into the gatehouse. Elomar and Dessa had moved on to another patient. Outside, around a small fire built at the rosc-covered wall, a few uninjured Mages and Prentices shivered in nightclothes and blankets. Taigan approached, picking out those who'd had the presence of mind to put on shoes, and flinched again as she heard a crash of timbers and masonry from the Hall five hundred feet away.

How could she have run away before trying to rescue her fellow Mageborns? Coward. Craven. Not at all worthy of the First Daughter of two brilliant lights of the Rising. Whatever of that brilliance she had inherited had deserted her. All she could do was listen as the others talked quickly among themselves. The consensus was that Mage Hall had been betrayed from within. No strangers had been seen in its precincts. Had the Mage on duty sensed any intrusions through her Wards, she would have called an alarm at once. But no one had infiltrated. The lethal Mage Globes had been set by one of their own.

Correction: one of Glenin Feiran's own.

Taigan gritted her teeth and gathered the able-bodied by snapping out their names (sometimes two or three times before they responded) and organizing them as they strode down the hill toward the burning wreck of Mage Hall.

"First, check the stables. We need horses and carts to transport the wounded. Akin, do what you can in the Prentices' quarters. Ketri, the Mages' wing. When you find any wounded, the rest of you take them back to the gatehouse. And everybody be *careful*. There haven't been any explosions for a few minutes, but there's no telling what's going to fall down next."

"Our duty is—" said one of the Mages, but Taigan interrupted him.

"*I'm* going for the Captal." To forestall any further discussion, she ran to catch up to Mikel. He gave her a fiercely challenging glare; she met his blue eyes levelly, and after a moment he relaxed and nodded.

"Joss went ahead." He gestured to the Oak Court with his right hand, wincing as his injured shoulder protested. The blaze leaped skyward from the sunken hollow like some great exotic fire-lily, the glow turning Mikel's curls to flames.

"What about Jored?"

"Haven't seen him since he carried Rennon to the gatehouse. They're probably looking for survivors." He gripped his wounded shoulder with his left hand, visibly repressing another grimace of pain. "Teggie—how did this happen? Who did this?"

"How should I know? But when I catch up with who-ever it was—"

"Assuming I don't catch up with 'em first. And don't

talk to me about being First Daughter either," he snarled suddenly. "Lirenza's dead in there."

She couldn't place the name for a moment, then recalled that he'd been carrying on a mild flirtation with their fellow Prentice.

"I'm sorry," she said, knowing how inadequate it was.

"I—I danced with her tonight," He wouldn't look at her. "And now she's dead. How could anybody *do* this?" A hand came up to swipe at his eyes, and Taigan didn't think it was because of the sting of blowing smoke.

They were nearly at the curving red-brick wall that guarded the sunken courtyard, and the noise of the fire and the sudden crashes of timber and masonry were deafening. The twins traded looks that refused to admit fear. Mikel preceded Taigan into the inferno, between wooden gates that blazed askew on their hinges, down the steep stairs to the courtyard. Taigan followed, choking at the sight of Granon Bekke—what was left of him. When she made as if to go smother the flames, Mikel hauled her back.

"It can't matter to him now!" he shouted above the furious roar of the fire. "Come on!"

There was another explosion then, not of a Mage Globe but a branch of the oak tree. They reeled back, Taigan brushing at the right side of her face where cinders scorched her skin. Suddenly Mikel slapped her head, nearly knocking her over. She pushed him away furiously. He plucked a long lock of blonde hair from her cloak, showing her the singed end. Taigan gasped and felt frantically at her head. Two or three more strands came loose in her fingers, the tufted ends sticking straight up at her crown.

He grabbed her elbow and dragged her toward the stairs. "Can we get out of here before we're *both* scarred for life and blistered bald?"

Taigan saw a cloaked figure on the balcony above, and thought it must be Jored. She screamed his name. There was no response. Mikel yelled, "Joss!" and the man turned from the entrance to the Captal's quarters, the sword swinging against his thigh.

"Is she in there?" Mikel shouted.

Josselin roared back, "Get out of here before you fry like all the rest! There's nothing you can do here but get yourselves killed—and then your mother would kill *me!*"

"Assuming *you* make it out of here!" Mikel yelled back.

Taigan's answer was more direct. She slithered past a burning trellis and raced up the stairs, the three burns on her face stinging like acid. Mikel was right behind her, both of them coughing and bleary-eyed with smoke. Josselin had vanished indoors by the time they arrived at the Captal's rooms. There was no fire within, and no windows had blown out, and once over the threshold the air was breathable. In the office, Mikel ran for a tall shelf, to what purpose Taigan had no idea. She went for the private inner chamber.

Beside the bed, Marra Gorrst rocked back and forth, crying softly into her husband's black hair. Taigan's grief gave way to fear when she saw the Captal, and Josselin, and felt a savage magic thicker and more deadly than the smoke outside.

The Captal stood in the center of the room, face streaked with soot and tears, eyes black acid as she confronted Josselin. He glared grimly back at her, a magnificent statue holding a sheathed sword.

"It's *mine,*" hissed the Captal, and her hand snapped forward as if she flung something at him. "I want it back!"

The magic—not even contained within a Globe, the Captal had no need of such visual exhibition of her power—crashed against Josselin's defense, which became visible only when the assaulting spell hit, arcing all the way around him in a spherical blast of crimson fire fully eight feet across. Taigan was caught in the backlash, reeling as the Captal struck again.

"Give it to me!" she shrieked. "How dare you take what's mine!"

Josselin shook his head slowly. He was breathing hard, sweat shining on smudged forehead and cheeks like rivulets of tears or blood.

"Give it to me!"

And Taigan heard echo of herself and Mikel from the first instants of their lives, when the Captal had taken their magic from them and they had rebelled against losing that thing which was most *theirs* of anything they were or ever could be. She had stolen it from them, and they had been hollowed by its loss—

No. She had Warded it up inside them. She had stolen nothing, taken nothing. She had protected them against its power until they were ready for it.

And that was exactly what Joss was doing now. That sword, Gorynel Desse's sword, one of The Fifty from St. Caitiri's own forge—in the hands of the Captal as she was now, it would slay anyone in its path. Josselin knew it; no one could look at her and not know it. Taigan shuddered as Joss barely resisted yet another onslaught. He would not survive many more. But he could not, would not, give up that sword, not to this raving madwoman whose life's work was burning to ashen ruin all around her.

Had all her power turned to Wild Magic? Taigan shuddered, for if this were true they were all lost—not just the people in this room but the Mage Guardians, forever. If The Bequest died with Cailet's insanity, the Mage Guardians would be destroyed.

Sidling along the wall of windows toward the bed, Taigan knelt by Marra and gripped her shoulder. Low-voiced, not wishing to draw the Captal's rage, she said, "Go—get out. We'll bring him. Hurry." When she received no responses other than an angry shrug of the shoulder she held, she dug her nails into Marra's flesh. "Joss can't last much longer, and I can't protect either of us against her—let alone the child you carry! Move!"

"The baby—" Sense returned to Marra's eyes, and with it terror for her unborn child. Exposure to powerful magic while still in the womb was risky at best; exposure to *this* kind of magic was tantamount to murder.

"Go!" Taigan said again, and then Mikel was at her side, dragging Marra to her feet. He'd grabbed the Captal's fur cloak from the wardrobe and wrapped her in it—using only his left hand. His right arm was hidden beneath his own cloak, drawn close to his ribs as if he'd been hurt again and was cradling the pain. But his eyes were clear, and he was neither flushed nor pallid beneath the soot on his cheeks, so Taigan decided he'd do until Elomar could do something for him. "Get her out of here," she ordered. "And don't come back for us!"

Her twin sent her a single eloquent glower over his shoulder and hurried Marra into the next room. Taigan stood, gulping back terror as Joss staggered within his Mage Globe.

"You have no right!" shrieked the Captal. "It's *mine!*"

Once again Josselin did nothing more than shake his head. It seemed to infuriate her more than any words he could have spoken.

Taigan bit both lips between her teeth. The Captal's back was to her; she was reasonably sure her presence had gone completely unnoticed. She jumped up onto the bed, stumbled across it, and launched herself at the Captal. Her adored Auntie Caisha. The madwoman who spun with the speed of a silverback cat to fend her off, and clawed at her as they plunged to the floor in a tangle of limbs and corrosive magic.

Her mind was scorched by that magic which burned without light. Self-born shadows that needed no fire to create them shrouded her in blackness. She couldn't even cry out, though her throat and lungs were as raw as if she'd screamed since the instant of her birth. Whatever magic was in her contracted to a tiny, terrified spark—but it was all she had against that smothering darkness. She clutched at it, and instinctively hid it from the sudden ruthless searching of that dark, rapacious magic.

Give it to me!

She Warded herself with frantic, mindless urgency. Black shadows swept over her like suffocating wings. There was no light anywhere except for that minuscule ember hiding within her—and all at once it was free to grow, to expand, to ensphere her totally and keep her safe.

Taigan was in someone's strong arms, her head lolling against a muscled shoulder. The rough wool of a cloak scratched her burned cheek and she tried to shift her head, but she couldn't seem to move. She inhaled, coughed, tried to suck moisture into her dry mouth, tongue shriveling and lips cracking and nostrils clotted with the heat. A masculine voice spoke her name. She couldn't reply. She couldn't move. The heat got worse, and the smoke, and for an interminable time she couldn't breathe. And then there was cleaner air, colder, and the shock of it to her lungs spasmed through her whole body.

She opened her eyes to more blackness, and whimpered. But it was only the night sky, and as her vision adjusted she could see the full Ladymoon and the pinpricks of brilliant stars. Craning her neck, she glimpsed the radiance of fire on billowing smoke. The light soothed her.

"Joss, don't let her wake up," said the man who held her, and Joss answered, "Mikel hit her so hard I don't think she'll wake up for a week."

Taigan came abruptly back to herself. "Jored?"

He tightened his embrace. "You're all right. So's the Captal—but for a slug on the jaw, courtesy your brother."

Oh, Sweet Saints—Mikel had hit the Captal? Then she remembered that she'd tried more or less the same thing, and subsided.

"And if you would," he asked mildly, "I'd appreciate a little less magic in the air."

"What?"

"You don't weigh very much, but you've put up Wards that feel—" He broke off, looking into her eyes "Didn't you know?"

She gulped, and concentrated, and the last of the protective magic faded away. Jored sighed and she felt his muscles relax. After a time, she murmured, "Jored? What did I do?"

He thought about it, then said, "Seems to me you're one of those Mageborns who can't *think* about their magic too much. You just have to *do* it without analyzing why or how."

Like Mother, the way she just *knew* things. It made sense. But it troubled her, too—for what was Wild Magic if not unrestrained instinct?

A little while later they entered the gatehouse. Truly told, Taigan had no wish to leave the warm, strong refuge of Jored's arms—a place prominently featured in her dreams and even more pleasing in reality. But the very shelter he offered suddenly grated on her nerves. How could she be selfishly safe while others were not? More, there was the rasp of pride to make her squirm slightly in his arms: she was Taigan Liwellan, she required no protecting and no help. So she told him to put her down, please, she was perfectly all right and there were things to be done. He set her on her feet, eyeing her warily in case she swayed. She was disgusted to find herself tempted to do just that, for the feel of his arms around her again.

Elomar Adennos, looking old enough to be Dessa's great-grandfather, had taken charge of the Captal. She had been wrapped in her fur cloak and a cushion had been found for her head where she lay on the floor. Kneeling at her side, the Master Healer put himself between her and the firelight, and conjured a tiny Mage Globe that hovered for a moment at her feet and then traveled up her body. Silvery-green to her waist, it blackened near her chest and stayed dark all the way to the crown of her head. Elo frowned, gnawing his lip as the Globe vanished, and said something to Lusira in a low voice. She shrugged in reply and used a damp cloth to clean the soot from the Captal's face—careful of the bruise beginning to swell on her chin.

"She'll be all right," Dessa whispered at Taigan's shoulder. "If Fa was worried, the Globe would still be watching over her."

"Oh," Taigan said for lack of anything else.

"You could use a wash," Dessa continued, eyeing Taigan critically.

"Wash?" she echoed incredulously. In the middle of this disaster, Dessa was concerned about whether or not Taigan's face was clean?

"You'll feel better, trust me," said Gorynel Desse's granddaughter. "Some cold water on those burns, then some salve—they're not serious, you won't scar, so don't worry. Mother's using the kitchen sink for soaking rags clean of blood, so try the spigot outside."

Marveling at Dessa's composure (and more relieved than she could rightly feel at the moment that her wounds

were not disfiguring), Taigan nodded and started outside—only to be startled, foolishly, by the neighing of a
horse. Somebody had followed her orders and rescued
some transportation: two wagons, big enough for nine or
ten wounded to lie down in reasonable comfort, were approaching, drawn by two horses each. Three more horses
were tethered to the wagons. Taigan turned on her heel to
count the injured inside—and when she finished, counted
again in sheer disbelief.

Of the one hundred and six Mages, Prentices, non-
Mageborns, and children in residence at the Hall, twenty-
two people lay in the gatehouse, too badly injured to sit
up, let alone walk. Add Lusira, Dessa, and Elomar; Mikel,
Joss, Jored, herself, and several more outside—

Were they all that was left? A faraway crash of pillars
and stone and timber brought tears to her eyes. Knuckling
them away, she counted once more inside, then went
around to the kitchen by the back door, then returned to
the front of the gatehouse.

Thirty-four. And that was all.

No. Thirty-three. She'd counted Aidan, whom someone had borne from the wreckage—Mikel and Marra together, probably, for Jored had taken her and Joss had
carried the Captal. Taigan scrubbed at her eyes, her
cheeks, smudging soot and tears, scraping her injured
face, ashamed that she'd worried about so trivial a matter
as a few scars.

"—south to Cantratown, it's the only way—"

"Through miles of populated countryside where
we'll have to explain that the Mage Guardians were attacked and the Hall destroyed?" Josselin gave a bitter
snarl. "North, Jored. To the Ladder at Peyres."

"How can we be sure of it—or of any Ladder, even
the Garvedian one in Cantratown? You'd have us take the
wounded over miles of *un*populated countryside—all
hills—where there'll be no help for them or us?" Jored
swept an arm toward the easy road south.

"And once we're in Cantratown? If the Garvedian
Ladder is still safe, it'll take us to Shellinkroth!"

"The one at the Affe mansion—" Jored began heatedly.

"—leads to Roke Castle, equally useless! But if we go north, the Ladder in Peyres goes to the Mage Academy, and from there we can go directly to Ryka Court!"

Taigan started toward them, incensed that the two men seemed to be deciding things not theirs to decide. Anger at them mostly served to hide—even from herself—that she was even angrier at herself for agreeing with Joss, not Jored.

Mikel beat her to it. He stood with the two older Prentices beside the rose-covered wall, both arms folded beneath his cloak—which wasn't his, she saw with some surprise. It was the old black one, collar stitched with snagged silver thread, that the Captal used for everyday.

"Seems to me," Mikel drawled, and for a moment he sounded so like Fa that Taigan's heart cringed; what would she have given to have Collan Rosvenir here now? "Seems to me Joss is right, and we can't be sure of *any* Ladders. If the Malerrisi were bold enough to attack Mage Hall, they won't stop at burning any Ladder they can get near."

"All the Ladders are guarded," Jored said.

"So were we," Mikel reminded him irrefutably.

"The question is which Ladder we chance." Joss shook his head. "Peyres is the best risk. If it *is* safe, we'd be in Ambrai. They already destroyed it once, why bother again?"

"Because they'd know it's the first place we'd go for safety," Jored argued. "Lady Elin is a close ally of the Captal—"

"And my mother," Mikel said suddenly, and Taigan shared his thought without even having to look at him: *What if the attack wasn't limited to Mage Hall? What if Mother and Fa—*

"All right, that's enough," Taigan snapped, as much to stop her own frightening speculations as to shut the men up. She strode forward to confront them, wrapped in the authority of a woman, a Blooded First Daughter, a Mageborn. "Nobody's going anywhere until the Captal wakes up and decides what's to be done."

"Teggie. . . ." Mikel bit his lip, then continued, "You

saw what she was like back there. If she wakes up in the same state—"

"Shut up!" Taigan discovered she was trembling. "How dare you!"

"He's right," Jored told her gently.

"You shut up, too!" Rounding on him, she felt dizzy for a moment before recovering herself—hoping they hadn't noticed. "She'll be fine. Dessa said her father isn't worried—"

"That's good to hear," Joss said, "but until the Captal's back with us, somebody has to decide what to do. We can't stay here."

"We're vulnerable," Jored agreed. "And we can't go into Heathering, it would put all those people at risk."

Mikel frowned at mention of the townsfolk. "Teggie, why haven't they come to help? Remember the brushfire near Wentrin Smallhold last Drygass? St. Lirance's rang the alarm, and everybody went to put out the fire before it could spread. But there's nobody here now—not a sign of a torch on the road to light their way, not a sound from St. Lirance's—where *are* they?"

No one answered him, because each knew that the only possible answer was magic. Everyone within ten miles of Heathering at been at the St. Maidil's celebrations tonight; it wasn't beyond a Malerrisi to spend the evening Working on every single one of them. A Ward against even looking in the direction of Mage Hall. . . .

"There'll be no help," Joss said softly. "And we can't put them in danger by asking. So we have to leave. North, for the Ladder at Peyres, to the old Academy."

"If we go south," Jored argued, "we'll at least be in range of a ship to take us wherever the Captal wants to go."

Taigan exchanged a glance with her brother, who shrugged his good shoulder. He nodded agreement with what was in her eyes, and she said, "We could go *both* places."

The two young men stared at her.

"We could send the wounded south. The rest of us could head for Peyres, and then Ambrai and Ryka Court. That's where the Captal needs to be." Where *she* needed to be. Where her mother and father were. At nearly eighteen, it might have mortified her to need them so much; but what was the shame in needing her mother's power and wisdom and her father's sense and strength? The Captal did. Taigan knew that without thinking about it. And as instinct reasserted itself, she gave a decisive nod.

"That's what we'll do, failing any truly brilliant suggestions." Turning to Mikel, finding renewed confidence in his resemblance to Fa—and sudden poignancy in how much older he looked—she went on, "Let Elomar know he's going south in the wagons with anyone who can't walk. Joss, you round up the able-bodied and find out who's got the best Folding spell. We'll have to take turns. It's a long way to Tillin Lake."

"Would a Ward of concealment help any?" Josselin asked. "I don't like the idea that everybody along the way will see us and—"

"—and ask what happened, and find out," Taigan finished, nodding again. "I agree. Get a list of those who can Fold and Ward, then—and if anybody has any other recommendations, I'll be glad to hear them. Mikel, what are you looking at me like that for?"

"I'm not going with the wounded, Teggie," he said flatly.

The notion of being separated from her twin made her jaw drop slightly; it was all the answer he needed. With a small, crooked grin, he went inside the gatehouse. Josselin followed, and Taigan nearly called him back before she saw that his hands were undoing the swordbelt from around his waist. As indignant as she'd been when she'd first seen him with it—it belonged to the Captal, no one else ought to touch it—she experienced a qualm at the thought of it within the Captal's reach. A sword responsive to emotion, acting in obedience to the deepest intent of its wielder—in the hands of that madwoman of an hour ago?

"I'll start getting the wagons ready," Jored said, and she gave a start. She'd forgotten his presence. "We'll need to leave before sunrise."

"Yes, of course. Dessa can drive a team, can't she? I know Lusira can, I've seen her, so she probably taught her daughter." She was babbling and couldn't seem to stop. "Take what you need from the gatehouse—food, blankets and so on—water jugs, something to cook in—"

"I know how to travel," he interrupted, smiling. "Don't worry, Taisha, it'll be all right."

Dumbfounded by his use of the diminutive—an endearment no one ever used—she saw his face change as his fingers lifted and hovered beside the mark on her right cheek.

"You're hurt."

She shook her head mutely.

"You should have the Master Healer take care of these."

She held her breath as his hand moved to her hair, lightly stroking the singed and tumbled mass of it.

"Promise me you'll get those burns seen to, Taisha."

She nodded, and watched him stride purposefully away to do her bidding about the supplies. And as oblivious as she had been to him a few minutes earlier, for the next hour she was so aware of him that he was like a second heartbeat—not quite keeping time with her own, leaping and fluttering every so often, taking some of her breath.

16

IN deference to a good night's sleep for its hard-working citizens, Heathering's clocktower was silent from Fourteenth to Fifth. By the time St. Lirance's rang the new morning, Mage Hall had burned to the ground. All its inhabitants not dead and burned to ashes within were miles away from Heathering, so distant that they never heard the five bright peals that greeted the sun. When, a day later, the Rimrunner rode up to the gatehouse to deliver the mail, a barren silence enwrapped her, carrying a

Warded warning: *GO NO FARTHER*. Being a sensible young woman, and possessing no magic with which to counteract the spell, she galloped north to Heathering. Only then did the townsfolk learn that the Mage Guardians had vanished, no one knew where or why.

THE CHASE

1

He stood before her, both of him, eyes Wraithen-gray, terrible in his beauty, tossing the sword back and forth. It circled endlessly, point-over-hilt, flying between his two selves, glistening with blood and glittering with fire, a moving whirling Mage Globe of crimson and steel and gold.

With it, she could kill him. Both of him.

"Give it to me!" she screamed. "It's mine!"

Both of him laughed and one of him said, "It was never yours, any more than the sum of The Bequest is yours."

And the other of him said, "You stole it all, like the ghoul Anniyas became as a Wraith—you even tried to steal an unborn Mageborn's magic—just as you stole this sword. It was never for you, never."

And the other of him said, "The one time you should have used it, you were too much the coward. So I still live—"

And the other of him said, "—and the sword is in my hand now, where it belongs."

Whimpering, her soul writhing, she saw Aidan come between him—Aidan, whose very first words to her had been, "You're the Captal. My papa died to keep you safe." But the child was now a man, and reached for the sword as it revolved in the air, and his quick hand—accustomed like his father Val's to swordskill—grasped its hilt. He cried out with the pain of magic. She tried to protect him from it, tried to move, to create a Mage Globe around him or the sword or both, but the Wards and Workings trapping her were too strong. Flames leaped up Aidan's arms, haloed his dark head in a blaze of light, burst from his eyes as he flung the sword straight upward, away from him—too late; he collapsed, the light around him dying as he died. A long, strong arm lashed out, dark fingers catching the sword's shining hilt. Once more it spun from one to the other of him, and he was laughing, both of him, and the world grew dark, dark, with only the sword a glistening, glittering, revolving circle of crimson and silver and gold in the blackness.

A sudden brilliant light came between him: magic. Clean, strong magic that did not yet know its own strength—such power, she needed it to replace her own that was feeble and frightened within her—there for the taking in her need, and this time she must do it, she must have that additional magic or be lost—

But this magic felt familiar, a variation echoing her own, and she knew that it was Taigan before her, not the raw untrained power of that unborn Mageborn child. She recoiled from her need, horrified. This was Sarra's First Daughter, the girl in the vision Anniyas had invoked years ago, the bright young magic that challenged her when she'd grown arrogant and complacent—

No—! Not Taigan—this was the other child, the true First Daughter, the one Cailet had killed within Sarra's womb—

There were two of Taigan, slender and blonde and powerful. And two of him, tall and gray-eyed and beautiful. One of her went to his side, took his hand, laughed with him. The other Taigan, the other of him—they began to fade, and the sword hung suspended in midair, arcing in a circle of crimson with the gold hilt at its center.

He grabbed for it once more. She joined him, blonde hair shining like golden flame, green eyes fired from without and within. But the other two crossed the empty air between and there were eight hands grasping that sword by the blade, adding to its crimson shimmer of blood and fire,

*struggling for possession of its magic. And all
the shadows merged into a deeper blackness,
and the laughter became Glenin's—*

"Cailet!"

Sobbing, she flailed against the hands that tried to restrain her.

"Cailet, stop!"

Her eyes opened, and with the end of the blackness came dazzling light, bright as the fires that had consumed Mage Hall.

She remembered, looking at Elomar's haggard face, and turned her head away to weep.

He left her alone. A little while later she heard his voice, and Lusira's, and Taigan's. She neither knew nor cared about their words and worries, though she thought Taigan might have said, "I didn't think Mikel hit her that hard." What she heard was the chaos of voices in her head—not Gorynel Desse or Alin Ostin or Lusath Adennos or Tamos Wolvar, but the newly dead, their Wraithen voices a thick cloud of meaningless sound. She turned over in bed and cried until she was senseless.

When she woke again, the smell of hot coffee made her gag. It was dark, and she was indoors somewhere, lying on a hard cot. Her body felt bruised from scalp to toes, with a particular ache in her jaw. For an instant she stared into the blackness—and then fear seized her, and she gave a low cry.

"Saints and Wraiths!" exclaimed a voice from the darkness. "I *told* you to leave a light burning for her!"

And light there was, and Marra came in like St. Miryenne herself, to place the single candle on a nearby table. The room had definition now—small, windowless, scant of comfort, with only the bed and the table below rafters the candlelight could barely reach. Cailet huddled into the soft fur cloak enwrapping her, wishing passionately for a hearthfire, a blaze to light this mean little room bright as day.

"Cailet?" Marra sat on the edge of the cot, weary and older, one hand on the swell of her belly. "Can you talk to me, dearest?"

"Dearest"? I killed your husband—Aidan will never see your son grow up— She averted her face, biting both lips between her teeth.

"Elo," Marra said, "do something."

Footsteps, then silence. She felt the gentle magic of his Healer's Globe pass over her body, and only then realized that the Ward concealing the wound Glenin had given her long ago was gone. She conjured it quickly, hoping Marra had noticed nothing beneath the cloak, knowing Elomar would keep her secret.

"She needs rest," he said.

It was reprieve from having to talk, from having to acknowledge what had happened and what she had done.

More footsteps—but only one set. Elomar stayed.

"We're safe for now," he told her. "The wounded are being taken to Cantratown. The rest are with you, heading north to Peyres."

With her, with the Captal, to ensure that she lived. That her precious, irreplaceable life was not lost. How many, just as precious, had paid for her criminal stupidity in not killing him, both of him, the instant she began to suspect what he was?

Elo waited, but when she said nothing he left her alone once more. She stared at her own candlethrown shadow on the wall, flinching at every flicker, until exhaustion overwhelmed her and she slept.

She woke for a third time the next day, and this time there was no reprieve from questions and worry and sympathy. A different room, with afternoon light streaming through the windows; a different house, low ceiling and whitewashed walls. And warm—she could feel the sun on her face, thinking how strange the heat felt. Certainly the chill inside her was such that not even sunlight or thick black fur could warm her.

"Sit up," Elomar ordered gruffly. "Drink."

She sat up, and drank. The tea was lukewarm and sickly sweet, with an undertaste of bitterness that nearly made her stomach rebel. But she finished the cup, avoiding his watchful eyes, and handed it back. "How many?" she asked quietly.

"Thirty-three living," he said.

"You know what I meant."

Slowly, reluctantly, as if every death had been his fault for not being there to heal their wounds: "Seventy-eight."

Cailet drew a long breath. "Who?"

There was a rustle of paper, and Elomar began a wooden recitation. "Adennos, Halla—Prentice. Adennos, Hallan—Prentice. Adennos, Sirran—Healer. Allard, Elina—Mage. Allard, Kanen—Warrior. Allard, Vallis—Prentice. Bekke, Granon—"

Cailet made a sound low in her throat and grabbed the paper from him. She read down the list, neatly alphabetized, written in Marra's hand. The names clawed at her. Rance Krestos, husband of Scholar Kella Doriaz, and the three young daughters they'd doted on. Aidan Maurgen. . . . All the men and women not Mageborn, all the children, all of them with no chance at all against murderous magic. Cailet read the names, strangling with guilt and grief, barely able to see the writing for the faces that came to her.

Elderly faces of Mages and Scholars and Healers and Warriors who, after surviving Ambrai and Anniyas's Purge and years of being hunted, had found peaceful retirement at Mage Hall, congenial work in teaching and study: Jenira Doriaz, Aifalun Escovor and her cousin Tirez, so many others.

Mages in the prime of their lives, who taught and wrote and explored what it was to be a Mage Guardian: Maidia Keviron, Viranon Maklyn—one of the Castle Dozen discovered on Bleynbradden the first year of Cailet's journeys in search of Mageborns—so many others.

Prentices just beginning to understand the gift of magic: Lirenza Mettyn, the two young Adennos cousins who might have become Healers, so many others.

The names went on and on. Lira Trevarin, the first Mageborn Cailet had found twenty years ago. Gavria and Kellos Wolvar, talented grandchildren of Tamos's beloved sister. Lirenza Gorrst, Cailet's elderly, blunt-spoken, scowling Scholar-Archivist. Worse still, First Sword Imilial Gorrst. Impossible to imagine life without Imi's blistering humor and full-throated laugh.

So many. So many.

She refused to wipe the tears from her eyes—though by now she should have no tears left to shed. Blinking rapidly, she felt the sting of them down her cheeks, as if they were not the water and salt of her own body but distilled from acid.

"Cailet, Taigan's been asking to see you."

Elomar's voice startled her. She crumpled the sheet of paper in her fist and told him, "No, I want to talk to Marra first."

"As you wish." He went to the door and murmured to someone standing outside. A few minutes later Marra entered, and smiled at seeing Cailet awake and sitting up and to all appearances recovering. Elomar left them alone at a glance from Cailet.

The young woman fell into her old role of taking care of the Captal. "You've some color back in your cheeks," she said. "I won't bring you anything to eat right now, but tonight, I promise you, you're going to have a four-course meal."

"Marra. . . ."

Paying no attention to her protest, Marra went on, "Do you know, Mikel did the oddest thing—and the smartest, too. While he was in your office, he grabbed up seven of those Globes you used to send messages. One broke on the way here, but the rest are intact. Trouble is, he didn't take any of the little wooden stands, so we don't know whose Globe he's got. And he doesn't recall exactly whose names were on the stands. But we're hoping he got a good geographical selection, and he swears that one of them is Telomir Renne's, so—"

"Send him to me," Cailet said. "After you and I have talked."

For the first time Marra's bright aspect dimmed a little, and in her eyes was wariness. What Cailet wanted to say was unwelcome, that was clear enough; but despite Marra's reluctance the thing had to be said.

"Marra, I—"

"No, don't bother yourself with anything right now. You're not recovered yet."

The coward in her made her say, "Tell me who's here, and what's been going on."

"We're almost to Peyres—it's been a little slower than we'd like, but the nine of us—"

"Nine?"

"You, me, Elomar, Lusira, and Dessa, plus Taigan and Mikel, and Josselin and Jored. Rennon wanted to come with us—being the only Warrior still standing—but Taigan told him he was needed to guard the wounded on the road south to Cantratown. Eighteen of them, with six to drive the wagons and tend their wounds and so on. Besides, Joss has your sword, as he pointed out to Rennon, and that's equal to a score of Warrior Mages in the right hands—"

"*Josselin* has my sword?"

"Until you're ready to take it up again, yes." Marra gave her a level look. "You weren't, you know."

"That's part of what I need to talk to you about. Aidan—"

She shook her head fiercely. "He was up late, making sure everyone was back from Heathering and in bed—he was outside the refectory when—" A pause. Marra again rested her hand over her belly. Then, quietly: "Gavria and Kellos Wolvar were taking care of the children while everyone was at St. Maidil's. They were all in the refectory."

Cailet nodded slowly. *They weren't worth keeping alive—not all of them would turn up Mageborn. But the Prentices—most of them survived. They're young enough to be converted to the Malerrisi viewpoint, once Glenin gets hold of them.*

Gorsha said, *There was planning in this, long nights of thought about where to place the Globes. I believe you're right about the Prentices—they're not "yours" yet, and still malleable. Most of the elderly are dead, those who remember the Academy in the old days. I'd guess that if there have been any attacks elsewhere, the dead will be the older Mages and the Warriors.*

The ones who remember, and the ones who know how

to fight, Cailet agreed. *What am I going to do, Gorsha? How do I salvage anything out of this?*

But he did not answer, and Marra was saying in a low, expressionless voice, "Aidan was about to have a cup of coffee with Gavria and Kellos when the windows exploded. There was fire everywhere, and the rafters collapsing—Gavria died instantly. Kellos tried to help Aidan get the children out, but the smoke was too much and most of the children were dead where they lay. They got a few out, but then the corridor was filled with fire as well. Aidan had—he had a splinter of glass in his chest, right near his heart. He got Kellos and two children out, and thought they were safe in the Oak Court—the tree hadn't begun to burn yet—and then came up to me. He lived long enough to tell me what happened—and then he died in my arms."

"But—the sword—"

"What? Oh—he took it from the wall, and had some idea of finding you and defending you with it—he wasn't thinking clearly by then, he thought there were attackers outside. But there weren't, were there? This was done by someone at Mage Hall. A traitor."

Again Cailet nodded, while trying to sort out her dream from the reality Marra reported. "And—Josselin? Jored?"

"They worked like slaves to feed us and keep us safe on the road—I don't think either has slept more than a few hours in the last two days."

"No, no, I meant were they there when Aidan had the sword?"

"I don't remember. What does it matter?"

"It's just—" She sighed. "I'm not very clear on what happened that night." But she must have sensed Aidan's hand on the sword when she got to her chambers—and the sword had remembered his desire to defend her, as his father had done. And he died, just as Val had died, to keep her safe.

But if Aidan's mark had been on the sword, then so must Jored's and Josselin's be as well, or she would not have had that dream—

Is that what it meant, Gorsha? Were they fighting

over who would take the sword before I came in? Or was it just Josselin at first, and Jored later? Do you remember?

My memories are yours from the time of your Making as Captal. But consider this. In your dream, each of them knew things they could not possibly know—about Sela Trayos's child, for instance. Or that you don't possess the entirety of the Bequest. Don't make more of the dream than it was, Caisha.

She said aloud, "I thought—I thought I'd killed Aidan. By not being able to defend him against the magic. I *did* kill him, you know. I killed all of them. I never saw this coming, and I should have. I should've put up Wards and—"

"How could you have known?" Marra took her hand, speaking urgently. "Cailet, it's not your fault."

She pressed Marra's cold fingers between both her own. "I'm so sorry. Marra, I can't begin to tell you how sorry I—"

"It was done by the traitor—and I hope whoever it was is dead of the magic used to kill my husband." Marra hesitated. "Cailet, I can't think who it might've been. Who could do this to us, at Glenin Feiran's orders?"

"I don't know." But she did. As confusing and surreal as her dream had been, her instincts were right. Josselin or Jored. And the sword was the power and authority of the Captal that one of them wanted to take from her.

Josselin now had the sword. To keep it, or to protect it while she mended?

"We'll find out who it was," Marra said. "And once we do, Imi will—" She broke off, recalling that her cousin was dead.

"I'd like to see Taigan now, please. And Mikel afterward, with the Globes."

"Only after you've had something to eat." Marra stood, paused, and said softly, "It wasn't your fault, Cailet. You must believe that."

Taigan came in shortly thereafter. With Marra's description of what had occurred, Cailet's own memory was a little more reliable—she still wasn't sure about who'd been where and when, but she was positive that in her greed she'd sought to steal Taigan's magic. So she only let the girl say how good it was to see her awake before apologizing.

"Sorry?" Taigan blinked startled green eyes. "What for?"

"What I tried to do to you." Hitching herself up in bed, with a lumpy pillow to support her back, she bit her lips together before continuing, "It's—something in me that craves power, when I can't rely on my own. I wanted yours, and nearly took it. I'm sorry, Taigan."

A frown, and a brief silence; then: "You weren't in your right mind, if you'll forgive my saying so, Captal. Mage Hall betrayed, so many dying—"

"That's no excuse."

"Maybe, but it's an understandable reason."

There was a calm in Taigan's eyes that had never been there before—Cailet saw that command had settled on her, and confidence in it, and consciousness of the rightness of her decisions. She trusted herself; perhaps she didn't fully trust her magic yet, but she believed in her ability to lead others. So like Sarra, this self-assurance—and so like Collan. So unlike the doubts and the shadows that plagued Cailet.

"It's happened before," Cailet murmured. "Once, when I was about your age . . . I tried to steal—"

"But you didn't mean to."

"In some ways I did. Stop looking at me as if I'm trying to guide you through a lesson," she added irritably. "I'm only telling you this because of what you did. You *fought,* Taigan—and I'm proud of you for fighting me. Your magic is yours, and no one can ever take it away or use it against your will, against what you know to be right. You refused to give in."

Taigan said softly, "I think it was because I knew what you'd do with it. So did Josselin. He still has your sword, by the way—and I don't think he wants it much. But he won't give it up to anyone but you."

Cailet nodded. "Let him keep it for now. I've no use for it." *Not when I can still barely think straight. St. Delilah only knows what I'd do with it if I had it to hand.*

"Marra says you want to see Mikel. About the Globes."

"Yes. I'm impressed that he thought of them."

"I'm disgusted that I didn't think of them myself. We saw Biren Halvos get a message at Roseguard once—I guess it stuck in Mikel's head." She frowned, picking at a snagged thumbnail. "I hope you aren't angry that I sent the others south. I don't know if I did right—"

"Yes, you did," Cailet interrupted. "You did exactly right, and you know it. You are your mother's daughter, after all."

The girl let out her breath in a long sigh, then smiled ruefully. "Yes, but Mother was a lot older than I am when she started giving orders."

"As I recall, she was just your age when she started ordering your father around. Not that it ever did much good."

"Oh, you mean in Pinderon? What *did* happen? They never told us the whole story."

"Well. . . ." Cailet ran a hand through her hair, wondering where to begin. She was saved from the recitation by Elomar, who entered carrying a bowl and a mug.

"Out," he said to Taigan, softening it with a smile and an "if you please."

Looking disappointed, Taigan rose. "I'll send Mikel to you in a little while."

"No, you won't," Elo corrected. "She'll be asleep."

"There are Mages I must contact," Cailet began.

"Later."

"Now."

They glared at each other; the Master Healer eventually gave in to the Captal, saying with poor grace, "*If* you finish this."

She sniffed at the soup, then the tea. "There'd better not be anything funny in it, Elo."

"Would I dare?" he asked as Lusira came in with a plate of bread and cheese.

"Yes," Cailet and Lusira said at the same time.

Taigan smiled and left the room. Lusira took her place in the chair, her husband standing nearby with arms folded, both of them with every evident intention of watching each sip and spoonful down Cailet's throat. She made a face at them and started eating.

"Felera went south," he said. Cailet nodded. Felera was an Adennos, a Healer with nearly ten years' experience. "And they've Rennon for protection." He paused, a tiny smile playing over his lips as Cailet's brows arched. "Taigan's doing."

Lusira elaborated. "He said his place as Warder was with you. She said the rest of us could defend you very nicely. He said Ketri Maklyn's arm would heal fast—which it will, don't worry—and anyway she could take on the Ryka Legion one-handed. She said if he didn't trust us to protect you, then maybe he'd trust your sword in the hands of a man he himself had helped train, so get in the damned wagon. He took one look at Joss, turned a rather interesting shade of red, and got in the damned wagon."

"Educational," Elo remarked. "Almost like Lady Sarra and Val Maurgen."

"I bet," Cailet said. "How far are we from Peyres?"

"Another day." Lusira sliced more cheese and put it into the empty bowl. Cailet opened her mouth to protest that she was full. Elomar scowled, and Lusira said, "All of it. You were unconscious for over two days."

"Send someone ahead to make sure the Ladder is secure—"

"Taigan already did. Jored should be there now, in fact. He left yesterday morning."

"Jored? He doesn't have a Folding spell yet."

"He learned," Elo said succinctly.

"They all did, even Dessa and Mikel." Lusira gave over the last slice of bread and poured more tea.

"Do I dare ask who's been carting me around like a sack of wheat?"

"Joss, of course." Lusira smiled. "He says his Folding is lousy, so he might as well make himself useful. Not that you're much of a burden—and Saints know he's got muscle enough to carry three of us without breaking a sweat."

Cailet drank off the last of the tea and pointedly

handed over the empty cup, plate, and bowl. "Are you happy now?" she asked Elomar.

"Deliriously."

"Then send Mikel in with those Globes. Any glimmers in any of them, by the way?"

"Nothing." Lusira stacked dishes, handed them to her husband, and brushed crumbs off the bed. "That could be both good and bad, naturally."

Good, if these Mages had nothing to report; bad, if these Mages had been killed. Unfortunately, Mikel didn't recall the names carved into the little wooden stands he'd swiped the Globes from.

"Just Telomir Renne's," he told Cailet. "I looked especially for his."

"Good thinking. Now," she said, settling herself cross-legged in bed with the six glass spheres on the bed before her, "picture the shelves in your mind. Close your eyes. This isn't magic, just memory. See what you saw when you entered the office." When he nodded, she went on, "You searched right off for Telo's. It was on the third shelf, right in the middle."

"I took it—and the one next to it. To the right."

"That'll be Pier Alvassy at Combel." Frowning, she examined the six orbs nestled in folds of her black fur cloak. Telomir's she had already set aside; it was one of the first she had made, and was larger than the newer ones. Besides, she contacted him rather often at Ryka Court, and so knew it pretty well by sight and touch. Pier's she wasn't so certain of, but of the five left three were quite small—no bigger than plums—so they must be for younger Mages. The other two were as big as Grand Roke apples, and so must have been made about the same time as Telo's. If she'd had half a brain, she told herself, she would've had the glasscrafter etch the names onto the orbs—but then she'd never anticipated any situation in which she'd have to guess which belonged to whom.

"Any more from that shelf?" she asked Mikel.

"No," he replied, eyes still squeezed shut. "One directly below Pier Alvassy's—and another from that row, but whether it was three or four to the left I can't remember. I'm sorry."

"That's all right. The one you're sure of is one I'm sure of, too—Nia Girre." Nia was a Scholar, Associate Dean of St. Mittru's College in Kenroke before her retirement—and for a long while had been the only Mage Guardian in that city. Cailet knew her Globe to be one of the oldest. The other apple-sized one must be Pier's, she realized; she'd made his and Elin's at the same time, about a year after Telo's. So that left the three small ones.

"I was picking them out pretty fast," Mikel said, opening his eyes. "Teggie went into the other room to find you—" He stopped, blushing all over his boyishly freckled cheeks—which bore a man's three-day stubble of amusingly carrot-red beard. Cailet nodded understanding, keeping a carefully expressionless face. "Anyway, things were crashing and collapsing all over, and I kept thinking about the fire getting upstairs. I looked over at the desk, I remember, and—" With a snort of disgust at himself he reached inside a pocket and produced a small bronze statue. "I took this, too. I thought you might want it."

Cailet turned the little St. Miryenne over and over in her fingers, then set it aside. "Thank you. Now think about the shelves again. You must've had some sort of idea who I might want to contact, or where—"

"One of them is Tiron Mossen's!" he blurted. "I remember because Kanen's his nephew, and we talked a few days ago about his being posted to Seinshir—Kanen, I mean, after he's Listed—so I thought it'd be important to find out if anything was going on at Malerris Castle."

"Better and better," Cailet approved, taking the very smallest of the Globes and setting it next to Telo's. "I made Tiron's last year, when I'd finally gotten the hang of the things."

Mikel blinked, then realized she was making fun of herself. He gestured to the largest Globe. "You mean of making them little enough not to need a crate to pack 'em in?"

"Insolent child. I still don't know how you juggled these things so long."

"I took that old cloak of yours that was lying across a chair, put it on, and wrapped the Globes as best I could."

"Dear me," she drawled. "What *would* your father say?"

"Huh?"

"The scandal of it, the damage to your reputation! How could you allow yourself to be seen in a cloak at least eight inches too short?" She waited for him to grin, then asked, "Which other Globes did you take, Mikel?"

Blue eyes squeezed shut behind dark copper lashes, but eventually he had to shake his head. "I'm sorry," he repeated. "I think Jored came in about then and distracted me."

"Jored?" she asked as casually as she could.

"Well, you wouldn't remember, I suppose."

"Not a thing after you clobbered me," Cailet replied cheerfully. "I really must have a talk with your mother about you. Though maybe it'd do more good to speak to your father—he has a tendency to the same disrespect. Did he ever tell you about the time he gave your mother such a slap on the rear that she couldn't sit down for a week?"

"He did?" Mikel's eyes were twice their usual size—and his chagrin over knocking Cailet out was forgotten, just as she'd intended.

"Why, yes," she replied blandly. "The time he kidnapped her."

"He *did?*"

Cailet smiled, seeing in Mikel's face that he didn't know whether to believe her or not. Remiss of Sarra and Collan not to have told their children family history. "I'll tell you the whole tale sometime," she promised. "For now, did you have other ideas about whom to contact?"

Again he blinked, and frowned, and said, "Somebody in Domburron—I thought that might be important, too, what with Vellerin Dombur coming to Ryka Court, to see if anything's happening down there."

Of the two Mages in the city of Domburron, only one had a Globe. "Lila Maklyn."

"I guess so—yes, that was it. But I don't remember the other one, Captal. I'm—"

"If you say 'I'm sorry' one more time—! Don't exasperate me, Mikel—though *that* comes naturally to a son of your father as well. You alone remembered to grab these things, and now you've given me enough information to figure out who almost all of them belong to. You may now leave me alone with them. I've work to do."

With a contrite smile, he rose and went to the door. Just as he opened it, however, he said over his shoulder, "I *am* sorry I hit you," and made his escape.

Cailet punched at the pillow behind her back and took pen and paper from the bedside table. She sobered as she wrote out a brief message four times: *Hall destroyed; 78 dead; advise your circumstances immediately.* Tearing the sheet neatly into four pieces, she set one beside each identified Globe and spent the next fifteen minutes spelling the messages into the glass spheres. She left Telo's for last, and to it appended, *Coming to Ryka. Twins safe.*

She picked up the little statue again, glad Mikel had obeyed his impulse to save it from the wreckage. But where once the Saint's serene smile had calmed her, now it seemed a smirking mockery. What if they were *all* dead? What if these Mages and Prentices with her now, and those on the road to Cantratown, were the only ones left alive? Could Glenin have done it, could she have wiped out so many at one stroke?

St. Miryenne stared back at her with a simper, holding the candle like a dare: *Light it again. Go on, try.*

Telomir's Globe began to radiate an almost blinding light. She averted her eyes, and saw two of the other spheres glimmer, then a third. She read Telo's first.

Refugees here from Wyte Lynn Castle, Neele, Havenport, Cantratown, Isodir—29 casualties— Tiron Mossen from Malerris waterfall Ladder, only survivor Seinshir Mages—what the hell is going on?

From The Waste, Pier Alvassy:

Are you safe? No trouble here but will find all Waster Mages immediately. Please advise your whereabouts and intentions.

From Kenroke, Nia Girre:

Malerrisi attempt failed, no casualties. Gather at Ryka Court?

From Lila Maklyn in Domburron:

Warrior, 3 Mages killed. Suspect Domburs with Malerrisi, no proof. Others, husbands, children gone to Ryka. I await instructions here.

Cailet sank into the pillow and closed her eyes. "So," she murmured aloud. "It begins."

Again, added Gorsha.

"I'm glad Telo's safe—and that he's the one in charge at Ryka. I can trust him to do what needs to be done." She looked at the clear, silent Mage Globe, the one whose owner she hadn't been able to name. Someone who was probably dead, and she would probably never know which of her Mages this sphere belonged to.

Elomar came in just as she finished writing her replics. He waited in silence while she sent them, asking nothing; her face must have been eloquent enough. He took each Globe from her hands as she finished with it, setting them neatly on the table. Finally, when she lay back once more, exhausted, he spoke.

"Jored has returned."

She met his gaze. "And all the Mages at Peyres are dead."

"Avin Sonne survives. As does the Ladder."

"Can we be there tomorrow?"

"Possibly. If you sleep tonight."

"Give me something, Elo," she said. "Something so I'll sleep without dreams. I can hear their Wraiths when I dream."

And see Josselin, his hands holding my sword.

Caisha—it was only a dream.

2

WHEN Chava Allard announced the visitor, Glenin was far from pleased. The woman had on occasion been of use, both in her home city of Pinderon and later in Roseguard where she could report the latest about Sarra and her whelps, but recent events had rendered her much too notorious for Glenin to receive—even at this late hour, and within the obscurity of a third-rate inn on the Bleynbradden coast.

"She's insistent," Chava warned when Glenin refused to see the caller. "I think if you don't let her in now, she'll come back in broad daylight wearing her Name colors and sigil for all the world to see."

Glenin chewed the end of her pen and looked down at the notes she was making for Ryka Court. Everything had to be perfectly timed, perfectly planned—perfectly staged. How she missed Chava's mother! Saris had possessed a gleefully devious mind and an uncanny understanding of how to prod and nudge using every emotion known to woman or man; the new Threadkeeper was a grimly dedicated individual with little imagination and no sense of humor at all. Glenin had left him at Malerris Castle.

In fact, it was just herself and Chava on this embassy to Ryka Court—and her son, of course, once Cailet did the expected thing and arrived to declare her grievances before the Council and Assembly. Saris had, in fact, long ago predicted her behavior based on what Chava had observed during his years in Heathering. This one throw of the dice, risking all and paying for all, had been in the plotting for fifteen years. Not that it would be much of a gamble; Glenin, with Saris's help and now Chava's, had anticipated and provided for everything.

"*A tweak to tighten the weave here, a pulled thread there—*" She could see Saris's cheerful smile, like a wolf on the hunt who smells success a long way off. "*—and of* *course one very important thread dyed a different color for a few years!"*

And now, on the eve of success, this irritating woman had come to pester her with some petty problem. Still, Chava was right. Glenin must speak to her, if only to get rid of her. She nodded curtly, and Chava—scratching at the beard she'd ordered him to grow—went to fetch Lady Mirya Witte.

She came upstairs to the tiny room wrapped in a nondescript brown cloak—threadbare, Glenin noted with irony. Mirya's place in the Great Loom had frayed, too, in recent years. Chava took the cloak from her shoulders, bowed, and left the women alone. As Mirya took a chair without being invited, Glenin saw that the spectacular figure was spectacular no more. Despite artful padding and propping, she was thin in all the wrong places and positively drooping in others. Never handsome, unless one had a taste for horses, her face showed reversals in public and private fortunes: bags and sags and dry, wrinkled skin that caved in below the cheekbones and stretched with the stretching of her lips in a smile. There was evidence of drink in the bloodshot eyes, and of sleeplessness in the dark smudges below them. She was forty-eight, a year older than Glenin, and looked closer to sixty.

"Well?" Glenin asked.

"You must help me," Mirya said. She folded stick-thin fingers around each other to hide their tremors, knuckle grating against knuckle. "Hear me out, and you'll find advantages to yourself in it."

Mirya knew how to capture her attention, even if the promised gains were doubtful at best. But she heard the woman out, and though most of the tale was already familiar to her, she had to struggle to keep eagerness from her face and posture as Mirya came to her conclusion.

The meat of it was this: she had been coerced several years ago into not divorcing her husband—and indeed into giving him freedoms humiliating to her and disgraceful to the institution of marriage. The person who'd wrung these concessions from her was Collan Rosvenir, infamous himself for the liberties he took in his marriage and in society at large.

Twenty-six days ago, on St. Pierga's, Mirya's husband was found dead in an alley outside the Silver Tankard, a tavern in Roseguard. He'd just come to Sheve from Brogdenguard, where he taught at St. Caitiri's, bringing Mirya's First Daughter with him; she had received her Certificate and was now ready to find a husband. After delivering the girl to her mother's house, Ellus had left his things at Wytte's and gone out for a meal.

The murder was particularly brutal—throat slashed ear-to-ear, so deep that an autopsy revealed that not only his windpipe but his spine had been cut. He was still bleeding when found, setting the time of death at just before Fourteenth. There were seventeen other knife wounds to his body made after the death blow, which to the Roseguard Watch indicated that even though his purse and personal jewelry were missing, this was not the work of a common thief. The vicious depth of the wound to the throat, the savage stab wounds inflicted as he bled into the gutter—these had real emotion in them: hatred, revenge, jealousy.

It had been a quick trial.

Mirya was unable to account for her whereabouts at the approximate time of the murder. Her sole remaining servant stoutly avowed in court that not only was the best carving knife vanished from the kitchen ("I keeps my knives sharp, so I do—and day after Saints' Days every week I whet them, so I knew immediate-like") but that the laundry hamper included a pair of black gloves soaked right through ("And before I do the knives, I puts the wash on to soak, so I do, and what were those gloves doing all damp as if someone'd already washed them clean?"). Mirya's own First Daughter coldly testified that she'd gone into her mother's rooms at Half-Thirteenth and again at Fourteenth, and found no one there. Mirya's original denial of guilt when arrested changed under this devastating evidence to justifiable manslaughter.

"For he was my husband," she told Glenin stiffly, "and defied me at every turn, even when I was generous to him—he ruined me in society, he mocked me by conducting himself in ways no decent husband should, he turned my mother and my daughters against me, he—"

"And you were convicted anyway of slitting his throat," Glenin interrupted.

"How could I get a fair trial in Roseguard? Everyone there is owned by Lady Sarra."

Mirya was taking her appeal to the High Judiciary at Ryka Court. Her defense now included a lawsuit against Sarra Liwellan and Collan Rosvenir for felonious interference between a woman and her husband, unlawful coercion, alienation of husbandly and daughterly affections, and instigating breach of legal contract.

"What?" Glenin eyed her, unsure whether to be appalled or amused.

"To begin with the first charge, they destroyed my marriage by sticking their noses in. Secondly, they forced me to give Ellus outrageous freedoms and allowing him to be employed in a distant Shir—taking my daughters with him! At the same time they forbade me to divorce him unless *he* consented!"

"Monstrous," Glenin said, knowing how it would play to conservatives.

"And then, as if all this wasn't enough, they deprived me of my last chance at happiness with a man perfectly willing to be my husband! They sent him to Mage Hall!"

Yes, I know, Glenin thought, hiding a grin. "You say they coerced you. I assume you mean they threatened to use their financial and political influence?"

"Of course. They drove me to this, it was my only escape from a hateful marriage to a man who'd lost all sense of propriety and decency—I was perfectly justified in what I did!"

"From what I know of Rosvenir, he's more likely to've threatened to give you the same bruises and broken bones you gave Ellus Penteon."

Mirya flushed—chagrined at what she'd done, but infuriated at the memory. "He said nothing to the point, but the look in his eyes—! The sheer effrontery—! I tell you I was terrified for my very life!"

"Yes, well, I suppose he knew that even he couldn't get away with outright intimidation. A woman's word is still worth more than a man's in the courts, after all." Not even Sarra had been fool enough to try to get *that* changed. "What else did he say?"

"Oh, it was all couched in roundabout terms, but he forced me to sell my estate at Shore Hill to the Ostins. For *thousands* below its fair price, I assure you. Thousands!"

So she was accusing the pair of using official position for private gain. This was delightful. In addition to all the other plans she had for Sarra, Cailet, and Collan, malfeasance of such core-of-society proportions was perfect.

"I'm out on bail pending appeal," Mirya went on bitterly. "Everything I own is signed over to the Roseguard Justiciary. My own mother wouldn't stand surety for me. Whatever happened to release on one's honor as a Blood—*and* a First Daughter?"

"Indeed." Glenin bestowed a benevolent smile on her guest. "My dear, you must come with me to Ryka. We'll travel with Lady Vellerin Dombur—who, like us, believes in the virtue of the old days. I'm sure she can help. She arrives tomorrow, and we sail the next day."

It was more than delightful. It was perfect. The Weaver had just supplied a new warp to the grand tapestry, and Glenin would have a marvelous time shuttling the unsuspecting threads back and forth to suit the design planned for years. Mirya's lawsuit against Sarra and Collan—and Cailet, if Glenin had anything to say about it—would bring up explosive questions of misuse of power to interfere in a woman's private affairs. Glenin hardly heard Mirya's words of thanks—stilted and resentful with wounded pride—as she envisioned the fine tangle of legal and emotional and political skeins that would end up throttling both her sisters. And it wouldn't even require any magic to accomplish, now that her son had proved himself worthy of being the next First Lord by using his magic to destroy Mage Hall.

3

AVIN Sonne was still in shock. He'd been in a mountain village for a week before and several days after St. Maidil's, visiting his only son, the boy's mother, her new young husband, and the family his son was about to marry into. Returning to Peyres on the fourth day of the week, he'd found Jored Karellos waiting for him with the horrible news that an unknown Malerrisi had killed the rest of the Sonne Mages. Jored had been shaken, too, only just having discovered the bodies before Avin arrived.

"No one came in," Avin kept saying as Cailet held his hands beside the blazing hearth. He hadn't slept since coming home yesterday morning, and looked it. "No one came into the shop to check on them. There must have been a Warding, don't you think, Captal? Everyone knows us. The shop sign was turned to 'closed' but everyone knows to ignore that if they need us. There must've been a Ward that sent them away. It's not possible that nobody needed medicine for so many days—how many was it? Three? Four? I don't remember. There must've been a Ward—"

"I agree. Here, Elomar's brought us some tea." She didn't drink; Elo's eyes warned her that it contained something to calm Avin's nerves. Not that Cailet couldn't use a little of the same. She watched him gulp the steaming brew, part of her wishing for another bout of temporary oblivion.

The bodies of Kanelto, Virenna, Dantia, her husband, and her two younger daughters would be burned this evening. The First Daughter, Jiora, was in Cantratown; Avin requested, and Cailet gave, permission to go there by Ladder once he'd taken them all through to Ambrai.

"A fortunate survival," Elomar said softly as the Warrior Mage's chin sank to his chest in drug-induced sleep. "For his sake and ours."

Cailet nodded. She knew all the Ladders, of course, but there were too many people to take through all at once to the Mage Academy, and she hadn't time to perform shuttle service. The four days it had taken them to get to Peyres, even with Folded roads, had cost precious time— her fault, for so utterly losing control of herself and her magic that it was a struggle for others to Fold even while she was unconscious. They hadn't told her that until this morning, when they'd set out on the last bit of the journey to Peyres. And they'd told her only because she grew curious about the relief on several faces as her efficiency got them twice as far in half the time. Gorsha's efficiency; her own magic was still mending after the trauma, and his bestowed expertise was all that allowed her to discipline herself to the spell.

"He'll wake clearheaded in two hours," Elomar went on. "His friends here sent food. I suggest we eat."

Again she nodded, and rose to ease the sleeping Mage into a more comfortable position in the big, soft chair. "Can someone local care for the shop? I'd hate for the town to go without medicines."

"Josselin arranged it."

When Avin woke, he escorted them all through Peyres to the opera house. Five Prentices, four Mage Guardians, and the Mage Captal made quite a spectacle on the streets at midafternoon. Cailet evaluated the glances they received. Inquisitive, certainly; toward Avin, compassionate; some frightened, some angry, some puzzled. But no satisfaction, no approval of what had been done. These people had lived beside the Sonnes, knew them, relied on them, were their friends. What they feared was a lack of Mages, not their presence in the community.

A girl of about sixteen approached from a bakery door, carrying a basket with something wrapped in a white napkin inside. "Will you see Jiora?" she asked Avin, and when he nodded she said, "Would you give her this? It's just some baking I did this morning, those butter-walnut cookies she likes. And please tell her how sorry I am about your family."

It seemed to be the signal for others to express sorrow and outrage, concern and pity. No, these people did not fear magic. They valued it and its practitioners, and urged Avin to come back soon.

Still, Cailet reflected as she walked down a theater aisle between rows of empty seats, there would be other places with other opinions. Large cities that didn't care if magic existed or not, because in the press of people contact with Mages was rare; small towns where magic was looked on askance even after so many years and so much effort; tiny villages unfamiliar with Mages because there simply weren't enough Mages to go around.

Backstage, she squeezed into the Ladder circle with Elomar, Dessa, Taigan, and Mikel, and wondered what the point had been. What had all her work and worry been for? What had nearly twenty years of her life accomplished? She was thirty-eight years old—what did she have to show for it but a duplication of what had occurred the year she was born? A handful of Mages who'd survived the wreckage of what should have been their stronghold—

"Well?" said Elomar, and Cailet gave a start. "Are we going, or aren't we?"

She closed her eyes and felt the Blanking Ward rise, and within moments they had left the afternoon behind in Peyres and were in a warm summer morning in Ambrai. Stepping out of the Ladder in the coldroom below the Academy kitchens, she didn't wait for the others to arrive from Peyres but instead climbed the stairs to a ruin just like the one she'd left behind her. Nothing accomplished, nothing built, nothing changed from all those years ago—she might just as well never have lived at all.

Now, that's the outside of enough, Gorsha scolded. *Feeling sorry for yourself will get you exactly nowhere.*

She didn't even bother telling him to shut up, spare her the clichés, and leave her alone. Striding across grassy, tree-dappled slopes that had once thronged with Mages and Prentices and were now a public park, she headed for the shell of the Warders Garrison. In it was the Ladder that led to Telomir Renne's rooms at Ryka Court—rooms that had belonged to Gorynel Desse when he was First Sword. She was just about to go inside, and to Ryka, when she heard someone shout her name.

Turning, she saw the tall, dark, elegantly clothed figure of Granon Mikleine running up the hill from the direction of the main city. Granon and Cailet had been born the same week in 951, and born too soon—for which the massacre in Ambrai was responsible. Cailet's mother had gone into premature labor on hearing what her divorced husband had done; Fiella, Granon's mother, had seen her own husband die. If not for the heroic efforts of a Healer Mage that had kept the baby in his mother's womb until Fiella was safely removed from Ambrai, Granon and Cailet would have shared a Birthingday as well.

As she waited impatiently for him to catch up to her, she heard Gorsha mutter, *St. Garony's Gilded Gavel, that boy looks more like his grandfather every year.*

Gorsha was sentimental about this grandson of his dearest friend. If one could believe his reminiscences, he and the first Granon had been rivals in everything from the appointment as First Sword to the bed favors of every beautiful, desirable young Mageborn woman at the Academy—none of which had prevented them from being boon companions. Granon Mikleine was the only man besides Tiva Senison that Gorsha had ever lost a woman to. But while Tiva had become Lilen Ostin's husband and the acknowledged father of her children, Granon, like Gorsha, had been wary of marriage and official fatherhood. He'd died that second day at Ambrai, protecting two Captals—Leninor Garvedian and Lusath Adennos— while Gorsha guided the transfer of the Bequest.

Before the younger Granon had seen his third spring, Gorsha Warded him in secret—without even Fiella's knowledge—to protect him just in case everything went wrong and the Mages were never restored to what they'd been. He owed it to his valiant old friend, and to the lovely Atheni Mikleine, Granon's distant cousin and Fiella's mother.

Cailet, who now had another Mikleine to worry about, recalled that Granon was now nearly the last Mage of that Name. She'd better tell him to watch himself, or he'd be dead, too.

If you persist in this, I swear that somehow I'll find a way to have Mikel knock you in the jaw again.

This time she did tell him to shut the hell up—and made sure of it by imagining the slammed lid of an iron strongbox with him in it. "Granon," she acknowledged as he came up to her, breathing hard. Technically, she could have greeted him as family—he was married to her cousin Elin—but that was of course impossible to admit. She usually greeted her Mages with the warmth that came of shared magic and the private ritual in the compass octagon—but for some reason she'd never grown to like Granon. He was pleasant and well-mannered, conscientious about his magic, a devoted husband and father, and able administrator with Elin of the city of Ambrai. But the latter position had in recent years given him a fine sense of his own importance, an annoying consciousness of rank and formidable magical heritage. Though Elin was of the Alvassy, Ambrai, Desse, and Dombur Bloods, *he* was descended from Adennos Healers, Bekke and Mikleine Warriors, and Garvedians who had produced a brilliant Captal. Whatever wide-eyed astonishment Granon had evidenced when Cailet entered him into the Lists in 972 was gone now, replaced by a pride that slid rather too often into arrogance.

Even at this hour of the morning—barely past Sixth—he was immaculately turned out in a summerweight velvet longvest of Mikleine purple and black, lace-cuffed silk shirt pinned at the throat with a gold device cunningly combining Alvassy Castle Spire and Mikleine Hearthfire sigils. Two earrings of onyxes and diamonds glistened in his left earlobe; one would have done, Cailet thought, seeing him with Collan's exacting eye. His boots were polished to a blinding gleam, and the only disorder about him was the spill of thick black curls imperfectly tucked into a black velvet coif.

"Captal! Thank all the Saints you're safe! Elin's brother arrived two nights ago with the news—and since yesterday morning we've had Mages coming by Ladder from all over Lenfell!"

"I assume they're all waiting for me to tell them what to do."

"No, Elin and I have been taking care of that. Most were sent to Ryka Court. A few were injured, and we've got them in the new Healers Ward across the hill."

Presumptuous, she thought, and wondered why she

reacted so pettily to an efficiency that spared her having to give orders. She struggled to put aside her aversion. "More might be coming, I don't know. I'm going to Ryka myself. Now."

"Elin will want to see you first."

Elin Alvassy was dictating to her in what should have been her own city? A woman who ruled Ambrai only because neither Sarra nor Cailet could admit to being its rightful heirs? A woman who, moreover, was a Mage Guardian and subject to Cailet's command?

Deciding she didn't much like Elin either, Cailet shrugged a reply and started once more for the Garrison. "I don't have time for Elin right now."

"Captal, she would very much like to discuss this situation with you."

Cailet pivoted on one heel. "Which situation did she have in mind? The situation where Mage Hall has just burned to the ground because we were betrayed from within? Or the situation that's made her order all the Mages who come here for refuge out of the city so Ambrai doesn't attract the Malerrisi? Or is it the situation regarding Vellerin Dombur—who sent a letter asking her as Blood kin to the Domburs and Ambrais to turn a blind eye when she and Glenin Feiran take over Domburronshir?"

All three "situations" were meant to shock. They succeeded. But that last sent hot, angry sparks into Granon's dark eyes.

"Do you *spy* on us, Captal?" he demanded witheringly.

"I notice you don't deny that the would-be Grand Duchess has contacted you."

"I notice that *you* don't deny the charge of spying! Who was it? Sirron Bekke?"

She lifted one hand in the ancient sign that meant she was not to be questioned. "Well? Does Elin care more for Ambrai than for her fellow Mage Guardians? Has she developed some family feeling for her long-lost cousins, the Domburs and the First Lady of Malerris?"

Granon's stiff-spined haughtiness as he denied it told her what she wanted to know. Contact from Vellerin

Dombur had been a guess, based not only on instinctive suspicion of Granon's arrogance but on information from Telomir Renne through his Mage Globe just today. Three Councillors and seventeen Assembly Members with Dombur Blood connections had been simply approached. They needn't actively support the bid for power; they need only not oppose it. Throw in with the Domburs, or at least keep your mouths shut, because the Mage Guardians are decimated and cannot stand against us. The sheer audacity of it, and what had dipped Telo's pen in acid, was that Sarra had received a private letter from Glenin making the same request, based on the same Blood claims. A slap in the face, of course—a supremely insolent, supremely confident challenge to Sarra: do what you like, Glenin Feiran didn't care.

Cailet interrupted Granon's protestations. "Maybe I'd better see Elin after all. Bring her to the old Library. I can spare her twenty minutes."

He went rigid with insult all the way to his coif, then informed her glacially, "My Lady is unable to leave the Octagon Court today for personal reasons. May I invite the Captal there? I assure the Captal her time will not be wasted."

She shrugged and followed him through the parkland, across the bridge, and down the wakening streets of Ambrai to the Octagon Court. Twenty years ago she'd walked this very path with Sarra, through a city destroyed, deserted, and heaped with rubble. She admitted—grudgingly—that Elin and Granon had worked wonders. Ambrai was no longer the greatest city on Lenfell, and never would be again. But it was a viable, working community, thick with commerce and Shir government. So what if Granon was overly impressed by accomplishment? At least what he and Elin had built still stood.

He took her into the Octagon Court by the front entrance, to the accompaniment of much bowing by servants and stewards amid the marble, tapestries, and bronzes. Once upstairs out of the public area, the decoration turned from suitably palatial to skimpy and in some places ragged. Carpets were threadbare, stained from lying for years under piles of fallen timber and stone;

walls and ceilings still showed smoke- and fire-darkened patches no matter how many times they'd been painted. Cailet was shocked; Sarra hadn't mentioned seeing any of this when she'd last been in Ambrai. But perhaps Elin had received her in the better rooms. These were the family quarters, and the contrast between the elegant first floor and these shabby hallways was a rebuke to Cailet's earlier disdain.

Elin presented the best possible face to the world, creating the illusion that the Alvassys were nearly as rich and powerful as the Ambrais had once been, that the Octagon Court was nearly the graceful showcase it had always been, and that Ambrai itself was nearly as great as in former days. Money attracted money; Webs invested in prosperity, not squalor. So the downstairs reception chambers must needs be replete with fine furnishings, carpets, tapestries—and neither Elin nor Granon nor their daughters must ever be seen in public without making their clothes and jewels a show of affluence and fashion.

Cailet was thoroughly ashamed of herself. She didn't like Granon any better, but at least she understood him more.

They were almost to the end of a long, drafty hall when Cailet stopped in her tracks. The towering oaken door to her right was Warded six ways to the Wraithenwood. She caught Granon by one silk sleeve.

"What in the Names of All the Saints is in there?"

"Elin."

"Is she ill? Why is it Warded like this?"

"It's a private matter. I'll take you to her sitting room, and fetch her for you—"

Shaking her head, Cailet strode to the door. The Wards, beneath the Go Away and You've No Business Here, were dire: Fatal Sickness Within, Open This Door At Your Peril, and the like. Surely too much, surely inappropriate—Elin had been panicky when she'd Worked them. Cailet walked right through each one.

The door gave into a long room with uncurtained windows twenty feet high at the far end, bare of furnishings except for an iron bedstead in the corner and a cushioned wooden chair beside it. In the chair sat Elin; in the bed was a child about five years old. Piera, Elin's young-est. Cailet bit her lip, then moved quietly forward. Was the child ill? No; Cailet smelled none of the usual medica-ments and saw no signs of sickness in her face—dark with Desse and Mikleine heritage, eyes huge and brilliant, glit-tering not with febrile light but a restless, constantly shift-ing agitation. As Cailet approached, that unquiet gaze fell on her—and the small body arched as Piera let out a terri-fied wail. Struggling, she flung herself back and forth be-neath a light sheet. Elin did nothing to restrain her; she didn't have to. The child's wrists and ankles were tied to the bedframe.

Elin looked around, saw Cailet, and rose from the chair. "Granon, calm her, please." He went to her at once, whispering a few words before he sat down and began to croon wordlessly to the little girl, stroking the black curls from her forehead.

Elin drew Cailet into the farthest corner, out of the child's sight. "Are you shocked?" she asked harshly. "We're both from old, proud families, Bloods and Mage-borns on both sides—but our daughter is everything the stories say a Fifth Tier used to be."

Cailet could only stare at her.

Elin gave a small, sharp shrug. "Physically, Piera is exquisite, if small for her age. You can see that for your-self. We didn't notice anything different about her until she reached the age for talking. We told ourselves she was just a little slower than other children—she was born four weeks early. She was never ill, she was always so beauti-ful—but she didn't speak. But sometimes she'd scream for hours and hours, and nothing I did was any good."

"Elin—" Cailet swallowed the thickness in her voice. "Why didn't you tell anyone? If it's to do with her magic, then maybe I can help—"

"It's not Wild Magic. Granon's seen that before. It's nothing like that in symptoms—and we don't think she has any magic at all. I hope she doesn't, because when she's old enough—who knows what could happen?"

"What can be done for her?" Cailet asked quietly. "Tell me what I can do."

"Nothing," said the mother, with the bleak certainty

of having tried everything to no avail. "We had to give her a room to herself when she was two. She'd wake screaming in the night, or get out of bed and—we found her one morning lying by the door, her forehead bleeding from trying to batter the door down." Elin glanced over her shoulder as Piera's cries faltered, then ceased. "Granon can almost always soothe her. There's nothing in this room but the bed and the chair because objects can suddenly frighten her, even if she's been around them her whole life. There was a tapestry, just a little thing, of cats playing. She loved it, she'd croon to it as if the cats were real. It was the only emotion she'd ever shown. So we gave her a kitten. For three weeks she wouldn't let it out of her sight. Then one day she ripped the tapestry off the wall and tore it to shreds, and then she tore the ears off that poor kitten and broke its legs and strangled it. She's incredibly strong in her frenzy." Elin reported it as if making an observation about the weather. "We don't dare leave Piera alone. She knows the two servants who tend her, but you're a stranger and when she saw you—"

"I'm sorry."

Elin shrugged away the sympathy. "She's lived in this Warded room for over a year. We explain her absences from the usual functions by saying she's still very young and terribly shy. I don't know what we'll do when we have to make excuses for not sending her to school. Grania's very good with her, she reads to her and sings, and plays finger-games. . . ."

"There must be some kind of help—someone who knows something about—"

She laughed bitterly, the numbness of continual grief broken. "Children like Piera aren't even supposed to exist! Who could we tell without ruining our entire family? Piera is living proof that my line and Granon's are tainted. I'm a Blood, this isn't supposed to happen to me."

Suddenly Cailet remembered that Sarra had said much the same thing after miscarrying her First Daughter twenty years ago. The brutal measures enacted after The Waste War had eliminated contamination from Lenfell's bloodlines. Or so it was avowed. Cailet looked over at the bed, where Piera lay calm again as her father's voice droned on and on, lulling her with meaningless sounds. And Cailet remembered a night long ago when Gorynel Desse had taken a newborn baby away from Ostinhold, and Lady Lilen had told her about places where these tragic children could grow up and live out their lives in safety.

Gorsha—tell me where. Tell me, so I can help this child and her parents and sisters out of this nightmare.

He was silent within her mind, but she could sense his sorrow. Granon Mikleine was the grandson of his old friend; Elin, the granddaughter of his own beloved sister. Cailet perceived no shock, no horror in him that such a thing could happen, only pain for them and the child.

"As you know, my cousin Glenin wrote to me," Elin was saying in a colorless voice, her brief emotion gone. She stared fixedly at her hands, turning around and around on her thumb a signet ring carved with the Alvassy Castle Spire. Cailet recognized it with a jolt; it was the family's First Daughter ring, centuries old. Sarra had worn it during her imposture as Elin's sister Mai. "She hopes I'll actively cooperate with her and Vellerin Dombur. There was an appeal to family loyalty—my grandfather was Telo Ambrai, Lady Allynis's brother. Glenin seems to have conveniently forgotten that she murdered my sister."

She also tried to murder me. *She'll try again. I'm too dangerous to let live, too old for childbearing—and she'll have Taigan and Mikel. But the only one she really needs is Taigan.*

"She also seems to forget that I'm a Mage Guardian, not a Malerrisi," Elin was saying, stubborn pride steeling her voice now. "My grandmother's brother was Gorynel Desse, Captal Garvedian's First Sword. Glenin will have nothing from me."

"Except your silence," Cailet murmured. "Because of Piera."

Shoulders sagging, she gave a weary nod. "If anyone found out—it would be the end of the Alvassys and the Mikleines, and of all we hope to accomplish in Ambrai. Children like her are born sometimes, but not to Bloods.

My brother wouldn't escape, or his children—can you imagine what Geria Ostin would do if she discovered her First Daughter's cousin is like *this?*"

"I understand." Cailet turned away, rubbing her face with both hands, then raked back her uncombed hair and faced Elin again. "I do understand. You couldn't risk so many Mages here, they might sense your Wards and find out about Piera. So you sent them to Ryka Court."

"Yes."

"And you can't oppose Glenin openly, in case she targets you the way she has me—and puts someone inside the Octagon Court the way someone got inside Mage Hall. I understand your silence, Elin, and the reasons for it. It breaks my heart for you and Granon and Piera. I won't tell anyone what I've seen here." Her cousin nodded slowly. "But there may be a small hope for her. There are places—"

"No! I won't have her taken away from me! She's my child, my baby—" Elin visibly controlled herself. "You're not a mother, you can't understand. Society tells me I should reject and fear this child, that when I suspected she wasn't—normal—I should've killed her and said she died in a fall, or a fever, or—but she's my *daughter.* I won't give her up."

"Forgive me, I should have realized." But one day it would become impossible to keep Piera at the Octagon Court. Elin already knew that; she already worried about excusing the child's absence from regular schooling. Eventually she'd see the wisdom of removing Piera to one of the safe places. And Cailet—as much a product of their society as Elin—suddenly loathed their world that offered mothers of such children two choices: murder or abandonment.

Cailet left them, and returned to the Mage Academy grounds. They were all looking for her—Elo and Lusira and Dessa, Taigan and Mikel, Jored and Josselin, all except Marra and Avin. The former had elected to stay in Ambrai at the new Healers Ward, in case the Ladder journey had adversely affected her unborn child. It was Elo's opinion that the baby was not yet developed enough for its brain to suffer any harm—if indeed it was Mageborn.

But Marra would not risk another Ladder, and Cailet didn't blame her. In a week or so she'd travel overland to The Waste, and live at Maurgen Hundred where Aidan had spent his childhood. As for Avir Sonne, he intended to go to Cantratown where his niece's daughter Jiora was.

So they were eight crammed into the Ladder to Telomir's rooms at Ryka Court. He was waiting for them, and the third early morning Cailet had experienced in a single day shone brightly through the windows as Telo told her that Glenin Feiran and Vellerin Dombur were expected at Ryka Court early next week.

4

THE Council regularly divided itself into thirds for discussion of regional matters. Subcommittees for North Lenfell, South Lenfell, and the Island Shirs met every other week while the Council and Assembly were in session, usually on an informal basis in one of the Members' suites. Sarra, as Councillor for Sheve, was hosting her colleagues for Tillinshir, The Waste, Ambraishir, and Cantrashir on this fifth day of Maiden Moon—and studiously ignoring their broad hints that after more than two hours of discussion, sustenance more substantial than coffee would be welcome. It was getting on for Half-Eighth and people were getting hungry. But it was Tarise's shrewd ploy to serve nothing except drinks: "Empty stomachs and full bladders—nothing will clear a room quicker."

The topics of discussion this morning, however, were much too urgent to abandon. The calamity at Mage Hall and the imminent arrival of Vellerin Dombur and Glenin Feiran: these and their possible relation to each other were thrashed out in all conceivable permutations by five women old enough to recall living under Anniyas's rule and young enough to have lived most of their lives free of it. They were not favorably disposed toward Vellerin

Dombur's ambitions—though they did not believe her goals included their own Shirs. On this they all agreed, except for Sarra, who intended to speak in private to Eskanel Rikkard of Ambraishir regarding Glenin.

The political dynamic of North Lenfell was skewed toward the Mage Guardians. Sarra's reasons for favoring the Captal were obvious (but for the true, secret ones). Lusian Wentrin of Tillinshir was not only infuriated that violence had been done in her Shir, but grieved the death of her nephew Jioram, a Prentice at Mage Hall. Though Grispina Wytte of Cantrashir had no Mageborn relations, Viko Garvedian had been her lover ten years ago and they remained close friends. Eskanel Rikkard held her Council seat by her own merits and the wholehearted support of Elin Alvassy. Maidine Karellos, youngest of them at thirty-six, counted among her friends her third cousin Mircia Ostin, First Daughter of Geria and her husband Mircian Karellos, whose husband was Pier Alvassy.

So it was pretty much all in the various families. North Lenfell's support fell to the Mages. Sarra never discounted the power of such relationships; they were the foundation of social order, the adhesive that glued the economic structure of the Webs, and the reason Shirs never went to war with each other.

She just wished they'd get out of her salon so she could go see Telomir and demand he send Cailet a message telling her to come to Ryka Court instantly.

Gradually, as Lusian Wentrin returned for the sixth time to her anger over what had been done not a hundred miles from the smallhold where she'd been born, the scents of fresh hot bread and spicily sauced beef drifted into the salon from the half-open door to the next room. Within minutes, the other Councillors excused themselves to their own suites—and lunch. When all were gone, Collan came in with a laden silver tray, looking insufferably smug.

"You did that on purpose," Sarra accused, grinning.

"You bet I did. Let's have lunch out on the balcony— and let's do it *now*. I'm starved." He laughed as her stomach growled agreement to the proposal. "Although if you don't stop stuffing yourself, you'll never get into that new gown and Timarrin Allard's heart will break."

Sarra stuck out her tongue at him.

"Don't do that unless you plan to use it."

She looked around for something to throw. Her fingers had just closed around a pillow when Tarise burst into the room from the antechamber, her husband Rillan right behind her, both of them practically dancing with excitement.

"Sarra! There's someone here who simply must see you immediately—"

Sarra groaned. "No. I refuse. I'm *hungry!*"

"Whoever it is can wait," Collan seconded.

Rillan laughed aloud. "You won't be saying that once you see who it is!"

"Who, then? And it better be good," Col warned.

"The best," Rillan promised, and turned with a flourish of one hand to the door.

Sarra half-rose from her chair, then sat back down hard. Her knees weren't working too well. Six people walked into the room, but she really saw only two of them. They'd washed their faces and combed their hair, but their clothes were so crumpled and soot-stained and travel-torn that they resembled derelicts from the filthiest slum on Lenfell. Both looked as if they'd slept perhaps four hours in the last four days. She had the confused impression that they'd grown at least two inches apiece. Maybe it was the way they held themselves now, with a poise that physically reflected the changes in thought and perception and experience that had created adults of the girl and boy she'd last seen.

For a moment she saw her First Daughter as she had been: a lovely sixteen-year-old with clear, fresh skin, and lustrous blonde hair, and green eyes by turns shrewd and candid. That Taigan disappeared, giving way to a young woman Sarra didn't know. There were small burn-scars on the right side of her face: one on her cheek, another at her temple near the hairline, a third at the angle of her jaw. Tendrils of hair shorter than the rest of her golden mane curled where locks had been singed off. The green eyes had lost all innocence.

And Mikel—where was that lanky boy with Collan's height but not yet his strength, Collan's handsome features but not his sleek good looks? What had happened to his cheerful humor and that ingratiating crooked grin in a faceful of freckles? This young stranger had broadly muscled shoulders, and a stubbly red beard, and a keen-eyed, uncompromising self-assurance that left her speechless.

Sarra felt the poignant ache of a mother who sees that her little girl has grown to a woman, and her little boy to a man. Ah, but such a woman and such a man as they had become! Pride surged up, flooding away her sense of loss. Her children, life of her life and her beloved's life, grown poised and strong with knowing their true worth, and with power awakened in their eyes—

Still, they looked so much older. She'd seen this same expression in Cailet's eyes at just this age, eighteen. Was the price of knowledge always to be paid in such grim coin?

Sarra couldn't seem to stand up, couldn't make her legs carry her toward her children who were children no longer. Collan had no such trouble. After a moment's silence, he let out a roar half-laughter, half-astonishment, and seized Taigan and Mikel in a fierce hug. Sarra watched him surround their children with his arms, hoarding them like a miser did gold.

Then she heard Cailet's soft voice at her side. "I guess they're kind of a shock, all grown up like this. I watched it happen, so I never notice the differences."

Sarra looked up, and sight of the weary grief in her sister's eyes was more of a shock than sight of her grown daughter and son. She rose, knees a bit wobbly, and hugged Cailet tightly, and for once in her life had no words.

Only a minute later, one word pierced Sarra's mindless hurt for Cailet's hurt. Taigan spoke it—Taigan, who hadn't said it since she was eight years old.

"Mama—?"

Cailet let go, then gave Sarra a little push. And Sarra found herself hoarded by her children, locked so fast in their arms that she could hardly breathe. Not that breathing seemed all that important right now.

"Mama," said Mikel, "are you *crying?*"

"Don't be silly, of course not," she mumbled into his shirt.

"Liar," said Collan.

Somehow over the next ten minutes Tarise organized them all for the noon meal. Food enough for twenty arrived, and they all sat around the salon with plates in their laps and big mugs of coffee at their elbows. Sarra was embarrassed to discover that the reunion had been witnessed by two others—Josselin Mikleine and Jored Karellos. She didn't mind about Telo, he was practically family himself, but she hated to have her private emotions seen by strangers.

Right off, Collan indignantly demanded to know why they hadn't come immediately here from Telo's rooms. Telo replied, "You had too many guests who'd ask too many awkward questions—and besides, they all look destitute, not at all fit for polite company. An old man's clothes don't fit any of these young bucks, and the days when I kept spare gowns for lady guests are long gone— along with the lady guests, I sorrowfully admit."

"Old man!" Tarise scoffed. "And to whom, might I ask, belong these crescent-shaped pearl earrings I saw on your bedside table the other day?"

Her husband arched his brows. "What were you doing in Telo's bedroom?"

Sarra wondered where all this light, teasing chatter had come from. It bounced among them almost giddily, like kittens batting a ball of yarn.

"Crescents?" Collan's very blue eyes went wide. "Outlined in diamonds?"

Tarise nodded vigorously. "The very same. They've been in the lady's family for at least six Generations—"

"I *still* want to know why you were in his bedroom," said Rillan.

"I know those earrings," Collan stated. "Telo, you old dog, you've been sleeping with the scrumptious Shonnia Somme!"

"You might very well think so," Telomir said serenely. "I couldn't possibly comment."

Everyone laughed—even Sarra, who now understood. But in Cailet's eyes was something Collan and Tarise and Rillan and Telomir had already seen, and acted on as if given prior instructions. Cailet was desperate to make things seem normal, to pretend they were all here only for a convivial meal. She had something to hide, something she didn't want to speak of just yet, and so wanted the conversation casual, amusing, as if nothing had happened. Mage Hall, Vellerin Dombur, and Glenin Feiran were not discussed. Not that anyone needed to say much; they all ate as assiduously as if this was their first good meal in a week. For some, it was.

Sarra contributed her share of informal chat while observing her children, getting used to them again. She watched the other two young men as well. Both were well worth study.

Jored and Josselin looked more like twins than the twins did. Both were tall, lean, muscular, and beautiful. From one head thick curling hair tumbled over the brow and down the collar; from the other, hair just as thick though not as curly was long enough to pull back into a plait at the nape. Eyes that in direct sunlight were tinged slightly green, like moonstones beneath wispy silk, were in the other face a sultry pewter gray. Sarra was genuinely awed that Josselin had become even more beautiful. Where most men would be haggard and splintered as an old stick by exhaustion, he seemed like ebonwood after a masterful hand had carved and refined him. Jored showed the effects of the ordeal more, but there was an almost luminous quality to his eyes that came from surviving a nightmare. Sarra couldn't decide which of them she preferred—and wondered if Taigan had come to prefer Jored as much as Mikel's letters had hinted. She must talk to Cailet about that.

At length, Tarise pried Taigan loose from the dessert plate. Rillan took charge of Mikel, Josselin, and Jored, and went to find them rooms. That left Sarra, Collan, Cailet, and Telomir—and Wards subtly reinforced by the latter two against eavesdroppers.

It was Telomir who narrated the story of what happened at Mage Hall and afterward, having learned it all from conversations over the last few hours with Cailet,

Elomar, and the twins. Cailet sat back in her chair, cradling a mug of hot coffee below her chin, eyes closed as she listened impassively to the tale of fire and death—almost, Sarra thought critically, as if she hadn't lived it herself.

When Telo had finished, Collan got up to pour him more coffee. "You've told us the 'what.' I can figure out 'why' for myself—and not because I'm even smarter than I look. Now I want to know 'who.'"

Cailet glanced up at last. "Meaning?"

"The usual Wards were in place—no problem. The sentry was on duty—no problem. Three possibilities: somebody took advantage of everyone's being in Heathering that night and sneaked in when you all came back. Second, the same somebody had an accomplice inside Mage Hall. Third, there was no outside 'somebody' and the traitor lived among you, maybe for years, waiting for this chance."

Cailet sipped coffee and said nothing.

"A Prentice," Sarra broke in, remembering what she'd seen that morning at Mage Hall, and her conversation with Cailet about knowing each new Mage Guardian. Collan frowned, and it was on his lips to ask how Sarra knew so definitely. But she shook her head a little, and he arched a brow in Cailet's direction, and subsided.

Sarra went on, "This person has a greater command of magic than anyone suspects. The setting and timing of so many Battle Globes presupposes formidable skill. The explosions were placed as precisely as if working to a map. We may also assume that this person is too valuable to sacrifice, too powerful to lose, and is therefore still alive." She heard Telomir draw a sharp breath, but before he could use it to speak Sarra silenced him, too, with a single look.

Cailet sat like a statue.

"But you already know all this," Sarra said quietly.

"Yes." Thin shoulders lifted in a shrug. "I just needed to hear somebody else say it, come to the same conclusion—to prove to myself I'm not totally insane."

"Which one?" Telo asked thickly.

Black eyes met Sarra's. "If I knew, I'd kill him."

"No, you wouldn't," Col said.

Cailet seemed to wilt in her chair. "No," she echoed softly. "I wouldn't."

But Sarra saw something else in her sister's eyes, and it startled her so much that she couldn't speak. Telomir proposed, and Collan encouraged, Cailet's taking a few hours to rest. Sarra watched the three of them leave the salon—Telo to escort his Captal, Col to find his children—and couldn't even move from her chair.

Cailet had lied. She did know who it was.

A Prentice—and still alive. One of the wounded sent to Cantratown? No. Cailet would keep the person close, to watch what happened next. What had she said about Vellerin Dombur? Wait and see how it played out?

A Prentice, still alive, and here at Ryka Court.

"If I knew, I'd kill him."

No one had reacted to the pronoun; it was common to use the masculine when speaking in the general negative. *"If I knew who the donor was, I'd name a hospital wing for her"*—but *"If I knew who cheated me, I'd hang him up by his balls."*

"Him." Jored Karellos. Josselin Mikleine.

Which of them was it? Which of those surpassingly beautiful young men was a traitor and a murderer and a Malerrisi?

And was Taigan in love with him?

5

CAILET broke the promise she'd made Elin, but only because Telomir's father might have told him where the sanctuaries were. Gorsha had been silent for what felt like a very long time now. She knew why when she made her request to Telomir: Gorsha's son turned away and stared out the arching windows of his office and said nothing for several minutes. When he faced her again, he looked like a hundred years of sorrow—and only then did she recall that he was family, too: his cousin Gerrin Desse had been Elin's father.

"I know such places exist, but I don't know where they are," he said slowly. "Lilen might. I doubt it. Gorsha took care of such things with one or two other Mages during the Purge, but all of them are dead now."

That set Cailet aback. "Do you mean that ever since I became Captal, these children—"

"—have been quietly killed, with no one the wiser? I don't know," he repeated. "Possibly someone else knew, and dealt with them, and passed along the knowledge. But it'd have to be a Mage. The sanctuaries must be Warded against discovery. There's been no rumor in any Shir."

"Find out," Cailet said. "I don't care what it takes, Telo—find out, because when Elin finally accepts that Piera can't live with them—"

"This goes to the foundation of what we are, Cailet," he said heavily. "We have so much invested in thinking ourselves free of the residual tragedies of The Waste War—"

"So much that an afflicted child is an affront to our arrogance and our delicate sensibilities," she snapped. "It's nauseating. Find a sanctuary for Piera. Just find one, Telo."

"I'll try. Now, I brought you here to rest, Captal, while rooms are being prepared for you. If you don't lie down, close your eyes, and sleep of your own choice, I'll bring in Elomar—and we both know he won't give you any choice at all."

"I don't have time—and I don't have any choice about not having any time either! There must be a hundred Mages roaming around Ryka Court, which is a stupid place for them to be if Glenin decides to get creative. I want to see all of them before I send them out by Ladder to—"

"—to where?" Telo asked. "We've lost Mages in every corner of Lenfell."

"Except Dindenshir, Kenrokeshir, and The Cloister. By Ladder and by ship and on foot if need be, they're going to be out of Ryka Court by the time Glenin arrives."

"If she *does* get frisky," he argued, "you'll need more than a few Mages and some Prentices to stand against her."

"I don't think much of this will have to do with magic at all. Think about it, Telo. This is Ryka Court. If Mages suddenly start dropping dead, the Council and Assembly will start to wonder who'll be next. Besides, Glenin has Vellerin Dombur to do her work for her, in large part. She'll present herself as the soul of prudence, and she'll only Work magic to keep the coffee hot. What I'm worried about is she'll find some nonmagical trap for all the other Mages, something I won't be able to counter. So I want them gone, Telo. Every last one of them."

"Except for—?"

"You, the twins, Elo—"

"Lusira won't like that much."

"I don't give a damn what she likes. She and her First and only Daughter are leaving. From your group here, keep Sevy Banian and Rillia Vekke—they're both young and Rillia can assuage your fears about my needing a Warrior to protect me."

"Speaking of which, I'd like to bring Sirron Bekke here from Ambrai. Other than the fact that he's damned good at what he does—which is everything—no Captal in memory has faced the Malerrisi without a Bekke Warrior at her side. And you need some new Warders."

Granon, she thought suddenly, painfully, and nodded. "Send Rillia away, then, and bring Sirron's cousin Ollia here from Neele. She's young for it, but quick and clever."

"And strong," he added with a faint smile. "I heard about your morning with her."

Cailet eyed him sidelong. "Will there ever be a similar morning for you, Prentice Renne?"

"Not a chance," he responded cheerfully. "I'm much too old. I'd curl up whimpering on the floor in two minutes flat. Now, who else stays?"

"Jored Karellos. Josselin Mikleine."

He cocked a graying brow. "The first for Taigan's sake, I suppose. But Josselin? Why keep him here?"

Cailet smiled thinly. "Surely you've noticed the distraction he provides. No woman can think about anything or anyone else for five minutes after he enters a room."

"*Ten* minutes, Captal! And you forgot to mention the men, who want to bed him or kill him! Well, Sevy Banian will be glad he's staying, anyway. He'll have a friend to talk to." When she looked blank, he explained, "He's a good lad, but a farmer to his toes. He's much more comfortable rusticating in Ryka's hill villages than wearing velvet regimentals around here."

"But wasn't he raised in Havenport? That's not exactly a barnyard."

"*Near* Havenport for his first thirteen years, then a year with an aunt who tried to hammer some culture and sophistication into him—without much success, though she did manage to get rid of his rural accent. Then Fiella Mikleine found him and took him to Mage Hall." He leaned back in his chair and pursed his lips meditatively. "Sevy's one of those Mages who're perfectly happy in a little farmhouse within reach of a dozen or so villages, not a Scholar or a Healer or a Warrior but knowing enough about each to teach school, help the local physicker, and defend whoever needs defending. They set Wards for the sheep in the high country, and set off Mage Globe fireworks on Saints' Days, and except for the times when people need magic they more or less forget that the woman or man living nearby *is* a Mage."

"The backbone of what we used to be," Cailet murmured. "Will we ever be that again? Will there ever be enough of us again to make magic a normal part of life?"

Telo shrugged. "It's a goal, Cailet. There rarely were enough of us to go around. That's why so many were itinerant. Mage, Healer, and Warrior, traveling great swaths of Lenfell to do what they could and hope nothing really awful happened when they were too far away to do anything at all."

"*That's* why there were Ladders. And Folding spells. And—" She stopped as a glow suddenly emanated from one of the crystal spheres cradled on Telomir's office couch. Avin Sonne had found a satchel to carry the Globes in and cloth to cushion them; Dessa had taken charge of the satchel and on arrival here emptied it onto the brocade couch. The six were lined up, each on its own pillow, like sleeping cats. But now one of them had awakened.

Not the one Cailet had hoped—the one she hadn't yet identified. She was afraid she would never know whose it was, which of her fifty-seven Mages who'd had one might now be dead. She hoped its owner was alive—but surely the Globe would have shone with a message by now, frantic and asking for help as the others had done. She'd visualized the shelves the way she'd told Mikel to do, trying to identify each and every glass orb, trying to match the names of the dead with the Globes that were now lost, trying to figure out from its size when it had been made and thus to whom it belonged. If she thought about it hard enough, she knew she'd be able to put a name to it, and send a message, and find out if that person still lived.

Cailet! Stop this obsessing and find out what Pier has to say!

Gorsha? she asked, confused for a moment.

No, the Wraith of Veller Ganfallin! Collect yourself and read the damned message!

Rising, she went to the couch and picked up the Globe.

Bringing Lenna Ostin Renig-Longriding-Ambrai-Ryka by St. Deiket's according to request. Any further information on legal developments, any/all documents, hearing date, please send soonest.

"Telo, who asked Lenna Ostin to come to Ryka?"

"Oh, shit," he muttered. "I completely forgot about that. Sarra and Collan have been named in a lawsuit before the High Judiciary."

"*Glenin?*"

"No. Mirya Witte divorced her husband, in a manner of speaking. She murdered him."

6

IT required vast amounts of patience to deal with Vellerin Dombur. During twenty years at Malerris Castle, Glenin had learned to tolerate the passage of time with a certain degree of calm, but she had never found it necessary to practice restraint with underlings—and everyone at Malerris Castle was her underling. Vellerin Dombur was not. Truly told, she fancied herself superior to every woman now living, and the only name that could spark any respect in her sapphire eyes was that of her ancestor, Veller Ganfallin. For her, Glenin and the Malerrisi were hammer and nails to be gripped firmly in her own expert hand; she would never admit to needing them, lest the hammer begin to think itself capable of driving home the nails under its own impetus. Without the Blood claims of the Domburs, Glenin was powerless.

Or so Glenin allowed the woman to believe. And it was hard, grindingly hard, to smile at her and Warm the day-old coffee sent up from the tavern and murmur the necessary things about how wonderful the world would be when all South Lenfell belonged once more to the Domburs, as it should.

"And then we'll see what we can do about Ambrai, my dear." A smirk dimpled her smug fat face. Fifty-two, she dressed as if she were still a skinny slip of an eighteen-year-old girl. Lace frills and silk ruffles meant to disguise the narrow shoulders of her youth now added bulk to already generous outlines; low-cut, tight bodices designed to make the most of very little now seemed in perpetual peril of bursting at the seams. Her extravagantly arched brows were dyed, as was her high-piled hair—augmented by bobbing false curls—and she wore precisely the wrong shade of plum-tinted powder on her eyelids. She looked like the vulgar mistress of a cheap whorehouse who took each of the boys to her bed thinking it was an honor for them.

But despite the fact that Glenin had youthful beauty,

taste, and elegance—everything Vellerin lacked—and ten times the brains into the bargain, this woman possessed an invaluable asset: the sheer, crushing *presence* that came of ambition even more ruthless than Glenin's.

Returning Vellerin's smile, Glenin dared for just an instant to loathe the Weaver's schemes that had given her this woman to wind so many threads around, and brought up the subject of Mirya Witte. Never one to suffer morons at all, let alone cheerfully, nevertheless Glenin suppressed her exasperation at having to explain everything three times before Vellerin began to see the point.

Invocation of Blood rights and dignity was not as potent as she'd thought it would be. Vellerin cared for no lineage but her own, which she traced in Bloods unsullied by Tiers (so she claimed) back to the First Census. Well, so could Glenin, but only on the Ambrai side. The Feirans were problematical; her father hadn't known the name of his own father, and the Feiran women hardly ever married and even less often named the men who sired their children. In any case, except for Glenin and her son, the Name was extinct, systematically targeted by a covetous Web throughout the last century. Glenin's grandmother had been the last female of the line until Glenin had taken the Name for herself. She didn't mention to Vellerin that she intended her own granddaughters to be called Feiran as well, no matter who their mothers might end up being. It was not something one discussed with a woman as determined to bring back every law and custom of the old days as thoroughly as Vellerin Dombur did—for her own glory and aggrandizement, of course.

Strangely, what gained her cooperation in Mirya Witte's cause was something Glenin hadn't expected: Sarra's misuse of her position to profit her Ostin friends. Glenin bit her tongue against the malicious observation that Vellerin had done much the same thing regarding her various land-grab schemes in Domburronshir. At first Glenin assumed the woman thought her intrigues secret, but after some thought decided that it went to basics of character. Just as the coward touted her own courage, the ignorant lout her powers of intellect, and the liar her veracity in all things, Vellerin Dombur would profess her-

self the soul of integrity and roundly condemn Sarra
Liwellan for being a cheat and a thief while she herself
cheated and thieved every chance she got.

The important thing was her agreement to support the
lawsuit. Chava had written down the detailed particulars
during a morning interview with Mirya. Glenin and Vellerin plotted strategy using this new gambit. It was galling
to pretend that almost every idea originated with the
would-be Grand Duchess, but she had the arrogance of
the supremely self-centered that would admit to no brilliance she herself did not propose.

At the end of the evening, Vellerin departed Glenin's
seedy lodgings, floorboards keening beneath her weight,
for the cliffside house owned by a wealthy supporter. Vellerin had condescended to invite Glenin to join the retinue
of fawning functionaries luxuriating at the mansion.
Glenin had declined. Humble as her above-the-tavern
room was, she preferred it to being one of dozens dancing
attendance on Vellerin Dombur and her disgusting husband with his ostentatious white clothes and frightful
poetry. It would take some doing at Ryka Court to establish her independence from Vellerin while subtly emphasizing their partnerships as equals in power—but she'd
already contacted a steward of chambers there who remembered her. He had assured her that her suite would
be at least the size and grandeur of Vellerin's.

A tap at her door distracted her from the beginnings
of a spell for sleep—excitement had perturbed her nights
recently. She rose from the narrow bed (Warded the instant she arrived to chase away bugs) and wrapped a
shawl around her shoulders. Chava would never disturb
her unless it was absolutely necessary, and only Chava
would dare disturb her at all.

"Lady, I am sorry," he said as he slipped into the
darkened room. Once the door was shut, he called up a
tiny Mage Globe, and by its light she saw that he was
fully dressed. "There's trouble downstairs. Someone's
heard about Mage Hall, and someone else heard Lady
Mirya say your name the other night, and put the two
together. It began with muttering, but it's about to esca-

late into nastiness. It's my opinion, Lady, that we ought to leave at once."

Run away, as Cailet had? Not damned likely. "Ridiculous," she scoffed. "In the first place, my Wards will keep us safe. In the second, there's no proof that any Malerrisi were involved with—"

"With respect, Lady, it's your very Wards that will drive them to a frenzy. Bleynbradden is staunchly for the Mage Guardians and hates the Domburs—they remember Veller Ganfallin's siege of Wyte Lynn Castle, though it happened centuries ago. And I must point out, again with respect, that 'proof' is incidental over that many bottles of Bleyn's Brown Ale."

She let the breath hiss out between her teeth. "If we run away, we confirm their every suspicion."

"Can that matter? All that is vital is to reach Ryka Court. Our ship docked less than an hour ago. You can be on it in twenty minutes."

Contending with the rabble would be to no profit at all. Nothing must be allowed to interfere with events at Ryka Court. "Very well," she said curtly.

Chava allowed himself a relieved sigh. "Please dress warmly. The baggage is already downstairs, and can be picked up tomorrow morning as scheduled. There's a back stair into the yard, and from there a short walk to the dock. I'll make sure the way is clear." With a scant bow, he left her room.

Glenin had just finished buttoning a woolen shortvest and was throwing her cloak over her shoulders when he knocked at the door again. She grabbed her coin-purse (the bulk of her money was sewn into the lining of her skirt) and followed him down the squeak-floored hall toward the back stairs.

And none too soon, for the mutterings in the tavern below had reached a boiling point. Glenin hadn't heard it from her room, but now the anger seethed up the stairs and she discovered she was frightened. Only for a brief, shameful instant; she was the First Lady of Malerris, she had no cause to fear anyone. Shaken more by her own reaction than the heavy tread of hobnailed boots on the stairs, she realized that she had ruled with absolute authority a community that gave her absolute deference for so long that the merest hint of disrespect would quite naturally upset her. Well, they would pay for it, and learn better—but not tonight.

The main staircase rose just beside the tavern's front door. The taproom ceiling soared to worm-eaten rafters, with the upper story bracketing it in an L-shape. The hall at the top of the stairs extended the length of the building and then turned a right angle at the back, with a second staircase at the intersection. Glenin and Chava were almost to this juncture when the tromping of many drunken feet announced the imminent arrival of aggrieved townsfolk. Chava swore under his breath, shoved his shoulder against the nearest door, dragged Glenin into a bedroom, and slammed the door behind him.

In a pair of beds shoved together for convenience frolicked two women and one man, all young and none wearing a single stitch. The man was profoundly occupied in pleasuring both women at the same time, and intense concentration on his task precluded his noticing the intruders. But one of the women, dark head lolling in transports of bliss, opened her eyes above splendid cheekbones Glenin wasted a moment envying, and saw them.

Chava gave her his most charming smile, white teeth flashing in his heavy brown beard. "Good evening. So sorry to have bothered you. Don't pay us any heed, just go on doing what you're doing. We'll be gone in a moment, vanished as if we'd never been here."

At the sound of his voice, the second woman jerked upright in bed, her short tawny hair every whichway. The dimples born of an ecstatic smile vanished from her cheeks as she opened her mouth to scream.

Glenin, who'd been preparing to make herself and Chava invisible within a Ward, cast a hasty spell instead. Not a sound issued from the blonde, who realized it, choked, disconnected herself from the man, and scrambled naked out of bed to huddle in a corner. The darker woman simply stared, too astounded even to attempt a scream. Their lover, whose conscientious attention to his duty Glenin rather admired, finally grasped that something was amiss. He rolled over, modestly clutching a scrap of sheet about his groin. Across his long face, capped by tousled dark hair, successive emotions played with comical predictability: surprise, indignation, irritation, wariness, and at last fear.

Footsteps went by outside in the hall. Glenin counted at least eight sets, all heading for her room. She made her voice gentle and reassuring as she said, "My apologies, ladies, for the interruption. We'll be going now."

Her turn to be surprised then—for the young man, deciding there was nothing to be scared about, was looking her over with new and flattering interest. "Honored if you'd join us, Lady," he purred.

Chava half-strangled on an outraged gasp. Glenin was so amused that she disregarded the man's impertinence. "I'm obliged to you, *Domni*. Perhaps another time."

"I'll count the hours, Lady," he responded with a rakish grin, and she couldn't help but grin back— especially when his remaining bedmate dealt him a resounding slap on the shoulder.

Chava opened the door, backed out, and Glenin spared a last wink for the young man before following. A glance back down the hall told her that her room had been invaded. The overflow crammed into the doorway, straining to see inside—and paying no attention to the rest of the hallway. She and Chava hurried down the back stairs and out into the yard. Trampling the vegetable garden on the shortest route to the gate, they wrapped their cloaks closer against the late-night chill and slipped through the quiet streets to the docks.

The captain of any ship was the only person who could authorize an unscheduled boarding. The captain of the *Gray-Eyed Lady* did not appreciate being woken up to check their credentials. While Glenin pointedly ignored her, Chava gave her to understand the Lady preferred to spend the night before a voyage in her cabin, to accustom herself to the roll of the ship so that seasickness did not plague her quite so much once they were underway.

The captain glanced meaningfully at the dead calm harbor. "We're at anchor."

"Yet the difference between a deck and a dock is

more than that of a single vowel," Chava suggested with another winning smile.

It did not impress; the captain scowled, grunted, grudgingly welcomed Glenin on board, and stomped back to her cabin.

The next morning saw the early arrival of Mirya Witte and her maidservant, and the late arrival of Vellerin Dombur with her retainers. Glenin spent the entire time in her cramped little cabin, furious with Vellerin for her tardiness and therefore unable to go abovedecks lest she snarl at the stupid woman. Galling, that she was compelled by necessity to behave as if she actually liked and admired that corpulent, condescending cow. She consoled herself with daydreams of Vellerin's death by slow starvation. It would make up for having to kill Sarra and Cailet so quickly.

Finally the anchor was weighed, the sails were unfurled, and the *Gray-Eyed Lady* moved into the open sea. Vellerin sent a flunky to invite her to lunch in her suite—the best on board, including a tiny bathroom with a tub and toilet (Glenin's cabin had an ewer-and-basin and a chamberpot). Glenin felt no compunctions about using Vellerin's servant to summon Chava—who arrived livid with fury.

"The trunks were never delivered. They never left the tavern storeroom—except to be unloaded into the innkeeper's closets! I waited and waited, then paid a runner to go find out what happened—and when he *finally* came back he said she greeted him wearing green velvet with seed pearls! *Your* green velvet with seed pearls! Forfeit, she said, for the unpaid bill—as if we hadn't paid her before we set foot in the place! Lady, if they hadn't been hauling up the anchor and if Lady Vellerin hadn't already made us so late we were in danger of missing the tide, I would've returned there and ripped your clothes right off her back!"

"What makes you think I'd let them touch me after she'd sweated her stink into them?" Glenin had already discovered that pacing this minuscule scrap of floorboards was an unrewarding occupation. So she settled for kicking the empty ceramic chamberpot to the other side of the cabin, where it shattered against the door.

"Lady, I—"

"Shut up. There's nothing to be done now about it. But I must have something decent to wear." Vellerin Dombur would have at least ten trunks filled with clothes, but not only were she and Glenin nowhere near of a size, her taste was hideous and Glenin refused to demean herself by begging for her help. Likewise she would not be seen in a dress belonging to one of Vellerin's servants. "Tell Mirya Witte that I require one of her gowns. Make sure it's her best—not that *that* will be very impressive, considering her poverty, but at least it'll be clean and it might fit without looking too dreadful. And the instant we get to Ryka Portside, find the nearest shop and buy me something to wear."

"At least there was no money in any of the trunks. When we get to Ryka Court, I'll discover the name of the finest dressmaker and get an immediate appointment. I'm positive it won't take long to get us both outfitted again."

And meanwhile Glenin would have to hide in her suite. Damn that woman, she'd have her eyes torn out.

It wasn't until after he'd gone that she remembered what else had been in her luggage. Her white velvet Ladder, her escape in case all her plans and all her preparations went awry. Loss of the original—*damn* Siral Warris!—had been painful enough. And nothing to the Work needed to replace it. Five solid years it had taken her, one just to memorize complex sequences of spells. Every silk thread, even before it was woven into velvet; every stitch of silver embroidery before the metal had even been spun to sewing thinness—and then while the weaving and spinning and sewing was done—all of it Worked and Worked again.

And the Ladder she'd struggled for five years to make had been packed in one of her trunks. By now its pristine white velvet would be spread beside that thieving innkeeper's bed to warm her filthy bare feet on cold mornings.

She'd tear that woman's heart out with her own fingers.

7

RYKA Court kept a quiet St. Deiket's (celebrations for the scholarly Saint were spirited only at colleges and academies) and in fact seemed to be holding its collective breath. Cailet stayed out of sight, available only to Lenna Ostin, Elomar Adennos, and Telomir Renne. She ignored her sister, her sister's husband and children, and anyone else who wanted to see her.

No one, not even Cailet, could permanently evict Tarise.

She began the morning of Ascension's third day with breakfast in her Ryka Court suite—the same luxurious rooms always kept for her use whenever she was forced to come. Tarise came in at Half-Fifth with a laden tray and the comment, "You'll love this, Cailet—it's simply too cute for words."

Cailet sat up against the oak headboard with its inlaid ebonwood feathers, kicked back the aviary embroidered on the quilt, and surveyed her meal. Some impish spirit in the kitchens had decided to match the menu to the surroundings. Six tiny hard-boiled eggs cuddled in a nest of asparagus tips, and a trio of flaky pastry swans sailed on waves of sliced grilled duck. The plate, cup, and coffeepot were of Rine porcelain with birds, the handles of the flatware were shaped like a rooster's tail plumage, and instead of flowers in a vase the tray was decorated with three white plums the size of goose eggs, out of which rose tall, iridescent feathers whose eyes seemed to wink at her.

"Sweet St. Alilen with Silver Wings and Golden Feathers! What Daftie is responsible for all this?"

"The Supreme Votary of Velirion's Vittles in Charge of Spectacular Presentation of Meals to Important Guests—he has some other equally ridiculous title, but that's his function." Tarise set the tray across Cailet's knees before seating herself at the foot of the gigantic bed.

"This place always did feel like a birdcage—does he have to rub it in?" She poured coffee, adding, "Besides, cute food is always awful. They spend so much time worrying about making it *look* good that they forget it should *taste* good."

Tarise smiled slightly. One forkful of duck later, Cailet changed her mind about cute food. It showed on her face, and Tarise said, "We're thinking of stealing him for Roseguard. Try a swan."

"Seems a shame to lop off its poor little head." But she did, and the pastry melted in her mouth. After a swallow of coffee and a long sigh, she eyed Tarise thoughtfully. "What is it you want to tell me that you intend to wait until I've finished because if you tell me now it'd spoil my appetite? Not that there's any danger of it—I'm starved and this is miraculous."

"Oh, it's only a little something I just happened to overhear."

"Ah. The same way you just happened to see the earrings in Telo's bedroom." She paused. "What *were* you doing in his bedroom, anyway? And don't say you were trying to seduce him, you haven't looked at another man since you first set eyes on Rillan twenty-five years ago."

"Twenty-seven," she corrected. "Though I could make an exception for Josselin Mikleine. And he's the one I overheard."

"Talking to—?" Cailet prompted.

"Mirya Witte! Her ship got in half a day early to Ryka Portside. She arrived late last night—and at the absolute crack of dawn went to find her former intended husband." Tarise selected a plum, removed the decorative feather, and began peeling it with her fingernails as she settled down for a good gossip. "I just *happened* to be in the hallway where your two gorgeous Prentices are sharing a room—no, truly told!" she protested as Cailet grinned. "I was going to get your breakfast. I stayed to listen from around the corner and that's why I'm late. Anyway, there they were, standing in the doorway, Josselin in nothing but a sheet—draped to cover *everything,* damn it—and Mirya the Mare trembling like a filly come into her first season. It seems he never replied to a letter she sent him back at Shepherds Moon. He said he didn't think there was anything to say. She said she'd drop the lawsuit if only he'd forget about being a Mage Guardian and come back to her as her husband, just as they planned. He said, 'Just as *you* planned,' and she said, 'You'd have everything I promised, and more,' and he said, 'All I'd have would be a mountain of debts and marriage to a woman jailed for murder.' Then *she* said, 'I'll win my appeal,' to which he said, 'If you drop the lawsuit against Lady Sarra and Lord Collan, what defense will you have for what you've done?"

"What defense, indeed," Cailet murmured. "To which Mirya said. . . ."

" 'You wanted me once, I can make you want me again,' and he said, 'Want you? Not in a million years. And nothing could make me want to end up like Ellus Penteon.' Smart boy." She took a bite of the plum, licked juice from her lips, and resumed, "Then Mirya threatened him. He'd better make his best deal now with her, because in a week his patron Lady Sarra will be ruined and he's got no money and no prospects other than what his pretty face can win him. He said he'd live on grubs for the rest of his life in the meanest hovel in The Waste rather than spend another two minutes with her. And then he slammed the door in her face."

"*That* wasn't very smart," Cailet commented.

"No, but what he did next was. After a moment or two he opened the door—the sheet had dropped from his shoulders to his waist, Mirya practically whinnied!—anyway, he said if she truly meant to drop the lawsuit against Sarra and Col, he'd think about coming back to her. She hardly heard him—he actually had to say it twice—and then she tried to paw him. He pulled the sheet up like a virgin bridegroom, wished her a good morning, and closed the door!" Tarise sucked the last juices from the plum pit, tossed it onto the tray, licked her fingers, and grinned. "Now what do you think of *that?*"

"Remarkable."

"And then some! But tell me what you think it all means, Cailet. You know the boy, I don't." She broke the tail off a swan and bit in.

"I think he doesn't want to go back to Mirya Witte."
If he was Glenin's son, the chances of his marrying that
woman were about the same as those of the Ladymoon's
falling out of the sky one night. Unless he was only what
he appeared to be, and the real traitor was Jored. In which
case Mirya Witte's lawsuit had absolutely nothing to do
with anything at all—except that it discredited Sarra and
Collan.

"Well, *obviously* he doesn't want to marry the Mare.
Who would?"

"But I think he wants Mirya to think he might."
Which made no sense, unless he truly intended to sacrifice himself for Sarra and Collan. They'd discovered he
was Mageborn, and spared him a distasteful marriage. He
was young, and the young were prone to grand gestures.

Unless the discovery had not been accidental at all.

Cailet, Gorsha warned.

"If Josselin plays Mirya right," Tarise was saying,
"she might drop those parts of her defense that blame it
all on Sarra. It's disgusting, truly told. Though I must say
Mirya's lust is enduring, if antiquated. Understandable,
of course—the boy is seriously gorgeous."

"A woman of nearly fifty ought to have more respect
for her own dignity."

"What's dignity compared to a face like Josselin
Mikleine's? Not his fault, poor thing."

"No. But I'll bet Glenin's really behind the appeal.
Sarra's the loser whichever way the High Justiciary decides. It's a lovely way to blacken a Councillor's character without Glenin's having to say a single word herself."

Tarise put down the remains of the pastry swan.
"Now you've spoiled *my* appetite! Finish your breakfast,
Cailet, do—or I'll be subjected to Elomar's gruesomest
glare!"

"All right, all right—but only if you go find Lenna
Ostin for me. We've already had one talk about this lawsuit, but I think she should hear this new wrinkle."

"I'll get Sarra and Col, too. And Josselin?"

"Mmm. . . ." Munching on an egg, she decapitated
the third pastry swan and nodded. "About an hour after
we begin our meeting, bring him in. And make sure he's

wearing something besides a sheet, won't you? Lenna's never seen him before—and she's not married."

8

THE twins looked in dismay at each other, then at Sarra, and then said in unison, "Do we *have* to?"

"Yes. And stop whining." Sarra looked them both up and down, finding fault with the too-casual drape of Taigan's turquoise silk shawl and the imperfect stuffing of Mikel's curls into his coif. "You need a haircut," she muttered, and he yelped as she forced a recalcitrant lock under the gray velvet.

Collan glanced at Cailet, who lounged against a table in the salon, trying not to laugh as her proud young Prentices were put in their proper place by their mother. "Get that smirk off your face," he told her. "You're next."

Sure enough, Sarra turned her critical gaze on the Captal, whose eyes widened at Sarra's frown. "What's wrong with the way I look?"

"You and all that damned *black*. It's much too harsh for your coloring—"

"She wants people to see her clothes, not her," Col said patiently.

Cailet suffered her sister to retie the silver sash around her waist. "I don't know what you're griping about. These are the regimentals *you* had made for me—"

"Twenty years, and you're still wearing the same ones!"

"At least she can still fit into 'em," Collan drawled. "Unlike some girls I could mention."

Sarra glared. "*You* try to keep a twenty-one-inch waistline after two children!"

"That's all right, First Daughter—I *like* my women nicely padded."

Her affronted scowl turned to a cloyingly sweet

smile. "Then you'll enjoy every minute you're going to spend with Vellerin Dombur."

Collan rolled his eyes. "I said 'padded,' not 'upholstered.' Cover her with brocade, she'd be a sofa."

Mikel snickered. Sarra gave him a quelling look before loftily ignoring all of them in favor of checking her own appearance one last time in a full-length mirror. Collan watched fondly as she subjected herself to the same scrutiny. Round Sarra might have become over the years, but between the firm swell of her breasts and the lush curves of her hips was a waist not *that* much bigger than the twenty-one inches of her youth. She wore an elegant ivory tunic subtly embroidered with brown and dark green arabesques, belted with a thin gold chain over brown silk trousers. Her jewelry was nothing more elaborate than a pair of small gold hoop earrings and Tarise had dressed her hair simply in a long tail down her back. She looked thirty of her forty-three years—except for the worry that shadowed her eyes.

"Come on, we're going to be late," she said at last.

"Aren't you going to put *him* to the test?" Cailet asked plaintively, pointing at Collan.

"Why bother?" he said before Sarra could reply. "I'm perfect."

This time Taigan giggled, and Col turned a reproachful eye on her. Hastily, she said, "Of course you're perfect, Fa, you always are."

Sarra snorted and shooed them all toward the door. And despite his claims to perfection, Col snagged a look in the mirror at himself. Just to make sure. His clothes were a skillful complement to Sarra's, combining almost the same shades of green, brown, and ivory. He was a little put-out that his latest innovation had not yet been commented upon: his longvest was a vest no more. It had sleeves to the wrists. Timarrin Allard had sent it from Ambrai only yesterday, with two others for more formal occasions. He fully expected to cause a sensation that would draw at least some of the attention from Vellerin Dombur—a small annoyance to the would-be Grand Duchess, but one Collan would relish.

"Do we *have* to go hear her speech?" Mikel said one

last time on their way through the halls. It earned him another stern look from his mother.

"Yes. And to the reception afterward. I want to know how people react in the gallery where you'll be sitting. I need all the eyes and ears I can get—and so does your Captal," Sarra added irrefutably, and the twins subsided—though Taigan kept touching nervous fingers to her hair, where Tarise's dexterity had *almost* disguised the singed bits. Collan felt an ill-timed rush of fury that anyone could put his little girl into such danger. Never mind that she was a little girl no longer. She was still and always *his* to keep safe. And he'd done a rotten job of it.

All thirty Councillors and three hundred twenty-five Members of the Assembly—plus anyone who could wrangle a seat—met in the Great Chamber on the fifth of Ascension to hear Vellerin Dombur speak. But until she made her appearance, easily the most remarked-upon attendee was Mage Captal Cailet Rille. (Collan came second on the to-be-stared-at list; the sleeved longvest had every man in the place making frantic mental appointments with his own tailor.) Rumors about Mage Hall had wildfired around Ryka Court all during Maiden Moon—and the grim facts had been known since the Captal's formal written report to the Council was read yesterday. Few were the families that had not lost a Mageborn relation in the murders all over Lenfell or in the destruction of Mage Hall.

But as to who was responsible . . . well, some had strong opinions and others had stronger fears, but everyone was waiting to hear what Vellerin Dombur had to say.

She surged into the Great Chamber—all three hundred and fifty-four pounds of her—wearing the Dombur white-on-white that matched the marble of the Speaker's Circle and the huge triangular Council table behind her. Once there had been fifteen red-cushioned chairs at that table; now there were thirty, and sometimes when the senior and junior Councillors for each Shir were not on speaking terms they gritted their teeth at being crammed together. When Dannin Rengirt had been Sarra's junior for Sheve, the close quarters embarrassed him so much he spent half his nine-year term apologizing to her for brushing against her shoulder.

This morning the vast table was bare of the usual pens, paper, crystal water pitchers and goblets, and other appointments of an official meeting; there would be no business done today and all the Councillors sat in the audience. Vellerin Dombur had the whole stage to herself, and as she entered by the side door, Collan realized that this was exactly the way she liked it. She positioned her bulk at the plinth as if it were a stepping stone to that usually crowded table—which Col figured she intended to sit at all by herself one day, not as First Councillor or even only Councillor, but as Grand Duchess of the whole damned world.

She was greeted by a polite silence, and immediately began her remarks. "Councillors, Members of the Assembly, citizens of Lenfell. I thank you for according me this opportunity to share with you my thoughts on the condition of our society and our mutual hopes for the future. I also bring greetings and best wishes from the people of Domburronshir, who have graciously named me to represent them here."

"Right," Col muttered. "They name her nightly in prayers to St. Venkelos for her quick death."

"Shh," hissed Sarra.

As Vellerin Dombur prated on, Collan glanced around the Chamber. There'd been changes made since the first time he'd sat here, the day Sarra had taken her oath as the newly elected Councillor for Sheve. The banners hanging from balcony rails and around the walls were still bright with the colors of every extant Name on Lenfell, but in the last nineteen years three Names had died out with the last of the female line.

"Nothing can bring back the old days—nor should they return. There was much to cause us chagrin about the manner in which our foremothers ruled Lenfell. Under the leadership of the new Council, many of these deplorable customs have been abandoned, and all to the good of our world. Yet there was much about the old days we can still admire, days in which strong and powerful and brilliant women worked hard for the greater good and glory of their Shirs."

She was referring to Veller Ganfallin, of course. But Col thought of Agatine Slegin. The Rose Crown banner was gone, there being no woman of that Name now living, and Collan regretted it—even though Agatine's lack of daughters meant Sarra's and therefore his own wealth. He'd liked Agatine and her husband Orlin Renne, for all that they'd dragged his unwilling self across half Lenfell during the Rising. If they hadn't, he never would have been tortured in that obscene white room; but if they hadn't, he never would have become Sarra's husband and father of her children. She introduced legislation at every Council session to allow third or fourth daughters to inherit a father's Name if it was in danger of extinction— both Riddon and Jeymi Slegin had fathered several daughters each—but she'd never even come close to the two-thirds majority necessary to take the measure to the Assembly.

"And let us not forget the humbler but no less important work of the majority of Lenfell's women, those who grew our crops and fished our waters, watched our flocks and herds, taught our children, guided commerce, crafted our necessities and our luxuries, supervised our mines and factories and estates, tended our flowers, and wove our garments and tapestries."

On Collan's other side, Cailet whispered, "Wonder how Glenin Feiran will like being lumped in with all the other good little drones."

"Shh!" hissed Sarra.

One of Dombur's images had caught Collan's mind: flowers. He'd given orders long ago that the gardens at Roseguard be restored to glory, but he hadn't the same feel for horticulture possessed by their former Master. Verald Jescarin had been his friend—chance-met, known for only a few brief weeks, but his friend nonetheless. His family's banner still hung from the wall, but the Trayos he'd married had been the last grown daughter of her Name. Collan's jaw hardened as he thought of Sela, and Verald, and their little girl Tamsa—all dead in the Rising. He'd seen Verald killed one cold night not fifty miles from where he now sat. Sela had died in childbirth; Tamsa succumbed to a fever after fleeing the attack on Ostinhold; the baby had vanished and was presumed dead. Col still had the jewelry Sela had given her husband—an amethyst earring, a wristlet of gold and dark green jade—and Verald's identification disk. He'd meant to give the tokens to Sela, but everything had happened so fast. . . .

Vellerin Dombur placed plump hands atop the plinth, and from one thumb winked a silver ring set with carved white onyx like a clot of snow. The sigils of every Saint in the Calendar marched in orderly rows up and down the upright block of marble; their presence was supposed to guarantee the truth and sincerity of the speaker's words. Collan had no doubt that this woman meant everything she said—and much more that she did not say.

"Nothing would please me and benefit Lenfell more than to restore the best of the old ways, the respect for tradition and craft and the finest of our customs. I know that opinions differ as to what we should retrieve and what we should not, but after the welcome I have received here and after meeting with several of you, I heartily believe that any differences among us will melt away like mist in the warm sunlight of understanding and cooperation."

"I may throw up," Collan whispered.

"Not here." Cailet nudged him with an elbow. "Sarra would never forgive you."

Sarra gave them both a look to paralyze a rabid rampaging grizzel in its tracks.

"But casting a shadow over this day is a terrible deed that has shocked and horrified us all. Treachery has obliterated Mage Hall. We all grieve at this calamity, which frighteningly recalls the slaughter perpetrated on the innocent citizens of Ambrai by the late unlamented Anniyas's votary, Auvry Feiran."

Col felt Sarra turn cold beside him. He sneaked a hand toward hers on the arm of her seat, covering the small, icy fist with his own.

"We all remember the Commander of Lenfell's armies—how he destroyed that great and gracious city in the course of three hideous days, murdering over thirty thousand, earning his odious title: Butcher of Ambrai. His crimes continued during that period known as the Purge, which all but wiped out the Mage Guardians—he who once had been one of them! But he could not completely extinguish their light. Cailet Rille, the new young Captal, built the Mage Guardians into a reality again—only to see her work destroyed."

All eyes had turned to Cailet. Col ground his teeth. He knew how she hated attention of this type. But it was part of her function to be a visible symbol, just as Sarra had deliberately played on her background as a daughter of two victims at Ambrai. But Vellerin Dombur was speaking as if Cailet were a relic and as if the destruction of Mage Hall meant the Mages were nearing inevitable extinction.

"We must resolve to right this terrible wrong," rang out Dombur's voice, drawing all attention back to her. "We must remember the evil of Auvry Feiran, who tried to exterminate the Mage Guardians in his lust for power. We must cast out such self-serving rapaciousness from among us, in whatever form it may appear, and nurture our Mageborns back to what they once were. For Lenfell *needs* magic. Those years we spent without it showed us this. The years since the Rising, when Mageborns have come among us again in our towns and cities and farmlands, have shown us this. Magic is one of the best things about the old days, and we must bring it fully back into our lives. With patience and hard work and a strong belief in a better future for our daughters, we can ensure that never again will Auvry Feiran's pattern of power-mad wickedness distort the fabric of our civilization."

Col listened to the applause and wondered what the hell the woman was up to. *Pattern* and *fabric* could only refer to Chevasto the Weaver, patron of the Malerrisi—but she'd just spent five minutes vilifying the father of the current First Lady of Malerris. Glenin Feiran (and where was she, anyway?) was supposed to be her ally; what was she playing at?

Then he recalled the insulting offer Pier Alvassy reported receiving from Glenin—they were cousins through the Ambrai line, and she had appealed to his family loyalty for support in her ventures. Pier hadn't replied—had been restrained only on his Captal's direct order from going to meet her ship and exploding a Mage Globe in her face—and the mere mention of her made his lip curl. But maybe Glenin was going to renounce the Feiran Name, take back Ambrai, and in that fashion claim the city of her birth. For the third missing banner was the Ambrai Octagon—Glenin, the last of that Name, had long since adopted her father's, so the Leaf Crown of the Feirans was present. Col wondered if Ambrai would soon replace it.

Everyone repaired to the Malachite Hall for drinks and nibble-food. Collan was immediately accosted by a group of young Ryka blades demanding to know the name of his clothes designer. After satisfying their curiosity (and grinning to himself again at their chagrin; not many could afford Timarrin Allard's prices), he moved smoothly through the crowd, picking up bits of chat here and there with expert ease.

He heard what he'd expected to hear. Speculation, admiration, suspicion, and a goodly dose of unrelated gossip about who was sleeping with whom, which Web would bid on which contracts/land/shipping routes, who was pregnant, who was getting married, and suchlike. On such rumors did the Minstrelsy build its reports and predictions—several of its members were in the crowd, and Collan expected to spend an interesting evening listening to all of it.

But the only thing of consequence he heard came from a tall, lean, good-looking young man whose ensemble, though fine enough for the occasion, looked assembled from five other men's wardrobes. Referring to one's Name in clothes and jewelry had gone out of fashion last year, so Collan had no convenient means of identifying him. A neatly trimmed beard concealed the lines of cheeks and jaw and lips, but there was something familiar in the arch of his nose, the deep set of his hazel eyes, and the poise of his head, even from twenty feet away.

The young man noticed Collan's regard, smiled slightly, and excused himself from the company of several fascinated, predatory ladies. On his way to where Col stood, he collected two full wineglasses off a passing servant's tray, presenting one with a dignified little bow.

"I don't doubt I seem familiar," he said in a low, unaccented voice. Up close, he wasn't as young as Col had thought—at least thirty, probably thirty-five. "I believe you met my father."

"Did I?" He cursed himself for revealing his puzzlement on his face, and now replaced it with a pleasant smile.

"At the time of the Rising." He sipped at the wine, then said casually, "His name was Vassa Doriaz."

Fifth Lord of Malerris, murderer of Taig Ostin. "Only once," Col said easily, his mind seething with remembered scenes in that white box Anniyas had called an *albadon.* "We didn't exactly warm up to each other."

"I was told you tried to drag him into . . . your own situation at the time."

"He wasn't inclined to join me."

"I can understand that."

"But now you Malerrisi want to join the party."

Stroking his bearded chin, he nodded. "It's a magnificent setting."

"With plenty of opportunities."

"Precisely."

They were not referring to the festivities in the Malachite Hall.

Collan said, "Today is your first opportunity to meet the Captal, as I recall? She's right over there, if you need to have her pointed out."

"You're right, I didn't have the pleasure of seeing her face-to-face that night at the Octagon Court—when Lady Sarra killed my father."

"After your father killed Taig Ostin."

The man nodded thoughtfully. "You haven't tasted your wine, Lord Collan."

"I'm picky about who I drink with."

"At least wishing to know their names? I've been remiss. I am Chava, son of Saris Allard—Threadmaster was her title among us. She was in the audience on the night the new theater opened in Roseguard. I—was not able to remain with her after she—" He hesitated, and there was a flash of something real and honest in his green-brown eyes. "I should very much like to know if she received a proper burning."

Such touching filial piety from the man whose mother had tried to kill Collan's children. He kept a snarl from his face and replied, "Lady Sarra ordered her disposed of in a manner appropriate to the circumstances."

Gold flared like fanned embers in his eyes.

With silken malice, Collan added, "What the fish couldn't chew up has probably drifted to Malerris Castle by now. Why don't you go back there and keep an eye on the tides?"

With that, he nodded and walked off.

Placing the wineglass on the nearest table, he took a moment to compose himself, then went in search of Sarra. He didn't see her on his first circuit of the huge Hall—not surprising, as she was so short she tended to vanish in a crush like this one—but he did catch sight of Vellerin Dombur, her simpering simple-minded husband beside her, holding forth to a group including many of the Dindenshir Assembly representatives and that Shir's senior Councillor, Ullin Dindennos.

The Minstrelsy reported that whereas Rinesteenshir, formidable mountains, and the mighty River Rine stood between Dindenshir and Vellerin Dombur's ambitions for South Lenfell, and nobody believed that the Iron City of Isodir would capitulate to her any more than it had to her ancestor, there was worry in the stone corridors of Dinn. Ullin Dindennos's frown confirmed that whatever Vellerin Dombur was saying, it was not soothing her very much. It had recently been discovered, and was not yet common knowledge, that persons fronting for the Dombur Web had bought up dozens of smallhold farms, at least one commercial building in every town in the Shir, and an entire block of prime waterfront businesses in Dinn itself. It was beginning to look as if the only Web capable of countering the Dombur's moves was Lady Lilen Ostin's—and, with a truculent First Daughter to contend with before nearly every transaction, Lilen had her own problems.

Collan made another round of the Malachite Hall, but

instead of Sarra, who seemed to have disappeared entirely, he found Glenin Feiran—to whom Granon Isidir was listening intently. Isidir, a secret supporter of the Rising, had been on the Council for Rinesteenshir since 952 and was Sarra's staunchest ally. Col didn't mind the alliance part of it; what he objected to—and had for twenty years—was the look in Isidir's eyes whenever he glanced at Sarra. At sixty-two he was as lean and predatory as ever, still handsome enough to catch any woman's eye. Col would have died rather than admit to Sarra that even after all this time he was still jealous—but every time he saw her with Isidir he couldn't help remembering the way they'd danced around the bonfire that night long ago. . . .

He doesn't matter—Glenin does. So he inspected the First Lady of Malerris. She was nearing fifty but even Col's prejudice had to admit she looked ten years younger. Tall, elegantly slender, she wore a honey-colored silk dress and ivory shortvest with as much effortless grace as if it had been made for her—which the inch-too-short hem indicated it had not. Dark-blonde hair only lightly touched with silver cascaded loose around her shoulders, the size and shape of her gray-green eyes were subtly emphasized with make-up, and around her throat glittered a chain of eight-sided gold links. *Octagons,* Collan noted sourly. *So she* is *going after Ambrai. Elin will be thrilled.* What she was saying as he edged near enough to listen, however, had nothing to do with the city of her birth.

"—enough Mageborns in this world that any of us can either hoard our gifts in isolation or neglect to educate ourselves in their uses. It's been wrong and prideful of me in the past, I see that now, to have kept aloof. We've all realized that whatever our philosophical differences with the Mage Guardians, we Mageborns must all dedicate ourselves to the service of Lenfell."

Councillor Isidir said, "In essence, you see yourself and the Mage Guardians as two shrines in the same city, each of value though dedicated to different Saints."

"Exactly," Glenin said. "We and they ought to be able to honor each other's shrines and applaud each other's good works, not be rivals for the devotion of the populace."

"And to this desirable, cooperative end—?" Isidir prompted.

"We're more than willing to go along with whatever would make the Captal feel secure."

"Inspection, for instance, of Malerris Castle and its methods of educating Mageborns?"

"Certainly. We have nothing to hide."

"And yet you've been in hiding there for the twenty years since Anniyas died."

"As I've said, that was wrong of me. I felt threatened and alone. But you must understand that in these twenty years, we've come to realize that the late First Councillor was an anomaly among us. She was a wicked, grasping woman who used everyone and everything to get what she wanted. Not what the Malerrisi wanted—what *she* wanted for herself." Glenin sighed. "I've never spoken of this, but perhaps you recall that in 968 I lost my First Daughter? It was not a miscarriage, as was put about at the time. Anniyas ordered me to abort the child."

For the second time that day, Collan felt like throwing up.

"Shocking," said Isidir. "I assume she wanted the girl dead because a grandson would not be able to challenge her in the way that a granddaughter could. You were deeply under her spell back then, to have agreed to such a thing."

"And have since freed myself of her influence and her viewpoint."

"Undemonstrated, unproved—and unbelievable, if you'll forgive my saying so." For the first time in his life Collan approved wholeheartedly of Granon Isidir's existence: the dark face suddenly lost its look of amiable interest and took on an aspect such as St. Venkelos must wear when judging the dead. "You Malerrisi have not changed your outlook since The Waste War. If others are so foolish as to be convinced by you, I will make it my task to disabuse them."

"I find it regrettable that you feel that way," said Glenin, and Collan could almost hear the Scissors click

as in her mind she excised Granon Isidir from the Great
Loom.

Isidir seemed to hear it, too. It daunted him not at all.
He gave her a nod so curt as to be barely civil, and walked
off. She turned her head slightly to watch him go, and met
Collan's gaze. One corner of her mouth tugged upward in
amusement. He realized then that she'd known he was
there, and intended her words to get back to Sarra and
Cailet. Unwilling to let her manipulate him so readily, he
pasted a half-smile on his face and approached her.

"Interesting speech Vellerin Dombur made today,"
he drawled. "How much of it did you write for her?"

"Everything but the adjectives," Glenin responded
calmly. "I find even I am unable to curb her tendency
toward the lurid."

"I agree, they were a touch overdone. Except in regard to your father." When that didn't even come close,
he paused and looked her down and up. "You and your
assistant appear to have had some difficulty with wardrobe."

She had her full share of vanity; this barb hit the
mark, though she showed it only in an almost imperceptible stiffening of shoulders and jaw. "Our luggage was
stolen."

"I'd be pleased to give you the name of a good dressmaker," he offered generously. "And I wouldn't worry
too much about the loss—you've been away from Ryka
Court so long the clothes you had were undoubtedly
twenty years behind the fashion."

The notion of this practically Nameless upstart Minstrel giving *her* advice—and in a place where what *she*
chose to wear and say and do had once set the style—
rendered her speechless with indignation.

Collan watched her eyes flash for a gratifying moment, then added, "Of course, everything about you is
twenty years out of date—including your jewelry."

Her fingers twitched involuntarily to the chain of gold
octagons around her neck. Then, mental Scissors snipping
again, she turned on her heel and walked away.

"What are *you* grinning about?"

Cailet's question made him turn. Taking her arm, he

escorted her through the crowd to a refreshment table, saying, "A woman stays a woman, no matter what."

She looked up at him blankly. "Huh?"

"Never mind. Have some of this, you'll feel better." He gave her a tall glass of golden bubbles. She sniffed at it, sipped, and made a face.

"We brewed better at Ostinhold. And what makes you think I need to feel better?"

"Masculine intuition. Drink up." Taking a glass for himself, he swigged half of it down.

"*Why* are you having such a good time?" she asked irritably.

"Because I might as well. It's another hour before I can sneak out of here."

"Where were you thinking of sneaking to?"

"A bar where they serve *real* drinks."

Cailet put down her glass. "Let's go. Sarra didn't even come in past the doors, you know. Why should she be the only one to escape all this?"

"Cai, we can't just—"

"Saints and Wraiths, you're dutiful today! I'm Mage Captal. I can do any damned thing I please, and I'm sick of this hothouse. Are you coming?"

9

THEY found Sarra outside in a corridor with the many reasons she hadn't even entered the hall. She'd been besieged—not by Councillors, members of the Assembly, Ryka Court bureaucrats, or even common citizens. When Cailet and Collan joined her, they were similarly surrounded.

"Lord Collan, a few minutes of your time? Shen Dalakard, *Island Shirs Press*."

"Excuse me, Captal, but if you could just answer a few questions—"

"The *Roke Castle Weekly Review* is running a story

on the destruction at Mage Hall—could I get a few comments?"

"Lord Collan, what was your reaction to Vellerin Dombur's speech today?"

"Lady Sarra, I'm Athni Golebirze of the *Isodir Record*—I have an artist waiting outside to sketch all of you for our broadsheet—"

"And what about this lawsuit brought by Mirya Witte? The man in question is a Prentice Mage, right, Captal?"

"Any reaction on tomorrow's court proceedings for our readers, Lady Sarra?"

"Yes," said Sarra. "No comment."

Collan shoved a way for the ladies through the throng of journalists. He hurried them down a side corridor—pursued at a run—and with the help of a sympathetic footman got them outside into the Council's private gardens.

It seemed they were not the first to take refuge there. On seeing them, Josselin Mikleine sprang up from a bench, broadsheets spilling from his knees onto the grass.

"What the hell are all those?" Collan asked, bending to snatch one from the ground.

"Punishment," Joss muttered. "Humiliation. Annoyance. Something to line the catbox with. Take your pick, my Lord."

Col read aloud from the headlines of the *Havenport Clarion*. " 'First Daughter's Secret Passion'—'Murderous Mirya Pleads with Mageborn Lover'—" He eyed Joss.

The young man winced. "It gets worse."

Cailet gathered more from the pile on the bench. " 'Councillor and Husband Named in Defense Appeal.' 'How Mirya Did It—Complete Reconstruction of the Crime.' This one has explanatory drawings," she remarked.

Joss opened another broadsheet to the inside pages and displayed them silently. Sarra felt her jaw drop.

WITTE-LESS FOLLY
THE HUSBAND SHE KILLED
THE MAGEBORN SHE KILLED FOR

Below the screaming headline were woodcut portraits. Mirya, Ellus Penteon, Josselin, even Sarra and Collan and Cailet, stared out from the pages, identifiable only because their names were printed at the bottom of the pictures.

"Does that look like me?" Cailet asked. "I don't think that looks like me."

"You think this is *funny?*" Sarra demanded.

"Doesn't look much like Josselin either."

"Laugh at *this,* I dare you," said Sarra, holding up a page for her sister's inspection.

COUNCILLOR AND HUSBAND CHARGED IN DEFENSE APPEAL
"THEY DROVE ME TO IT" SAYS MIRYA WITTE

"Did you? Drive her to it, I mean."

"Here's one," Col said. " 'Mikleine Foster Mother's Whole True Story!' "

"I've never even *heard* of that woman!" Josselin moaned.

Cailet peered at the accompanying woodcut. "This one doesn't look much like you, either. It could just as easily be Jored."

"Doesn't this bother you?" he asked in bewilderment.

"Should it? Whatever truth may be in any of it will die of loneliness amid the lies."

Then Collan showed her the *Pinderon Perspective.*

"THEY STOLE MY HUSBAND, THEN STOLE MY LOVE"
MIRYA'S COMPLETE EXCLUSIVE STORY!

Josselin looked as if contemplating suicide.

Cailet gave him a half-smile. "Relax. There's worse to come, if it hasn't already."

"Such as?" Collan asked, genuinely curious.

"Oh, probably something about how I lured him with pernicious magical spells away from his happy prospects with Mirya Witte for my own vile, depraved, degenerate purposes."

Col snorted. "Yes, you're known worldwide for your omnivorous and perverted sexual appetites."

Sarra had had enough. "Stop this right now," she declared. "It's not funny. You're showing absolutely no consideration, Cailet—think how Josselin must feel. You and Col and I are used to having our names in all the papers."

Her sister shrugged. "Sorry. My main consideration is how very craftily all this nonsense distracts from Vellerin Dombur and Glenin Feiran."

Josselin, who'd looked startled when Sarra gave the Mage Captal a dressing-down, now frankly stared. "You mean it's all been *planted?*"

"Some of it. But certainly it's all been planned. How many broadsheets does the Dombur Web own these days?" She stretched her arms wide, looked around the deserted garden, and said, "I don't know about you, but I'm going to go lock myself in my bathroom. The one advantage to Ryka Court is the plumbing. A hot bath here is the closest I've ever come to a true religious experience. Good afternoon, all."

She strolled away. Sarra glared after her, then glanced at Josselin. He was busy collecting the broadsheets—probably for burning in his bedchamber hearth. Sarra went to him and patted a shoulder (Holy St. Geridon, the boy has muscles!), saying, "We'll expect to see you tomorrow at dinner, Josselin. Thirteenth, my suite, casual—just family and Mages."

"Thank you, Lady Sarra. I—" Straightening, he visibly steeled himself to say, "I'm extremely sorry I've caused you and Lord Collan so much trouble. If I'd known anything like this would happen, I'd just've married her and—"

"Don't you ever say anything like that ever again," she scolded. "You're a Mageborn, a Mage Guardian, and to have wasted yourself on someone you didn't love—let alone someone like Mirya Witte!—would have been murder just as surely as she killed poor Ellus Penteon."

Collan smiled. "And now that you've been told what to think by the Lady who knows what *everyone* ought to think—"

She slapped playfully at her husband's arm—just as nicely muscled as Josselin's, she noted with approval. Well, perhaps not *quite* as nicely, but more than adequate for her own vile, depraved, degenerate purposes.

"—we'll see you tomorrow at dinner," Collan finished.

Josselin hesitated, then blurted, "If it had been like that with Mirya—like it is between you, I mean—" He caught himself and although a blush was invisible beneath his dark skin, Sarra was positive he was blushing. Smiling, she nudged Collan toward the garden gates.

"He's so young," she murmured when they were out of Josselin's hearing. "He blushes as if he were still sixteen."

"Did you see the look on his face when Cailet mentioned her disgusting sexual proclivities? No, I guess not. You were too busy being provoked by your sister's sense of humor—admittedly odd—just as she intended you to be."

"What?" Sarra tilted her head back to see his face. "She did?"

"Of course. She can play you like a lute, First Daughter dear. There's something about that boy she doesn't like—or doesn't trust, I haven't decided which. But the look he gave her just then. . . ." Collan laughed softly.

"*What* look?" Sarra repeated.

But however she coaxed, cajoled, and commanded, he only laughed at her all the more, and would give no details.

10

"ALL right," said Lenna Ostin the next evening, folding her ink-stained hands atop the open galazhi-leather portfolio spread before her. "This is where we're at."

Dinner had been cleared away. Coffee, dessert, and brandies had been handed around, though few partook of liquor because everyone wanted a clear head. They were eleven around Sarra's oval table that night; she had arranged the seating so she could watch two particular faces—Lenna's as she explained what they could expect in the courtroom two days hence, and Josselin's as he reacted.

Not that there was much to see. Lenna, wearing the "lecture face" she used in the classroom—for she also taught law at the fledgling Renig College in addition to her lucrative practice—gave them a short course in changes in the legal system since the Rising. Court proceedings on the local level were very different now, reforms allowing a more adversarial approach intended to get at the truth. The Justice at the bench no longer presented the Shir's case against the accused; that was now the duty of an Advocate in private practice hired for that specific purpose. Most of the Advocates in any given community had a legal specialty—anything from theft and murder to commerce and contracts—and prosecutorial assignments were made on this basis (unless, of course, the lawyer had already been engaged to defend the accused). No Advocate got rich off litigating the Shir's cases, but few ever turned down the chance if offered; civic responsibility was taken very seriously.

However, the appeals process was just the same as it had been in 951 when Captal Leninor Garvedian had petitioned for reversal of her conviction. The High Judiciary, consisting of five Grand Justices, would hear arguments from the convicted criminal's Advocate, retire to consider, and render a verdict within a week or so.

"This case is more complex," Lenna said, "because Mirya Witte's defense includes a lawsuit against Sarra and Collan." She paused for a sip of coffee. "We're looking at four charges. First, interference between a woman and her husband. Nonsensical, of course. Collan, you only knew Ellus Penteon from a few conversations at Wytte's. Sarra tells me she saw the man on one or two social occasions, and spoke to him maybe three times, all in Mirya's presence. So much for interference in the marriage."

Lenna took a pair of spectacles from a pocket of her skirt, set them on her nose, and consulted her notes.

"Next, the more serious allegations of coercion and use of public position for personal gain—we'll get back to that one in a minute. Third, alienation of husbandly and daughterly affections. Same response as in the charge regarding the husband. Neither of you ever even saw the daughters, let alone talked to them. And we have a counter to this as well, in an affidavit—damn, where'd I put it? Oh, here it is. An affidavit provided by Mirya's own First Daughter, who asserts that her mother's behavior disgusted the three girls. Let's see—a pretty much endless succession of different men, all much younger and extremely handsome—" She looked over the top rim of her spectacles at Josselin. "I believe this is where *you* begin to figure in the proceedings."

There was no change in his frozen expression.

"Yes. Well." Lenna cleared her throat. "This leads us to instigating breach of contract. She can't sue for alienation of Prentice Mikleine's affections, because he wasn't her husband and she had no legal right to his affections or anything else. But this item avows that in paying for his residence and, um, training at Wytte's, a contract between them did in fact exist. Basically, she wants her money back." She took off her lenses and grinned. "The lovely part about this is that the bill from Wytte's amounts to about the cost of a middling-good horse."

"No reflection on you, Joss." Collan gave a low chuckle as he walked around the table to replenish the coffee cups. "The Wyttes can't stand the Wittes. The original invoice was comparable to the cost of a whole herd of Maurgen Dapplebacks. Mirya didn't pay it. When Pierigo Wytte heard about this lawsuit, he made a great show of going over the books to get an accurate estimate—and what d'you know, it seems they'd overcharged!" He poured a triumphant dram of brandy into a glass and raised it to the young Prentice, grinning.

"So even if she wins that part of it," Lenna said, "she'll end up with not even enough to pay her Advocate." Eyeing Josselin, she added with a twinkle, "Personally, I have trouble believing that a big strong young blade like you costs two cutpieces a day to feed, but that's what the invoice says."

"A horse," Josselin muttered to his fists on the table. "I'm worth the price of a horse—and not a very good horse at that." Then he glanced up, a rueful twist to his lips. "Well, I guess she *did* consider herself to be purchasing a stud."

Sarra, pleased to see the Prentice had recovered his sense of humor, smiled her approval. Everyone else chuckled appreciatively—all except Cailet, Sarra noted in puzzlement. She was turning a spoon over and over in her hands, not looking at anybody.

Lenna continued, "Now, to win on this charge she'd have to prove there was a binding contract. As I see it, paying for the, um, time of a young man not licensed either to a bower or in private practice, as it were, is called slavery. Josselin was never so licensed, never applied for a license, and therefore any attempted purchase becomes attempted enslavement. Paying for Wytte's constitutes a gift, much as one would pay for someone's tuition, books, and so forth. Whatever Mirya expected in return is moot. End of item."

"Which leaves us with coercion and that other stuff," said Collan.

"Right. Especially 'that other stuff.'" Lenna pinched the bridge of her nose between her fingers, then leaned back in her chair and frowned at Collan. "I know all about it, of course. I drew up the deed of sale. You got her to sell Shore Hill at roughly half its real worth by threatening to expose publicly Mirya's abuse of her husband. That would have been enough, you know. But then you had to threaten her with legal proceedings—which, considering Sarra's position as a Councillor, implied not just the Sheve legal system but all the weight and resources of the government at Ryka Court! That was stupid, Collan. Really, really stupid."

"I never said a damned word directly!"

"Who'd believe that? Someone of your rank and influence can start a fashion in sleeved longvests or a run on a particular wine—or the process of changing a law. Everyone'll believe you threatened Mirya. And from all I've heard, you couldn't have been all that oblique about it or she never would've understood what the hell you were talking about."

Sarra did not come to her husband's defense. He'd been wrong, and she'd told him so at the time. But she didn't say *I told you so* now; instead, she flashed a look at Lenna meant to end the castigation. Collan had been a fool; he knew it, and Sarra knew it, and now they all knew it. Sarra didn't want him berated in front of everyone any more than strictly necessary. Pointing out his mistakes was Sarra's prerogative.

"Well," Lenna said with a sigh, "it's not fatal, anyway. We can work around it. After all, you have no official position outside of being Sarra's husband. And to win this point Mirya would have to prove that Sarra knew in advance and planned with you to coerce using her status as a Councillor. Such proof, naturally, is impossible."

"There's something else," Josselin said. "There's what *I* planned to do."

"I was about to get to that." Leaning forward once again with an elbow on the table, Lenna rested her chin on her fist, brown eyes staring across the candle stumps and wilting flowers at Josselin. "Your foster mother—whichever one it was, and the broadsheets have interviewed at least seven by my count, but that's not the point—anyway, there *was* a contract of sorts, between your foster mother and Mirya Witte, legal until you reached your majority in 987. Your plan, as I understand it, was to put Mirya off until the Autumn Equinox freed you from that contract, at which time you'd tell Mirya thanks-but-no-thanks."

Jored spoke for the first time. "Joss, didn't you say you were going to try and get work at a jeweler's?"

Josselin nodded. "I'm no hand at cutting gems, but I'm pretty good with clocks and gears and machinery—I'd've paid her back for Wytte's with the money I earned."

"Admirable," Lenna remarked sourly. "Can you prove it? Did you talk to any Roseguard jewelers about a job?"

"No—in case she heard about it."

"Did anyone else know what you planned to do when

you reached eighteen?" When he shook his head, she gave a shrug. "That's that, then. We can bring it up in court, but it'll sound dreamed up well after the fact. And in any event, you arrived at Mage Hall—when?"

"Two days before St. Caitiri's," said Cailet.

"Ah, yes," Lenna smiled. "Your Birthingday. Remember the year Miram and Tevis and Lindren and I sent you on a scavenger hunt for your presents? You were eleven, I think."

"Nine." Cailet smiled back. "And I ended up halfway to Longriding because I'd mistaken the clues!"

"I can still see Mother's face when she couldn't find you and sent us out on our horses. We yelled our lungs out all afternoon."

"Oh, I heard you after the first hour—but I figured you needed to be taught a lesson, so I followed along behind you, hiding in the rocks, and let you keep looking."

"Miserable child! It wasn't *our* fault you misread perfectly straightforward clues!"

Sarra felt something she hadn't felt in a long time: sadness that she and Cailet had been cheated of growing up together. The Ostin women were more like sisters to Cailet than she was. Her gaze strayed to her children, and the sadness became anger at herself for missing so much of their growing up. Then she noticed that Taigan—and Joss next to her, and Mikel and Jored besides—were all trying to hide two kinds of shock: that Lenna teased the Captal so openly, and that the Captal had *ever* been nine years old.

"But the point is," Lenna was saying, "that Cailet's Birthingday is a full week before the Autumn Equinox, which means that Josselin really had no legal right to skip out on Mirya Witte and his foster mother's contract. I don't suppose there's any way to prove that you were born at the *Spring* Equinox, is there?"

Again he shook his head. "Both my parents were dead before I was six weeks old. Like Jored, I got passed from family to family for a long time."

Cailet said, "Even if you swore in court that your Birthingday was Spring Moon, there are so many tales of your early years being published in the broadsheets that they completely confuse the issue. Nobody would believe you."

"I wouldn't swear to something I don't know to be true," he said stiffly.

"Of course," Cailet replied, pouring herself more coffee.

There's definitely *something going on here,* Sarra told herself. *Can she really believe Josselin is the traitor?*

Lenna sorted more papers. "All these charges are in aid of getting Mirya's murder conviction overturned—at least that's what *she* wants. My feeling, correct me if I'm wrong, is that Vellerin Dombur intends to use this case to reinstate some of the more delightful of our old marriage laws. A woman's absolute dominion over her husband, his complete lack of rights, her unchallenged privilege of parading as many men as she likes in and out of her bedroom—all those venerable traditions that made Lenfell great during the days of Veller Ganfallin." Her lip curled and she drank a large swallow of coffee as if to get a bad taste out of her mouth.

"We see it the same way," Sarra told her. "Apart from the coercion charge, the rest of Mirya's case is easily dealt with, if I understand you correctly. And yet it's those other charges that are the most potent with the reactionaries."

"Who," said Telomir, "will despair all the more of the perilous state of our society when those charges are thrown out of court as irrelevant."

"A mess," remarked Elomar, with his usual succinctness.

"All we can do is let it play out," Cailet said. "Lenna, you defend Sarra and Collan every way you know how. Let me worry about Vellerin Dombur and Glenin Feiran."

"Now, that's the one person we haven't yet mentioned," Lenna said. "What's her stake in all this?"

"Sheer amusement," Collan growled, sloshing more brandy into his glass.

"I think she wants to be seen as the voice of reason." When Jored said that, everyone turned to stare at him. He glanced around the table, seeming slightly startled by his own boldness, but continued his thought at Cailet's nod of encouragement. "Lady Sarra and Lord Collan on one side, seen as radicals by the conservatives—Vellerin Dombur and Mirya Witte on the other, championing laws and customs everybody with sense knows were wrong. If Glenin Feiran takes the middle and says 'Preserve the best of the old, but treat husbands fairly—'"

"Then she'll go a long way toward establishing herself as an exemplar of moderation," Telomir said, "canceling much of the suspicion of her Malerrisi beliefs."

"No one ever said she was stupid," Pier said acidly. "Her letter to me was a work of art."

"Don't you go anywhere near her," Cailet warned.

"No fears, Captal—I'll hold my temper and my tongue. There are more important concerns here than my personal desire to strangle her with that octagon chain."

Lenna tidied papers and closed the portfolio on them. "I'm ready. I suggest the rest of you go to bed, get some sleep, spend a quiet day tomorrow, and on the seventh let me do all the talking—unless Mirya's Advocate calls you to the witness box, in which case say only what I told you to say during preparation. All right? All right. Prentice Mikleine, I have a few things about your testimony I'd like to go over again."

They left, and Sarra's gaze traveled slowly from face to face around her dinner table. Mikel, thoughtful and subdued; he hadn't said a word all evening. Next to him, Elomar, who'd said exactly two words that summed up everything: "A mess." Taigan had toyed with her food, barely glancing at Jored. Though Josselin's chair was empty, his humiliation lingered. Telomir, seated between Joss and Collan, was conscientiously pleating his napkin. Col himself, sullen and withdrawn, halfway through a third glass of brandy; beside him, Cailet had gone through twice that many cups of strong coffee and would probably be awake all night, doubtless her intention. Then came Lenna's empty chair, Pier's proud and defiant face, and Jored—who hadn't looked at Taigan either, as far as Sarra could tell.

Saints and Wraiths, what a cheery group! Rising, she

speared her sister with a stern look. "Cailet, don't you dare drink more coffee, you'll be up until dawn. Taigan, Mikel, it's past your bedtime, and *don't* tell me you're too old for a bedtime. You're not yet eighteen, I'm still your mother, and when I say go to bed, go to bed. As for the rest of you—you're all adults with presumably enough sense to follow Lenna's excellent advice and get some sleep."

"Yes, Lady," Telomir murmured with every indication of seemly masculine meekness.

When they were all gone but Collan, turning his brandy glass between his long hands, Sarra sat down again. "Well?"

"It *was* stupid of me," he said quietly. "I'm sorry."

"Neither of us ever thought it would come to this."

"No." He brought the glass to his lips but didn't drink. "I'll have to testify, you know. Lenna says it's inevitable. And up there in the witness box I'll offend just about everybody with my immodest, unnatural, unmanly ways. Y'know what I overheard the other day? I don't know who it was, I didn't recognize the voice. But she said, 'Don't be fooled by those sweet, submissive murmurings in public! Collan Rosvenir is a terrible example to our young men! Why, he seems to think he can pee sitting down!' "

"Col—"

"I haven't been the sort of husband you need, Sarra. Oh, not you personally, as a woman. I mean you as a Councillor and a Blooded Lady and all that."

"Don't make me say that you're the only husband I ever would have chosen. Don't make me say that if not for you—"

"If not for me you wouldn't be in a mess, as the eloquent Elomar rightly termed it."

"If not for you," she repeated deliberately, "I wouldn't be alive. And I don't just mean that you saved my life during the Rising. I mean that you showed me how to *live*. With everything Agatine and Orlin taught me, somehow they never got around to that. I suppose they thought I'd just learn it along the way—or find somebody to teach me, the way they taught each other. But you—" She dimpled. "You dragged me into it kicking and screaming." She saw his wide mouth curl into a hint of a reminiscent grin. "I love you, Collan. I wouldn't know how to live, without you. Everything I value most, you gave me." She got to her feet again, circled the table, and arranged herself quite deliberately in his lap. "Minstrel dear, if you want to pee standing up, sitting down, or into Vellerin Dombur's coffee cup, you go right ahead."

He gave in and smiled. "Don't tempt me, First Daughter."

Sarra traced the curve of his ear with a fingernail. "But that's what *I* do best."

11

ON Cailet's personal scale of desirable activities, attending Mirya Witte's appeal hearing before the High Judiciary was roughly equivalent to riding all the way from Ostinhold to Combel during an acid rainstorm. Dressed in her second-best regimentals, she went to the courtroom only because she couldn't avoid it. Lending the dignity of the Mage Captal's presence to the proceedings irked her; she must be seen to support Josselin, however, and through him the right of all Mageborns—female or male—to be trained in magic if they chose.

So on the morning of the seventh day of Ascension she chose an aisle seat near the back, arriving after Sarra, Collan, and Josselin, but before the crowd of spectators who crammed into the courtroom—an appropriately somber chamber lined in leather-bound volumes of the Statutes of Lenfell and decorated with a large map of the world to the right of the bench. The Seal of the High Judiciary hung above the bench behind the Justices' chairs: a spread-winged eagle above a thorn tree within a hollow circle, all of it in solid gold. The rest was oak paneling and benches, brass-railed witness box, and a podium of white marble reminiscent of the Speakers Circle

on the other side of Ryka Court. There were no tables or
chairs for Advocates and their clients; they were compelled to stand for the entire proceeding, on the theory
that sore feet equaled brief speech. Mirya Witte and her
Advocate stood on one side, Lenna Ostin alone on the
other, their backs to the audience as if no one else existed.

The clerk called for order. The Grand Justices entered: four women and one man, none under the age of
eighty, wearing brilliant crimson robes with their Seal on
heavy gold chains at their breasts. All the Justices were
members of formerly Blooded Names: Nunne, Doyannis,
Irresh, Feleson, and Maklyn. Cailet knew none of them
personally, and of their politics and prejudices knew only
what Sarra and Lenna had told her. Which wasn't much;
unless one had an appeal before the High Judiciary, one
never came into contact with its members, who were all
but invisible outside their courtroom. Most people
promptly forgot about them after final exams in the obligatory Government classes in school, except when a sensa-
tional case such as Mirya Witte's came up. The Justices
had nothing to do with the making of law, only with its
application, and whole years went by without their hearing more than two or three appeals.

Yet they had one very important privilege: their decisions were absolute and final. And they could base these
decisions on the Statutes or not, as they pleased. They
were beholden not only to the written law but to the un-
written code of morals and ethics and traditions—
whatever the individual Justice might conceive that code
to be. Which meant that they didn't get a lot of work
because, fearing their sometimes capricious rulings, people settled cases at a lower level. If the current sitting
Justices were fire-breathing reactionaries, Sarra and Collan didn't stand a chance and there was nothing anyone
could do about it.

The clerk bade everyone sit down—except the Advocates and their clients, of course—and read out a sum-
mary of the Roseguard proceedings in a deathly
monotone. Cailet supposed the emotionless recital was
designed to present facts in a nonprejudicial manner—but

not even wooden diction could disguise the horror of this crime.

"On St. Pierga's Day last Ellus Penteon husband of Lady Mirya Witte arrived at Roseguard with Lady Mirya's First Daughter and upon conveying said First Daughter to her mother's house himself went to the establishment known as Wytte's and thence to the Silver Tankard Tavern where at approximately Fourteenth of that night he was found in an alley outside said tavern, his purse and jewelry stolen, himself dead of a deep slashing wound to the neck and seventeen stabbing wounds to his body done with a knife."

Cailet had to admire the man's lung capacity, if not his implied punctuation; only now did he pause for breath, and hadn't paused at all for commas.

"The Roseguard Watch for reasons of the multiple wounds inflicted after the victim was already dying of a slashed throat concluded that the murder was done not for theft but for passion and subsequent questioning of witnesses at the residence of Lady Mirya Witte revealed firstly that she was unable to account for her whereabouts at the time of the death; secondly that her First Daughter had looked for Lady Mirya at Half-Thirteenth and again at Fourteenth and found no trace of her in the house; thirdly that a knife of the size and type that inflicted the stabbing wounds was missing from the kitchen on her premises; fourthly that a pair of black gloves reaching to the upper arms of the type worn on formal occasions was found in the laundry already having been washed and still damp. Upon this evidence being given in the Roseguard Court of the Shir Lady Mirya Witte pleaded justifiable manslaughter but was convicted on a charge of murder subsequent to which sentence was postponed subject to this present appeal before the High Judiciary. These are the facts of this case."

Amazing, commented Gorynel Desse. *Semicolons!*

I thought I heard periods.

I have ever regretted your deficiencies in grammar.

"Now come before Their Honors in this court is Lady Mirya Witte with her petition of appeal augmented by litigation against Senior Councillor for Sheve Lady Sarra

Liwellan and her husband Lord Collan Rosvenir for firstly felonious interference between Lady Mirya Witte and her husband Lord Ellus Penteon; secondly unlawful coercion and use of public position for personal gain; thirdly alienation of husbandly and daughterly affections; and fourthly instigating breach of contract between Lady Mirya Witte and the legal foster mother of Prentice Mage Josselin Mikleine."

My apologies, Gorsha, you were right. Definitely semicolons.

"To answer these charges against Councillor Liwellan and Lord Rosvenir is come before Their Honors *Domna* Lenna Ostin Advocate of Renig, The Waste. To present the appeal of Lady Mirya Witte is come before Their Honors *Domni* Chava Allard Advocate of Seinshir."

Geridon's Golden Stones! That's the young blacksmith—

Seems he's added the law to his other accomplishments. Shh. I want to hear this.

But nobody spoke, because at that moment Vellerin Dombur entered the court. All five Justices looked displeased at her untimely interruption, and even more annoyed when all eyes followed her ponderous progress to a front-row seat held for her by a flunky. She settled her considerable self on the bench, waving a hand to indicate the court could continue—and for a moment Cailet thought eighty-eight-year-old Justice Irresh would have an apoplexy.

Lenna Ostin, clad in a subdued gown of her family's gray with thin orange piping at cuffs and hem, took the white podium for an opening statement that refuted Mirya's accusations, using much more formal language than she had the other night. When she was finished, she called Lord Collan Rosvenir to the witness box.

He wore the most dismally sober clothing Cailet had ever seen on him: trousers, shirt, longvest (without sleeves), coif and boots in five exquisitely boring shades of brown. Not a single coppery curl escaped confinement; not a single piece of jewelry shone gold or silver from ears or throat or fingers.

A little ostentatious, don't you think? Gorsha commented.

The Grand Justices don't know him by sight, only by reputation. He's decently covered and modestly dressed, and that will influence them whether they know it or not.

Hmph, said Gorsha. *He'd better not look at them straight on, then. Nobody could mistake what's in those blue eyes of his.*

Lenna took him through the sequence of events in his brief acquaintance with Ellus Penteon—which gave her the opportunity to introduce evidence about the injuries Mirya Witte had inflicted on her husband. Collan spoke calmly and quietly, and when Chava Allard protested that his testimony was hearsay, Lenna had Col read aloud sworn statements by three Roseguard physicians. Justice Maklyn's ferocious silver eyebrows were bristling by the end of it, his wrinkled map-of-the-Kenroke-Delta face cramped so tight that there were white dents at the corners of his mouth.

"If it please Your Honors," Lenna said then, "I should like to recall this witness later, and now bring to the stand someone who will provide expert testimony regarding the medical questions in the case."

Collan resumed his seat in the audience next to Sarra; the clerk swore in a Ryka Court physician with credentials up one side and down the other. The most famous non-Mageborn physicker on Lenfell, Lusine Ferros was sixty-nine years old and had practiced medicine in seven Shirs, treated injuries resulting from everything from farm accidents to street fights, performed a thousand operations, set a million bones, and spent three years before her retirement to academic work as adviser to the Council on public health. She reviewed the pages read aloud by Collan, confirmed that the inquiries described were consistent not with accident but with attack, and added that in her learned opinion Ellus Penteon was lucky to have gotten his teaching job in Brogdenguard, far away from Mirya Witte.

"Protest, Your Honors! It is by no means established that Lady Mirya ever laid a finger on him, much less a fist!"

"Your witness, Advocate," said Lenna, and returned to her post near the podium.

Chava Allard stood with his tall, lean back to the audience, long fingers laced behind him. "*Domna* Ferros, these statements refer to three cracked ribs and a broken jaw. Could such injuries have been caused by a fall—say, down the stairs?"

"Not all at the same time."

"What about several falls downstairs?"

"Advocate, do you know anyone *that* clumsy?"

Justice Nunne smirked.

Chava Allard wasn't finished. "But if, for example, someone fell down a half flight or so, staggered to his feet, tripped, and fell again—"

"Or was pushed?"

"Your pardon, *Domna,* but I ask the questions here. Is it possible for these injuries to have occurred at the same time, by means of an accidental fall such as I have described?"

"Highly improbable. Ellus Penteon was by all accounts an athletic man."

"But it is *possible* that even such a man, when, for instance, under the influence of too much alcohol, might become clumsy?"

"The Roseguard physicians made no mention of intoxication when he was treated for his injuries."

"Do they mention that when asked about how he'd come by his injuries, he repeatedly told others that he'd fallen down the stairs?"

"No."

"Would you be so kind, *Domna* Ferros, to read aloud the following statements, sworn by several eminent citizens of Roseguard?"

She read, unwillingly. Cailet silently congratulated Allard on his cleverness in obtaining such documentation. When the physician had finished, Allard was finished with her, and Lenna strode to the podium again.

"*Domna* Ferros, in your forty-five years of medical practice, how many husbands whose injuries were obviously the result of physical attack in your expert opinion have ever admitted that any such attack occurred?"

"None."

"Not one? Can you tell us why?"

"The husband is ashamed of the incident, and moreover believes he brought it on himself—that it was his own fault. He is fearful of retaliation, and feels powerless. He has few legal recourses—and until and unless the abuse is proven and the law begins to protect him, he is compelled to remain in the household where further attack can occur at any time."

"And he never fights back?"

The physician looked shocked—and so did the Justices. "Of course not! We all know what the penalty is for striking any woman. Five public lashes on the first offense."

"And for a second offense?"

"I've never heard of a second offense. And very few instances of a first either. Men do not raise their hands against women."

"Quite so. Thank you. You're excused. If it please Your Honors, I will now call Lord Collan Rosvenir back to the witness box."

After a few more questions regarding Ellus Penteon's injuries, claims of clumsiness, and Collan's own reactions, she asked him why he had intervened.

"To keep the man alive."

"Protest, Your Honors. Speculation."

Justice Feleson shook her head. "I want to hear it anyway. Go on."

"I'm the husband of a Councillor. I have a passing familiarity with the law. Somewhere the Statutes say that every citizen has a right to be secure at home. To me, that means safe. Ellus Penteon wasn't. He was beaten on a regular basis. The last time—the one those medical reports are about—he was hit with something big and heavy, like the cudgels the Watch uses. His ribs could've splintered and punctured his lung. I *knew* he was in danger of being killed."

"So you helped arrange a prestigious position for him at St. Caitiri's, where he went with Lady Mirya's three daughters for their education—and with her complete approval. And kept it all quiet, as he obviously wanted."

"Yes."

"Thank you. No more questions."

Now it was Chava Allard's turn. He stroked his beard with a thumb for a moment, then said, "Lord Collan, I'm going to ask several questions that require only a 'yes' or 'no' answer. First, did you ever see Lady Mirya Witte strike her husband?"

"No."

"Did Ellus Penteon ever complain about her treatment of him in any particular?"

"No, but—"

"Did you ever hear Lady Mirya scold, chastise, humiliate, or become angry with her husband?"

"No," Collan replied tightly.

"Did he ever complain of verbal abuse on her part?"

"No."

"Did he have any explanation for his occasional bruises—such as a fall, or knocking into a door, or some such?"

"Yes."

"Were the bruises ever inconsistent with his explanations? In other words, was it physically apparent on his body that someone had been deliberately striking him?"

"I'm not an expert in medicine."

"Oh, I believe you have an opinion about this, given that you have opinions on everything else to do with the marriage of Lady Mirya and Ellus Penteon."

"Keep it civil, Advocate Allard," warned Justice Maklyn.

"Of course, Your Honors." The Advocate consulted his notes. "Did you visit Lady Mirya in her home to discuss the property known as Shore Hill?"

"Yes."

"Was a price discussed? A price lower than fair market value?"

"Lady Mirya was experiencing financial—"

"That doesn't answer my ques—"

"—difficulties and needed any money she could get her hands on. The price offered was fair enough—and she accepted it, didn't she? So she must've found it fair."

"If she didn't accept, you'd accuse her in court of

abusing her husband! Even though he made no public complaint, nor even complained in private to his friends, and all his injuries could be accounted for by—"

"—by being clumsy? Anybody that accident-prone couldn't even button his own longvest without breaking his fingers! She beat the shit out of him and everybody knows it—"

"Lord Collan, didn't you threaten to destroy Lady Mirya's good name and financial dealings if she refused to sell Shore Hill to you?"

"No."

Technically correct, Gorsha mused. *He didn't offer to buy it himself, he was acting on Miram's behalf. It's unlike the Allard boy to make a mistake. He's too clever.*

Mmm. Quiet, I'm listening.

"May I remind you of the penalty of perjury, Lord Collan?"

"I never offered to buy Shore Hill. Neither did I threaten Lady Mirya with financial ruin. She was doing a great job of *that* all by herself."

"No further questions."

Lenna Ostin read Mirya's First Daughter's affidavit into the record, told the court that never in the nearly twenty years of Lady Sarra's tenure as Councillor for Sheve had she ever used her public position for private gain—hers or anybody else's—and offered sworn statements to that fact by Councillors past and present (politely declined, out of deference to Lady Sarra; if she said she was honest, then the court would assume she was). Then Lenna reiterated her opening statement in abbreviated form, reminding the Justices that she'd shown a total lack of substantive evidence for any of Mirya Witte's charges. The "interference" had been nothing more sinister than offering Ellus Penteon a teaching position. That he had accepted and taken the three Witte daughters with him had been done with Mirya's agreement and approval.

Justice Irresh spoke for her colleagues. "We'll decide these charges after we've heard Lady Mirya's appeal. Advocate?" She looked at Chava Allard, who once more approached the podium. "You may present your case."

"Thank you, Your Honors. I call Prentice Mage Josselin Mikleine to the witness box."

Good-looking boy, no doubt about it—but a little ragged around the edges.

Cailet silently agreed with Gorsha. She knew she wasn't sleeping well; Josselin's slightly hollowed eyes showed he wasn't either.

"Prentice, when and where were you born?"

"One of the Equinoxes of 969, I'm not sure which. Or where. Probably The Waste."

"Probably?"

"I was orphaned as a baby, and it was a confusing time, what with all the refugees. A lot of families were separated, and a lot of people died."

"Do you know your Mother's Name?"

"No."

"So you don't even really know if you're a Mikleine."

"I'm sure I'm not. I was adopted by that family."

"And how many foster mothers took you in?"

"I don't know."

"More than two? More than ten?"

Josselin shrugged broad shoulders.

"So in effect, Prentice, you are Nameless, an orphan passed from family to family with no idea who you really are."

"Though I hesitate to contradict the learned Advocate, I know exactly who I am. A Prentice Mage."

"Of course. Your pardon." Long fingers smoothed the beard. "Now, Prentice, please contradict me further if I say anything inaccurate about the events of your seventeenth year. You caught the attention of Lady Mirya Witte, your foster mother, Geriana Escovor, contracted with Lady Mirya for your education at Lady Mirya's expense, you came to live in Roseguard, discovered you were Mageborn, and went to Mage Hall in late summer of 987."

"True."

"But because you're not sure which Equinox is your Birthingday, technically you were in breach of contract when you left for Mage Hall before the week of Autumn Moon. You were not yet eighteen."

"That's a matter of opinion. I might have been born in the spring."

"But you're not certain."

"No."

"So, I repeat, you were in breach of contract."

Josselin looked at Lenna; she said, "Protest, Your Honors. This is irrelevant. He didn't sign the original contract, being underage and thus with no legal authority to sign anything. If Lady Mirya sues anyone for breach and restitution, it ought to be Geriana Escovor."

"Agreed," rumbled Justice Feleson. "What's this to do with anything, Advocate?"

"Merely establishing that a contract did exist, Your Honors, and was not consummated."

Someone in the audience giggled.

"So to speak," Chava Allard added.

Now there was outright laughter.

"Get on with it," Justice Feleson growled.

"Now, Prentice, it is my understanding that you were to marry Lady Mirya."

"There was some talk of it," Josselin admitted.

"More than some, I should say. Did she love you?"

"You'd have to ask her."

"If she was willing to divorce her husband to marry you, wouldn't you say she must have been in love with you?"

"I suppose."

"Did she ever tell you so?"

"She may have said something like it."

"And yet you doubted her word?"

"I don't define love as possession."

"How *would* you define it?"

Justice Maklyn interrupted, shaggy eyebrows twitching irritably. "This is a courtroom, not a philosophy class."

"I was only trying to discover if Prentice Mikleine's definition of love applied to whatever feelings he had for Lady Mirya. Did you love her, Prentice, as you define love?"

"No."

"Were you willing to marry her?"

"No."

"And yet you *were* willing to accept her protection. You *were* willing to accept a snug roof over your head, good food on your plate, fine clothes on your back, and an expensive education in the manners and duties of a First Daughter's husband—all of which she paid for. You *were* willing to discuss marriage. And yet you did not love her."

"No."

"Why did you accept all this from a woman you didn't love?"

Josselin said nothing.

"The witness will answer the question," Justice Nunne directed.

After a moment, Josselin said quietly, "I was seventeen. I had nothing. No dower, no prospects, no craft, no Name. She was a Blooded Lady who offered my foster mother favorable terms with her Web if I agreed to be . . . taken under her protection. Geriana Escovor and her husband were good to me—they took me in when no one else wanted me."

"And I would imagine a big, strong youth such as yourself costs quite a bit to feed."

Joss ignored him. "I worked hard, but I couldn't begin to repay her—either in money or kindness. So when Lady Mirya's offer came. . . ."

Allard finished for him, "You took advantage of *her* money and kindness."

"If you want to see it that way—"

Chava Allard spread his fine hands wide, addressing the Justices. "Is there any other way *to* see it? He led her on, made her believe her love was returned, that he would become her husband—that he was, in short, a young man possessing all the masculine virtues of integrity, obedience, and honesty, as well as remarkable beauty. Instead, he turned out to be a liar, a cheat, and as rebellious as he was ungrateful after all she'd done for him."

Justice Irresh cleared her throat. "Is there a question for the witness anywhere in our future?"

"My question is this: Prentice Mikleine, did you always plan to defraud Lady Mirya, destroy her hopes, and break her heart, or did you get the idea after you met Collan Rosvenir?"

"I made no such plan. Lord Collan had nothing to do with anything, except that through him and Lady Sarra came the discovery that I'm Mageborn."

"And becoming a Mage Guardian was more important than becoming a husband to a kind and generous woman? Ah, but I forget—you never loved her, you never intended marriage. That will be all, Prentice. You may step down."

Caisha, that poor boy got mauled.

I thought he gave a rather good performance.

She expected Allard to call Lady Mirya to the witness box next. He did not. Instead, he addressed the High Justices in summation.

"Your Honors, for thirty-eight Generations we trusted the Bloods to do what was right, wise, and proper. Surely so many hundreds of years of inbred sagacity have a powerful influence on the thinking of our own Generation—it has not been so very long, truly told, since the Bloods and Tiers were abolished at the behest of Lady Glenin Feiran. Lady Mirya Witte must be understood in that context. Because a Blooded First Daughter is by the very reason of that Blood a more valuable person than any other, whatever she does for whatever reason must be more carefully considered than the actions and reasons of any other person.

"Even more important, however, is that she is a *woman.* Why else do we celebrate the coming of 'Wise Blood,' when a young girl leaves behind the amusements of childhood for the serious responsibilities of adult womanhood? We see here a First Daughter, yes; a Blooded Lady, yes; but most importantly, we see a *woman.* For Generations only women could own and manage property; only women could hold office and participate in civic affairs; only women could decide the great questions of power and faith and magic.

"Lady Mirya Witte was accused and found guilty of causing the death of her husband. Two hundred years ago she would never have been brought into court. Charges would never have been filed. Not because of any alteration in the laws or customs of Lenfell from that day to this—but because two hundred years ago, Lady Mirya would never have found *reason* to cause the death of her husband. Her husband would never have *given* her reason."

Two hundred years—around about Veller Ganfallin's era, shall we say?

He doesn't have to say it, Gorsha. The dates are in all the history books and we all went to school.

"Times were simpler then, more direct, less complex, and there were injustices. But I'm not sure that change is always for the better. And I am positive that in Lady Mirya Witte's case, too much change, too rapidly, too threatening to all she holds to be sacred and true—change caused the death of her husband."

Not bad, Gorsha remarked. *From blaming Sarra and Col, he's gone on to blame society at large. Vellerin Dombur must be hugging herself with joy.*

I doubt her arms can reach that far. And it's better than that. It's an indictment of all men who do so much as express an opinion of their own, as if they had brains to think with just like women do.

Careful, Caisha—you're starting to sound like a radical.

Fuck the "middle path" Telomir set me on twenty years ago! she responded venomously. *I know what's right and what's wrong, and I'll do what I have to—*

Even to murdering Josselin Mikleine or Jored Karellos without any proof of guilt?

"Now, there will be some who will say, 'The ungrateful villain deserved what he got.' Lady Mirya took Ellus Penteon from nothing—from poverty, obscurity, a life without prospects and without hope—and made him husband of a First Daughter, with the right to be called a Lord. She gave him three beautiful daughters to raise. She allowed him to work at a profession he enjoyed. Early in their marriage, she paid for further schooling that qualified him for that profession. She didn't believe in keeping her husband ignorant and simple. She agreed to his taking a prestigious position at St. Caitiri's, even though it took him far away from her—and her daughters with him."

You took both Jored and Josselin from nothing, didn't you, Cailet? You taught them, made them part of Mage Hall—and look how one of them repaid you. Is that how your thoughts go? Does one of those young men deserve to die because of what you think *he did?*

Gorsha, do *shut up,* she responded tiredly.

"And look how he repaid her, some people will say. They will say he was ungrateful in his independence and disobedient in his good fortune, taking all the advantages she offered and selfishly pleasing himself through them without thought to the pain it caused her. They will say he drove her to it—that he should be held up as a warning to other men similarly minded. They will even say that he deserved it because he was of a lower Tier and he dared first to marry a Blooded First Daughter and then to flout her will.

"I am not one of those who will say such things," said Chava Allard. "What I say is that Lady Mirya was left without anchorage in law. All she had was tradition and custom, and when she saw these things endangered by the behavior of her husband—" He broke off and clasped his hands behind his back again, shaking his head. "She is like a bird who nests comfortably in a particular tree with her chosen mate, raises her chicks, and is perfectly happy. And then one day she flies back to her tree to find it has been cut down, and lies dead in the forest, leaving her homeless and bereft and her children without a home. If the bird flies about in a panic, unable to comprehend the magnitude of her loss, then who can blame her?

"Ellus Penteon was her husband. There was a time when a woman had every right over her husband, including life and death. I do not urge a return to that time, but I do urge Your Honors to consider what effect nearly a thousand years of such rights have on a woman who tries to make her husband happy, only to find he wants more, and more, and still more.

"Contributing to her afflictions was Prentice Mikleine's treachery. Some of us may find it inappropriate for a woman of mature years to seek out a boy of seventeen, but a gap of even twenty years between a woman and her husband is not unusual. Indeed, it greatly benefits a man to marry a woman older and more experienced than he, so that he may learn from her.

"But Ellus Penteon—and, later, Josselin Mikleine— did not see themselves as having anything to learn. Penteon defied her, took her daughters from her home, lived apart from her for years. She eventually was unable to bear life without the comforts and consolations of a husband living in her home as a husband ought. She fell in love with a handsome youth, and took him under her protection with every expectation of marriage. I ask Your Honors to note that she did *not* initiate divorce proceedings against Ellus Penteon before ascertaining whether or not Josselin Mikleine would indeed marry her. It was, truly told, her intention to settle a certain amount upon Penteon, in addition to his salary at St. Caitiri's, and to allow him full visitation rights with her daughters.

"But she was betrayed by an opportunistic young man. Again, note that she did *not* divorce Ellus Penteon. She still had hopes of their becoming a family once again. In times past, he never would have left. But in these times, it was impossible for Lady Mirya to know exactly where she stood. Nearly a thousand years of tradition and Blood rights kept telling her there were certain things she should expect of marriage and a husband—and of a young man who willingly entered into her protection. The defiant disobedience of Ellus Penteon, the craven deception of Josselin Mikleine—these things shattered her inherent beliefs, and in her torment and confusion she acted upon her oldest instincts."

You know, it's quite amazing, Gorsha mused. *Here's an educated, clever man, arguing for the return of a social tradition that would never have allowed him to learn there even* was *such a thing as the law.*

At least he wasn't harping about Joss and Jored anymore. She decided to forgive him—it wasn't easy being mad at somebody who shared your skull—and replied, *Yes, it's been quite a show. But it's not yet over. Lenna's turn next.*

Don't these people ever get hungry? They've been at this since Half-Sixth and it's damned near Ninth!

She nearly laughed aloud. *Gorynel Desse, you're a Wraith! You haven't got a stomach to be hungry with!*

But you do, and if it doesn't get fed soon it'll start to growl, and then you'll embarrass me.

Don't be ridiculous—nobody even knows you're here!

That, he replied disdainfully, *doesn't matter. I know I'm here.*

Y'know, she teased, *I'm still trying to figure out why all those women found you so charming. I'm surprised any of them invited you to dinner, let alone into their beds.*

I resent that. And you're suspiciously cheerful, Capital.

Oh, I'm just a cheerful kind of girl. How many children were there, anyway?

Haughty silence.

Chava Allard was finishing up. "Circumstances for which she was not responsible led Lady Mirya to such frustration and unhappiness, and threatened her deepest beliefs so violently, that she felt herself cornered. Trapped. Unable to see beyond the source of her unhappiness—the man who should have been the joy and comfort of her life—she fixed on his removal from her life as a solution. Though we may not condone her killing Ellus Penteon, we cannot be so lacking in understanding that we do not know why she did it. And because of this, I humbly petition Your Honors to set aside her conviction and pardon her, for she was not responsible for what she did."

"Thank you, Advocate Allard." Justice Irresh lifted a glass of water with fingers skinny as sticks, sipped, and leaned back in her chair. "Advocate Ostin? Have you anything to add?"

"Nothing but this, Your Honors." Lenna didn't bother to take the podium. "I must say that it was an affecting image, that of the poor homeless bird who has lost her tree. But if I recall correctly, Lady Mirya not only allowed the tree of her marriage to Ellus Penteon to be chopped down—and sent to St. Caitiri's Academy on Brogdenguard—she imported a new young sapling to plant in its place. If she flew about chirping and squawking, she did so in private—and for almost seven years between the time Ellus Penteon left for Brogdenguard and the night she slashed his throat and stabbed him seventeen times." After a brief pause, she said, "I thank Your Honors for your attention."

At a signal from Justice Irresh, the clerk called for all to rise. The Grand Justices departed to chambers. Spectators filed out, discussing the proceedings in low voices—and Cailet was willing to bet that despite the many hours since breakfast, it would be a while before anybody could eat lunch. Lenna had left them all—including the Justices—with the image of Ellus Penteon lying in a dark alley in a pool of his own blood.

Cailet waited for Sarra and Collan near the back door. Josselin went past without even seeing her—head high, gray eyes glazed with weariness, mouth taut with strain. Cailet thought it genuine; Saints knew her own was real enough. Josselin was getting tired of playing his part, and Cailet was getting tired of watching him do it so well.

Would the same stress begin to show soon in Jored's face?

Which one of them was it? Damn it to All Saints, *which?*

Sarra and Collan approached, and Cailet fell into step with them, murmuring to her sister's husband, "Nice work—but aren't you utterly mortified by those clothes?"

He nearly snarled at her, sense of humor defunct. Sarra shot her a reproving look. She shrugged and accompanied them down the long corridors back to the Council's portion of Ryka Court, and Sarra's own suite. Tarise, hurrying back before them, had mulled wine waiting, saying it was guaranteed to cheer a dismal day. Cailet glanced out a window, startled to see rain. One could spend weeks inside Ryka Court without ever setting foot out of doors.

"*I* thought it went very nicely," Tarise said as she ladled their cups full. "And not just because we're going to win and Mirya the Mare is going to lose."

"Oh?" Cailet said, for lack of anything else, and almost burned her tongue on the wine.

"Yes," Tarise continued, determined to be optimistic. "It's a vindication of everything we ever wanted to change about the legal system. Listening to Lenna and that other Advocate argue their sides of the case—zealous defense and zealous prosecution, just what the judicial system ought to be."

"Wonderful," Collan muttered. "My taxes at work."

"What are you complaining about? I thought you came off rather well."

He almost snarled at her, too, and took his glass and his grumpiness over to the windows to watch the rain.

"How long before they reach a decision?" Cailet asked Sarra.

"Who knows? It could come tomorrow, or next week, or next Thieves Moon. They take their time and nobody rushes them."

"I hope the rain lets up soon," said Tarise. "They've asked Rillan to help with a hunt scheduled for the ninth, but he says if the ground's too soaked for a safe gallop, it'll have to be postponed a few days."

"Imagine my disappointment," Collan grunted over his shoulder.

"Nobody invited *you*," she snapped back. "And we have to do *something* around here while we wait for the Justices to hand down their aggregate wisdom—not to mention I don't intend to sit and knit socks while Vellerin Dombur and Glenin Feiran take their time doing whatever it is they came here to do."

"Any ideas what that might turn out to be, Cailet?" asked Sarra a bit testily. "Or are you still of a mind to let it happen as it will?"

She could have given a short lecture on the strictures imposed by her position and her ethics: that she could take no action until the enemy did. She could, for instance, kill Josselin or Jored now as a preventive measure, forcing Glenin's hand—but she had no proof. And even if she did, killing either was not an option unless he threatened her life, or the important lives around her. She was, in a word, stuck. But she said none of this. She only shrugged and took her cup of mulled wine with her for a walk in the soft, relentless summer rain.

12

THAT evening Glenin saw her son alone for the first time in more years than she cared to think about. She'd glimpsed him at the reception in the Malachite Hall, and watched him pass by at a distance with the Captal and the other Mages and Prentices. But now, tonight, she was alone with him, her emotion too deep for words.

They did not meet openly. They could not be seen together, and he'd told her the Captal suspected something. So they stood together beneath a dripping tree in the depths of the commons, where anyone could walk of an evening. Quite a few people did, even at this late hour. The air was still rain-misted, allowing the concealment of cloaks. She wished they could have met in the private Council Gardens, but too many people who could recognize either of them, despite their hoods, might be about. Though the light was bad, with only the dim glow of tall lamps to illumine the nearby paths, still she saw at once that he had grown more beautiful than ever. The practice of magic agreed with him.

She told him so when she finally found her voice. He laughed and gave her a full account of setting the Mage Globes at the Hall, and the Captal's deranged behavior over the sword, and apologized that he hadn't been able to kill everyone.

"You did brilliantly, darling. What did you think of the little courtroom comedy today?"

"Weaver have mercy, I'd rather not discuss it! But Chava was magnificent, wasn't he? By the way, when did he grow the beard?"

"This winter, and for the same reason I had *you* grow one before you met with your cousins that time."

"Of course, I should've realized." He put an arm

around her waist and leaned close, rubbing his cheek against hers.

"Mmm—smooth as silk," she purred. "You're looking remarkably well for all this time spent with the enemy."

"And you're as beautiful as ever. I've missed you so much!" He drew away, taking one of her hands. "So, Mother, what happens next?"

She smiled and with her free hand tucked a lock of hair back into his coif. "We've conducted our hunt, my love, and located the quarry. We've chased her to where we want her to be. And once she's cornered and helpless, then comes the kill." She described her plan—formulated many years ago with Saris Allard's help, honed and rethought and reworked and revised constantly since then, and now ready for culmination. Before she was halfway through he was grinning, white teeth flashing in the darkness.

"Perfect." He glanced around as someone hurried up the walk, and urged her more deeply into the sheltering trees. "I'd love to stay—it's been so long since we've talked, and I do miss you dreadfully—but I have to get back or my roommate will begin to wonder where I am."

"What do you think of him? Should we spare him?"

"He's an idiot," he said at once, then paused and added, "a magically gifted idiot, though. Spare him if you like—he may amuse you. At the very least, he can father a few Mageborns."

"I'll consider it." Glenin took his face between her hands; he closed luminous gray eyes and smiled. "I've missed you, too."

"Another week. Then we can be together always."

"Just be careful, darling."

He circled her wrists with his fingers, turned his head from one side to the other to kiss the hollows of her palms. "You, too, Mother."

And they went their separate ways back to Ryka Court, to anticipate the kill.

THE KILL

1

CAILET sat bolt upright in bed when the earthquake hit, grabbing frantically for something to hold onto. The "earthquake" grinned down at her, gave the carved bedposts another shake, and asked, "Planning to sleep all day, kitten?"

She fell back into the pillows, dragged the quilt over her head, and moaned. "Go *away*, Collan!"

"Come on, get up. Everybody's awake but you."

"Good for everybody," she muttered. Then, as the bed quivered ominously once more, she threw back the covers and sat up. "All right, all right! I'm awake!"

Col tossed her a bedrobe and wandered over to the windowside table, selecting an apple from the bowl of fruit left there. "Sun's shining, but Rillan's postponed the hunt until the eleventh. Not that he cares about the riders breaking their necks, but we're going after triplehorns." He said this as if it ought to mean something to her. When he saw that it didn't, he added, "They're smart, and lead the chase through the swampiest ground they can find. So we have to wait for things to dry out a bit."

"Oh." She slid her arms into the robe and rolled to her feet.

"Come on, it's too nice a day to sit indoors and wait for somebody to do something."

Cailet stretched, yawned, and glanced at the little gilt clock on the mantelpiece—Saints, nearly Seventh—before wandering over to inspect the fruit bowl. Nothing particularly appealed to her, but she picked up a bunch of grapes and began popping them in her mouth anyway. "I'm getting a little tired of pacing the Council Gardens, myself."

"You weren't there last night. I looked."

Cailet grimaced. "*Don't* tell Sirron or Ollia. Warrior-type Mages hate it when they don't know exactly where the Captal is at all times. I hiked halfway around the lake last night—felt like it, anyway—so I hope you're not planning anything too strenuous this morning."

"You frail little thing, you," he mocked. "Get dressed. The twins are waiting."

"And Sarra?"

He shook his head. "Meetings. This is Ryka Court, remember? She'll be with the Council from Sixth to Fourteenth." He didn't sound as resentful as he once had; Cailet surmised his own work with the Minstrelsy occupied so much of his time that he and Sarra were about even.

A short time later, Cailet was back on the shores of Council Lake, watching the trio race toward her across the beach. Col sprinted the last fifty feet and did a nosedive into soft sand (imported at great expense from a Seinshir island beach). Three steps behind him, his daughter attempted to avoid a suddenly out-thrust paternal foot, failed, and went sprawling. Mikel, a half-step behind Taigan, tried to swerve sideways on ridiculously short notice, only to have his ankle caught in his father's strong grip. He, too, measured his length in silky white sand.

Taigan levered herself up, whooping for breath. "No fair! You tripped me!"

"But you fell for it," Collan laughed, earning groans from his offspring. "Still think you can outrun the old man?"

"No, y'Lordship—not me, y'Lordship," Mikel panted piously.

Cailet strolled over to stand at the waterline. "You three have all the precision and grace of hobbled galazhi."

"What a sweet thing to say," Col observed pleasantly, and exchanged a quick glance with the twins.

Too late, Cailet backed off. Going down under a triple assault, she yelled a protest as they dumped her in the shallow surf. She struggled to her feet, spitting water, only to be caught behind the knees in a gentle wave that sent her staggering. She barely caught her balance in time, and glared, dripping, at her three grinning tormentors. Proximity to their father had evidently reinfected the twins with his total lack of decorum—but all at once Cailet cherished their rowdy spirits. When Taigan and Mikel were little, she'd been their adored Auntie Caisha. . . . Ah, but it was with their father that they played—Sarra said once that their favorite toy was Collan—not her. Not the Mage Captal. Still, she wasn't about to argue with the results. Saints and Wraiths, how she'd needed to laugh!

"What was that about precision and grace?" Col enquired.

Slicking wet hair back from her face, she concentrated for a moment. Collan blinked, developed a look of alarm, twitched a hand toward his groin, fisted his fingers, and at last was compelled by Cailet's playful—if slightly sadistic—spell to scratch.

"Damn it, Cailet—! Stop that!"

She opened her eyes to their widest and most innocent. "Stop what?"

Taigan and Mikel were howling with laughter. Cailet unWorked the spell—only to be rushed in a tackle that sent her and Collan into knee-deep water with a splash.

"Truce!" Cailet shouted, surfacing only to be pushed under again and tickled. When she came up once more, she went for Collan's ribs.

"Need some help?" Mikel asked his father.

"Doing fine, thanks." He twisted, and somehow Cailet found herself arcing over Col's shoulder to land flat on her back in the shallows. "No more magic?" Col asked warily.

"Would I do that to you?"

"Yes!"

She regained her footing, and lost it again as Col swept her legs out from under her. She lifted her hands in surrender, fully aware of the ludicrous picture she presented—sprawled in lapping waves, soaked to the skin—and not minding a bit. "I'm never setting foot out of my own rooms again without a Warrior Mage to protect me!" Then, fixing the twins with a terrible gaze, she demanded, "And what about *you?* Aren't you supposed to get into this on *my* side?"

"Against *him?*" Mikel shook his head. "Not if I want to live to see my eighteenth Birthingday."

Col held out a hand. Cailet took it, watching for signs of another somersault into the lake. He grinned, pulled her to her feet, and slung an arm across her shoulders as they staggered back up the beach. All four collapsed on a grassy hillock, and Cailet hauled off her boots and dumped the water from them—giving her sister's husband a sour look that inevitably dissolved into laughter. Col was as good for her as he was for Sarra; she could almost forget there were such things as threats and betrayals and murders by magic.

"Why don't you show some consideration for the old folks," Collan said to Mikel, "and get us something to drink from the boardwalk stands up there?"

"Old?" Mikel turned to his sister. "Did he say 'old,' Teggie?"

"I think so. Which old folks is he talking about?"

"Us, after that race."

"He cheated," Taigan announced.

"He *always* cheats."

Their father threw a handful of sand at them. "This is the respect I get? I thought I taught you some manners."

"Who, us?" Mikel's eyes widened. "Did you ever learn any, Teggie?"

"Not that I can remember."

"Well, find some, fast," Cailet said regretfully. "We're about to have company."

She nodded in the direction of the boardwalk, where a tall, stately blonde woman was approaching across the grasses. Mikel started to get to his feet, but Collan stopped him with a hand on his arm.

"Manners are the fool's refuge," Col said quietly. "You've got wits, both of you. Use them."

"Yes, Fa," Taigan murmured, green eyes glinting with the light of battle.

Glenin pretended very prettily to notice them, and portrayed surprise even better. Cailet consciously untensed her shoulders, forcing herself to lean back on her elbows with legs casually outstretched. Her eldest sister was impeccably dressed in casual plum-colored trousers and a white shirt, with leather sandals on her feet. Her hair was drawn back by a pair of silver clips that emphasized the gray of her gray-green eyes. Their father's eyes; Cailet remembered them in his face, filled with loving pride in her as he died for her sake.

She hadn't looked into Glenin's eyes since that night at the Octagon Court. Between the callow girl she'd been and the woman she was now had come twenty years as Mage Captal. Years of authority and power, of teaching young Mageborns the full use of their gifts, of anticipating this moment—not these precise circumstances, but this very instant when her eyes met her sister's. For Glenin, those same twenty years had brought the same authority, the same power, the same teaching. And the same anticipation. But Glenin was eager. Cailet was plagued by dread. And Glenin knew it.

"Good morning, Captal. Lord Collan. Lovely day, isn't it?" She appeared to notice their drenched clothing for the first time. "But perhaps I'm interrupting a lesson for your Prentices."

"Not at all," Cailet said smoothly. "We were only discussing tactics."

Col's voice was a classic drawl. "Nice day for it. Lots of examples to draw on."

"Indeed." Glenin smiled, deepening the lines framing her mouth and raying out from the corners of her eyes. Cailet was startled by the evidences of age—even more by the realization that Glenin would be forty-seven this year. She knew her own face had changed, that she also looked much older. But at not quite thirty-eight, she was still in the prime of her life. Glenin had passed it, and must see old age looming, and fewer years ahead of her than behind. She might present a serene face to the world, but within her the impatience must be growing.

"Speaking of examples," Glenin said, "the Captal seems constantly attended by such exquisite examples of masculinity! Including Lady Sarra's son, whom I'm delighted to meet," she added with a graceful nod for Mikel. "If it's permitted, I'd like to be introduced to the others so I may offer my compliments."

"I'm sure they'd be honored," Cailet said in a voice

to match her sister's for sweet insincerity. Taigan was frowning slightly at the oblique reference to Jored, but what annoyed Cailet was the implication behind *attended*. After what Glenin had done to her twenty years ago, she could hint that these exquisite young men were the Captal's lovers?

Glenin was smiling still, her eyes glistening as if at some private joke between herself and Cailet. "On the contrary, the honor would be mine. I should also be honored," she continued smoothly, "if at some point during my visit here Lady Sarra would consent to allowing Lord Collan to sing for me."

Col stretched his lips over his teeth and Cailet saw something dangerous and unpardonable coming. So before he could speak, she said, "His duties to Lady Sarra's Web are such that he has little time for music anymore."

"Indeed? A tragedy." Then her expression altered to one of sadness. "I was sorry to hear about Mage Hall."

I just bet you were. "Thank you," said Cailet.

"Have you any idea who was responsible? There's talk of a rogue Mage, succumbing to Wild Magic."

As if you don't know who did it. "Investigation continues," said Cailet.

"Will you rebuild?"

Collan answered that one in a properly controlled voice that nonetheless dripped acid. "The Malerrisi have tried to wipe out the Mage Guardians before. You haven't succeeded yet."

Glenin shook her head. "Those grievous years were Anniyas's doing. These days, we——"

"Only met her once myself," Col interrupted. "But once was more than enough. Whatever she touched, if she didn't kill it, she corrupted it. But you'd know—you were married to her son."

Score one for the Minstrel, Cailet thought.

"We are all fortunate to have survived contact with the late First Councillor," Glenin replied blandly.

"But the Captal *won*," Mikel said, blue eyes guileless.

"Yes, she did. And when she was about the same age

you are now." Glenin gave Cailet a respectful nod. "It's humbling to be in the presence of a legend."

Saints, how she hated being referred to as if she were a million years old and not quite real. It was time to end this verbal duel before somebody drew blood, and she'd never been opposed to a strategic retreat in good order. Accordingly, she glanced at the sun overhead and pulled on her boots. "Forgive us, but we do have appointments. Even though Mage Hall is gone, Prentices still must be taught."

"I'm sure that every moment with the Captal is a valuable lesson." She nodded again, her eyes laughing at Cailet, and continued her stroll along the beach.

"Delightful woman," Collan muttered as he got to his feet. "Utterly charming. It's going to be a real pleasure killing her."

Taigan frowned. "But—"

"But nothing. You don't think it'll end any other way, do you?"

"Then why don't we just have it out with her right now?"

"Because this whole mess has more twists than a back alley in Longriding."

"Fa—" Mikel hesitated, then went on, "Will it really come to a fight? Will we have to—"

Col ruffled his son's curls, bare to the sunlight and shining coppery-gold. "Whaddya mean, 'we'? You leave the fighting and the worrying to us old folks. That's what we're for."

Taigan sighed. "Old folks." Then, with a wicked grin, she sprang to her feet and called out, "Race you, Fa!"

2

" . . . ASSIST the unfortunate and disadvantaged if the same percentage of taxes as is expended upon them by each Shir was returned to each Web, so *they* could use it to—"

An explosive "Hah!" sounded from the far end of the Council's private conference table, startling Sarra from the random designs she was drawing on her notepad.

"You had a comment, Councillor Maklyn?" said this year's Chief of Council, Brishina Eddavar of Gierkenshir.

"She's joking, right?" Vasha Maklyn of Brogden-guard was a mere sixty-eight to her cousin the Grand Justice's ninety, but they had the same unmanageable white eyebrows and unmitigated disgust for pretension. Vellerin Dombur, four chairs away from Sarra, leaned forward and glared down the length of the rectangular table. Vasha glared right back down a long, narrow nose. "You really expect the Webs to take the tax money we refund to them and spend it on good works?"

"If it's made a matter of law. . . ." ventured the junior Councillor for Ryka, Miriel Gorrst. Sarra marveled that the same family could produce a vigorous lion like Imilial and a flinching lamb like Miriel. Her own junior for Sheve was a Jescarin—and the only thing glum and gloomy Deiker had in common with the blithe former Master of the Roseguard Grounds was a Name.

"It is my belief," intoned Vellerin Dombur, "that charity should not be coerced. Indeed, it must spring from the very deepest parts of our compassionate souls. Those less fortunate than we must be provided for, but how can the central government or even the Shirs know exactly what is needed in small, remote villages? Only the Webs who have family members there or who do business in such places can be certain of—"

"Lemme get this straight," interrupted Vasha Maklyn. "Webs're supposed to provide for all family members in the first place, right? But a lot of 'em can't, so you propose the rich Webs take up the slack by contributing the same amount of money the Council and Assembly and Shirs now spend on the indigent, right?"

"Yes."

A second emphatic "Hah!" made Sarra hide a grin. Vasha's frown drew her eyebrows into a single swath of white above her nose. "What world are *you* living in?"

"The world I would *like* to live in is one in which everyone fortunate enough to have a secure place in society also has the compassion to assist those less fortunate."

Sarra kept her face straight, but she was thinking, *Translation: everybody with her own specific pattern in the Great Loom, and those who don't fit are "assisted" out of it. Vellerin actually thinks she'll be directing the weaving. She doesn't know Glenin very well yet.*

"An admirable goal," said Councillor Eddavar. "And one we must be sure to work toward. But for the present, I believe the Public Aid Fund should stay as it is. Councillors? A voice vote will suffice."

They voted, and yet another of Vellerin Dombur's—and Glenin Feiran's—proposals was defeated. That made nine in the last two days, some of them critical points of law and governance, others with more philosophical than practical consequences. Vellerin seemed disappointed, but not overly so, confirming Sarra's opinion that she and Glenin had something in mind that would make all of these presentations, discussions, and votes meaningless.

The Council adjourned for lunch at a reasonable time—Half-Eighth—and as Sarra consulted with her junior she saw Vasha Maklyn trying to catch her eye. An invitation to lunch was accepted, and they walked through the halls talking idly of Sarra's children and Vasha's grandchildren. But once inside the suite—done in a sea-creatures theme as relentless as Cailet's birdcage—Vasha dismissed her servants so they could talk freely.

"Y'know," she said over shrimp casserole and salad, "I heard a story about Vellerin the other day. When she and her cousins were little, they'd play a game in the streets of Domburron. They'd pretend they were beating her up, and leave her sprawled on the pavement. A kind-hearted pedestrian would stop and bend over to help her—and she'd leap up and yell 'Surprise!' in her unsuspecting victim's face." She paused to sip wine. "These days I keep wondering when she's going to start playing dead."

"And which of us will try to help."

"Oh, I think we can count on Mittrian Shelan for that. He's a credulous little moron, truly told." She let out a snort of laughter. "Do you know, five years ago when we were overhauling the Web regulations for the millionth time, he actually believed that because I slept with him once I'd vote his way?"

"So how was he?" Sarra teased.

"Not worth the bother. Great body, but incapable of using it for anything inventive. Speaking of great bodies, how's that luscious lug of a Minstrel of yours?"

"Inventive, Vasha," Sarra purred. "*Very* inventive."

"You're merciless," she groaned.

"So's Brishina," Sarra said frankly. "She lets Vellerin speak her piece—barely—then cuts off debate and takes a vote. None of these proposals will ever get to the Assembly for discussion. And I don't think that's wise. It makes the Council look as if we're ruling Lenfell all by ourselves."

"Not to mention it gives the broadsheets the chance to editorialize pompously about free and open debate among the Assembly's three hundred and twenty-five, instead of our own paltry thirty." She poured more wine for herself and Sarra, shaking her head. "At least if things got to the Assembly, we'd have more time."

"For what?"

"To see what's really going on here. Tell me, Sarra, d'you think Brishina's rushing through things on purpose?"

She thought that over, sipping a crisp golden shabby—Vasha's family's private reserve from its vineyards below Caitiri's Forge—and at length said, "I've heard nothing of any lucrative new deals between their Webs. They trade, of course. We all do with each other to a certain extent. But nothing special is going on. And I'm fairly certain Brishina doesn't subscribe to the turn-back-the-clock theory. If not for profit or philosophy, why would she do it?"

"Well, if she's not working *with* Dombur, she's working *against* her—which is just as dangerous." Vasha ruminated for a time. "Have your husband's Minstrelsy nose around a bit."

Sarra pasted a blank look onto her face. "My husband's—?"

"Oh, please!" Vasha snorted. "My favorite grandson is strutting around Dindenshir this very minute, warbling lewd ballads in disreputable taverns by night and spying for your husband by day!"

"I didn't think you knew—and I'm sure Collan will be annoyed that you found out." Sarra smiled. "And even more annoyed to hear you called it 'spying.' How did you learn what Savachel's up to?"

"His postage bills to his cousin at Mage Hall are a family scandal." Her dark eyes gleamed merrily below bristling white brows. "The very least Collan could do is reimburse us."

"I'll discuss it with him!" Sarra laughed. "Speaking of my husband, thank you for lunch but I really must go. I haven't seen him in two days."

"As if when you get him alone you spend the time *talking!*"

Sarra laughed. "Normally, no! But when I get back at night from meetings, he's asleep, and when I leave in the morning for more meetings, he's *still* asleep!"

"Well, go find him while he's awake, then, and give him a flourish for me. Are you hunting on the eleventh? There's a little farmhouse not five miles from the proposed route—and the farmer cooperatively vanishes after you contribute an eagle or two to her coffers."

"I'll keep it in mind," Sarra promised, returning Vasha's grin.

Not even Tarise knew where Collan and Cailet and the twins had disappeared to for the day. Feeling lonely and left out, Sarra spent the afternoon going through her mail—mainly letters from Roseguard about the Slegin Web that Col hadn't had time to deal with yet. But there was one envelope with a return address she didn't recognize, and on opening it she could scarcely believe what she read.

The First Daughter of the Liwellan Name was coming to Ryka Court. Sarra, who had never even met another Liwellan, always thought of *herself* as holding that position. But in fact she was legally beholden to the Cloistered ancient who had decided to come visit.

Since the Thirty-Eighth Census in 950 the family had thinned from nearly a hundred members to just forty: fifteen adult women (four childless, three whose daughters had died, and eight who had borne only sons), eighteen adult men (eleven married, seven elderly widowers), five unmarried boys (including Mikel), and Sarra and Taigan. Gorynel Desse had chosen that Name because there *were* so few of them. Of course, that worked in reverse as well: the fewer the members of a Name, the greater probability that they all not only knew each other but were very closely related. The Liwellans, however, were the exception: scattered all over Lenfell, the common ancestor dated all the way back to the Thirty-Second Census in 800. So there was small chance of Sarra's ever meeting another Liwellan, and even less chance of her status as one of them being questioned; the branches were few and thin. Presumably, at the time of Ambrai's destruction Desse had also had some sort of secret agreement with the Liwellan First Daughter, distant cousin of the present eighty-year-old who was now coming to visit Sarra. And, after a moment's thought, Sarra knew why.

The venerable Lady Alinar had for the last thirty years lived at The Cloister, glad to leave the running of the negligible Liwellan Web to her granddaughter, dead this winter in a carriage accident with her daughters, the last two unmarried girls of the Name. Thus Alinar was coming to Ryka for a look at Taigan, on whom hope of the Liwellans' survival depended.

Alinar's mother had died in 958, taking with her the secret of Sarra's irregular membership in the family. There had been polite letters congratulating her at her marriage and at Taigan's birth, acknowledging her yearly contribution to the Dower Fund, and announcing family marriages, births, and deaths—sometimes a year or more after the event, as the Liwellans were not a closely woven Web and communicated with each other only as strictly necessary.

But now Lady Alinar had left The Cloister and was on her way to Ryka Court, wishing to inspect the last Liwellan daughter. Sarra sighed and wondered how soon she could push through legislation to permit transfer of a dying Name to a woman descended from that family through a male of the line. A third or fourth daughter could easily be spared from their mothers' families to continue their fathers' Name.

Sarra had been fighting battles over inheritance laws her whole public life, first addressing the Council twenty years ago when Lady Agatine petitioned to make Sarra her heir. She'd felt guilty then over what she saw as robbery from the Slegin boys, and felt guiltier now over her false status as a Liwellan. And that wasn't even considering what Taigan would say when she realized she was expected to breed up lots of daughters to replenish the Name. With another sigh, Sarra set Lady Alinar's letter aside in favor of less troublesome correspondence.

At Twelfth she was still working, and still alone in her suite. When the wall clock chimed the hour, she stretched, yawned, and decided she'd had enough and wanted some fresh air. After changing into casual trousers and shirt, she wandered the Council Gardens, pausing to admire the sunset. The sky was a hundred different shades of rose, to which a few downy clouds added accents of ruby-red and gold. Sarra sat for a time on a wooden bench, alone with her memories of how astonished Cailet had been when first shown these gardens, so wholly different from the bleak landscape of The Waste. She recalled, too, how much fun it had been introducing her little sister to the civilization and culture that The Waste so thoroughly lacked. Sarra still rebelled at circumstances that had forced an Ambrai, a granddaughter of Lady Allynis, to grow up in a provincial backwater without the education and privileges that would have given her confidence in herself. Operas, concerts, plays, books, restaurants, conversation—with wide-eyed relish Cailet devoured new experiences, as long as Sarra or Collan had been there to guide her through them. Even so, she always escaped as quickly as possible from Ryka Court, her shyness unable to support the attention the Mage Captal always attracted.

Rising from the bench as dusk deepened, Sarra thought of returning to her suite—the air grew chilly with the evening breeze off the lake—but instead resumed her wandering. After a time she caught sight of a faint glow down by a copse of white poplar trees. A Mage Globe—and to judge by the pure silvery-white of the light, Cailet's. As Sarra approached, she saw that Cailet was giving Josselin Mikleine a lesson in self-defense. Their audience was Taigan, Mikel, and Jored Karellos; as Sarra neared, Mikel turned and smiled, moving to one side on a stone bench to make room for her.

She sat, glancing at her daughter and Jored on the opposite bench, and wondered if perhaps Taigan wouldn't be so hostile after all to the idea of marriage and daughters. Then, with a mental admonishment not to be an interfering mother, she watched the lesson.

Cailet took Josselin through several basic challenges and responses, using barely glowing Globes that held nothing of real power in them. It was more of a dance than a training session, the spheres glancing off each other, their light muted and mellow. Sarra was pleased to see that Cailet was relaxed and easy in her movements and her magic. Josselin was more tense, and after a time caught his lower lip between his teeth in the effort to concentrate.

All at once one of his Globes burst in a shower of gold sparks, and he flinched back with a startled exclamation. Cailet's Globe immediately extinguished, and she folded her arms and shook her head.

"Stop *thinking* so hard," she said. "Listen to your magic, let it anticipate for you."

"Yes, Captal," the young man said, doubt shading his voice.

"There's a kind of rhythm to it, like swordskill," Cailet went on. "But only the greatest are as one with their blades, whereas magic is always an expression of the self."

"The colors?" Josselin guessed.

"Partly. They're an indication of emotion and intent. That last one of yours was tinged with scarlet, which showed you were getting annoyed—but there was also a flash of muddy green and that meant you were getting tired."

Sarra, who had seen neither color, was impressed anew by her little sister.

"I couldn't relax into it," Josselin admitted.

Cailet shrugged. "If you had, you'd be capable of going on all night."

Sarra hid an untimely grin at the thought of the ribald reply Collan would make to that.

Cailet turned, nodded to Sarra, then looked at each of the three other Prentices in turn. "Well? Who's next?"

Mikel sighed, got to his feet, let his cloak drop to the bench, and said, "Everybody stand back. I'm not very good at this yet."

"Why do you think the whole copse is Warded?" Cailet asked, smiling.

Sarra saw in her son's face that he didn't know enough to know that Sarra should have paused at the Ward; only family could walk through each other's spells so easily. She supposed that if anyone asked, Cailet would explain that as she worked with Josselin, she'd sensed Sarra's approach and adjusted the Ward accordingly.

But that led Sarra to wonder how so many people had walked so freely through the Wards around Cailet's rooms at Mage Hall that horrible night of St. Maidil's. The Wards were keyed for Marra and Aidan, of course; Taigan and Mikel were family, though they didn't know it; but what about Josselin and Jored?

It hit her then, right in the stomach, twisting her insides: *One of them is family. One of them is Glenin's son.*

No. Impossible. But her instincts were screaming at her, so fiercely that she felt dizzy, ill, the small glowing spheres conjured by Cailet and Mikel suddenly so bright that her eyes burned.

One of them is Glenin's son. My nephew.

She squeezed her eyes shut and breathed with exquisite care. It didn't help. Denial was frantic within her mind and heart.

One of them destroyed Mage Hall. One of them killed all those people.

She felt a terrible quaking begin deep inside her bones, and locked every muscle taut to prevent a convulsive shiver.

One of them is courting my daughter.

She forced her eyelids open, aware that someone was staring at her. Josselin stood by a tree, a bewildered frown shadowing his moonstone-gray eyes. Jored sat beside Taigan, and his eyes were wide open and silvery in the dusk and the glimmer of the Mage Globes.

And at her breastbone, next to the tiny birthmark (*"Where a Saint kissed you to start your heartbeat, Sasha love"*), the little Globe Cailet had given her long ago was a shard of ice against her skin. She was in the presence of threatening magic and she didn't know from whom it came. Despite her efforts, she did shiver, and the chill glass sphere trembled with the pounding of her heart.

Then there was warmth around her shoulders. Jored had come to her side, and draped his cloak about her. She couldn't thank him, couldn't even look up at him. The warning cold at her breast was suddenly gone.

Him? Or the other? Does Cailet know? Of course *she knows, damn her! Why didn't she say anything?*

"If I knew, I'd kill him."

She's not certain which it is, any more than I am.

Sarra made herself look at each young man. But as relentless as her instincts had been a few moments ago, now they were silent. And the little glass ornament beneath her shirt was only an ornament, warm now with the warmth of the cloak she clutched around her—certainly not with the warmth of her shivering body.

Mikel begged off further instruction, claiming that if he tried one more time to increase the size of his Mage Globe without increasing its power, he'd incinerate himself—and, more vitally to the son of Collan Rosvenir, the brand new sleeved longvest Fa had given him. Cailet dismissed her Prentices with a smile and came to sit beside Sarra.

"Why didn't you tell me?" Sarra asked quietly when they were alone. "Which of them is it, Cai? Josselin or Jored?"

Cailet stared into the blackening distance. "I don't know."

"Which of them betrayed you, killed all those people—*which of them is Glenin's son?*"

"I don't *know*—not for certain, I can't prove it—"

"Proof?" Sarra gaped at her sister. "You suspect one of them, you're sure in your own mind of which, I can see it in your face—and you're waiting for *proof?*"

Cailet leaped to her feet. "And what would you have me do? Would you order Vellerin Dombur assassinated for what you *suspect* she wants to do? Would you have us all return to the good old days she wants to bring back, when her ancestor had all rivals in the Dombur family killed because she *suspected* them of disloyalty?"

"One of those men butchered Mages and Prentices and children—"

"And one of them didn't! What if I'm wrong? What if I suspect Jored, when it's really Josselin? Or Joss, if it turns out to be Jored?"

Sarra blanched when she heard which name Cailet spoke first. "Jored? Is he—? Cailet, Taigan's half in love with him—"

"I don't *know!* I told you before—if I *did* know, I'd kill him!"

Sarra tugged at the chain around her neck. Drawing the glass sphere from her shirt, she held it up in the darkness and said, "When I realized a little while ago who one of them must be, they both looked at me—and this turned to ice. Then Jored put his cloak around my shoulders, and the cold from this was gone."

"Is it him?" Cailet said for her. "Sensing your emotions because you're his aunt, forming some kind of connection that triggered the Globe—and then severing it? Or was it Josselin, from a distance, feeling that you knew something—and then repressing his magic?"

"It could be either," Sarra replied numbly. "It could have happened either way."

"And now you see why I'm not sure which of them

it is. I feel filthy suspecting either of them, even though I know it has to be one of them. I *saw* Josselin return early to Mage Hall that night. I didn't see Jored do the same, and neither did Taigan—but that signifies nothing. They both survived. You'd expect that, of Glenin's son." She paced a few short, sharp steps, then spun around. "I *taught* them, Sarra—they sat with me beneath the oak and listened to me, questioned me, *learned* from me—and turned what they learned against me."

"He already knew," she murmured. "He came to you, knowing."

"Josselin saved my life, did you know that? That poor little boy Collan brought me last year—his magic went Wild and he attacked me, and Josselin took up my sword—" She choked on the rest.

"Caisha—" Rising, she put her arms around her sister. Cailet tried to shrug her off; Sarra held fast. At length the thin, tense body seemed to wilt, and Sarra rocked her as if she were still a little girl—the child-Cailet Sarra had never known.

"I want to kill him," Cailet whispered against her shoulder. "If I could only be certain, I *would* kill him for what he's done."

"I know, dearest."

"But I can't. Not until I'm sure. He has to do something, say something—*anything*—that would—but he'd know it the instant I *knew,* and Ward himself so that not even I could—"

"Hush."

"He murdered them, Sasha—in their beds where they slept, in their cradles—he killed Gransha, who loved me—I never knew it until the moment he died, but he *loved* me—"

"I know."

"How could you know when I didn't?"

"It doesn't matter. Caisha, you were right. We must let this play itself out. There'll be proof, just as there'll be proof of what Vellerin Dombur plans, and what Glenin's purpose here is, and when there is and we *know,* when we're *certain*—"

"—then *we'll* become murderers, just like the Malerrisi we despise."

"No. There will be justice, and retribution. And if they die as they deserve, I won't waste any tears. I'm not especially civilized when it comes to my daughter, or my son, or my sister."

Cailet shook her head, but did not leave the shelter of Sarra's embrace. After a long time in the darkness, they turned as one and slowly made their way back through the Council Gardens, and separated in silence.

3

"WHAT I *still* don't understand," Collan said as he yanked on his boots, "is why the Council's giving Dombur a hearing in the first place."

Sarra twisted the long rope of her braid into a tidy knot at the nape of her neck, securing it with a mouthful of hairpins. "Appeasement," she replied succinctly.

"Give her some of what she wants and hope that satisfies her?" He shook his head. "Stupid idea. Like a little girl who asks for candy and gets it, she'll always be back for more."

"I agree. We haven't given her anything she wants, so she's starting to get frustrated." She paused. "At least, she *ought* to be frustrated. She's not. She's waiting for something."

"Glenin Feiran's move."

"Probably." She slid a pair of tiny silver hoops into her ears, not wishing to lose anything larger or more expensive on the hunt. "If only we could figure out what that will be."

"Any ideas from the other Councillors?"

"Nothing substantive. Senasta Dombur keeps smirking behind her hand, or so Granon Isidir says—he sits opposite her at the far end of the table. We compare notes on who reacts how to what."

"Convenient," he remarked. "Maybe I should get myself elected to the Council, so *I* can have intimate private meetings with you, too."

"Minstrel mine," she laughed, plying her dimples at him, "I sincerely doubt we'd ever get around to discussing business!"

He said nothing. He sprawled across a nearby chair, elegant in fawn-colored riding leathers, one long leg hooked over the chair arm. All his dichotomies were visible in his position and expression: a pose that should have looked awkward but was instead inherently elegant; eyes that saw with piercing clarity even when they sulked; a cynical twist to lips that never lost their tender curve; lean body casually slumped yet constantly alert.

"You're being ridiculous," she chided softly.

"Ah, but you *expect* me to act jealous, and I learned long ago that it's always wise to oblige a lady." He rose and brought her boots over, kneeling to help her on with them. "What's Cailet say about Dombur?"

"Let it play out. I've come to see the wisdom of her way of thinking—more or less," she added wryly as his brows arched.

"So we all make nice on the happy hunt, and hope somebody doesn't 'accidentally' shoot an arrow our way."

Sarra shrugged. "I don't intend to be anywhere near the hunt. I've heard about a little cottage along the way, owned by a very obliging farmer—"

Taigan's entrance interrupted her. "Mother, there's a woman here to see you—she says she's the Liwellan First Daughter."

"She is." When Taigan's green eyes widened, Sarra added, "I hope you remembered your manners. She's here to look you over, you know."

"How could I know?" Taigan complained. "Nobody ever tells me anything. And why would she want to—oh, Saints!"

"Uh-huh," Col said, not without sympathy.

"Lady Alinar's early—I didn't expect her until tomorrow," Sarra went on. "Well, that's the end of the hunt for me." She extended one leg so Col could remove the boot he'd just put on it. "Teggie, find me something else to wear, quick, then go tell her I'll be with her directly."

"I'll play lady's maid," Collan offered. "Go charm Lady Alinar, pixie."

"Oh, thanks! I love you too, Fa!" Taigan stuck out her tongue at him, grinned, and departed. A few minutes later, Sarra's riding clothes had been exchanged for a turquoise silk dress and soft leather slippers. She added earrings and a bracelet of lapis, complimenting her visitor by wearing the Liwellan colors.

"Nice," Collan approved—he never let her out of their bedroom until he'd evaluated her clothing. "Could use a little something in your hair, though."

"Bring me back a talon, and I'll have it made into a comb," she teased.

He snorted. "I don't need to find an eagle's claw to win me my own true love. Though I suspect Taigan will be scouring the forest floor. I wish Mikel would find somebody, too."

"I don't."

"What's the matter, Sarra? Going all motherly?" He smiled and tapped her nose. "Maybe a bit jealous yourself at the idea you wouldn't be the only woman in your son's life anymore?"

"Not at all," she replied serenely. "It's only that I'm *much* too young to be a grandmother." The wall clock sounded Half-Fifth. "You'll be late for the hunt, and I should go rescue Taigan from the appraisal."

"They can wait."

And for the next few minutes, time didn't matter in the slightest.

Someone knocked on the door—probably a servant sent by an increasingly desperate Taigan—and Sarra drew reluctantly out of her husband's arms. "You know," she said, bending over at the dressing table mirror to tidy her hair, "I won't mind not being the only woman in Mishka's life one day—just so long as I'm always the only one in yours."

"Truly told?" He wore that whimsical, crooked little smile that had felled women from Dindenshir to The Waste, and she simply had to kiss him again.

"Never more truly." Then, with a private promise to find that cottage *very* soon, she went to greet her august visitor.

4

"THE main objective, my dear," Lady Alinar said, "is to find a man who reacts the right way when you tell him to sit down and shut up."

Taigan blinked.

Fine-boned, with skin fine as parchment and gestures as wispy as the pale gray silk shawl around her shoulders, Lady Alinar Liwellan sipped daintily at the tea in a Rine porcelain cup before continuing her lecture. Every time she moved, Taigan nearly flinched, for the thick curls piled atop her head seemed too heavy for so delicate a neck to support. It was amazing hair, like spun silver without a trace of white; unpinned, it must fall to her hips—quite a distance, for she was a tall woman. Indeed, she seemed made entirely of silver, hair and gray eyes and the sheen of her plain, high-collared dress. Even her voice was a melody of thin silvery wind-chimes. In her high-nosed, heart-shaped face could still be seen the great beauty she had once been, and in her sudden quirk of a smile was yet a hint of a winsome, flirtatious girl.

"Some men," said Lady Alinar, "will do exactly as told and never think a thing about it. Avoid them at all costs. Nothing more boring than marriage to a sheep! And nothing more depressing than to become mother to meek little lambs just like him. Some men will indeed sit down and shut up, but resent you for giving the order. Avoid them, too. Any man without the spirit to speak his mind isn't worth allowing into your home, let alone allowing to father your children. Now, some will shut up but not sit down, indicating thereby displeasure at your command, and some will sit down but not shut up, and neither kind has any manners, and your children won't learn any either. And if he'll neither sit down *nor* shut up, he's too contentious to live with and will father noisy, disobedient, regrettable offspring."

Confused, Taigan ventured, "But that's the end of the options, isn't it?"

"Not at all." Alinar laughed soundlessly. "You've forgotten the kind who will simply walk out of the room!"

"And that's the kind of man to marry?"

"Gracious St. Gorynel, child, of course not!" Lady Alinar sipped again at her tea, silver curls gleaming as her head moved on a long, exquisite neck.

Hopelessly bewildered now, Taigan could only stare.

"Consider, my dear. What kind of man *requires* being told to sit down and shut up?"

Suddenly Taigan laughed. "The kind you shouldn't marry in the first place!"

"Precisely." Her eyes danced merrily. "Have you ever heard your mother say such a thing to your father?"

"Not in a million years."

"So. A man with manners enough not to need correcting, who knows when to talk and when to stay quiet, but who will inform you in no uncertain terms of his opinions. That's the kind of man you want—and few of us are lucky enough to find."

"That's very good advice, Lady Alinar," Taigan said. "I'd never thought of it quite that way before."

"Most young girls don't, until it's too late. May I trouble you for some more of this excellent tea, my dear? And after your mother comes, I promise you'll be released to join this hunt that sounds so enjoyable."

Taigan was beginning to think the hunt would not be half so enjoyable as a morning in the Lady's company, and so it was with mixed feelings that she saw her mother enter the room. Staying long enough to hear herself declared a good, sensible girl by Lady Alinar—and to see her mother give her a sidelong glance of wry approval—she politely withdrew and went to the courtyard. Mikel held her horse, a fine smoke-gray Tillinshir hunter borrowed from the Ryka Court stables and grudgingly approved by Rillan Veliaz for her use. Brother and horse both were chafing at her lateness.

"This is the end of my obligations for the day," Mikel warned as he boosted her up into the saddle. "If you expect me to rein in so you can keep up, forget it."

"Try and keep up with *me*," she retorted, fingering the saddle-charm tied to the pommel. Geranium leaves for protection, a sprig of cedar for strength, and two roses— one red for love, one yellow for perfection. The whole was secured with humbly anonymous white string, but the colors told her who it was from.

Mikel sighed a vastly tolerant sigh. "Guess who."

"I can't imagine," she said demurely.

He gave a complex snort and vaulted easily into his saddle. "The string's white—you could always say it's from one of the Domburs," he said as his parting shot, and heeled his stallion into a canter out the courtyard gates.

They'd found a horse for Vellerin Dombur to ride. A gelding half-Tillinshir and half-Clydie with hooves that could fill soup tureens, it lumbered along at a gait made remarkable for speed as well as thundering awkwardness. Her Ladyship had packed herself into riding clothes of sulfurous yellow, an orange scarf tied under her chins to secure a towering black hat. Looking at her hurt Taigan's eyes; she could just imagine what her father would say about this ensemble. The rule in a hunt was to wear bright colors so there could be no accidents in the woods. The field was gaudy in reds, blues, and purples. Taigan herself wore a turquoise shirt and shortvest, and even the Captal had abandoned her usual black for an outfit of bright crimson. But Vellerin Dombur's attire seemed calculated not only to alert other hunters to her presence but to terrify any animal in a ten-mile radius.

Clattering from the courtyard down to the lake, the riders had attracted cheers from passersby and the traditional calls of "Good hunting!" and "Fielto favor you!" It would have been more appropriate to hold the hunt on the Saint's Day, but that was weeks ahead and Gery Canzallis, Director of Diversions, was a passionate equestrian who damned well wanted a hunt, out of season though it was.

"Do them all good to get out of this hothouse," she'd told Rillan when enlisting his aid, "into the fresh air, clear their heads of politics, see the world as it is instead of how they want to see it." So hunting they went, and as Taigan cantered up to join her father and brother, she was glad of it. She had a fine mare, a whole day ahead of galloping across the hills and through the woodlands, and the blessed prospect of leaving all troubles behind at Ryka Court.

And, just maybe, some time alone in the forest with Jored.

5

"GRACIOUS St. Gorynel, you do lead a busy life, my dear Sarra! Mine is so placid at The Cloister, all this talk of politics and government and scheming quite exhausts me—though I'm glad the Liwellans have so eloquent and influential a voice." Lady Alinar paused, pale eyes suddenly twinkling. "Even if you're not, strictly speaking, a Liwellan."

Sarra allowed not a flicker of reaction to show on her face as she tried to think up something to say. Alinar spared her the necessity.

"Of course, neither am I."

This time, despite her best efforts, Sarra felt her jaw drop. Happily, her teacup did not—though it was a near thing.

"Alinar Liwellan is a cherished friend who allowed me to borrow her identity for this journey. She hasn't been outside The Cloister in thirty years, so there's no risk of anyone's discovering my little imposture. I *do* live at The Cloister, under another Name not my own—you'll forgive me if I don't share it with you, my dear."

Her smile was so warm and intimate that Sarra forgave her on the spot, no matter how loudly curiosity clamored for satisfaction.

"I'll add that I've Warded this room against ears that shouldn't hear what we say."

Now Sarra was truly in shock. This woman was Mageborn? A Mage Guardian, living in retirement at The Cloister—

But there was more than one kind of Mageborn.

Instantly she dismissed the notion. This woman was no more a Malerrisi than Cailet was. The magic Sarra barely knew how to sense held the distinct overtones of a Mage Guardian in its application of Silence to the sitting room. Besides, the tiny glass sphere over her heart was warm, not icy cold. And she trusted it more than she trusted her magic—but not more than she trusted her own instincts, which said this woman was her friend.

"So we can speak freely, of things that haven't been spoken of in many long years—not since Alinar confided to me the deception of the Name." She leaned forward to put her teacup down. The action dislodged the gray silk shawl, and as she wrapped it around her again Sarra saw that the decoration was on the underside—black and gold and silver embroidery finely done but randomly patterned.

When the old woman sat back again, her aspect had altered. All the spun silver had changed to steel. "Sarra," she said, "you are in more danger than you can be aware of."

Sarra placed her own cup on the table, hearing the porcelain rattle. "Lady, tell me what you know."

6

THE forest-dwellers in the hills above Council Lake fed peacefully in the morning stillness, concerned only with the summer bounty. Jumpmice taught their nestlings how to leap high for choice insects; rainbow beetles the size of a man's fist scuttled along, looking for unguarded late eggs; red-dappled squirrels raced each other around and around the trees, almost forgetting in their fun that they'd come for the best new nuts and seeds. Birds spun in and out of the branches, feathers flashing in glints of bronze and green and gold. Presiding over all were triplehorn deer, grazing on lush dewy grass and flowers.

Mikel had only seen pictures of them, and cherished no great hopes of actually viewing one today—the hunt was too large and made too much noise. But Gery Canzallis knew her business, and at the forest's edge had split the field into a dozen groups of eight or nine each to minimize their noise and fuss. Mikel rode with Taigan, their father, the Captal, Jored, Josselin, Granon Isidir—and Chava Allard and Glenin Feiran. It hadn't just fallen out that way either; the latter pair had sorted themselves into the field near Taigan and Jored before they were halfway to the woods. Mikel, noticing it at the same time his father and the Captal did, joined them deliberately. As the groups separated at *Domna* Canzallis's direction, Isidir ambled over on his big Dappleback mare with a graceful request to be included. Mikel was glad of another ally—no matter what opinion Fa held of Granon personally, all the Isidirs of Isodir were on their side.

At least they were spared Vellerin Dombur's raptures—shared at the top of her lungs—on the glories of the day, the beauties of the forest, and the skills of her husband, who had brought along a secretary to record poetic inspiration as it occurred to him. He was engaged to give a performance at the banquet tomorrow night of the verses composed in the saddle today. Mikel, who thanks to his father and Falundir knew poetry when he heard it, had no expectation of hearing anything resembling it from Stene Dombur. He wondered as he rode into the trees what sort of pretext he could come up with for not attending the Hunt Banquet. But he was damned if he'd include Taigan in his escape. Let her think up her own excuse.

The nine of them were just inside the woods when another rider came up—one of Rillan's grooms, who consulted in whispers with Fa and then withdrew to wait. Mikel arched a brow, and his father shrugged.

To the rest, he said, "I'm afraid I'll have to ride back. Slegin Web business."

Mikel knew at once that he was lying.

"Nothing dire, I hope?" asked the Captal. Mikel blinked at realizing she knew it, too.

"Nothing I can't handle. Trouble is, I'm the only one who's authorized to handle it."

Glenin said smoothly, "Your Lady allows you extensive control over her holdings, Lord Collan. I see her trust is not misplaced. To forgo your own pleasure in favor of work—not many men would be so conscientious. No wonder you have scant time for singing."

Mikel saw his father's mouth stretch in a rather sour smile. With a respectful half-bow to the Captal that pointedly did not include Lady Glenin, he gestured for Mikel to ride with him a little ways. When they were out of hearing range, he said, "Minstrelsy report—about time, too."

"I thought that might be it."

"Maybe now we'll know for sure what's happened around Lenfell. What the surviving Mages had to say wasn't much political help."

"That's what the Minstrelsy's for."

"Right. I'll meet the courier away from Ryka Court. Don't look for me anytime before dark. Tell your mother when you get back."

"I will, Fa."

With a brisk nod, he started to rein his horse around, then turned back again. "Keep an eye on your sister—and the Captal, too."

"And *both* eyes on Glenin Feiran."

"Smart boy."

Mikel shrugged, mouth quirking. "Your son."

Collan grinned, slapped his shoulder fondly, and rode away.

7

"I came to give warning, Sarra, and what help I can. I'm genuinely interested in your charming Taigan, of course, and it will please me to bring a favorable report back to Alinar. I must congratulate you and your husband, by the way. Taigan is everything she ought to be—and in time she will become an accomplished Mage Guardian."

"Thank you," Sarra said automatically.

"It is no accident that she is the last young woman of the Liwellan Name. You are, in short, being manipulated."

"Glenin Feiran," she heard herself say.

The Lady nodded her elegant white head. "Her Malerrisi were responsible for the deaths of Alinar's granddaughter and her children. There is but one strong young Liwellan Thread now: Taigan. I strongly suspect that Glenin Feiran knows she is not a Liwellan at all."

"She does," Sarra confirmed without elaborating.

"So?" Her eyes sparked with fascination, quickly disciplined. "When Alinar dies, you will rule not only the Slegin Web but the Liwellan—which, by the way, owns land on which a rather interesting event occurred this winter. Few have heard of the discovery of gold in a very obscure stream that runs into the River Rine—"

"From Domburronshir?"

Another nod. "Vellerin Dombur is one of the few who know. Alinar received an offer—Saints, an insult! When she refused, the only surviving Liwellan women met with 'accidental' deaths. The Domburs are notoriously unsubtle."

Instincts howling, Sarra exclaimed, "Glenin wouldn't dare try to throw suspicion onto me for those deaths!"

"Would she not?"

"With the Slegin Web, I'm so rich that not even the biggest gold mine on Lenfell could make a difference!"

"Ah, but 'gold' is a word that carries much magic. Who would believe anyone indifferent to such wealth?"

Sarra thought that over. "Mirya Witte's appeal, now this—Glenin has a mountain of so-called evidence all ready to shovel onto me, doesn't she?"

"Indeed she does. It's all of a piece. Think long and hard, my dear," she said earnestly. "What are her reasons for wishing to discredit you? What does she *want?* It is not what Vellerin Dombur wants. She's only Glenin's tool."

"Obviously. And what she wants is power. But how does she plan to attain it? The people don't trust the Malerrisi."

"And with good reason," the Lady said. "As I myself know well."

8

THEY left their horses a half-mile into the forest, reins tied to fallen logs, and proceeded on foot. Taigan, as eager to see a real live triplehorn as her brother, concentrated on making no noise whatsoever, and by and large succeeded. A few feet away from her Jored slid silently through the underbrush; just beyond him was Josselin, who moved almost as quietly. Chava Allard was ten feet away, showing a surprising knack for stalking prey in the forest as well as in the courtroom. Taigan hadn't attended the appeal, but she'd heard all about it.

To her left, Mikel had broken twigs at an alarming rate when they'd started out on foot. Then the Captal took him aside, murmuring a few words. After that he made no more sound than a slight breeze—and Taigan realized he'd Warded himself. She wished she'd had the foresight to ask the Captal how, but she wasn't very good at Wardings yet. Maybe if she just let it happen, trusted to her magic and the way it felt—

No good. She sighed and resigned herself to the application of woodcraft rules learned on childhood visits to Sleginhold. The woods here were very different, being

mainly oak and brambles, lacking the majestic redwoods
of Sheve Dark, but the principles were the same.

At least Gery Canzallis had managed to keep them
well away from the marshes. Not even Mikel's Warding or
Allard's skills would silence the squelch of muddy boots.

She couldn't see either *Domna* Feiran or Councillor
Isidir, though she could occasionally hear the latter, over
to her far right. The seven of them had fanned out, well
within calling distance of each other, to sneak a slow mile
or two toward a glade marked on *Domna* Canzallis's map
and shown to the Captal before they split from the other
groups. Taigan hoped the rest of the field was far enough
away so their own stalk would be undisturbed; she very
much wanted to see at least one of those deer in the wild.

And there they were—more than a dozen of them.
Eight does almost ready to birth their fawns were guarded
by a stag whose three spiraling horns were three feet long,
ridged in places where they'd grown back after breakage
in combat. Two immature males hovered anxious and resentful on the edges of the herd; lacking anything more
impressive than bony ridges where next year their horns
would grow, they could not challenge the stag. Four females too young to be bred cropped grass and swished
their short black tails contemptuously at the junior stags.
None of the animals was under six feet tall at the
shoulder.

Triplehorn deer were in that small category of creatures known for certain to have been altered by the results
of The Waste War. Wall frescoes and tile mosaics in several shrines confirmed that once they had been very much
smaller, nearly the size of galazhi, with cloven hooves
like horses' and only two horns, which moreover
branched into four or more points. A Scholar Mage—
Taigan forgot his name—had concluded after much study
that those dainty deer had been transformed into what she
saw before her now: single-hoofed, three-horned, but with
the same white bellies and golden-brown backs, the same
faces, the same social organization, the same diet, the
same everything, with one other exception: few predators
dared approach.

And scant wonder: those spiraling spikes were poisonous. The stag, catching scent or sound of the intruders, trilled low in his throat. Reaction was instantaneous and disciplined: the females all gathered in the center of the clearing, and the two young males took up positions on either side. At another signal from the stag, the does swerved to form a tight circle of deadly horns. The stag strode the perimeter, muscles rippling beneath his sleek hide, making sure their defenses were in order, snapping at one doe who broke the silence with a frightened bleat. He then planted his hooves in the dirt, threw back his gorgeous head, and let out a cry that sent ice down Taigan's backbone.

9

COLLAN got directions from the groom and told him to ride back to Ryka Court. He met the Minstrelsy courier outside a little domed shrine about four miles from the forest. He wanted badly to pace the cobbled court—though Cailet could protect the twins better than he could, who knew what Glenin Feiran would be up to?—but limited his nervousness to rubbing the nape of his neck where a by-now unfamiliar coif had tugged his hair the wrong way. He'd taken the damned thing off on leaving the forest; no need for its bright blue color that warned hunters to point their arrows in another direction.

"This is certain," he said to the courier.

"Yes, Lord Collan," Savachel Maklyn replied. "The residue of magical energy around the known Ladder at Malerris Castle indicates it was used quite a bit the week before St. Maidil's Day. Tiron Mossen investigated with three others, and they all agree on the amount of activity and the timing. At least two hundred Malerrisi are gone from the Castle."

This was a new one to him; Cai had never bothered to inform him that a Mage could tell when someone had recently gone through a Ladder. There was probably a

Scholarly formula for calculating the length of time since a Ladder's use and how many had used it. Something complex, taking into account the magic needed to transfer someone the specific distance of the Ladders involved, how much residue would be left by ten or twenty or a hundred, the rate of decrease over time—the part of his mind that loved playing with numbers nattered away, and he wished he could indulge it. There was something comfortingly definitive about mathematics; you always got an answer. Of course, what answer you got depended on the accuracy of the numbers themselves and your own skill in working out the equation.

"And it's certain that no Malerrisi have come back?" he asked Sava.

The young man shrugged. "We've kept the Ladder under constant watch." He smiled slightly. "Warding themselves as rocks. I didn't know they were there until one of them stood up right in front of me."

Again Collan felt the need to pace. Again he restrained himself. This Malerrisi equation did not add up. Other than those killed at Mage Hall, sixty-three Mage Guardians had died at twenty-one locations across Lenfell. It didn't take two hundred Malerrisi to murder sixty-three Mages. One was enough in each place—as amply demonstrated at Mage Hall.

"Sava, how current is this information?"

"About two hours old. One of the Mages brought me back through the Ladder to Captal Bekke's Tower, then to Ryka. I sent the groom to find you, and here we are. Nobody saw me or suspects me of being here, if that's what you're worried about."

"Why were you in Seinshir? Your patrol is Dindenshir."

"My grandmother Vasha's Birthingday is coming up. She sent me a note weeks ago telling me to come to Ryka Court by way of Seinshir and see what I could see at the Castle. I got there yesterday morning, walked up to the waterfall, and the rest you know."

"Before your grandmother knows it?" he asked wryly.

Savachel didn't see the humor. Stiffly, he replied,

"Yes. I'm part of the Minstrelsy. Whatever and whomever else you suspect, my Lord, you can't possibly suspect Councillor Vasha Maklyn!"

"Geridon's Stones, of course not! She's one of our best friends on the Council."

"Then what are you getting at?"

"I'm not sure." Nothing odd about Vasha Maklyn's request to her grandson—Sarra had said she knew about the Minstrelsy. But this time he did pace, the heels of his riding boots digging into the soft earth between cobblestones. Something was wrong here besides the discrepancy of Malerrisi to Mage deaths, but he couldn't figure out what.

Collan went on pacing, right hand clenched around the gold sigil pin that had fastened his coif. The crossed daggers of the Rosvenirs were barely an inch long, but their points dug into his palm almost as sharply as the real things. Another reason he hated the damned coif—whenever he looked down, the pin dug into his neck.

Where had all those Malerrisi gone to? And why so many from that Ladder?

Suddenly he swung around. "They're watching the Ladder east of the waterfall, right?"

"Yes. The western side is the one to Captal Bekke's Tower. The Mages found a good spot a little ways up the trail where you can see over to the other side quite clearly."

"But why that Ladder? It goes to a shrine in the hills above Havenport—miles from anywhere." Twenty years ago he'd played every version he knew of "The Ladder Song" for Alin Ostin, who'd postulated that there were three great hubs: Ryka Court, the Mage Academy, and Malerris Castle. Extrapolating from events before and during the Rising, there had to be at least ten Ladders at the Castle. So why had two hundred Malerrisi used that particular one?

"Does it have something to do with the shrine?" asked Savachel. Then, cheeks suddenly flushed, he exclaimed, "No—it's near Havenport! They could disperse by ship as anything from passengers to hired-on crew. They wouldn't even have to use magic. Why bother? A third of Lenfell's shipping goes through Havenport. They could be *anywhere* by now!"

"And probably are," he replied grimly. For it finally fit together, neatly as one of Cai's magic puzzles that became a different picture every time you worked it. Start with Vellerin Dombur's piece, and only South Lenfell showed in the final scene. Start with Glenin Feiran, and you got Ambrai. But pick the Havenport piece, and the result was a map of the world with cutpieces all over it. Third-largest shipping center, fourth-largest banking center. In the Slegin Web's dealings with the Dombur Web over the last few years, all the drafts had been drawn on the St. Tirreiz Mercantile Bank of Havenport. When Collan attempted to buy into it—to make transfer of funds simpler and untaxed—he was politely informed that no new investors were being considered. The Minstrelsy had nosed around at his request and come up with nothing very substantial, except that the Domburs and their surrogates owned about half the shares in the St. Tirreiz. But add this to the accounts opened all over Lenfell, discovered by the Rennes and used to buy up pieces of Domburronshir for Vellerin Dombur—

Now that the purchases were completed, the accounts would be used another way.

He fixed a narrow gaze on Savachel. "What happens when a lot of money is withdrawn from a bank in a short period of time?"

"How should I know? I'm a singer, not an accountant."

"The education of young men," Collan said severely, "is criminally deficient in practical matters. What happens is that word gets out, people think there's a reason *not* to keep money in that bank, so they withdraw their cash as well. The bank starts to run short on coin—nobody keeps more sacks of cutpieces and eagles than are necessary for normal business, the rest of it's on paper. They begin to borrow from other banks to cover the shortfall—which lets the other banks know there's something wrong. They won't lend the cash. Depositors want their money in coin, the bank shuts its doors before it runs out of coin, the depositors panic, the bank's investors want out, there's not enough money in cash *or* on paper to cover their investments—and the bank is doomed."

"So?" Savachel said, impatient with this lecture.

"So two hundred people withdrawing two hundred cutpieces each equals forty thousand cutpieces—"

"Four hundred gold eagles," the young man whispered, awed. "You could buy a house on the best street in Firrense for that!"

"Add in a hundred or so who want their savings in cash—some of them having considerably more than two hundred cutpieces. . . . " He shrugged. "There are at least fifty banks across Lenfell that've been set up to fall."

The excited color faded from Savachel's sharp cheekbones. "But what for?"

Collan sighed. What *did* they teach in schools these days? Taguare had taught him better at Scraller's Fief. "To unbalance the banking system, that's what for. Not severely, she doesn't want to wreck it, but enough to make people nervous. What do you want to bet that over the next few days word starts coming in from all over Lenfell that there's been a run on such-and-such a bank—everywhere but Domburronshir, of course," he finished dourly.

"Because Vellerin Dombur has such a wonderful grasp of finance and regulates *her* Shir's banks to perfection."

"You're getting the idea. But next comes the really fun part. The bank failures will bite into quite a few Webs. The Dombur Web won't be exempt. Vellerin will lose money, too, poor thing. But in her generosity and goodness, she'll buy up the remaining shares from frightened investors—and pretty cheap, too—"

"—and end up with half the banks on Lenfell doing her bidding!"

"Not that many—not to begin with, anyway. But the important thing in immediate terms is that the people will hail her as their financial savior."

Sava thought this over, then shook his head. "That's an awfully big leap of conjecture."

Col grinned tightly. "It's called 'gut-jumping' and I learned it from an expert. Sava, go back to Ryka Court.

Find Telomir Renne. Tell him what you've told me and as much as you can remember of what I've told you. Tell him as well to get the word out by Ladder to as many Mages as he can that the Malerrisi are out and intend to set themselves up in every city and village on Lenfell."

"Huh?"

"Oh, use your brains, boy! Why else would Glenin Feiran lend Vellerin Dombur her Malerrisi to start runs on selected banks all over the world unless they get to keep the money as start-up funds for entering general society?"

"Oh!" Another blink of big blue eyes, then another.

"After you've seen Telo, find Lady Sarra and let her know what's going on."

"And when she asks where you'll be?"

"I'll ride back to get the Captal. She can use those Mage Globes of hers to reach a few Mages, who can get the word out to a few more. And have Telomir get Mossen and the others the hell away from the Castle."

Despite a deficiency in basic economic theory, Savachel Maklyn was no fool; Col would never have hired him for the Minstrelsy otherwise, no matter how sweetly he sang the Bardic Canon. He looked Collan right in the eye and said, "It's possible that you're wrong about the banks, my Lord—and that those two hundred Malerrisi have all come to Ryka."

"I'm not wrong," he replied. "But I'll admit you may be just as right. There may be too many of them here for the Mages we have now to deal with."

"I'll tell this to *Domni* Renne as well—and Lady Sarra."

"Do that. And hurry, Sava."

The young man gave a crisp nod, turned on his heel, strode to his horse, bent to unwrap the reins from the shrine's tethering plinth—and straightened up very suddenly, spinning around with a startled expression on his face. The steel tip of an arrow protruded through the middle of his chest—an arrow shot with enough vicious strength go all the way through him.

Col started for him, wits thick with shock. Savachel

waved him back, gasping as movement shifted the arrow within him. "No—get out of here—"

"Appropriate, don't you think?" asked a casual voice behind him. "Killed with an arrow, symbol of his Name Saint. As it happens, he was wrong. What need have I of a hundred or even a thousand Malerrisi when I am here, and Chava, and especially my son?"

Collan whirled, damning his mind that wasn't Mageborn and his knives that would never penetrate the Wards rising in layer upon layer around the tall, elegant form of Glenin Feiran. Sauntering from the concealing curve of the shrine's walls, she shouldered her bow—nowhere near the drawing weight that could have produced such lethal power, undoubtedly spelled as well—and smiled.

"You may die now," she said to Savachel. "I have no further use for you."

But he was already dead, even before he collapsed to the cobblestones.

"With you, however," she told Collan, "I have unfinished business. We have no *albadon* and no Pain Stake, but I've learned quite a bit since then. *This* time, Minstrel, you'll sing for me. *A'verro,* you will."

10

CAILET froze where she crouched behind a berry bramble, dismally aware of the scantiness of her shelter. The stag seemed to be staring straight at her, despite every Ward she could think of. Maybe they were like horses, and refused to admit the existence of magic.

She remembered something Gorsha had told her long ago—something about sending a teasing little tickle into the brain, a technique he *said* he'd used in attempts to find the part that stimulated desire in beautiful ladies. She'd always suspected he'd experimented in other ways, too, looking for places that would temporarily blind or deafen or paralyze an opponent; he'd been First Sword, after all, and authorized to use his magic in war if necessary.

Could she do that now? Stun the deer somehow so they could escape before the animals charged? For Tamos Wolvar's memories told her that was what would happen next. The stag would attack the threat perceived as the most serious, and the dominant females—having no new fawns to protect—would take on the lesser dangers, allowing their sisters to flee.

But even if she could do it without harm to the triplehorns, she had no assurance that some of their hunting party wouldn't take it as a Saints-given opportunity to fire arrows into every single deer in the glade.

Well, if she couldn't stun them, maybe she could reassure them. And she needn't tweak their brains with magic to do it. There were Wards and spells she could use—

—which the Malerrisi here present could counter if they so chose. That this hunt was the opportunity given by a specific Saint—to wit, Chevasto—was as glaringly apparent to Cailet as the glisten of amber-gold poison oozing now from the tips of all those beautiful spiraling horns.

She could sense Taigan and Mikel nearby, and see Granon Isidir's bright yellow coif. Of Glenin, Chava Allard, Jored, and Josselin, she neither saw nor felt any trace—which wasn't unexpected. The only Mageborn in the group not Malerrisi-trained for concealment was the only Mageborn who had neither gone through the Ritual of the List nor been born an Ambrai.

Jored? Josselin? *Which?*

Time seemed suspended. Cailet's legs cramped with the strain of keeping still. The stag did not relax vigilance—indeed, he paced more rapidly around the circle of his does, snapping at the two young males who stood guard, a low gravelly whine vibrating his long throat.

They couldn't continue here all day. But any movement from anyone hidden in the brush would bring the stag slashing and spearing with those horns. An arrow would have to pierce directly to the heart with incredible force to fell him before he could kill.

Cailet never felt it coming. All at once it was simply *there*—a mocking echo of whatever had terrified the pakkas back at Mage Hall, magic that now made no attempt to hide its malice. The stag roared, fury made worse by fear in an animal that feared nothing. Lowering his head, he charged.

Cailet Warded herself, cast frantic spells. Implausibly, she felt someone else's magic wrap around her, too—Mikel? No. Taigan. Acting on instinct, just like her mother—

The stag was upon her. Magic had no meaning for him. His frenzied eyes loomed above her and then he ducked his head and stabbed, all his weight behind the amber-tipped horns. She threw herself to one side, rolling over and over in thorns.

Taigan's magic was gone. The girl screamed Jored's name—Cailet heard it over an oddly distant thunder of hooves. She pushed herself to her knees, bleeding from a thousand bramble scratches. The stag's neck and withers bristled with five and then six and then seven arrows, and then an eighth that sank deep into his left side at the heart. Swaying, he slashed lethargically with his horns—eyes still angry but knowing himself mortally wounded—and crashed to the forest floor.

Granon Isidir, bow still in hand and another arrow nocked, ignored his magnificent kill and ran for Cailet. Dropping the bow, he knelt, tearing off his yellow coif to wipe desperately at her upper right arm. She looked down, bewildered; she couldn't feel the scrape of cloth. Her sleeve was torn, a shallow furrow carved across her skin.

"Lie back," the Councillor ordered. "Breathe slowly, stay quiet."

Fuzzily, she knew what he meant. If her heartbeats calmed, her blood won't flow as fast, and maybe the poison wouldn't spread before . . . before Elomar could . . . could. . . .

Elomar was supposed to do something, she was sure. He could cure anything. But the numbness seemed to go right to her brain, and she couldn't recall what Elo should do or why he should do it. Neither did it matter. The dark-

ness—the shadows—closed in around her, and she knew
nothing more.

11

"WHAT are the means to power?" asked the Lady
who was not Alinar Liwellan. "How does one overthrow
a government?"

Sarra shrugged. "I gave a lecture series on political
theory at St. Caitiri's—and though it's been a while, I
remember my notes. The long, hard way is to get like-
minded revolutionaries elected, then legislate your aims
into law. Another method is to buy yourself enough legis-
lators—risky if your enemies have just as much or more
money than you have."

"The trouble with buying people is that so often they
don't stay bought. Once for sale, always for sale. A third
way is military—but an army's hard to hide." She
paused. "I've always thought Anniyas's ploy was one of
the cleverest."

"Create a threat in the would-be Grand Duke of
Domburronshir, defeat him as planned, and receive the
title of First Councillor from a grateful world. She did
roughly the same thing with the Mage Guardians in 951,
using Lady Allynis and Captal Garvedian as her manufactured threats. Is that what Glenin is doing?"

"Possibly. If so, she's going about it backward. The
Council is the threat, she and Vellerin Dombur are the
voices of reason and tradition. The real irony, of course,
is that Allynis Ambrai and Leninor Garvedian were defending the oldest of traditions, that Mages do not hold
public office, against Anniyas's insistence that they
should. All done for Auvry Feiran's sake, of course.
Which leads us to another path to power, Sarra. Magic."

"Which Anniyas didn't dare use, but which Glenin
will if she gets the slightest chance."

"My dear, she has already used it to excellent effect. The Mage Guardians are once again crippled."

Sarra smiled bleakly. "Not for long, if I know the present Captal."

"A remarkable and energetic young woman. I believe the methods being used now are a combination of all those we've mentioned."

Sarra ticked them off on her fingers. "Money, Vellerin Dombur certainly has. Magic, in the person of Glenin. Friends in Council and Assembly. A manufactured threat to frighten people into believing she's their only hope—but where's her army?"

"Truly told, she has two. Neither can be seen drilling in secret locations with swords and spears, but both are exceedingly well-armed. One is an army of obedient little soldiers within the Dombur Web, buying and managing buildings, businesses, and farms. What they do not purchase outright, they control through trade. The other army—"

"The Malerrisi," Sarra breathed. "Who don't need swords or spears—not when a single person can destroy Mage Hall."

"The ethic of the Mage Guardians, older than The Waste War, dictates the use of magic in service to Lenfell. The Malerrisi serve themselves."

"No," Sarra said. "They serve the pattern they wish to impose on the world. Everyone locked in place, Bloods and Tiers and Mageborns, according to the design of the Great Loom. We've always known this is Glenin's aim. Now we see some of how she means to accomplish it. Vellerin Dombur is expendable—indeed, highly undesirable as an ally, for she has ambitions of her own. But I suppose Glenin used what she had. She'll take Ambrai first, then use it as her personal power base to take the rest of Lenfell."

"But not for philosophy's sake," the Lady warned. "This is the danger of Malerrisi thought. Society must have order or it does not function. There must be methods of interaction, of settling differences—agreement on what is correct and just behavior in whatever situation may arise. We term it 'law,' made up of custom, tradition, and innovation in response to new circumstances. But it must be an agreement among the majority. This is what we believe. The Malerrisi take upon themselves the decision of what is correct, and deem themselves the *only* persons capable of deciding. And at the end, it is one person who decides: the Warden of the Loom. If she is sincere in her beliefs and unselfish in her aims—no matter how wrong-minded we may think them—then at least there is the advantage of dealing with someone of integrity."

" 'Integrity' and 'Malerrisi' are mutually exclusive terms," Sarra stated.

"Not really. There have been some . . . but I digress." Sighing, she picked at the fringe of her shawl for a moment, while Sarra silently begged, *Digress, digress!* But when she resumed, it was not to speak of the past. "The point is that if the Warden of the Loom is a person of appetites rather than ideals, we get an Avira Anniyas. Or a Glenin Feiran."

"Who is intent on righting what she perceives to be multiple wrongs." Sarra shook her head. "Her hunger is for Ambrai, and what she sees as her rightful place."

"And for breeding up in orderly, directed fashion every new Generation of Mageborns."

Sarra thought of Taigan, and shuddered.

"A dictatorship of magic—a thaumatocracy, if you will. A concentration of power in the hands of those who need not threaten with swords or financial ruin to make people obey. A spell here, a Ward there, and which of those *not* Mageborn could resist or rebel?"

After a moment's silence, Sarra said, "They have only to place themselves in strategic locations across Lenfell, establish their identities as workers of magic, and let it be known that there are objectives to be met in the grand design. And to think people used to be afraid of Mage Guardians! They don't know what fear of magic is!"

"They will, if Glenin succeeds."

"But what's her criteria of success? Not one of Vellerin Dombur's proposals has been agreed to by the Council."

The Lady spread her delicate white hands, revealing

again the strange embroidery on the reverse of the shawl. "And is that not the evidence she needs to frighten people? Dangerous departure from cherished traditions will wreck our world. Radical elements in control of the government. Necessity of a strong hand to correct excesses."

"Glenin's hand."

"Eventually. Not just yet. Once out of the cities, the Shirs are quite conservative, you know. They're not yet used to the abolition of Bloods and Tiers—though that happened nearly twenty-five years ago. For example, my dear, every time you propose allowing a Name in danger of extinction to be passed to a third or fourth daughter, they mutter."

"But—"

"Yes, I know. It's right and just. But it's not *tradition.*" She poured the last of the tea into her cup. "Vellerin is fifty-two this year and has a First Daughter to succeed her. An ambitious young woman, though at the moment blunted by anger at her mother for compelling her to divorce a husband she still loves. But in time she'll get over him, and even if she doesn't, she knows where her future lies. Glenin may have Ambrai with Vellerin's blessing. She's only a temporary nuisance. She has no First Daughter. When Glenin dies, Vellerin will give Ambrai to her own daughter Linsel. Lacking in subtlety as the Domburs are, they know how to wait. They've sometimes taken a century and more to ruin certain families in the Shir."

"But Glenin *does* have a child. A son."

"I know," she said, without saying how she knew, which fretted intolerably at Sarra's curiosity. "And whether he is called Lord of Ambrai or First Lord of Malerris, he will be both. Vellerin's ambitions will be thwarted."

"And then," Sarra blurted, "Linsel will challenge for Ambrai—that's when the Malerrisi will seize total power."

"It's a likely extrapolation. Even if Linsel decides she can do without Ambrai, the Dombur-Malerrisi alliance will fall apart. Sides will be chosen, the Malerrisi in their towns and villages will dictate which way to weave their allegiance, and we both know who will win." Leaning back in her chair, her sigh this time seemed to drain her of strength. But only for a minute. "Glenin, too, knows how to wait. She could not act until her son was old enough to participate in her plans."

"That's exactly what Cailet said."

"It's an advantage to have a wise Captal of Mage Guardians."

"She doesn't see herself as wise."

"She is wrong." The Lady smiled briefly. "Oh, Sarra, how very wrong she is."

12

THE layers began to peel from his Wards. Like a great wind roaring through him, like the wind remembered from early childhood that knocked him into the ditch, leaving him there stunned while the reivers killed his family and burned down his home—

No.

There never *was* any wind. Nor ditch. Nor reivers nor mother nor cottage nor family nor anything else remembered from that life. It was not his life. They were not his memories. They were as the wind he couldn't grasp or feel—

—because the wind was magic.

Sweeping over him, a tempest that blew away everything he'd been born, wiping away another life, leaving nothingness where other memories were substituted for the ones that belonged to him.

The ditch? Ah, that was where his true self was hidden while the magic blew past, sweeping all before it.

The cottage? All his life before the magic wind, burned to the ground, unrecognizable for what it had once been.

The reivers? They were the ones who had stolen his

true identity and caged his memories. The imprisonment had not been of his body, but his Self.

And he'd escaped them once. He knew that now. Something about a cat, bronze fur that his mind had seen clinging to the nonexistent bars of a nonexistent cage—the smell had reminded him of his own cat, and the memory of getting out of the cage was his memory of escaping their magic. For a time. A very short time.

He saw the faces of those who were the true reivers—and suddenly he began to laugh. He recognized them all, knew them all. His mother, soft-voiced and beautiful, with her black hair and green eyes, holding a lute, wearing a silver bracelet set with a blue onyx in which a sliver of gold resembled a candleflame. His father, tall and strong and serious, with blue eyes and red hair just like his own, just like Mikel's. His grandparents, all four of them, from four different yet equally powerful Names. These were the reivers, not wicked at all, who had taken him from what he had been. Each was almost as deeply loved as he loved Sarra Ambrai.

"Of course!" he exclaimed, the first and only words that had left his lips since a different magic had wrapped around him. "*Of course!*"

The layers were all swept away, down to the last Warding that had been the first to be set on his mind a lifetime ago, and he could feel himself rising from that frozen muddy ditch where he'd hidden for so long. *This* was who and what he truly was.

But he knew that he must not stand before this woman and let her see.

And so, laughing at her frustration and her rage, he reached for that portion of her magic that would obey her deepest impulses the way one of the Fifty Swords obeyed the deepest intentions of its wielder. And he used it, this ravaging need of hers for his death, to die.

13

CAILET came awake slowly, groggily, lying on a bed not hers in a room not hers; no birds. No hangings or carvings or decorations at all, in fact—just a small, bare, functional room painted a shade that reminded her of coffee with far too much cream. There wasn't even a window to look out of—or, she suddenly realized, for anyone to climb through. The reason for her unconsciousness abruptly returned to her memory, and again, as long ago at Ryka Court, she knew her life was in grievous danger.

She winced slightly to think of the gibbering panic this had caused in her twenty years ago. Had she faced death so often since that she could shrug off this new threat? Certainly not. Perhaps it was the feeling of inevitability that accompanied the attempt on her life. In a way, it was a relief that it had finally happened.

Which did not relieve others of responsibility for its not happening again, with the desired results this time.

Her right shoulder was still numb, but her head was rapidly clearing and she felt, on the whole, not all that bad. Truly told, she was so free of pain that she suspected Elo of doing something to dull the bramble-scratches as well as the cut from the poisoned horn.

"So. You're back."

Another inevitability: Elomar, stern and glowering, coming over to stand over her bed. She smiled up at him. "Didn't go very far," she answered.

"You might have. I heard what happened. You haven't—nor what came after."

"After what? Oh, you mean after Granon Isidir killed the stag."

"Reluctantly. Refused the trophy horns."

"He didn't look happy," she admitted. "So what happened after?"

"A stampede. Everyone's safe but Jored—a horn caught his thigh. He'll live. It was no accident, any more than that," Elo said, gesturing to her shoulder.

"No. But I'm still here." She tried to push herself up in bed, failed, and looked up at him in surprise.

"Stay put," he growled. "You weren't mortally poisoned—thanks to Isidir—but it's bed for another two days, Captal."

"Impossible."

He merely folded his arms, silently daring her to try. Subsiding, she glared at him. "Where's Sarra?"

"Cursing her husband, vanished on Minstrelsy business."

"He's lucky he found an escape from this mess—and if I know Col, he'll take as long about it as he possibly can." She reached for a glass of water with her good arm. "Who's Warding me?"

"Pier Alvassy."

"Get Sirron or Ollia Bekke."

A brow arched.

"Pier is family," she said deliberately, and a flicker of startlement passed over Elo's long face. She almost smiled; he was one of the very few who knew who she and Sarra truly were, and most of the time he forgot. But because Pier *was* a close cousin to the Ambrais, Glenin and her son could almost certainly pass through any Working he set. "Besides, it's the Bekke Name's privilege, Warding the Captal."

Cailet sipped again at the water, and settled back into the pillows. All at once she realized Elo was waiting for something—and from her lips there issued a string of feeble curses when she figured out what it was.

He was unimpressed. "In bed you stay, Captal." Taking the glass from her limp fingers, he drew the blanket to her shoulders. "And Bekkes to Ward you it will be. Sleep well."

And for the second time that day she slipped into the darkness.

14

TAIGAN, deprived of her father's common sense, sought out her mother's cool practicality instead. Once assured that both the Captal and Jored would live and be none the worse, mother and First Daughter silently sought the privacy of the Council Gardens that night.

There had once been a wooden summerhouse here; Anniyas's favorite haunt, and because of this torn down and replaced by a gift from the Isidirs of Rinesteenshir. An airy circular fantasy of wrought iron painted white, the little trellised room was twenty feet high and twenty feet across, with a stained-glass roof whose full beauty vanished with the sun. But on nights such as this, with the Ladymoon one day away from full, silvery light was enough to bring pallid life to the colors and shapes overhead. Taigan sat in one of the three velvet chairs and stared upward, picking out the sequence of the story: Falinsen Crystal-hand, Maurget Quickfingers, and Caitiri the Fiery-eyed inventing the art of glass.

"Ward us, please—for silence only, unless you don't wish to be seen," said Sarra, and Taigan did—inexpertly she knew, but it was harder because of the iron. She had to huddle the Ward close around herself and her mother, and felt the sting of the metal the whole time.

Sarra sat down, putting a cushion behind her back—unnecessarily. Her posture was so rigid that her spine never came within six inches of the pillow. For a long while nothing was said. At last Taigan could bear it no more.

"Why did you ask for Silence, if neither of us is going to talk?"

Her mother roused herself and met Taigan's gaze. "You're in love with him."

She nodded helplessly. "Mikel doesn't understand."

"You've been close all your lives. But you're grown now, with different paths to follow."

"It's not just that."

The beautiful black eyes were opaque, lustreless, set in a pallid face framed by moonlight-whitened hair. "Then what is it, Teggie?"

"He doesn't trust Jored. I saw it in his face today, after the stampede." She'd told the story once; now she told it again, with the personal things this time. The feelings. "When the stag charged, Joss ran from cover. Jored held him back. They got all tangled and then the herd panicked and ran straight for them. I've never been so scared in my life—I thought we were all going to die. I think I tried to Ward the Captal, I'm not sure. It all happened so fast. Mikel grabbed me and practically wrapped me around a tree—I saw Granon Isidir start shooting, and Mikel try to get to the Captal, and Jored hold *him* back, too—Mother, he saved both their lives! They would've had to go right through the herd and all those poisoned horns to get to her, it was insane even to try—oath or no oath! And Isidir was firing arrows quicker than I could see—but still Mikel and Joss both tried to get to her. Jored did right to stop them. They would've been killed."

"Even so, Jored was injured."

"They were struggling against him—Joss literally threw him halfway across the clearing, and one of the does grazed him with her horn as she passed."

"I see."

Taigan sat up straight. "You think like Mikel, don't you? That it was wrong of Jored to keep them safe."

"I wasn't there. I have no idea what happened. But I'm more interested in why you think Mikel hates Jored."

"I didn't say that."

"Come now, Taigan! It was in your voice and your eyes, if not the specific words. I'm your mother. I know you."

Putting so stern a name to the look in Mikel's eyes made her reevaluate the look itself. "Not hatred," she said slowly. "He was angry—first because Jored kept Josselin from the Captal, and then because he did the same thing to Mikel. A Nameless nobody from nowhere, daring to interfere with a Liwellan of Roseguard—"

"You're not being fair. Your brother's not that kind of person."

Taigan shrugged. "He *looked* like that kind of person."

"Is that your love for Jored talking? I certainly don't recognize my daughter's voice."

"I can't help that I love him!" she cried, jumping to her feet. "Mikel liked him at the beginning! I don't know what happened!"

"Ask him."

"I can't. I'm scared to. If he answers the wrong way, it'll ruin everything."

"Between you and your brother, or you and Jored?"

"Both. You're so lucky, you and Fa—you don't have any siblings or even any other relatives to worry about whether they like the person you married—"

"Taigan." Sarra's voice was very soft. "Do you wish to marry Jored Karellos?"

Marry him. Live with him, lie in his arms at night, have him father her children. . . .

"I don't know. Maybe. I'm not even eighteen."

"A year ago, you would've said you *were* eighteen, so few days before the fact. Does that tell you something?"

"That I'm not ready to be married—yes, I can see that, thanks," she snapped.

Sarra said nothing for a few moments. Then, rising to her feet: "It's getting late. I have a great deal to do tomorrow. And no one will be helped by lack of sleep."

"I'm not tired."

"I didn't think so. But don't stay out here too long."

Sarra came over to Taigan and bent to kiss her brow. "You think I don't understand, but I do. I love you so much, my darling. I only want you to be happy. Good night."

Several astonished minutes later, Taigan found her voice and whispered, "I love you too, Mama." But by then Sarra had vanished into the darkness of the Gardens.

A short while after that, Taigan left the lacy circle of iron. She paced aimlessly along gravel paths into the more public areas, but no one was out—everyone was too busy gossiping about the morning's near-tragedy. Only this morning? So short a time since she'd sat with Alinar Liwellan while that venerable Lady frankly looked her over for worthiness to be First Daughter of the Name?

All at once she wondered what Alinar would make of Jored as a husband. And how Jored would respond if she ever told him to sit down and shut up.

She managed a smile at that, her mood finally beginning to ease. She was surprised to find she'd walked all the way down to the lakeshore—again, deserted, and so quiet that she nearly leaped out of her skin when someone spoke from the shadows behind her.

"Cailet?"

Taigan turned around, moonlight shining full in her face, squinting. For just an instant he looked like Jored. But of course it wasn't. It was Josselin.

"Taigan," he said. "How stupid of me. Of course she wouldn't be here—she's still resting. Has there been any change? Have you heard anything?"

She'd never heard him babble. Why so nervous? "She'll be all right. Elomar's the best."

He came a few steps closer. "Can't you sleep either?" When she shrugged, he went on, "He'll be all right, you know." No need to identify *he*. "You care a great deal for him. Forgive me if it's rude to say so. I—I believe he cares for you as well. As much as he dares."

"Because of who I am? How ridiculous!"

"That's probably part of it. It's more like—caring isn't something either Jored or I ever learned how to do. Or maybe we did know, once, and taught ourselves not to. We're orphans, Taigan. His life has been as unsettled as mine. We've talked about it—we're a lot alike in that way, almost the twins in experience that people sometimes call us in looks. He'd ask what my childhood was like, and almost everything I said was something matched in his life."

"You both had it rough when you were growing up. I know that."

"You try not to care about any person or place, even something so simple as a cat or dog, because you never know when it'll be taken away, or you'll be sent away—" He stopped, shoulders hunching in a shrug, and a smile flashed whitely in his dark face. "I'm sorry. That sounds disgustingly self-pitying, doesn't it? Please tell me to shut up now!"

Now, there was something Lady Alinar hadn't figured on: a man who *asked* to be told to shut up! Taigan smiled, thinking she'd have to share this new alternative in masculine character with the old woman tomorrow.

"Joss, neither you nor Jored ever had a family—and that's a rarity in our world, where *everything* turns on family one way or another. But if you're looking for people to belong to, you've already found them. Your fellow Mageborns."

He nodded gratefully. "But it's tough to get past childhood training. If Jored sometimes seems to back away from you—" He broke off again. "I've bothered you enough for one night, Taigan. If you'll excuse me?"

She watched him walk away along the pebbled beach, then shook her head and started back for the lights of Ryka Court. But she was barely to the first stand of trees when she saw a figure she could never mistake for any other striding down to catch up with Joss.

What was Mikel doing here at this hour?

Well, for that matter, what was *she?*

Sleeplessness, she decided, was endemic tonight. For a moment she debated talking to her brother as their mother had recommended. But her nerves were wound almost as tight as Josselin's, and she'd likely say something she shouldn't. So she trudged back to her room, and sat up for most of the night with a book she would never remember having read.

15

"BUT why'd he do it?" Mikel asked again, and again Josselin shrugged.

"To protect us. You especially. It wouldn't endear him to Lady Sarra, to be presented as her First Daughter's future husband—the man who let her son be gored by triplehorns."

Mikel kicked at a rock. "You really think Teggie will marry him? What do you think of him? As a person, would you want him for a brother?"

"You're worried about your sister."

"No, just *him*. Why don't I trust him?"

"Because he doesn't trust anybody else. I tried to tell Taigan the same thing a little while ago. Jored's like me. He doesn't care easily. He doesn't trust."

"He probably saved my life today. Yours, too. So why don't I trust him?"

Joss sighed, hunkering down on the stones, long fingers scooping up flat stones to skim across the lake. "Mikel, feelings are just *there* sometimes. They happen, and there's nothing you can do about them."

"You mean I can't help not trusting Jored, and Teggie can't help loving him."

"Maybe when you get to know him better—"

Mikel shook his head, surprising himself with his answer. "I don't *want* to."

Another rock sailed out across the water before Joss looked up, gray eyes frosted by moonlight. "The Captal accepted him at Mage Hall. Can you trust *her* judgment, at least?"

"I have to, don't I?" Mikel muttered.

Joss flung his handful of stones into the lake, and rose with a rueful laugh. "Don't we all? Which of us could possibly out-think the Captal? She scares people to death. But she's just a woman, Mikel. Not all-powerful, not omnipotent, not a candidate for future Sainthood."

He sounded somehow as if trying to convince himself. Mikel found that very strange. Wryly, he remarked, "Couldn't prove it by me. She was different when she was our Auntie Caisha than she is these days as Mage Captal."

" 'Auntie Caisha'? Joselet's Silver Shovel!" He laughed low in his throat. "Auntie Caisha! I can't imagine ever calling her that!"

"If you tell anyone I told you that, I'll deny it in a court of law to my last breath!"

Josselin grimaced as they started back up the slope. "And here I'd almost managed to forget about the Grand Justices."

"They're taking their sweet time about a decision."

"The longer they think it over, the more uneasy I get. They won't dare acquit, but they'll have to throw a sop to the conservative faction. And that means I'll have to find some way of paying back the money Mirya spent on me."

"I'll lend it to you—Saints, I'll *give* it to you!—in exchange for one thing."

"What?" he asked warily.

Mikel grinned. "Tell me what it was like at Wytte's. Spare no details. I want all the facts and all the gossip."

Joss shook his head emphatically. "Your father would skin my hide for a fingerpick pouch, hang my hollow bones for wind chimes, and use my guts for lute strings if I soiled your innocent young ears with such things. And that's if there was anything left of me after your mother got finished!"

"Then it *is* a—"

Joss interrupted silkily, eyeing him sidelong. "Don't say it, Mikel. The last man to do so ended with a black eye. I swore then that the next would have his balls presented to him on a fork. Fried. With plum-brandy sauce."

Abruptly Mikel felt the two years' difference in their ages—and not just the difference between the last of adolescence and the first of manhood. For all the humor of the threat, threat it definitely was. Joss might not know what Name to call his own, but the one he did have he would defend. And it had taken quite a beating at the appeals court.

"Sorry."

"Forgotten. And don't worry too much about Taigan and Jored. I have a feeling that it's a marriage that will never happen."

"She's eighteen in three days, just like me. She can do as she pleases then—just like you."

"Yes—and look at the trouble it got me into."

16

THE Malachite Hall was arrayed for a Hunt Banquet—usually held the night of the chase, when all the riders bathed, applied liniment and liquor as their weariness dictated, and dressed for the occasion in an hour and a half. This time the feast had been postponed. To hold one grand affair the day before Midsummer Moon celebrations would be both exhausting and redundant. The delay was fortuitous in that it was certain by evening that the Mage Captal and her Prentice would recover fully from their shocking accident—though neither was yet well enough to attend the festivities. Holding a showy entertainment with their fate undetermined would have cast a pall over the whole evening.

Accordingly, at sunset on the night of Midsummer Moon four hundred sumptuously clothed and bejeweled diners gathered in the Malachite Hall. The same genius responsible for Cailet's bird-themed breakfast chose to work with the gorgeous striations of the stonework; the company was inundated in green. Full-grown willows stood in massive copper tubs rusted green with age. Ivy-twined trellises framed every door and window. The centerpieces were potted ferns. Candles of every conceivable shade from lime to pine squatted beside each celadon porcelain plate atop grassy table linens, and the chairs cushioned backs and bottoms in moss-colored velvet.

"Lucky the knives and forks aren't green, too, or we'd be groping all over the tables to find them," commented Telomir Renne as he escorted Sarra in Collan's absence. "And pity anyone wearing that color tonight—they'll vanish, too."

"It's like being inside a bottle of parsley sauce," she replied. "Where are we sitting? And *please* tell me it's near a door. Stene Dombur is supposed to inflict us with a recital tonight, and I'm hoping to slip out before he finishes dessert."

"We'll have to settle for sleeping with our eyes

open," Telo replied with sympathy. "We're directly opposite the Domburs."

The scattering of round tables usually used for banquets had been replaced by a gigantic horseshoe arrangement of rectangular tables, with the diners seated all along the outside so everybody could see everybody else. The center—an area thirty feet wide—was left free for the servants to deliver and collect dishes, for the entertainment (musicians, singers, and one very bad poet), and for displaying the trophies of the hunt.

Sarra arranged her gown to prevent wrinkling the bronze silk, and sat in the place Telomir indicated. She wished Collan's taste in this particular instance had not run to a high-buttoned collar; it was bound to grow stiflingly hot in the Malachite Hall over the next few hours. But she had to admit the dress was magnificent. Sleeveless and cut in at the shoulders, its collar fanned out two inches to frame her jawline. Tarise had done her hair up off her neck, secured with black onyx hairpins that matched the buttons down the front and simple earrings.

Vellerin Dombur was, predictably, wearing white. Mile upon mile of white. She looked like a walking, talking Winter Wraith such as children built of snow. Would that she'd melt away and take trouble with her, as, according to folklore, Winter Wraiths were supposed to do.

Vellerin's husband, along with most other men with any claim to fashion, had adopted Collan's innovation in longvests with frantic haste; the results ranged from the attractively tailored to the too-tight-for-movement to sleeves so loose they dragged in the soup. Sarra was reminded of the inane style favored by Garon Anniyas twenty years ago: long ribbons sewn to his shirtsleeves, supposedly emphasizing grace of gesture but instead tangling in everything from doorknobs to his own rings.

And why would she think of him now? Perhaps because the woman whose husband he had been entered the room, pausing as if to find a friend's face or her assigned seat but really to let all admire her. Glenin did not wear white, though she probably wanted to. It was the Malerrisi color. The colors she did wear stiffened Sarra's spine: Ambrai's black and turquoise.

The diners were seated. The first course was brought out. Conversation began—naturally, a rehash of yesterday's hunt. A lone flutist played delicate airs from a corner. Sarra dipped her spoon into the soup, rearranging vegetables by color, pushing them around in little flotillas until they sank.

On her left, Telomir tucked in to the meal. On her right, Taigan and Mikel evidenced as little appetite as Sarra. The twins were barely on speaking terms, and their mother knew why, and as much as she wanted to tell them either to stop this nonsense or have it out in a shouting match, she did not. There was a constriction in her throat and a trembling unease in her chest that made it impossible to speak.

She *knew* that whatever Glenin had planned, it would come tonight. Sarra's forces had been divided. She was not at her full strength. Collan was off Saints knew where doing Saints knew what for the Minstrelsy; Cailet was still recovering from poison. Sarra was on her own. And Glenin knew it.

Soup was removed, and replaced by tidbits of fruit and cheese with toasted slices of bread. "Eat something," Telo whispered. She tried. She really did. But she couldn't.

The flute gave way to a mandolin. It had been an instrument much favored by Lady Allynis, and the songs now being played were Ambraian folk tunes. Sarra began humming one melody under her breath while the musician's quick fingers picked it out on quivering strings. It had been her grandmother's favorite. Sarra recalled well the first time Col played it for her. No voice gave the lyrics tonight, but she could hear her husband as clearly as if he sat beside her. Just thinking of him gave her ease.

Wear me not as a ring on your finger—
Your hand needs no adorn.
Wear me not as a circle of jewels at your throat—
To jewels and wealth you were born.
Wear me not as a song on your lips by night—
For such are forgot by morn.

"You know that one, Mother?" Taigan asked.

"From a long time ago. It's not much performed anymore." In her childhood, they'd played it whenever Grandmother made a formal appearance. The musicians of the Octagon Court had made it into an anthem of proud dedication to Ambrai itself, but the single mandolin rendered it as Collan always had: intimate, infinitely sweet, a song from a man to a woman.

> *No, not as a ring on your finger—*
> *Removed for washing, and lost.*
> *No, not as a circle of jewels at your throat—*
> *So others may see the cost.*
> *No, not as a song on your lips by night—*
> *To still with the dawn's cold frost.*

"Where'd Glenin Feiran go?" Taigan asked. "I don't see her."

"She won't be gone long," Mikel predicted. He shared Sarra's intimations, then. Interesting.

"You know everything, don't you?" Taigan snapped.

"Stop it," Sarra commanded. "I won't have it. Not here. In private if you must, but not at a state banquet."

Her sharp tone had the intended effect. She sipped from her wineglass, eyes fixed on the centerpiece of humble woodland flowers, trying to calm the quiver that had begun again in her breast. The crystal Globe beneath her bodice was warm still, but she knew it would turn to a lump of ice before the evening was over.

> *Wear me instead as a woolen cloak,*
> *To keep you warm and dry.*
> *Wear me instead as a Saint-forged sword,*
> *And keep me always by.*
> *Wear me instead as this vow on your heart:*
> *"Yours until I die."*

That had been Grandmother Allynis's promise to Ambrai. She'd tried so hard, done so much—and ultimately been defeated. It had been years before Sarra understood that. She'd been only a child—innocently, ignorantly happy, leading a charmed life of wealth and love and indulgence until those last few weeks, when not even a child could fail to discern her elders' tension. Sarra felt as lost and alone now as she had then. She reached for the memory of Collan's deep voice singing this same song and could not grasp it.

Why did it have to be that way? Why did Ambrai have to die? Why did I have to grow up so far from home? Why did Cailet have to grow up a nobody? Why was so much stolen from us? Collan—I need you, Minstrel mine. I have Collan, and Cailet has no one—

Third course: delicacies made from livers and tongues of the thirty deer killed yesterday. But not the one Granon Isidir had felled with eight arrows shot impossibly fast. He had ordered the stag left in the forest with horns intact. Sarra admired him for it; not many would forgo so splendid a trophy.

All at once Vellerin Dombur got to her feet. She was no more the smiling, affable guest. Her expression was serious and in her piercing sapphire eyes was the avidity of a bird of prey among the flaunting, fluttering denizens of Ryka Court.

"My friends," she said, having caught everyone's attention, "I regret to disturb this delightful occasion with news that has shocked me profoundly."

Her cousin and ally, Councillor Senasta Dombur, sat forward from her place at the head table, necklace of diamonds and sapphires dangling in her plate. "What news is this, Lady?"

"My staff has been conducting careful research into a matter which has been troubling me for some time. I have only now been informed that my suspicions were correct." She gestured heavily to a young man effacing himself nearby. Sarra hadn't seen him come in—but she did see Glenin return, slide back into her seat five chairs down from Vellerin Dombur, and stare resolutely at her plate.

She knows what's coming. She planned *what's coming. Collan, I need you!*

Vasha Maklyn held up a hand for silence. "Please tell us the source of this trouble."

"I must preface it. Please be patient, and you'll soon understand."

"You have our attention," Senasta assured her.

"A lifetime ago, the Mage Guardians were a powerful force on Lenfell. They performed a vast number of services for our world, and were honored for their generosity with their magic. There was only one stricture upon them in this dedication: they must never hold political office.

"Now, why was this so? Ostensibly because it had been dictated at the time of their founding, long before The Waste War. But, truly told, it was because everyone knew magic's power, and everyone feared that in high office—or indeed in any office—magic would be used to further the aims of the Mage Guardians.

"The events of 950 to 951 were predicated on a struggle between First Councillor Avira Anniyas and Lady Allynis Ambrai over just this issue. Allied with Lady Allynis was the Mage Captal, Leninor Garvedian. The details of the conflict have become muddied in the years since by the tragedies it brought about. But the basics were these: Anniyas wanted a specific person to become Chancellor of Ambrai. This person was Mageborn, trained in his craft by Mage Guardians—including the most renowned of First Swords, Gorynel Desse, who was his friend—but he never advanced beyond the rank of Prentice Mage. We will leave aside the question of 'why' for a moment. This Prentice Mage was husband to Lady Allynis's First Daughter, Maichen, and father of two lovely little girls. He was respected and celebrated in Ambrai, and possessed everything a man could possibly hope for. But he wanted more. He wanted power. And the way he saw to get it was to become Chancellor of Ambrai.

"This, as a Mageborn, he was forbidden. But Anniyas wanted it, and he wanted it, and thus there came a series of moves that led to the deaths of Lady Allynis and her family, thousands upon thousands of citizens of Ambrai, Captal Garvedian, Mages too numerous to count, and the destruction of the Mage Academy, the Healers Ward, Bard Hall, and most of that beautiful city. But long before these catastrophes, Maichen Ambrai and her younger daughter fled to a location that is to this day unknown."

"Great," Mikel muttered. "A history lesson and a mystery story. Just the thing for the digestion."

"Shh," Taigan hissed.

Sarra, frozen in her green-velvet chair, heard the tautness in her son's voice, and knew that he was fighting instincts that told him to run—just as hers were doing. Taigan wasn't yet aware of what was really going on. But she would be, very soon.

"Eighteen years passed. Auvry Feiran, the man whose ambition to become Chancellor of Ambrai caused all this, became Anniyas's most feared minion. He all but obliterated the city that had once honored him, and became known as the Butcher of Ambrai. He all but obliterated the Mage Guardians—the fellowship of Mageborns to which he could never fully belong, for he was only a Prentice. He all but obliterated the Malerrisi in their Seinshir Castle—*or seemed to*. For the reason he was never more than a Prentice was the same reason Anniyas favored him, and the reason Malerris Castle had to *seem* destroyed. Auvry Feiran was one of them. He always had been. And so was Anniyas."

Absolute, breathless silence.

Vellerin looked mildly disappointed for an instant, then resumed with fresh vigor. "Now, little of this will be news to you—except that Auvry Feiran was from the very beginning a Malerrisi. He did not dare become a full Mage Guardian, for in the process of the Ritual of the Lists a Captal comes to know the deepest heart of the candidate. There is no deception, no Warding, no spell that can hide what someone truly is."

Sarra remembered Ollia Bekke standing in the compass octagon. No one knew of the Ritual but Mages. Or Prentices preparing for it. Like Jored and Josselin.

Or Prentices who refused it. Like Josselin.

"Should any more proof be needed of Auvry Feiran's true magical allegiance, I offer the sight of his daughter, who took his Name in preference to the one her Blooded mother gave her, and even now sits at the pinnacle of Malerrisi power as Warden of the Loom." She flung a hand in Glenin's direction. Glenin sat with shining blonde head bowed. "Yet there was another daughter, born in 946. Her name, all but forgotten now, was Sarra. It's a common name, honoring the Virgin Saint who is mistress of flowers and jewels and patron of young girls, usually given to one born in St. Sirrala's own week of First Flowers."

The sapphire gaze swept around the horseshoe of tables, coming to rest directly opposite her own place. "Lady," she asked silkily, "when is your Birthingday?"

Sarra felt Taigan and Mikel react, but could do nothing, say nothing. She sat like a stone carving, white to the lips, her eyes fixed on Vellerin Dombur as she spun the fatal truths like a shroud. *The Wards are gone. Whatever Gorynel Desse did, it's gone now. Everyone will know. Glenin has known for years. She told Vellerin Dombur. And the Wards are gone.*

Sarra, born on the third day of First Flowers, knew she ought to speak. Deny, refute, scorn, reject. *Speak.* But she couldn't. She only wished she'd been struck deaf and blind as well as turned to frozen stone.

It occurred to her that *she* had become the Winter Wraith now. She was snow to her marrow. Frost covered her skin, encasing the stone in ice. Everything she had been, everything she was, everything that was truth and half-truth and lie and Warded for her lifelong safety would soon melt away.

Vellerin Dombur shrugged. "Very well. We will leave that for the moment and consider other circumstances. We all know the tale of how Lady Sarra Liwellan—" Was there the slightest emphasis on the Blood Name? "—and Collan Rosvenir escaped from Renig across The Waste to an unknown location, where they spent several days in hiding—until Auvry Feiran found them. He took Collan Rosvenir away with him—*but not Lady Sarra.* Why?"

He didn't know I was there. I stood in the upstairs shadows like the coward I was, the coward my silence confirms I still am, while Collan went with him to be tortured by Anniyas and Vassa Doriaz and Glenin—

"Lady," said Vellerin Dombur, "who was your father?"

Collan! I need you! She felt Taigan's muscles tense, preparing to rise, her young body quivering with fury and insult. Mikel shifted, too, ready to stand beside his sister. Sarra moved at last, her frozen bones cracking through the ice, and clasped her First Daughter's slender wrist in her fingers.

"This is ludicrous!" roared Granon Isidir. "I don't wonder Lady Sarra refuses even to acknowledge such ridiculous questions!"

Dear Granon. A good name, that, for good men: Elin's beloved husband, Cailet's devoted Warder, Sarra's own loyal colleague. What a pity that faith was about to be betrayed.

"*Can* she acknowledge such questions and remain among us?" countered Vellerin. "I would hear an answer to them, Lady Sarra, and so would the rest of this eminent gathering."

"No need," Glenin said in an emotion-strained voice. "I can spare her the strain of speaking." Not rising from her seat, she looked at Sarra across thirty empty feet of space—thirty-eight empty years of time—her face pale and solemn. "Her father was also my father. Auvry Feiran."

Extraordinary, Sarra thought, oddly detached, feeling almost nothing. *How can so many people stay so completely quiet? If an eyelash fell right now, we'd all hear the echo.*

"Lady Sarra Liwellan is, truly told, my sister—Sarra Ambrai."

"Mother," Taigan said in a strangled whisper, "*say* something!"

She tore her gaze from Glenin's gleaming, laughing eyes and looked at her children. Her proud, brilliant, beautiful Mageborns. Grandchildren of Auvry Feiran.

Daughter and son of Collan Rosvenir.

"You hear no denial," said Vellerin Dombur. "It is the truth!"

"Yes," Glenin said. "But there is more."

And news to her ally, Sarra saw that at once.

Glenin rose slowly to her feet, tall and stately in her black-and-turquoise gown. Her fair hair was upswept, giving her additional inches she didn't need, held at the crown by a comb of onyxes and turquoises cut as octagons. She suddenly dominated the gathering in a way different from Vellerin Dombur's sheer force of ambition. Glenin had sheer physical presence, like Lady Allynis had had, a magnetism that had less to do with beauty than the ingrained belief that she was a person worth looking at, listening to—and heeding without question. Sarra had not inherited it; she used her will and her words. Cailet's bearing was of yet another kind—as instinctive as Glenin's, as resolute as Sarra's, subtler than either, it was based not on personality but instead on the magic at her command and the position she had been given.

It occurred to Sarra then that the three of them, the three Ambrai sisters, had never been in the same room at the same time. Twenty years ago, Sarra faced Glenin alone in Renig, the night Mai Alvassy died; Cailet confronted her at the Octagon Court, the night Anniyas and Auvry Feiran died. Glenin was not present for Vellerin Dombur's speech to the Council and Assembly, only the reception afterward—which Sarra had not attended. Sarra had not ridden out yesterday with the hunt. And tonight Cailet was in a windowless, Warded room, sleeping off the effects of killing poison and healing potions.

Never together, not once. Sarra wondered if, had they ever inhabited the same room at the same time, everyone would have seen years ago what Glenin chose to reveal now.

"I am, as Lady Vellerin has said and all here have always known, the First Daughter of Maichen Ambrai and her husband Auvry Feiran. I am also the First Lady of Malerris, and have been since the death of Avira Anniyas. These twenty years I have tried to untangle the Malerrisi from her dominance and tyranny. I believe I have succeeded. But the taint attached to my name precludes my leading the Malerrisi back into the world. You do not trust me, and I understand this completely. You have every right not to trust a daughter of Auvry Feiran."

Like her, Sarra thought. *Like me. Like Cailet.*

Glenin paused to glance around the hushed chamber. "I am willing to give up my position. I am willing to give up my magic. Let someone else, someone of the Council's choosing, lead the new Malerrisi and oversee their return to society. I will ask the Mage Captal to Ward me as so many persons have been Warded against their magic. I wish to renounce my Mageborn powers. I wish to be an Ambrai again, and live in peace in the city of my birth."

As Glenin concluded her speech, Vellerin Dombur drew in a long breath that threatened the seams of her white gown. "This brings us to the question of the other Ambrai here present. Lady Sarra, as a Mageborn—"

She got no further. The successive revelations and shocks had gripped them by the throat, and before anything new could be considered the fist must loosen so they could breathe. With one loud cry the four hundred expelled their astonishment—not at Sarra's true identity, not at Glenin's offer of renunciation, but at the simpler and more comprehensible information that Sarra was Mageborn. A Councillor, sitting in the highest seat her Shir and her world could bestow, she was Mageborn.

She had lied for twenty years.

She knew it would never occur to them that she had never used magic. Had the Mage Captal been here to swear to it, they would not believe that she knew nothing of *how* to use magic. They saw a Mageborn who was a Councillor—a position even more powerful than Auvry Feiran had aspired to in Ambraishir—against all tradition and custom and an edict older than The Waste War.

"This is madness!" shouted Granon Isidir, springing to his feet. "If she *were* Mageborn, why hasn't she used her magic to reorganize the whole world to her liking? Better still, to rid Lenfell of vermin like you?"

Now that their throats were freed, they could gasp at this outrageous insult—bad enough from a woman, intolerable from a man. Proof of fracturing social order, proof of growing disrespect for age-old traditions.

"Not Mageborn?" Her honor having been defended by the reaction of her audience, Vellerin Dombur seized on his denial. "*Not* Mageborn? With a sire and a sister two of the most powerful Mageborns who ever lived? She *is* Mageborn, and I'll prove it! She's Warded this Hall herself tonight—have you seen a door open or a servant enter since I asked who her father was? Go on, try to leave!" she flung at Isidir. "Try!"

Granon Isidir strode to the door opposite the head table. He reached for the gilt handle and could not touch it. He tried to take a step closer to the door and could not. He turned, and the convulsion of anguished betrayal on his face when he looked at Sarra cracked her heart open a little wider. *I* cared *for you*! his eyes cried out. *I've mourned my whole life that Collan was yours and I was not—*

Mikel was on his feet, with nothing and no one to stop him. He circled the tables, went to the door Granon had been unable to open—and turned the gilt handle, and opened the door, and swung around to stand beneath the lintel staring at Glenin.

"There *are* Wards here—but not hers," he said, biting off the words. "My Lady Mother could no more Work a Warding than she could fly!"

Glenin shrugged. "You're her son. Family can pass through Wards set by family."

He accepted it then. Sarra saw it in his face. *"Family."* Grandson of the Butcher of Ambrai, nephew of the Warden of the Loom.

Taigan did not accept it. But she would, very soon.

Vasha Maklyn stood, angry and disbelieving but in full control of her temper. "I've heard a lot of conjecture and innuendo based on things those of us not Mageborn can't claim to understand. What I want is *proof.* Can you offer that, Vellerin? Or you, Lady of Malerris?"

"Have you heard her deny it?" demanded Domhur.

"Proof?" Glenin walked slowly around the long tables, taking all attention with her. "My sister's birth was a joyous occasion in Ambrai, a great relief that child and mother were safe. My mother hadn't been well throughout her pregnancy, and was attended during labor by six Healer Mages. I wasn't yet four years old, and I remember how frightened I was, that long day and longer night at the beginning of First Flowers."

She was now at the bottom of the horseshoe, where Mikel and Granon Isidir still stood, both of them tense with loathing. She smiled at Mikel as she neared him. He took an involuntary step back from her when she passed.

"My sister's Naming was attended by a hundred times as many people as attended her birth. All commented upon a certain mark on her body—a tiny, round, rose-colored birthmark."

She stood in front of Sarra now, looking down on her as she'd done in their childhood: the all-knowing, all-wise, all-powerful, adored elder sister, who'd vanished one day with their father never to return. But the fond smile was malicious now, the gray-green eyes alive not with affection but with triumph.

"We shared a room as children," Glenin said. "When you were very little, I used to dress you, like a doll—you were so lovely, Sarra, and have become more beautiful still. But the birthmark remains."

She jerked back from Glenin's reaching hands. But not fast or far enough. Glenin leaned across the table, oversetting a wine glass with one elbow, and tore open the collar of the bronze velvet gown. Black buttons went flying. Glenin stood back with a sweeping gesture.

Sarra sat absolutely still, breasts half-exposed, the birthmark clearly visible. Someone gasped. She could feel the women's shock at what Glenin had done competing with the men's admiration that no stricture of manners could stifle. She felt their eyes like spiders on her flesh.

"Sarra, my sister, daughter of Maichen Ambrai and Auvry Feiran." Glenin looked at her again, and her smile wavered for a moment. Swiftly she reached again and yanked the crystal sphere from Sarra's neck. The chain resisted, broke, leaving a red welt at her nape.

Three things happened then. Mikel was there, wrapping around her his sleeved blue longvest, raw linen scratching at her exposed skin. Taigan shifted her stance at Sarra's side, and Glenin, the tiny Globe clenched in her palm, suddenly gave a blurt of pain and dropped it shattering onto the malachite floor.

"Taigan!" Sarra cried. "No!"

"She deserves—"

"Not by your magic! Taigan, please!"

The girl trembled and looked down into Sarra's eyes.

She was so beautiful in her flowered blue gown, so grown-up—but her face was the face of a bewildered child. Sarra held her gaze, silently imploring where once she would have commanded. Taigan did grow up then, suddenly and completely. The last of the little girl was gone. She shuddered and sank into her chair, utterly defeated. She believed now. She had no choice but to believe.

There was a crimson mark in the center of Glenin's palm—a burn not of fire but of ice. She stared at it, then at Taigan. A slow smile began on her face. She held her hand up for all to see the mark. "Magic. From a Mage Globe she's worn for who knows how many years—used this time by her Mageborn First Daughter." She paused, then concluded in a ringing voice, "Given her by her Mageborn sister—*our* sister—the Captal!"

This was too much. Whatever had held them before, and eased its grip just enough for throats to fill with air, now strangled them. The silence deafened.

"Why did Maichen Ambrai abandon the city of her birth long before its destruction? Because she was again pregnant and wanted no one to know—especially not the father. She left in secret—so desperate to be gone that she traveled by Ladder, endangering the child in her womb, who was certainly Mageborn, for Ladders can be perilous to the unborn. Where did she go? To Ostinhold, where she died giving birth. But that third daughter lived. And just as Sarra took the name Liwellan and was fostered by Lady Agatine Slegin, Cailet took the Name Rille and was fostered by Lady Lilen Ostin. But their true Name is *Ambrai*, and they are my sisters, daughters of Auvry Feiran—"

"A Malerrisi!" Granon Isidir managed, his last try at denial. "Just as he taught *you* to be!"

"*I* have never concealed who and what I am. *I* have never lied to the Council, the Assembly, the people of Lenfell—or to the Mage Guardians. I am Glenin Ambrai, Mageborn of Maichen Ambrai and Auvry Feiran, trained in the Malerrisi Tradition." She pointed one long finger at Sarra. "*She* is Sarra Ambrai, Mageborn of the same parents. And the woman you know as Cailet Rille is

Cailet Ambrai, Mageborn like her two sisters, Mage Capital for twenty years. *I* have not lied."

The last hope had faded from Taigan's voice as she whispered, "Mother—is it true?"

Mikel answered her. "Yes. It's all true."

True. Sarra accepted it all at last. The Mage who had been her father and the Malerrisi who had become the Butcher of Ambrai were one and the same. And she knew, almost impersonally, that her failure to accept that truth in the past had cost her the future.

Why hadn't she and Cailet seen this coming? Whatever they had thought Glenin might do or say, this had never even occurred to them. Thirty-eight years of trusting to Wards set by Gorynel Desse had made them complacent. Fatally so.

Vellerin Dombur—who had taken a little more time to recover from this new shock, for which Glenin had obviously not prepared her—spoke once more. "Who speaks to contradict these facts? Not Sarra Ambrai—she says nothing. Not her children, who have shown themselves as stunned by these revelations as the rest of us. She even lied to them! And not her devoted husband. A man married to a Mageborn Ambrai, who begot more Mageborn Ambrais—is Collan Rosvenir even aware of their true ancestry?"

Collan, she whimpered inside. *Oh, Minstrel, forgive me—* What she had seen in Granon's eyes would be a million times worse when seen in Collan's.

"Considering all these newly revealed facts," Dombur went on harshly, "I think you will understand why all my conversations with the Council these last weeks are now suspect. I am wary even of remaining on Ryka while *she* is among you—Councillor for Sheve, Mageborn of Auvry Feiran, sister to the Lady of Malerris and the Mage Captal!"

Vasha Maklyn thumped her fist on the table. Dishes and goblets rattled. "A birthmark and some unsubstantiated allegations! Again I demand, present your proof!"

"And again I ask, have you heard her deny it?"

The silence drew out, thin and taut as a string tuned

to the breaking point. Sarra said nothing. There was nothing she could say.

"And what will they do to us now that their secret is common knowledge? What other secrets are they hiding?"

Her cousin Senasta called out, "Please, Vellerin! Don't let this spoil everything we could accomplish! You must know that *most* of the Council is sincere—that we do not share the private ambitions of these Ambrais!"

"How is anyone to know how much policy is the work of Sarra and Cailet Ambrai?"

Vasha yelled, "And how much of *yours* can be traced to Glenin Feiran?"

She was shouted down. Senasta glared at her and said to Vellerin, "Any of us would be willing to accompany you to a place of your own choosing, to continue our discussions—"

"While the rest of you come under their spell again?" was the scornful reply.

"Take *them!*" someone shouted.

"Out of the question!" Vasha exclaimed, but her rebuke was drowned in the chorus of approval.

"Take them all!"

"Feiran's get—Mageborn traitors—"

"How do we know Mage Hall wasn't destroyed on the Captal's own order?"

"The way Malerris Castle *seemed* to be destroyed! What trick is this?"

"Has anyone even *seen* Mage Hall?"

"Twenty years of lies—"

"Take them!"

Sarra's frozen facade finally shattered. Her children's future was lost. They should have been Mage Guardians, working in defense of all Lenfell; they should have been honored, respected, revered. Instead—

Vellerin Dombur was allowing herself to be persuaded, her sapphire eyes half-hooded by her painted lids to hide sparkling triumph. "Very well. As a sign of good faith—"

There was a coldness at Sarra's side where Mikel had been. She leaned forward, fingers tangling in the green tablecloth, darkly wet where spilled wine soaked it. Her lips soundlessly formed her son's name as he strode around the tables to the center of the Malachite Hall.

"You?" Vellerin Dombur smiled.

"Yes," Mikel said quietly. "I'm not even half a Mage Guardian yet, but I am my mother's son and the Captal's nephew. And," he finished proudly, "an Ambrai."

"Mikel!" Taigan called out. "If you go, I go too!"

"No!" Sarra cried. "I forbid this! You're the last—"

"The last *what?*" shouted Senasta Dombur. "The last Ambrais, the last hope for domination over Ambraishir and the Council and the Assembly and the Mage Guardians—over all Lenfell! We need Sarra *Ambrai* and Cailet *Ambrai* here in order to discover their plans. Yes, take the boy, Vellerin. Lady Glenin will see to it that he behaves himself."

Sarra saw disappointment in Glenin's eyes, swiftly masked. It was Taigan she wanted—and Sarra knew why.

"As you wish." Vellerin gestured, and two tall, muscular young men with the sapphire Dombur eyes left their places at table to approach Mikel.

He lifted one hand. "No. I've given my word. I won't be led away like a criminal."

"The word of an Ambrai!" came a derisive shout.

"Yes," Mikel replied, but his arrogance was nothing of Ambrai and all of Collan Rosvenir.

"He's yours, Vellerin—and welcome to him," said Councillor Dombur.

The would-be Grand Duchess nodded to four hundred astonished faces in the Malachite Hall and nudged her equally startled husband in the ribs. He followed her to the door near which Granon Isidir still stood. There she turned her head, looking over her shoulder at Sarra.

Sarra looked up at Glenin. Who gave a tiny shrug and a tinier smile, joined the Domburs and Mikel, and walked through the open door. *Family.* Vellerin prodded her husband forward, and warily he took a step, then confidently joined Glenin on the other side of the threshold.

"Thank you," Vellerin said with sweet sarcasm to Sarra, "for canceling your Wards."

And they were gone.

"Sarra Ambrai," intoned Senasta Dombur, "you and your First Daughter will proceed under guard to your chambers, and wait there at the Council's pleasure until we decide what to do with you."

Agony resolved itself into simple hatred. Sarra rose to her feet, pulling Mikel's longvest around her, and glared at her fellow Councillor. When she spoke at last, all the carefully learned casualness of Roseguard vanished in long, liquid vowels and clipped consonants. The haughty, unmistakable accent of Ambrai. The accent of her childhood.

"And what do you propose to do with us?" Her voice rang through the Hall like a temple bell on a winter night. "Imprisonment? Execution? Do you really think you could pronounce either on a Mageborn Ambrai—and enforce it?"

"Take her away!"

Granon Isidir came forward. "*I* will act as escort," he said, and there was that in his tone that dared anyone to object. No one dared.

As he took her and Taigan out of the Malachite Hall, Sarra tried not to see the grief and broken faith in his eyes. She was so horribly afraid she would soon see the same in Collan's.

17

"SO. You didn't know your ancestry," said his aunt. "I trust you're suitably impressed."

Mikel shrugged. They'd taken him to Vellerin Dombur's huge suite, put him in an antechamber between bedrooms, and left him alone with Glenin. Both of them had Warded themselves six ways to the Wraithenwood.

"You spoke bravely enough back in the Malachite Hall. What's happened to your voice? It's considered civilized to make conversation."

"Conversation is correct in *polite* company."

"So much for the elegant manners of an Ambrai."

" 'Manners'? After what you did to my mother, in front of all those people—?"

"I assume you mean the birthmark. Histrionic, I agree, but I had three excellent reasons."

"First and foremost, to humiliate my mother."

"Of course." She shrugged. "Besides, there's no surer way of infuriating middle-aged women than seeing someone your mother's age with such pretty breasts. And no better way of catching men's attention than by showing them those breasts."

"My father will kill you for it," Mikel observed quietly.

"He would if he could, I'm sure. You know, Mikel, I think we'll have an interesting time of it while I decided whether to kill you or keep you alive to breed more Mageborns."

Mikel smiled. "Why do you think I offered myself?"

"Before your sister could?" Glenin laughed. "Do you sincerely believe I won't end up with her as well? But you present the greater challenge. Drug you, and you're incapable. Keep your head clear, and you'll resist. I might be able to spell you into it, but—"

"—but family can walk through each other's Wards, so I could probably counter your other magic as well. Yes, I'd say I'm definitely a problem," he finished with more complacence than he felt.

"Ah, but your sister. . . ." Glenin smiled. "Restrained by drugs or magic or rope around her wrists and ankles, all she has to do is lie there."

Taigan. Raped.

He resolved then and there to kill Glenin himself.

Vellerin Dombur invaded the tiny room, red-cheeked and huffing. "Ambrais! All of them! Why didn't you tell me?"

"It wasn't necessary for you to know," Glenin responded.

"Think again, my fine Lady of Malerris! And why didn't you let me get around to Mirya's trial, and the Liwellan deaths, and—"

"You mean there was more?" Mikel interrupted, eyes

as wide as he could make them. "Considering all the rest of it, don't you think that would be a little over the top?"

Vellerin snarled at him. Glenin looked amused.

"Which is not even to mention your timing," the wrathful Lady continued. "When you gave me the signal, I was completely unprepared! I thought we'd agreed to begin *after*—"

"—dessert?" said Mikel. "I agree—a despicable lapse. Not even half a dinner, no dancing—and not a couplet of his Lordship's sterling poetry."

"Close your mouth, boy, or I'll have the Weaver's servants sew it shut!" To Glenin she said, "There's other work to be done—we'll discuss this later," and slammed the door.

"Fascinating woman," Mikel observed.

Glenin shrugged. "One works with what one has."

"Tell me if I've got this right," he continued conversationally. "She had to know enough to convince her this would succeed, so her speech would be convincing. But she couldn't know all of it, because there was always the chance she'd blab."

Glenin nodded. "And her shock was necessary, as it created fellow-feeling among everyone else when *they* were shocked."

"I understand. I don't think *she* will, though. By the way, has she consulted a physician about her blood pressure?"

"She won't die of an apoplexy, if that's what you mean. I have something else in mind for her—something I intend she'll live to enjoy."

"Truly told?"

"Never more truly. She's about to be ruined financially."

"How will you do it?" he asked, genuinely curious. His father's son, truly told.

"By destroying confidence in every bank in which she has a share. She thinks we're working together on this. My Malerrisi have been withdrawing large sums planted for the purpose all over Lenfell—"

"—to cause a panic," Mikel said, "after which the same money—*her* money—will buy up the tottering banks cheap, so she can run the banking system pretty much as she pleases."

"So she believes. Instead, the money to purchase bank shares will not be forthcoming. I intend to use it to establish my people in positions of influence all over Lenfell."

"And Vellerin Dombur—?"

"She'll have to sell large portions of her personal property to complete the planned purchases of banks, at which point she'll be suspected as the instigator— especially when the original account deposits are traced back to her. She'll then be found liable and have to sell nearly everything to make good to depositors."

"And as she dismantles her own holdings, the rest of the Dombur Web will suffer."

"Collapse," she corrected. "She wove her affairs so tightly with the rest that they're compelled to support her in her ambitions—and will join her in her downfall." She laughed softly, avidly. "So much for the Domburs!"

Mikel was both awed and appalled. It wasn't just Vellerin Dombur she'd ruin; the panic would affect every Shir. Fa had educated him in the finer points of finance, with an eye to his one day becoming a husband who oversaw business affairs and maybe a whole Web. He'd learned how to add and subtract sitting on Fa's knee, "helping" with the account books. Mikel understood how the economy fit together, and that the wheat harvest in Brogdenguard could affect not only the price of bread at Wyte Lynn Castle but also something so seemingly unrelated as the production of leather in Cantrashir. *"Hell, Mishka, why d'you think they call 'em 'Webs'?"* And nothing was more entangled in itself than the banking system.

"But why?" he asked.

Glenin only smiled.

"No, truly told, I want to know," he insisted. "Why ruin her?"

Gray-green eyes darkened grimly, the smile gone. "Because her family ruined the Feiran Name. We were originally from Domburronshir, with vast lands and wealth. The Domburs coveted what we had, and set about obliterating us."

"No wonder I never did like any of them," he remarked, and she nodded approvingly, but he was thinking furiously behind his casual manner. The panic that would sweep Lenfell, the economic troubles that would follow, all those Malerrisi with all that money . . . and all that magic. With Mage Guardians censured and despised because of their Captal, the Malerrisi would move in to fill the gap.

"So you see why I tolerated working with Vellerin Dombur," finished Glenin.

"Yes. Have you decided about me yet?"

"Oh, I'll let you live—for a while, anyway. You're quick, and I find you almost as entertaining as your father." She laughed. "And every time I think of your mother's agony as she imagines you in my tender keeping. . . ."

"I can take care of myself. I'm my father's son— *that's* no secret."

She eyed him speculatively, head tilted to one side. "Secrets, Mikel, are the most important things in the world. When you know the secrets of others, you have power over them—and you guard and cherish those secrets as a miser does her gold. When you have secrets of your own, you guard them just as scrupulously, in case others should find them out and use them against you. My sisters' mistake was that they thought their secrets locked and Warded from everyone but me, and that I couldn't denounce them without endangering myself. After all, I am also a daughter of Auvry Feiran."

"But that was never a secret," he replied. "I bet you have a few left to use, just in case."

"Two," she agreed readily. "The first is my son. The second—ah, but I'll save that for the right time. That's the other thing about secrets, nephew dear. Knowing them isn't enough. Knowing when and how to use them is the trick." She stretched her arms wide, then got to her feet. "Speaking of which, it's just about time for you to meet your cousin. I've enjoyed our chat. You won't do anything foolish, like trying to escape, would you?"

He shrugged. "Nobody's made any secret of those four big Domburs outside."

"Good boy. I knew you wouldn't be stupid."

"By the way," he said sweetly, "if I were you I'd have that burn on your palm treated. My sister's magic can be a little severe at times."

Her eyes glittered appreciation of the remark. "Thank you. Very kind of you to be concerned about your auntie's health and well-being."

Truly told, he hoped it festered and she died of it. But as she left him alone, he reflected that whereas words had gotten him into this, and could be a telling weapon against some enemies, words wouldn't get him out. Brute strength in the form of those big, dumb Domburs stood watch on both doors to the antechamber; no chance of overpowering them on their terms. He sat there in his shirtsleeves with nothing up them. He had his wits and his magic, and that was all.

Come to think of it, considering the former came from his father and the latter from his mother, not a bad arsenal.

18

"YOU'LL wish to change clothes," said Granon Isidir in a stiffly formal voice that nonetheless conveyed the depths of his misery.

Taigan didn't care how he felt. She waited for her mother to acknowledge the words—to say something, look at him, go through to her bedroom, anything that indicated she was paying attention. Sarra stood in the center of the reception salon, apathetic and silent.

"Mother." No response. Taigan glanced at Isidir. "Councillor, if you'd leave us for a moment?"

"With regret, *Domna,* I cannot."

Not "Prentice" or "Lady"—unworthy of the first, and no longer the First Daughter of a First Daughter. . . .

"Mother," she said again, ignoring Isidir, "come with me."

Sarra did as told, shivering intermittently. Taigan chose a warm woolen shirt and trousers for her. The mother was dressed not as the mother had once dressed the daughter, but as a child dressed a rag doll. Taigan paused only to find salve for the reddened welt at Sarra's nape where the chain had scraped delicate skin. She bundled the bronze velvet gown in a corner of the closet. Then she sorted through her father's clothes, knowing she wouldn't be allowed to go to her own rooms. Shirt, trousers, and sleeveless longvest replaced her silken dress—a Timarrin Allard original, the kind of dress she used to dream of wearing. How long ago that seemed. And how unimportant. She gave the gorgeous blue flowers a last look, doubting she'd ever wear anything remotely like this again.

Execution was unthinkable. Imprisonment . . . all Fa's droll stories of being thrown into jail whirled through her mind. It wouldn't be like that. Nothing at all like that. It would be a dark, damp cell in Ryka —or a suffocating cubicle in The Waste—

But for Mikel, a block of windswept ice in Domburronshir.

She slammed the closet doors shut and leaned her forehead against the carved wood, squeezing her eyes shut against tears.

"So you finally feel it, too," said her mother, and she turned to find the black eyes looking at her, knowing her for the first time since they'd left the Malachite Hall.

"Feel what?" Taigan asked thickly.

"How hopeless it is. I've fought for or against one thing or another almost all my life. I can't fight this. I can't fight anymore."

Taigan knelt before her where she sat on the bed. "Are you ashamed? Do you think Mikel and I—" She took the small, icy hands in her own. "You're the daughter of a First Daughter of Ambrai!"

"And of the Butcher of Ambrai."

"What does that have to do with us?"

"We're his get. The shadows are in us, too. Haven't you ever felt them?"

"If I have, I didn't give in to them."

"How young you are. What do you know of evil and ambition?"

"Enough to recognize them in others. We were told by the Captal—" Aunt Cailet in truth as well as affection. She strangled on the rest.

"My sister is full of Mageborn clichés."

"You're Mageborn, and an Ambrai! Start behaving like it!"

Sarra gave her a look to shrivel her flesh. "Don't presume too far, child."

Taigan had never heard that tone of voice before. She flinched. "Mama—" But if she hoped for soothing words and assurances that she hadn't meant it, she hoped in vain. Taigan stood up, letting go her mother's hands. "Why didn't you see this coming?" she demanded harshly. "Between you and the Captal, you ought to've known Glenin would—"

"Would do what, exactly? And what, exactly, should we have known to do?" Small shoulders in dark-brown wool shrugged. "Perhaps we thought Gorsha's Wards were so strong and so thorough that nothing could make anyone believe, even if they guessed—or were told outright, the way Glenin did tonight."

"Or maybe that's what you *wanted* to believe."

"They held for thirty-eight years, Taigan. Why should we think that one night they'd become useless?"

"You should have known!" Taigan cried—unfairly, she knew, but right now she wasn't disposed to be fair.

"Maybe we should have. Cailet's strategy was to let it play itself out. She learned long ago not to run headlong into a problem and hope that her strength matched it without really knowing how powerful it might turn out to be. A straight line isn't always the best way to get from one place to another. It's better to go around a wall than try to slam your way through."

"*Now* who's speaking in clichés?"

"You presume again, daughter," said Sarra, but this time without much rancor. Truly told, she just sounded tired. "I believe that what Cailet wanted was to bring Glenin out into the open—and Vellerin Dombur, too. Well, that's happened. And not in any way that either of us could have anticipated, so please don't run on about it anymore."

"But she *knew* who you are—both of you—didn't it ever occur to you she'd use that?"

"Gorynel Desse's Wardings, remember?" Another tiny shrug. "Nothing, not a hint of suspicion, in thirty-eight years. Of those who knew—Lady Lilen is the only one unWarded. Her children don't even know, not anywhere in their minds that they can reach. I've always been very careful not to make too many references to Ostinhold—of course, Mother and I weren't there very long before Cailet was born. Mother died a day or two later."

Taigan was torn between wanting to ask about that time—and about the Octagon Court and her grandparents and great-grandparents and a million other things, questions she'd never even considered asking before (Warded against them?)—and the equally urgent need to find some reason for all this. Some explanation for why her entire life had ended before it had even begun. Two days short of eighteen, and her future was in a jail cell.

And Mikel—

"I don't suppose there's any real accounting for it," Sarra said, as if she'd read Taigan's mind. "Except that things happen because they happen. Perhaps that's an excuse for being stupid and blind. I don't know. But it's done now. There's no way out of it."

"There *has* to be a way out! I won't spend the rest of my life—"

"When Cailet and I make a mistake," Sarra interrupted, "we don't do it by halves."

This infuriated Taigan so deeply that for a moment she thought she might slap her own mother. The impulse had barely been fought down when the door was flung open and Lady Alinar came in, leaning heavily on a silver-headed cane. Granon Isidir stood behind her.

"I had to see for myself," Lady Alinar said querulously. "Isidir tells me it's true. Is it?"

"Yes," Taigan answered, and even though she had

never knowingly deceived anyone about her lineage, she writhed inside with shame.

"Stop hovering, Isidir," rapped out Lady Alinar. "I doubt they'll murder me—why bother? And even if they do, what do I care? The Liwellan Name is well and truly dead now. And I should have been, long before I found out about *this*."

"Lady," he said, bowing his head and withdrawing.

She hobbled in, and suddenly lashed out a foot to hook around the door and slam it shut. Nothing about her now was fragile or elderly as she came rapidly forward to the bed. "There's not much time. We have to get you out of here."

"Why bother?" asked Sarra.

"Because I assume you have no wish to die, and your sister and your children with you—or do you entertain any illusions that this is precisely what Glenin plans?"

"She won't kill Taigan. She *needs* Taigan," Sarra said bitterly.

Lady Alinar gave a start, then nodded briskly. "Yes, of course. Be that as it may—"

"Why me?" Taigan demanded.

"Use the wits the Saints gave you," her mother snapped. "You're a Mageborn Ambrai—the only young woman in the world who can say that until you have a daughter."

Taigan nearly gagged.

Lady Alinar let the shawl drop from her shoulders. Gathering it, she unfurled the heavily woven gray silk to show its embroidered underside. "I'm getting foolish in my old age—I meant to give you this at our last meeting, Sarra, and forgot. It's very, very old, made by Cloister women from a pattern of tiles in a shrine to St. Mikellan."

Taigan peered at it. "You mean the Ladder Saint?"

She smiled slightly. "On the walls of Firrense, he looks like Alin Ostin—or so I'm told. I gather that's why your brother's name is Mikel. 'Alin Liwellan' *would* be quite a mouthful. Take this and give it to the Captal."

Sarra made no move to accept it, so Taigan did, trying to work out the design of black and silver and gold. It made no sense to her—until she recalled whose shrine the pattern came from. "Ladders," she whispered. "All the Ladders on Lenfell."

"Most of them. I haven't tried them all, no one has since The Waste War. But the pattern is here, and requires only a map laid under it—and the correct version of 'The Ladder Song,' of course." She glanced over her shoulder. "Someone's here—one hopes it's my idiot son at long nerve-wracking last. He certainly didn't inherit his father's sense of timing."

The salon door crashed open and a familiar voice called urgently, "Are you decent? Hurry up—we have to get out of here!"

Josselin Mikleine, wild of eye and black curling hair, filled the doorway. Jored was right behind him, just as agitated and even more disheveled.

"My mistake," murmured Lady Alinar. "Great-grandson."

Taigan barely heard her. She stared at the two young men, not understanding for a moment. Then, with a rush of loving gratitude for Jored, she gave him a dazzling smile.

"Come on, Mother!" She yanked Sarra to her feet.

"No," Sarra replied, stepping toward the bed. "Not with him. *Never* with him! Don't you understand?"

"Lady Sarra," said Joss, taking a few more steps into the bedchamber, "I have no idea what you're talking about—and no time to discover what it is. Councillor Isidir very kindly let us in, and very kindly invited Jored to knock him out—not *too* hard, I hope?" he asked over his shoulder, and Jored shook his head. "Good. We can escape with a clear conscience. But we must escape *now*." He noticed Lady Alinar then, over by the windows, and gave a start.

"Oh, don't mind me, young man," she told him almost merrily. "It would scarcely require fisticuffs to subdue me."

"I would never dream of it, Lady," he said, bowing.

All at once Sarra stood up and caught Taigan's gaze. "Mageborn Ambrai, am I? All right, then."

Grabbing the shawl, she hurried to her dressing table. Taigan's eyes popped when, at the touch of a finger here and there, a drawer appeared where there shouldn't have been a drawer. From it Sarra extracted a small wooden box—one Taigan had seen before, long long ago. Sarra opened it, dumped its contents—some dried flowers, some jewelry, a black silk glove—into the shawl, and knotted the material around the hoard. Taigan could suddenly hear her father: *"Never be without something small and portable to sell, pixie, preferably jewels—a lesson I learned the hard way!"*

"Well?" Sarra demanded, black eyes fierce as she went to where Taigan stood gaping at her. "What are you all standing around for? Let's get the hell out of here."

"What about Fa?" Taigan said.

"All in good time," said another voice, and all eyes went to the slim, black-clad figure of the Captal. She strode past Jored in the doorway, nodded politely to Lady Alinar—who, Taigan was by now convinced, was no more a Liwellan than she herself was—and said to Sarra, "I've been very well informed by Elomar and the Bekkes—before I ordered them to get the hell out of here by Ladder. You're right, we don't have much time. Jored, move away from Josselin."

"Captal—?"

"Do it." And a Mage Globe appeared, dark crimson and shot with silver lightning.

Josselin stared at her. Jored backed away toward the writing desk in the corner, gray eyes huge. They glanced at each other, then at the two-foot Globe, then at the Captal.

Taigan saw three things then. First, that allowing for green eyes and certain traits inherited from Collan Rosvenir, she herself was a pretty fair rendering of what the Captal must have looked like at eighteen. Second, that the Captal was not angry, despite the bloody glow of her Mage Globe; sadness was in her eyes, and regret, and a flicker of uncertainty. Third, that Joss had the Captal's sword buckled around his hips.

The Captal had seen it, too. "I'd like that back now," she said.

Bewilderment was scrawled all across his face. But

he unhooked the fastening and wrapped the leather around the hilt.

"Taigan, if you'd be so kind—?"

She went forward a few paces, but stopped when the Captal spoke again.

"That's far enough. Slide it across the floor to her, Josselin."

"Captal, I don't underst—"

"Taigan. The sword." Her voice had sharpened.

She did as told, after Josselin crouched and pushed the sword half the distance between them. Lady Alinar was smiling a little. As Joss straightened, he looked surprised for an instant and glanced around the room. Taigan knelt where she was, reaching—half-expecting someone to make a grab for it. But it came into her hands, and she held it in its scabbard, and even through tooled leather it spoke to her magic in fleeting tremors of power.

The Captal sighed quietly.

"Cailet. . . ."

"Not now, Sarra." The Mage Globe hovered again equidistant between the two young men. "Too clever for me, aren't you?" she asked them. "The one who had the sword gave it up, the one who didn't have it didn't try to take it. I'd hoped—ah, but you *are* too clever for me, truly told."

Neither said a word.

"Captal," asked Lady Alinar, "what is this little exercise intended to prove?"

"Which of them destroyed Mage Hall."

Taigan caught her breath.

"And which of them, therefore, is Glenin's son."

This time she blurted out, "No!"

"Yes, dear, it's quite true."

Jored and Josselin spun half around as Glenin came in. Before her eldest sister could speak, the Captal said, "And now we are all here—excepting Mikel, of course. What did you do with him, Glenin?"

"He's perfectly safe." She gave the Mage Globe a bored glance and walked around it to stand beside the dressing table. "Yes, now we're all here."

"For the first time," Sarra said conversationally.

Glenin looked surprised. "It is, isn't it? All three of us in one room. Tell me, Lady Whoever-you-are," she directed at the old woman by the windows, "as a disinterested observer, is there a family resemblance?"

"Certainly," replied Lady Alinar at once. "But I assume you don't need an opinion on which most favors your mother and which your father."

"You knew them both?" Sarra enquired, still in that calm, everyday tone.

Lady Alinar only smiled.

Glenin smiled back. "There are traits of each in all of us. My son inherited nothing but his grandfather's height."

"It happens that way sometimes in families," said Lady Alinar. "My own progeny resembles me in no particular, and in his children and grandchildren I've seen quite a bit of the other side of their breeding lines."

"Where *did* you find this wordy old fossil?" Glenin asked Sarra.

Cailet spoke impatiently. "Enough, Glenin. Do what you came to do—if you can."

"You've been singularly inept at anticipating me so far—what can you possibly know about what I came here to do?"

"Get Taigan, of course, to complete your matched set of Ambrais."

"You're learning!" She turned to Taigan. "Tell me, dear, how does it feel to know who you really are?"

With a great effort at casual calm, she replied, "I'm still not clear on exactly why it matters so much. I'm the same person I was yesterday."

"It matters," Glenin said flatly.

"To you," she shot back.

"Yes. And to my son—whom I would never allow to father Mageborns on any but the finest lineage."

Glenin was too late to shock and horrify, but Taigan had to struggle to keep loathing from her face. She shrugged one shoulder and tried to look bored. She didn't dare look at either Jored or Josselin.

"Oh, now, what girl *wouldn't* want to bed so charming and handsome a young man?" Glenin asked playfully.

"After all, you've already shown a decided preference for him."

Him.

Jored.

Smiling at her, ignoring the Mage Globe as he went to stand beside his mother. Jored. Who at Mage Hall had shown himself the true grandson of the Butcher of Ambrai.

In the next instant he spoke her name, and a darkness so vast she physically staggered swept over her. She fought it off wildly, unable even now to believe it came from him. Instinct flung up Wards—Wards his darkness stormed through as if they had not existed. Family. He was family. He could get through any Ward she used.

And all at once she understood what her mother had tried to tell her. His shadows called to a facet of her being she hadn't known existed. The beauty of Jored's face and body were as nothing compared to the seduction, the sweet allure, the *power* that filled her mind and heart and made her want nothing else than to be with him, be one with him in the darkness.

She knew then what had happened to Auvry Feiran, how it had happened. She was his granddaughter. With his grandson, she formed a unity of strength and magic, body and will, to make them invincible. And for the space of a heartbeat, a lifetime, she joyously agreed.

"Taigan!"

Cailet's voice. Jored, still smiling, conjured visions in the darkness—of the Captal as a bloodless ruin, of Taigan's mother, father, brother dead. She could escape the carnage by joining with him. Only by joining with him.

Taigan drew the sword at the same instant Cailet struck. Hate exploded in her simultaneously with the Mage Globe's explosion of righteous fury and terrible fear. Taigan heard her mother scream, and briefly wondered why Lady Alinar didn't, nor Josselin. Not that she could be bothered to care about any of them; she wanted Jored's throat. She wanted it hewn, severed, gushing blood. She wanted his death, and the sword knew it.

She put the whole weight of her body behind the blow that would strike him down. But the blade crashed into another Mage Globe—so darkly red it was nearly black, crawling with black lightning. It erupted as the sword slashed through it. Taigan reeled but did not fall.

"Careful, Mother," said Jored, as if cautioning her against a rain-slick step. "She's uneducated as yet, but stronger than she knows."

"As strong as you or I? Don't make me laugh. This is serious work. We have to take care of them all, right now. And don't forget that senile wreckage by the windows."

Another Globe—this one the Captal's, intended for Jored. And another, Glenin's, intended for Sarra. And yet another, hurtling toward her from Jored's magic.

"Don't make me hurt you," he said as she sheared into it with the sword. "I care for you, Taisha, but not enough to let you get anywhere near me with that thing."

She'd been wrong; the Captal's Globe was not meant to attack Jored. It was meant to protect him from her sword. It hovered in the magic-charged air between them, guarding him.

Why? Why would she prevent Taigan from doing what had to be done?

"Taigan!"

She turned her head and saw her mother, clinging to a bedpost for support, gasping. Glenin's magic was dissipating all around her, malicious but strangely inadequate.

"Why can't I kill you?" Glenin said irritably. "There's no Ward, no spell to prevent me—"

"Mother!" Jored had fallen back with two Mage Globes—one his, one the Captal's—casting blackened crimson light on his face, turning his gray eyes to red coals. Glenin turned to defend her son. Taigan ran to her mother, putting the sword between her and any more magic—but the sword knew what she wanted. It crooned and chanted, and when seduction failed it began to shriek for Jored's throat.

She heard it. Obeyed it. Broke free of her mother's clutching hands. Started for Jored. His back was against a wall, gray eyes with their subtle hints of green darting in real terror from the Captal to the two Globes to Glenin.

She would have his blood. The sword agreed, and of its lengthy experience even told her how to do it.

19

MIKEL got it right at the same time friends came to rescue him.

Glenin's Wards must be to keep others out, because she knew they couldn't keep him in. *Family.* But he couldn't just walk out. He had to provide a diversion for the Domburs. He needed to cast a Ward of his own. He'd made Joss teach him the Kyyos in the Bushes that had so startled him back at Mage Hall; reviewing in his mind the configuration of the room beyond for a good place to put it, he decided on the gold-and-marble table by the windows. *"Stone, silk, and pure metal—these hold a Warding most strongly,"* the Captal had told them.

The Captal. Auntie Caisha.

Hard work it was, visualizing in detail a table glimpsed in passing. It was big, gaudy, meant to attract attention, and he wouldn't have noticed it but for the huge crystal vase of white flameflowers atop it. Mikel knew his history; sigil of the Renne Name, the flower had been the symbol of the Rising. The bouquet was either an innocent tribute to the Dombur color, or a not-so-innocent visual message that a *new* Rising to rectify the excess of the old was now to begin, and it would be led by the Malerrisi. Or maybe, he suddenly thought, it was a mockery meant for Cailet, whose Name Saint's flower it was.

His first effort yielded not a sound from beyond the door. His second—with eyes squeezed shut and tongue bitten between teeth—was no more successful. Then he remembered what Taigan had said about magic: that when she *tried,* it didn't work very well, but when she just let it happen. . . .

So he just let it happen.

The big, brawny Domburs screeched. Mikel kicked

open the door, smashing the lock with his bootheel, in time to see their fleeing backs. He left the Ward where it was—ugly piece of furniture, it deserved to be thrown out. He was out in the hall in a trice.

Telomir Renne, Ollia and Sirron Bekke, and Sevy Banian were there, flattened to a wall to avoid the stampede.

"Sorry we're late," Telo said.

"Don't worry about it," Mikel replied. "I was just about to start wondering where to escape *to*."

"Thought so," Ollia told him, nodding her satisfaction. "Our timing was perfect."

"Brilliant," he agreed. "Since you know where we're going, can we please go there *now*?"

20

CAILET knew what was coming. Glenin conjured a third sphere, flinging it toward the hovering pair; all three collided in a shower of sparks and the dressing-table mirror shattered. Cailet lurched against a table, overturning it, stumbling to keep her balance. Josselin moved to hold her up, and she cast him a single mute glance of apology before righting herself and shaking free of his grip.

"I can't Work," he said rapidly. "I'm Warded—and it's not my doing! But I can't help you, Cailet, I can't!"

She shook her head, meaning it didn't matter, but wondered just the same where those Wards had come from. They surrounded him, let him move and touch her but allowed no magic in or out. Excellently done, the work of an expert. But she couldn't worry about that now.

Glenin hurled another flashing black sphere. Cailet fought it off—this time more easily, without the backlash that had nearly felled her before. The mother's magic weaker than the son's? No—the difference was Jored's lethal intent. Glenin's spells were not killing spells—and Glenin's knew it. Her eyes bled confusion and the beginnings of panic. Cailet wanted badly to laugh at her, to unbalance her further, but she was too busy repelling another assault by Jored.

Glenin turned, looking for Sarra. But Taigan was between them—intent on one thing only. It was in her blazing green eyes, the sword's insidious spells working with her deepest desires. She would kill him if she could—and with that sword, she most definitely could.

Which Cailet could not allow. Jored's blood on Taigan's hands would blight her whole life. She knew it as surely as she knew that had her father not tried to protect her from Glenin twenty years ago, his Wraith would have been pent in the Dead White Forest, condemned for eternity—and Anniyas would have devoured him along with all the rest, and that extra strength might have been just enough for her to kill and kill and kill as she wished.

Auvry Feiran's had been an act of will to *do*. Taigan's must be an act of will to stop.

Cailet thought all this in a single heartbeat. Josselin suddenly stepped between her and Jored—and a Mage Globe black as a fragment of unmitigated evil slammed into Joss's strange, inexplicable Wards.

Jored's sphere ruptured. Magic spewed out. Cailet recoiled from its backlash, knowing that if it had hit her or even one of her own Globes she might very well be dead. Josselin moaned, falling to his knees. And that peculiar old woman collapsed on the carpet, a thousand jewel-toned shards of window glass raining down onto her silvery head.

"Jored!" Glenin cried. "I can't kill them—*any* of them! It's gone!"

Cailet stood only because she could lean both hands on Josselin's broad shoulders where he knelt before her. His head was bent and his breath came in heavy gasps. The Wards around him were gone. Cailet, too, fought for air, for sight of Jored and Glenin and Sarra—

"He took it from me!" Glenin cried frantically. "He took all the *killing* out of me and used it to kill himself!"

But she saw only Taigan, like St. Delilah with Her Sword come to life. Cailet had to stop her or the shadow that was Jored would darken the rest of her life. She pushed herself away from Josselin, who staggered to his feet. Before she could conjure another Globe, he strode straight to Taigan—unWarded, unarmed—and closed both strong hands around the sword. Blood dripped down the blade from his sliced palms and fingers.

"No." Very quietly. "Give it to me, Taigan. Let it go."

She snarled at him, and struggled, and even though he was nearly three times her slender size he could not wrest it from her. The blade cut more deeply into his hands, and he grimaced, but he would not let go.

Yet another of Jored's murderous Globes flew toward them. Cailet countered it, but this time could not make it explode; it was pushed back, but try as she might, she could not use her own Globe to shatter it.

And if she had, she realized suddenly, with all the force of fatal magic inside it, everyone in this room might die.

21

MIKEL ran with the others for his mother's suite, trusting to the two Warrior Mages for safety. Ollia Bekke was ahead of him, sword in one hand and throwing knife in the other, ready to cut down anyone who got in their way; Sirron Bekke followed behind, casting defensive Wards at each intersection so no one would or could come after them. The only resistance they met was in the tall, lean form of Chava Allard, standing guard outside Sarra's chambers.

"Out of the way," snapped Ollia.

"I'm very sorry," he said politely, "but I'm afraid you can't go in there right now. My Lady and her son are rather busy, and do not wish to be disturbed."

Telomir Renne seemed in the grip of some powerful emotion. He stared at the younger man for a moment, as if looking past the bearded face and hazel eyes to something inside Allard's very soul, then said very quietly, "You know I can get past your Wardings."

Mikel gaped, briefly stunned out of his fury. Telomir Renne, the world's oldest Prentice Mage, could get by a Malerrisi?

Allard blinked, then smiled and unwittingly provided Mikel with the answer. "You know, I believe you could. There's little I'd put past a son of Gorynel Desse."

Ollia caught her breath; so did Sevy. Sirron had no reaction at all.

"Will you stand aside?" Telomir asked.

The Malerrisi shook his head. "I sincerely regret, *Domni* Renne, that I must decline. Orders, you know."

It was a silent battle, and invisible but for the strain on both faces. Mikel looked at Ollia and Sirron and Sevy, seeing that they felt what he felt: exactly nothing. The intensity of the struggle was so finely directed between these two that not a hint of magic spilled over. If Mikel hadn't been so frantic, he might have been impressed.

Chava Allard gave a little sigh, and without warning his long body folded to the floor, unconscious. Telo sagged against Sevy Banian, squinting as if even the gentle light of the hallway lamps pained his eyes.

"We'll Ward the door," he managed, peering at Mikel. "Go."

Mikel went.

Granon Isidir was sprawled across a carpet. Mikel had no time for him, left him to Sirron and Ollia. He saw a wild crimson glow from his mother's bedroom, and felt the backlash of power, and for the first time understood the "taste" of Malerrisi magic. And recognized it from the night of St. Maidil's, when Lirenza Mettyn died in his arms.

22

CAILET gathered strength, knowing for a certainty that if her magic clashed with Jored's, people would die. But Glenin was vulnerable; for some reason, she could not kill even though she desperately wanted to. So Cailet called on Tamos Wolvar's consummate mastery of Mage Globes, and while maintaining the sphere that kept Jored's at bay constructed another one to aim at Glenin.

Not to kill her. Only to enfold her as Josselin had mysteriously been enfolded, allowing no magic in or out.

Glenin conjured a small, compact Globe between her hands, ready to fling it at Sarra—unprotected while Taigan and Joss grappled with the sword. Within ruby depths something gold shimmered and trembled. When the sphere left her hands, Cailet wasn't yet ready to counter it.

But it did nothing. It shot a few feet toward Sarra, then stopped like a ball slamming into a barn. Glenin tried again, again to no avail. A storm broke over her face, contorting beauty into feral rage. She turned—not toward Cailet, but toward the splintered windows. The old woman sat with her back to the stone wall, bleeding from cuts on her cheeks and hands. On her lips was a serene smile.

"I really can't allow this, you know," she said softly. "You can no longer kill, but you could do great damage."

Glenin cursed savagely. "Let me go, you old witch!"

"Mage Guardians," the Lady informed her, as if speaking to a dull-witted child, "do not obey Malerrisi."

"Mage Guardians"—? was all Cailet had time to think before Glenin screamed at her son:

"Jored! Leave me! I command it!"

"No—Mother—"

He *was* Malerrisi, and yet he did not instantly obey. Cailet saw his anguish, felt him vacillate—watched his Mage Globe weaken and fade away. But before she could Work to hold him, he gave a terrible cry and fled.

And within the nullifying sphere the mysterious Lady had set around Glenin, the blood-red Globe with its quivering golden center exploded.

23

MIKEL grunted with the impact of colliding with Jored. He reeled, knocking over a chair. He had barely gained his balance, and Jored had barely raced past him, when he heard screams both from within his mother's bedchamber and outside in the hallway. He staggered again, buffeted between two overwhelming gouts of magic. He righted himself and lurched toward the open door.

Sarra, the Captal, Taigan, Josselin, some silver-haired lady—all sprawled on the floor, stunned but still breathing. Glenin was a tangle of long limbs and turquoise silk and black lace and blood. Her arms had been blown away to the elbows.

Yet she lived. Mikel went to her, looked down into her face: scorched to blackness, crisped skin peeling from cheeks and brow, wounds oozing blood and clear yellowish fluid. He gagged, swallowed bile, and stepped back. His heel caught on something; he bent, picked it up, caught his breath as it singed his fingers, dropped it to the carpet. But he'd seen what it was. Twisted and bent, half-melted by the blast of magic, still he knew what the little piece of gold was. A coif pin. He'd last seen it yesterday, riding out on the hunt. He recognized it easily.

Not that Fa had ever worn it much.

Tears stung his eyes and he went to where his mother lay. Gathering her up, he placed her gently on the bed. She seemed at once older and younger than her forty-three years: fear aged her, drawing her face into lines of anguish, but with her golden hair tumbled around her cheeks she looked like a little girl. He knuckled his eyes and locked the sight of her in his heart, a memory to be taken out later, after grief turned her into an old woman once she learned that her husband was dead.

Taigan was stirring. Mikel got her into a chair, looking hard into her groggy eyes. "Teggie? Come on, Teggie, come back to me."

She shook her head violently, moaned, and sat up straighter. "Mother—?"

"She'll be all right. As soon as you can, help Joss." He glanced down at his fellow Prentice, giving a start. "What happened to his hands? There's blood all over them."

Taigan pushed him away. "I'll take care of him. You go to the Captal."

He did, to find her huddled now on the carpet, the heels of her palms pressed tight to her head as if she would crush her skull between them. "Captal?" he said softly. Then: "Cailet?"

She looked up, black eyes tearing and bloodshot, her skin like bleached linen. "Glenin," she said in a voice that shook with the pounding of her heartbeats.

"Dying, if not already dead." He knew better than to ask what the hell had happened. She'd tell him when he needed to know.

"Help me."

He half-carried her to where her eldest sister lay. Cailet knelt, one hand still rubbing at her temple, and with the other touched Glenin's blood-smeared hair.

Lashless, blackened lids peeled back from gray-green eyes untouched by the explosion. Luminous, beautiful, they stared up at Cailet with loathing and triumph and hideous pain.

"My son lives," Glenin whispered through seared lips.

"Yes," Cailet said.

"He loved me best," Glenin breathed, and Mikel thought she was talking about her son until she added, "He took *me* with him."

"Yes."

"But in the end. . . ." She coughed. Blood trickled from her mouth.

"In the end," Cailet echoed steadily, "it was all for nothing."

Glenin's body stiffened. "What I did, I did to save a world."

"To rule it. To remold it as you wanted it to be."

"As it *should* be. As—" She whimpered low in her throat. "Oh, Weaver, it hurts—"

Cailet went on stroking her hair. "It'll be over soon, Glensha."

A spark lit her eyes. "Nobody's called me that since—" Then her face drew taut with pride. "How dare you call me that."

"You're my sister."

"As am I," said another voice, strained and trembling. Mikel flinched at the sight of his mother. She knelt, placing a hand on her sister's shoulder. "I'm here, Glensha."

Glenin blinked charred eyelids to clear her vision of blood. "No one I *want* around me when I die."

"Sisters who would have loved you," Cailet said. "If you'd let us."

"Loved me? For what?" Her lips stretched in a smile. "For killing Collan Rosvenir?"

Sarra recoiled with a little cry. Glenin's arms moved, the stumps twitching grotesquely at her sides. Mikel knew what she wanted. He bent, picked up the sigil pin—cool now to the touch—and held it out to his mother.

That terrible smile still on her face, Glenin said, "My final secret. Remember, Mikel? Secrets must be used at just the right time—"

Sarra's hand lashed out and knocked the sigil pin from Mikel's fingers. "No! He's not dead—he's *not*—"

Taigan was there suddenly, arms around her mother, rocking her like a child as she cried. Taigan was crying, too. Sarra abruptly wrenched away from her, rasping out, "Don't touch me! Just—don't *touch* me!" But Taigan embraced her again and hung on tight, and Sarra slumped into her daughter's arm.

Mikel fought his own tears, throat too tight for speech. *Fa—no, not Fa—* he repeated mindlessly, because seeing his mother's and sister's grief made the death real to him at last. *Not Fa—please—*

He looked at Cailet, whose hand had stilled on Glenin's hair. The First Lady of Malerris had died with no one but the Mage Captal to notice her passing.

"Yes, Gorsha," he heard her whisper. "I know. Another minute."

"Gorsha"? Mikel stared.

He had no time to puzzle it out. Footsteps made him look up in time to see Telomir, Ollia, Sirron, and Sevy come into the room. Ollia went to Joss, exclaimed over his hands, and ripped the sheets off the bed for bandages. Sirron swept up the sword that lay bloodied on the carpet and took up post at the door. Sevy stood gaping, not believing the evidence of his own eyes.

But Telomir, after one quick glance around, hurried to the shattered windows where the mysterious elderly woman still sat amid the rainbow of colored glass shards. "Mother! What the hell are *you* doing here? Are you all right?"

"Don't fuss, dear," she said. "I'll be fine."

Cailet's head snapped around. "You're—"

"Jeymian Renne," she said as her son assisted her to her feet and then to a velvet couch. "Forgive me for not introducing myself earlier. I wish there was time to get acquainted, but I'm afraid you must all get out of here as soon as possible."

Mikel too felt the need of a chair. He locked his knees together so he wouldn't fall over, and managed, "But where will we go? And what about everybody else?"

"Unless my son has completely lost the wits his father and I bestowed on him, all the Mage Guardians on Ryka are currently in this room."

Cailet scowled at Sirron and Ollia. "I thought I ordered you—"

"Sorry, Captal," said Granon Bekke's nephew. "Elomar Adennos and the rest went to Ambrai—one step ahead of the Domburs and the Council Guard. Every Ladder in the Court is unavailable to us now."

"There are alternatives," Telomir said, then turned to his mother. "You'll come with us, of course."

"Saints, no, dear," she said. "I'm still Lady Alinar Liwellan—who can delay them here while she gives some sort of suitably garbled account of this. I'm worth more to you in sheer confusion here than I ever could be running about Lenfell."

"That's all we can look forward to," Mikel blurted. "Running. For the rest of our lives—until they catch up to us."

"No," Cailet said suddenly, but would not elaborate. She got to her feet, swaying slightly. "Lady Jeymian, I am deeply honored. Gorsha spea—spoke of you with high regard."

"I'll just bet he did," she replied, eyes twinkling. "Help me up, Telo."

He did, supporting her with an arm around her delicate waist as she walked to where Josselin sat, having his hands bandaged by Ollia. Jcymian looked down at the young man for a long moment; he returned her gaze with bewilderment. And Telo—his eyes went from his mother to the Prentice and back again before he bent his head to hide powerful emotion.

Caressing Josselin's black curls, Jeymian Renne murmured, "I sought you twenty years ago, and finally found you—ah, such a journey for a woman nearly seventy years old, searching for a single tiny baby in all that madness in The Waste! But I did find you, and Ward you, and then lost you again until tonight."

"Lady—" he began in a choked voice.

"Your great-grandfather was dead by then, or he would have done it. And your grandfather, not being a Listed Mage Guardian, had not the skills. He—"

Cailet interrupted as a clocktower rang Fourteenth. "Lady Jeymian, *who is this man?*"

"Great-grandson of myself and Gorynel Desse," she said proudly, still gazing down into Joss's moonstone-gray eyes. "Grandson of Telomir Renne and Mauren Trayos."

Telomir could barely speak, but he supplied the rest. "Son of my daughter Sela Trayos and Verald Jescarin."

24

CAILET turned away.

"Born the first day of Spring Moon," Jeymian said, smiling at her great-grandson.

—whom Cailet had suspected of being the traitor at Mage Hall—Gentle St. Miryenne, a descendant of Gorynel Desse, traitor to the Mage Guardians!

"Just so you know," Jeymian went on, "you *are* a Mikleine—your grandmother Mauren Trayos's father was Gorsha's dear friend Granon Mikleine. Her mother was Josea—which is where 'Josselin' comes from. I arranged for Mikleines to give you the Name. But the 'Josselin' is truly your own—your mother wrote it down before she died."

—died giving birth too soon, because Cailet had tried to steal her child's magic while he was yet unborn.

Gorsha—damn you, why didn't you tell *me?*

You think I knew*? It's exactly as Jeymian says—I was dead before the boy was born, how could I know who he was when he showed up at Mage Hall?*

But how did she *know to go find him?*

What Jeymian Renne doesn't know isn't worth the knowing.

That's no answer!

Then ask her.

Joss rose unsteadily to his feet, towering over the frail old woman. Bending, he put his arms carefully around her. She held him, saying softly, "As tightly as you please, my dearest. Love won't break these old bones."

Telomir put a shaking hand on his grandson's shoulder. The young man shifted, one arm reaching to enfold Telomir as well in his embrace.

Sirron Bekke cleared his throat. "Captal—"

"Yes. Of course." Cailet glanced at Sarra, still weeping in Taigan's arms. *Collan—I knew something was wrong when he didn't come back from the hunt—no mat-*

ter what he learned from the courier, he would have sent word—oh, Saints, Savachel Maklyn must be dead, too—

"Captal, I think we'd better leave. Right now."

Sirron's right, said Gorsha. *Just—just let me look at Jeymian once more, Cailet.*

You loved her best of them all.

I adored her. Still do, he replied gruffly. *Let me look at her again, and then let's get the hell out of here.*

Cailet said Taigan's name. The girl—woman now, her face older than her years—looked up. "Take care of your mother," Cailet said, and she nodded. Then, to Ollia: "You and Sirron get Granon Isidir—"

Sirron shook his head. "He's dead, Captal. Broken neck."

"Jored's doing, on his way out." Mikel came to her side. "He and Chava Allard must be long gone by now."

"Not necessarily." Telo moved away from his mother and grandson, wiping his eyes. From beneath his buttoned longvest he pulled a crumpled white cloth. This he spread onto the carpet—revealing gold and silver stitching on a three-foot-wide circle of velvet. "I relieved Allard of this before Jored shoved through and escaped with him."

"That's Glenin's," Cailet said. "What was Chava Allard doing with it?"

"Probably keeping it close to hand in case they had to escape quick. We can use it, you know. We've read their *Code.*"

"The *Code of Malerris?*" Jeymian Renne asked in astonishment. "You have a copy?"

"Back at Mage Hall—and ashes by now, Mother. But the Captal and I have read it, and what she doesn't remember I probably do."

"You really must write to me more often," Jeymian scolded. Then, after a few more quiet words to Josselin, she walked unaided back to the windows, where she arranged herself on the floor as she had been. "Much as I'd love to become a Mage Guardian again, I'll play my part of Lady Alinar and then return to the Cloister. Now, you'd better hurry, Cailet dear. Those Wards won't last forever outside."

"Become a Mage Guardian again?" Mikel echoed. "When we're about to be hunted all over Lenfell?"

"Where will we go?" Taigan asked.

"Ambrai?" Telo suggested. "It's where I sent the others."

Cailet was about to say *No,* because by now there would be Malerrisi all over the city. But then she remembered a locked and Warded room at the Octagon Court, where only a few people ever went. "Ambrai," she agreed.

Back to the beginning?

For a day or two. I have someplace else in mind as a final destination.

How final?

Can I take a few years to think it over?

Mikel was eyeing the circle of embroidered white velvet. "That thing's too small to take more than two people at once."

"I'm a fair proficient at Ladders," Ollia said. "Once the Captal shows me where we're going, she and I can trade off taking the rest of you."

Cailet nodded. Gathering Sarra from Taigan, she held tight to her only remaining sister and gave Gorsha his last look at Jeymian. The Lady was smiling at Cailet—who wished she could know who else she smiled at this one last time.

Cradling Sarra's head to her shoulder, she took her own last look at Glenin. *Her Wraith must be with Anniyas's now, in the Dead White Forest. Why did it have to happen this way? Why couldn't she—*

—change? Gorsha asked sadly. *You know why. Your father knew what we Mages were, and turned his back on us. Glenin never learned. She had nothing to turn* toward. *Consider her last act, her last words—gloating that she'd killed Collan, knowing it would break Sarra's heart. Grieve if you must, Caisha, but for what was, not what could never have been.*

And her son? Do I grieve for him, too, or hope that in his time with me he learned another way?

He paused a moment, then replied, *Take a few years to think it over.*

EPILOGUE

1

"**HERE?!**" Sarra stared at her sister, horrified out of her lethargy. "You're crazy!"

"Why *not* here? It's remote, uninhabited—"

"Uninhabitable!"

"Well, you've got me there," Cailet replied cheerfully. "Scavengers have probably cleaned out everything. There won't even be beds to sleep in."

Taigan, studying the immense—and immensely ugly—structure of Scraller's Fief, walked up a few of the three hundred and eighty-six steps. "We need a base. This will do."

"It's definitely defensible," stated Ollia Bekke, who seemed to have taken Imilial Gorrst's place if not yet her title as First Sword.

"And it'll hold a lot of people," Mikel added. "That'll be a help in the future."

"Future?" Sarra exclaimed. This time Cailet grinned at her. "You're *all* crazy! My children used to be fairly rational—what have you done to them, Cailet?"

Josselin leaned a hip against the low retaining wall. "I always thought the Mage Guardians should have a really imposing sort of headquarters again. And as sanctuaries go, this one looks pretty secure."

"No one in her right mind would choose a place like this to live in—especially *this* place!" Sarra cried.

"Exactly," said Cailet.

Sarra glared at her sister. She couldn't live here, where Collan had been a slave. She wouldn't do it. Cailet couldn't ask it of her. "I thought you *hated* The Waste! You couldn't wait to get away twenty years ago, and every time you came back to visit you couldn't leave fast enough! And now here you are again—*by choice!*"

"Truly told, it makes you wonder," Cailet mused.

"About your sanity—yes!" She narrowed her eyes at

the endless steps and thick walls of gray granite and acid-scarred blue-tiled roof. She hated it. She had never seen it before and had hoped never to see it in her life—and now Cailet was proposing that they *live* here.

She could feel all of them watching her—Taigan's and Dessa's eyes, different but equally intense shades of green; Mikel's as pure a blue as his father's; Josselin's calm gray (surely *too* calm, considering only two days ago he'd learned who he truly was—perhaps he simply didn't believe it yet). The dark, thoughtful gazes of Lusira and Elomar and Telo (standing near his newfound grandson and looking as if he couldn't quite believe it either); Ollia Bekke's bright turquoise eyes that frankly assessed both Sarra and Scraller's Fief; the other Mages, Sirron Bekke and Sevy Banian and four more whose names she'd probably heard but didn't remember, who didn't look directly at her but instead cast little glances of speculation or apprehension that annoyed her unbearably.

How could she possibly live in this hideous place?

But there was nowhere else, and she knew it.

Turning her glare on the group as a whole, she said briskly, "Well? What are you all standing around for? If you're so determined to stay, then get busy. Mikel, organize the other men and get our supplies up these damned steps. Telo, find us someplace at least passably livable—a working hearth will do, and a clean floor. Elomar, you and Lusira and Dessa set up a room for your medicines. We're going to have everything from sore backs to smashed thumbs in the next few days—if we don't sneeze ourselves to death from the dust first."

She saw a quick smile flash from Telomir to Cailet, the message clear: *That's our Sarra back again!* She chose to ignore it.

Passionately glad to have something to do, she had everyone installed in reasonable comfort by dusk. After Scraller's death, departing slaves had cleaned the place out of anything portable; in the twenty years since, scavengers had taken whatever was left that wasn't nailed down, and plenty of things that were. But nothing short of two teams of Clydies could have moved the huge cast-iron ovens, so at least there was both warmth and a place to cook their provisions. Sarra hoped that when other Mages began arriving they'd have the sense to bring along something to eat. Preferably fruit, vegetables, and grain; there was game aplenty for the hunting, but woman did not live on galazhi steak alone.

Tarise surely would bring provisions when she finally got here; dear, practical Tarise. But what would Rillan do without any horses to tend? Perhaps Riena Maurgen would let them buy a few Dapplebacks. . . .

And so her thoughts ran, until almost without her knowing it she soon didn't think of anything but what the hell they were going to do to make this awful place habitable. Until bedrooms could be found, cleaned, and furnished, she ordered their bedrolls arranged in the kitchen. Collan had spent part of his childhood—no. Don't think about that. The treadmill that turned the machinery of the cooking spit was long gone, probably in some other gigantic kitchen or broken up for scrap metal. But every time she glanced at the hearth, she could almost see a redheaded four-year-old slave.

Glad as she was for the work, she was gladder still to have something to occupy her mind. She hadn't thought about much at all these last two days. Truly told, she remembered little about them. She went where she was told, walked while Mages Folded paths, stood still for Cailet to take her through Ladders—she had no idea how many— ate when food was put before her, slept when a bed presented itself. Any thought would lead her to Collan, so she dared not think at all. She didn't trust herself.

Worse, she no longer knew who she was.

Councillor for Sheve, Lady of Roseguard—gone. No more would she help to direct the fate of the government she had done so much to build. No more would her words command instant respect. No more would she guide her adopted city and Shir to prosperity and justice. The woman who had done all those things was gone.

She had been a woman husbanded; now she was a widow. There were times when she'd catch sight of Mikel from a distance, and the coppery curls would make her heart lurch—it was all a mistake, Collan wasn't dead, he would come back to her. But he was gone. She wondered if it would have been any easier to accept had she seen his body, seen him die. Because she had not, for her he still lived—until those piercing moments when she remembered he was dead.

This wasn't the ending she'd had in mind—if she'd ever even thought about ending at all. She looked forward down empty, bitter years, seeing herself grow old without him.

She was yet a mother, but her children were grown and didn't need her. There'd been so little time with them; always her duties and responsibilities and endless work had taken her from her children. She saw now that she had lived as if she had a thousand years in which to do everything, be everything, without pausing to savor along the way.

She had done so much, all of it using one title or another, one identity or another—Councillor, Lady of Roseguard, a woman husbanded, a mother—all of them honest enough, but ultimately based on a lie. Now all titles and identities were gone, and the Name she bore for the first time in thirty-eight years would become synonymous with treachery. She had lost everything because of that Name, the only thing that truly belonged to her in the end.

The Name, and the heritage of magic.

She was a Mageborn Ambrai. And that was all she was. Her gift lay dormant and unused within her, Warded and then denied and now, finally, the only thing she had. The only thing she was.

She looked around at the people in Scraller's kitchen—seated on the floor, on the sink counters, on the massive butcher's table that, like the ovens, was simply too heavy to move. Of them, she was the only one without any knowledge whatsoever of magic.

Well, she told herself, now Telomir would have a companion in his title of Oldest Living Prentice Mage.

2

"IT'LL feel more like Mage Hall when the rest get here, I suppose," Mikel remarked as Josselin handed him another blanket. They'd found a suite of rooms in an upstairs hallway that Mikel thought his mother would like—once it had real furniture and the plumbing worked again. Tall windows in every chamber gave views of rugged mountains. The only drawback was that some of the glass was broken, as was the case in most of the keep. Glazing was high on Sarra's list of things-to-be-done, but stretched cloth would keep out the wind until then.

For the moment, the two young men were building Sarra a bed out of empty crates and thick blankets. Now that she was behaving more like herself, Mikel knew she'd want some privacy. He hadn't seen her cry once since that initial outburst two nights ago; she had been stony-faced and silent ever since. When she did weep again, he didn't want her to have to search through the whole of Scraller's Fief for a place to be alone.

Joss shook out another blanket, bandaged hands making him clumsy. "Taguare Veliaz should have some useful advice about this place—he lived here for a while, didn't he?"

"Until Lady Agatine bought him, freed him, and made him her sons' tutor." Fa could have told them all about Scraller's Fief, too. *Fa—no, please—* Quickly, for something to say, he asked, "How long do you think it'll take to get everybody here?"

"Depends on who decides to come. Lady Elin said they'll stick it out at Ambrai—there'll be other Mages in lesser positions who'll denounce the Captal and be allowed to stay where they are."

"Under Malerrisi supervision."

"There's that, yes. I suspect plenty will come here after they've had a taste of what it's like to be watched all the time."

"How many will *mean* it when they forswear themselves?" Mikel asked bitterly.

"A few." Joss shrugged. "It'll be interesting."

"And then some. And all over Lenfell. I don't think Glenin understood what she was really doing with that run on all those banks. I hope Vellerin Dombur *does* get blamed for it—between them, they damned near wrecked the whole economy."

The Ambrais had traveled one end of Lenfell to the other in the past two days—a tactic meant to confuse and confound those searching for them—and at every Ladder they'd heard the same thing: banks were failing, cash was being hoarded, and prices were going up and down and up again. Added to the panic Glenin had created were rumors created by the panic. Crop failures, forest fires that destroyed valuable timber, outbreaks of disease among cattle and sheep and galazhi, loss of Dindenshir's entire fishing fleet in a storm, a freeze blighting Gierkenshir's citrus groves—Mikel didn't know what to believe, and neither did anyone else. People unsure of what their money was worth were wary of spending it—except to buy up all the basic necessities, which meant stores and warehouses were running short, which only added credence to the hearsay reports of disasters. Every Web was selling off its nonessential holdings—or trying to; prices had plummeted on properties that a week ago would have brought twice and thrice what was offered for them now. Contributing to the confusion were reliable reports of a new vein of gold struck on Liwellan lands in South Lenfell—and any time more of a scarce commodity was discovered, the value of that commodity went down.

Fa will be up all night in his office with his steward and factor over this, Mikel thought, then bit his lip. *Am I ever going to stop thinking of him as still being alive?*

Joss was watching him, and he realized he hadn't said anything for several minutes. That was a good thing about Joss: he pretty much let you be quiet if you wanted to be, and waited until you were ready to talk.

"I've never been poor," Mikel said with a shrug. "That should be interesting, too."

"It's not," Joss said flatly.

Embarrassed, Mikel finished smoothing the blankets on the makeshift bed. "She's used to better, but this is better than the floor."

"Exactly the right attitude," Josselin approved. Then, after a brief hesitation: "I never got the chance to tell you how sorry I am about your father."

Mikel nodded once, uncomfortably.

"And Lirenza Mettyn. I know you cared for her."

He shoved his hands in his pockets, one fist closing around her bracelet of gray agates and yellow topazes. There'd been no one of the Mettyn Name at Ryka Court to give it to. Maybe that was for the best. He couldn't have found words to explain anyway. And he wanted a reminder—not of her (forgetting was impossible), or the pleasure they'd given each other (*"Whatever you do, Mishka, don't swipe a souvenir token—a lot of men do, but it's impossibly vulgar!"*). He deserved to be reminded that he hadn't grieved her as she deserved. Before Fa's death, he hadn't known *how* to grieve.

"I didn't love her," he said abruptly. "I should have, but I didn't. We did it—"

"Mikel. 'Doing it' is what happens in a bower. Trust me, I know. She may not've been the love of your life, but you did love her. You're not the type to be with a woman unless—"

"I'll never get the chance to find out if I really did love her. She's dead."

"And you're alive, and you think you could have saved her? Think, Mikel. Jored didn't want to kill you— from what I've heard, your room and Taigan's weren't even touched. Lirenza had a better chance being with you than with any man at Mage Hall."

"But we weren't in my room. We—we were in the hayloft." He hadn't told anyone that. Not even Fa. He'd been too ashamed. "I think—I *know*— if I'd held her differently—the glass would've hit *me*—and—"

"That's enough," Josselin said firmly. "It was an accident. A tragedy that wasn't your fault—unless your real mother was Elinar Longsight, who knows the future."

"I suppose," he said with a shrug. Some of the guilt drained off—which paradoxically made the grief all the worse. He rebelled for a moment, then realized it was more like what he felt when he thought of Fa—not nearly so intense, not nearly so terrible, but a grief that was somehow cleaner. Sorrow for *Lirenza,* not for himself and his shame.

"Come on," Joss said, interrupting Mikel's puzzled thoughts. "We still have the Captal's room to do."

They gathered up extra blankets and Cailet's black fur cloak, going down the hall to the staircase. Spiders and even less savory inhabitants scuttled out of their way.

"Cats," said Joss. "We need a whole family of cats." He stopped at the landing, looking surprised. "I had a cat when I was little. Feathers—silly name for a cat with a mane like a lion's. I haven't thought about him in years. He was the only thing I ever took with me to a new family . . . I never had anything else. Not a single thing that belonged to my real family."

"Saints and Wraiths! I forgot!" Mikel dug in the pocket that didn't hold Lirenza's bracelet. Into Josselin's white-swathed hands he poured three items of jewelry: an identification disk, a gold-and-amethyst pendant earring, and a wristlet of gold with chips of dark green jade carved into flowers.

Joss looked at them blankly. "What—?"

"My father kept them for years—ever since your father died." He explained how, right after the Rising, Collan had hired people to search for the children of Sela Trayos and Verald Jescarin: a little girl of four named Tamsa and an infant boy, name unknown. Eventually it was reported that Tamsa died of a fever in some village near Maidil's Mirror.

"But no trace of you was ever found," he concluded. "I guess Fa kept hoping that one day he'd see somebody who looked like his friend—they *were* friends, even though they didn't know each other very long. I wish he could know you're alive."

Joss cradled the mementos in his bandaged palms. "Did—did your father ever say much about my parents?"

"A little. I'll be glad to tell you everything I know."

"I've heard some of it from *Domni*—I mean, my grandfather—" He broke off, shaking his head. "Do you

know how bizarre it is to have family you never even—
but of course you do, I'm being an idiot."

Mikel grinned ruefully. "I probably can't add much
to what Telo says. But whatever I can remember is yours.
Though you've already seen your father's heart and soul,
in a way. He created Roseguard Grounds."

Josselin awkwardly pocketed the jewelry and glanced
around the dim, heavy-vaulted stairwell. "I don't think
I'll be following in his footsteps. Can't grow roses in The
Waste."

"I've never seen a place that needed roses more than
these do—not even that awful wall! And we'll have to
have a greenhouse to grow food. You can probably sneak
in some flowers."

"I'll give it a try. That was always the one thing that
even brought me close to resigning myself to Mirya
Witte—the gardens at their house in Pinderon are famous!"

That reminded Mikel of something. "That letter," he
said suddenly. "From her?"

"Letter?"

"The one that got mixed up with Jored's that time."

As they continued up a flight of stairs, Joss said,
"You saw that? You don't miss much."

"Only if it's shoved under my nose."

"It was from Mirya's Advocate in Roseguard, telling
me she was about to start proceedings for breach of contract and to recover the money she spent on my 'education.' I was ashamed—especially when Jored saw it—"

"And his letter? Did you see anything?"

"That's what was so odd. The frank on it was Roseguard, just like mine."

"Mirya was Glenin's creature," he mused. "I heard
Mother say that Glenin probably got her information
about Teggie and me from Mirya, the time she tried to
kidnap us."

"Jored's letter could've been the message telling him
when to destroy Mage Hall."

"Written in the most innocuous possible terms, I'm
sure, in case someone got hold of it by accident—the way
you nearly did. He didn't dare Ward it after he received

it, in case someone sensed it—probably burned it that night, in fact."

"Nobody ever suspected him," Joss said, shouldering aside a door half off its hinges. The room they entered was the antechamber of another suite, this one with windows (only a few panes missing) that overlooked the vastness of The Waste.

"The Captal did," Mikel said, and regretted it at once. She'd suspected Josselin, too. "Does any of the landscape look familiar? You spent a few years in The Waste, didn't you?"

"If one reads the broadsheets, I lived in every corner of it," he replied dryly.

Mikel nodded. "All those interviews with people who said they knew or fostered you—they probably won't be so eager to claim the acquaintance now."

"And they confused my background so completely that it's no wonder nobody knew what to think. If I *had* been the traitor, that would've worked in my favor."

"Why didn't you say anything? Why didn't you ever tell your whole story?"

"What could it matter to anyone but me?" Joss went into the bedchamber. Mikel followed. "If I'd given all the details, it would've been seen as a play for sympathy. Poor orphaned Nameless child, passed from family to family—not knowing who he was or where he came from or anything at all about himself—"

"Hell of a shock when you *did* find out, huh? I can definitely empathize." He said it with a smile, and Joss smiled back.

There was no need to construct a bed here; a deep, wide-arched alcove was fitted with a shelf obviously meant to hold a mattress. Blankets wouldn't do as well, but they *were* better than sleeping on the floor. On the stonework above the bed were charming frescoes of local flora and fauna done by an amateur but talented hand.

"I think she'll like this," Mikel said.

"If she doesn't, there are lots of other rooms to choose from. They say Scraller's own chambers were something to behold. Evidently the guest rooms were more subdued. This one's rather pretty." He began shaking out another blanket. "Why so far from your mother, though? It's three flights of stairs and a very long hallway back to the third floor."

Mikel took a cloth from his back pocket and began sweeping the dust from the alcove. "They've never lived together before. Both of them are used to running their own houses. I figured that if they had adjoining rooms, they'd *really* get on each other's nerves!"

Josselin eyed him thoughtfully. "Y'know, for your age, you know a lot about women."

3

"I'M confused about Avin Sonne," said Telomir as Sirron poured coffee. "Jored must've killed all the others at Peyres when he arrived—but why not Avin?"

Cailet nodded at the Bekke who would take Granon's place as Master of the Captal's Warders—though Sirron didn't know it yet. "Thanks. You can sit down now for at least five minutes," she added teasingly. "Consider it an order."

"Yes, Captal." He bowed gravely, and obeyed.

Cailet sighed. She'd have to teach him to have a sense of humor. "Avin Sonne? That's easy," she said to Telo, drawing her knees up to her chin. They sat on the floor, near enough to the vast hearth so Telo's bones wouldn't ache. "Avin was gone when Jored killed the others. Jored didn't dare kill him, too—somebody could've seen Avin return to town. Besides, he was the only person besides me who would use that Ladder—and Jored had no idea whether or not I'd be capable by the time we reached Peyres."

"If only we'd known about Joss earlier—" He broke off and shook his head. "A grandson. I have a grandson."

"How did Lady Jeymian know about him? And how did she know *to* know—if you know what I mean!"

"Nothing so dramatic as a birthmark. Mother came

to Roseguard when little Tamsa was born—though not as Jeymian Renne, of course—to see her first great-grand-daughter. Sarra might remember her visit, back in 965, an evening at the Residence with my brother Orlin and the boys. He tried to get her to come clean on who she was, but she wouldn't do it. Safer at The Cloister, she said, even after the Rising." Telo sighed and shook his head. "Anyway, when Sela became pregnant again, I wrote Mother about it. She was on her way from The Cloister when we all had to leave Roseguard. Then came the Rising. Verald was killed, Sela died giving birth to Josselin at the Ostin house in Longriding. Lilen took both children to Ostinhold. So much we already knew."

"But your mother—?" she prompted.

"After Ostinhold burned, she went looking for them." He paused for a sip of coffee. "A little girl with a kitten, a newborn baby boy, all that chaos—it must've been a nightmare. But she found them. Joss, anyway. Tamsa had died. Mother Warded Joss and gave him to a Mikleine woman, along with some money and a letter to give me. The woman ended up dying, too, somewhere between Ambraishir and Sheve. After that he was lost to us. Until two days ago." He shook his head again.

"Lilen knew his name—the 'Josselin' part, anyway. It's not common."

"How could she be expected to remember one baby in the midst of everything that happened next?"

"Well . . . I see your point. But Lady Jeymian should've been able to track him, if he was always known as Josselin Mikleine."

"Joss told me yesterday that the first foster-mother he remembers was a Mikleine, widowed on the flight from The Waste, with no other children, though she did talk sometimes about a son who would've been his big brother. She died when Joss was about four. Now, imagine your husband and your only child died on the trek across The Waste and Ambrai. All at once a baby is abandoned, alone, and available. You take this baby in, love it as your own—maybe move to a new location where no one knows you and therefore can't know that the baby isn't really yours. One day someone comes to your village asking about just such a child as you took in and made your own."

Cailet nodded. "She would've gotten rid of the letter as soon as she could—if she ever even had it at all."

"That's how I see it." Telomir rubbed a shoulder. "What's really bothering me is something that happened back at Mage Hall. I thought only close family could get through one's Wards. How did Joss get into your chambers there that night?"

"That *is* intriguing," she agreed, not having considered it before. "Other than my own, the Wards were Granon Bekke's, arranged so Marra and Aidan could come and go at will. But he was dead by the time Josselin arrived upstairs, his magic dissipated. Jored got in because he's family, of course—same thing for Taigan and Mikel."

"But Joss? The nearest you and he are related is—" He thought a minute. "Your great-great-grandmother married a Desse, and that's as close as it gets. And that's not close enough. So how'd he do it?"

Cailet was about to say she hadn't the first clue when she heard Gorsha chuckle inside her head. *And what, First Sword dear, are you about to amaze me with now?*

Nothing really. Only that Joss isn't your family, dear—he's mine. And I taught you all the Wards you know.

She damned near dropped her coffee mug. *You're kidding. The family resemblance in* magic *let him enter where he shouldn't have?*

That's essentially it.

To Telomir she said, "I think—I think it was probably because I wasn't exactly in my right mind that night. It certainly could have affected the Wards."

The explanation seemed to satisfy him.

Good recovery, Caisha.

No thanks to you! It's not as if I could tell him you're here, and invite him to have a talk with his father!

You could try, and see what happens!

She was distracted by a minor bustling at the kitchen door—and scrambled to her feet when Lady Lilen Ostin came in, flanked by her daughters Lenna and Miram and her granddaughter Mircian. Riddon Slegin and Pier Alvassy followed, arms full of packages.

"What's all this, then?" Lilen asked. "Here I've made my poor grandson-in-law Fold us all the way from Longriding and nobody's even at the front door to welcome us!"

"Speaking of Wards," Telo murmured as Cailet helped him to his feet. "I know, I know—Pier's a cousin, and your grandfather was an Ostin, so they can all get through. Remind me to find somebody who isn't related to *anybody* to Ward this place!"

Lilen, Lenna, and Miram were busy greeting Sarra. Mircian—who resembled her mother Geria in every superficial physical feature and in no substantial character trait whatsoever—nodded shyly at Cailet. "Cousin," Cailet said with a smile, and held out her hands. "I *can* call you that, can't I? It doesn't utterly humiliate you to be related to me?"

"To so desperate a character as the Mage Captal, you mean?" Mircian laughed, her lovely face that was so like Geria's made lovelier for the humor and sweetness Geria utterly lacked. "I'm crushed and despondent, you can be sure."

"What about your mother?" Cailet winked.

Lenna came up in time to hear this, and snorted. "Having conniptions this very instant."

"Personally," said Mircian, "I find that conniptions take up too much time and energy."

"I wish First Daughter health of them," Cailet said. "Come meet Sarra and Taigan—Mikel's around here somewhere, too."

"Did I hear Mikel's name mentioned?" asked Lady Lilen, coming up to Cailet with arms spread wide. As they hugged, she went on, "He and Taigan are the reasons we're here!" More softly, for Cailet's ears alone, "How are you, Caisha?"

"Better. Feeling safe helps. And coming home." She drew away, smiling.

"Home to The Waste—Saints help you." Lilen glanced around the kitchen. "Not *too* dreadful—but I can just imagine what the rest of it must be like. We'll stay a day or two, if that suits, and help."

"You're more welcome than I can possibly tell you. But what's this about Taigan and—oh, no!" she exclaimed.

"I had a suspicion they might've been forgotten in all this bother. Send someone to find the boy, would you? We can't begin until he's here." Lilen turned to the door. "And I've brought someone else as well—without whom we couldn't possibly have a party."

Cailet craned her neck to see past Miram and Sarra, and all at once tears came to her eyes. Falundir smiled at her from the doorway. Cradled in one arm was his lutc-case—containing the instrument given to Collan long ago. Rescued from Roseguard, brought all this way, now it would belong to Mikel: like his father, a gift on his eighteenth Birthingday.

4

THE party began with Mikel's return—after Ollia ran upstairs yelling for him and Josselin so loudly that they thought the Ryka Legion had arrived to do battle. Lilen had provided eighteen gifts for Mikel and eighteen for Taigan, as was customary. The twins opened sixteen parcels and two envelopes while everyone else gathered around the kitchen hearth to admire the presents and sip the wine Riddon had brought from Longriding.

There were practical gifts of clothes and galazhi-hide boots, and thoughtful gifts of books (*Lives of Famous Ambrais* for Taigan; *Ambraishir: A Personal View by Dirken Halvos* for Mikel), and a dazzling gift of a Maurgen Moonstreak Dappleback each, promised by notes from Riena. Other envelopes from Jennis contained the information that saddles and bridles went with the horses. Cailet smiled then, telling the twins that she'd received exactly the same from Lady Sefana on her own eighteenth.

Taigan also received a necklace and bracelet of carved sand-jade—Cailet gave a start and told her they were the work of "Rinnel Solingirt"—and Mikel a wristlet and earring of the same material by the same maker. Bottles of wine, crocheted coverlets in Ambrai's turquoise and black octagons, and small marble statues of their Name Saints completed Lilen's gifting.

Falundir presented Mikel with the lute, and Taigan with twin throwing knives to replace the ones she hadn't been wearing with her formal gown on Midsummer Moon night. They were very old knives, inscribed with strange sigils down the blades, the hilts wrapped in new gold wire. Sarra then opened the velvet pouch Lilen had provided, and came forward to place small shining objects in her children's hands. Taigan gulped on seeing a pair of sapphire earrings; Mikel caught his breath at the thin wristlet of carved moonstones and turquoises.

"These," Sarra said in a steady voice, "are from your father and me. There was more—"

"This is enough," Mikel interrupted, his voice not at all steady. Taigan could only nod.

"Eighteen years ago," their mother said softly, "I saw you for the very first time. I won't say it seems like yesterday, because it doesn't."

"Well, I should hope not," Cailet drawled. "Yesterday we were running for our lives in Kenrokeshir. Or was it Bleynbradden?"

"Both—I think," said Telomir.

"And five other places besides," added Mikel.

"Only five?" asked Taigan. "I could've sworn—"

"Oh, stop it!" Sarra laughed. "I'm trying to tell you that you've lived good lives in these eighteen years, and I'm proud of you—though I had little to do with it." She held up a hand as they began to protest. "You are the children of your father, and an honor to him."

For the first time in thirty-eight years, Falundir used his crippled hands to applaud his approval. Others began to join him, clappping louder and louder until Cailet went to stand at her sister's side and raised a hand for silence.

"My gift isn't exactly the one I intended, but it's the most important thing you'll ever own. I give you, Taigan, and you, Mikel, your true Name—*our* Name. Ambrai."

"Taigan Ambrai!" Riddon called out, raising his glass of wine. "Mikel Ambrai!"

And amid the cheers and toasts they started to get used to their own names.

A little while later, Mikel drew his sister aside, finding a corner of the kitchen where they could talk in comparative privacy. "Happy Birthingday," he said, and kissed her cheek. "You know, I clean forgot what today was. Do you feel as weird as I do?"

"That it's not at Roseguard, and Fa's not here?" She nodded, and kissed him back. "We're surrounded by strangers who're really our family. Miram's the genealogist in the group, she's offered to draw us a map of—" She broke off. "Like the map Jored drew of Mage Hall. Mishka, I *helped* him do it! I helped him plan out how to destroy Mage Hall!"

"That's enough," he said, echoing Josselin's chiding of earlier. "How could you know?"

"I should have. So much for any instincts I may have inherited from Mother," she added bitterly.

"Teggie, I think your *magic* is absolutely instinctive," Mikel told her.

"And that's just the problem! You'd think there wasn't any brain at all behind it—"

"You just have to learn to think it through."

"*Think* about an *instinct?* Oh, that just makes piles of sense!"

"That's not what I meant. Your magic comes without your having to think about it, in response to a threat." He paused as a burst of merriment nearby filled the kitchen with the best kind of noise. Pulling her a little ways further from it, he went on, "What you need to learn is why your brain *perceives* a threat—if you think about it beforehand, and sort out the serious from the trivial, then your magic will be under much better control."

"I'd understand it better," she said slowly, "and trust it more when my instincts call on it."

"Right," he agreed. "And remember, you're not a

Listed Mage yet. You can't be expected to know everything."

"But I *should* have known to tell someone about Jored's map of the Hall," she insisted.

He shook her arm and said severely, "If you say 'If I had, then Fa wouldn't be dead,' I'll kick you into the middle of next Candleweek! Jored planned what he did, and Glenin planned to kill Fa. There's nothing anybody could've done."

"I wanted to kill him," she whispered. "I had that sword in my hand, and—why did Joss stop me? Why did he do that?"

"Because it wasn't right for you to kill him, and Joss knew it."

"But his hands—" Her gaze shifted to where Josselin stood, clumsily cradling a wineglass in both gauze-wrapped hands. "Elo says they'll heal, but he'll have scars the rest of his life."

"Maybe he did it because he cares about you."

"Me? Joss?"

"You never saw anyone but Jored. Maybe Joss found a chance to make you see *him*."

"Josselin?"

Riddon came to fill their glasses, and talked about when they might go up to Maurgen Hundred to select their horses. "My little brother Jeymi has several in mind, real beauties. And none of them close enough related to preclude your starting your own herd here."

"Here?" Taigan asked in much the same tone her mother had used this morning. "Where would we put a herd of horses?"

Riddon laughed. "Do you have any idea how *big* this place is?"

"Not yet," Mikel said, "but I get the feeling we'll find out as soon as we start getting lost. Miram says Lenna will play with the title deeds for us so one of the Ostins owns the place. Make sure she keeps track of how much it costs—sooner or later we'll liberate some money out of the banks in Roseguard."

Riddon grimaced. "If *any* bank is still standing after

the mess going on now. But we're not talking about un-
pleasant things tonight."

Mikel nodded, but wondered privately just how un-
pleasant things might become for the Ostins—who had
sheltered Cailet Ambrai in childhood and were closely
allied to the Mage Guardians.

"Our First Daughter, Tevis, wants me to make particularly sure to tell you she and Alyn and Cailie helped me
work your coverlets—and I freely admit I never would've
finished in time without them."

"Thank you so much," Taigan said warmly. "And I
hope to be able to thank my cousins in person soon—we
are all cousins, aren't we?"

"One way or another," Riddon replied, smiling, and
Mikel recalled that Orlin Renne's father had been an Alvassy, so that made them all related . . . somehow. Definitely Miram would have to draw them a map for
navigation of the genealogical waters. Riddon continued,
"We're all in the same wagon, you know—I'm told my
Uncle Telo's grandson is here."

"Josselin Mikleine," said Mikel. "Don't tell me you
haven't met him? Come on, I'll introduce you. *He's* a
little overwhelmed by sudden mobs of relatives, too."

5

"HOW did you manage this in only two days?" Sarra
asked Lilen, who smiled.

"We'd intended giving them a few things anyway. It
was only a matter of doing a little more shopping—and
Riddon and his girls sitting up late to finish the coverlets."

"They're beautiful." After a brief hesitation, she
said, "Lilen, did Dellian Vekke come with Falundir from
Roseguard?"

Lilen hesitated. "I'd hoped not to tell you until tomorrow."

It was a moment before Sarra found her voice again. "How—?" was all she could manage.

"I'm not precisely certain, but Falundir told me as much as he could with that song about Shen Escovor— 'The Fourth Lord,' I think it's called. When the Malerrisi seized him to execute him, he was kneeling beside his hearth, burning his letters from Captal Caitirin Bekke."

Yes, Dellian would have been conscientious about that—she'd get rid of all Sarra's most personal records before seeing to her own safety.

"I've written to her mother," Lilen added softly.

"Thank you. I'll do the same tomorrow."

"You can't, my dearest. You *can't*. No one must know you're still alive."

Sarra's nails cut into her palms. "I'd be better dead. Dead and burned, with Collan—" And then she choked, because she didn't even know if Glenin had given his body honorable burning.

"You forget I am twice a widow," Lilen said stiffly. "Don't expect to get over him. But don't desecrate the living you did together by hating the living you have left to do." Then, because a group of people had drifted within hearing range, she said brightly, "I'm told that delicious young man over there was born in my very own house in Longriding."

Sarra bit back a bad-tempered reply and lifted one hand, and Joss excused himself to Riddon and came to where the ladies stood by the sink. With scant grace, Sarra said, "Lady Lilen Ostin, Josselin Mikleine."

Joss's smile could have lit Scraller's Fief from cellar to roof. Bowing profoundly to the old woman, he said, "Lady, forgive the presumption, but in the last two days I've come to realize I had three mothers—and one of them was you."

"No presumption at all," Lilen told him. "You and I must talk about Sela—she was a lovely girl and I wish I'd known her better. But who is your third mother?"

He turned to Sarra. "This Lady here—who sent me to Mage Hall."

"Mother!" said Miram, approaching with a frown. "Cai's being stubborn again. Come talk some sense into her about supplies, won't you? I'm not making any progress."

Lilen sighed and excused herself, leaving Sarra and Josselin by themselves.

"I would have thought Cailet would be your third mother," she said.

His gaze flashed to Cailet and back again. "No," he said. "Not at all."

Sarra felt her jaw drop, just a little, and in one of her least diplomatic speeches said, "Why, you're in love with her!"

"That would be pretty stupid, wouldn't it?" Joss snapped. An instant later he bit both lips between his teeth and shook his head. "Forgive me, Lady, that was unconscionably rude. I'm sorry."

Sarra's brows arched. "*I'm* not," she said.

6

CAILET, muscles aching with unaccustomed housework—there was plenty to be done and Sarra had spared her not at all today—and head buzzing a little with wine, slipped away from the Birthingday celebrations to explore a bit. Cartloads of dirt, debris, and nestings would have to be removed and the whole place scoured before the stale smells faded, but aromas of fresh bread and spicy stew and woodsmoke banished mustiness all the way up to the third floor.

She paused on a landing, her candle flickering in a breeze through broken windows, as laughter echoed up from the kitchen. Laughter and vigorous new life was just what this decaying old corpse of a keep needed.

A light burning from inside a doorway attracted her, and investigation showed her why Mikel and Joss and vanished for so long this evening, and what they'd been up to. Soon enough everyone would have private rooms—though real beds and other furniture would take more time. Lilen had told her that she was thinking of redoing some of Ostinhold, the obvious implication being that in ordering new furnishings she could give Cailet the old and no one would be the wiser. Cailet nodded blandly, determined to pay for the cast-offs. Somehow.

She climbed further, wandered down corridors, was startled by scurrying, scuttling noises that greeted the light of her candle. From a closet on the fifth floor, a baby bat whined impatiently for its mother to come home with dinner. *Sorry, little one,* Cailet thought. *You and everybody else currently in residence are about to be evicted.*

On the sixth floor another fat candle burning in a wide dish led her to another suite, one she knew was meant for her: the fur-lined cloak was draped on the alcove-shelf bed. It was thoughtful of Mikel and Joss to arrange her comfort. The room lacked only a desk, a chair, and hooks to hang clothes on. Although there'd unquestionably be quite a bit more by the time Lilen and Sarra were through.

Just down the hall was a door leading to a balcony. Cailet stepped outside into the night, found a stone bench, brushed it off, blew out her candle, and sat down to watch the bleak starlit landscape below. The Ladymoon and her small companion had set, leaving the sky a dazzle of stars in the darkness. A Saint's Spark flew from west to east in a stream of silver light, vanishing behind a ridge of mountains. Wind ruffled Cailet's hair and after a time she was surprised to feel it drying tears on her cheeks. She hadn't known she was crying.

How had it come back to The Waste? This harsh, unforgiving land that had nonetheless sheltered Maichen and Sarra, the place where Cailet had been born and her mother had died, where Gorynel Desse had posed as Rinnel Solingirt—the mad old man of Crackwall Canyon— and waited for Cailet to grow up.

None of the people she'd brought with her today, and few of those who would come over the next weeks, had any idea of how to live here. But if anything were true, it was this: people were infinitely adaptable. Hadn't the ancestors of everyone now living somehow survived The Waste War, adapted to its hideous aftermath, adjusted to new social and environmental conditions, and eventually thrived?

The Mage Guardians would do no less. There would be those who could not accept this place, Cailet knew. She'd give all the help she could, but in the end it would be their choice. She would make the transition as easy as possible, but she could not smoothe everyone's way, comfort all hurts, provide solace for everything lost. Those who could adapt, would. Those who could not—or would not—must not be allowed to hinder the rest.

And wasn't that just what the Malerrisi proposed to do? How could she even think such a thing, after seeing Piera Alvassy again, hearing her scream at the invasion of strangers again, not forty hours ago?

She fought with it, as they had fought after The Waste War: survival of the many against the needs and troubles of the few. Those who could survive, would. The strong would always adapt, change, adjust—if not themselves, then the world around them. But did they not have a responsibility to help those who could not do the same?

The glow of another candle behind her frayed the star-thrown shadows, and a soft footstep made her head turn. "Sarra. I thought you'd be up here soon."

"I can see right through you, little sister." Seating herself on the bench, she adjusted Lady Jeymian's shawl about her shoulders and blew the candle out. "Anyone could see how you maneuvered me into this, giving me so much to do that I wouldn't have time to think."

"Did I do that?"

She snorted. "Sweet innocence!"

They were quiet for a time, looking out at the stars.

"I'm ashamed of myself," Sarra said at last. "Forgetting their Birthingday."

"Everyone did—including them."

"This isn't what I had in mind."

"No."

"Not just tonight. This." She swept a hand out to indicate The Waste. "It's not what they ought to have had."

"You keep saying that—first about me, now about them."

"It's different now. There'll be prices on all our heads, you know."

"What did our parents plan for us, Sarra? Do you ever wonder?"

"You would've been Captal. Your gifts are too powerful for you to have become anything else. As for me—"

"Politics."

"Maybe. But that's lost to me now. So—" She drew in a long breath. "Will you take me on as a Prentice, Captal?"

"Gladly." Cailet took her sister's hand between her own.

Sarra nodded. It was proposed and accepted; they would speak of it more fully later. For now, she asked, "What do you think Glenin planned for Jored? Although I suppose that matters less now than what *he* plans to do next."

"I'm sure we'll find out."

"If only Taigan—"

"She'll need soft handling," Cailet mused. "But she won't permit it."

"I just wish—" Sarra bit her lip and turned her face away.

"Collan?" Cailet said softly. "I know. I wish, too. But could you see him confined to this rock, his wings clipped?"

Sarra shook her head. "No."

"I worry that way about you, too, you know."

"I have my children. And soon, my magic." She paused. "And you? What do you have?"

"What I need."

"Do you?" Sarra wore a small, secretive smile. "Sister dear, do you even know what you truly need? Would you know it if it stood in front of you?"

All at once they both sat up straighter: voices were singing downstairs, audible even up here, with Mikel's strong tenor leading.

I know of a garden not far from a river,
A temple of roses, gold sun, and green shade,
Where dawn diamonds misted the grass of a morning,

And evening's soft breeze laced a shadowy glade.

Sarra murmured, "That's the old version of 'The Long Sun.' "

The one about Ambrai; that one that had so enraged Anniyas. "Was Ambrai truly like that?" Cailet asked.

"For me, as a child—I suppose so. But I was *only* a child, Caisha." Rising, she patted the pockets of her shortvest, feeling for her matchbox. Cailet obliged her by lighting both their candles with a flicker of magic. Sarra made a face at her. "Braggart."

"You're just irked because you can't do it yet. But you'll learn how soon enough." She smiled. "Just think, Sasha—no more cold coffee ever again!"

"What magnificent compensation for all *this*," was the tart reply, with another sweeping gesture at The Waste.

"Speaking of cold, it's freezing up here." Cailet stood and stretched, marking the fall of another Saint's Spark across the sky. Scraller's Fief was too far south, but she couldn't help wishing that one glimmer of iridescence, just one, might drift down from the Wraithen Mountains one night . . . surely it would be accompanied by the clear, sweet notes of a lute. . . .

"It's colder anyway," Sarra said suddenly. "I've noticed that, since Collan died. It's so much colder." Her eyes squeezing shut against tears, she whispered, "And the music is gone."

Cailet didn't say that the music was still there in Collan's son. It would be a very long time before Sarra heard it.

Circling her sister's shoulders with one arm, Cailet murmured, "Come inside, Sasha."

And together they went into their only sanctuary.

SELECTIVE GENEALOGY

```
Birella Ostin      /—Taigrel Ostin    /—Lilen Ostin     /—Geria Ostin
=————————/  =————————/  =————————/  =————————————— issue
Taigan Vekke       /   Lenyr Ellevit   Tiva Senison     /   Mircian Karellos
                   /                                     /—Taig Ostin
                   /                                     /—Margit Ostin
                   /                                     /—Lenna Ostin
                   /                                     /—Tevis Ostin
                   /                                     /—Miram Ostin
                   /                                     /  =————————————— issue
                   /                                     /   Riddon Slegin
                   /                                     /—Alin Ostin
                   /                                     /—Terrill Ostin
                   /—Gerrin Ostin                        /—Lindren Ostin
                   /                                         =————————————— issue
                   /                                     /—Biron Maurgen
                   /                   Sefana Maurgen    /—Vallrion Maurgen
                   /—Jener Ostin       =————————————/  /=/———————— Aidan Maurgen
Tevis Vekke        =—————————————— Sollan Vekke     /   Rina Firennos
=—————————————    Solla Vekke                          /   Jeymi Slegin
Mittrian Solingirt                                      /  =————————————— issue
                                                       /—Riena Maurgen
                                                       /—Jennis Maurgen
                                                           /=/1———————— issue
                                                           Tamaso Obreic
                                                           /=/2-———————— issue
                                                           Biren Halvos
                                                           /=/3-———————— issue
                                                           Steenan Oslir
```

━━━

=marriage
/—/liaison

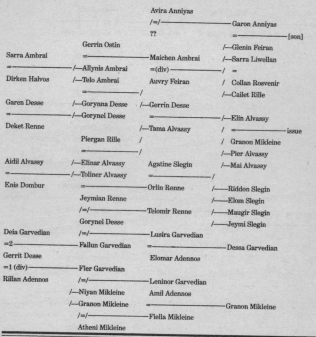

=marriage
/=/liaison

INDEX OF SAINTS

Flerna The Weary. Patron of accountants. Sigil: abacus.

Garony The Righteous. Patron of lawyers, prisoners. Sigil: gavel.

Gelenis First Daughter. Patron of pregnant women, childbirth, First Daughters. Sigil: carved chair.

Geridon The Stallion. Patron of fathers, horses, domestic animals. Sigil: horseshoes.

Gorynel The Compassionate. Patron of grief, widows, cripples, judges, printers. Sigil: thorn tree.

Ilsevet Waterborn. Patron of fish and fisherfolk. Sigil: crossed hooks.

Imili The Joyous. Patron of joy, newlyweds, new mothers, old lovers. Sigil: flower basket.

Jenavira Rememberer. Patron of memory. Sigil: open book.

Jeymian Gentlehand. Patron of wild animals. Sigil: open hand.

Jeyrom Bookcounter. Patron of librarians. Sigil: lion.

Jiorto Silverhelm. Patron of armorers. Sigil: helmet.

Joselet Green-eyes. Patron of gardeners. Sigil: shovel and hoe.

Kembial The Veiled. Patron of fugitives. Sigil: veil.

Kiy The Forgetful. Patron of wine, vintners, toothaches, lawyers. Sigil: spilled cup.

Lirance Cloudchaser. Patron of wind. Sigil: tower.

Lusine and Lusir The Twins. Patron of innocents, children, shepherds. Sigils: bow (Lusine); shepherd's crook (Lusir).

Maidil The Betrayer. Patron of new lovers, fools, unfaithful husbands. Sigil: mask.

Maurget Quickfingers. Patron of jewelers, gemcutters, artists, beggars, tax collectors, politicians. Sigil: quill pen and purse.

Mikellan Startoucher. Patron of Mage Guardians. Sigil: ladder.

AUTHOR'S NOTE

Humble apologies to the Wraith of Guiseppe Verdi for mangling his magnificent *Rigoletto*.

While I'm on the subject, a word about music. There are a hundred songs I'd love to include (in forms altered by time, space, and societal needs, as with the opera), but whereas by the time these novels take place the lyrics will in public domain, I'm writing in the 1990s and there's pesky thing called "copyright" to be considered. So e assume that Collan's repertoire includes versions r own favorite songs, the ones you just know will wherever our species may wander; it's just that pertinent to the story occurs on the occasions happens to sing them!

s as ever go to Russell Galen and Danny Baror; helan and Audrey Price-Whelan; Sheila Gil-tsy Wollheim; Jennifer Roberson and Alis

ratitude to Nora and Joanne, my friends ue Elementary School (more years ago admit). This one's for you.

o all the friends (and friends' charac-arbled into cities, geographical fea-ot that any of them *qualifies*. John one of my professors at Scripps island. . . .

Miramili The Summoner. Patron of bells, weddings. Sigil: Miramili's Bells.

Miryenne The Guardian. Patron of light, candles, magic, Mage Guardians. Sigil: lighted candle.

Mittru Bluehair. Patron of rivers. Sigil: sheaf of reeds.

Nialos The Bargainer. Patron of merchants. Sigil: Raised first finger.

Niya The Seamstress. Patron of tailors. Sigil: scissors.

Oseth Hammerer. Patron of carpenters. Sigil: nails.

Pierga Cleverhand. Patron of thieves, condemned p⟨ris⟩ers, divorced husbands. Sigil: broken lock.

Rilla The Guide. Patron of travelers, coachmen⟨,⟩ Mage Guardians. Sigil: white sparrow.

Shonne Dreamdealer. Patron of shrines⟨.⟩ Sigil: triangle.

Sirrala The Virgin. Patron of flowe⟨rs,⟩ girls. Sigil: flower crown.

Sollian The Generous. Patron ⟨of⟩ kard.

Steen Swordsworn. Pat⟨ron⟩ gauntlet.

Tamas The Ma⟨p⟩ and rope⟨s⟩

Telomar T⟨⟩ Sig⟨⟩

Tir⟨⟩

Ve⟨⟩

Velireon⟨⟩ farme⟨⟩

Venkelos Th⟨⟩ Wraithena⟨⟩

Viranka The Gray⟨⟩